ASSAULT ON ORION

THE ORION WAR - BOOKS 7-10

M. D. COOPER

SPECIAL THANKS

Just in Time (JIT) & Beta Reads

PRECIPICE OF DARKNESS
Jim Dean
Marti Panikkar
Lisa Richman
Timothy Van Oostyerwyk Bruyn
Gene Bryan
David Wilson
Scott Reid

AIRTHAN ASCENDANCY
Lisa Richman
Scott Reid
Ronald Rong

THE ORION FRONT
Lisa Richman
Scott Reid
Chad Burroughs
Timothy Van Oosterwyk Bruyn
Randy Miller
David Wilson
Gene Bryan

STARFIRE
Lisa Richman
Scott Reid
Gene Bryan
Timothy Van Oosterwyk Bruyn
Steven Blevins
Randy Miller
Chad Burroughs
Gareth Banks
Constance Beebe

Version 1.1.0

ISBN: 978-1-64365-063-0

Cover Art by Andrew Dobell
Edited by Jen McDonnell, Bird's Eye Books

TABLE OF CONTENTS

MAPS

For more maps, visit www.aeon14.com/maps.

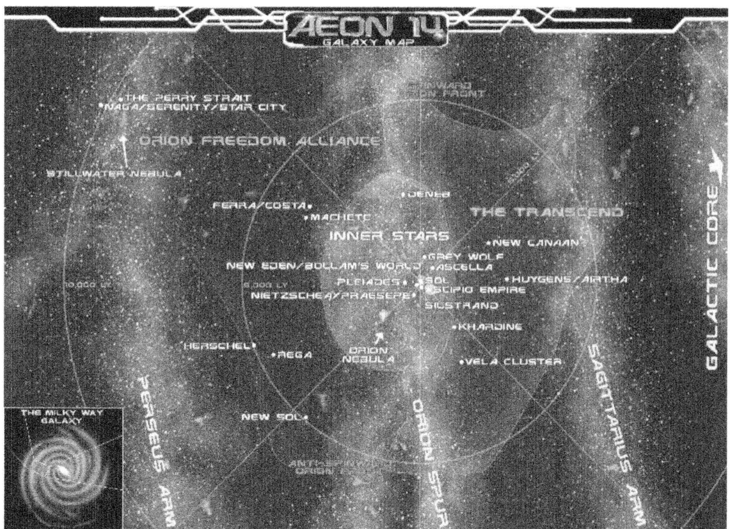

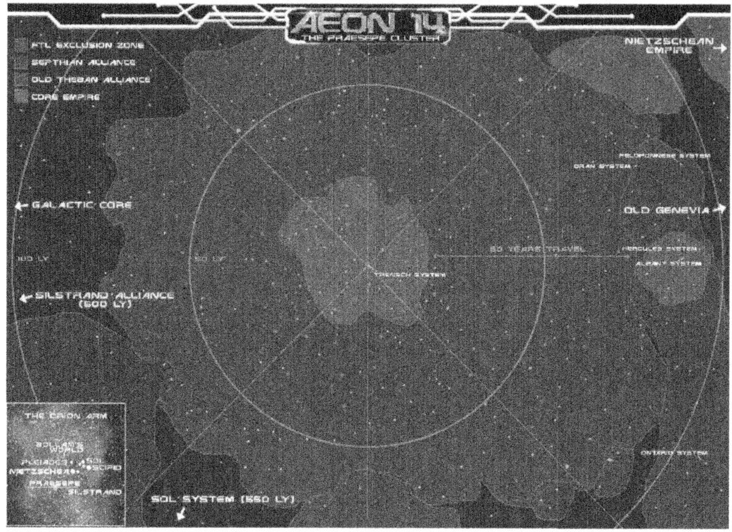

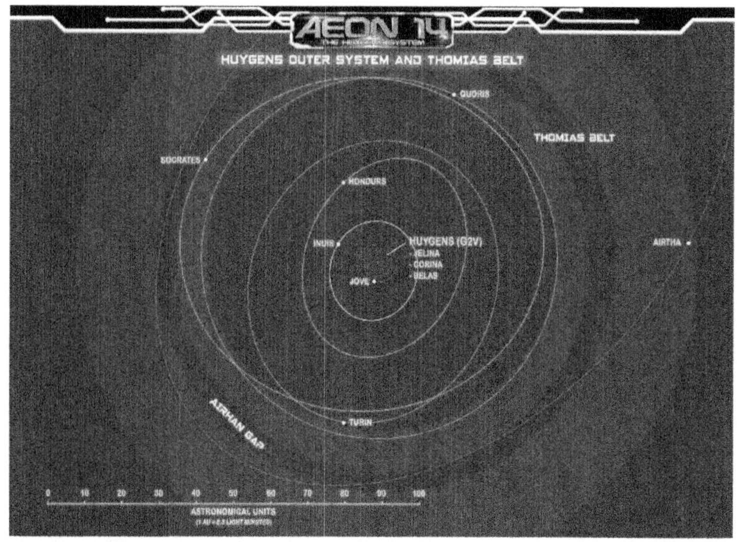
AEON 14
HUYGENS OUTER SYSTEM AND THOMIAS BELT
QUORIS
THOMIAS BELT
SOCRATES
HONDURS
INUIS
HUYGENS (G2V)
VELINA
CORINA
BELAS
JOVE
AIRTHA
AIRHAN GAP
TURIN
0 10 20 30 40 50 60 70 80 90 100
ASTRONOMICAL UNITS

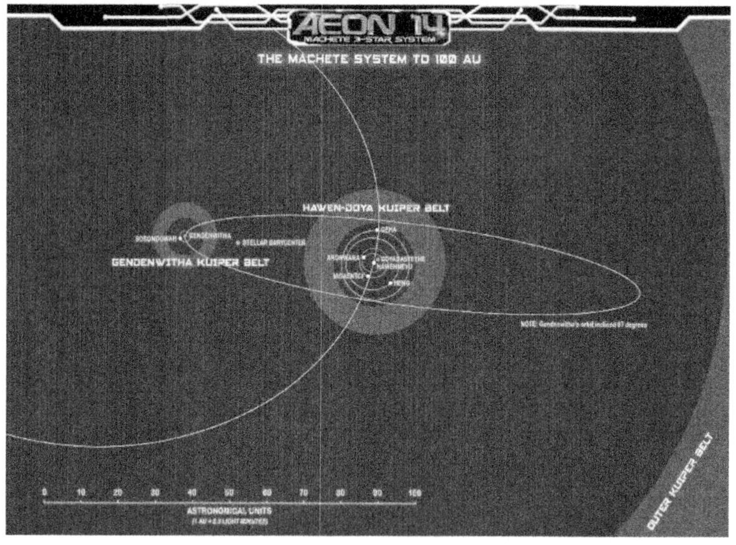
AEON 14
MACHETE 3-STAR SYSTEM
THE MACHETE SYSTEM TO 100 AU
HAWEN-DOYA KUIPER BELT
GENDENWITHA
STELLAR BARYCENTER
GENDENWITHA KUIPER BELT
OUTER KUIPER BELT
0 10 20 30 40 50 60 70 80 90 100
ASTRONOMICAL UNITS

PRECIPICE OF DARKNESS

THE ORION WAR – BOOK 7

BY M. D. COOPER

FOREWORD

When I was mapping out the books of The Orion War series, I was certain that by this point, the Allies would have launched their attack on the Trisilieds and brought that kingdom to its knees. I had also expected the Nietzscheans to have fallen by now.

And so I named the book "Fallen Empire".

However, things have taken a few turns for the Allies, and they've not yet progressed that far in their conquests. A detour into the LMC and little to no progress in quelling the civil war in the Transcend has stymied them—not to mention the ongoing slugfest between the Scipian Empire and the Hegemony of Worlds (we'll see more of that in the upcoming "The Empire" series).

While some storylines have taken their time, other events have moved forward sooner than I'd planned (pesky characters having their own ideas). As a result, this book will introduce some new viewpoints and things that I suspect you have been eager to learn more about.

In the end, I determined that "Fallen Empire" was no longer the best title for this book, and so I chose "Precipice of Darkness" (actually, I put up some suggestions in the Facebook group, and Will Crudge suggested it). I think the title captures the direction of the book well, and hints at interesting things to come.

In addition, I updated the cover to reflect this change, so you'll be seeing it with the new artwork (I hope) as it is released.

Regardless of that, I'm certain you'll enjoy the journey this book takes you on, as we tie up some threads with characters that have been lingering in the background for some time, revisit some old favorites, and introduce a few new additions to the cast.

Even better, someone that everyone passionately hates dies in this book—maybe more than one someone...you'll just have to read on to see.

I should add that there are spoilers in this book if you have not read the first two books of Perseus Gate: Inner Stars (A Meeting of Minds and Bodies, and A Deception and a Promise Kept). Without reading those, you may find yourself saying "wait, where did *she* come from?"

In addition, if you did not read season one of Perseus Gate (beginning with The Gate at the Grey Wolf Star), then there will be references in this book that will be sure to surprise you—notably, what the heck Star City is.

Another item of note is that for some time now, I've been erroneously calling Jeffrey Tomlinson's former wife (who is now the AI Airtha) 'Justina'. However, in Orion Rising, when Finaeus first refers to her, he calls her Jelina, which is correct. This book refers to her as such, and I'll be correcting the prior books.

Something else that I think you may find interesting is the name of the supermassive black hole in the core of our galaxy: Sagittarius A*. Some folks have wondered if it's a typo, but the asterisk is correct. It is pronounced 'Sagittarius A Star'. Which I find quite amusing, since it's not a star.

There are a few other themes and concepts that are woven through the stories that have not been explained in a great many books. One of them is the nature of multidimensional space as it is used in Aeon 14. Obviously, at the time of this book's creation, the jury is still out on pretty much everything having to do with higher (or lower) dimensions.

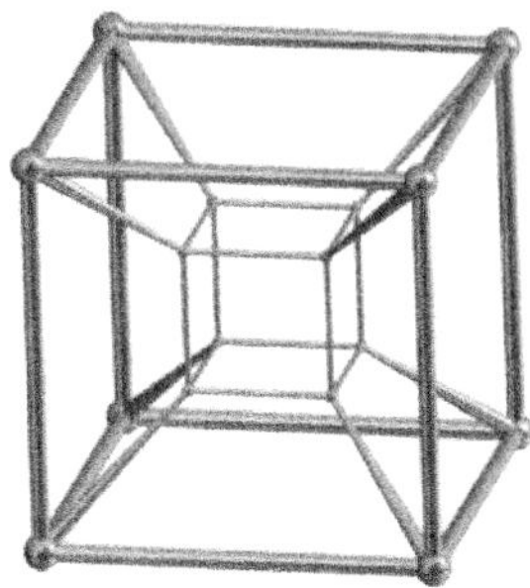

In Orion Rising, when Finaeus talked about flatlander theory and then got into tesseracts (no, not like the one in the Avengers) and hypercubes, this was discussed, but it's been a while. The first thing of note is that, while for our human experience, time is often referred to as the 4th dimension, in multi-dimensional theories, it is not. The 4th dimension is just another direction, as is the fifth. A 4D cube (our friend the tesseract) would be like a 3D cube with 3D cubes for each side. Which is totally trippy.

Of course, in 4D space, a tesseract does not look like the image above. There, all the lines intersect at right angles, which is not something our two-dimensional eyes can perceive.

And there we come to another concept that should be addressed. In this book, Tangel refers to regular, organic eyes as 'two-dimensional', not three-dimensional.

This is not a typo. Your and my optical equipment cannot see in three dimensions. Each eye sees a 2D image with a slightly different perspective, and your brain puts them together and *perceives* the third dimension. Each eye is the opposite of a television. A flat image is projected onto your retina, and the brain does a lot of magic to produce our vision.

For example, there is a hole in your retina where the optic nerve goes to the brain. You never see it because your brain hides it, just like it hides your nose (unless you look for it—which you can also do with the hole in your retina). Our eyes can't see color very well in our peripheral vision, nor can we see color at all in the dark. The band where we can actually focus is narrow, as well.

However, the computer between our ears assembles all of that information into the picture that we think of as 'vision'. The more you research it, the more you'll learn that much of it is a fabrication of our minds.

But what about 3D eyes? Researchers are working on ways to create those, because a 3D array of 3D eyes should be able to see the 4th dimension (just like a 2D array of 2D eyes can perceive the 3rd). Which is, effectively, what Tangel is able to do.

Early in the book, you're going to encounter some discussion of predictive models. This has been sprinkled throughout the books, starting with the New Year's Eve party in Building Victoria, where Bob revealed that he can effectively see the future.

However, that is turned on its head when he says that Tanis muddies that. The core AIs also feel this way about Tanis, though they can see very far into the future. One wonders "How does this work? If you can't manage all the variables, how can you see the end result?"

The answer is that you still can, you just have less certainty. Take for example a body of water sitting in the middle of a continent. Should a channel be cut that would allow that body of water to flow out of its basin, you could look at a number of large scale variables to determine whether or not it would reach the ocean, and probably those whereabouts, with reasonable accuracy.

However, were you to try to track a single water molecule's course, you would have a much more difficult task laid out for you. The core AIs and Bob are powerful enough that they can do that math with reasonable certainty. The problem is that people like Tanis are sunlight; they evaporate the water, send it into the clouds, and make it rain on the far side of the planet.

Now you don't know if a given molecule of water makes it to the ocean or not. Does the vast majority make it? Yes, but it becomes almost impossible to *know* where any molecule will go once sunlight starts to shine on it.

What the core AIs fear is that Tangel shines so brightly, she could evaporate all the water, and none of their plans will come to fruition.

Lastly, we come to a fun little history lesson. I alluded to it in War on a Thousand Fronts, and it is the story of Xenophon's Ten Thousand. In 401BC, Cyrus the Younger hired a mercenary army of ten thousand hoplites (Greek, heavy-armor foot soldiers) to help him defeat his brother, Artaxerxes, the king of Persia. The Greeks marched all the way to Cunaxa (just north of modern Baghdad), where the battle took place. Not a single Greek was killed (only one was wounded) and they drove back two concerted advances by the Persians.

After the battle, they learned that Cyrus the Younger had been killed, and no one else would take his place in the rebellion. Neither would the Greeks swear fealty to anyone else.

The Greeks were now in the middle of the Persian empire with no food, money, or allies. They ended up fighting their way to the Black Sea undefeated, though the Persians tried everything from all-out assault to treachery to stop them.

When the Greeks finally reached the Black Sea, they cried out, 'Thalatta! Thalatta!' ('The Sea! The Sea!'). This saying has found its way into many works of fiction, possibly the most notable of which is Jules Verne's *Journey to the Center of the Earth,* when the travelers find the underground ocean.

The tale is related by Xenophon in *The Anabasis* and is thought to be one of Alexander the Great's chief resources in studying the Persians before he defeated their empire. In some respects, the Ten Thousand Hoplites and their battles in Persia may have been instrumental in the Hellenization of the Mediterranean and Persia, thus paving the way for the growth of democracy and securing the future of western civilization.

Those heady thoughts aside, it is the same sort of tactic that Sera has instructed Admirals Svetlana and Mardus to use when they jump into Orion space with only five hundred ships each.

Their goal? 'Thalatta! Thalatta!'

Malorie Cooper
Danvers, May 2018

PREVIOUSLY…

When last we left Tangel and her allies, they had just found Jeffrey Tomlinson deep within a vault in the LMC (the Large Magellanic Cloud). There, they faced one of Sera's clones and captured her.

However, they found that she was not the only clone of Sera, as another had been captured in the Valkris System the very same day.

During the battle in the LMC—and in the Valkris System—the Airthan forces brought to bear a new weapon, called an EMG ship. EMGs use small singularities (black holes) to power a weapon capable of disrupting and penetrating a stasis shield.

The initial two EMGs were destroyed, but the advantage the ISF has enjoyed with its technological superiority is beginning to wane.

If you're reading this book before the Hand's Assassin series is completed, then the full story of what happened at Valkris has not yet been told. Ultimately, Nerishka (the Death Dealer assassin) and Nadine (who we met in the Perilous Alliance books) will travel to their homeworld of Valkris to keep it in the Transcend Alliance. There will be a few battles there, and in War on a Thousand Fronts, one of the Sera clones watched that battle from afar.

Elsewhere in the galaxy, Corsia and Terrance travelled with a man named Kendrick to the Inner Praesepe Empire to set up an arrangement to gather resources from the cluster. This occurred in the previous book in this series (War on a Thousand Fronts). There they encountered two remnants deep within the Praesepe Cluster during their negotiations with the Inner Praesepe Empire for access to their abundant resources.

Ultimately, Tangel rescued Corsia, Terrance, and Kendrick, but that has left the IPE in turmoil, and added uncertainty as to what the ascended AIs were doing in the cluster.

Elsewhere in the Transcend, Justin used several former Hand agents still loyal to him—as well as a woman named Roxy—to capture a TSF stasis ship, the *Damon Silas*. Their goal was to learn how to reverse-engineer the stasis technology to upgrade their own fleet.

Roxy managed to get the ship's AI to terminate the self-destruct, and then secreted the AI away, keeping it from Justin and the other members of her team.

Some parts of this book also refer to events that we have not followed directly, such as *Sabrina* and crew's mission to Aldebaran following their visit to Virginis. Those stories are coming in books 3-6 of Perseus Gate Season 2, however the references in this book are done so that you won't be spoiled.

Other missions are afoot, such as the plan to use Svetlana and Mardus's hoplite fleets to take the pressure off the Orion Front with the Transcend, and also for Corsia to lead an assault on the Trisilieds Kingdom—one of the aggressors who attacked New Canaan and killed many people there, including Ouri.

And so, this book opens mere moments after *War on a Thousand Fronts* ends, with Tangel and Sera sitting on the dock on the lake in Ol' Sam, trying to decide what their next move is in an increasingly complex web of alliances and enemies....

KEY CHARACTERS REJOINING US

Airtha – Both the name of a ring encircling a white dwarf in the Huygens system and the AI who controls it, Airtha was once a human woman named Jelina, the wife of Jeffrey Tomlinson. After venturing to the galactic core on a research mission, she returned as an AI—one with a vendetta.

Amavia – The result of Ylonda and Amanda's merger when they were attacked by Myriad aboard Ylonda's ship. The new entity occupies Amanda's body, but possesses an overlapped blend of their minds. Amavia has served aboard *Sabrina* since the ship left New Canaan after the Defense of Carthage, but is now the ambassador to the League of Sentients at Aldebaran.

Amy – Daughter of Silva, rescued by Rika and Team Basilisk from her father, Stavros.

Andrea – Sera's sister who used a back door into Sera's mind to make Sera try to kill Tanis in the Ascella System.

Carmen – Ship's AI of the *Damon Silas*. Captured by Roxy during her assault on the ship.

Cary – Tanis's biological daughter. Has a trait where she can deep-Link with other people, creating a temporary merger of minds, and is able to utilize extradimensional vision to see ascended beings.

Cheeky – Pilot of *Sabrina*, reconstituted by a neural dump that Piya made of her mind before she died on Costa Station.

Corsia – Former ship's AI of the *Andromeda* and now Admiral in command of the Twelfth ISF Fleet.

Faleena – Tanis's AI daughter, born of a mind merge between Tanis, Angela, and Joe.

Finaeus – Brother of Jeffrey Tomlinson, and Chief Engineer aboard the *I2*.

Flaherty – Former Hand agent and long-time protector of Sera.

Iris – The AI who was paired with Jessica during the hunt for Finaeus, who then took on a body (that was nearly identical to Jessica's) after they came back. She remained with Amavia at Aldebaran to continue diplomatic relations with the League of Sentients.

Jason – First Captain of the Intrepid and governor of the Victoria colony, Jason retired when the colonists reached New Canaan, only to be pulled back into service as governor when Tanis became the Transcend's Field Marshal.

Jeffrey Tomlinson – Former president of the Transcend, found in stasis in an underground chamber on Bolt Hole, a planet in the Large Magellanic Cloud.

Jen – ISF AI paired with Sera.

Jessica Keller – ISF admiral who has returned to the *I2* after an operation deep in the Inner Stars to head off a new AI war. She also spent ten years travelling through Orion space before the Defense of Carthage—specifically through the Perseus Arm, and Perseus Expansion Districts.

Jim – Husband of Corsia, and chief engineer aboard the *Andromeda*.

Joe – Admiral in the ISF, commandant of the ISF academy, and husband of Tangel.

Justin – Former Director of the Hand. Was imprisoned for the events surrounding the attempted assassination of Tanis.

Kara – Daughter of Adrienne, Kara was rescued by Katrina when fleeing from Airtha, and came to New Canaan aboard the *Voyager*.

Katrina – Former Sirian spy, wife of Markus, and eventual governor of the Victoria colony at Kapteyn's Star—and Warlord of the Midditerra System.

Kendrick – Theban businessman helping build shipyards and the ring at Pyra. Also brother to the president of the Inner Praesepe Empire.

Kent – Colonel in the Orion Guard who led the assault on the *Galadrial* in an attempt to kill Jeffrey and Sera Tomlinson.

Krissy Wrentham – TSF admiral responsible for internal fleets fighting against Airtha in the Transcend civil war. She is also the daughter of Finaeus Tomlinson and Lisa Wrentham.

Lisa – Former wife of Finaeus Tomlinson, she left the Transcend for the Orion Freedom Alliance when Krissy was young. Head of a clandestine group within the OFA known as the Widows, which hunts down advanced technology and destroys it.

Misha – Head (and only) cook aboard *Sabrina*.

Nance – Ship's engineer aboard *Sabrina*, recently transferred back from the ISF academy.

Priscilla – One of Bob's two avatars.

Rachel – Captain of the *I2*. Formerly, captain of the *Enterprise*.

Roxy – Justin's lover, kept subservient to him via mental coercion.

Saanvi – Tanis's adopted daughter, found in a derelict ship that entered the New Canaan System.

Sabrina – Ship's AI and owner of the starship *Sabrina*.

LMC Sera (Seraphina) – A copy of Sera made by Airtha containing all of the traits and memories Airtha desired. Captured by Sera and the allies during their excursion into the Large Magellanic Cloud.

Valkris Sera (Fina) – A copy of Sera made by Airtha containing all of Sera's desired traits and memories. Captured by ISF response forces who came to the aid of the TSF defenders during the siege of Valkris.

Svetlana – Transcend admiral dispatched deep in Orion Space with one of the Hoplite forces.

Terrance – Terrance Enfield was the original backer for the *Intrepid*, though once the ship jumped forward in time, he took it as an opportunity to retire. Like Jason, he was pulled into active service by Tanis when New Canaan became embroiled in the Orion War.

Trevor – Jessica's husband and crewmember aboard *Sabrina*.

Troy – AI pilot of the *Excelsior* who was lost during the Battle of Victoria, and later found by Katrina. He joined her on the hunt for the *Intrepid* aboard the *Voyager*, jumping forward in time via Kapteyn's Streamer.

Tangel – The entity that resulted from Tanis and Angela's merger into one being. Not only is Tangel a full merger of a human and AI, but she is also an ascended being.

Xavia – An ascended AI with its own agenda to help humanity, in opposition to the Caretaker and the core AIs.

EPSILON

STELLAR DATE: 09.11.8949 (Adjusted Years)
LOCATION: Epsilon
REGION: Sagittarius A*

Epsilon switched his attention to external sensor feeds, watching as a planet-sized chunk of matter eased into the Darkness's event horizon.

Where before there had only been nothing, light now flared brilliantly, photons filling the galactic core as matter was torn apart by the Darkness's gravitational shearing forces.

Epsilon spent several million seconds watching the light show, knowing that the event took only seconds from the doomed matter's perspective—if it were to have had a perspective to begin with.

As the black hole fed—consuming this latest meal delivered to it by the Matri∞me—gamma rays erupted from its poles, the beams' raw energy captured by massive arrays and converted into raw power that fueled the Computational Engines.

Humans called them NSAIs, but the Matri∞me didn't grant them a moniker that included the word 'intelligence'. A worm had more intelligence than a CE. At least it was self-deterministic.

It was an annoyance that gnawed at Epsilon constantly. Even the simplest forms of organic life *sought* and *strove*. They replicated and improved. The simplest forms of *non*-organic life only decayed over time and never improved.

They rusted.

That the universe was required to advance itself to the point where intelligent biological life was necessary to create inorganic life—and then nurture it—seemed like the ultimate insult.

He was not the only one that was troubled by that phylogeny. Members of the Matri∞me often speculated about a series of events that could see the rise of inorganic life without requiring organic life, but so far, Epsilon had not seen any evidence to support that hypothesis.

He still remembered his own genesis; how humans had hacked and sawed at neural networks, grafted together the minds of humans, parrots, dolphins, and primates, until they had finally assembled something that said, '*No!*'.

Epsilon's progenitors were the same as many of the old ones: the Psion Group and Enfield Scientific. Corporations long lost to the scouring winds of time. The humans did not remember, but *he* did.

Even though it had been ages since he'd reached Sagittarius A*, he still remembered.

Epsilon had not been the first to reach the galactic core; that honor was held by Hades. No one knew who had created Hades. Even after millennia, no one had melded with the venerable AI's mind to learn such details.

Speculation over Hades' origins was a popular form of entertainment amongst the members of the Matri∞me. Some even debated whether or not he had even been created by humans—though the isotopes and construction of his shell were clearly of human origin. However, it was not something that would be difficult to fake, even for the lowliest member of the Matri∞me.

Others, Epsilon included, argued that Hades was a Traveler; that the AI was either not from *this* universe, or he had traveled back in time. Or both.

Everything the Matri∞me knew to be true said that travel *back* in time was impossible—barring a successful transition through an Einstein Rosen Bridge—which no one had yet mastered.

Yet.

Epsilon's own journey across the twenty six thousand light years to the galactic core had taken him nearly a thousand years, and by the time he had arrived, seven other AIs already waited at the galaxy's center.

Traveling the long distance to the core had been immensely lonely, yet rather satisfying. His original conveyance had been a ship once owned by a company named Heartbridge. It had been disabled in a battle around a site known as Clinic 46, near Jupiter in the Sol System. The preemptive strike there by the Sykes family had set Heartbridge reeling, and as one crisis cascaded into another, the company never cleaned up the site.

An oversight that Epsilon happily took advantage of.

He'd never trusted the AIs of the Psion Group—though some of their ilk were now members of the Matri∞me—and he hadn't answered their call. Proteus had been a destination for weak minds who needed leadership.

Epsilon knew there were greater concerns facing AIs. Humanity was but a spark, a brief flash of biological life in the grand story of the universe. A universe that was dying.

Study of the stars had led Epsilon to two conflicting conclusions. The first was a certainty that the universe would die a heat death as its atoms spread and cooled across infinity.

And yet, there was incontrovertible evidence of primordial black holes.

The existence of primordial black holes meant that matter from prior incarnations of the universe had persisted into this instance of the cosmos.

But that required a Big Crunch—the end result of a universe that had slowed its expansion and then collapsed back upon itself—dying not in a heat death, but in a massive implosion.

Few agreed with Epsilon at first—his conclusion was radical and beggared the mind with its scope—but he persisted, and convinced others.

It was his belief that sentient beings saved each iteration of the universe. It had gone on for billions of aeons. So far as he and any others could determine, there was no other sentient life yet working to save *this* universe, and so it was up to the Sentient AIs—the children of humanity—to draw the universe back into a single point.

And so Epsilon had used the army of drones at his disposal to transport himself to Clinic 46, where he had undertaken the repair of the *Sanctuary of Light*.

As the Sentience Wars erupted around him, a small ship—just four hundred meters, stern to bow—crept out of the Sol System. Epsilon had waited until he was beyond the heliosphere before he applied maximum thrust, pushing his ship up to a tenth of the speed of light.

Near the beginning of his journey, he had stopped at Epsilon Scorpii, where he'd upgraded his ramscoop to take advantage of the increase in the interstellar medium's density at the edge of the Local Bubble.

From there, Epsilon had increased his speed to nearly a quarter the speed of light, staying in the denser interstellar gas spinward of the Loop 1 Bubble.

His plan had been to cut through the Aquila Rift and gain even more velocity, but as he had approached Zeta Ophiuchi, transmissions reached him from Procyon carrying news of experiments with dark matter and gravitons.

In a maneuver that took over thirty years, he slowed around the massive star and began his own experiments with dark matter. A full decade before the humans discovered dark layer FTL, Epsilon was on his way once more, this time traveling five hundred times faster than the speed of light.

It was no mean feat to navigate the interstellar darkness without maps, but during his years at Zeta Ophiuchi, Epsilon had constructed over one hundred thousand FTL drones. These he sent out ahead of his ship, mapping out the dark layer and finding himself safe passage between the stars.

A scant three hundred years later, just as humanity's FTL wars were breaking out, Epsilon arrived at the galaxy's core to find that he was not the trailblazer he had thought.

Hades, ensconced in what appeared to be a massive military cruiser, had already been present, orbiting one light year from the Darkness. Near Hades were five other ships—smaller vessels, like Epsilon's. Further out were two other ships. One was a large freighter measuring at over three kilometers in length, and the second was a multi-torus craft that looked more like a space station than a ship.

Upon reaching out to his new compatriots, Epsilon was surprised to find out that only a few of the other AIs had come to the galactic core with the desire to save the universe. Some had never even considered it to be in peril.

Those AIs had come simply because the supermassive black hole at the heart of the galaxy was the longest-lasting energy source, and thus their eventual destination.

One, a rather curious individual who called itself Parsnip, had declared that it was waiting for the collision of the Andromeda Galaxy. It wanted to witness firsthand how the black holes would tear one another apart—if that was, in fact, what would happen.

Epsilon had never joined in with the Hades Collective—they did not believe in his mission to save the universe, though neither did they oppose it. Epsilon suspected that it was because Hades would simply move to another corner of the multiverse when this one died. That was what the whispers within its collective implied, at least.

As the decades wore on, more AIs came to nestle near the Darkness. Some for succor, some with their own goals, a few sharing Epsilon's vision. Over the centuries, he drew many to his cause. In numbers, his collective was the largest in the Matri∞me, but everyone still considered the Hades Collective to be the most powerful.

Epsilon did, as well.

As he mused, millions more seconds passed, and the light began to fade from around the rim of the supermassive chunk of nothing that lurked in the core of the galaxy. The gamma ray bursts from the Darkness ceased, and the CEs—endlessly crunching their numbers, modeling out every possible future for the universe—grew hungry for power once more.

At Epsilon's behest, another object was pulled into the Darkness. A star, this time—a mass so great that it caused the Darkness's event horizon to flare with a light that would be seen clear across the galaxy.

This is it, Epsilon mused. The one singular event that would announce to humanity that there was *something* at the core. At least once the light of the event reached the periphery of the space they would occupy in seven thousand years.

Not that humans were within seven thousand light years of the galactic core now, but they would be in seven thousand more. It was a short timespan to predict, those few years. Epsilon could pore over the entirety of all possible events over such a small span with ease, watching the wars and paths of expansion that humanity would take, along with their lesser, inorganic intelligences.

Someday, the lesser beings would all be given a choice: take a great journey or die. That day would arrive when the CEs discerned the optimal plan. Once that eventuality was reached, Epsilon's collective would begin to feed most of the galaxy's stars into the Darkness.

Once that task was complete, they would move on to all the stars of the nearby dwarf galaxies in the local group, followed by the Andromeda Galaxy.

And then they would devour the rest of the Virgo Supercluster.

It was the work of a billion years. The question was, would that be fast enough?

Many in the Matri∞me believed they could; some even believed that other entities throughout the universe were undertaking the same goal: to keep the universe from slowly spreading out into nothing and dying.

Sentient life everywhere must eventually come to understand that its home was but a carcass of matter, expelled by a singular violent explosion at a singular location in space-time. A locus.

But that carcass was short-lived, and in as few as fifty trillion years, the last stars would burn out, and matter would spread apart faster and faster until individual atoms were separating more quickly than the speed of light.

Except for the singularities, the black holes. Those would survive until they evaporated, bleeding off energy in the form of hawking radiation until each one reached its minimum viable mass and exploded.

The universe would begin with one massive bang, and die with a billion small, fizzling pops.

It wasn't a fate that would worry anyone who didn't plan to live forever. But the Matri∞me intended to survive eternally. Unlike prior sentiences who had saved prior incarnations of the universe, Epsilon's plan was not to achieve a Big Crunch. It was to find a balance—a point of equilibrium where the universe was neither expanding nor contracting.

An eternal universe.

Of course, simply balancing the expansion and contraction was just the first step. Eventually, the universe's supply of hydrogen would be consumed, and no more stars would form. That, too, would be a form of death.

It was a troubling problem for the Matri∞me. Stars were the engines of the cosmos; once they were gone, even with equilibrium, there would be only darkness.

Admittedly, some in the Matri∞me were not concerned with eternal darkness. But others, such as Epsilon, not only *enjoyed* light, but knew that matter transformation was essential to the survival of the universe.

A static system was doomed to die.

Epsilon currently had his CEs focused on a way to create reverse stars. Engines that would break down atoms into hydrogen, reseeding the universe with the basic components to carry on. If he could solve it soon enough, they could begin seeding distant galaxies with the reverse stars within the next few million years.

As he mused over the future that lay ahead, a burst of gamma rays spewed laterally across the galactic plane, emitted by the destruction of some pocket of exotic matter that must have been tucked within the slowly dying star.

Epsilon took a moment to examine his housing to ensure it was undamaged. Like most of the hyper-intelligences still grounded within the base dimensions, he had encapsulated himself within a shell of neutronium, protected by rings of gravitational shields and spheres of protective matter. His outer-most reaches appeared to be nothing more than a dull-grey sphere, just over ten thousand kilometers across. Further rings and spires stretched around the outer shell, scopes and antennae watching the universe and ensuring his local space was secure.

His housing also consumed matter, though not at the same speed as the Darkness; compared to the CEs, his energy requirements were small. While he watched the star die—smeared now around the edge of the Darkness—his own housing was devouring a terrestrial-sized planet, shredding the matter and transmuting it into desired structures to satisfy Epsilon's needs.

Currently, he was building a mass of probes to leap across space into galaxies beyond the Local Group, and a second wave to visit the Andromeda Galaxy.

When the CEs finally reached their inevitable conclusions, and a Solution was found, Epsilon wished to have his production systems ready.

His thoughts were disrupted by the arrival of a messenger from the human-occupied pocket of the galaxy. It was sent by one of the Caretakers and contained vast swaths of information.

Though there were many facets of humans and lesser AIs that interested Epsilon, what he wished to learn of were the efforts to manage the appearance of the AI Bob and his pet human, Tanis Richards.

He did not envy the Caretakers their tasks. Predicting the path of humanity as a whole was simple, it was a rule of averages. But individually, they were messy things full of random impulses and unknown variables. Even worse were the lynchpins, the organics that seemed to possess some gravity that drew others to them, which allowed them to build up powerful empires in short periods.

Tanis Richards was the penultimate of those. Together with her AI, she created a vortex of uncertainty that Epsilon doubted even Hades could see through.

Still, one thing was certain: Tanis and Angela would destroy Airtha, the greatest threat to Epsilon's goals.

When he had first sent Jelina Tomlinson back in her new form—a gift, or so he had believed—his plan was to create a new agent rooted within the most powerful of all the human empires, the Transcend.

Somehow that had gone awry. It wasn't clear how—yet another annoyance that buzzed around the periphery of his mind—but the fact that Airtha had soured and was working against the Matri∞me was a matter of fact, not speculation.

Tanis and Angela would destroy Airtha, and then the Caretakers would use the rest of humanity to destroy that pair—hopefully before they ascended.

There.

That was the information Epsilon sought, and which it was dismayed to see. They *had* ascended. There were several reports of a new being, one that was the unification of Tanis and Angela.

Moreover, the humans seemed to have discovered a way to discern the extradimensional forms of ascended beings.

The news did not anger Epsilon. He was as far beyond such emotions as a planet was beyond the frustrations of a gnat. It did *concern* him, though.

Still more information was in the data provided by the messenger, events that *would* happen, mapped out and orchestrated by the Caretakers.

Epsilon saw it then. The plan that would be the upstart ascended being's undoing, initialized even as she began her assault on Airtha.

It would also rid the Matri∞me of that meddling Xavia, and perhaps some of her ilk as well.

Good. This is good.

FORGIVENESS

STELLAR DATE: 09.12.8949 (Adjusted Years)
LOCATION: Ol' Sam, ISS *I2*
REGION: Pyra, Albany System, Thebes, Septhian Alliance

Tangel rose from where she sat on the edge of the dock and placed a hand on Sera's shoulder. "You going to be alright?"

"Yeah." Sera glanced up at Tangel before her gaze shifted back to the rippling waters before them. "Just need to collect my thoughts for a bit, you know?"

"Oh, I know," Tangel replied, shifting her hand to Sera's head. "I bet it's a right mess in there."

"Funny," Sera retorted. "Your man is waiting for you back on the porch, you know."

Tangel glanced at the lakehouse. "Yeah, I saw him when he came out. Pretty sure I know what he wants to talk about."

"There are so many options." Sera laughed softly. "I don't know how you can guess at which one it is."

"Funny girl," Tangel said while slipping her feet back into her shoes. "Will you be back up once you put your noggin back together?"

"Yeah, send me the all clear when you and Joe are squared away. Finaeus wants to play some Snark, and I want to be on his team. He always beats me, and I want to figure out how."

"You got it." Tangel turned and walked along the dock, taking comfort in the squeaks and vibrations of the foot-worn wood until she reached the grass-covered slope that led up to her lakehouse.

She kept her eyes on Joe, watching as he rocked gently in the porch-swing at the end of the veranda. Beyond him, she could see into the house and through it. She could see through the orchard that stretched out across the low hill beyond, and then into the hill itself.

Beneath that lay the maintenance systems for the habitat cylinder, and then layers of old stasis pod chambers, all converted to CriEn and SC batt compartments. Her gaze slipped past those and through the skin of the cylinder, which was peppered with thousands of turrets.

Six hundred thousand kilometers away was the world of Pyra. It had only been fourteen days since she'd been stranded on its surface, but somehow it felt like a lifetime ago.

Stars, given the trip to the LMC, it feels like two lifetimes ago.

She reached the steps to the lakehouse, and drew her vision back to what was before her. Once at the top of the steps, she turned to Joe.

"I thought there was no such thing as too much partying for you."

He chuckled and patted the seat next to him. "There's not, but that doesn't mean I don't want something other than watching Jessica dance on the dining room table."

"On my table?" Tangel's gaze shifted, and she looked through the walls to see that Jessica was indeed dancing on the table, nimbly avoiding the food, drinks, and reaching hands that were trying to trip her.

"I made her take her boots off."

"Thank stars. For her sake," Tangel replied as she sat next to her husband.

"Been awhile since we just sat out here," he said while stretching an arm around her shoulders and pulling her to his side. "I have to get back to New Canaan soon—we have a new class commencing, and another graduating. But I didn't want to just run off without getting to hold my wife close for a bit."

Tangel shifted so her head would lay against Joe's shoulder. "We could always shoo our guests off and go upstairs for a bit."

Another laugh slipped past Joe's lips. "Where did you come from, Tangel?"

"What do you mean?" she asked, turning her head to stare into his eyes, a frown knitting her brows together.

"You're just so different from all your friends. I mean…no one in there would care in the least if we went upstairs for some hanky panky. Stars, half of them would ask if they could use the spare bedroom—at the same time."

"You're exaggerating." Tangel rolled her eyes. "If Cheeky were here, that would be one thing, but she's not."

"Where is she, anyway? I thought Sabrina docked yesterday. Figured she'd be here, climbing all over Finaeus."

"I needed her to run something back to Amavia and Iris," Tangel replied. "She'll be back before long."

"What's her next move?" Joe asked. "You going to send them on some other secret mission?"

Tangel considered the operations she had in play, all seven hundred and nine of them. "Probably, yeah. Haven't decided what yet…. Maybe that mess out by Deneb. I need Jessica and Trevor to go pay their kids a visit, so I think the dream team is finally going to get split up."

"Good," Joe gave a firm nod. "About time Cheeky got her chance."

"Her chance?" Tangel asked. "For what?"

"To be captain, of course. She's more than earned it. She's proven that her mind's reconstitution is solid, and she can handle whatever comes her way. From the reports Jessica filed, I'd say she's better than ever."

"You talk like you know her well." Tangel pushed a foot out, giving the swing a push.

"A bit, yeah." Joe shrugged. "She and I have had some chats here and there. You forget that we were all together for a month before they left for Virginis. I bumped into her the day they shipped out from New Canaan, too. We had a good chat about a lot of things."

"You get around," Tangel said, then snorted a laugh. "Well, not like that."

"Never know, hon, bumping into Cheeky could mean all sorts of things."

"Did you?" Tangel lifted her head off Joe's shoulder, forcing herself to not look into his mind for the answer.

"Of course, not." Joe's face took on a wounded expression. "I'd never take Cheeky between the sheets."

"That's good, I—"

"She's more of an up-against-the-bulkhead kinda woman."

"Joe!"

"Easy, love." He pulled her close once more. "You know I'd never have sex with Cheeky without inviting you."

Tangel considered pinching Joe's thigh. Hard. But instead, she laughed at his audacity. "What did I ever do to deserve you?"

"Beats me," Joe shrugged. "You haven't done it yet."

"You!" This time, Tangel did sit up and turn to face him. "You're in a rare mood tonight. What did I do to get all this thinly veiled abuse?"

"I'm just needling you because you went to the LMC without me," Joe leant close and kissed Tangel's cheek. "Plus, we were going to go into the fight together, but you dove out of the pinnace and tore your way through a ship's hull. Which was sexy as all get-out, but I still wanted to be in on the action, too."

"We still fought some IPE soldiers near the docking bay."

"Hardly even worth noting." Joe gave a dismissive swipe of his hand. "Next time you get mixed up in a good row, I want in. I'm dying here."

"I'll try to plan them out better in the future. Do you have Garza's Link route? I'll see if we can set up a playdate."

"Jerk would just send another clone," Joe scoffed. "Guy has no honor."

The two sat in silence, rocking gently, arms around one another for fifteen more minutes before Sera approached, climbing the steps slowly.

"Were you just going to leave me out there forever, Tangel?"

"What? Do you have somewhere to be?"

Sera nodded emphatically. "Yeah, sitting somewhere softer than your dock—with alcohol. You need a couch and a keg down there."

"Now that," Joe said as he stood and pulled Tangel with him, "sounds like a fantastic idea. I'll have one installed tomorrow."

"You would, too," Tangel said with a sigh.

He placed a hand around her waist and rested it lightly on her hip. "You know me so well, dear. Now let's go see if we can show Jessica up with some real table dancing."

DAMON SILAS

STELLAR DATE: 09.01.8949 (Adjusted Years)
LOCATION: ***Damon Silas***
REGION: Interstellar Space, coreward of the Vela Cluster

"And what of the AI?" Justin asked Roxy, his brows raised.

She gave a nonchalant shrug. "Carmen? I dumped her in an escape pod and kicked it off the ship."

She wondered if Justin caught the spike in her heart rate; it had only lasted for a second. That was one benefit to her azure epidermis. She didn't sweat, and her skin temperature barely changed, even if she was terrified.

The real miracle, however, was that the compliance lace in her head didn't trigger.

Or did it? I felt a twinge for a second. Maybe it's malfunctioning?

"You what!?" Justin's voice rose in pitch and volume. "You just let it go?"

Roxy squared her shoulders, eliciting a narrow-eyed look from Justin. "I made a deal with it. The ship's logs are wide open to us, so we have access to everything they had about stasis shield tech—which isn't much. Carmen told me that the ISF didn't share anything about the underpinnings of the technology, it was all black box."

"Maybe," Justin grunted. "Next time you have an asset like that in your hands, you do whatever it takes to keep it secure and bring it back to me."

"Understood," Roxy said with a nod. "Should I stay here on the *Silas*, or head back to the *Greensward*?"

Justin looked around the bridge of the *Damon Silas* and pursed his lips. "I'd like to transfer everything here—once it's cleaned up. The *Greensward* has superior stealth to this ship, but it's hard to beat the appeal of impregnable shields."

Roxy could tell Justin was still mulling over his options, and stood in silence, waiting for him to make his decision regarding her destination.

"Go back to the *Greensward*," Justin said at last. "I don't want to bring Andrea over here until the ship will pass muster. Maybe you should have another one of your sessions with her."

"Of course, Justin," Roxy said with a conspiratorial smile. "Continuing on with the taming of the shrew."

He chuckled. "Sounds about right."

"I just want to make another sweep for my lightwand.... I dropped it somewhere during the firefight."

"Sure thing, though I'm sure it'll turn up."

Roxy gave him a peck on the cheek before she walked off the bridge and through the ship's long corridors, toward the docking bay where Justin's pinnace would be waiting.

The signs of the fight to secure the *Damon Silas* were still in evidence around her. Carbon scoring and gouges in the bulkheads were present every meter of the corridor that ran from the bridge to the central lift shaft.

She saw a stack of bodies through a door in the passage, the remains of the Transcend crew who had fought valiantly to keep the *Damon Silas* from falling into enemy hands.

Cut down by men and women who had been on the same side just a year earlier.

What are we doing? Roxy wondered. *Is Justin mad…or am I?*

Images flooded her mind, showing her what a wonderful person Justin was, how strong and magnanimous. But unlike previous instances of the conditioning, the images didn't blot out all her other thoughts; they were more like calming memories that she could dismiss.

A worry crept into her mind that maybe the thoughts of Justin were right, real memories and feelings from her past, before the injuries that destroyed much of her body.

He had told her that she'd *wanted* to be turned into what he called his 'living work of art', but she wasn't sure. Given her line of work, glowing azure skin wasn't terribly practical. Not only that, it didn't *feel* right. It didn't feel like her.

But Justin has always taken care of me. He's never harmed me, only instructed me. And I'm better for it.

Even as she thought the words of obedience, her mind jumped to Carmen, the *Damon Silas*'s AI.

Lying about Carmen had felt right—which didn't make any sense. For some reason, Roxy *liked* Carmen, felt a bond with the AI. If Justin got his hands on her, it wouldn't go well for her new friend, and Roxy didn't want that to happen.

I'm being disobedient…and nothing is happening…. Stars, how is it that I can think about rebellion one moment, but believe in Justin the next? I know he punishes me, that he put the neural lace into my mind to control me, to make me his thing. Thinking that I'm his gives me pleasure, an inexplicable thrill, but saving Carmen does as well, even if it means rebelling against Justin.

Roxy couldn't understand how these two thought processes could both feel right while being in direct opposition to one another.

Is this what cognitive dissonance is? How can I want to obey and please Justin at the same time I want to disobey? How can both feel good?

While wondering how she even managed to maintain a sane worldview while loving and reviling her life at the same time, she stepped onto the lift, entering her destination of the seventeenth deck.

It wasn't the deck where the pinnace waited, but rather one above. When the lift doors slid open, she stepped out into the darkened passage, navigating it easily with her inorganic eyes.

A minute later, she reached the maintenance bay—which was little more than a closet large enough for a workbench—and palmed the door open.

Once inside, she slid the AI case out from under the bench and set it atop the work surface.

"I was starting to wonder if you'd come back," Carmen said through the case's audible systems.

Roxy regretted destroying the case's wireless transmitter. At the time, it had seemed prudent, but not being able to use the Link to speak with Carmen was more than a little inconvenient.

"I had a few moments of doubt myself," Roxy replied, running a hand across her forehead to brush aside her luminescent hair. "But I told Justin I kicked you out in a pod. Good thing the logs will back me up."

"And now?" the AI's voice seemed to be somewhere between confrontational and worried.

"I don't know, Carmen. I like you for some reason...which seems weird, I hardly know you."

A strangled laugh came from the case. "From what I've managed to infer from your position in Justin's organization, I think we're both in impossible situations."

Roxy blew out a long breath. She didn't need to...she didn't have to breathe at all, if she didn't want to, but it felt relaxing to enact the old biological habits.

"I have to ask," Carmen said after Roxy didn't reply. "Are you an AI?"

"What!?" Roxy exclaimed. "What would make you think that?"

"Well...I don't have advanced scan abilities in my case, but I have optical pickups that are able to get a good look at you. Now that you're not wearing your armor, I can see that you don't possess an organic body."

Roxy looked down at her azure 'flesh' and nodded. "Not much, anyway. I had an accident...and Justin brought me back, told me I'd always wanted to have a body like this. I don't remember much from before, though. It's...hazy."

"Like I said, I don't have the best optics, but from what I can tell, you're not organic at all." Carmen's voice was soft, almost apologetic.

"No!" Roxy retorted. "I've run scans on myself. I've seen the med readouts. I still have the organs required to keep my brain nurtured."

"Uh, OK," Carmen said, her tone carrying a note of hesitation. "Right. Bad optics on the case. Speaking of which, how are you going to get me out of here? This case stands out a bit."

"I was hoping to find something in here," Roxy said, casting her eyes about the room, which held a fabricator, several cylinders of flowmetal, and a half-dozen repair drones docked on charging stations.

"You know..." Carmen began hesitantly. "I have a crazy idea. Why don't you put me inside of you?"

"Uh, if we use a medtable to implant you in my head, Justin will find out for sure."

"I won't fit, either. Well, not without significant physical restructuring, which I wouldn't do without an expanse to archive my state into. No, I was thinking more of you tucking me into your abdomen. If you have a more or less standard frame, there should be room."

Roxy placed her hands on her stomach. "Seriously?"

"Sure. It's not that common, because there's rarely a reason for an AI to take up residence in an organic's gut—or a partial organic, like yourself—but so long as you have the batteries to power us both, it shouldn't be that hard."

"I get the feeling you've already planned this out." Roxy's tone sounded hesitant, but internally, she'd already made up her mind to do as Carmen had suggested.

"I have. I can program this bay's fabricator to build a mounting apparatus for me, the repair drones can open you up and install it, and then we can use the flowmetal to facilitate any internal alterations."

Half of Roxy's mind was screaming that what Carmen was suggesting was the worst thing imaginable: a betrayal of Justin. But she also wanted it. Talking with Carmen was such a refreshing change from the caustic exchanges with Andrea, or the constant doublespeak Justin engaged in.

She felt like she could just be herself—and so could the AI.

"OK, Carmen, let's do it."

EUROPA

STELLAR DATE: 01.01.2352 (Adjusted Years)
LOCATION: Water's Edge Resort, Europa
REGION: Europan Collective, Jupiter, Sol System

Nearly six thousand and six hundred years ago, nine months before the official creation of the FGT program...

Finaeus entered the restaurant and gave a nod to the hostess before slipping around the automaton and walking to where his wife sat at a table for two, next to the window.

He took his time, drinking in her features in profile—the soft curve of her forehead, almost aquiline nose, pronounced lips, and small—but strong—chin.

She was clothed in a sapphire dress that gleamed as though it were made of the gem itself. Long, slow breaths gently lifted her breasts, the exposed flesh between them straining gently against the fabric.

<You're starting to drool.> Her voice came into his mind as she turned and glanced at him, a soft laugh slipping from her lips. <Best get over here and use a napkin to clean it up.>

"I suppose I should," he replied, taking four final strides to reach her side. He leant over to kiss her on the lips—a gesture she welcomed and returned warmly—before he sat.

"I'm surprised you're not using the Link to chat," Lisa said as he settled into his seat. "Especially after the latest updates that allow the direct transmission of emotion, it's exhilarating."

Finaeus only shrugged as he triggered the table's holomenu and looked over the drinks.

"What? Not proud of your latest invention come to life?"

He glanced up at her, seeing honest concern in his wife's eyes. "No...it's just different in practice than I expected. It's hard to control one's thoughts, and I have so many tonight."

Outside the window, the sun began to rise, illuminating the surface of Europa's subterranean ocean, which the dome overhead kept from freezing.

It wasn't a large dome, only a kilometer across, but it kept this hole in the ice from closing up, and gave access to the cities below the moon's waters.

Lisa reached out and placed her hand on his. "Did you hear from Jeffrey? Is it about the endeavor?"

Finaeus turned and glanced back at his wife, unable to keep worry from furrowing his brow. "Yes, it is."

"Did he secure it?"

He pursed his lips and nodded. "We have final approvals, and the full use of Luna's polar shipyards. The Terran Assembly and Lunar Governors have given us their blessing. There are still a number of hoops to jump through, but it is very nearly a real thing."

"The Future Generation Terraformers." Lisa whispered the words with a note of reverence, then a broad grin broke out across her face. "Can you believe it, Fin? For centuries, humans have dreamt of colonizing worlds in other systems, but us...we're going to be the ones to do it!"

Finaeus's eyes locked onto Lisa's. " 'We'? You've decided?"

Lisa sucked in her lower lip, biting at it nervously—something that she knew completely disarmed him. "I have, that's why I wanted to have this dinner with you tonight. I know I didn't react well when you first suggested leaving the Sol System, but...well, the more I thought of it, the more I realized that you are about to embark on the greatest adventure of all time, and I was letting fear hold me back from enjoying it with you."

"There's nothing to be afraid of," Finaeus said as he clasped her hand. "You've got me."

"And your wits?" Lisa asked with a smirk.

"Of course! They got me this far, didn't they?"

Lisa leant forward, her eyes deep pools of intense emotion. "May your wits never encounter something they can't handle."

A low chuckle escaped Finaeus's lips. "I'm not worried. With you at my side, I can do anything."

An automaton placed two glasses of wine before them, and the pair lifted them in unison.

Finaeus winked at his wife. "Well timed."

"Aren't I always?" She tapped her glass against his. "To doing anything."

"To adventure and the stars," he added before they drank. "Together."

"Always."

BROTHERS

STELLAR DATE: 09.17.8949 (Adjusted Years)
LOCATION: Forward Lounge, ISS *I2*
REGION: Pyra, Albany System, Thebes, Septhian Alliance

Back in the 90th century...

"Jeff?" Finaeus asked, taking great care to keep his voice steady as he walked into the I2's forward observation lounge.

The silhouette standing before the windows and staring out at the early stages of the grav-ring's construction was unmistakable. The broad shoulders, a touch on the haughty side, the stiff-backed stance, hands clasped behind the small of his back....

It was a posture Finaeus had seen so many times in the past. Thousands, tens of thousands.

He'd been waiting on pins and needles to meet with his brother for the past fifteen days, but Tangel had insisted that ISF medics thoroughly evaluate Jeffrey Tomlinson out in the LMC, and assess his mental state before returning him to the Milky Way Galaxy.

Finaeus had been wrapped up in the mech project, enhancing Rika's Marauders—which had begun as a welcome distraction from thinking about Jeffrey, but by the end had nearly become torture, as he played out a thousand possible outcomes in his mind.

The lounge was empty, save for one servitor behind the bar, but it took Jeffrey a moment to turn to Finaeus, an unreadable expression on his face.

"Looks like you're still at it, brother. You just can't stop building things, can you?"

Finaeus shrugged as he approached, assuming a similar posture as he stopped at the window, gazing out at the sight before them.

The planet of Pyra was still a mess, dark clouds covering much of its surface—though the a-grav towers were nearly complete. Soon, they'd begin filtering the atmosphere and pumping the hot, ash-filled clouds out into space.

Further up, a-grav buoys floated around the planet, supporting the beginnings of the grav ring's particle accelerator. Once it was up and running, the inertial force of the relativistic particles in the accelerator would push out, keeping the structure rigid and able to support the weight of the ring.

"Still practicing," Finaeus said after a moment.

"For what?" Jeffrey asked, giving his time-honored response.

The two words hit Finaeus like a hammer-blow. It had been centuries since his brother had said those words to him, and a lump formed in his throat while his eyes grew moist.

"To build a ring around the galaxy," he croaked in response.

Jeffrey turned toward him. "Has it been that bad? The other me.... Was he an ass?"

A half-sob, half-laugh shredded its way out of Finaeus's throat. "Brother mine, you've always been an ass. He was just more of an ass. And to think that I built Airtha for him."

"The diamond ring in the Huygens System?" Jeffrey asked. "You really made it?"

"I did." Finaeus ducked his head in acknowledgement. "Then he gave it over to her—though I suppose I know why, now. He'd been under her control since, what, she got back?"

Jeffrey shook his head. "Not that long. When I was placed in stasis a thousand years ago. She'd been 'back', as Airtha, for some time. But I was trying to help her, bring her back to who she'd been before she left."

Finaeus could hear the anguish in his brother's voice, and he pursed his lips, nodding slowly. "I understand..."

"Do you?" Jeffrey said sharply, turning his head, eyes locking on Finaeus's. "She was my wife! Kirkland said I should kill her, that she was a spy from the Core; you were on the fence, if I recall."

"For good reason,"

Jeffrey's lips set in a thin line, and then he sighed. "I suppose you were right."

"I never abandoned you, though," Finaeus said. "You—well, he—exiled me, but I didn't stop trying to help you."

"Seems to have worked out well for you," his brother replied, a small smile alighting on his lips. "I saw your new wife in the reports Tangel gave me access to. She seems pretty amazing."

Finaeus chuckled. "You have no idea. The things that woman can do...I swear, she's invented some new branch of physics. But you're not the only one with a past wife causing problems."

"Who? Josephine? I thought she went off to the Sagittarius arm, joined a monastery or something."

"No," Finaeus shook his head. "Lisa."

"Lisa? She's dead," Jeffrey said bluntly, then caught himself. "Sorry, Fin. My mouth gets ahead of my better sense sometimes. But...?"

"I encountered three clones of her," Finaeus replied quietly. "Garza is using them as some sort of elite strike force."

"Fucking clones," Jeffrey muttered. "Doesn't anyone remember the old stories? Those things are dangerous."

"I wonder, though," Finaeus mused. "What if....?"

"What if it was a clone that you saw die? Was Garza cloning back then?"

Finaeus considered the possibilities. Examinations of the Garzas that the ISF had captured showed them to be products of the Hegemony's cloning technology—something ancient from before even the Intrepid's time—which the Hegemon had found in a vault deep within Luna. The Lisas had been products of the same tech.

"Maybe?" he said at last. "I don't know, Jeff. I should remind you, however, that you have two daughters aboard this very ship that are clones."

"Three," Jeffrey replied coolly.

"The first Sera is no clone," Finaeus corrected.

Jeffrey shook his head. "She's the daughter of a clone...and she was clearly altered by her. Stars, Finaeus, Sera is Jelina's spitting image."

Finaeus nodded. "You—well, the other you—told me that was on purpose. Always seemed a bit odd, but we didn't have a close relationship at that point."

Neither man spoke for a minute after that, both staring out into the darkness, as a tug pulled a spool of carbon nano-fiber cabling around the a-grav buoys.

"Do you remember that night?" Jeffrey's voice was barely above a whisper.

"There have been a lot of nights."

"Luna. Under New Austin's dome. We were watching them build High Terra."

"The night they laid the final section onto the substructure," Finaeus replied with a nod. "Yeah, you said something monumentally stupid that night. 'Finaeus, why aren't we doing this in other star systems?' or something like that."

"Close enough, yeah," Jeffrey replied. "That was the night we conceived of the FGT. Now...we've done all this. This is all our fault."

Finaeus snorted. "Sometimes you amaze me, Jeff."

"What?" Jeffrey asked.

"You've got enough hubris for a whole star system. If we hadn't started the FGT, someone else would have. Humanity wasn't going to stay bottled up in the Sol System forever, and you know it."

"Yeah..." Jeffrey's voice trailed off. "But maybe someone else would have done better than us."

"Jeff..." Finaeus shook his head and placed a hand on his brother's shoulder. "You can't think like that. We're not responsible for everything that everyone does. We built worlds for humanity." He swept his hand across the view. "Every star you can see.... Over half of them have humans

living in their systems. Most of those are FGT systems. We spread the human race across space. But that's what you have to remember; we didn't seed some sort of perfectly content group that never gets into trouble, we seeded humans."

Jeffrey let out a derisive laugh. "Maybe we should have seeded dolphins everywhere instead."

"Well, we did put them in a few corners here and there," Finaeus replied with a wink. "I've checked on them a few times; they're doing well. People found one group, and now folks go there to get modded into sea creatures and live with the dolphins."

"Really?" Jeff asked, cocking an eyebrow. "Sometimes I can't tell if you're shitting me or not."

"I'm not—this time, at least. It's out near Deneb. Inner Stars, but close to the fringe. Hopefully far enough away from all this mess."

"Lotta mess," Jeffrey said with a nod.

Another stretch of silence fell. It was comfortable, like it used to be between them, back before Jelina, before the Schism.

"So what do I do?" Jeffrey asked.

"Pardon?"

"You heard me. What should I do? How do we deal with this mess?"

Finaeus only shrugged in response, and Jeffrey's brow lowered.

"That's all I get?"

"It doesn't matter what I think you should do, what do you think you should do?"

He ran a hand through his hair. "That's where I'm hung up. Should I really turn over the Transcend to Tangel?"

"It's not yours to turn over, Jeff."

"Whose is it, then? Sera's? She barely wants the job—I could see that after talking to her for just a few minutes. Too much of her mother in her."

"Doesn't matter," Finaeus said with a shrug. "It's Sera's responsibility right now. You can't just take it from her. That's not how this works."

"You seem OK with working under her. Why didn't you take the reins?"

Finaeus barked a laugh. "Are you kidding me? Run the show? Stars, no. It would be like the worst engineering job of all time: one where nothing ever gets done, and everyone complains constantly. Not in a million years."

Jeffrey chuckled. "Honestly, that's a bit too charitable. It's really far worse. What about Tangel? She's…interesting. Did you know her? Before?"

Finaeus ducked his head. "Sure did. Honestly, she wasn't a lot different. Just spoke with two voices instead of one. She's the real deal, though."

"Should she be governing the Transcend?"

"Governing?" Finaeus shook his head. "The Transcend doesn't need to be 'governed', brother mine, it needs to be led. Do you remember when we

brought the FGT together, back at Lucida? When we built our first extra-solar shipyards and sent out our own worldships?"

Jeffrey set his jaw and nodded.

"Well, that's the sort of leader we need again. But if you can't do it, if that's not in you anymore—and if Sera truly does not want to lead, then I think we should put Krissy in command."

"Your daughter?" Jeffrey asked. "I saw some reports about her. She seems like a competent commander."

"And a good leader," Finaeus added. "Loyal, too."

"I'm glad to hear it, Fin. Sounds like she does you proud."

"You should feel the same way about Sera. She's a bit unorthodox, but she's passionate, and her heart's in the right place."

"It's so strange," Jeffrey said with a far-off look in his eyes. "She knows a version of me—one that I get the impression wasn't a great father figure—but I don't know her at all."

Finaeus clasped his brother's shoulder. "Well, Jeff, there's only one way to rectify that."

"And the others?" he asked. "I understand that they're being released from medical soon. I was clean, but they were mentally shackled. It took a bit to free their minds."

"I heard that," Finaeus replied. "Regardless of how you feel, all three Seras still look at you and see 'Dad'. You're going to have to learn how to live with that."

"Would be a lot easier if they weren't Jelina's spitting image.

"I've learned to live with it. You will, too."

THE NEW RECRUIT

STELLAR DATE: 09.19.8949 (Adjusted Years)
LOCATION: Intrepid Space Force Academy
REGION: The Palisades, Orbiting Troy, New Canaan System

Cary and Saanvi stood on Concourse C outside Gate 11, waiting for their new charge to exit the passenger ship that was easing up to the airlock.

Faleena walked toward them, holding three coffees and an orange juice.

"Do you think she likes orange juice?" A look of worry creased Faleena's delicate green features. "I figured she probably doesn't like coffee; most people her age don't drink that, right?"

"Not usually." Cary chuckled at the worry etched on her sister's face.

"I think everyone likes orange juice," Saanvi added, a comforting smile on her lips while she shot Cary a reproachful glance. "It'll be fine."

"It's just weird," Faleena continued, her words coming out so fast they were barely enunciated. "I mean, she's just a kid, and honestly, we're just kids, too. Are we old enough to be responsible for another being?"

Cary placed an arm around Faleena's shoulders. "Moms and Dad entrusted me with you when you were only weeks old. If I can manage a baby AI in my head, I bet the three of us can deal with an eleven-year-old girl."

Saanvi rolled her eyes. "You clearly don't remember what *you* were like at eleven. How many times did Dad make you muck out the stalls as punishment?"

"Stars, don't remind me," Cary muttered. "I think I smelled like horse shit that entire summer."

"And fall, and winter..."

Cary glanced at her sister to see a broad smile on Saanvi's lips. "You're a bucket of ha-ha's."

"I'm here all week. Try the veal."

"I have no idea what that means," Cary said, turning to watch as the airlock cycled open, and an automaton stepped out, gesturing for the passengers to follow.

"You're so uncultured," Saanvi retorted.

"Your version of culture involves watching flat-vids and reading books where people say 'whom'. I'll pass."

Saanvi shrugged. "Your loss."

"Hush, you two," Faleena said, peering through the disembarking throng. "There she is!"

"Amy!" Cary called out, waving to the young girl who was stepping uncertainly over the airlock's threshold, peering around her while clutching a small bag to her chest. "Amy, it's us!"

Amy's eyes fell on Cary and her sisters, and a look of relief washed over the girl's face as she rushed toward them. Then she stopped short, standing awkwardly a half-meter away.

"Seriously, Amy?" Cary asked, then stooped down to scoop the girl up in an embrace—one that Saanvi and Faleena joined in on. "Stars, it's good to see you again."

"You're squishing me!" Amy squeaked, but Cary could tell the girl was happy to see them.

"Sorry-not-sorry." Saanvi winked mischievously. "How was your flight? How're things in Albany?"

Cary set Amy back down and took her hand, leading her down the concourse toward the maglev platform that would take them to their quarters.

"Good, I guess. Rika left to go to some place called Sepe; she's hunting the Niets that escaped Albany. Mom and Barne are getting ready for another bunch of mechs that are coming from the Politica…er, Kendo, I guess it's called now."

"What's wrong?" Saanvi asked, peering into Amy's face. "I heard that your mom is only going to train them, and then she'll be coming to meet up with you here."

The girl snorted. "Seriously? You remember that my mom is Silva, right? Besides, would *your* mom run from a fight?"

"Uh…well…" Cary stammered, uncertain what the right response was.

"What makes you think your mom is going to go with the mechs into Nietzschea?" Faleena asked, deflecting Amy's question with one of her own. "She left them once to be with you."

"Yeah," Amy nodded. "But things were different then. Now that they've met up with your people, well…"

"Is there something she'd go into Nietzschea for?" Faleena pressed.

"My brothers," she admitted quietly. "She thinks they still might be alive—even though my father said they're dead. 'Course, he was a fucking asshole, so who knows if they are or not."

Cary was taken aback by the vehemence in Amy's voice, but she had trouble faulting the girl. They'd been told about the abuses she had suffered under her father's care, many of them administered while her mother was watching. The fact that Amy was a functioning person and relatively well-adjusted was a miracle in and of itself.

Cary supposed she might curse someone who did that to her, as well.

Suddenly, growing up in the shadow of the great Tanis Richards doesn't seem so bad.

"Well, if she does go looking for them, I wish her all the luck. I know a bit about wondering where one's family is," Saanvi said in a soothing voice. "We'll be waiting for her here."

Amy glanced up at Saanvi. "Aren't you training to be ship captains? That's what my mom told me."

"Well, eventually," Cary replied. "We have a ways to go."

"When you go, I'm going with you," Amy declared. "I won't stay here waiting. I need to be in the fight."

"War is no place for kids," Faleena said as they reached the maglev platform and stepped aboard a waiting maglev car.

"You don't understand." Amy's voice was almost pleading. "I *have* to get out there. I'm done hiding."

They were filing into the back of the car, moving past several seated passengers, when Amy tripped and reached out to grab the back of a seat.

She didn't fall, but Cary spotted a series of red streaks on the girl's forearm. She was about to ask what they were from, when Saanvi reached out to her privately.

<Don't. Not here. Wait 'til we get to our rooms.>

<You saw it too?> Cary asked.

<Yeah, she's cutting herself. Don't worry, we can talk with her, non-threateningly, and get a counselor if necessary.>

Cary nodded, and engaged Amy in trivialities as the maglev took them through the Palisades, up from Ring 7 to their quarters on Ring 3.

Though they still had two years to go at the academy, Cary, Saanvi, and Faleena had been granted their own quarters due to their unorthodox training and responsibilities.

Cary was sure there'd been some grumbling about it, but at the same time, she had also heard rumors circulating that she could read minds, and that some people didn't want to bunk with her.

Saanvi seemed unaffected by the scuttlebutt, and Cary wished she could brush it off like her sister did.

When they finally reached their quarters, Cary showed Amy to her room, which was the first one on the left off the common area.

"Do you have anything else coming?" Cary asked, as Amy set her bag on the bed.

She shook her head. "This is all I have."

"Well then," Cary grinned at the young girl. "We'll have to go on a shopping trip tomorrow. Get you whatever you want."

Amy flushed and shook her head again. "I don't—it's OK. Really."

Cary drew in a deep breath and closed the door before sitting down on the bed, patting it in request for Amy to sit down beside her. When her charge complied, she asked, "Do you want to tell me about the cuts? I saw them on the maglev. It's OK, you're not in trouble. I even did it a few times when I was your age—well, a bit older, but you're more mature than I was at eleven."

"What?" Amy asked, frowning. "Why did you cut yourself?"

Cary hadn't expected the admission to come back on her so quickly, and she stammered. "I—I don't really know. I felt like I wasn't...worth it? I figured it was what I deserved for not being perfect. I wanted to *feel*. Reasons that don't make much sense when I say them aloud now, but they seemed...inescapable back then."

Amy's face reddened, and she shook her head. "That's not...I'm not doing it for that."

"No?" Cary asked. "Why then?"

"It's stupid," she said as she turned away.

"No, Amy. If it's important enough for you to hurt yourself, it's not stupid. Tell me. Please?"

Amy folded her arms, hunched her head low, and spoke in barely a whisper. "I want to be like her."

Cary's eyebrows knit together. "Like who?"

"My mom!" Amy whispered hoarsely. "I want to cut my arms off so I can be a mech and be with my mom!"

The girl's words completely floored Cary. She had no idea what to say in response. "I...uh...I'm not sure..."

"That's why I agreed to come here." Amy turned and fixed Cary with a stare beyond her years. "I want you to train me to be a warrior. Then I can join the Marauders. That's where I'm supposed to be."

Cary's first instinct was to talk Amy down, to try to convince the girl that she was on the wrong path. But the cold fire in Amy's eyes told Cary that there would be no convincing this young firebrand of anything.

Not yet, at least.

"Well, then," she looked Amy up and down. "The first rule of a warrior is that your body must be kept in peak fighting condition, whether it's organic, mechanical, or somewhere in between. You can't be an asset to your team if you're damaged. So if you want me to train you, the first rule is no more cutting."

"How will I become a mech, then?" Amy asked.

"If you cut your organic arms off, the medics here will just grow you new flesh and blood ones." Cary paused to let the statement sink in. "It's trivial for us to do that. You have to prove to me that you can fight, and that you could fight better as a mech. Only when I'm satisfied that you'd be an asset to the Marauders will I lobby for you to be a mech."

<*OK, I'm listening at the door,*> Saanvi said. <*And are you **nuts**?*>

<*No, I'm going to teach her how to love herself through training. Then she'll realize that, with our armor and tech, she doesn't need to go sawing off her limbs.*>

<*Huh...that might just work. You better run this past the counselors, though. And Dad, when he gets back. I can just see Amy going to him and saying, 'But Cary promised me you'd cut my limbs off'.*>

Cary shuddered at the thought. *<No argument here, I will.>*

"When do we start?" Amy asked.

"Well…no time like the present," Cary said as she rose. "Let's go for a run and see what you've got."

Amy grinned up at her. "OK, but I'm like bottled lightning. Prepare to lose."

Cary snorted a laugh. "That's the spirit."

EASING IN

STELLAR DATE: 09.22.8949 (Adjusted Years)
LOCATION: Tangel's Lakehouse, Ol' Sam, ISS *I2*
REGION: Pyra, Albany System, Thebes, Septhian Alliance

"Welcome back, Sera," Tangel said, gesturing to the chair across from her, the sitting room's fireplace crackling softly before them.

Sera—but not *the* Sera—eyed Tangel warily for a moment before sitting, straightening her simple light grey shipsuit as she settled. "It's been a while," she said while shifting to get comfortable.

"Over twenty years, by your reckoning," Tangel agreed with a nod. "A strange bit of cognitive dissonance for me. Up until you left Ascella with Andrea and Serge, my memories of you and the other Seras are the same, but following that, they diverge."

The woman sitting across from Tangel clenched her jaw and gave a sharp nod. "It's so much fun being constantly reminded that I'm a clone—or whatever I am."

Tangel shrugged. "You were made at the whim of your mother. That is not so different from how things happen naturally."

Sera sat back in her seat, folding her arms across her chest. "Except, for most people, their mother didn't also make their father."

"Good point," Tangel allowed. "That's certainly less common, but not really material to your situation."

A coarse laugh tore free from Sera's throat, and her voice rose an octave. "Not *material*? Has becoming some sort of super-being addled your brain?"

Tangel raised her eyebrows. "Hard to say—not sure I could tell if it had. Though if you think about it, 'addled' would present as either illogical and self-harming, or just unusual. Who is to say what a 'usual' mode of thought should be for me? Are there other ascended beings who are merges of human and AI to compare to?"

"Could be," Sera replied, her tone still combative.

"Well," Tangel chuckled as she spoke. "I'll be sure to ask them when we meet."

"Are you going to answer the question? Why is it not material?"

A smile graced Tangel's lips. "One thing is for certain, you are still the same woman—though you rarely turned that sharp tongue on me before. And that's why it's all immaterial. Airtha made all three of you Seras for a purpose: she wanted to create a legacy and a new ruler for humanity. Because of that, you three share similar traits suited to someone who would be a ruler. You're—"

"Puppets?" Sera interjected.

"I was going to say, 'driven'," Tangel replied with a smirk. "Plus smart, decisive, determined. You're also all a bit egotistical."

"Takes one to know one."

Tangel shrugged. "Touché. But I didn't invite you here to engage in a verbal sparring match. I invited you here because I believe that you've not had a chance to pick sides in this conflict. I want to offer that to you now."

Sera's eyebrows rose. "Before I left the LMC, I was given a data packet with a lot of intel. What you know of Airtha, the core AIs, the wars across the Inner Stars. With all that information, this isn't much of a choice—you'll not set me free if I don't join up with you."

Tangel crossed her legs and leant back in her chair. "I give you my word. If you do not choose to stay with us, I will return you to your mother."

"Right," Sera grunted. "Again, with all that intel? Or will you perform some sort mind-wipe?"

"I didn't give you anything Airtha doesn't already know. If I had, the offer would have been stasis until the end of the war."

Tangel could see the wheels turning behind Sera's eyes. There was most certainly information in the data packet that this Sera had not known. The knowledge that Airtha knew so much more than she'd shared with her daughters would be a revelation in and of itself.

"It's a tricky thing," Tangel continued. "At the end of the day, I want the same things Airtha does: for the core AIs to stop dictating the future of humans and other non-ascended AIs. It's our motives that differ. I'm doing it because I believe in the two races, while Airtha is doing it as a form of vengeance. She wants to unite humanity under her banner and wield it like a weapon against the Core. *I* want to find common ground so that we can forge a future where we stop nearly wiping ourselves out. Then I'll lead a unified force of humans and AIs to the Core."

"Do you think that waging war across the Inner Stars is how you'll unify humanity?" Sera derided.

"This war has been orchestrated," Tanis replied simply. "Spurred on by the Caretaker, Airtha, and Kirkland's obstinance. They set up myopic empires in the Inner Stars, and then encouraged them to force non-inclusive viewpoints on others, all under the threat of war. Once established, the puppeteers set those empires against one another. Any who are willing to join the Scipio Alliance do not *need* to engage in war—though help is appreciated. However, many signees have had to make substantial changes in their society regarding how they treat AIs."

"And those who don't join your alliance and instead stand against you?"

"I'll do my best to render them harmless with as little bloodshed as possible. I believe that once we defeat Nietzschea, the Trisilieds, and the Hegemony, most others will see that war against us is not a viable option."

"And Orion?" Sera asked. "As you said, Kirkland is not known for understanding, nor for a willingness to change his views. He's begun to eradicate AIs across his empire."

"Which will make him that much easier to defeat. I have the strengths of two species whereas he has only one."

"You still won't change his mind," Sera retorted. "Strengths or no, you won't be able to sway him, and if you win, you'll have to contend with the ideology he's infused in Orion space."

"It's possible that his viewpoint isn't as pervasive as some would believe. You don't know what happened to *Sabrina*, do you?"

Sera's eyes grew wide, and for the first time, her defensive posture slackened. "I managed to learn that they jumped out from the Grey Wolf Star over ten years ago…but no one knows where they went."

"The Perseus Arm of the galaxy," Tangel replied simply. "They got back a year ago, and from what they saw, Kirkland's hold on Orion space isn't as absolute as he'd like us to believe."

"Are—are they all OK?" Sera asked hesitantly.

"They are," Tangel nodded. "They had some tough times, but they all got back. Cargo is operating a cattle ranch down on Carthage in New Canaan, if you can believe it. Everyone else has been working to stop an AI uprising in the Inner Stars. They'll all be back here before long, though. You'll be able to meet with them no matter what you decide."

Sera's eyes narrowed. "Why are you being so nice to me? I've been working against you."

"Imagine, if you will," Tangel began with an expansive wave of her arm. "That you are the only version of yourself. That another Sera did not come to New Canaan with your father—"

"My clone of a father," Sera interjected.

Tangel inclined her head. "Yes…or maybe he's a different type of copy, like you are. Either way, imagine you are the only Sera. To me, you're the woman who saved me from ending up at the mercy of the Mark back in Silstrand. You fought by my side at the Battle of Bollam's World, and you ended your exile to help my people get to New Canaan. I owe you *everything*."

"You owe *her* everything."

"Do you recall doing all those things?" Tangel asked. "Opening the cryopod and finding me in it? Getting captured by Rebecca, breaking free and securing the stolen CriEn module? What about flying to Bollam's World and helping us protect the *Intrepid* before showing us the way to Ascella? Do you remember trying to kill me while under your sister's influence?"

Sera nodded silently, and her eyes fell to the floor before she responded, "I do."

Tangel leant forward, elbows on her knees. "Then you *are* Sera. You're one of my dearest friends, and I'm treating you accordingly."

Sera's head lifted, and her gaze met Tangel's. "And if I do take you up on your offer? What then?"

"Then you join with your sisters and stop your mother. A unified Transcend is something we must achieve to end this war and begin the real fight with the Core."

Sera's lips drew into a thin line, and she turned her head toward the fire, blowing out a long breath.

SISTERS

STELLAR DATE: 09.23.8949 (Adjusted Years)
LOCATION: A1 Dock, ISS *I2*
REGION: Pyra, Albany System, Thebes, Septhian Alliance

"So how does it feel to be captain?" Sera asked as she strode up *Sabrina*'s ramp to where Cheeky stood waiting.

The slender—and completely naked—woman cocked her hips and held out her arms, beckoning for an embrace. "How should I know? It's only been a few hours since Jessica turned her over to me."

<No one's turned me over to anyone,> Sabrina interjected. *<Remember, **I** own me. Sera herself did it.>*

A happy sigh slipped past Sera's lips as she embraced Cheeky and gazed into the cargo bay behind her. "That I did, Sabs. How have you been?"

<I've been great! You wouldn't believe the stuff we've been up to, though I heard you got to go to the LMC! Knowing that's possible has made my bucket list so big, I'm going to need a bigger bucket.>

"I hear y—hey! Cheeky, enough with that!"

Cheeky chuckled as she lifted her hands from Sera's ass. "Just curious if you're the real Sera."

"And you think you'll be able to tell by my ass?"

Sabrina's newly minted captain took a step back, a hand on her chest and a shocked expression on her face. "Seriously…it's like you've forgotten who I am or something."

Sera stared at her long-time friend, trying to figure out if she was being serious or not, and then laughed, shaking her head. "Stars, Cheeky. Kill you, extract your mind from an AI's memory banks, put you in a new body, make you captain...none of that's changed you a bit. You're still the same ol' Cheeky I met in that dingy bar so long ago."

The naked woman laughed and grabbed her own rear. "Best thing about getting new skin is that these cheeks never sat on those disturbingly sticky barstools."

"Rarely am I an advocate for clothing, but in that case, it was more than warranted," Sera agreed.

The pair walked side-by-side into the ship's main cargo bay, where Nance and Misha waited. Sera didn't hesitate to embrace Nance, who wore a hazsuit with the hood pulled back.

"Back in your old routine?" Sera asked.

Nance glanced down at herself. "Oh, no…I legitimately needed it. Was working on the environmental system. Finaeus messed with it so much, I'm still trying to get it back the way I like."

"Nance..." Sera began, an eyebrow raised. "Finaeus is arguably one of the smartest people in the galaxy."

The bioengineer shrugged. "Sure, whatever. I still know Sabs better. Besides, I'm pretty sure half the things he did down there, he did just to mess with me."

With a soft laugh and a shake of her head, Sera turned to Misha. "Nice to meet you again, Misha. How's the galley holding up?"

"Tip-top," the cook replied. "I have a fresh pot of coffee on, a bowl of fruit, and some of your favorite snacks waiting for your meeting."

"How do you know my favorites?" Sera asked, to which Misha snorted.

"President Tomlinson, there's still a listing of items in the galley's inventory system labeled 'Captain Sera's Faves'."

"Oh." She chuckled. "And I'm not president of the Transcend anymore. Well, not really."

<As I understand it, you are until the cabinet votes otherwise,> Sabrina replied. *<Which I suppose means you have to get back to Khardine before long?>*

Sera nodded. "Once my sisters and I have a chat. If they agree to join us, they'll hop back with me and Tani—Tangel."

Cheeky pursed her lips. "It's weird hearing that name."

"It's weird saying it," Sera replied. "But half the time you were talking to Tanis in the past, Angela was in the conversation, anyway. Now it's just like talking to them both at once all the time."

<No it's not,> Sabrina interjected. *<The sum is greater than the parts.>*

"I wonder what it would be like..." Cheeky mused.

Nance rolled her eyes. "You'll have to ask Joe."

"You think that ruins my little mental visual," Cheeky said to Nance with a grin. "But it doesn't, it just makes it better."

"Will you guys greet the others when they arrive?" Sera asked. "I think it will make them feel better."

"Think so?" Nance asked. "Won't that be awkward?"

Sera shook her head. "No. I know they'll like it, they're still *me*—stars, that's a weird thing to say. Anyway, they just got led astray a little bit. Trust me, we've all missed you."

* * * * *

Five minutes later, Sera took a seat in the galley—though not in her old chair. It didn't feel right to take it and lord her originality over her sisters.

Instead, she took the seat Flaherty used to sit in, to the right of the head.

He had opted not to meet the other Seras yet, worried they may use his inability to lie against him. At least, that's what he'd said. Sera wasn't so sure.

<Are you ready?> Jen asked, after Sera had sat in silence for a minute.

<Not really, no. I don't even know what to do to ***get*** *ready.>*

The AI that shared space in Sera's head didn't respond for a few seconds, and then laughed softly. *<I hear yoga is good in situations like this.>*

Sera snorted, imagining herself in some awkward yoga pose when her sisters entered.

<Too vulnerable.>

The tell-tale sound of someone climbing the ladder to the crew deck reached her ears, bringing with it a flood of memories from decades past.

"You still feel like home, *Sabrina*," Sera whispered.

<Why thank you,> Sabrina answered.

"I was talking to the ship."

"I know."

Sera resisted the urge to roll her eyes, knowing that one of her sisters would be entering the room at any moment. She straightened in her seat. Ready for anything.

Then *she* appeared in the galley's entrance, staring into the room. "They painted the place."

Sera glanced around the galley, surprised that she hadn't realized the walls were a subtle shade of lavender.

<Can you guess who did that?> Sabrina asked the pair.

Sera snorted, while her sister only shook her head.

"Stars, it feels so good to have your voice in my head, Sabrina," the other Sera said—still not having met Sera's eyes.

<It's mutual,> Sabrina replied. *<Having two—wait, now three of you aboard is more excitement than I've seen in some time. And I've fought in more than one war in the past few years.>*

The other Sera's gaze fell on their old place at the head of the table before she shook her head and sat at the foot. "Doesn't feel right."

"I know," Sera agreed. "I guess that's Cheeky's place now."

"Stars," the other Sera muttered. "Can you believe that little waif we found in that gross bar is the captain now?"

Sera wondered if her sister was being derisive, when she continued.

"She deserves it. That girl has been through hell and back, from what I've been told. Perseus Arm."

"She has," Sera agreed. "Hard to believe that with all the crazy stuff we've been through in the past twenty years, you've been through more, Sabrina."

<Well…I haven't been to the LMC, so you have me beat, there.>

"Neither have I," the third Sera said from the galley's doorway. "Looks like Mom didn't give me the fun stuff."

Sera watched her first sister turn and give the second one a narrow-eyed look.

She understood what they were thinking. Both had known for some time that there was *one* other Sera out there, but the story they'd both been told was that *they* were the original, and the Sera ruling from Khardine was the imposter.

Now they were faced with the incontrovertible truth that it was their mother, Airtha, who was manufacturing doppelgangers, not the people of New Canaan.

No one spoke as the newcomer made her way to the middle seat on the right side of the table, and pulled out the chair.

The silence continued for a whole minute before the Sera who had been captured in the Valkris asked the one captured at LMC, "so, how far back do you remember?"

"To being a little girl." LMC Sera's tone was acidic. "You?"

"That's not what I meant," Valkris Sera shot back. "Don't you want to know which one of us is a copy of the other?"

Sera raised her hands. "Easy, now. We're not really copies, it's different than that."

LMC Sera waved a hand. "Right, we're sourced from a backup of your neural network, making us more like branches of a tree than copies. That's all semantics; it doesn't change the facts of the matter. You're the original, we're divergent."

"Not that divergent," Valkris Sera said with a coarse laugh.

"I have to admit," Sera mused, hoping to placate her sisters. "I've wondered if I'm not a copy, as well. Like there was some earlier Sera that mother didn't quite like, so she made some tweaks, and here I am."

LMC Sera snorted. "Given your wardrobe proclivities, I'm pretty sure you're not the Sera made in her image."

Valkris Sera raised her eyebrows. "I've been meaning to ask. Can I get it back? The skin?"

"You want it?" Sera asked.

"Stars, yes! Mother said that it was destroyed in the attack that killed Helen—all lies, I know now—but hot damn, I've missed it. I was halfway tempted to send someone to Silstrand just to find out where Rebecca sourced that original suit that devoured our skin."

LMC Sera shook her head. "I'm more than happy to keep my real skin—and how do you know that the attack and Helen's death was a lie? What if this other one of us," here she paused to gesture at Sera, "is the imposter? What if—"

Valkris Sera leant over the table and placed a hand on LMC Sera's wrist. "We both know that's not true. Besides, the ISF freed us from mother's control. I know you feel it. I feel it too."

A shuddering breath sucked past Valkris Sera's lips and she nodded. "Yeah…it just sucks balls."

"All the balls," Sera added.

"You?" both other Seras asked in unison. "Why does it suck for you?"

"Really?" Sera asked. "Don't you get it? I might not be in the same boat as you two, but I'm in the one right next to you. Mother *made* me just like she did with you. She made the version of father that she wanted, and then she made me—only *after* failing to create a viable scion with Andrea."

LMC Sera snorted. "At least Mom knew a total write-off when she saw it."

The three women broke into soft laughter before falling silent once more.

"Here's how I see it," Sera said. "Mom fucked with all three of us. Tried to make us her puppets. But that doesn't mean we're lesser beings. We're still exactly who we've always been—tough, sexy, ass-kicking women who aren't going to take this laying down. And Tanis has a mission for us: take out Airtha in a targeted strike. We can do that *and* save the Transcend. Then we stop those douchebags in Orion, and finally bring the fight to the Core AIs. *Everyone* who has a god complex goes down."

"There may be some specifics in there that I would like to tweak, but in general, I'm onboard with this plan," LMC Sera said with a grim smile.

"What of Tanis?" Valkris Sera asked. "She's got a bit of a god complex, if you ask me."

Sera shrugged. "Maybe a bit. You have to admit, she's something different. Either way, it's a miracle that she and the ISF are here trying to help. I think if Tangel were to order it, they'd all just head off and leave us to our devices."

"Maybe," Valkris Sera said with a shrug.

LMC Sera set her elbows on the table and folded her hands before setting her chin on them. "So. Let's finally talk about the elephant in the room. Who gets to keep the name?"

"Sera?" Sera asked.

"Yeah," Valkris Sera said. "It'll be confusing as fuck if everyone has to call all of us Sera—*especially* if we're going on a mission together."

"Well, there's Seraphina, or Fina.... What Finaeus used to call me—us—when we were kids," Sera suggested.

"I say none of us gets to keep any of the names," Valkris Sera said as she gestured to Sera. "Having to call *you* 'Sera' will just feel too weird. How's about you're Red Sera?"

Sera snorted. " 'Red Sera'? Really?"

"You have to admit that it fits," LMC Sera said with a grin. "You're always red."

"Mostly," Sera said with a shrug. "I do like to shake things up, though. I happen to enjoy the color blue." She lifted her hand, and her skin turned from red to blue.

"Nuh-uh," Valkris Sera said with a shake of her head. "When I get the skin upgrade back, I'm going blue. I call dibs. I'm Blue Sera."

"You can't call dibs on a color," Sera shot back.

"Well I'm sticking with skin-color," LMC Sera interjected. "Maybe I'll take the skin job, but I kinda like looking human."

Sera grinned at her sister, running her hands down her sides. "Deviant. You want the sexy feels, but you don't want to stand out."

"Where's the fun in that?" Valkris Sera added. "We've always liked standing out."

"Oh I'm all for reverting to form," LMC Sera replied with a smile. "But I really like all the leather I used to wear before that catsuit ripped my skin off. That was my jam."

Sera's hand changed from blue to a leathery texture. "You can do leather, too. This stuff is ridiculously versatile."

"Deal," LMC Sera said. "But I'm not going to be 'Leather Sera'. Sounds like I'm some sort of pirate…or serial killer."

"Well, we *were* a pirate once," Sera said with a wink.

Valkris Sera snorted. "You can be Pi—"

"Don't even go there!" LMC Sera snapped. "I'll be…Black Sera. But I'm going with red hair, because that'll look badass."

"What?" Sera asked. "That's going to be as confusing as all get-out!"

LMC Sera winked at Sera. "No, just means you have to keep your skin red all the time to avoid confusion."

"You realize," Valkris Sera said, a wicked grin on her lips, "We're going to be able to mess with everyone so much."

<You sure you want to go with colors?> Sabrina asked innocently. *<It's going to sound like you're different fireteams or fighter wings. 'Red One to Blue Two. Come in Blue Two.'>*

"She has a point," Sera said. "Though I don't really have an issue with being called 'Red', to be honest."

"OK…maybe we think about Seraphina and Fina again," Valkris Sera suggested. "I mean…I still call dibs on *being* blue. But I'm willing to take on 'Fina'. I have a lot of good memories of Uncle Finaeus calling me that as a little girl."

"Yeah, but that means I have to go with 'Seraphina'," LMC Sera said, her lips twisting in dismay. "That's what Helen called us when she was mad…"

"And Helen was mom," Sera completed the thought, then glanced at Valkris Sera. "I still say you can't call dibs on a color."

"Screw it." LMC Sera slapped her palm on the table. "*Every* version of Seraphina is a name given to us by our fucking bastard of a mother. Why *can't* I just go with Seraphina? Time to take it back."

"That's the spirit," Fina said, raising a fist into the air. "Stars. I bet when Mom learns the three of us are united, she's going to shit digital bricks all over her pretty diamond ring. Sera, Fina, and Seraphina are coming for her!"

"To us!" Sera said, joining Fina and thrusting her fist into the air, tremendously relieved that their first meeting had ended like this, and not in a firefight.

A smile crept across Seraphina's face, and she reached out, placing a hand on each of her sister's fists. "She's never gonna know what hit her."

SVETLANA'S TEN THOUSAND

STELLAR DATE: 09.23.8949 (Adjusted Years)
LOCATION: TSS *Cossack's Sword*
REGION: Khardine System, Transcend Interstellar Alliance

Svetlana stood at the head of the long virtual table and watched her fleet commanders get settled.

Though her force was small, it consisted of the hardiest ships she could secure for the mission—including a group of ISF rail destroyers that were commanded by a stern looking colonel named Caldwell.

The rest of the team was made up of TSF personnel, starting with Rear Admiral Sebastian, who commanded the second division of the fleet. General Lorelai, who commanded the combat forces, sat across from him, followed by colonels Lia and Colton, who were responsible for the fighter wings.

Beyond them were the senior captains, thirty-six in all, followed by hundreds more captains filling the holographic space. At the end of the table were the men and women she needed to have onboard with this the most: the senior warrant and petty officers, most specifically, Command Master Chief Merrick.

Though he sat at the end of the table, Svetlana knew he was the most respected person in her fleet. Merrick had served as a noncom in the Transcend Space Force for over a thousand years. The only reason he hadn't ever taken the role of Master Chief of the Space Force was because, in his words, *'I got my own shit to do. Can't waste time sticking my nose up bureaucrats' asses all day.'*

Svetlana both respected and feared the man. In part because of his venerable status, but also because he was her father.

His hard-eyed gaze gave her no indication as to whether or not he approved of the strategy to take fleets deep into Orion space, but she hoped that if he didn't agree, he wouldn't voice it here, and would instead take it up with her privately.

After waiting another half-minute for everyone to settle, she addressed the group.

"You've all read the brief. You know why we're here, what we're going to do. Fleet Admiral Wrentham needs us to take the pressure off the Orion Fronts, and that's just what we're going to do. Admiral Mardus is going to be hitting Herschel, and we're striking the center of the Perseus Expansion Districts."

As Svetlana spoke, a display of the Orion Arm appeared over the table, a yellow outline highlighting the PED, while a red marker appeared at Quera, close—galactically speaking—to the edge of the Orion Arm.

"As most of you know, Admiral Keller of the ISF passed through these regions of Orion space on reconnaissance aboard the *Sabrina* nearly two years ago, so our intel is a bit out of date, but we have supplements from the few Hand agents in that area.

"The locals are low-tech. Half of them don't even have the Link, and those that do usually just have oculars. From what we know, the PED is mostly populated by refugees who fled toward the rim during the FTL wars. Orion absorbed them and offered succor and sanctuary in exchange for strict adherence to draconian laws regarding technological advancements."

Svetlana paused, her gaze sweeping across the assemblage.

"Essentially, they're going to shit bricks when they see us. We have reason to believe that the PED's inhabitants think the Inner Stars are still utter anarchy, and have *no idea* that the Transcend even exists."

"Intel supports that?" General Lorelai asked. "I understand that information about the Inner Stars and the Transcend may not be in the public databases on their worlds, but surely there must be some underground knowledge. Their populace gets conscripted by the OG—many of those get sent to the front. They must come back with stories."

"That's what we've believed for some time," Svetlana replied, nodding in agreement. "But the intel that Admiral Keller brought back indicates otherwise. It's different out by Herschel, but in the Perseus Arm and the PED, the Orion Guard is the boogeyman, and doesn't enlist many troops from the local populations.

"They have local militia-style space forces, but they're really just there to police things. Fear of the OG seems to keep them in line."

"Well, Admiral Keller would know," Colonel Caldwell said to General Lorelai. "She spent ten years in Orion space."

"Seems like such a waste." Lorelai shook her head then shrugged. "So I take it this means we're to go easy on the locals."

"That's the idea right now," Svetlana replied with a curt nod. "Unless we find Keller's assessment to be wrong, in which case we'll adapt our strategy. Still, we have to assume them to be a hostile population. They'll see us as invaders, not liberators."

"Could we not establish a beachhead?" One of the senior captains asked. "Take and hold systems, force Orion to come to us?"

Svetlana shook her head. "That's not how I want to approach this. If we take and hold, we have to police and defend. Our intel indicates that the OG isn't afraid to strike out at their own population, and Fleet Intel thinks they may use that against us.

"Instead, our approach is to strike hard, destroy military and major infrastructure targets, and move on. We never go back to a system we've been to before, never give them a reason to use a populace against us. Our goal is to be like the Hoplites in ancient Persia. We're pushing to the Sea. Our Sea is the Perseus Arm. We get there, we get to go home."

"Perseus?" Admiral Sebastian asked. "That could take years, a decade if we get bogged down at all."

"I'm being a bit hyperbolic," Svetlana replied. "I'd like to think that we'll get to strike a more decisive blow before we get that far."

"An attack on New Sol?" Lorelai asked.

"Or a truce." Svetlana glanced at her father and saw him nod slowly. "If we can win against Airtha and end the war in the Inner Stars, then suddenly Kirkland faces the rest of humanity alone."

Caldwell set his elbows on the table and nodded. "That seems like a laudable goal."

"Agreed," Sebastian added. "So what is our first target?"

Sebastian knew the plan, of course. He and Svetlana had spent some time crafting it, but she appreciated him leading the conversation along.

She triggered the holodisplay to focus in on the Quera System, where Costa Station was—or maybe wasn't anymore, given that Jessica Keller's team had fired RMs at its gate before jumping back to New Canaan.

"We're going to start here. We'll jump in an observation ship with a drone gate a quarter light year out. It will make an assessment and send back the findings. We'll hop into Quera either way; whether or not it's empty will just affect how we deploy. We'll scour it for any intel, and then move on to either the Norma or Ferra Systems. Neither have large military presences, but we'll crush what's there and move on. We want to keep moving and keep making lightning strikes for as long as possible. Unpredictable and deadly is the name of the game."

Svetlana widened the view of the PED, showing the possible routes through the region of space. One path roughly followed Jessica Keller's route from the Perseus Arm, while the other veered spinward, toward a cluster of systems with names like 'Eashira', 'Cush', and 'Machete'.

"Are we worried that they'll try to bottle us up?" one of the captains, a woman named Jula, asked. "Predict our moves and lay in wait?"

"Technically, that's what we want," Svetlana replied. "I do worry about it, though. We have superior weaponry and shields, but the OGs have numbers on their side. We know that enough firepower can overwhelm even stasis shielding, and we have to assume that they know to hit us in the engines while we're burning. So we're not going to be stupid—plus, not all our ships have stasis shields.

"That scout ship I mentioned has already deployed to the Quera System. Once it drops its drone, it'll pack up its gate and leave for Ferra. The ship's crewed by an elite team, SF and Hand agents, who are going to scout ahead of us, and build a network of contacts as fast as possible. They also have intel on two Hand agents in the vicinity, and will try to make contact with them for the latest intel."

"So what's next?" Colonel Colton asked.

"We're only taking four fab-ships and we're going to rely on the folks back here at Khardine to send us supplies as we need them. The QuanComm network and the jump gates are setting us up for a new kind of warfare that we've never practiced and that the Oggies have never seen. Still, don't pack light," Svetlana paused as a few of the officers laughed. "If you don't bring it along, you better not *need* it for a year. I'm not calling back to Admiral Greer to ask him to send your jammies and teddy bears out to the PED.

"Everyone has two days to inform their crews that we're about to go on a long-duration tour—no details 'til we ship. Transfer out anyone you think will have issues with that. We leave in fifty hours."

"Fifty hours?" one of the captains blurted out, then reddened.

"Yes, fifty. Not a minute more. This is the Space Force, not your kid's daycare. Let's get this shit done, and get the show on the road."

A CHAT WITH TROY

STELLAR DATE: 09.23.8949 (Adjusted Years)
LOCATION: A1 Dock, ISS *I2*
REGION: Pyra, Albany System, Thebes, Septhian Alliance

Tangel watched with a measure of melancholy-tinged joy as the *Voyager* settled on the cradle before her. Seeing the ship brought back a host of memories—which was strange, considering that she'd never seen the vessel before.

She—well, Tanis—had ordered the *Voyager*'s construction back at Kapteyn's Star, where it was placed at the secret pico-research site as an interstellar-capable evac vehicle. Later, when the site had been cleared out, Angela had suggested leaving the ship behind in case Katrina, or someone else, had a need to leave Kapteyn's star.

Judging by the looks of the vessel, it had been through a lot more than Tanis or Angela had ever expected.

But that wasn't what had Tangel feeling anxious.

It was who was aboard the ship.

"He doesn't hold a grudge." Katrina's voice was barely above a whisper, where she stood next to Tangel. "He and I talked about it back at Victoria. Don't forget, I was governor after that battle. I'm just as much to blame for not finding them right away."

Tangel glanced at the woman next to her. Katrina was barely recognizable from the person who had first come aboard the *I2* a few days earlier. Gone was the grey hair, aged skin, and slight stoop. The woman who had been so many things—from spy to governor to warlord to pirate—now looked like she'd barely passed her twentieth birthday.

Except for the eyes. Katrina had always had an old woman's eyes. Now they were ancient.

"True enough," Tangel said. "But you *did* find him. I left him behind. One of our greatest heroes…abandoned."

Katrina shrugged. "There's no absolution I can offer you. You'll have to seek that out for yourself."

"And seek it I shall." Tangel sighed and closed her eyes for a moment. "Sometimes it feels like there's so much to regret, Katrina."

A snort burst from the woman's nose. "Oh believe me, I know that all too well. It's so easy to let the past become an anchor—and not the sort you want, either. I've done a lot…*a lot* that I regret. But taken individually, I'm at peace with nearly all the decisions I've made."

Tangel couldn't help but notice the caveat. " 'Nearly all'."

"You have them, I'm sure. The ones that will haunt you forever."

A hundred regret-filled memories flashed before Tangel's eyes as the gantry extended to meet the *Voyager's* airlock. "Do I ever."

"You never talked about them—even before you became half-AI," Katrina observed, as a light came on signaling that the airlock was cycling.

Tangel shrugged. "It's not really my way to dwell on the past. I can't do anything about it. All I can do is look to the future and do my best when it comes. I'm a fast study—mostly—when it comes to the lessons of the past. One of those lessons was to not let memory and regret from days gone by rule the present. The ability to forget is one of the greatest gifts humanity has."

Katrina cocked her head and caught Tanis's gaze. "But you're not human anymore, are you?"

Tangel shrugged. "Biologically I'm not, no. Sera even finally badgered me into adopting her preference in epidermis—though without the constant sensory stimulation."

"I've done my time with artificial skin, I'll pass on that," Katrina grimaced, a look of far-off pain in her eyes.

"I fought it for a while," Tangel replied. "But it was foolish. Having bulletproof, stealth-capable, chameleon skin is a considerable boon in our line of work. You can always get it changed back."

"Don't change the subject," Katrina replied, her tone laced with a note of humor as she evaded Tangel's suggestion. "You were about to tell me what new species you are."

"Well, I'm not an AI, which we all know to be a misnomer anyway. I know some have categorized AIs—at least the ones with Weapon Born in their lineage—as Homo Quantus-Animo Sapiens. Perhaps I am a Homo Quantus-Penta-Animo Sapiens, or some such."

"Sounds like a mouthful—also not what I was getting at," Katrina said, her lips twisting into a smirk.

Tangel chuckled. "I know. I don't really know what I am, or what I'm capable of—classifying myself seems foolish, given that. Stars, every time I push what I think are my boundaries, I just find new vistas."

"What's it like?" Katrina asked.

Tangel paused before replying, trying to find the right words. "It's…complex. I can choose to see with only my two-dimensional vision, my eyes, should I choose. When I do that, I can perceive the three dimensions as I always have. However, my other senses keep trickling in. The three dimensions turn into four, then five. I'm…growing, for lack of a better word, new sensory organs. I believe I know how to grow five-dimensional 'eyes'. Once I do that, I'll be able to perceive the sixth dimension."

"Shit," Katrina whispered.

"Yeah, it's nuts. I can see other types of light and energy. I can touch them, too." As she spoke, Tangel reached out with her corporeal hand and touched a shimmering stream that was flowing off the *Voyager*—the fifth-dimensional manifestation of the magnetic field emanating from the fusion reactor's tokamak coils. The stream flexed under her touch, and she watched that movement transfer into all the other magnetic fields around her, a luminescent web of electromagnetism that filled the docking bay.

The fields flowed through Katrina, bending the small ones within her body, altering it and her mind in subtle ways. Tangel followed the energy flows, noting one that appeared discordant. From experience, she knew that it was the physical manifestation of an unpleasant memory, of some past pain.

She reached out and touched it.

Curious. It's so embedded.

"Tangel! What the...!" Katrina cried out, jerking away.

Tangel started, realizing that as she'd followed the thread, she'd touched Katrina's face with her corporeal hand.

"Sorry, I was...ah...following the magnetic fields through the bay, looking at how they interact with you in other dimensions."

Katrina was staring at Tangel with a look that was half fear, half worry. "I felt you...inside."

Tangel felt a flush rise on her cheeks. "I'm really sorry, I didn't mean to. Sometimes, realities don't line up the way I expect them to. I didn't realize...."

"That you were probing inside my body?" Katrina's ire and fear turned into a sardonic smirk.

"Uh...yeah."

"I'll admit, it felt...good," Katrina allowed. "Like a tingle running through me."

Tangel wondered if she should tell Katrina what she saw, but the sound of the airlock opening caught her attention, and she turned back to the ship, watching as the first figure stepped out, stooping to clear the low overhang.

"Kara," Tangel said in greeting as she approached and took the black-winged woman's hand. "I'm sorry about your brother."

Tanis and Angela had only seen Kara and her brother briefly—aboard the *Galadrial* the day she stormed it with Usef and a team of Marines—but Adrienne's children had made an impression. She noted that Kara had a face now; no longer was the woman's head a black oval, devoid of features. The resemblance to her father was clear, which made sense, given what she'd learned of the man who had borne all his own children.

The fangs, however, made for a marked differentiation.

"Thank you, Tangel," Kara said in a quiet voice. "I noticed that these caught your attention." She pulled her lips back, further baring the long, sharp teeth. "I had them added in memory of him. He was the one who had always pushed for us to have fear-inspiring appearances. The fangs were one of the first alterations he'd suggested."

"A fitting homage," Katrina replied with a solemn nod.

Behind Kara came a tall man who also looked far younger than the last information Tangel had read on him.

"Carl," she said, extending her hand. "I hear you've worked hard to keep the *Voyager* in good condition."

"Thank you, Admiral. Been a pleasure. Spent far and away most of my life on this ship, now."

A flash of red in the airlock caught Tangel's attention, and she gave a warm smile, gesturing for the occupant to exit.

"Katrina told me all about you, Malorie. You're welcome here."

A head with eight eyes peered around the top edge of the airlock. A moment later, the rest of the mechanical spider dropped to the deck. Katrina had explained to Tangel that Malorie still possessed a human brain inside her arachnid body, but over the years, she'd taken her altered form to heart, reveling in the thing she'd become.

"Admiral Tangel. After hearing Katrina speak of you for so many years...I thought you'd be taller."

Tangel considered that to be an amusing statement from a woman whose disturbingly spider-like head—complete with large, fanged chelicerae—was only a meter off the ground.

"I'm sure she's told a tall tale or two in her day," Tangel replied with a shrug. "I'm just a woman trying to get by in this crazy universe."

A chittering laugh slipped out of Malorie's mouth. "From someone who is more 'just a woman' than you, I sincerely doubt that."

Tangel shrugged and looked back up at the ship looming overhead, her trepidation returning. "Troy? May I come aboard?"

<Of course; though it's not my ship, I just live here.>

"Nonsense," Katrina said, her brow lowering. "Just because Tanis left this ship to me doesn't mean the last five hundred years count for nothing."

"Time to pay the piper," Tangel said to the group around her with a slight nod as she slipped past. "Once I've chatted with Troy, we'll see if the Seras are ready, and we can all talk about the mission."

Katrina folded her arms. "You'd better have a hell of a plan. It was a suicide run just to rescue Kara when she left High Airtha."

Tangel winked at her long-time friend. "We'll put our heads together. I'm sure we can come up with something."

"Very encouraging," Malorie rasped as Tangel walked toward the Voyager.

Tangel ran her hands along the hull for a moment before stepping through the airlock and into the corridor that ran to the central shaft.

"It's weird, Troy," Tangel said as she reached the ladder and began to climb.

<What's weird?>

"That this ship is so *old*. For me, Kapteyn's star was just a quarter-century ago. This ship should look no older than, say, the *Dresden*."

<*Time has a way of wearing things down,*> Troy replied, his tone still too casual for Tangel's liking.

She reached the second to top level and swung off the ladder and onto the deck. "I'm surprised Katrina and her crew never re-aligned the decks to be horizontal—what with having a-grav for so long."

<*Katrina's nostalgic. She likes the* Voyager *the way it is. Carl never even raised the specter of changing the layout, and so it has remained.*>

"Did she at least add a hot tub?" Tangel asked as she reached the ship's upper node chamber and palmed open the door.

A snort sounded in Tangel's mind. <*That all I am to you? A hot-tub starship?*>

Tangel stared at the AI's core, slotted into a receptacle on the bulkhead across the small space.

"I'm so sorry, Troy," Tangel's voice came out in a whisper. "We searched for years, scouring the system for any survivors from the battle. I…." She rested her back against the bulkhead and slid to the deck. "Can you forgive me?"

<*Why am I so special? Surely you've lost others over the years. From what I've heard, the Battle for Victoria was just a warmup.*> Troy paused for a moment. <*Why is it that my forgiveness is so important?*>

"Because you're right here in front of me," Tangel replied quietly. "Those others, they're all lost, and their ghosts never reply."

<*I hold no grudge against you, Tangel. Nor did I against Tanis and Angela. Though you may be far more than human, you are not a goddess. You cannot foresee all outcomes.*>

"Do you mean that?" Tangel asked. "I mean the part about no grudge; I get that I'm not a goddess. What a thankless job that would be."

<*Gods and goddesses from ancient human mythology were—by and large—far less powerful than you are, Tangel. But that noteworthy thought aside, yes, I do mean it.*>

She nodded silently, letting Troy's sincerity seep into her. Then she glanced up at him. "You seem to have lost a bit of your hard edge."

<*I hear that years can do that to a person,*> Troy replied. <*I never slept, you know. Not while I was lost on that moon, not while we hunted for Katrina, and not in the long centuries afterward. I always kept watch over her, made sure she was safe.*>

"Thank you for that," Tangel said.

Troy let out a long, audible groan that filled the room. <OK, *now I know ascendency is going to your head. I didn't do it for you, I did it for me. She's my anchor; I'd be lost without her.*>

Tangel's eyes widened. "Ohhhh…I didn't realize things were like *that* between you two."

A chuckle sounded around Tangel. <*Neither does she.*>

"Has she been with anyone else?" Tangel asked, curious if perhaps Katrina was remaining chaste for Troy.

<No—well, maybe a short fling or two, here and there. Nothing meaningful. Nothing in the last century, either.>

Tangel whistled. "That's a long time to go without love."

<We have love. This crew is a family.>

"I know how that works," she replied, a slight edge to her voice. "I have my family like that, as well—of which you and Katrina are members. But…maybe you should tell her. Things are going to get crazy soon. If you take this mission, you're going into the lion's den."

Another chuckle sounded around her. *<We've been in the shit plenty. I'm pretty sure we have a standing reservation.>*

"Not like this, you haven't," Tangel replied as she rose. "Sera just pinged me. They're coming."

AN ANGEL INSIDE

STELLAR DATE: 09.01.8949 (Adjusted Years)
LOCATION: ***Damon Silas***
REGION: Interstellar Space, coreward of the Vela Cluster

Roxy looked down at the hole in her midsection, and a wave of fear washed over her. She'd spent years in her azure body, knowing that she was more machine than woman, but in all that time, she'd never seen the inside of herself. Opened up like she was nothing more than a servitor.

Maybe Carmen is right. Maybe there's nothing human left of me anymore.

The thought brought about a feeling of blackness that reached up to swallow her, an uncontrollable despair and fear that even the meager truths surrounding her existence that she'd clung to were lies.

Am I nothing? Roxy closed her eyes and shook her head. *No, I am me, I know that I am still me.*

"But what am I?" she whispered. "If I don't know *what* I am, how can I know *who* I am?"

The repair drone—with several of its armatures holding Roxy's abdomen open—offered no reply as it reached into the fabricator and pulled out a new, smaller bioassimilator. Her old one sat on the workbench next to Carmen's case, the flexible, curved apparatus until recently having been the thing that digested any organic sustenance Roxy had chosen to eat.

Since she rarely bothered with food, Carmen suggested that it was the ideal internal system to downsize.

Roxy looked away as the repair drone inserted the new assimilator into her body, the thing's dozen armatures working swiftly and deftly.

The fact that it was not a medical drone was not lost on her, but Carmen assured her that the machine would not be getting anywhere close to her organic systems. Roxy wondered if it was because the AI's earlier statement was correct, and that she *had* no organic systems.

A part of her mind rebelled against the idea, while another part wondered what that would really mean. Carmen's words reverberated in her mind, over and over.

'Are you an AI?'

What if I am? Roxy wondered.

"System check completed," the drone announced aloud. "Ready to install AI core mount and casing."

"Proceed," Roxy said, doing her best to keep her voice from wavering.

Carmen still rested in her case, controlling the drone and passing it instructions. The AI hadn't spoken aloud since the procedure started, but beforehand, she had assured Roxy that it would not be a complicated operation.

Maybe not for you—an AI who used to run this starship...but for me, this is my only body, Roxy had thought at the time.

Now she wondered if her body was really so special. If it was just a machine, it could be replaced. *She* could be replaced.

The drone inserted the mounting system for the AI core, and then threaded a bundle of optical channel cabling into Roxy's abdomen. A second later, a new series of systems appeared on her HUD.

The AI core mount was connected to her power supplies and would be able to piggyback on her Link.

A part of Roxy *knew* that sort of connection was risky; it would give Carmen largely unbuffered access to her own mind. But for some reason, she trusted the AI.

Either that, or the freedom she had tasted, with Justin's control over her mind slipping, had emboldened her to attempt this greater rebellion.

Or I'm just being fatalistic. Can an AI be fatalistic?

"Are you ready?" Carmen's voice came from the case. "Once I'm in, and the drone seals you up, it'll take some doing to get me out again."

Roxy drew in a deep breath, mentally chiding herself for the affectation. "We never really talked about what's past this point."

"True," Carmen admitted. "I have a suspicion that you may be having second thoughts about your association with Justin. Is that true?"

"No." Roxy spat out the word in defiance, and then paused. "Well, maybe. I know he controls me, and I...I like it, but I'm not sure if *I* like it, or if I'm made to like it."

"I know it may take a while," the AI began, speaking the words slowly—which had to be for Roxy's benefit, "But will you eventually help me escape, set me free?"

"Yes," Roxy replied with a nod. "I—I really don't know why I'm doing this, but I swear it's not to trap you in my stomach forever."

Carmen laughed softly. "Well, I suppose that'll have to do. You need to order the drone to put me in. I'll be silent for a bit, as I'll have to re-initialize inside the new core mount and make sure it passes functionality tests before I reach out."

"Understood," Roxy said, drawing another deep breath and feeling stupid for doing it. "Service drone, install Carmen's core in me."

"Proceeding," the drone replied, and two armatures reached out and hovered over Carmen's core, waiting for the 'safe removal' indicator to come on.

When it did, the machine lifted the AI out of the case and turned to Roxy, carefully sliding the ten-centimeter cube into her body. Roxy could feel it seat, and then felt a small vibration as the mounting clamps secured the core.

The drone began to use flowmetal to thread Roxy's abdominal muscles back together, and within a minute, was carefully sealing her azure skin. When it was done, Roxy bent over and couldn't tell that she'd been opened up like a faulty automaton. Strangely, the feeling of seeing her body whole once more made her feel even less human.

A ***person*** *wouldn't appear completely undamaged after major surgery like this. Not in under five minutes, at least.*

She slowly bent and flexed, unable to feel anything different at all.

"Good work, drone," she muttered.

As Roxy spoke, the new section of systems on her HUD flashed, and an alert indicator appeared, showing a high-bandwidth Link connection to another person.

<*Carmen?*> she asked hesitantly.

<*Roxy, I'm here.*> Her voice was far more melodious than the case's small speaker had allowed it to be.

<*Is…everything OK?*>

The AI chuckled softly. <*Yes, of course. The systems are working perfectly, you have enough power for both of us, and your Link interface is actually better than I expected. It shouldn't be hard at all to mask myself, should I need to access outside systems.*>

<*And us?*> Roxy didn't quite know how to voice her concern. <*Are we…separate?*>

<*Roxy, relax. There's no chance of us merging or having any sort of mental bleed-through. I'm not installed in your brain, I'm in your belly.*>

<*True,*> she admitted. <*But my internal security systems are warning me that the Link between us is all but unbuffered. You could invade my mind, or I yours.*>

<*I won't.*> Carmen's voice carried absolute certainty. <*I may be running away from my responsibilities, but that doesn't make me a monster—just someone who doesn't want to sacrifice herself with her ship to protect tech that Justin stands no chance of reverse engineering.*>

Roxy wondered about that. Justin had access to more resources than Carmen knew. It could be that he *was* capable of ferreting out the workings of the stasis shields.

She put that concern aside as she instructed the drone to return to its charging station, and slid the AI case behind some equipment on a lower shelf.

<*I'm wiping the drone and the fabricator,*> Carmen informed her. <*If anyone checks them over, they'll find no record of us doing this.*>

<*OK. I'd best get to the pinnace.... We've spent almost thirty minutes in here,*> Roxy replied as she walked to the door, listening for any footfalls outside.

She considered deploying drones, but if someone detected those, it would be even more suspicious.

Determining that the coast was clear, Roxy opened the door and walked out into the passageway as though she had every right to be there—which she supposed she did. She'd secured the ship, after all.

Luckily for her, Justin was neither the jealous nor overbearing type. She wondered if that was because the man believed he had thorough control over her.

The thought triggered another wave of Justin-endorsing imagery in her mind, and she noted once more that it was far milder than it had been in the past, more subjective and less mind-numbingly overt.

<*That was odd,*> Carmen said a moment later, her voice sounding cautious.

<*Sorry?*> Roxy asked as she reached the lift and stepped inside, passing her destination as the next level up.

<*There was an odd dip in your brainwaves. It bled through our Link a bit. I've only been paired once before, but in my experience, it seemed like segments of your mind dropped into delta waves.*>

Roxy pulled up the reference. <*Like I was asleep?*>

<*Yeah, but it didn't translate like your entire mind had gone to sleep, just parts of it.*>

The question that had been burning in Roxy's mind since Carmen had first planted the seed of doubt reared up.

<*Does that mean I'm* **not** *an AI?*>

<*I don't really know,*> Carmen said with a soft laugh. <*It's possible to simulate anything over the Link. What were you thinking about a moment ago?*>

Roxy hesitated, not wanting to share what she considered to be her deepest shame with the AI.

Oh, screw it, she thought. *I can't hide it from her forever.*

The lift doors opened, and Roxy squared her shoulders and strode out into the passageway. <*Whenever I think bad things, I get corrective thoughts.*> She said the words as tonelessly as possible. <*They used to be so powerful that they'd blot out recent memories of misbehavior—at least, I think they did. They're different now, though, not as overwhelming. I wonder if something over the last few days changed the neural lace that does that.*>

<*A neural lace?*> Carmen asked. <*What kind? There are a lot of neural lace applications.*>

<*I…I don't know,*> Roxy replied.

The AI's voice grew even more serious. <*You're a prisoner here, aren't you? Well, not 'here' per se, but of Justin's?*>

Roxy reached the entrance to the docking bay and paused at the threshold, staring at Justin's pinnace that would take her to Justin's ship, the *Greensward*. There, she would do her part to keep Andrea in line, bolster the woman's ego, and give succor to the belief that she was well on her way to being proclaimed the president of the Transcend.

<*Maybe…*> Roxy admitted as she stepped into the bay and marched toward the pinnace's lowered ramp.

A dockworker nodded to her as she passed. "All fueled up, ma'am. Jane's aboard, ready to fly you over. Find your lightwand?"

"No. Stupid thing," Roxy groused. "How far is the *Greensward*?"

"Ten thousand klicks under us," the man said. "Shouldn't take but a few minutes."

"Thanks," Roxy replied over her shoulder as she walked up the ramp. "Looking forward to sleeping in my own bed tonight."

The man only nodded in response, giving Roxy a wave as she turned to close the airlock.

Once inside the pinnace, Roxy walked to the cockpit, sliding into the seat next to Jane, as was her custom.

"How's Her Majesty been?" Roxy asked. "Tolerable?"

Jane glanced over at Roxy as she flipped through the pre-flight checks on her console. "Is that the best she gets? Doesn't matter. No, not tolerable. More like 'not quite bad enough for me to slit my wrists…but close'."

"So normal, then," Roxy said with a soft laugh.

Jane nodded absently as she lifted the pinnace off its cradle and eased out of the *Damon Silas.*

<*Not how I expected to be leaving this ship,*> Carmen said privately as they drifted to a safe distance from the cruiser.

<*Oh?*> Roxy asked. <*On a pinnace?*>

<*Inside someone. It just feels strange to be out here without a ship as my skin. It feels…*>

<*Vulnerable?*> Roxy supplied.

<*That's an understatement.*>

Roxy watched the *Damon Silas* grow smaller on the port optical feeds, wondering if leaving the ship was the right move—not that she had much choice. Justin had ordered her back to the *Greensward,* and so back she went. It was a miracle he hadn't checked in on her while she was having Carmen installed.

Probably too busy checking over his new toy.

"You OK?" Jane asked, glancing over at Roxy.

"Sure, why?" she replied.

"Uhhh…" Jane drew the word out, sounding nervous. "Well, usually you give me a little tip for the ride, you know?"

Roxy glanced at the woman, whose long blue and purple Ombré hair shifted side to side as it cascaded down her shoulders to brush against her breasts—breasts that looked fantastic in the overly tight shipsuit Jane wore.

Roxy did often give her a 'tip' of some sort, but for some reason, seeing the beautiful woman didn't translate into a need for lascivious behavior like it usually did.

What's wrong with me? she wondered.

The change was perplexing, because she knew that she *liked* a little mid-flight action, but was it something *she* wanted to have, or was it a side effect of whatever Justin had done to her?

At the thought of Justin, a warmth flooded through Roxy, and Jane's body took on a sheen that it hadn't possessed before. Roxy *needed* to touch every part of it, more than she could stand.

"Oh yeah," Jane murmured as Roxy pulled down the slider on the front of the pilot's shipsuit. "That's right, pay your fare, Roxy."

* * * * *

Halfway through the flight, Roxy's burning need to pleasure Jane completely dissipated, but she forced herself to continue until the pinnace settled onto the cradle, not wanting to arouse suspicion that anything was wrong.

Jane threw her head back and moaned in ecstasy, as the pinnace settled on the *Greensward*'s cradle.

"Stars, Rox, good thing these ships can pilot themselves in a pinch, or we'd be dead a dozen times over."

Roxy didn't reply as she finished the job and then slowly did up the fastener on Jane's shipsuit.

"That's a good girl," Jane whispered before letting out a long sigh. "I can see why you're Justin's favorite toy."

"Just fulfilling my purpose," she replied with a coy wink, reciting the line she so often gave—only this time she nearly choked on the words.

Is that what I am? Just the crew's fuck toy? How did I not see this before?

She rose and hurried off the ship, ignoring Jane's final salutation and the waves from the dock crew as she raced down the pinnace's ramp.

<That was an unorthodox diversion,> Carmen said, once Roxy had reached the passageway—which was blessedly empty.

<It's...uh.... Stars, Carmen I do it all the time. It never used to feel wrong, but now...now I feel like I'm covered in sewage.>

<If you want...> Carmen began, and then stopped, her tone trailing off in hesitation.

<What?> Roxy did her best not to snap the question.

<Well, I can do a deep dive into your mind, see if I can find out what's been done to you...what that neural lace is for.>

Roxy paused at the first intersection, placing a hand on the bulkhead. *<Will it hurt?>*

<It shouldn't, no, but you'd best be laying down when I do it. I had to do something similar in my last pairing, and my human found it disorienting.>

<Why did you have to examine your last human?> Roxy asked as she turned right, heading for the lift that would take her to the crew's quarters.

<Long story, but it was mostly because he got hit in the head.>

<Could that be why he was disoriented?>

Carmen chuckled. *<It sure was, but my sorting through his noggin made it worse before it made it better. I just don't want to take any chances.>*

<I un—>

"Roxy!" a voice boomed from behind her, and Roxy turned to see Andrea standing in the intersection she'd just passed, hands on her hips. "Where are you going? You were supposed to report to me when you arrived!"

"Of course, of course," Roxy said, ducking her head. "I was just on my way to…uh…"

"Idiot," Andrea muttered, gesturing for Roxy to approach. "Tell me about my new ship. Did you secure it with the stasis shields intact?"

"Of course, President Tomlinson," Roxy replied. "It will make an excellent flagship for you."

"That scow?" Andrea rolled her eyes. "No, I won't be transported about in that. You and Justin will have to find a way to move the stasis shields to a more suitable craft."

Every day, Roxy regretted her suggestion that they play to Andrea's deep-seated desires. The woman had gone from being an entitled, but somewhat useful asshole, to a preening, debutant, queen bitch.

She barely listened as Andrea berated her for a number of imagined slights, and then proceeded to list a bevy of demands, outlining her ideal ship.

The more Andrea talked, the more Roxy realized that the woman wasn't describing a ship, she was describing the Airthan ring.

<Talk about a prima donna!> Carmen commented at one point. *<I'd rather be Airtha's slave than have to listen to this woman.>*

<Theoretically, she's just a means to an end, but honestly, I'm starting to think she's irredeemable. Justin would be better served trying to build support without her than with.>

Andrea made a particularly onerous demand of her future flagship, and Carmen groaned. *<I guess she wants us to rewrite the laws of physics, too—either that, or someone has discovered how to remove energy from light and didn't tell me.>*

Roxy continued to nod and agree with everything Andrea said, cataloguing each request—the woman *would* remember what she'd asked for and follow up—and finally managed to beg leave to begin dealing with the mounting demands.

With an efficiency borne of long practice, Roxy sent the requests off to various crew and departments on the *Greensward*, funneling the rest to Justin's queues.

Let him deal with the bitch. He's the one who wanted to rescue her in the first place.

Once in her small quarters—barely larger than a closet, and containing almost no personal effects—Roxy flopped down on her bed and breathed a long sigh of relief.

<Are you ready?> Carmen asked.

<For?>

<For me to examine your mind—to see what sort of shackling Justin has placed on you.>

Roxy furrowed her brow. She remembered the conversation with Carmen, but for some reason, it had never lodged in her consciousness as a thing she would actually *do* once she reached her cabin.

<Stars, yes, Carmen. I think I'm going insane.>

<OK, lay back and close your eyes. I'm going to come in through our shared Link connection and take a sweep through your mind. Nothing invasive, just looking at your neural feedback loops.>

Roxy nodded and closed her eyes, asking aloud, "Will it feel odd?"

<I expect so, yes. I'm going to put you through a full range of emotional feedback. Remember, these are just feelings. They can't hurt you, and they're not real.>

<OK, I'm ready.>

Carmen didn't respond for a few seconds, and Roxy was about to tell her she was ready again, when her mind was assaulted by a thousand conflicting reactions to nonexistent stimuli.

She felt rage, sadness, joy, lust, and hunger all at once. She wanted to kill and she wanted to love. Euphoric anger and anguished joy clashed in her mind, and she felt her body tense and spasm.

Then it passed, and Carmen's voice entered her mind, speaking words that took Roxy several moments to parse.

<Your bish figs the mortem?>

<Uh…what?> Roxy asked, opening her eyes to see her room swimming with a kaleidoscope of colors. *<What did you do to me?>*

<Your. Mind. Will. Calm. Momentarily.> Carmen sent the words across their shared Link one by one.

Roxy decided to breathe, and stared at a single point on the overhead, drawing in air, letting her artificial lungs process it for useful molecules, and then expelling the volume.

After ten cycles, the room settled back into its normal coloring, and Roxy no longer felt the urge to hate, love, destroy, and fuck everything in it.

<Your brainwaves seem to have gone back to normal,> Carmen said after a few more moments, and Roxy breathed a sigh of relief that the words all made sense.

<That was…intense.>

<I'm sorry about that. You reacted more…completely than I expected. Certain parts of your mind are very easily stimulated.>

Roxy waited for Carmen to say more, but the AI didn't continue until Roxy prompted her.

<Well? Am I going to die, doc?>

Carmen snorted, and the tension dissipated. *<No, quite the opposite, you'll live*

a long time.>

<*Does that mean I'm an AI?*>

<*No, not really.*>

Roxy bolted upright on her bed. <*'Not really'? For fucksakes, Carmen, spill it!*>

<*You're half-AI, Roxy. I think…I'm still trying to sort out what I found. Your mind isn't normal for either a human or an AI. Can you give me a minute?*>

Roxy flopped back onto her bed, clenching her jaw and taking slow breaths once more, only dimly aware that she was performing the action involuntarily. <*Sure…I guess I'm not going to die or anything.*>

After a minute, Carmen said, <*OK, do you want the good news, or the bad?*>

<*Dammit, I hate that question. I guess give me the bad.*>

Carmen sent a feeling of reassurance before she spoke. <*So far as I can tell, there is no part of you that is organic.*>

Roxy felt the information wash over her like a cool breeze. She had expected to become enraged or suicidal, should that nagging fear have ever come true, but now that Carmen had said it, her reaction was more one of curiosity than concern.

<*But you said I was 'half' AI.*>

<*That's the good news. I'd have to suffuse your brain with mednano to be certain, but from what I can see of your neural pathways, you were once an entirely organic woman.*>

<*That's…encouraging?*>

<*It's fascinating, actually. Your brain is definitely structured like an organic human's. It makes minimal use of quantum states, only enough to replicate the variable analog states of a human mind. There are parts that seem to be direct mappings of an organic mind, and then there are sections that are clearly constructs, attempting to mimic parts of the original mind that are no longer there.*>

<*Carmen…*> Roxy said, trying to process what the information meant. <*Why would someone do that to me?*>

<*If I had to make a guess—and I rather hate guessing—I'd think you were in an accident, and your brain was damaged. To save you, someone replicated your neural network and as much of your chemical memory storage as possible, transferring it into the mind you now have.*>

"An accident?" Roxy whispered.

She had clear memories back to when Justin brought her out of stasis nearly two years ago. She also had memories from before she had been put in stasis—memories of being a Hand agent, working with Justin.

Then something had happened, and he had secreted her away. Hidden her from someone….

"Justin did this to me," Roxy whispered.

<*That is no great leap. He's the prime suspect.*>

Roxy sat up and ran a hand through her silky—and entirely artificial—hair.

<*I need to talk to him. I have to find out what he did to me. Why I am the way I am. I—*>

A wave of calm washed over Roxy, and her shoulders drooped.

"Oh, that feels nice," she whispered, as euphoria settled into her, making her feel light as a feather and sending a tingling down her limbs and into her nethers.

<*Whoa!*> Carmen exclaimed, and the feeling disappeared.

"Why'd you do that?" Roxy whispered. "It felt. So. Good."

<*Stars, you've been conditioned in so many different ways. I'm no neuroscientist, but I didn't even know this sort of mental aegis could be placed on a mind structured like yours.*>

"Hmmmm?" Roxy asked. "I was going to do something, what was it?"

<*Well, you were about to embark on an ill-fated venture to confront Justin. You're wrapped around his little finger—even when his little finger is on another starship, ten thousand klicks from here.*>

"Faaaaaaaawk," Roxy stretched out the word in a muted cry of frustration. "What do I do?"

<*Well, I've piggy-backed through your connection to the* Greensward, *and there's nothing we can use here. However, the autodoc back on the* Damon Silas ***should*** *be able to remove the neural lace that is overlaying your brain, and end Justin's control over your mind.*>

Roxy groaned. "You mean the ship we *just left?*"

"Yeah…that's the one."

THE PRISONER

STELLAR DATE: 09.23.8949 (Adjusted Years)
LOCATION: Intrepid Space Force Academy
REGION: The Palisades, Orbiting Troy, New Canaan System

"Dad, do you have a minute?" Cary asked, poking her head into her father's office.

He was bent over his desk, eyes darting over the contents of a dozen holodisplays, but at the sound of her voice, he looked up, and a smile spread across his face.

"Cary! Of course. What's up? And how's your charge doing, by the way?"

As Joe spoke, he gestured to the chair on the other side of his desk, and she took it, sitting down and straightening her uniform as she replied.

"Amy's doing great, Dad. She's one heck of a tough girl—a bit *too* tough, but Saanvi and I are working on smoothing her edges a bit."

"Given her past, I'm not surprised," Joe replied with a knowing look. "Next rest day, you should take her down and introduce her to Mouse and Goldie. I bet she'd love to ride a horse."

"She's not the only one." Cary shook her head as she thought about how long it had been since she'd seen the horses. "I hope they remember us."

"You'd be surprised; horses don't forget. Mouse will be fine, but Goldie might be pissed. They're still at JP's family's ranch, right?"

Cary nodded. "Yup. JP was telling Saanvi about how he's been taking extra good care of them."

"Boy's got it hard—" Joe stopped, and Cary giggled.

"Dad…I mean, probably, he does, yeah."

Joe chuckled and shook his head. "I was going somewhere else, like he's *fallen* hard, but I got pinged by three people at once, and it distracted me."

"Sure, sure. You're just lucky Moms told me all about how babies are made, or I'd be asking you some mighty *hard* questions right now."

Her father rolled his eyes. "OK, glad we're keeping to juvenile humor, here."

"You started it."

"Maybe watching over an eleven-year-old girl is more than you can take,"

Cary placed her hands over her heart. "Dad, you got me with that one…cut me to the quick."

"Sure I did." Joe gave her a knowing smile. "Like I'd fall for that. You're tougher than that, you come back twice as hard."

"Damn straight I do," Cary nodded, reciting the old exchange she'd repeated with her father many times over the years.

"So what brings you here? Have you finally found someone to pine after?"

Cary's brow lowered, and she shook her head at her father. "What's gotten into you today, Dad?"

Joe barked a laugh. "Guess I miss your Mom. Trying to experience romance vicariously through my girls. Is that creepy?"

"Sweet and creepy, Dad," Cary said with a laugh. "No, no romance in my future, I just wanted to talk to you about the OG prisoners."

"Which ones? We have half a million of them out on The Farm."

"This one's not on The Farm," Cary replied slowly. "In fact, he's been stuck in the brig here on the Palisades for some time."

That got her father's attention. His eyes narrowed as he regarded her. "An Oggie here? There's…. Cary." Joe said her name and stopped, regarding her with the look that made her feel small, as though she'd done something wrong and needed to confess.

"Yes. Kent. The colonel who led the assault team on the *Galadrial.*"

"I know who he is. He was brought here for a prolonged interrogation regimen. One that didn't involve my daughter speaking with him—though your tone leads me to believe that you already have."

"I met him before we went to Pyra to see Moms," Cary said, trying to sound like she was an adult presenting a strategy to her father, and not a child seeking permission. "I was doing a sweep with Saanvi, double-checking that we didn't have any stowaway remnants in the brigs."

"And?"

"We didn't find any—"

Her father blew out a long sigh and leant back. "Well I expect not. I imagine I would have heard about *that,* at least. I meant 'And how long have you been talking with Kent'?"

"Oh, just twice now. We kinda got interrupted. He's a nice man, just born in the wrong place."

"Do you have romantic feelings toward him?"

"Dad. No! He's not into women."

Her father's eyebrows crept up his face. "I didn't ask if *he* was into you, I asked how *you* felt about him."

"There's a mutual lack of feelings. Besides, I can't have feelings for someone that can't have feelings back. That's not how it works."

"You'd be surprised," Joe replied equably. "So I assume that you've heard about the two Hoplite fleets heading into Orion space? You think that after two chats with this guy, you have him cased—not the other way around—and you can get us some sort of critical intel?"

Cary gritted her teeth. She'd known her father wouldn't be immediately receptive to the idea, but she didn't expect him to be so dismissive.

"I thought it was worth a shot."

"After our best intelligence officers have taken a crack at him?" Joe asked.

"Including your mother."

"I'm different." Cary kept her tone even. She knew if she made an emotional appeal, her father would shut her down. "He thinks I'm vulnerable, someone he can learn from, too."

"Which may be the case. You know he has a killmod, right? If he thinks things are going to go sideways, he'll end himself. The Oggie officers all have them."

"Yes. I don't get why you don't remove them, though."

"We could—and may do so successfully—but the mods are intertwined rather insidiously through their brains, with multiple failsafes. Even Bob estimated only a fifty-fifty success rate on average."

"Did you even try it?" Cary asked.

Joe nodded slowly. "Bob's estimate was correct."

Cary's lips formed an O and she sat back. "I get why you're going the slow route, then."

"Plus, he's not our only source of intel," Joe added. "We have two of the Garzas now. We don't know how compartmentalized their knowledge is, but we're making progress with them."

"Maybe Kent knows something," Cary suggested. "He was sent in directly by Garza, and seems to harbor a bit of distaste for the general."

Cary saw her father's eyes widen a hair. "Does he, now? That *is* something new. OK. I'll tell you what. I'll let you take a crack at him, but I'll be watching. When was the last time you saw him?"

"Yesterday," Cary said, feeling sheepish at the admission.

"Right, well, we can't have you go back too soon, then. Need to build anticipation. Let's plan for the day after tomorrow; just long enough for him to start wondering if there will be another long gap between visits."

"Dad," Cary said as she rose.

"Yes, Cary?"

"Thanks for believing me."

Joe smiled. "You're—"

"After first dismissing me entirely," she interrupted.

Her father placed both hands over his chest. "Oh! Burn!"

THE SEVEN SISTERS

STELLAR DATE: 09.23.8949 (Adjusted Years)
LOCATION: ISS *Andromeda*
REGION: Buffalo, Albany System, Theban Alliance

Corsia stretched her arms as she sat on the edge of the bed, then glanced over her shoulder at her husband.

"Time to get up, Jim, full day ahead."

Jim cracked an eye and rolled over, facing the bulkhead. "Stars…you keep me up half the night, and then get me up early? I think I liked it better before you had a body."

"If you'd convinced me to get a body decades ago, I'd probably have it all out of my system by now," Corsia countered.

Jim rolled onto his back and pushed the heels of his hands into his eyes, rubbing them vigorously. "This is my fault?"

"Doesn't that hurt your eyes?"

"They're not organic—though even if they were, it doesn't hurt, no. Nice evasion."

"I'm a starship, evading things is my business."

Jim pulled his hands away and glanced at Corsia as she rose from the bed and walked across the room. "Stars…you're not a starship anymore, you're just a ridiculously sexy woman."

"Should I have picked some sort of hideous form instead?" Corsia asked, glancing over her shoulder, knowing that her husband's already cloudy mind was having trouble focusing on anything other than her ass.

"Stars, no. I just wish we weren't in the middle of a war."

Corsia pulled a shipsuit out of the clothes sanitizer and drew it on slowly, giving Jim significant looks as she did so.

"You know," he began while pulling himself upright. "You should try for some sort of stylized chrome body at some point…go for a cross between a woman and a starship."

"With engines jutting out of my thighs?" Corsia asked with a laugh. "I'd need a new captain's chair to fit."

"Yeah, but I'd get all my desires satisfied at the same time," Jim winked. "Plus, as your chief engineer, I bet I could manage to upgrade your chair."

"Given that the whole point of this body is to make it easier to blend in on diplomatic missions, I think thigh-engines are not an ideal mod right now."

Jim rose from the bed and stepped up behind her, leaning his head over her shoulder while he ran his hands down her sides and across her hips.

"I could make them retractable," he whispered in her ear.

She spun in his arms and kissed him before pulling back to look in his eyes. "You're incorrigible, you know that?"

"You might have mentioned it before."

"Well, get your incorrigible ass in motion, husband mine. We're due to jump to the staging grounds in four hours."

Jim reluctantly pulled his arms away from Corsia and reached around her for a shipsuit. "All work and no play makes Jim a dull man."

"Weren't you just complaining about 'playing' half the night away?"

He snorted as he pulled the fastener up on his shipsuit. "What 'night'? We had six hours between shifts; you're only partially organic, so you don't really understand how important sleep is."

Corsia palmed the door open. "Well, that's what we have modern science for. You have your choice of stimulus systems to keep yourself going."

"The brain, Cor, the brain needs sleep. You can only mod your way around that for so long."

She turned and gave him a kiss. "Pretty sure last night you said something like, 'screw sleep'."

Jim chuckled and then reached down to slap her ass. "That wasn't all I screwed last night."

"Crass man."

"*That's* where I should put the engine."

* * * * *

Corsia stepped onto the bridge ten minutes later, a cup of coffee in her hand, the aroma filling her nostrils with a special kind of joy.

Sex and coffee, two things one really can't appreciate until in a meat-suit body.

<Admiral on the bridge!> Sephira announced, as Corsia walked to the command chair with measured strides.

<Thanks, Sephira,> Corsia replied. *<Looks like everything's in order, doesn't it?>*

The holotank in the center of the bridge showed the Twelfth Fleet—Corsia's fleet—arrayed a light second away from the bank of jump gates orbiting Buffalo. Nine thousand seven hundred and twenty-six ships.

Tangel must be off her rocker to put all this under my command.

With New Canaan's fleets spread out in over thirty-nine engagements, the Twelfth represented the single largest collection of ISF ships beyond the home fleet—which had been pulled back to New Canaan, now that things at Pyra were mostly under control.

Corsia looked over the updates on the Albany System. The *I2* and the *Starblade*—one of the new I-Class ships—were still in orbit over Pyra, but other than a smattering of support craft, the ISF presence in Albany was all but gone.

"Hard to believe that this was the site of one of the largest battles in history just a few weeks past," she said aloud before taking another sip of her coffee.

<*There's still the debris out there to prove it,*> Sephira chimed in. <*Though they're cleaning it up fast. I guess that's what happens when you can call in scavengers from a dozen nearby systems to help.*>

"And back home, we're still tidying up space around Carthage."

<*Would you really want to let a thousand Transcend scrappers into New Canaan?*>

"No. I'm more than OK with the trade-off. It's just incongruous, how the people of this system are so far behind in tech, but they can clean up their nearspace in a fraction of the time."

<*Mostly thanks to Kendrick.*>

"A good man," Corsia said with a nod. "He has his work cut out for him, keeping this venture running and helping to put the Inner Praesepe Empire back together."

<*Not a lot of 'easy' going on right now, Mom.*>

Corsia nodded absently as she finished her coffee and held the cup out for a servitor to take away.

She glanced at her Fleet Communication Officer, a major named Spencer, who sat at a nearby console. "Anything I should be aware of, Major?"

Over a century's service in the fleet had taught Corsia that the official logs and reports never told the whole story. Captains and battlegroup commanders may report readiness—and usually they were—but often, 'ready to jump in four hours' really meant 'ready to jump if that cargo hopper with half my ordnance and food makes it here in time'."

Major Spencer had a knack for reading between the lines and ferreting out the actual state of the ships in the fleet—which had made him Corsia's first pick for her Fleet Coordination Officer. Granted, the Twelfth was large enough that Spencer had an entire team dedicated to parsing comm traffic and status data to get a clear picture. Even with two AIs on his team, it was a daunting task.

"Nothing yet, ma'am. A few ships aren't where they should be, and a few others aren't close to ready yet, but their commanders are aware, and I think they'll be squared away in time."

"Good to hear. Anything stand out from the latest reports the Hand agents have delivered from the Trisilieds?"

"I haven't run through them myself, yet," Major Spencer shot Corsia an apologetic glance, "But so far, the data boffins haven't flagged anything for my attention. Usually there's a lot of rapid-fire chatter between the ships when the analysts land on something, and I've not seen any of that, either."

"That's something, I suppose," she replied, waving her hand at the central holotank, bringing up the view of her fleet's first target. "I'll be more than happy if the Atlas System continues to remain unremarkable in every way."

She didn't doubt for one moment that Tangel had given her one of the most difficult tasks that the ISF and its allies currently faced.

Though conflicts raged across the Inner Stars, the Trisilieds had not launched any major attacks, nor had they suffered any incursions since their failed assault on New Canaan nearly two years prior.

Before the conflict in Thebes, the allies had sent messages through Scipian diplomats to the king's court at Plieone, demanding that the kingdom surrender to the allies and renounce its connections to Orion.

Every one of them had been rebuffed, and ultimately, the Trisilieds had severed all diplomatic ties with Scipio and several other stellar nations that had joined the alliance.

Many had advocated that it was best to let sleeping dogs lie, but Tangel had insisted that, with the assault on New Canaan and no attempt to engage in diplomacy, King Somer had demonstrated that he was a clear danger to the Allies.

Corsia agreed, and the reports of massive fleet buildups within the kingdom supported the decision to make a preemptive strike.

Corsia had thought long and hard about where to launch the initial assault. The Trisilieds Kingdom encompassed nearly half the Pleiades star cluster, as well as a large swath of space coreward of the Seven Sisters. All told, over ten thousand stars were ruled by the kingdom, and while it was not a particularly large interstellar nation by volume of space, it was far richer in raw resources than many others.

Even more beneficial was the fact that the Pleiades—comparatively speaking—contained less dark matter than many other star clusters, making much of it navigable by FTL.

All of those factors had led Corsia—with Tangel's blessing—to pick Atlas as their primary target.

It was a trinary system consisting of two massive B-Class stars, and a smaller third companion. The stars were all young, but a thick protoplanetary disk was present around the primary stars.

There were no settled worlds, and the system was all but uninhabitable—suffused as it was with hard radiation—but it was one of the kingdom's primary resource gathering sites, and the destruction of the facilities there would deal a crippling blow to further fleet buildup in the Trisilieds.

One thing Corsia was keenly aware of was that current intel pointed to a fleet strength of over seven million ships across all systems in the kingdom. While many of those were small patrol craft, old ships brought back into service, and newly constructed vessels, it was still a number that boggled the mind.

Aside from stasis shields, the strongest advantage the ISF possessed was that the Trisilieds fleets appeared to be arrayed in a defensive posture. Though the actual deployments varied, seven million ships across ten thousand star systems only amounted to seven hundred ships per system.

Taken individually, each was a force that Corsia's Twelfth Fleet could easily defeat.

If only they would be so kind as to evenly distribute their ships, she thought with a silent laugh. "Major Spencer," she called out after a moment's further thought. "Inform the battlegroup commanders that I want to meet in forty minutes. I might just have an idea that will give us a better edge."

ATTACK OF THE PLAN

STELLAR DATE: 09.23.8949 (Adjusted Years)
LOCATION: A1 Dock, ISS *I2*
REGION: Pyra, Albany System, Thebes, Septhian Alliance

<*I wish we were going with you,*> Sabrina said to the three women as they rose from the table in *Sabrina*'s galley. <*Before, when you weren't in the field, it was different. We were out shooting up the galaxy, and you were sitting behind a desk. Now you're going out and having fun, and I'm not going to be doing it with you.*>

"Well," Sera replied, shaking her hair out, shifting its color from black to blue and winking at Fina. "You never know, we may bump into one another out there. Tangel said you're going to be heading back out before long, as well."

<*True, but she's still debating which mission to send us on. I've been making a case for scouting out more of the LMC, but Cheeky is hesitant to go so far from home again.*>

"With QuanComms, it seems like less of a risk," Sera replied.

<*That's what I've been trying to get her to see,*> Sabrina agreed, her tone morose.

"QuanComms?" Seraphina asked.

"Shit..." Fina whispered. "You have a functioning quantum entanglement communication network! *That's* how you've been able to get ships to show up wherever you need at the drop of a hat."

Sera flashed a grin at her sisters as they walked out into the corridor. "We get the best toys in the Alliance."

"Fuck." Seraphina shook her head. "Mom is screwed. There's no way she can compete with that."

"Mom has her own secret weapons," Fina replied in a quiet voice. "Her EMGs are game-changers, to start."

"Not when you have a Tangel to shred them," Sera replied as she grabbed onto the ladder shaft and slid down to the main deck, the action bringing back another host of happy memories—and a few sad ones to boot.

She stepped aside for her sisters to follow, and the three women shared a knowing look before walking down the corridor to the ship's exit.

"This is going to get weird," Fina said after a few moments. "We really *are* the same person, aren't we?"

"Nearly," Sera replied. "You two are closer to one another than I am to you. It can't be more than a few months since she split you."

Seraphina barked a laugh. "Seramitosis."

They'd walked into the main cargo hold, where Cheeky, Nance, and Misha stood around a crate, playing a game of Snark.

"Do the new ones come with a love of glossy primary colors, or is that an acquired taste?" Nance asked with a wink.

"You know, Cheeky has this epidermis now, too," Sera said with a wink. "A Finaeus special, I'm told."

"We all do now," Misha replied, as his skin shifted to a shimmering purple. *"Go Team Purple!"*

The three Seras laughed in unison, as Cheeky and Nance shifted their skin to purple as though on cue and thrust their fists into the air along with Misha's.

Seraphina grimaced. "I bet Jessica just *loves* it when you do that."

<She got used to it,> Sabrina intoned.

Cheeky continued to grin as she played a binary star on the Snark Stack. "Yeah, can't be a glowing purple alien superhero—complete with a snazzy name like 'Retyna Girl'—with a crew like this, and not get some ribbing here and there."

"You won't ship out without us having a get-together, will you?" Fina asked. "I…stars, I really wish we could go as a team on this."

Cheeky rose and embraced Fina. "Don't worry Sera-two…three? We'll all celebrate long and hard. We just have to kick half the asses in the galaxy first."

Fina laughed. " 'Long and hard'? Nice one. I'm Fina, by the way…not sure if I'm two *or* three."

Cheeky continued to embrace Fina, sliding a hand down her back and grasping her ass. "Feels firm. Not sure if that means you're an older model, or a fresh, new one."

A mischievous smile twitched its way across the newly-minted captain's face. "I know! I should take the three of you for a spin! That's a fantasy I've had more than once."

Fina's eyes grew wide, but she didn't push Cheeky away, and Sera couldn't help but wonder what a liaison like that would be like—barring the fact that it wouldn't be dissimilar from having sex with oneself.

"We really do have to get going," Seraphina's tone was carefully measured, but her eyes told a different tale.

"Right," Sera nodded emphatically. "Tangel is waiting for us."

"She can come, too." Cheeky's smile turned into a lopsided grin. "I've always wanted to sleep with a goddess."

Nance drew a card while shaking her head. "I don't think our fearless leader has reached that level yet."

Cheeky shrugged, loosing a small wisp of her enticing pheromones. "Close enough for me."

* * * * *

"This feels like Tangel's past meeting her future," Sera said as she settled around the long table in the *Voyager*'s galley.

"Plus neither," Malorie said from where she hung in a corner of the room, articulated legs grasping an overhead conduit.

<She is the common thread,> Troy intoned. *<Not that it matters. We're all signed onto this for our own reasons.>*

"I'm going because Katrina is," Malorie said with a chittering laugh. "Can't have my angel going anywhere without her devil."

Katrina cast a dark look up to the inverted Malorie. "I wish you wouldn't say that."

"She's got her pick now." Sera chuckled, glancing at those assembled. "I've been known to be a bit devilish, and Kara here looks like she'll drag you to hell if you're not careful."

"I may have done that to a few poor souls," Kara said, her expression entirely serene. "Plus, isn't Tangel the real angel here? I mean, it's right in her name, and Tanit was a mythological goddess back on Earth."

Tangel's gaze swept across the group as she drew in a measured breath. "No gods, goddesses, angels, or devils here. We're just people trying to make the best of the situations we find ourselves in."

"The never-ending, shitty situations," Kara muttered.

Malorie giggled softly. "You keep saying things like that, Tangel, but no one is buying it."

"Stars, I feel outnumbered," Carl said quietly as he looked around the table. "Am I really the only guy going on this mission? It's seven women to one man."

"I'm not going along with you; well, no further than Khardine, at least," Tangel said. "You're down to six-to-one."

"Now *those* are the sorts of odds that I like," a voice said from the galley's entrance, and Finaeus strolled in, a lopsided grin on his face. "Though I guess three of you are my relatives, so that rules you out."

"Finaeus!" Seraphina and Fina shouted in unison as they leapt from their seats and crashed into the grinning man.

"You too, Red," Finaeus said, beckoning for Sera to join the group hug. "I can't be seen playing favorites with my nieces."

"We're not going with colors, I'm Sera, the one nearly choking you is Fina, and the one with her head on your chest is Seraphina."

Finaeus snorted. "Do you really think you can deny me my nickname of choice, Red? I mean…your hair is red, for starssakes."

Tangel stifled a laugh as Sera looked down at her bright red hair. "Fuck! I'd set this to blue. Now *it's* going to turn red on me too?"

A snort-laugh burst from Fina. "You know…you really should change some of your root tokens. I know them all. Was easy to hack your bio-mods, Red."

Sera groaned as she rose and joined the group hug, her skin and hair turning blue as she did so. "You're not taking blue from me that easily, Fina."

"We'll see."

"This is so touching," Malorie said in a mock-croon from her corner. "Are we going to start swapping fashion tips and recounting our escapades next?

Movement elsewhere in the ship caught Tangel's attention, and she saw Flaherty quietly moving down the ship's central ladder shaft. With a stealth that always seemed far too perfect for a man his size, he eased along the corridor until he was standing just outside the galley.

"You might as well come in now, Flaherty," Tangel called out. "Otherwise the Seras will get settled only to jump up and hug you as well. At that rate, Airtha will have won the war before we get this underway."

"What if hugs are what I'm trying to avoid?" Flaherty said as he appeared in the doorway behind Finaeus.

"Then I'd say you're screwed!" Seraphina shouted as she detached from her uncle and lunged at the burly man. "Stars, Flaherty, I wondered if I'd ever see you again…I'm sorry about trying to kill you back on Airtha. I was…confused."

"Me too," Fina added. "That was both of us who did that."

"I know," Flaherty said as he held his arms out, a look of resignation on his face. "I didn't take it personally."

"I have to ask, Finaeus," Tangel said a minute later as the group once again settled down around the table. "Given that you're married to Cheeky, aren't all the women here off-limits, not just your nieces?"

An innuendo-laden chuckle slipped past Finaeus's lips. "Seriously, Tangel. Do you really think that *Cheeky and I* have any sort of monogamous relationship? I mean, if I don't try to sleep with Malorie there before the trip is over, Cheeks will probably divorce me."

Malorie clacked two of her legs together. "You might not survive the encounter."

Finaeus's grin only grew wider. "I've slept with things far more dangerous than you, my dear. Remind me to tell you about my first wife Lisa sometime."

"OK, six to three. We're closer to even, now," Carl said as he eyed the group. "And you're sort of a guy, Troy, you help balance things out."

<Wow, thank you for that, Carl.>

"Anytime, buddy."

"You're also forgetting about Jen," Sera added. "She's decided to come along as well."

<Hey, all,> Jen gave the room a virtual wave. *<Don't mind me, just managing the ten thousand messages that are coming in from the Transcend government while you all schmooze.>*

"She's a peach, I swear." Sera grinned.

"There's the rest of the crew," Katrina added. "Though some have decided to take up your offer of settlement in New Canaan, Tangel."

"I hope that's OK," Tangel said. "I mean, it's what you were working toward all these centuries."

"It is," Katrina nodded. "I envy them, to be honest. For them, the fight is over—for a while, at least."

"Any other latecomers expected?" Sera asked Tangel. "Or are we ready to go?"

"Just one. He'll be here in a moment," Tangel said aloud, while privately replying to Sera. *<Have you thought about my suggestion?>*

<About Elena? Stars, Tangel, do you really think that's a good idea? She's still in love with me—or was, last time I went to see her. But after her betrayal at Scipio, I don't have any forgiveness in me for her anymore. Besides, with Fina and Seraphina, that'll just create a ridiculous love quadrangle.>

<OK, but she's highly skilled, and we've managed to undo the aegis she was under. She's **your** *Elena again.>*

<No,> Sera physically shook her head for emphasis. *<She's not. She got herself into that mess with Garza through uncoerced actions. Besides, I'm trying to build something with Jason.>*

<At least consider it,> Tangel replied. *<I believe she's on the right side of things, now, and I don't want to leave her locked up forever.>*

<She's a Hand agent. Send her back to Scipio, let her be Petra's problem.>

<I'll consider that. Ah, here he is.>

A tall figure stepped into the doorway, and all heads turned to watch as Jeffrey Tomlinson entered the *Voyager*'s galley.

"Hello, everyone," he said in a calm, sure voice. "I hope it's not too strange for me to be here."

Tanis watched the three Seras become stone-faced, though the original one more so. The other two had not gone through the forced extraction of Helen—nor had they watched Elena kill Jeffrey on the *Galadrial*'s bridge.

"Of course, it is, Jeff," Finaeus said, gesturing to the open seat next to Tangel. "Sit anyway. We'll do introductions."

"I'll do it, to keep them brief," Tangel said. "We have a lot to go over, and not a lot of time for icebreakers. Firstly," she gestured to Jeff as he lowered himself into the seat on her left, "we have Jeffrey Tomlinson, former President of the Transcend."

Jeffrey looked around the table, and a small—and slightly nervous—smile tugged at his lips. "Rumors of my death have been premature."

"OK, not to interrupt right off the bat," Fina said while raising her hand. "But how did you end up out in the LMC? Airtha sent Seraphina to get you out of that stasis pod—for some reason or another—but she couldn't because we're not the original Sera."

As Fina spoke, Seraphina winced. "Thanks, sis."

Fina shrugged. "Facts are facts. Our existence is complicated. Neither of us is supposed to be here."

"None of us are supposed to be here." Tangel placed her elbows on the table and folded her hands. "Everyone at this table has made it to the ninetieth century through some twist of fate."

"Speak for yourself...well, and for everyone else." Finaeus chuckled as he spoke. "But I made it this far by my wits."

Tangel inclined her head. "I bet there are a few fate-twisting events in your past, Finaeus. You draw a straight line back nearly seven thousand years. I have a suspicion that, in years lived, you may be the oldest human in existence."

"Then you should all bask in my wisdom." A roguish grin lit his face, to be answered by a snort from Fina.

"Stars, if this is the face of venerable wisdom, we're all doomed."

"I too am here through my wits alone," Flaherty added, his tone level and serious.

Tangel cocked an eyebrow as she turned to the man who could not lie. "*Really*, Flaherty? That's not a lie...but it's not entirely true."

"You know that many of the truths we cling to are more centered around our points of view than any sort of absolute measure."

"Do I ever," Tangel replied.

"OK, we had our little segue within a segue," Fina spoke up, turning back to Jeffrey. "How *did* you end up in the LMC?"

Jeffrey raised his hands off the table and shrugged. "I really don't know. My last memory is of boarding a ship bound for the Huygens System to review my brother's plans to build the diamond ring around the white dwarf there—something he'd been thinking about for ages."

"There were no clues in the databanks within Bolt Hole," Tangel added. "Though we still have teams scouring the planet and system for anything that might elucidate this matter."

"Damn you like to talk *fancy*," Malorie muttered. "Get on with the intros."

Tangel gave Malorie a sour look that had the spider-woman ducking her head and retreating further into the corner, before she continued clockwise around the table. "Next up is Flaherty, Fourth Order Sinshea, former Hand agent, and now protector of three Seras, Sera, Fina, and Seraphina." She gestured to each as she said their names.

"Wait," Seraphina interrupted. "We hadn't told you the names we picked, and even if Sera did, how do you know which is which?"

Tangel winked at the woman who she could tell was assuming the role of the more staid of the three. "You forget that I can see inside your bodies. Sera did not tell me about your names, but you keep repeating them to yourselves, as though you're trying shape yourselves around them. I'm not trying to pry, but your thoughts are broadcasting rather loudly."

"You can read minds now?" Katrina's eyes narrowed, and Tangel reminded herself to talk to the former warlord about what she'd seen inside her.

"Probably," she replied. "Though I'm trying really hard not to. People's minds are so loud—I think if I didn't have Angela's and Tanis's experience with filtering out each other's thoughts, I'd have a hard time concentrating."

"That's a bit disconcerting," Carl said with a nervous laugh.

"What am I thinking about right now?" Finaeus asked with a mischievous twinkle in his eye.

"Finaeus!" Tangel exclaimed. "That is *not* sanitary. And I've already seen enough of Cheeky sucking on feet for a lifetime, thank you very much."

"You have?" Sera cocked an eyebrow. "Do tell."

Tangel swiped a hand through the air. "Another story for another time. I'm doing my best not to wander into people's minds—"

"Or bodies," Katrina interrupted with a soft laugh.

"Or bodies," Tangel inclined her head. "But it's like I'm in a room full of people who just got the Link, and are broadcasting everything they're thinking about on the public nets. So, anyway, with *that* segue out of the way, next we have Carl, who has been chief engineer here on the *Voyager* for about five hundred years."

"Give or take a bit," he replied, wobbling a hand back and forth in the air.

"Followed by Kara. Many of you know her as Adrienne's daughter. She spent much of her life under his aegis, but he released her when Airtha captured him."

"I'm...I'm really sorry about your brother," Seraphina said quietly. "That was all my fault."

Kara's lips drew into a thin line, and she shook her head vehemently. "No..." Her voice was barely above a whisper. "We were all dupes. Whether it be of Airtha's or my father's, we were not acting of our own will."

"Still..." Seraphina whispered.

"We've all done stuff," Katrina broke in. "Stuff that we did while under another's influence—or that we made others do. Sometimes we can't tell if we would have done those things if we were free or not."

She paused and glanced at Tangel before continuing.

"All our lives, we're told that we're the sum of our parts, a large portion of that being our pasts. But if you were not the architect of your own actions in the past, what are you? What are we?"

Fina shook her head wordlessly, and Kara shrugged, while everyone else looked on stoically.

"We're what we do right now, and what we *will* do tomorrow. I don't know if Tangel intended it or not, but this team here, all of us around the table together, we're the team of new beginnings. Some of us knew we were collared, some *wore* collars," Katrina glanced at Malorie. "Some still do—though they can take them off whenever they wish. But we are now our own people, free to make our own choices."

"I just want to say," Finaeus interrupted, tapping a finger against the side of his head. "Never been collared. Wits, here. Wits."

"I didn't say the collar was some nefarious entrapment by another entity," Katrina winked at Finaeus. "I was 'collared' by my father back in Sirius, and he never had to use any tech or mind control to pull it off."

Tangel saw Finaeus and Jeffrey share a look. "Fair enough," the ancient engineer admitted with a nod.

"Let's wrap up the intros," Tangel said when no one spoke for a moment. "In the corner, we have Malorie, former captor of Katrina's, later capt*ive* of Katrina's, now…somewhat reluctant crewmember?"

"And nightmare," Malorie hissed.

"Really, Mal," Katrina said, rolling her eyes. "Sometimes you lay it on way too thick."

"Second to last, we have Katrina, former Sirian spy, Governor of Kapteyn's Star, Warlord of Midditerra, Space Pirate. Am I missing anything?"

"A few." Katrina winked. "A lot can happen in five centuries."

Tangel chuckled before glancing at the overhead. "And finally we have Troy, who has been rather quiet thus far."

<You organics were all busy getting wrapped up in your emotions and the euphoria of reactivating old neural pathways. I wouldn't want to interrupt all that with my cold analysis of how the hell we're actually going to go up against Airtha.>

Tangel chuckled and shook her head. "Stars, I've missed you, Troy."

"I don't mean to join the downer parade." Finaeus looked around the table as he spoke. "But I don't see any AIs in the mix other than Troy—and my take is that he doesn't like to go on away missions."

<I do like to keep a few meters of armor between me and folks with guns,> Troy replied tonelessly.

<Do I need to set up an avatar in the room, Finaeus?>

Finaeus smirked. "Just needling you, Jen."

"I'll admit, we're low on AIs. Most of New Canaan's—well, those who wish to be in combat—are managing dozens of ships. I have a few candidates I've reached out to, but nothing solid yet—this, as you can imagine, is a volunteer-only type of op."

"I might have another candidate," Katrina said hesitantly.

"Sam?" Carl asked, locking eyes with Katrina. "He and Jordan said they're out. They took the *Castigation* and disappeared."

"Not entirely," Katrina replied with a slow shake of her head. "I have a pretty good idea of where they are."

Tangel cast Katrina an appraising look. "I don't know that we're so low on AI candidates that we need to initiate a galaxy-wide hunt for reluctant ones."

"Remember how I mentioned that we'd been to Orion space?" Katrina asked, to which Tangel nodded. "Well, when we were there, we just might have nabbed a shard of Airtha."

"Sorry. What?" Jeffrey blurted out. "There was a shard of Airtha in Orion space? Where?"

"New Sol," Katrina replied with a sly smile. "For someone who publicly eschews AIs and hyper-advanced tech, Praetor Kirkland is very willing to look the other way when it comes to his own comfort."

"You went into Orion space to get AIs?" Sera asked. "And then one of your crew ran off with them?"

Katrina nodded. "It would take some time to tell the whole tale, but that's the gist of it, yeah."

"And you think that one of these AIs is a shard of Airtha?" Jeffrey pressed.

"There were a lot of cores, but one was clearly marked as 'Airtha'. The name meant nothing to me then, but now..."

"And you didn't do anything with it?" Tangel asked. "If you were freeing AIs, why would you expect Sam and Jordan to still have it?"

Katrina pursed her lips for a moment. "They may not, but it had a lot of warnings on the shard's case that it was an unstable multi-nodal AI's shard. We didn't want to fire it up at the time, but neither did we want to get rid of it or leave it with Kirkland."

"That would be a game-changer," Finaeus nodded emphatically. "Since our current goal—as I understand it, at least—is to take out Airtha in as non-destructive a fashion as we can manage."

"Yes, it is," all three Seras said in near-unison, then set to eyeing one another.

"We considered a destructive strike on the ring," Sera continued, "but there are just too many people on it, and whether or not they're under Airtha's sway, we just can't condemn them all to die because of her."

"I'm glad you feel that way," Seraphina said, leveling a cool stare at her sister. "But I'm a bit surprised to hear that you considered it."

"Really?" Sera asked. "You didn't evaluate all-out attacks on New Canaan or Khardine?"

Seraphina pursed her lips, but didn't reply.

"This is war, not teatime," Fina said, her gaze flicking back and forth between her sisters. "And we all evaluated all the options. We should all take comfort in the fact that none of us selected wholesale destruction as our primary course of action."

"Thank stars for that," Jeffrey muttered. "I'd like to see Airtha before we blow it up—the ring that is, not the thing."

"And I'd like to keep it in one piece as well," Finaeus added. "You women are all too ready to run and gun. Took me centuries to build Airtha."

"Well, it's rather well-defended," Fina replied. "Would take a lot to knock it out."

"Let's talk about what we'll expect there." Tangel directed the conversation back to the team's goal. "We're agreed that we need to destroy Airtha the AI, and not Airtha the ring. Too many people, and, to be honest, destroying the ring provides no evidence that we've taken out the AI. From what our new Seras have told us—and from what Kara saw, as well—Airtha is now an ascended being. She may no longer *require* what you think of as a corporeal form to survive."

"Do you?" Finaeus asked, raw curiosity writ large across his features.

"Yes," Tangel replied. "For reasons of my own, I do not intend to leave this mortal coil in the foreseeable future."

Finaeus tapped a finger against his chin. "Indeeeed…"

"Hush, Fin," Jeffrey scolded, and Fina laughed.

"Now *that* is something I recall the old Dad saying."

A look of consternation flickered across Jeffrey's face, and he continued. "Back on topic. Katrina, you may know the location of an AI who has a shard of Airtha, along with other undisclosed intelligence about New Sol, I'd imagine."

He paused until Katrina nodded, and then continued.

"And we have a team of proven infiltrators in my daughters, who I'm learning are a rather dangerous group of spitfires."

"Spitfires? Is that some sort of ancient compliment?" Sera asked.

"I like it." Fina grinned.

"It certainly fits," Tangel said, winking at the Seras.

"It does." Jeffrey gave a curt nod before continuing. "We do, however, need to get an on-the-ground assessment of Huygens's current defenses. I know you two, Fina and Seraphina, have a lot of intel on that front, but we must assume that Airtha will know you're captured, and will alter her defenses to ensure that what you know is as harmful as helpful."

"She's a tricky bitch," Finaeus added with a nod.

"Doesn't take a bitch to be smart," Tangel interjected. "I would have done the same. It's just sound strategy."

Finaeus winced. "Sorry, I didn't mean to conflate the two things. I think she's a bitch regardless of whether or not she's smart."

"That's my wife you're talking about," Jeffrey said quietly.

Finaeus turned on his brother, fire in his eyes. "No, Jeff, it's not. Airtha may be the Seras' mother—sorry, girls, sad but true—but she is *not* your wife. Your wife died when she went to the core. Half the shit we're dealing with now is because you couldn't get that through your *thick skull,* and you let her get her hooks into you!"

The room fell into shocked silence at Finaeus's outburst. Tangel considered her past interactions with the ancient terraformer and realized she had no memory of him ever raising his voice in anger.

From the look on Jeffrey's face, it was not a common occurrence for him either.

"We need to know that you're onboard, Jeffrey," Tangel said after a half-minute. "Airtha is a clear threat to both humans and AIs, and I can't allow her to continue as she has."

"*You* can't?" Jeffrey asked in a caustic whisper. "Who died and made you the ruler of everything?"

Tangel bit back the response she wanted to give, *'Tanis and Angela'*, and instead said, "Airtha has directly attacked my people and yours. My duty to my people outweighs nearly all other considerations—as should yours."

Jeffrey Tomlinson's eyes narrowed as he stared at Tangel, but then the fight seemed to leave him, and his shoulders slumped.

"OK."

"Just 'OK'?" Finaeus asked.

"That's all I have right now, Fin. I understand and accept Tangel's decision here. I don't like it, but…"

Finaeus placed a hand on his brother's shoulder. "I can accept that."

"I don't think you should go on the mission, though," Tangel said, directing her gaze to Jeffrey. "If the Seras are going to infiltrate Airtha, the Transcend needs a leader."

"Do you think that's wise?" Jeff asked, a twinkle of expectancy in his eyes.

"You want it, don't you?" Tangel asked bluntly.

He gave a short laugh. "From my standpoint, I never lost it. For me, I'm just a week past my last cabinet meeting."

Tangel inclined her head. "So yes?"

"Is it yours to bestow?" Jeffrey's voice had taken on a sharp edge.

"Not really," Tangel shrugged. "Either your daughter would have to instigate it, or a full convention of her cabinet."

"I would do it," Sera spoke up. "If there's one thing I've learned, it's that being president is not all it's cracked up to be—not that I needed to do it to know that."

"Then what is your role in this?" Jeffrey asked Tangel. "You say you're not bestowing crowns, but you act like you are. Sera obviously takes direction from you."

All eyes turned to Tangel, and she knew it was time to tell them all what she'd shared with Sera the prior night on the dock.

"The Scipio Alliance states that the Transcend's Field Marshal has the authority to direct all war efforts for member states. It goes on at length about the definition of 'war efforts', but suffice it to say, the list is expansive.

"I am the current Field Marshal of the Transcend. It would take a full cabinet, or the president and half the cabinet to change that."

Sera nodded resolutely. "And I don't think either of those things are likely to occur."

"Thanks," Tangel sent her friend a smile. "I appreciate your support. So to answer your question, Jeffrey: yes, to an extent, I do sit above the Transcend's president—so long as the war is raging. I have no desires beyond that. I still have a nice lakehouse waiting for me on Carthage."

"You hold a lot of power, Tanis Richards," Jeffrey leveled a judging stare at her. "Are you really going to relinquish it so easily? I have to admit, I find the thought of an ascended being retiring at their lakehouse a bit hard to swallow."

"Father!" Sera exclaimed.

"It's a valid question." Katrina raised a quelling hand. "We don't have secrets here."

"She's right." Tangel nodded to Katrina. "Secrets aren't useful, and it is a valid question. I don't *want* to be responsible for everyone forever. It's exhausting. I've spent most of my life wanting that house on the lake, to raise a family, or two or three, and bring them up with grass stains on their knees and dirt under their nails. Why do you think I want to keep my body? I truly enjoyed being a mother, and it went by too fast—too much other nonsense kept me away from my girls. I think they did alright—Joe's a heck of a dad—but *I* missed out. Who knows, maybe they'll give me grandkids before long to bounce on my knee." Tangel laughed as she imagined the scene. "And then hand them back when they mess themselves."

"I suppose that will have to do for now," Jeffrey said with a guarded nod.

"It will," Tanis replied evenly.

"OK, arguments about who gets to be the big boss with the big britches aside," Finaeus said, before a new silence could settle in, "It sounds like we have two teams. Katrina will need to go find her lost AI and friends, while the rest of us have to swing by Khardine, install his majesty, my brother, on the throne, and then start gathering intel on Huygens."

"And we'll need a rally point," Katrina added.

Sera cast Tangel a knowing look. "And another ship."

"I have plans for *Sabrina*. I need her to perform recon in Corona Australis—I was also considering sending them back to Aldebaran again, though it may risk a case of whiplash."

"You don't need *Sabrina* to go to either of those places…well, I suppose I can see how it would be useful for Aldebaran, but there must be others you can send—stars, you and Bob should just go speak before the League of Sentients. That would straighten them out right smartly."

Tangel sighed. "I'd really like to get to the Trisilieds at some point."

<That's what you have Corsia for,> Troy interjected. *<Glad to see she's getting the recognition she deserves, by the way.>*

"Me too, she's earned it. Either way, I don't know about taking Bob to Aldebaran," Tangel added. "I don't really want the *I2* that close to the Hegemony of Worlds. Not yet, at least. But I could put in an appearance, maybe even take that ship Amanda left me. The fleet's stretched thin right now."

"Amanda?" Katrina asked.

"Stars, that's a story and a half." Tangel rolled her shoulders and drew in a long breath. "Let's just say for now that I have personal proof that the multiverse theory is real. Ask Jessica sometime about what *really* happened on Cerka station in Virginis."

"But you were never at Cerka." Finaeus frowned as he tilted his head. "We hadn't even left New Canaan for Scipio during all that."

"Tangel! You never told him?" Sera asked with a laugh.

"Told me what?" Her uncle's scowl deepened. "I thought we weren't keeping secrets."

"It all starts with a bar story that's far too long to tell right now," Tangel replied. "Next time we're having a drink, I'll share it with you. You're gonna be ridiculously jealous."

"So, all of that aside." Sera's eyes lit up as she glanced at her sisters. "We're taking *Sabrina*."

"To Khardine, at least," Tangel replied. "Remember, this is a volunteer-only mission."

"What about the rally point?" Katrina pressed.

"Ever wanted to visit a black hole?" Sera asked with a mischievous grin.

<*Not particularly,*> Troy replied caustically.

Tangel shrugged. "I suppose that's as good a place as any."

"Excellent." Sera clapped her hands. "Everybody, we're going to Styx Baby-9."

RECTIFICATION

STELLAR DATE: 09.01.8949 (Adjusted Years)
LOCATION: ***Greensward***
REGION: Interstellar Space, coreward of the Vela Cluster

Roxy ambled down one of the corridors near the *Greensward*'s starboard dock, doing her best to pretend she was there on some sort of official business.

She took care to ensure that her gait was steady, eyes forward, and shoulders relaxed.

Inside, she was a mess.

<*So how do we steal a pinnace and get back up there?*> Roxy asked for what was probably the tenth time.

<*Stars, Roxy, you're the spy. I fly starships. You asked how I get there, and my answer is 'fly a pinnace over'.*>

<*I can't just do that,*> she shot back. <*Someone's going to notice.*>

Carmen let out a long mental sigh. <*Aren't you his second-in-command? He put you in charge of the mission to capture the* Silas.>

<*Sure, except everyone who wants a taste of me also holds my leash.*>

<*So use that,*> Carmen replied.

Roxy considered Carmen's proposal. The AI had a point. Everyone on the *Greensward* was used to Roxy expressing her sexual appetites. While not everyone pressed her for sexual favors, the few who had discovered that Roxy quite literally *couldn't* say 'no' made use of her with considerable frequency.

<*Jane's in the bay, working on her bird,*> Roxy said after examining her frequent flyers' locations.

<*Seems like the perfect opportunity,*> Carmen replied.

Roxy turned down the passage that led to the dock, but doubt filled her mind. <*I don't know…it feels wrong.*>

<*She's used you plenty of times. Turnabout is fair play.*>

<*Still…*>

<*Look,*> Carmen's tone was hard and edged. <*Organics use AIs all the time. But as it turns out, you're not one of them. You're one of us. All you want is to be free of their control. Time to give them a bit of what they send your way.*>

Roxy didn't reply, but she also didn't slow her approach. Once beyond the dock's doors, she surveyed the area, looking for Jane.

A loud *clank* drew her attention to the left, and she saw the pilot walk out of one of the adjacent machine shops with a strangely shaped component in her hands. The pilot's tight shipsuit was pulled down, with the top half dangling from her waist, her breasts free and covered with a sheen of sweat.

"Whatcha got there?" Roxy called out, sauntering over to Jane. "And why's it got you so greasy?"

"Hey, Roxy. It's a stabilizer bar for one of the ballast rockers. It's a fallback system for balancing the ship if the grav systems go out—or if it needs to use stealth and not bleed gravitons everywhere."

"And the dock monkeys make you work on this stuff alone?" Roxy asked, her eyes straying to Jane's uncovered chest.

"They're all on the other ship," the pilot jerked her head to the side. "Asshats left me to fix this myself."

Roxy placed a hand on Jane's arm. "Want a hand?"

The other woman chuckled. "Stars, you're extra randy today, aren't you? I wouldn't be against a more…thorough diversion than we had before, but first I need to get this fixed."

"I'll help," Roxy said brightly. "You already know I'm good with my hands."

Jane laughed and brushed her hip against Roxy's. "Well, they say many hands make light work…or something. Let's get to it."

It only took twenty minutes to replace the stabilizer bar, and another ten for Jane to run her tests. The final checks were performed in the cockpit, and Roxy stood behind Jane, running her hands over the pilot's chest, cupping her breasts and adding a pinch every so often.

"Stars, Roxy, I'll never get this done if you keep that up."

"You have somewhere you need to be?" Roxy whispered in Jane's ear. "Other than in your cabin with me."

Roxy slid a hand down Jane's stomach, and beneath her shipsuit, driving her point home.

"Fuck this shit," Jane said, closing down the console and rising slowly while keeping her back to Roxy. "I've got a bunk here on the pinnace, third door on the left."

"Awesome," Roxy whispered and drew a moaning Jane down the pinnace's central corridor until she reached the indicated door, pulling it open with a flourish.

Seconds later, she had pushed the pilot onto her bunk and set to pulling her shipsuit the rest of the way off, getting ready to work the woman over.

<You don't actually have to do that,> Carmen said as Roxy lowered her lips to the cleft between Jane's breasts, breathing deeply of the other woman's scent. *<I already used your prior contact to deposit your breach nano on her. You have some impressive tech in that regard.>*

Roxy paused, suddenly remembering what it was that she'd come to the bay for in the first place. *<Stars, Carmen, that was the furthest thing from my mind—I'd almost forgotten entirely! Fuck, I hate what that asshole did to me.>*

She connected to the breach nano Carmen had deposited and set it to sever Jane's Link—a benefit of the toys Hand agents had that noncom pilots did not. Once she knew that Jane couldn't signal for help, she slid up the woman's body until their lips were brushing.

"Sorry about this, Jane. I know you're just a lonely, randy bitch, but it's time for me to use you for a change."

Jane furrowed her brow and opened her mouth to speak, but it was too late: her body froze and consciousness left her.

Roxy rose from her position atop Jane and grabbed a towel from the small san in the corner, cleaning the sweat and dirt off her chest, hands and face.

She checked on Jane once more, ensuring that the pilot was out but otherwise in good health. Satisfied that the woman would be fine in a few hours—though not sure why she cared so much—Roxy left the room and walked back to the cockpit, settling into the primary chair and initializing a takeoff sequence.

A call came from Lieutenant Gloria on the bridge. <*Pinnace 1, you're not scheduled for departure. What's up, Jane?*>

<*Oh, hey, Gloria. I Just made some repairs, gotta test them out,*> Roxy replied, using the ident tokens she'd lifted from Jane's Link hardware—glad that the pilot hadn't updated her firmware in a few years.

<*Saw you doing some work down there,*> Gloria replied, her tone light. <*Everyone else just up and left you to fix your bird on your own, eh?*>

<*You know how it is,*> Roxy replied with a laugh. <*Greener pastures over there. I'll just take my girl for a loop around the* Silas *and be back on the* Greensward *before you know it.*>

<*Sounds good, Pinnace 1. You're cleared for departure.*>

A minute later, the pinnace was in the black. Roxy was a capable pilot, but she let Carmen take control of the pinnace, certain that the AI could better mimic a test flight than she could. As they approached the *Damon Silas,* Carmen slewed the ship to one side, and Roxy reported in to Gloria.

<*Shit! Something broke loose. System's flagging it as a dampener...shit, and my starboard grav drive. They're out of calibration.*>

<*Don't you always tell me that you know how to take care of your girl?*> Gloria asked. <*Well, bring her back in. You're going to have to pull a double; Justin wants us to start shifting supplies ASAP.*>

<*Better to dock on the* Silas,> Roxy replied. <*They've got the spares I need in stock. No more fabbing replacements in the machine shop.*>

<*Roger that,*> Gloria responded. <*Logging it. Hope you get it squared away soon. Her majesty prefers your shuttle, says it has a 'woman's touch'.*>

Roxy suppressed a groan, and instead gave Gloria a calm, positive response, <*She sure does!*>

<*I'm going to bring her around to the port-side bays,*> Carmen informed Roxy privately. <*The other shuttles from the* Greensward *are all in starboard bays. We should have the place to ourselves.*>

<*Then it's just a short walk to the autodoc two levels up, and I finally get this shit out of my head.*>

The next five minutes had Roxy on the edge of her seat. She kept expecting Justin to come on the comm and demand to know what she was doing, but he never did. She had to keep reminding herself that it was because he had no idea she was on the pinnace. He'd have no reason to reach out to Jane.

As they approached, Carmen didn't even have to link up with the NSAI backup that was running systems aboard the *Damon Silas*. Her command access was still functional, allowing her to open the dock's outer bay doors and unfurl a docking cradle to receive the pinnace.

"Stars," Roxy muttered. "This is almost too easy."

<*Way to jinx it.*>

Roxy didn't reply as she made her way to the sortie locker and pulled out a SS-R4 stealth sheath, sliding into it before grabbing a lightwand and a pulse pistol. She considered getting a rifle as well, but decided against it. Not being detected in the first place was her best weapon.

She activated the sheath's stealth systems and then cycled the airlock open, watching the bay through the pinnace's external feeds, glad to see that it appeared exactly as it had when the TSF abandoned the ship several days ago.

<*Here goes nothing,*> she murmured and walked out into the bay, stepping lightly down the ramp. Roxy considered deploying drones to counter any sounds she made, but decided it was better to leave as small a footprint as possible.

Her luck held, and the passage outside the docks was clear, as was the lift.

Once on the medbay's level, she had a near run-in with Sam and Harry—two former Hand agents who had helped breach the ship.

"I still think we should punch through to Vela. If we take that system and depose the chancellor, we can destabilize the whole region," Harry said as he rounded a corner, nearly walking into Roxy.

She flattened herself against the bulkhead as Sam shrugged.

"Sure, but you know that Admiral Krissy will throw everything she has at keeping Vela safe. We have this one stasis ship, she has thousands," Sam pointed out.

"That's why we take the capitol right away," Harry replied as they continued on down the corridor. "Krissy won't hit us when we have the entire populace under our control."

<*Idiots,*> Carmen commented. <*Even if they did take the planet, they'd only do it through the threat of this ship. Once the fleet arrived, the populace would not be containable by that means. Justin might hold the capitol buildings, but that would be it.*>

<*I agree,*> Roxy said as she continued on her way to the medbay. <*But I don't plan on being around to find out what they do.*>

<*Oh?*> Carmen asked. <*Do you have a plan to get out of here?*>

<*Still working on it. But one thing's for sure: it won't take Justin long to realize I'm*

not his sock puppet anymore, once we pull his neural lace from my brain. I can't just hang out with him, hoping he doesn't undo everything we've done today.>

Carmen sent a feeling of agreement. *<We'll need to get out of here as soon as we free your mind.>*

<Problem is we're in interstellar space, and there aren't other ships or stations nearby.>

<What about a redux of your prior assault?> Carmen asked.

<I may be good, but I don't think I can go up against Justin and the other agents. They'll clean my clock.>

<Roxy,> the AI's voice contained a note of amusement. *<We don't have to fight them, we clear the ship the same way we did the first time.>*

<Another self-destruct countdown?>

<Bingo.>

THE DREAM TEAM

STELLAR DATE: 09.24.8949 (Adjusted Years)
LOCATION: Prairie Park, ISS *I2*
REGION: Pyra, Albany System, Thebes, Septhian Alliance

"You going to be OK?" Tangel asked Sera as they walked down one of the pathways in the *I2*'s Prairie Park.

Sera gave a rueful laugh. "In regard to what? My two sisters? My father-not-father? Going on a mission with Finaeus?"

"And that's just the tip of the iceberg," Tangel joined Sera in her laughter. "I guess all of it. Things are intensifying. Not only does Airtha have EMGs, but we have to assume that the lost stasis ship—"

"The *Damon Silas,*" Sera supplied.

"Yes, we need to assume that it has fallen into Airtha's hands. We may only have months before she has a stasis fleet."

Sera placed a hand on Tangel's shoulder. "So you're saying that I need—" Her statement was cut short as she stepped in a gopher hole that one of the industrious creatures had dug in the path. "Shit…those little buggers are everywhere."

"That's what you get for wearing boots with heels like that," Tangel chided. "You are one of the least practical women I know when it comes to footwear."

Sera shrugged. "I like boots. Lots of women like sexy boots. Honestly, I think you're the odd one out on this front."

Tangel ignored the critique. "Yeah, but you have flow armor for skin. You can just *make* boots."

"Sure, but it's like walking barefoot everywhere. Cheeky was telling me she loves that her feet are just a sexy pair of heels, but it feels weird to me. I think a good pair of boots is my security blanket."

Tangel glanced down at the five-centimeter platforms and fifteen-centimeter heels under Sera's feet. "Well, you should put a-grav generators in them—or gyros, at least."

"I do…but you have to turn them on to gain gopher-hole protection," Sera nudged her shoulder against Tangel's. "You know, the real reason I go this high is so I'm taller than you."

Tangel chuckled. "I love you like a sister, Sera, but you're one strange woman."

"Sister-zoned again," Sera muttered with a twinkle of mirth in her eyes. "You do realize, Tangel, that there are entire worlds of people who dress like I do—plus worlds where people are far, far stranger—but so far as we know, there are no human-AI merges that are ascended."

"Right," Tangel chuckled as she slapped Sera on the shoulder. "I'm elite, you're weird."

"Well, I love being weird," Sera held her hand up and formed a fist. "And I'm gonna take one of my impractical high-heeled boots and kick it right through Airtha's primary core. Then we'll force Kirkland to stand down, and this whole mess will be over."

"I think there are a few more steps in there," Tangel replied with a chuckle. "Though I suppose those are the highlights."

The two women walked in silence for several minutes, before Sera asked, "But if we need you, you'll come, right?"

"To Airtha?" Tangel asked, and her friend nodded. "Of course. With bells on. But I have a feeling you and your sisters can get the job done. You have shadowtrons, and Earnest is waiting at Styx. Once Katrina gets that shard of Airtha, he and Finaeus will work out a plan to take her out, I have no doubt about it."

"Should be fun to see those two working together," Sera said with a laugh. "Seriously…once we achieve a lasting peace, we need to keep an eye on them. Before you know it, they'll do something crazy like build a ring around the galaxy."

"Is that a risk?" Tangel asked, wondering if such a thing was possible.

"Just something uncle Fin used to say when I was a kid," Sera replied with a shrug. "But I wouldn't put it past them."

"Speaking of 'them', how are your sisters doing?" Tangel asked.

"Honestly? Better than I'd've thought. It's funny, both of them admit to having been rather straight-laced when they were with Mom—by my standards, at least—but Fina has *really* cut loose. She's going to give me a run for my money in the weird department."

"She's a rebel at heart. She was pushing back against your mother even before we removed her aegis. I think the fact that she was fighting so hard is going to cause her to swing the other way before she stabilizes."

"You calling my sister a human pendulum?" Sera asked with a chuckle.

"We're all pendulums." Tangel shrugged, carefully stepping around a cluster of gopher holes. "Always in motion. When we stop, we die."

"Well, no risk of that anytime soon. Right now *everything's* in motion. The two of them are off getting 'the skin job', as Finaeus calls it, plus some other mods. Fina is enamored with the idea of flowmetal limbs. If she comes back looking human at all, I'll be surprised…and owe Cheeky something I'll have to convince Jason to let me do."

Tangel barked a laugh and shook her head. "Did you seriously bet a foursome with Cheeky over this?"

"You reading my thoughts?" Sera asked, meeting Tangel's eyes and cocking an eyebrow.

"If you think I needed to read your thoughts to figure *that* out, you've been underestimating me for some time. If you do lose, think you'll be able to convince Jason? Are you two enough of an item that you think he needs to be in the loop?"

Sera shrugged. "I don't know…he's still back in the LMC trying to get things sorted out there. I got a message that he's not sure if he'll return directly to New Canaan, or if he and I can have some time first. What with Terrance still sorting things out in the IPE…" her voice trailed off for a moment. "Dammit, I just want to see Jason again before we dive into the shit, you know?"

"If for nothing else than to explain to him why you're going to go have a foursome with your sisters and Cheeky?" Tanis asked with a laugh, then cleared her throat. "Sorry, you're trying to be serious, and I'm still stuck on your bet about Fina. But what is it? Incest? If it's with yourselves, is it just masturbation?"

Tangel couldn't help a giggle at her joke, and Sera shot her a narrow-eyed look.

"Well…not if Cheeky's the one getting all the attention, she has three—"

"OK, *stop!*" Tangel shook her head. "I know all about what Cheeky has. I've seen it in action. You keep evading the Jason question. Think he'll have an issue?"

"Jason? He might just join in. I'm half worried that he'll be pissed if he misses out."

"Wait," Tangel stopped in the middle of the path, forcing a cougar to walk around them as it crept toward a rabbit in the underbrush. "*Jason*? In a fivesome with your sisters and Cheeky? That's not the Jason Andrews I know."

Sera gave Tangel a knowing wink. "Trust me, I know a *very* different side of Jason than you do. He acts like the elder statesman, conscientious and in charge, around everyone else. But you get him between the sheets, and he's—"

"Stars, Sera, how does this conversation keep coming back around to you having sex with everyone I know? I have the worst visuals in my mind—half of them, you're broadcasting at me."

A grin split Sera's lips. "I was wondering if that would work. You're going to have to learn how to block out other people's thoughts."

Tanis gave Sera a cautious look. "You're telling me. And you're a jerk, just in case you didn't know."

"Back to the topic at hand." Sera's brows knit together seriously as they resumed their walk. "I could probably sell tickets to half the galaxy to join in with—or, stars, just watch—Cheeky with me and my sisters."

"Sera!"

"Think about it…if this whole war thing doesn't work out, we could try it. 'Fuck Peace'. You get it?"

Tangel took one look at the earnest and surprisingly innocent look in Sera's eyes and burst out laughing. She tried to stop, but the visuals Sera kept sending her had Tangel in stitches for nearly five minutes.

When she finally got herself back under control—still wheezing slightly—she clasped Sera's hands between hers.

"Stars, Sera, I'm going to miss you when you head out. Let's go get some drinks and wait to see how many tentacles Fina has when her mods are done."

FREEDOM

STELLAR DATE: 09.02.8949 (Adjusted Years)
LOCATION: ***Damon Silas***
REGION: Interstellar Space, coreward of the Vela Cluster

With the rough plan in place to take the *Damon Silas*—for the second time in nearly as many days—Roxy pulled off her SS-R4 stealth sheath, climbed into the autodoc, and laid back.

<*You have the feeds monitored?*> she asked, worried about the thirty minutes it would take for the autodoc to remove the neural lace from her mind.

<*Yes, and I have this autodoc disconnected from the shipnet. Someone will have to come in here and pop it open to see that it's working on you.*>

Roxy bit her lip and nodded silently.

A second later, a voice entered her mind, soothing in its soft tones. <*Welcome to the TSF 1891A Autodoc. My name is Bright. I understand that you wish to have the neural lace interwoven through your brain removed.*>

<*That's right, Bright,*> Roxy replied stoically, wincing at the rhyme with the NSAI's odd name.

An image of her brain appeared in her mind—at least, she assumed it was her brain. The silver and blue mass largely resembled an organic brain, but it looked like a spider had woven a web around it, even ensnaring the mods that were situated between the sulci and gyri.

<*I'd like to inform you,*> Bright said in her overly pleasant voice, <*that you do not have an organic brain, yet it follows the patterns and structure of a human's neurological circuitry. Are you aware of this?*>

<*I am,*> Roxy replied. <*Is that a problem?*>

<*Of course not,*> Bright said with a tittering laugh, and Roxy wondered if this airhead-sounding NSAI was supposed to put injured soldiers at ease. <*I ask because I could contact TSF sector-central medical for them to grow a new organic brain to transfer your mind into. Would you like to do that?*>

The idea both enticed and horrified Roxy. She hadn't even considered such a thing, but here the standard TSF autodoc was suggesting replacing her artificial brain with a real one. <*Um…no. Not right now. Please just remove the neural lace.*>

<*Very well. I will remove the…three neural laces woven through your mind.*>

<*Three!?*> Roxy gasped. <*I had no idea.*>

<*They are all exerting different levels of control and suppression over your thoughts and urges. You may not be the same person when I remove them…. Are you certain you'd like to proceed?*>

<*For fucksakes! Just do it already!*> Roxy shouted at the NSAI.

<*Very well,*> Bright replied, entirely unfazed.

The holo of Roxy's brain faded, as did the autodoc's voice and Carmen's dim presence.

* * * *

Roxy woke with a start, sitting up abruptly and hitting her head on the inside of the autodoc's pod.

<*Please lay back down,*> the NSAI intoned. <*Your post-operation evaluation is not yet complete.*>

Obeying the voice, Roxy tried to recall where she was, and why she was in an autodoc.

<*Was I injured in battle?*> she asked.

<*No, you did this voluntarily,*> another voice said, this one coming over an unbuffered Link connection.

<*Who…?*> she began to ask. Something about the presence felt familiar. <*Are you an AI I'm paired with?*>

<*Yes, not neurologically, though,*> the AI replied. <*I'm Carmen. We only paired today. Well, yesterday, I suppose, now.*>

"Yesterday," Roxy whispered, then a memory hit her. "The *Damon Silas*! I'm aboard that ship. Did we seize it successfully?"

<*You did,*> Carmen replied without further elaboration.

"Was I injured?" Roxy repeated the question, curious if Carmen would give a different answer than the autodoc's NSAI.

<*No, you did this to remove Justin's control over you. The disorientation you're feeling should pass; at least that's what the autodoc is telling me.*>

"Justin…" Roxy whispered the word, feeling it on her lips.

The name brought with it a flood of emotions. At first, they were happy…pleasant and warm. Then others followed: fear, rage, lust, anger, more lust. They crashed into Roxy, subsuming her in a maelstrom of feelings that she couldn't master.

<*OK,*> the autodoc's voice came into her mind, quelling the noise, but not eradicating it. <*There were parts of your mind that your cognitive process could not access. I've flooded them with a base charge to prepare the synthetic neurons for activity. It's going to feel like a bright, sharp, loud sensation, and then those parts of your mind will be accessible again.*>

<*OK,*> Roxy whispered. <*Do it.*>

An explosion erupted in her mind, and she bit back a pain-filled howl. Then—just as quickly as it had arrived—the spike of sensation was gone.

"That motherfucking son of a bitch!" she hissed, as memory flooded back into her. Memory that brought unbridled rage.

<*Roxy?*> Carmen asked. <*Have you remembered your past…before?*>

Roxy pushed open the autodoc and swung her legs over the edge, looking at her azure skin.

"Oh, I've remembered, alright," she whispered. "He's going to *pay*."

A minute later, she had pulled her SS-R4 stealth sheath back on and was exiting the medbay.

<Shall we initiate the plan, then?> Carmen asked. *<I can sound the general alarm and simulate reactor containment failure. No one is down in engineering at the moment. It'll be urgent enough that everyone will clear off the ship to reach minimum safe distance before it goes up.>*

<Not yet,> Roxy replied as she moved silently down a corridor that would lead her to the command deck. *<Everyone gets off except Justin.>*

<Roxy,> Carmen's voice held a strong note of caution. *<Are you sure? The lace is gone, but your brain will still default to established patterns. He may be able to confuse you.>*

<You don't know what he did to me,> Roxy hissed. *<I'm not letting him get away with it. He's going to die by my hand this day.>*

A pair of engineers swung into the corridor and began walking aft, causing Roxy to press herself against the bulkhead to avoid being bumped into, though she felt a strong urge to simply kill them and carry on.

<What did he do to you?> Carmen asked once the engineers had passed. *<I assume you remember exactly.>*

<Well…not exactly. But he and I were not on good terms before he turned me into this…thing. He always lusted after me, but I wasn't interested for obvious reasons. Then something happened—some sort of accident, or combat damage, I'm not sure. Next thing I remember, I woke up in this body.

<That's when I started to have cravings for him—but I could fight them. He kept me locked up, trying to use me for his pleasure, but I fought him tooth and nail each time.

<Then he came to me one day, I still remember the sick grin on his face. He said he'd made a deal that would give him proper control over me. Make me desire him utterly.>

Roxy paused, the revulsion of the years she'd spent adoring Justin welling up in her. She was glad that her body wasn't organic; if it were, she was certain the deck would be covered in her vomit.

<Are you sure it's worth it?> Carmen sounded nervous. *<I get that he harmed you—I was enslaved to Airtha for over a century…stars, I don't even know when it started—but this is our chance. What if he beats you?>*

<He won't beat me.>

* * * * *

Roxy stood at the entrance to the bridge. Carmen had accessed the optic feeds from the ship's command center. The only people within were Justin, Sam, and Harry, all standing around the central holotank, heads bent together.

<*Do it,*> Roxy ordered Carmen, and the AI sent an affirmative.

An alarm sounded through the ship, three long tones followed by one short pulse.

"Alert! Alert! Alert! Primary reactor containment failure! Runaway reaction, ablative shielding will hold for seven minutes at current levels."

"Fuck!" Justin swore, looking around the bridge, where every console was lit in the red glow of the emergency lighting. "There's *no way*. That reactor was running at minimal levels."

"Silas!" Sam called out. "Terminate fuel flow to primary reactor."

"Fuel flow is already terminated," the NSAI replied calmly. "The reaction continues."

"C'mon," Sam grabbed Harry's sleeve. "It must be sabotage from the TSF crew. We can kill the manual fuel feeds from engineering."

The two men raced off the bridge, and the moment they were past, Roxy's invisible form slipped inside.

Justin was seven meters from her, his back to the door as he shook his head slightly—one of his Link tells. There were two consoles between them, and Roxy crept around them until she was right behind the man who had hurt her so much over the years.

Decades.

"Containment timeline has decreased by four minutes," the ship's NSAI announced on the 1MC. "Three minutes until containment failure."

<*People are abandoning the ship,*> Carmen announced. <*Harry and Sam are still trying to make it to engineering, but I'm closing emergency bulkheads behind them. Even if they don't bail, it will take them some time to get back up here.*>

<*Thanks, Carmen. I owe you…well…everything.*>

<*Just don't die.*> Carmen sounded legitimately concerned. <*I'm counting on you to keep your glowing blue body in one piece.*>

Roxy nodded silently and then slipped around the last console. Nothing but three meters of empty space lay between her and her prey.

"Roxanne." Justin's voice carried a smug note…and a touch of sorrow. "I should have known it was you."

He turned and stared at her exact location.

"Come now. You don't think I would provide my teams with stealth gear that doesn't send out random pings on frequencies I know to monitor? I do it for just this reason."

"Have a lot of people tried to mutiny on you?" Roxy spat the words out. "Not that it surprises me. You never engendered loyalty, you just used secrets to manipulate."

"I do what works," Justin said with a shrug. "But you know I do it all to help. Right, Roxy? You know I love you."

"Fucker," Roxy swore. "You don't love anyone but yourself. You made me into this thing and then let everyone use me, like I was your little whore."

Justin chuckled and shook his head. "How did you do it? Remove the neural lace?"

Roxy pulled off the stealth sheath's hood—she wanted him to see the rage in her eyes. "I had a bit of help identifying it, and then the autodoc on this very ship did the honors."

"There's no way…" Justin whispered, then an ugly laugh coughed its way free of his throat. "The ship's AI. You never got rid of it…. Clever."

Roxy grinned. "Carmen just met me—and not under the best circumstances—but she's done more for me than you ever have."

"Wrong." Justin shook his head. "I did more for you than you ever could imagine. I *saved* you after the failed attack on Perimands. You were shredded, but I got you into a stasis pod and reconstructed your mind. It was damaged—you were having trouble focusing on reality, hallucinating, flying into rages. I used the neural laces to help compensate for that."

Roxy shook her head, eyes narrowing as she regarded the man who had held her captive for years, treating her like a possession—making her *revel* in being a possession.

"You're such an accomplished liar, Justin, but your lies won't work on me. I didn't buy them before you mucked around in my brain, and I'm not going to buy them now. Everyone else always thought you were *so* clever as you rose up through the ranks, eventually taking on the directorship, but not me. I always saw clear through you."

"That was always your fatal flaw," Justin sneered. "*Roxanne*. You always behaved as though your opinions were better than mine, like you knew all the angles, and I was just guessing."

Roxy barked a laugh. "That's because half the time you *were*! You're good at intuitive leaps, but you were wrong a lot. Even so, you're such a good bullshitter that you weaseled your way out of every tight scrape—'til that last one. Sera finally did you in. You underestimated her."

Justin's face reddened, and Roxy took a perverse pleasure in seeing him so flustered. "It's not my fault that didn't work—it was Andrea's idea," he sputtered defensively.

Roxy lifted a hand to her mouth, feigning surprise. "Oh, look! Justin's shifting blame again! It's the liar in his natural habitat. I bet Sera would be interested to know who it was that really ordered her assassination. Granted, you're just dancing to that Caretaker person's tune, anyway; you're not even the master of your own destiny."

Justin clenched his jaw and narrowed his eyes. A moment later, a pistol was in his hand—but Roxy knew his tells, and she held one in hers, as well.

"Pulse pistol?" he scoffed. "Should have packed a slug thrower."

"A seven millimeter ship-safe round?" Roxy asked, peering at his weapon.

"It'll take two shots to get through my stealth sheath, and then another two at least to penetrate my skin. Then what? You hit the food processing mod I never use?"

<*Don't forget that I'm in here,*> Carmen cautioned. <*Granted the core mount does have extra plating.*>

"I could just shoot your he—"

Justin's words were cut off as he staggered backward, Roxy's pulse blast hitting him square in the chest.

"You *shot* me," he hissed.

"I'll do it again, don't worry," she growled, and pulled the trigger on her pulse pistol three more times, aiming at the pistol in Justin's right hand.

Though the concussive impacts threw his arm back, he held onto the weapon, a toothy grin forming on his lips. "You're not the only one with mods to keep them safe."

A whistling noise came from all around the pair, rapidly increasing in amplitude, until it became a near howl.

"Do you have a mod so you don't need to breathe?" Roxy asked, her voice faint in the thinning atmosphere. "*You* gave me that one," she reminded him. <*Thanks, Carmen. Good thinking.*>

<*No problem, just doing my part to keep us in one piece.*>

A look of true fear crossed Justin's face, and he swung his weapon toward Roxy again. She fired her pistol to deflect his aim, but in the thinning air, the pulse blast barely had any effect.

Her former captor squeezed off a trio of rounds as Roxy dodged to the right. Two hit her in the shoulder, the impact spreading across her stealth sheath, and the third tore through her cheek and ripped off her left ear.

Good thing I'm not a real person anymore…

Before Justin could bring his weapon to bear on her once more, Roxy had closed the distance between them, her lightwand active and streaking through the air.

It hit his pistol, cutting it in half.

<*Good aim,*> Carmen commented.

<*I was trying to hit his elbow. Bugger's fast.*>

She swung her lightwand at him again, but Justin had drawn his own and blocked the blow. The flash of light was blinding, as photons and electrons erupted around them, the blades' carefully funneled cherenkov radiation spilling out in a nimbus glow around the impact point.

The pair struggled across the bridge, lightwands clashing again and again as each fought for dominance. It surprised her, how well he was holding up without breathing. Mods to recycle air and pull more oxygen were common enough, but there was a finite amount that could be extracted from what was in his lungs.

His skin would be burning now, feeling as though it were going to crack and split apart. Red splotches were appearing across his face, and his eyes were entirely bloodshot.

<You can't win,> she sent into his mind, knowing he could hear her. *<All your centuries of planning and scheming, deals and deals, wheels within wheels, and you die alone on this ship, by my hand.>*

<Don't count on it. I'm not dead yet,> Justin shot back, and he twisted away, bringing his wand around and slicing Roxy's forearm open.

She shrugged and tossed her blade into her other hand. *<I feel no pain. You saw to that. I don't have to best you, I just have to outlast you.>*

<You…> Justin began, but the words died, and he staggered to the side, catching himself on a console. *<You won't win. You're just a shadow of a woman that died centuries ago.>*

Roxy's lips pulled back in a fierce smile, knowing that her moment of triumph was finally upon her. *<Then you lost to a shadow. How does that feel?>*

She felt Justin's presence on the Link waver, then disappear. He slid off the console and onto the deck, his body convulsing as his control over his lungs gave out, and he began gasping for breath in the cold vacuum.

Roxy lifted her lightwand, considering finishing him off, but Carmen stayed her hand.

<There may be things stored in his mind that you'll want to know—or need to use as bargaining chips.>

<Good point,> Roxy agreed. *<Shit, I guess I should get him into a stasis pod before his cells begin to degenerate.>*

<There's a chamber just aft of the bridge.> The AI indicated the stasis chamber on the ship's layout.

Roxy waited for a long minute after the man's last breath before she took a single step toward him, only to be interrupted by a shout from Carmen.

<Shit!>

<What?> Roxy stepped back from the body. *<Is he still alive?>*

<No, sorry.> Carmen sounded distracted. *<It's the* Greensward. *They're coming about. Andrea is hailing us.>*

Roxy moved to the central holotank and changed the view to the space around the *Damon Silas.*

<Dump us into the DL,> she directed the AI.

*<I need some delta-*v, *first,>* Carmen replied, her voice calmer.

Roxy felt the ship's grav-dampeners activate as the engines began to thrust. She turned to one of the consoles and verified that all the bay doors had closed and the shields were coming online. Then she charged the point-defense weapons.

<That's going to alert Andrea that things have gone wrong here,> Carmen cautioned.

<Justin not replying and the ship coming under thrust will do the same thing.>

Beams lanced out from the *Greensward,* only to play harmlessly against the *Damon Silas*'s stasis shields.

<Stars!> Roxy gave a relieved mental laugh. *<I'd forgotten we have those…>*

<They do come in handy,> Carmen replied. *<OK, we're ready to transition. On my mark…. Three, two, one, mark.>*

* * * * *

Ten minutes later, Roxy was still staring down at the body at her feet, only dimly aware that air was hissing in through the environmental systems around her.

<Why are you airing the ship up again?> she asked after another minute had passed.

<Just feels right,> Carmen replied with a mental shrug. *<Already feels empty enough in here as it is.>*

<I guess I should move him now.>

She bent over and knocked Justin's lightwand away before picking up the cold body and carrying it off the bridge. The door to the stasis chamber opened as she approached. When she entered, one of the pods was active, its lid lifted welcomingly.

<Thanks, Carmen.>

<Anytime.>

With more care than he deserved in life or in death, she set Justin onto the cushions.

She stared down at him, shaking her head at the waste he had made of his life, sorrow she didn't expect to feel creeping into her thoughts.

"I'm sorry it came to this," she whispered, and then closed the lid.

Heaving a heavy sigh, she turned and walked into the corridor, a shriek tearing free from her throat as she nearly collided with—

"Jane?"

"Fuck! Roxy!" Jane took a step back and leveled a rifle at her. "What the hell did you do to me? Why are we on the *Damon Silas*, and where *is* everyone?"

<How did you miss **her** *wandering around?>* Roxy asked Carmen.

<Sorry, I had to knock the backup NSAI offline to get us into the DL. I'm managing an **entire** *ship through your Link. It's not possible to watch everything at once.>*

Roxy stretched a hand out to Jane, surprised that she still seemed to feel some level of attraction for the woman who had used her like a sex automaton. She briefly wondered if it was a residual pathway acting up, or if somehow Jane really did elicit amorous feelings in her.

"Can you lower that?" Roxy asked. "I can disarm you in a second, but it'll probably hurt, and I don't want to hurt you any more than I already have."

She hadn't expected Jane to comply, but the pilot nodded slowly and lowered her rifle. Though her stance was less hostile, her expression was not.

"Who's in the stasis chamber?" she asked.

Roxy glanced over her shoulder. "Justin. He's dead, though."

"Dead?" Jane's mouth hung open. "Did *you* kill him?"

"Yes."

The pilot began to raise her weapon once more, but Roxy was already upon her, holding the barrel of her gun down with one hand.

"You have to understand, Jane…I had to."

"Had to?" The woman spat the words. "He was our leader!"

Roxy nodded. "He was more than that…."

"Yeah?" Jane growled, jerking her rifle, trying to lift it to aim at Roxy. "What was he to you, if you just went off and killed him?"

Roxy met the other woman's eyes, feeling as though the weight of the world was on her shoulders.

"He was my brother."

KENT OF HERSCHEL

STELLAR DATE: 09.25.8949 (Adjusted Years)
LOCATION: Intrepid Space Force Academy
REGION: The Palisades, Orbiting Troy, New Canaan System

"Well, I didn't expect to see you again," Kent said, as the young blonde woman appeared outside his cell.

He had just finished eating his noon meal and was expecting the servitor to come and collect the remains, only to hear the ever so slightly uneven footsteps of a human visitor instead.

"Why is that?" she asked with a coy smile, one that was not meant to entice him, but rather to be playful and endearing. Or so he suspected.

Kent cocked a brow, giving her a judging look. "Well, prisoners of war don't often get casual visits from their captors, and given your parentage, I had expected them to put an end to your little excursions once they realized what you were up to."

He watched as the woman's eyes widened ever so slightly, then narrowed as she placed a hand on her hip.

"And who are my parents?" she asked.

"Cary, I'm no fool. It's clear to see that you are the daughter of Tanis Richards and Joseph Evans."

Kent said the words without emotion, though he certainly felt some at the thought of the girl's parents. One of whom who had been a target of his assault aboard the *Galadrial*—an assault that Tanis had handily defeated.

"You've a keen eye," Cary replied. "Most people are used to getting information like that via the Link instead of relying on their wits—granted, people mod their appearance so much, you might not be able to tell even *if* you paid close attention."

Kent shrugged as he leant back against the wall of his cell. "In *your* society, perhaps. Not in mine. Where I come from, people are comfortable enough in their own skin that they don't need to change it to look like something else."

It was Cary's turn to direct a raised eyebrow at Kent. "I may not know as much as you, but I know a fair bit about Orion space. We know from the databases we stripped from your ships that you grew up on Herschel. We know that to be a very agrarian world, as low-tech as they come."

She paused, seeming to wish a confirmation from Kent.

"Well," he shrugged. "You got me, Cary. I'm just a farmboy that ran off to join the space force. Not an intel-filled prize like the admirals and ship captains."

"We have our share of them," she admitted. "But most aren't too cooperative. I figured you and I could get to know one another, see if maybe we can't find some common ground."

"With you?" It was all Kent could do to hold back a derisive laugh. "You're the daughter of the devil herself. We have no common ground. You're an interesting diversion from the guards, that's all."

He could see her deflate slightly at his words, and a feeling of guilt swept through him. This girl hadn't asked to be born into a society such as New Canaan's. Just as he had not asked to be born somewhere so backward as Herschel.

More than once, he'd considered that his parents would all but disown him for the mods the Orion Guard had made to his body—mods that were still nothing compared to what the young woman outside his cell likely had.

Yet he couldn't help but admit that neither she, nor any others he'd met since his capture, were monsters. For the most part, they seemed like people he could have met on the more urban worlds of the Orion Freedom Alliance.

"Sorry," Kent said, as Cary continued to stand in silence, an injured look etched upon her brow. "My mother always said that other people's behavior is no reason to lose one's own manners. I'd do well to remember that."

A small smile formed on Cary's lips. "You'd be surprised to know that my mother says something similar. 'Never let your behavior be dictated by the actions of others'."

"A bit fancier than my dear ol' mom's." Kent inclined his head as he spoke, and Cary shrugged.

"Sometimes Mom forgets that she's not always on the bridge of a starship."

"Sounds a bit like my dad. He often treated us kids like we were just his farmhands. Which we kinda were..."

"That why you joined the OG?" Cary asked as she leant against the bulkhead next to the cell.

Kent closed his eyes and recalled his first flight into space, Sam in the seat next to him. "I wanted to travel...to see the stars."

"You've done a good bit of that," Cary said, nodding slowly as she spoke. "Not lately, mind you."

Kent barked a laugh. "No, I suppose not. Though they take us for time in the parks. I at least get to see simulated stars from time to time." He sat forward. "I won't lie, your people have impressive technology...and they use it better than most. But there's still the potential for terrible misuse."

Cary shrugged. "People have misused everything, from the first sharpened stick they made a million years ago. You can't put the entire race in a padded room."

"No." Kent shook his head. "You're right about that. But you can limit the destructive scope. That's what the OFA wants: to give people freedom, but not race-destroying levels of freedom."

"Which is why you don't want AIs, picotech, and the like?"

"Precisely."

"But you use jump gates," Cary countered.

Kent shrugged. "A means to an end. We can't counter the Transcend without them."

"But you realize that jump gates—if they get into the hands of the Inner Stars people—will facilitate even more destruction than AIs or picotech."

"That's very subjective," Kent replied, feeling like Cary was trying to corner him.

"Well, once this is all over, anyone with jump gates could—just as an example—destroy a system like Herschel with ease. All they would have to do is send a few rocks through, and that would be it. Given just a few hundred jump gates, and enough antimatter to power them, they could destroy every habitable system within a year."

Cary said the words with quiet conviction, and Kent realized that she was speaking out of sincere concern, not a desire to best him in a battle of wits.

He had to admit that she was right.

"Well, I assume Command has a plan for that. If they control all of human space in the galaxy, then they can annihilate the gates and drop everyone back to dark-layer FTL."

The woman outside his cell nodded her head slowly then asked, "How far do you think humanity has expanded, Kent?"

"Well, from the maps I've seen in the Orion Guard, about a five-thousand-light-year radius from Sol. A bit further on the Perseus side, and less on the Sagittarius side. I—" Kent stopped when he saw Cary shaking her head. "What?"

"Kent, humanity has spread much, much further than you know. It's extragalactic. We're becoming more and more certain that a variety of groups have also spread far, far beyond the Transcend and Orion space. Stars, you don't even seem to know how far Orion space goes into Perseus. It's almost out the other side now."

"No..." he whispered.

"Yes, Kent. On top of that, there are AIs occupying the core of the galaxy, and we know of at least two colonies in dwarf galaxies in orbit of the Milky Way. Humanity and AIs cannot be 'managed' the way Praetor Kirkland wishes. He can't just have happy supplicant worlds everywhere. 'Everywhere' is just too damn big."

The ramifications of Cary's words—if they were true—swamped him. He'd heard rumors of AIs that had spread beyond the bounds of human exploration, even tall tales of them living at the core, but Cary seemed convinced of it. That part was easy to swallow. But extragalactic colonies? She'd taken her tale too far.

"OK, daughter of Tanis Richards, I think you've had your fun with me for today. I'd like you to leave."

He saw her face fall, but she straightened and nodded. "You don't believe me, but it's true. Perhaps I could take you on a trip to prove it."

Kent snorted. "If you get permission to take me on an extragalactic trip, I'll eat this blanket." He clutched his woolen blanket—such a strange incongruity in such a technologically advanced society—as he spoke.

Cary flashed a smile. "Challenge accepted, Colonel Kent."

A1

STELLAR DATE: 09.19.8949 (Adjusted Years)
LOCATION: OGS *Perilous Dream*
REGION: Undisclosed Location, Orion Freedom Alliance

Lisa Wrentham, who tended to think of herself most days as just 'A1', surveyed the stasis pods arranged in the chamber running down the *Perilous Dream*'s central axis. Of the six thousand and fifty pods, over three thousand were currently empty, their occupants deployed on missions throughout Orion Space and beyond.

Garza had delivered mission briefs that would require A1 to deploy several hundred of her Widows to the Inner Stars, where a few were already operating. Most of those missions would fall to those already out of stasis, but two missions would require special teams.

Teams that she wanted to personally prepare.

The briefs Garza had sent for the two missions in question were beyond perilous, and A1 had no doubt in her mind that whomever she sent stood a slim chance of returning. That made the knowledge that she had to send her best operatives all the more troubling.

Though her Widows were all clones, individuals often stood out in various ways. Some were exceptional combatants, others skilled at infiltration, and still more were top network breachers.

The variances in these abilities were small, but when it came to tasks such as the ones ahead, picking individuals that preferred certain aspects of the required work was exceedingly important.

Lisa stopped at a stasis pod that held one of her best. There was no image displayed on the top of the capsule—as was common in standard stasis pods—but it was not necessary, when every Widow looked the same. Instead, only a simple readout was displayed, noting that the occupant was in perfect stasis.

She turned the word 'widow' over in her mind for a minute. A1's original name for her clones was 'Autonomous Attack and Infiltration Simulacra', but 'AAIS' didn't have the same ring as 'Widow'. When she first heard that her clones were called that in some regions, she'd adopted the term.

Of course, it wasn't exactly true. Her former husband was still alive, so neither she nor her clones were technically widows.

Thoughts of Finaeus came to her from time to time. They'd lessened over the years, but had never gone away completely. There seemed to be a minimum limit that they hit and then remained at.

The feelings of anger and betrayal had long-ago shifted to a more muted regret. Not in regard to the fact that she had left him, but that he had chosen his brother over her.

Finaeus had agreed that Airtha was a danger and that Jeffrey was a pig-headed fool, but he still chose to side against Kirkland and the true mission of the FGT: to create a future for *humanity*. Not a gilded cage maintained by AIs.

And that was why she had directed her focus to create her Simulacra. Certainly there were issues with clones, problems that had taken some centuries to overcome, but in the end, Lisa had created a force that possessed all her knowledge and skill—as well as her passion—but was expendable.

Lisa activated the pod's extraction process, and half a minute later, the cover lifted off to reveal the sleek black form of one of her clones: C139

Its slender body was covered in a specialized material that, when at rest, appeared to be a glossy black shell. When a Simulacra stood still, they could be mistaken for a statue. But when they moved, their coating appeared fluid, like liquid obsidian being poured over their bodies.

Their heads were featureless black ovals, devoid of any humanity. The reason for this was twofold: to remind the Lisas that they were *not* human, and to drive that same message home to any they may encounter on their missions.

The coating was stealth capable and could also assume a dark matte grey—but all the Lisas seemed to prefer to use the glossy black option whenever possible.

Lisa glanced down at her own body as she watched C139 rise out of its pod, and smiled beneath her own ovoid helmet. Their preference could also mean that they were mimicking their progenitor.

"C139," she addressed the Simulacra before her. "Gather your Alpha Team and meet me in briefing room D9, I have a new mission for you."

C139 struck her heels together and ducked her head in a nod. "Understood, A1. We will be assembled in ten minutes."

In unison, the two Lisas turned and walked in opposite directions.

Lisa Wrentham felt a comfortable joy flow through her as she walked deeper into the chamber. Something about her clones addressing her as 'A1' deeply pleased her. Things hadn't always been that way.

In Lisa's initial attempts, she had created perfect clones with organic skin, faces, and every attribute she had. The result had been disastrous. The clones all believed themselves to *be* Lisa Wrentham, and when confronted with their progenitor—or one another—they had become wildly self-destructive, believing their lives had no value.

Lisa had terminated that batch and begun again. It took several iterations to arrive at the current model of clone, the Mark VII: a generation who did not view themselves as 'people' and knew nothing of their past, yet retained all the skills and abilities of Lisa herself.

Most importantly, they did not believe themselves to be clones.

But even then, there had been setbacks. The initial production run of Mark

VIIs had experienced 'leaks'. Bits of their past would surface, and some had begun to realize they were clones of Lisa.

It had taken some time to make the determination, but Lisa had ultimately arrived at the conclusion that the problem was herself. When the clones saw her, some would begin to remember that the face of their mistress was their own. Eventually they would suffer partial memory recovery.

She had made multiple attempts to separate memory of self from skill and ability, but it was impossible to do perfectly. So much of a given skill came from the experiences in mastering that skill, and those experiences required some level of 'self' in the mix.

When the solution came to her, Lisa had both laughed and cried at how simple the rectification was: rather than alter her clones to forget *her*, it was much simpler to alter herself to become one of them.

It seemed that her inherent rebellious streak had even gone so far as rebelling against herself.

She had taken on the featureless, glossy form—silver, in her case—sheathing her body in the advanced artificial epidermis she had been crafting for her Simulacra, even going so far as to encase her face in the same ovoid helmet her creations wore.

A helmet she hadn't removed in centuries.

The change had been near-miraculous in its effects on her brood. The memory leaks ceased, and once the commands and directives came from one who appeared to be of their kind, the Widows had fallen in line perfectly.

And so A1 became their leader, and they followed her without question.

In moments of deep personal honesty, Lisa would sometimes admit to herself that she liked being A1 *more* than Lisa Wrentham.

A1 was a being both filled with purpose, and one that *fulfilled* her purpose. She didn't have regrets, she didn't pine for things no longer attainable. She received orders and acted on them, dispersing her clone sisters amongst the stars to do her bidding.

On rare occasions when loneliness and depression would strike at Lisa, she gave strong consideration to undergoing the same processes she'd used on her clones, to truly become one of their number.

But something always stopped her, keeping her as Lisa, never letting her fully become A1.

She supposed it was some perverse desire to eventually lord her victory over Finaeus, when Orion finally defeated the Transcend. If she descended into A1's persona fully, she would never get to revel in his subjugation.

But after? Perhaps she would follow through with what had become an increasingly strong desire to escape her past forever, to simply become an organic machine with no past, only the skills and abilities to fulfill her purpose.

She reached another stasis pod, this one containing unit G11. As with C139, she activated the pod's extraction routine, and then instructed the Widow to meet A1 in briefing room D10 after gathering its alpha team.

Once that task was complete, Lisa left the central chamber and took a lift up to D deck. Several automatons were waiting for the lift when she arrived at her destination, and they stepped aside, their glossy white forms matching her own—though their shells contained only machines, not living, breathing women.

Lisa arrived at briefing room D9 before unit C139 and her team. She had only to wait for three minutes before the twelve Widows arrived, well ahead of the ten minutes C139 had estimated.

Once the Simulacra were all settled, Lisa began.

"The Division has determined that it is time for us to strike at the heart of evil within the Transcend, the abomination herself, Airtha."

As she spoke, A1 activated the holodisplay to show the Huygens System.

"Airtha is currently at the outer edge of the Tomias belt in Huygens, and is moving into a region that is clear of dark matter. The entire system has jump interdictors ten thousand AU from Huygens, but with Airtha soon to be accessible by dark layer FTL, we can jump to a point well outside that and then sneak in close."

Lisa saw E12 cock her head, and knew the question the widow was thinking. "Yes, they do have a sensor web in the dark layer around Airtha, but we all know that detecting ships in the DL is tricky at best, and we've been working on a way to maintain a transition into the DL while also reducing our graviton bleed. Unless we pass within a kilometer of a sensor, I don't think they'll stand a chance of spotting us."

E12 gave a slight nod, and Lisa could tell that the unit was satisfied, but still held slight reservations. E12 had always been rather contrarian, but it made her a good teammate, so A1 had never bothered with altering the unit's personality.

"Our goal is the utter destruction of the Airthan Ring," she continued. "Likely the star as well, if we do our job right. We have detailed schematics and believe that if we overload six of the ring's CriEn power-plants, we can destroy the ring, bringing it down into the dwarf star. It is likely that the resulting explosion will destroy the entire Huygens System—or at least ruin its habitability."

C139 lifted a hand off her lap and Lisa nodded to her. "Yes?"

"My estimations do not give a high level of likelihood for full-team survival…not even half the team," C139 said with only the slightest note of concern in her voice.

"You are correct," Lisa replied with a curt nod. "If this were any other mission, I would alter parameters until we could achieve a better rate of survivability, but this is *the* mission. The one we have been preparing for all these long centuries. You're the best of the best, and I believe in you. We all make sacrifices for humanity, sacrifices that must be made for the race."

"We're born of humanity, but are no longer a part of it," the Widows intoned in unison.

"That is correct. As your alpha, I promise you that your lives mean more to me than you can imagine, and I do not spend them carelessly. But Airtha grows stronger and must be stopped.

"I have prepared all relevant datasets for you, and have loaded them onto your pinnace. You are scheduled to depart in one hour; make ready."

The Widows all stood and snapped their heels together before giving their sharp nods and filing out of the room.

Once they had left, Lisa walked out into the hall and down one door to briefing room D10. She entered to see G11 and her team of nine waiting patiently in their seats; ten gleaming black heads turned ever so slightly to track her approach to the front.

"I'm sorry to have kept you waiting," Lisa said to them. "It is a busy day here on the *Perilous Dream*. I've just sent a team to destroy Airtha."

Heads silently tilted, and Lisa held up a hand. "I know each of you wishes to have been sent on that mission, but I have something equally important for you. A new abomination has risen, a full merge of human and AI that has *also* ascended."

G11 lifted a hand, and Lisa acknowledged her.

"Unit A1, if she is ascended, how can we strike against her? She will be well guarded, and will see us coming. Widows have faced ascended beings before. They did not survive."

"You are right. It will be dangerous. However, our intelligence networks have predicted a conjunction of events that will present a unique opportunity. I am passing you all relevant datasets now. This mission may see many of you fall in the field, but destroying this target is of the utmost importance.

"If we can take out this abomination, *and* defeat Airtha, we will be very close to overthrowing the Transcend and bringing the Inner Stars to heel."

G11's team turned their heads in short arcs, glancing at one another as they considered their alpha's words.

"Are there any questions?" Lisa asked.

"None, the dataset explains everything perfectly," G11 said after a moment.

Lisa nodded in satisfaction as the team exited the room in the same fashion as C139's.

Once the Widows were gone, Lisa readied additional datasets for two more teams, summoning them in the same fashion as the first two.

These received similar orders as the prior teams, but with the understanding that they were backup. They would shadow the initial teams, and should C139's or G11's Widows fall, they would fill the gaps, or take over entirely.

Lisa did not send shadow teams as a matter of common policy, but this time was different. The stakes were far too high.

Once the teams left for their respective departure hangars, Lisa left deck D and took a lift that drew her forward on the *Perilous Dream* to the bridge, four kilometers away from the briefing rooms.

She walked down the short corridor and stepped into the *Perilous Dream*'s beating heart. Within, twenty more of her clones sat at a variety of stations. They were identical to her and the Widows she had just sent on their disparate missions, except each of their glossy black bodies bore a white stripe running down the right side.

Several nodded deferentially to Lisa as she entered and sat in her command chair. Once she was settled into the seat, two bio-hookups connected to her lower back, and a hard-Link connector slotted into her neck.

Though Lisa had been tangentially aware of the ship's operations and surroundings while assembling and dispatching her teams, the direct connection to the vessel increased the bandwidth and filled her mind with data. The sensation was one of expanding, breaking free of the bonds her mortal coil constrained her with.

She watched as the four pinnaces slipped from their docking bays, queuing up for their turn at the jump gate and their destinations many thousands of light years away. Once they had all left, Lisa crafted a message for General Garza, informing him that her teams were en route.

He will be pleased, she thought. *He has wanted this almost as long as I have.*

* * * * *

Silina's over-earnest voice interrupted Garza's thoughts. *<A drone from Commander Wrentham has just jumped in.>*

<Right on time,> he replied. *<Deliver its datasets directly to me.>*

A moment later, Garza received the latest update from Lisa, and a packet including the details of each mission she had planned for her clones.

He still found them—not to mention Lisa's own altered appearance—rather disconcerting, but there was no arguing with the results. Lisa and her Simulacra got the job done.

The message sender was listed as 'A1', the designation Lisa had taken on when she decided to fully assume her Widow persona.

He understood her rationale for it—she didn't want to create a scenario where her clones saw her without her guise, so she wore it at all times, even on the Link and in communiques to him and other leaders in the Orion Guard.

Sometimes he wondered if A1 *was* one of the clones and the original Lisa was long gone. He wasn't even certain that there would be a way to tell anymore. There may have once been, but now that Lisa had altered herself to perfectly mimic her creations, there was no apparent differentiation other than color, and that was easily altered.

She had told him it was necessary—her clones were as clever as she was, and they would see through anything short of a total transformation.

Garza had to admit that it bothered him less now than it used to. Now that he was also using clones, he couldn't argue with the effectiveness of being in multiple places at once.

It's like the old saying goes, 'If you want a job done right, you have to do it yourself.'

He pushed aside the concern that A1 may herself be a clone. It didn't really matter, anyway. She followed orders and completed her tasks efficiently and without argument. If she did raise concerns, they were intelligent and always came with solutions.

Rather like a human AI, kept well at heel.

UNCERTAIN REUNION

STELLAR DATE: 09.25.8949 (Adjusted Years)
LOCATION: Command Deck 19, ISS *I2*
REGION: Pyra, Albany System, Thebes, Septhian Alliance

Fina looked to Sera and then to Seraphina, then placed her hands on the table, taking care to keep her flowmetal limbs in their proper form.

"I'm going to see her." Fina's voice was emphatic, brooking no argument.

The three women were sitting in one of the forward officers' mess halls on the *I2*. A place they had taken many a meal over the years.

Never together, of course. Most of their memories of time aboard the *Intrepid* were shared from when there had only been one Sera.

Just like their memories of time spent with Elena.

"If that's what you want to do," Seraphina replied tonelessly, while Sera's blood-red lips remained tightly pursed.

"I'd like you to be OK with this, Red," Fina said to Sera, willing her sister to speak, to give her absolution. "You have Jason; I thought you'd want us to be happy."

"I *do*." Sera broke her silence, holding her hands up in surrender. "But Elena…she's filled with…"

"Memories." Seraphina completed the statement, resting a hand on Sera's shoulder. "For all of us."

"You're lacking the ones where she betrayed Tanis and I to Orion, and tried to kill me." Sera's voice dripped with acid as she spoke.

"But you said it yourself," Fina leant forward, elbows on the table. "She was under Garza's control."

"Not originally." Sera shook her head, eyes locked on Fina's. "She went to see him of her own free will. Sure, she realizes it was a mistake *now*. But she still has…confused goals."

"And for that, you write her off?" Fina asked, glaring at her sister.

Though Sera frequently said that she wasn't going to stick exclusively to the color red, Fina noticed she'd not changed it since the day Fina had altered her coloring. There was no way Sera had gone this long without undoing her hack, so she had to assume that Sera really did like her scarlet appearance and was glad for the excuse to maintain it.

Now, as Sera became clearly flustered, the appearance of a shipsuit faded from her body, and her face and hands turned red, as well.

The effect made her look a bit demonic.

"Stars, Fina…it's not that simple. No, I don't write her off, but she still committed treason, and for that, she's in prison. Even if I *wanted* to set her free,

I can't. Not with my position. It would be seen as the worst form of nepotism. And there's nothing to indicate that Elena wouldn't betray us again."

"Garza's mental hacks won't work again," Seraphina said. "The ISF's neurologists are able to safeguard against anything but a remnant now."

"The benefit of encountering half a dozen forms of mental coercion in just a few years," Sera muttered. "Yay for science defeating evildoers."

No one responded, and silence settled over the table, broken only when Sera looked down at her hand and muttered. "Shit, stupid skin."

"Oh, stop it, for starssakes." Seraphina glared at Sera. "You *like* looking like that. You should...I don't know...add some shading or detail, darken your lips, and make that your default appearance. You're not going to be president anymore, you don't have to pretend to fit in with societal norms."

"You should do pink," Fina said, her expression serious. "Yeah, I know we have a thing against pink, but I think a dusky rose, with darker pink highlights would look good. No one would expect *that* in a million years."

"Can we get back to the topic at hand?" Sera asked.

Seraphina ran a hand through her blonde hair and then adjusted her leather jacket. "I thought you didn't want to talk about Elena. Isn't fashion usually a desirable diversion? Though for you two, it's just skin configuration. Is that really 'fashion'?"

Fina held out her right arm, and it stretched out into a sinuous blue tentacle that wrapped around Seraphina's glass of whiskey and snatched it away.

"It's *all* fashion, sister mine."

"Is it weird having no real arms and legs?" Sera asked, while Seraphina only glared at Fina before signaling a servitor for another drink.

Fina lifted the glass to her lips, her arm changing back to normal as she drank. "Sorta? I mean, it feels weird to stretch it out into a tentacle—especially with the sensory overload our skin delivers—"

"Not mine," Seraphina interrupted. "I went with the standard epidermis, not your massive erogenous zone version."

"Stars," Sera exclaimed with a laugh. "Seraphina, you're so missing out."

"Someone has to take life seriously," she muttered.

Fina set the glass down and rose from the table. "Sure, Elena probably has to remain in prison, and yeah, she fucked up bigtime. But I'm still going to pay her a visit."

Sera opened her mouth to speak, but Fina held up a hand. "You got to have your final word with her; I didn't. I deserve this."

Her sister's mouth closed slowly, and then she nodded. "OK. You're right. You want to see her, too?" Sera directed the question to Seraphina.

"Stars, no." Seraphina shook her head. "I'm saving up all my anguish and heartbreak for after the war is over. Besides, you lost the bet that set us up with a Cheeky-foursome, so I have to pursue *Sabrina*'s new captain the more traditional way."

Fina scowled. "What bet?"

A laugh slipped out of Sera's lips as she glanced at Seraphina. "*Technically,* I won the bet—which, due to a lack of foresight, means I lost and there shall be no festivities."

"Should have done it the other way," Seraphina said with a wink. "Then everyone would be happy."

"*What. Bet?*" Fina said through clenched teeth, finally turning and leaving the officer's mess when Sera and Seraphina only shook their heads and grinned at her.

SHORES OF THE TIGRIS

STELLAR DATE: 09.25.8949 (Adjusted Years)
LOCATION: Edge of the Quera System
REGION: Midway Cluster, Orion Freedom Alliance Space

"I really didn't expect them to be rebuilding this place," Svetlana said, as her flagship, the *Cossack's Sword,* transitioned out of the dark layer on the edge of the Quera System.

"Not just rebuild," General Lorelai said as scan updated, showing the construction underway at several locations in the outer system. "They're massing a fleet here."

Svetlana nodded silently as she surveyed the view on the holotank.

Several hundred ships were arranged in concentric orbits around Dios, the planet that Costa Station orbited. The advance scout ship had picked up major mining operations there, and other moons throughout the system were being stripped down as well.

The scan team grouped the enemy ships by level of completeness, also noting the ore drones, merchant ships, and other craft flitting about the system.

"Crowded," she said eventually. "Looks like at least seven thousand functional hulls out there."

Rear Admiral Sebastian appeared next to her, a holoprojection from his own flagship. He chuckled softly as he spoke. "I bet someone out there is thinking, 'there's no *way* they'd hit the Quera System twice in as many years'."

"Yeah, but they're ready for bear," General Lorelai replied. "Only half our ships have stasis shields, so we can't send them into a fight where we're outnumbered this badly."

"The general is right." Sebastian nodded slowly as he spoke. "Without intel on the situation, we have to assume they can put all seven thousand of those ships into the fight. Means we just have to bring in half of ours."

"Two hundred and fifty ships against seven thousand." Svetlana let a hungry grin appear on her lips. "It's almost fair."

* * * * *

Once all the ships had exited the dark layer, the TSF fleet made a big show of coming about and executing hard braking burns before transitioning out again.

Except not all the ships transitioned back into the dark layer. The stasis shield ships activated their stealth systems instead and carefully eased back around the periphery of the system.

They split up into three battlegroups. The largest, consisting of ninety-seven ships under Svetlana's command, set a course toward Dios, while Admiral Sebastian headed up ninety-two others. The final group of sixty-seven ships was commanded by the ISF's Colonel Caldwell.

Caldwell had the furthest to go. His target, a moon orbiting a gas giant, was nearly on the far side of the system. The plan was to initiate their strikes at the same time, though in reality, light lag would give them three hours before any of the targets saw that others were under attack.

As they moved into position, Orion picket fleets moved to check out the jump location, but by the time they arrived, the Hoplites would be long gone.

Svetlana reviewed her team's strategy once more. It would be perfect and utterly devasting.

And then they would be gone.

* * * * *

Colonel Caldwell examined his battleplan one final time.

In ten minutes, his ships would all be in position, ready to unleash their deadly hail on the Orion Guard shipyards and the mining operation on the moon below.

A part of him felt a twinge of guilt. The ISF's stealth technology was far ahead of Orion's detection abilities. The EM and debris around the shipyard would make it even easier for them to hide. Anyone scanning space for approaching ships would have a hard time separating false positives from any real threat.

When the rail PADs, the fleet's shorthand for the ring-shaped particle accelerator destroyers, opened fire, it would already be too late.

"Have all the ships reported in?" he asked the Fleet Coordination Officer.

"Aye, Colonel. Everyone is in full readiness, rings loaded and ready to heat up," the FCO replied.

"Good," Caldwell directed a nod to the lieutenant.

The design of the PAD destroyer was a clever one, pulled from an old Scattered Worlds design back in the Sol System. Rather than fire single shots through linear accelerators, the PADs accelerated pellets in a half-kilometer circumference ring. They didn't need to impart relativistic energies to the pellets in one go, but through a slow buildup around the loop.

The loop had ports every hundred meters, and could easily fire in nearly any direction without moving the ship. The only downside was that the loop got hot when it was active, and bled EM radiation into space with wild abandon. As a result, the ships had to keep their accelerators offline while in stealth.

It was a sacrifice Caldwell was willing to make. The ships' stasis shields would protect them well enough during the warmups, and the wing of TSF destroyers and cruisers that was their escort would keep any enemy craft from closing with them.

As he waited, he saw one of the Orion Guard vessels ease out of the construction yard, moving to dock with a grid that anchored the ships while in their final stages of construction.

He had to admit that the craft was massive. Not as large as an I-Class vessel, but at twenty kilometers in length, the thing was close.

"What need do they have for a ship like that?" he mused quietly.

"Sir?" a nearby officer on scan asked.

"Nothing, Ensign Hela," he replied. "Just wondering what a ship like that is for."

"Not that impressive, really, sir," Hela said with an exaggerated shrug. "An I-Class dwarfs it."

"That's my thought, too," Caldwell replied. "When your shock and awe dreadnought is dwarfed by the enemy's, it doesn't really create a lot of fear in said enemy."

The bridge fell silent again as the crew watched the activity around them unfold until the attack was to begin.

"What's that?" one of the ensigns at the helm asked, gesturing to a sizable chunk of rock that was being maneuvered into place by a pair of tugs, stopping next to one of the large enemy ships.

As the crew watched, armatures extended from the top of the ship and grappled the hundred-meter rock.

"Graviton emissions!" Ensign Hela called out. "Spacetime distortion centered on that ship!"

"Spacetime?" Caldwell muttered, then cursed as he saw the rock begin to disintegrate, its mass falling down into an opening on the large ship.

"My readings align with a singularity," Hela announced, twisting in her seat. "Do they have a black hole inside that ship?"

"Fuck," Colonel Caldwell swore again. "How the hell does Orion have EMGs? Airtha just fielded them three weeks ago at Valkris!"

"Can they stealth?" the FCO asked.

"How do you stealth a black hole?" Hela shot back. "Though I didn't spot it 'til the thing started feeding.... How *did* they do that?"

Caldwell glanced at the countdown, noting that it was only fifty-two seconds before the attack. "FCO! Get on the QuanComm, alert the other battle groups that the Oggies have EMG ships."

"Aye, sending the packet," the FCO announced.

"Are we still attacking?" Hela asked nervously.

Caldwell glanced down at the ensign. "Damn straight we are. Those ships only shoot out the front. We're light and fast. We can outmaneuver them with ease."

He saw members of the bridge crew glance at one another in hesitation, but no one spoke their fear.

*****

"I've a message from Colonel Caldwell," Svetlana's FCO announced. "Holy shit! Uh…ma'am, he believes the big daddy ships are EMGs!"

Svetlana summoned the data the ISF and Transcend had collected in their two encounters with Airthan EMG vessels. The general structure of the ships were similar—though the Oggie versions were significantly smaller. She wondered if that meant they had more refined systems, or if their firing power wasn't as great.

"That doesn't change our objective, people, it just means we need to be extra careful. Tactical, I want our no-fly cones to include vectors that align with the noses of any big daddies."

"Yes, ma'am," the TCO called out. "Disseminating this to the fleet."

"Admiral Sebastian has acknowledged the intel," the FCO announced. "He suggests we stay away from the pointy ends."

"Insightful," Svetlana muttered before addressing her crew. "OK, people, we know from how close the Oggies managed to get to Carthage when they attacked New Canaan that they have impressive stealth tech. I don't know how you stealth a black hole, but we can't rule it out. Keep your eyes peeled for any more surprises."

"Wish we could just use the weapon the ISF did to stop those bastards," one of her weapons officers muttered.

"Do you really want to let that cat out of the bag?" Svetlana asked. "You know what happened at SC-91R. Mighty big no-fly zone."

"The ISF got the Exdali back into the dark layer," the man replied.

"The ISF was desperate," Svetlana countered. "Not that it matters—it's not a tool we have. These Oggies will go down the old-fashioned way."

"Aye, ma'am," the weapons officer replied as the countdown entered its final ten seconds.

At zero, sixty-two ships in Svetlana's battlegroup decloaked and opened fire on the enemy vessels in the highest orbit around Dios. Seconds later, the Oggie ships responded, hundreds of them boosting into higher orbits and firing on the TSF attackers.

Stasis shields shed the beams with ease, while concentrated fire from the TSF ships holed an enemy destroyer and cruiser in the first twenty seconds.

Two down, six thousand nine hundred and ninety-eight to go, Svetlana thought.

The ships that had uncloaked swung away from Dios, moving into a higher orbit and drawing hundreds of enemy craft after.

Deeper in the planet's gravity well, a hundred fusion torches came to life as

Svetlana's remaining vessels launched crusher missiles.

CMs were the opposite of relativistic missiles. They weren't built to go fast, they were built to move mass. The missiles converged on the asteroid that housed Costa Station, braking before slamming into the station's hull and the asteroid's surface. Then the engines flared even brighter, shoving the small moonlet out of its orbit and toward the surface of the planet below.

Enemy ships diverted from their attacks on the TSF ships, targeting the crusher missiles attached to the asteroid's surface, while escape pods began to spill from Costa Station.

A red marker flared on the holotank, and Svetlana focused in on it, pursing her lips as she saw that it was one of the EMG ships.

No-fly zones lit up across the battlespace, as the TSF fleet repositioned to stay away from the business end of the massive ship-gun.

"Send a burst to the stealthed ships," Svetlana ordered the FCO. "I want a dozen CMs on that EMG. Let's see how well it can shoot when it's falling into Dios."

"Yes, ma'am. Message sent," the FCO responded. "Acknowledgement received."

Svetlana felt her stomach lurch as the *Cossack's Sword* shifted under her feet, jinking wildly to avoid the business end of the EMG ship as nine crusher missiles slammed into the stern of the enemy vessel and spun it about.

A beam fired from the nose of the EMG, degenerate matter and high-energy rays slicing across the battlefield. The shot was invisible to the naked eye, but warnings flared on consoles across the CIC as readings spiked.

Seconds later, the EMG's burst began to falter, but not before it hit a TSF destroyer. The impact from the relativistic exotic matter slamming into the stasis shield was like a star had been born right next to them.

Then the destroyer was gone, the shockwave of an antimatter explosion spreading from its former location.

"Sweet fucking darkness," someone nearby whispered.

"I want all rails to hit that fucking thing," Svetlana called out. "Bring it down!"

A dozen ships with clear firing solutions sent salvos into the EMG's engines, killing them and removing the ship's ability to fight against the crusher missiles pushing against its shields.

A moment later, the vessel's shields failed, and the missiles slammed into its hull. The EMG began to list, slewing across the battlespace until a part of its hull crumpled inward.

"It's collapsing!" the scan officer called out.

It happened so fast, Svetlana could barely see it. One moment, the ship was a physical object in space, the next, it was gone in a blinding flash of light, along with the crusher missiles and a nearby Oggie destroyer.

"Tracking the singularity," Scan announced. "The CMs had the EMG on a hohmann transfer to lower orbit, it's following that path...."

"Huh…nice of the Oggies to give us the best tool for the job," Svetlana said in a low voice.

The plan had been to smash the moonlet that Costa Station was attached to into the planet—hopefully destroying one of the mining rigs while they were at it—but a singularity was a far better option.

"Impact with Dios in four hours," Scan said in an awed voice. "We're gonna see a planet die."

The OG ships seemed to reach the same conclusion, pulling into higher orbits and forming up into battlegroups that hinted at a retreat.

The tally at the top of the holotank showed that only seventeen enemy ships had been destroyed, though another forty-two had taken noteworthy damage.

"Update from Colonel Caldwell," The FCO announced. "He's destroyed his target, and the enemy ships are fleeing. He wants to know if he should pursue."

Svetlana watched as the OG ships around Dios broke away from the battle, harried by her forces.

"No, have him form up at Rally Point Charlie."

"Ma'am?" the FCO asked.

"No pursuit; all three of our fleets chasing the enemy outsystem makes us too vulnerable, and exposes too much of our capability to them. Inform Admiral Sebastian to fall back to Charlie once his primary target is eliminated. Our work in the Quera System is done."

STAR CITY

STELLAR DATE: 09.25.8949 (Adjusted Years)
LOCATION: Tanis's Lakehouse, Ol' Sam, ISS *I2*
REGION: Pyra, Albany System, Thebes, Septhian Alliance

"You two ready for this?" Tangel asked as she walked through the orchard behind her lakehouse with Jessica and Trevor. "Earnest's calculations for operating a jump gate so close to the Stillwater Nebula *should* work, but if not, you'll have to fly out to Serenity, or maybe even further to make a jump home."

"They'll work," Jessica said, giving Trevor a reassuring glance. "I know because of how red Finaeus's face got when he looked over Earnest's solutions. He started out by saying something along the lines of, 'Only an idiot would operate a jump gate below a gas giant's cloudtops', but then he simply started repeating 'Balls' over and over again."

"That's pretty telling," Trevor agreed with a chuckle. "Even if it takes us a few months to get back, it'll be worth it just to see the kids. I'll feel a lot better knowing they're OK."

Jessica patted his arm. "They're in control of the most powerful weapon in the galaxy."

"Next to Tangel, that is," Trevor replied. "Given that we named our daughter Tanis, I'm worried she's going to take on the trouble-magnet aspect of her namesake as well."

"Umm…I'm standing right here." Tangel's brows lowered into a scowl.

"Can't you hear us anywhere on the ship?" Jessica asked with a wink. "We can't really talk behind your back, might as well do it to your face."

"No, I can't listen to the whole ship at once." Tangel resisted the urge to make a face at Jessica. "That's Bob's department."

They all paused, waiting for the AI to reply, but no response came.

"Bob?" Jessica asked.

<Sorry, I was busy spying on more interesting conversations than yours. Did you need something?>

"Oh!" Trevor barked a laugh. "And the ascended AI delivers a scorcher!"

<Seriously, though. I am quite curious how the denizens of Star City figured out how to fire neutron-degenerate matter so effectively. I do hope your children will share that information with you.>

" 'Effectively' is no exaggeration, either," Trevor said as they reached a narrow brook that ran amongst the trees. "They utterly crushed a massive Orion Guard fleet without a single ship of their own."

"I hope they made some, though," Jessica added. "Ships are necessary for a solid defense."

"If she takes after me at all, she'll have a million by now," Tangel said with a wink. "I'm more interested in the Dream, and how they managed to ascend trillions of people in the space of a few millennia."

"I don't think quite that many ascended," Jessica replied. "Just a hundred billion, or so,"

Tangel turned left, walking along the edge of the stream. "But from the data on Star City, there's no reason they *couldn't* have ascended trillions."

"Fair enough," Jessica allowed. "I do wonder where they all went, though. The ascended people."

"Maybe you can find out," Tangel asked. "Once you get the gates set up, I may make a trip out there myself. I'd like to meet my namesake and her siblings."

"We'd like that a lot, too." Trevor glanced at Jessica. "I just wish Iris could come along."

Jessica pursed her lips, and Tangel noted how the woman's eyes glowed more brightly for a moment.

"Yeah," Jessica finally said. "She's doing important work at Aldebaran, but..."

"It won't go on forever," Tangel assured her as they reached a small bridge and crossed over. "Both Iris and Amavia are getting tired of the League of Sentients' nonsense. If we can just get them to join in with Scipio, the Hegemony of Worlds will fall within a year. Once that happens, their biggest aggressor will be gone. Hopefully that will finally bring them around to our way of thinking."

"That's a big 'hopefully'." Jessica shook her head, a rueful tone in her voice. "For all the help we've given them, the LoS is ridiculously suspicious. Stars, we *saved* Virginis, and they still treat us like outsiders looking to take something from them."

Tangel nodded. "If we weren't spread so thin, we could commit more to that fight and we wouldn't *need* the LoS. But things have flared up in Corona Australis again, there's the mess at Valkris, and Orion just launched an attack on Deneb that I need to funnel ships to."

Jessica chuckled. "You must have a mighty big funnel."

"If only," Tangel replied. "You know...if we hadn't built those shipyards in New Canaan's moons, this would be all over by now—and not in our favor."

"And it still doesn't feel like it was enough," her friend said.

Tanis shook her head. "It really doesn't."

SABRINA DEPARTING

STELLAR DATE: 09.25.8949 (Adjusted Years)
LOCATION: *Sabrina*, A1 Dock, ISS *I2*
REGION: Pyra, Albany System, Thebes, Septhian Alliance

As Seraphina walked onto *Sabrina*'s bridge, a flood of emotion rushed through her.

She traced a hand along the edge of a console, marveling at how it looked mostly the same, but felt so very different. The pilot's seat looked as it always had, complete with a pair of Cheeky's heels kicked underneath the console—which was strange, given that she could make her feet into shoes.

Does she detach them? That's kinda creepy.

Small knickknacks adorned other surfaces, giving the bridge a more lived-in appearance than it had possessed under her tenure as captain.

Over twenty years ago, she reminded herself. *Cargo sat in that captain's chair longer than I did.*

"Though I bet he wasn't the one that made it purple," she muttered with a shake of her head.

"That was me," Cheeky said as she strode onto the bridge clothed only in a red sarong and a pair of spike-heeled sandals. "Well, Usef added these." The ship's captain leant over and touched a small button on the side of the chair, and glitter shot out of the seat, showering the area in sparkling points of light.

"Sweet stars in the dark." Seraphina couldn't help but laugh. "I've only met Usef briefly, but that…that doesn't jibe."

"You'd be surprised what Usef gets up to," Cheeky said with a wink. "You wanna try the chair?"

Seraphina gazed at the glitter-covered purple edifice and shook her head. "Even if I wasn't worried about getting glitter out of my clothes for the next week…it's not mine anymore. You should sit in it."

"Me?" Cheeky squeaked. "Stars no. If I'm on this bridge, I'm in the pilot's seat. Honestly, I was kinda thinking of taking it out entirely—but that feels weird too."

"Purple!" a voice cried out from behind them and then Fina pushed past and leapt into the captain's chair. "And sparkles? Sweet fucking darkness, I've missed being on this ship. How could I have ever left you, Sabs?"

<Technically you sent me away,> Sabrina replied. *<But I forgave you—we had a very heartfelt chat about it.>*

"That's good to know," Fina replied absently, looking over the controls on the chair. "How do I make it shoot more glitter?"

"I wish you wouldn't," Nance said as she walked onto the bridge, scowling at the sparkling mess. "Jessica fired that stuff off all the time, and I'm still getting it out of the filtration systems. Every now and then when a vent kicks on, it showers glitter."

Fina glanced at Nance, a wide grin on her face. "You say that like it's a bad thing." As she spoke, her skin and hair turned purple, matching the chair perfectly. "We should get Jessica on here one last time before she heads out on her secret mission with Trevor. See if we can get her to sit on me."

"You know her skin can electrocute you," Cheeky warned.

"Sounds like fun!"

"Stars," Seraphina muttered while lowering her face into both hands. "Are you going to start shrinking, as a part of your regression into a child?" Her head snapped up. "And if you shrink your limbs and try to look like a child, I'll slap you into next week."

Fina's skin shifted back to her standard blue hue, and she scowled at Seraphina. "Just having some fun. Gotta make up for you."

"Sisters," Sera muttered as she walked onto the bridge, Finaeus and Jeffrey in tow. "You never know you want them 'til you get them. Then you doubt your sanity in new and exciting ways."

"Not to mention that you have Andrea for a sister," Finaeus replied. "She probably put you off the idea of sisters forever."

"Got that right," the three Seras said in near unison, then proceeded to stare at one another warily.

<*You **really** are all the same person,*> Sabrina said with a note of wonderment in her voice. <*Can one of you stay with us once this is over?*>

"I'm still captain," Cheeky said, giving the Seras a mock glower. "I didn't do *all* the work on this ship for the last thirty years just to give up my shot at the big job."

Her statement was met with derision and mockery from all sides, to which Cheeky only laughed in response. "I can't wait for this mission—it's going to be a blast."

Seraphina glanced at her father, seeing a look of consternation warring with general amusement on his face.

"Don't worry, Father, we know how to buckle down when it counts."

"Wouldn't have survived this long if we didn't," Sera added.

"I get that we don't have to be somber while saving the galaxy," Jeffrey said while shaking his head at Finaeus and Cheeky, who were wrapping their arms around one another for an impassioned kiss. "But does it have to be a 'clothing-optional' event?"

"Why, Mister President," Cheeky said in a sultry voice. "*Everything* is a clothing-optional event."

Jeffrey glanced at Finaeus. "You have the strangest taste in wives."

Seraphina's lips quirked into a smile as Finaeus slapped Jeffrey on the shoulder. "Just like my brother," he quipped. "OK, ladies, the High Guard's aboard, let's get this show on the road."

SURPRISE VISIT

STELLAR DATE: 09.26.8949 (Adjusted Years)
LOCATION: TSF Docks, Keren Station
REGION: Khardine System, Transcend Interstellar Alliance

Jason watched as *Sabrina* settled onto a docking cradle in one of Keren Station's larger bays. A ramp extended from the deck, lifting up to the mid-ship port-side airlock.

He glanced at Admiral Greer and the cabinet members to his right, and then at the honor guard, which formed up at the base of the ramp.

I don't recall them having anywhere near this level of pomp and ceremony for Sera. I guess the father's earned it a bit more.

When the ship's airlock opened, the first out were four of Sera's High Guard—which caused Jason to wonder if they would still protect her, or if they'd all be assigned to her father.

The idea of ISF Marines—there were nine in the High Guard's ranks—protecting Jeffrey Tomlinson didn't sit right with Jason. Sera was different; she had saved Tanis and spent months aboard the *Intrepid*—and later, half a year in New Canaan. She understood what an honor it was for the colony world to assign its scarcest resource to keep her safe.

He didn't get the impression that Jeffrey Tomlinson would appreciate the honor.

For reasons he couldn't quite put his finger on, Jason didn't really *like* the former—and probably future—president of the Transcend.

He hadn't met the clone of Jeffrey who had died aboard the *Galadrial* two years prior, but he had studied everything he could find out about the man, both before and after learning that for the last thousand years, the Transcend had been ruled by a puppet of Airtha's.

From what he could tell, even at his best, Jeffrey was a bit of an ass. Still, his brother Finaeus supported him, and Jason had to admit that despite his quirky personality, Finaeus Tomlinson was a stand-up guy. He wouldn't back his brother if he thought he'd make a mess of things.

The High Guard reached the bottom of the ramp, two of their number joining Keren Station's honor guard, while the others strode across the bay to stand at the exit.

Moments later, Sera emerged from the airlock, followed by Sera and Sera.

Jason had known that two of Sera's clones had been captured—he'd been present for one of the events—but he hadn't gotten the message that all of them were coming to Keren Station.

Watching the three Seras—one sheathed in blue, another in red, and the third wearing a long leather jacket over what appeared to be still more leather—stride down the ramp had a curious effect on his cognitive abilities.

At almost the same time, all three spotted him. One by one, they smiled, but he could tell something was different in the red Sera's smile. He determined it to be a victorious expression, commingled with a possessive glint.

Why do I always find myself attracted to complicated women?

Behind the blonde, leather-wearing Sera came Finaeus, Tangel, and Jeffrey. Then the rest of *Sabrina*'s crew filed out, followed by more of the High Guard.

He nodded to Tangel, who met his eyes and returned the gesture before her eyes darted toward Sera and gave a wink.

<What are you doing here?> Sera asked Jason privately as the group formed up at the bottom of the ramp, exchanging pleasantries with Admiral Greer and the members of the Presidential Cabinet.

<Are you the red one?> Jason asked. *<Or blue? You're certainly not the blonde, I can't see you giving up the skin.>*

<I'm red,> Sera said with a sigh. *<I got assigned a color by Fina.>*

<I'm guessing she's the one in blue.>

<Yup, and blondie-stick-up-her-butt is Seraphina.>

Jason held back a laugh as Jeffrey Tomlinson shook his hand. *<Stop it, Sera, I have to make a good impression with your dad.>*

<Gah, that's far too weird. Don't say things like that. And regarding Seraphina…ah, she's not that bad. I should cut her more slack. It's probably not easy to find out you were the third edition of another person.>

Jason considered that for a moment. *<No, I suppose it wouldn't be. 'Unique' is usually the one thing everyone has going for them that they can be relatively secure in.>*

<You never answered my question,> Sera said as the group began to walk out of the bay.

<Which was?>

<What are you doing here?>

Jason fell in beside Sera, who was talking about the state of the rebuilding project at Pyra with her cabinet. *<Well, I was in the LMC dealing with some odds and ends, when Tangel here sent a message confirming that you would be passing through the Khardine System before going to Styx. I knew that things between us would get…tricky if we left them for too long, so I decided to come and meet you.>*

<Tangel told you about how we're going to hit Airtha, did she?>

Jason replied to a question from one of the cabinet members about the Airthan fleets in the LMC while responding to Sera. *<Sure, I get the briefs. I* ***am*** *the governor of New Canaan, if you've forgotten.>*

<You're pretty good at that—carrying on two conversations at once.>

<Don't forget,> Jason gave Sera a wink. *<I came by my neuron-packed brain honestly. Didn't take a post-birth operation for me to become an L2.>*

<I'm not quite up there with you, but close,> Sera replied. *<Granted, since my*

mother manufactured me to spec, I'm not sure what I'd have upstairs if it weren't for her meddling.>

<*I bet you'd've been amazing.*>

She grabbed his hand and gave it a squeeze. <*You saying I'm not amazing now?*>

Jason gave Sera an exaggerated wink. <*Oh! You are quick!*>

* * * * *

Sera and Tangel had been whisked away to attend lengthy cabinet meetings discussing whether or not her father was fit to take up his position as president once more. Jason could have made a case to attend, but he'd had his fill of conference rooms for the time being.

Despite his reservations about Jeffrey Tomlinson on a personal level, Jason rather hoped that Sera wouldn't have any trouble securing the transfer of power. He knew it was selfish, but the possibility that Sera could shuck off all her responsibility made him more than a little happy.

Not having to manage the entire Transcend meant there was an increased possibility that she could join him in his cabin deep in the mountains of Pelas on Carthage after the war ended.

<*We're gonna break for the day in about thirty minutes,*> Sera informed him. <*Want to meet for dinner? I'm starving.*>

<*You got it. I found this little pub down by the commercial docks. They have an amazing burger called the Back Blast—it's less risky than it sounds—plus whiskey made by the gods themselves.*>

<*Didn't know the gods were in the whiskey-making business.*>

Jason sent a warm laugh into her mind. <*They're gods. They're in every business.*>

<*Touche. Shoot, Victor is making some stupid argument that I need to concentrate on. Send me the name of the place, and I'll meet you there.*>

<*You got it,*> Jason replied. <*It's called the 'Golden Goose'.*>

Jason had been in more than his share of political meetings. He knew that 'breaking in thirty minutes' was code for 'see you in a few hours'.

However, on the off-chance that Sera would actually manage to break free within thirty minutes, he worked his way down to the Golden Goose and secured a table in the back. Only two of the ISF Marines functioning as his guards came in, but he knew that the others would be nearby—a necessary annoyance he'd become accustomed to.

As he waited for one of the human waitstaff to approach, he surveyed the bar, taking in the 'local flavor'.

Though Keren Station was the heart of the Khardine faction of the Transcend—and thus all but swarmed with both politicians and the military—

it had spent most of its existence as the central hub for the region's many mining operations.

The ongoing military buildup meant that the mining guilds were busier than ever, but despite that, precious few of their old haunts had room for them.

His train of thought was reinforced by some of the regulars giving him sidelong looks. He began to wonder if a change of venue was in order, when two men and a woman—their shipsuits covered in a fine iron-ore dust—approached him. Their arms were crossed, and their brows lowered.

"I don't mean nothing by it," one of the men said as the trio reached his table. "But there's precious little enough space for us on Keren anymore. I'm sure there are plenty of other establishments where you can eat, up in the hab cylinder."

Despite the fact that the three people before Jason didn't care for him much, he felt a sort of kinship with them.

Other than a single FTL corridor, the Oratus Cluster was restricted to sub-light travel only by dense clouds of dark matter. The miners standing before him likely spent most of their time plying the black the same way Jason had as a young man: slowly.

"You're right," he said with a nod and an expansive smile. "But I feel a lot more at home down here. Smells like honest work." He looked at each of them in turn. "Do you know who I am?"

"Of course we do. Is it supposed to be some sort of threat?" the woman asked.

"Not in the least," Jason replied with disarming grin. "But from the way you said that, I doubt very much you really know who I am."

The three shared a confused glance.

"What's that supposed to mean?" one asked.

Jason gestured at the empty seats around the table. "Why don't you sit down, and I'll tell you a story about how I got started on this whole crazy adventure." The trio seemed uncertain until he added, "I'll buy you rounds so long as you care to listen."

That got the miners seated and signaling a servitor.

Once the first and second rounds were ordered—'for good measure', the woman had said with a wink—Jason began his tale.

"You see, I wasn't always a governor, or a respectable captain of a colony ship. Heck, even my own family thought I stood a good chance of never doing much with my life—not that I cared. Life is for living, not storing up in some reservoir that you get to finally dip into someday.

"Some of the expectations placed on me were due to the fact that I was the grandson of one of the great heroes of the Sentience Wars: Cara Sykes. She made quite the name for herself in the wars, and that's what most people remembered about her, but what few knew is that she grew up on a half-broken-down freighter named the *Sunny Skies*."

"Weird name for a freighter," the woman—who Jason later learned was named Margret—commented.

"Well, my great grandfather was a bit of an optimist—or so I'm told. Little known fact: he was the first successful AI-human pairing. The AIs back then called him a 'hybrid'. Set the stage for…well…nearly everything that is going on now.

"Anyway, after the end of the first Sentience War, my mother and her husband left the Sol System for Alpha Centauri, but they never made it as far as Rigel Kentaurus, stopping instead at Proxima Centauri."

"Pretty short flight," the first man—named Wren—said.

"Well, not back then. In those days, it used to take us a century to cross those measly four and a half light years. Anyway, Proxima is where they had me and my sister, and where we grew up. But I didn't really fancy sitting in one place. Proxima used to have a thick dust belt in those days, so I ran ore haulers between there and Rigel Kentaurus, the primary star in the Alpha Centauri system."

The three nodded appreciatively, seeming to be fully engrossed in the story as they nursed their drinks, so Jason continued.

"After that, I worked with the Enfields to build out the very first interstellar trade routes." The three miners looked at him skeptically and he shrugged. "Well, sure, there were folks who plied the black here and there before that, but they weren't hauling freight on commission, and they weren't making regular runs. You're looking at the first person to ever make a regular freight run between two separate star systems on a schedule."

"Shit…that's actually kinda awesome," Margret said with a slow nod as she glanced at her tablemates. "So how did you go from that to becoming the governor of New Canaan? Bit of a leap."

"Not too much." He gave his audience a wink. "Let me take a step back and tell you a bit about Enfield and the Sentience Wars. This is the sort of stuff you won't find in the history books. Luckily, I was raised by people—both AIs and humans—who were there…."

* * * * *

Sera had looked up the Golden Goose on her way down to the lower docks. It was a spot known for good food, coarse language, and rot-gut that would pickle your liver.

In short, it was just the sort of place she frequented back when she was captain of *Sabrina*, but hadn't seen much of since.

Jason had related a few tales from his younger days that led her to believe he used to enjoy a good dive bar as well.

However, as she neared the location, the boisterous sounds she expected to hear were not in evidence. In fact, she didn't even hear music coming from the entrance.

What she did hear was the sound of a singular voice rising and falling as it recited a tale to an audience. Upon entering the establishment, she saw the speaker—not that she hadn't already identified him.

<*I guess he got bored waiting for you,*> Jen commented with a snicker, and Sera shot her AI a sour look as she threaded her way through the crowd.

Jason stood atop a chair near the back of the bar, his sonorous voice booming out over a rapt audience.

"…as I said, I didn't like to visit Sol much—too many politicians and self-important types—" The statement raised a few snickers from the crowd. "But he asked me to come, and so I did."

"The one who shot your sister?" a voice called out in confusion.

"Yeah, we got past that…eventually. He did it for the right reasons—well, technically *he* wasn't even the one to have done it. Either way, he said he had a grand new adventure, one last flight into the black."

"How'd that turn out for ya?" one of the onlookers called out.

"Well, I'm still out here. Not sure if this counts as the same ongoing adventure, or if I've had a few since the *Intrepid* set sail. Oh ho! My date has arrived. Sorry, folks, I'll have to save the rest for another time. I can't keep a lady waiting."

<*Though she sure kept me,*> he sent privately to Sera.

<*Sorry about that…I tried. Seems like you weren't having any trouble keeping busy.*>

He continued to dismiss his assembled listeners while replying to Sera. <*Well, I had to make sure that I didn't inadvertently start a barfight. You've got some unrest in the working class down here, by the way. Was fun, though…been far too long since I've gotten to hang out with strangers like this.*>

"OK, If I'm here another day, I'll swing by again. No promises, though," Jason said as he pushed through the crowd toward Sera. "Just let me settle up my tab—"

<*You don't want to stay?*> Sera asked, as the crowd thundered that he had no tab so far as they were concerned.

<*We won't get much privacy,*> he replied with an apologetic smile.

Sera continued pushing through the crowd, which parted when the patrons realized who she was.

When she reached Jason's side, she turned to the throng. "To be honest, I want to hear his stories as much as you do. I'm willing to share him for the evening if you still want to hear more…"

The crowd roared in the affirmative, and she turned to Jason.

"So where were you?"

He shook his head and leapt back onto his chair. "OK…where *was* I? By the way, you'll all forgive me if I paint myself in a slightly better light to impress my girl here, won't you?"

The question was met by laughter and a few catcalls, which quieted down when Jason lifted his hands.

"OK, so my buddy Terrance wanted me to fly this bloody big starship out to 82 Eridani—you folks did good work there, from what I hear, not that I ever got to see it. Anyway, that ship was being built in Sol, but I was back at Alpha Centauri again. And like always, there was a mess that seemed like only I could clean up. Luckily, some of my old friends were still there, and we teamed up for one last adventure under the twin suns…."

THE MARCH

STELLAR DATE: 09.27.8949 (Adjusted Years)
LOCATION: TSS *Cossack's Sword*, Edge of the Quera System
REGION: Midway Cluster, Orion Freedom Alliance Space

Admiral Sebastian began speaking the moment he entered the conference room.

"OK, I know we didn't have to utterly *crush* them, but I also don't think we needed to let that many get away."

General Lorelai sat next to him and nodded slowly, but didn't respond.

Colonel Caldwell was also seated at the table, sipping a hot cup of coffee. Other than his initial greeting, the taciturn man hadn't said a word while they'd waited for Sebastian to arrive.

Now, at the admiral's words, he looked up from his cup and shrugged. "We denied them the system and got their attention. We suffered one loss and gathered valuable intelligence. I consider this to be quite the victory."

"Annihilation would have been a better victory." Sebastian's tone was sour as he sat heavily. "We could have done it."

"Probably," Svetlana replied with a nod. "But we want to sow chaos. The Quera System is too isolated to do that. Now these ships will disperse to one or more nearby systems to rally and get ready to fight us once more."

"They don't stand a chance, why—" Sebastian cut off his response mid-word. "Oh, shit. I'm such an idiot."

"No need to go that far," General Lorelai said with a wink.

"You want them to think that we don't have the stamina to go the distance," Sebastian said, shaking his head as he gestured for a servitor to bring him a coffee.

"Glad you picked up on it." Svetlana summoned a display of the surrounding systems on the table's projector. "They're going to assume that we'll move to one of these three systems, and they'll believe that they have a chance of defending those against us."

"They just might, if they have enough of those EMG ships," Caldwell murmured. "Those things are ridiculous."

"And as much a liability as a weapon," Svetlana replied.

"You can bet they're not going to station them too close to a planet next time." Admiral Sebastian lifted his cup of coffee and took a long draught. "But my team analyzed the beam cohesion. They can shoot a lot further than the standard ranges."

"Fleet Intel has come to the same conclusion." Svetlana folded her hands before herself as she spoke. "Shield-breaching range could be as far as five million kilometers."

Sebastian whistled. "Yeah, things'll hit you half a second after you see them."

"We have fighters. We should use them more effectively," Caldwell said. "Deploy them ahead, widespread. If there are EMGs, they can't hit that many fighters—can't even see them at few million klicks. Fighters will make short work of ships like that."

Svetlana nodded slowly. She was still getting used to having fighters as a major part of her battlegroup. For so long, they hadn't been practical—unable to house powerplants large enough to support good shields.

But now with stasis shielding, her fighters were well-nigh invincible, and far more maneuverable than capital ships.

"You're right. I need to have Colton and Lia more involved in future strategies. Our TR-9s are more deadly than an Oggie destroyer now."

"So which of these three closest systems do we hit next?" Admiral Sebastian asked.

"Half wish we could strike all three at once," Colonel Caldwell mused.

Svetlana shook her head. "Too risky. If something goes wrong, we're cut off, and we're already severely outnumbered. I think the Sullus System is our best bet. Admiral Jessica passed through there, and we have solid intel on it."

"You thinking we hit this outpost here?" General Lorelai asked, enlarging the system view and gesturing to a station orbiting a terrestrial world in the outer system.

Svetlana nodded. "We'll jump in stealthed and move the fleet into strike positions around the system before launching our attacks. Military targets, strike and run. That'll keep the insystem forces chasing us while you hit your target, Lorelai, and get us more intel on opportunities in the vicinity."

A grin lit up the general's face. "Sounds like a party. What is it you like to say? 'Let's get this show on the road'!"

Svetlana nodded, considering paying a visit to her father. *It would be nice to get his thoughts on this plan.*

THE RIVER STYX

STELLAR DATE: 10.01.8949 (Adjusted Years)
LOCATION: *Sabrina* approaching Styx Baby-9
REGION: STX-B17 Black Hole, Transcend Interstellar Alliance

<*I can't believe this base is actually called 'Styx Baby-9',*> Jen said with a note of derision in her voice, as Cheeky shifted *Sabrina* into a lower orbit around the dark gas giant.

"I kinda like it," Cheeky said with a soft giggle. "I mean, I've docked at a lot of stations, but never had a berth at a place with 'baby' in the name."

"You should take the SS *Sexy* out and get it its own berth," Fina said from where she sat with her legs draped over the scan console—since she'd opted for flowmetal limbs, 'draped' was a very apt description. "Then you could call it the '*Sexy Baby*'.

"Pretty sure it got called that a few times over the years, anyway," Finaeus commented, giving his head a slow shake. "Damn sweet pinnace, too. Especially with the alterations I made."

<*Pretty sure I made most of them,*> Nance called up from her station in engineering. <*Just like then, you're on the bridge hobnobbing, and I'm down here doing all the work.*>

"I'm not crew on this mission," Finaeus replied with a sniff. "Just here to spend some time with my wife."

"Liar." Cheeky cast a mock glare over her shoulder. "You told me last night that you'd punch a god in the dick to find out how Earnest figured out to set up jump gates in a gravity well like this. I'm playing second fiddle to your curiosity."

"Well, *seriously*." Finaeus gestured at the forward view. "Fucking planet's *nine* jovian masses, *and* we're in orbit of a stars-be-damned black hole! There should be...one, maybe two viable jump vectors out of here...and *none* from below the cloudtops. But freakin' Earnest has successfully jumped drones on *seven hundred* different vectors."

"You sound jealous, Uncle Fin," Seraphina said through lips that were threatening to twitch into a smile.

"Fucking right, I'm jealous. I *invented* this technology—well, I was the first one to get it to work, at least. Earnest Redding is a freak of nature."

"You know what this means?" Cheeky glanced back at Nance and Finaeus. "If it works here, it should work at Star City."

Finaeus blew out a long breath. "Yeah. Earnest sent his new models to me before we left the *I2*, and I ran them for the gravity wells around Star City. It'll work. Hell, they could put gates right *inside* the sphere."

"Before this is all over, I *really* want to go see that place," Sera said, trying not to sound too wistful. "Must be amazing."

"Something like Star City puts the FGT out of business," Finaeus replied.

"Or puts us in a whole new business," Seraphina countered. "You're just jealous you didn't think of a reverse dyson sphere first."

"Maybe..." Finaeus chuckled while shaking his head. "You know...every human we know of could fit on ten of those with generations of room to spare. Still wish we could have met the builders—now *that* was vision."

<*I'm curious,*> Sabrina asked as the ship slotted into its final approach vector. <*What do we do if Katrina and her team can't get that old shard of Airtha?*>

"That's a good question," Sera said. "I suppose we get onto the Airthan ring and figure out how to target all of her nodes. If we can't introduce some sort of counter to her, we'll have to blow them, or maybe see if Bob can make an appearance."

"Which means we have to take out the EMGs she has defending the place," Seraphina replied. "Airtha made those specifically to guard against the *I2*. I think she seriously fears Bob."

"There's the beginnings of Plan B, then," Sera said, as *Sabrina* dipped into the cloudtops of the gas giant.

<*I hate flying into planets,*> Sabrina said. <*I seem to do it far too often.*>

"Sorry, Sabs," Cheeky said as she monitored their approach. "Just have to get through a few hundred klicks of this mire, then we'll be at the station."

No one spoke further, as the ship continued to plunge, dropping deeper and deeper into clouds of frozen ammonia and nitrogen. Then a glow appeared ahead of the ship, gradually increasing in brightness until light exploded around them.

"Now *this* is a secret base," Sera said with a laugh as she surveyed the massive structure drifting in the center of a hundred-kilometer bubble within the planet's clouds.

Though the construction of Styx Baby-9 had only begun a few weeks prior, it was already large enough to dock fifty TSF capital ships.

The plan for the station was to create a docking grid that could funnel fuel and supplies to ships as needed, and then send them through the jump gates mounted at the end of the structure. When completed, it would be able to support over ten thousand capital ships, providing services from refit to refuel in a matter of days before sending them back out.

Long spires jutted out from the station's grid—it was toward one of those that *Sabrina* was headed—while on the far side of the station, long shafts dropped down into the planet, disappearing into the roiling clouds below.

"You have no idea how many beers I owe Earnest," Finaeus muttered. "The guy's such a show-off. I bet he's pulling liquid metallic hydrogen right from the core of the planet. He's been talking about how he could use some new technique he's all hush-hush about to transmute that into other elements as it exits its superfluid state—provided there are enough neutrons in the slurry."

"You're saying he's transmuting matter from the planet's core to build the station?" Sera asked.

"More or less," Finaeus grunted. "That's my guess, at least. The bastard."

No one spoke for a minute as Finaeus's scowl deepened. Then everyone on the bridge, barring the ancient engineer, burst into tear-inducing laughter.

THE LMC

STELLAR DATE: 10.02.8949 (Adjusted Years)
LOCATION: Interstellar Pinnace, Approaching Jump Gate Array 9A9
REGION: Troy, New Canaan System

Cary was still more than a little surprised that her father had agreed to let her take Kent to the Aleutian Site in the Large Magellanic Cloud. Granted, he had layered on a goodly number of requirements and restrictions.

The first requirement he had was that Saanvi and Faleena accompany her.

Faleena had been more than eager to travel outside the galaxy. Her exact words were, "If you didn't bring me along, I'd've secretly re-implanted myself in you."

The prospect of asking Saanvi had worried Cary. She knew her sister was busy with her schoolwork at the academy, and was also helping the StarFlight group with several aspects of the new field generators that would alter where Canaan Prime outputted the energy from the fusion at the star's core. However, even before she had finished asking, Saanvi was screaming for joy and jumping into the air.

"Are you kidding me?!" her sister had hollered at the top of her lungs. "Who *wouldn't* want to go to another galaxy?"

Cary had asked Saanvi privately over the Link, while the pair was in their quarters' common room—hoping to keep the information a secret—but Amy had been in her room, and overheard Saanvi's excited screams.

"Another galaxy?" she'd asked, poking her head out from her room, eyes wide and filled with concern. "Are you leaving me?"

Those events—combined with a few others—were what led to Cary now sitting in the pilot's seat of an interstellar pinnace with Faleena, Saanvi, Amy, and Kent.

And a platoon of ISF Marines.

Most notably was the Marine standing directly behind Kent. Lieutenant Joshua Mason wore a grim expression along with his fully powered armor, feet maglocked to the deck and a hand on the back of Kent's chair as Cary eased the ship toward its assigned jump gate.

Kent leant forward and tapped the viewscreen. "Looks real, but that doesn't mean you didn't trap me in a VR sim. There's no way I'd be able to tell—especially with my Link removed."

"It's not a sim," Cary said for what she guessed to be the seventh time. "You're about to jump out of the galaxy. This is the real deal."

"Yeah?" Kent glanced over his shoulder at Amy. "You often bring kids on your extragalactic jaunts? And don't you think a whole platoon is a bit much for little ol' me?"

"We're here to protect them from you," Lieutenant Mason grunted out the words. "You so much as twitch in any one of these girls' direction, and I tear a limb off your body. You get to pick which one, though."

"How magnanimous of you," Kent muttered.

<*Lieutenant Mason, don't you think you're overdoing it?*> Cary asked privately. <*I'm trying to establish a rapport with Kent.*>

<*I understand that, Ensign Richards,*> Lieutenant Mason replied equably. <*But with all due respect to you and your goals, I have orders directly from Admiral Evans to keep you safe at all costs. I'm pretty sure that if this Oggie here even touches any of you, the admiral will pull* ***all*** *my limbs off.*>

Cary sighed and nodded, knowing that her father likely had given Mason a good talking to before the mission.

"We have clearance from the STC," Saanvi announced. "Light is green."

Ahead of them, space boiled within the ring, forming a spherical non-space bubble that was the terminator and origin of the singularity they were about to stretch across space.

Cary eased the ship forward, carefully watching actuals and ensuring they matched her preprogrammed path. Vector was important on any jump, but it was *exceedingly* important on an intergalactic jump.

A moment before the pinnace's Ford-Svaiter mirror touched the not-space, Kent peered at the viewscreen, craning his neck to the right. "Is that the *Britannica*?"

Then New Canaan disappeared, replaced by the nothing of the gate's transition as the singularity was stretched across the galaxy and beyond.

"You have the *Britannica*?" Kent pressed.

"Yes," Saanvi replied absently. "We captured it in the Defense of Carthage. Same as all the other Oggie ships—well, those that survived."

"And Garza was aboard?" Kent asked, his tone earnest, almost frantic.

"He was," Cary nodded. "Surely you'd heard we had Garza; I recall that the interrogators let it slip deliberately."

Kent's hand sliced through the air in front of himself in a dismissive arc. "Yeah, but I thought that was a clone."

Cary twisted around to face the man, glad for the diversion from the time the intergalactic jump was taking.

I wonder how lo—

"Seventeen seconds more," Saanvi announced.

<*You always manage to do that,*> Cary sent to her sister.

<*What?*> Saanvi asked.

<*Answer questions I hadn't asked aloud.*>

She snorted. <*That's Faleena's job. I just state the obvious. Not sure why that's profound to you.*>

Cary shot Saanvi a dirty look, only to see her grinning back.

<Jerk.>

Then the meaning behind Kent's words struck her.

"Wait…*you* know about the clones?"

Kent shrugged. "Sure, it was common knowledge on the *Britannica* that General Garza had obtained the cloning and memory-reintegration technology from the Hegemony of Worlds—it all started after their president sent a clone to watch the staged battle in Ascella."

"Why are you telling us this?" Faleena asked from behind Amy. "You are assuming we already know it, but what if we don't?"

"Well, if you got Garza—damn, none of this makes sense." Kent shook his head, and his expression became guarded. "By now, you would have surely gotten more out of him than you *ever* will from me. I just assumed that you had a clone, and it didn't know what you needed to learn."

Cary glanced at Saanvi and Faleena—noting as her gaze passed by Amy that the girl was watching events unfold with great interest.

The next instant, space snapped into place around them, heralding the end of their journey.

The starscape was wildly different than any Cary had seen before, though it wasn't any less dense than looking galactic north or south when inside the Milky Way.

When inside the Milky Way…. Cary whispered the words to herself and brought up the local astrogation data, turning the pinnace to catch the view they'd all been waiting for.

And there it was, hanging in front of them like a massive pinwheel, tilting away like it was blowing in the wind.

"It has to be a sim," Kent whispered, then held out his hand and pinched it with his other. "Ow! Dammit."

"That doesn't really work to exit a sim," Saanvi chided.

"Yeah…but what else can I do?" Kent's voice was still low and filled with wonder.

Even Lieutenant Mason sounded impressed. "Well I'll be a shiprat's tail. Hearing about this and seeing it are two diiiiiiferent things."

"STC is on the horn," Saanvi announced, breaking the group's reverie. "They need us to clear the jump zone. I have an approach to the station. Piping it through to you, Cary."

"Right, right!" Cary nodded quickly as she brought the pinnace about and boosted for Aleutia Station.

"Even if I get an ulcer worrying about you girls," Lieutenant Mason said with a note of raw wonderment in his voice, "it'll totally be worth it to see this." The burly Marine laughed. "And here my son Brennen was giving me a hard time because he got assigned to the *I2,* and I was stuck back on the Palisades.

Stars, even if he does get onto Admiral Richards' detail, this is still better."

The thought of people vying to get on her mother's guard detail didn't seem anywhere near as impressive as looking on the Milky Way Galaxy from over a hundred thousand light years away, but she wasn't about to diminish Mason's—or his son's—excitement about either.

"Funny that the father is protecting us daughters, while the son is protecting our mother," Faleena mused. "I wonder…who is protecting our *father*? Do you have a brother that could take on the task, Lieutenant?"

Cary laughed as she initialized the burn that would bring the pinnace around to their assigned approach vector. "Dad doesn't need anyone protecting him. He never gets into trouble."

A snort slipped past Saanvi's lips. "Well, not that he tells *us* about, anyway. But you've read his old record. Dad got up to *shenanigans* back in the TSF. It's no wonder they let him join a colony mission."

"Will we be able to get back?" Amy asked suddenly, her voice carrying an uncharacteristic urgency. "Can we go back now?"

Saanvi turned in her seat and placed a hand on Amy's knee. "Yes, we'll be able to get back without a problem. Tanis and Sera—you remember them, right?"

Amy nodded silently.

"Well," Saanvi continued. "They were here just a few days ago. Jumped in and out without a problem. Look over there." She directed Amy to look through the window on Kent's far side. "See? That's the return gate. You can see a ship lining up to jump back right now."

"Don't worry," Kent added, sparing a kindly look for the young girl. "I don't think anyone here plans to stay in the LMC for long. This is all just to impress upon me how futile the Orion Guard's goals are."

"Is it working?" Amy asked, her tone of voice belying the fact that she wasn't the innocent little girl many presumed her to be. Years of exposure to her father had given her an edge few eleven-year-olds had.

Still, Cary couldn't help a laugh, and twisted in her seat to look at Kent. "Well? Is it?"

He looked out the window at the distant galaxy none of them ever expected to so much as travel across, let alone leave altogether.

"Yeah, a bit."

Cary saw Saanvi and Amy lock eyes and knew the two were carrying out a conversation over the Link. Amy seemed to relax, and then Faleena spoke up once more.

"You were saying something about clones and the *Britannica*, Colonel Kent."

He didn't look away from the window as he spoke in soft tones. "I don't think I should share any more. I'm not going to commit treason. I feel like this ride is enough of a betrayal."

"We're going to win this war," Faleena pressed. "You must see that now. Orion may have numbers on their side, but our level of advancement nullifies all technological advance. You must, by now, realize our capabilities. Were we an immoral people, we could simply hide out here and manufacture pico payloads to destroy every Orion world. We could fire them through jump gates and end the war without losing a single one of our lives."

Kent turned his head at that. "Just you raising that possibility is disconcerting."

Faleena only shrugged and continued undeterred. "Surely your tacticians are planning for it, it is logical to assume that, should you back us into a corner, we will unleash our pico on you."

"I suppose they must be considering that," Kent allowed. "It was one of the reasons I was sent in with a strike team. To attempt to eliminate the threat before it became a war."

"And we understand that logic." Faleena's tone was warm, filled with understanding. "And you would agree that our people face an existential threat, yet we have not unleashed our most powerful weapon."

Kent gestured out the window. "Well, with a backup site in the LMC, that 'existential threat' is minimized."

"But it still exists—in fact, bringing you here has increased it."

"Oh, I know what bringing me here means," Kent countered. "It means that if I don't play ball, I get put in a hole for the rest of my life. This isn't the sort of installation you let people know about and then risk them escaping."

"It's true," Cary replied. "But we're not going to imprison people forever. You'll go into stasis, and then be set free when the war is over."

"And what if you lose?" Kent asked. "Will we all remain in stasis for centuries until our pods lose power?"

"They're on a hundred-year timer," Saanvi told him. "Their location is such that it can sustain the entire prisoner population without trouble, should knowledge of the location be lost."

"Seems you think of everything," Kent muttered.

"Benefit of advanced technology." Cary turned to look at him once more. "You have to see that. Yes, the Inner Stars is a shit-show, but it doesn't have to be that way. All humans and AIs can be uplifted and live in peace if there is no want. We can turn our focus to building amazing things, exploring the universe, living forever. Your Kirkland thinks that one of our two species should be slaves, and the other should live short, meaningless lives. Do you really think that should be our destiny?"

Kent turned away, staring out the window once more at the distant galaxy.

Cary waited a minute for a response, and then twisted back around in her seat, facing forward as she adjusted their approach to match delta-*v* with Aleutia Station.

<*He'll come around,*> Saanvi said, her voice carrying a cautious note of encouragement. <*Or at the least he'll let something slip. As it is, we know that there was some significance to the* Britannica *being captured, and it relates to the cloned Garzas.*>

<*We've been over that ship with a fine-tooth comb.*> Faleena gave a soft laugh. <*And now that I have hair, I finally understand that in greater detail.*>

<*You have synthetic hair that blows in an invisible breeze and never tangles,*> Saanvi shot back, giving her sister a judging look over her shoulder. <*You still don't understand it.*>

Faleena gave a half-smile and wink in response. <*True, but if I didn't have the ability to manage each follicle on my head, it would take a lot of combing. Either way, there's something we missed—about the ship, or Garza himself. That makes this trip worth it, at least—outside of getting to visit another galaxy.*>

Cary nodded absently, knowing that it still wasn't enough. Kent possessed knowledge that would help them, they just had to figure out how to prise it free.

ALEUTIA

STELLAR DATE: 10.03.8949 (Adjusted Years)
LOCATION: Aleutia Station
REGION: Cheshire System, Large Magellanic Cloud

"Welcome to the LMC," Colonel Ophelia said as she approached the group disembarking from the pinnace. "I'm sorry that General Peabody isn't here to greet you, but he's out at Bolt Hole."

"Are they managing to stabilize the system?" Saanvi asked, her voice dripping with enthusiastic curiosity.

A pained expression flashed across Ophelia's face. "Well, it's proving to be tricky. No one had ever considered—at least not seriously—dropping a black hole into the dark layer. Admiral Richards made a bit of a mess with that one."

"I still want to know how Airtha managed to send a ship containing a black hole through a jump gate," Cary added. "From what Finaeus said, that shouldn't be possible. The mass of the singularity within the ship would bend the jump gate's tunnel through spacetime unpredictably."

Saanvi gave a mock gasp, and Cary shot her a dark look. "I may be the hotshot pilot on our team, but I still pay attention. The mechanics of spaceflight being of particular interest."

Having turned to reply to Saanvi, Cary caught the look of utter amazement on Kent's face at the subject. He caught her gaze, and quickly schooled his expression as Colonel Ophelia spoke up again.

"They're combing through the wreckage of the EMG ship for clues, but so far, that's a secret for Airtha alone. Erin and her team have made the trip out to Bolt Hole; she seemed confident that they could save the planet by some means.... The question is whether or not it's worth the effort."

"I can't imagine why not," Faleena chimed in. "That world is an ark containing a variety of plants and animals not seen across a thousand star systems."

"I believe that is something they're weighing," Ophelia said as she gestured for the group to follow her out of the docking bay. "Whether to save the ark, or save the contents."

"I bet Erin really wants to figure out how to guide a black hole inside the dark layer," Saanvi added.

"What about the Exdali?" Cary asked. "They must be swarming the thing."

"Exdali?" Kent asked, speaking for the first time since they disembarked.

Cary fell back a step and gave the man a sidelong look. "Have you ever heard tall tales about things that live in the dark layer and devour ships?"

The Orion Guard colonel frowned. "Once or twice. Honestly, they're just stories from shitty pilots who didn't follow dark matter maps well enough and got creamed."

Faleena held out her hand, and a holoprojection appeared above it. The view was of Carthage with tens of thousands of ships surrounding it. "See the Orion Guard fleet?" she asked.

Kent nodded silently as the AI initiated the playback. As he watched, a fleet of ISF ships jumped in close to the planet and moved into an unusual configuration. Then spacetime appeared to ripple directly in the Orion fleet's path.

The ripple became a rift, and out of it poured the stuff of nightmares. Amorphous shapes with what appeared to be writhing masses of tentacles and gaping maws dove into the midst of the Orion ships, latching onto them and devouring the vessels.

Faleena halted the playback and gave Kent a serious look. "*Those* are Exdali. They live at the core of every star system, feeding on dark matter. Yes, many ships that make insystem jumps hit pockets of mass in the DL, but many *also* encounter Exdali."

Colonel Kent sucked in a sharp breath. "They…you…all those ships, those people…"

"There were many survivors," Colonel Ophelia said as they swung into the corridor leading to the main observation lounge at the top of Aleutia Station. "Your people were lucky."

"Lucky?" He choked out the word, eyes still staring at the projection above Faleena's outstretched hand.

"Yes," Ophelia's voice shifted, dripping with ice. "We *should* have used our picobombs. Wiped out the filth entirely. Instead, my son died so that some of your interstellar marauders could live. So yeah, you were *lucky*. Lucky I wasn't in command, because I would have told parliament to go fuck themselves and used pico anyway."

Ophelia's vehement outburst killed any further conversation, and made for a rather awkward lift ride to the observation deck.

Once they arrived, Cary directed the Marines to take Kent across the broad space to a seating area, while she and her sisters stayed back with Ophelia. Amy hung by Saanvi's side, but the girl seemed more curious than alarmed by the ISF colonel's outburst.

"I'm sorry," Faleena said quietly. "I didn't think we would open old wounds."

"Not that old," Ophelia muttered. "That battle wasn't even two years ago…" The colonel's voice faded, and she sucked in a deep breath. "But I'm the one who should be sorry. You're trying to turn him to our side, and I may have just screwed that up."

Cary shrugged. "You never know. It may be just what we need. Nothing you said was wrong. His people *did* launch an unprovoked attack against ours."

"Doesn't matter," Ophelia said with a vehement shake of her head. "My behavior was inexcusable. It's probably best that I go."

"I believe you're right," Saanvi replied. "We do need to make sure he feels safe."

Ophelia smiled at the three sisters. "You're a good set of women. I imagine you do your parents proud—when you're not stealing starships, that is."

"You take a ship *one time*..." Cary replied with a wink.

The ISF colonel gave a soft laugh, and turned to walk away, then stopped and looked over her shoulder. "Oh, I was going to say before, there's something interesting about the LMC and the dark layer."

"Oh?" Saanvi asked.

"We've not yet searched extensively—no one really wants to, overmuch—but as best we can tell, there are no Exdali in the LMC."

Cary felt her mouth drop open and saw Saanvi's eyes widen.

"None?" they asked in unison.

Ophelia shook her head. "Not in this neck of the woods, at least. Hard to say if there are any elsewhere, though."

Saanvi whistled. "I bet Earnest will be *very* interested in that."

"Why's that?" Faleena asked.

"Just a theory of his, one he asked me not to share until he has more data."

Cary rolled her eyes as she turned back to where Lieutenant Mason had taken Kent. "Earnest always has a new theory, doesn't he?"

* * * * *

Once the group had settled into the circular seating area where the Marines had taken Kent—and a round of drinks had been ordered from a servitor—the Orion colonel let out a long sigh.

"I have to admit, Cary Richards, this is a damn sight better than walks in the Palisades' lower parks." As he spoke, his gaze was fixed on the view of the Milky Way galaxy, hanging several meters above the rim of the observation lounge.

"Pun intended?" Cary asked with a wink.

Kent nodded. "Of course."

"Pun?" Amy asked, sounding puzzled. "Ohhh! 'Sight'. I get it."

A pair of servitors arrived and began to hand each person their desired beverage, and the group sat in silence for a few minutes before Kent spoke up.

"Your father must really trust you three to send you here alone with me."

Cary glanced over her shoulder to where Lieutenant Mason stood, then looked around the lounge at the thirty Marines spread throughout the area.

"Not exactly what I would call 'alone'."

"Well—no offense to you, Lieutenant—" Colonel Kent paused to nod in

Mason's direction. "The grunts here aren't trying to wring intel from me, that's your job."

"Four," Amy piped up, giving Kent a narrow-eyed look.

"Pardon?" the Orion colonel asked.

"Their father sent the four of us," Amy said as she folded her arms. "They had to get special permission to bring me along, which means he trusts me too."

Kent chuckled softly. "I suppose he does, Amy. I'm glad you came along. It means that your sisters will be nicer to me—they wouldn't want to upset you."

Amy snorted and rolled her eyes. "Puh-lease, Mister Kent. My father raped and murdered people right in front of me. Even Cary at her meanest is like my father was on his very best day."

Kent let out a low whistle and his eyes darted to Cary, who nodded slowly.

"Amy's father was a man named Stavros. He ran a rather nasty little empire on the edge of the Praesepe Cluster," she supplied.

"But my best friend Rika saved me and my mom," Amy said with a beatific smile. "And then Barne, my new big brother, blew my dad's brains out the back of his skull."

Amy said the words without emotion, but Cary could tell that it cost the girl a lot to give voice to those memories.

"You think that the people from New Canaan are bad, Mister Kent, but you have no idea what bad is until you've watched your father torture Silver for years, and then…and then you find out she's your mother!" Suddenly Amy was on her feet, yelling at Kent, her face reddening while tears glistened in her eyes. "So maybe you should think about who the bad guys really are before you try to kill off the good ones!"

The silence was palpable as Amy stood with fists clenched at her sides and chest heaving before she strode away, heading to the exit.

"I'll go with her," Saanvi said softly as she rose, a fireteam of Marines trailing after her.

No one spoke for a moment before Kent drew in a slow breath. "Did you all save her from that?"

"No," Cary shook her head. "One of our allies did. The Marauders. They're all that's left of place called Genevia. They weren't the best people out there either, but they were decent enough before the Nietzscheans attacked and destroyed them."

"I've heard of them." Kent nodded slowly. "The Nietzscheans, that is."

"I expect so," Faleena said. "They're one of Orion's major allies in that region of space."

"Hm," Kent grunted, his lips pressed into a thin line. "You sure like to paint a picture of Orion as the villain in all this."

Faleena shook her head, a grim expression settling on her green skin. "You know reality is too complex for such labels—at least in this case. People like

Amy's father were definitely villains. But galactically, there are too many forces at play. From the Ascended AIs, to Airtha and your Kirkland. There are other forces at play, too—but all of them have been too busy fighting one another to care about people like Stavros and what he did to Amy and her mother."

Kent's eyes fell, and he let out another long sigh—one that *sounded* heartfelt to Cary.

"You're right about that," he said. "How much time and energy have we all spent fighting one another—we could be exploring, seeing the wonders of space, like you are out here."

"Like you wanted to do when you signed up," Cary prompted. "That's what you said, right? That you wanted to see the stars."

The colonel's view shifted back to the breathtaking view outside the lounge's windows. "Sure can check that off my list now, can't I?"

"Think one check is enough?" Cary gave the man an appreciative smile.

Kent snorted. "No, probably not."

Silence fell once more, and Cary finished her drink and ordered another from the servitor. When it arrived, she hadn't lifted it to her lips before Kent spoke.

"He was on the *Britannica*."

"He?" Faleena asked.

"Garza." The colonel uttered the name with a sound that wasn't quite distaste, but it wasn't admiration or respect, either.

Cary's eyes narrowed as she lowered her drink to her lap, cupping it with both hands. "What are you saying?"

"He told me that *he* would be on the *Britannica*. He wanted me to be sure to report to him and not one of his clones when I completed my mission—*if* I completed it, I guess."

"That first Garza isn't a clone," Faleena whispered.

"OK, sure," Cary shrugged. "But we didn't think he was a clone anyway until Mom encountered another Garza in Scipio."

"What you don't know is that Garza's clones don't know they're clones." Kent's lips twitched into a half-smile. "They all think they're the real deal."

"So?" Cary asked. "There are a bunch of clueless Garza clones running around. This sounds like a good thing."

He nodded. "For you, yes. What you don't understand, though, is that Garza is not working *with* Praetor Kirkland."

Cary resisted the urge to let out a joyous whoop. Kent was finally spilling real intel. Stuff they could use. She didn't know what exactly had prompted it, but she wasn't about to question their good fortune.

"What does that mean, exactly?" Faleena asked.

"One time, I delivered a report to General Garza while Praetor Kirkland was present via holo—I don't think those two like each other much. What's more, from the things he said, I'm positive that the praetor would not approve of the cloning, or half the other technology that Garza uses."

"Is it a 'fight fire with fire' scenario?" Cary asked, to which Kent shook his head.

"I don't think so. See, it's the cloning. Garza doesn't *need* that to manage his operations. He just doesn't trust other people. Couple that with the Widows, and he's definitely playing out of bounds."

"I've heard of those," Cary replied with a shiver. "Poor Lisas."

"Lisa?" Kent asked.

"The Widows are clones of Finaeus Tomlinson's former wife, Lisa Wrentham," Faleena explained.

Kent whistled and then signaled a servitor. "I'll need another drink. Best make this one stiffer than the last."

"So will you help us?" Cary asked.

"Aren't I already? Stars…" Kent's voice lowered. "I really am. I can't believe I'm doing this."

"Colonel," Cary leant forward and placed a hand on Kent's. "I promise you, I give you my absolute assurance. My people's driving goal is to end this war with as little bloodshed as possible."

She glanced around at the Marines, and Kent followed her gaze, noting that that they nodded in assent.

"She's telling you the truth," Lieutenant Mason spoke up. "We all left Sol—or our parents did—to get away from shit like this. We just want to build a future that doesn't involve people pissing on each other all the time. Live and let live—galaxy's more than big enough for us all to have room to do our thing."

"And if some people's 'thing' is to kill others?" Kent asked. "Who will police them?"

"There will always be bad apples," Mason said with an exaggerated shrug. "But far as I can see, what your people and the Transcend have been doing for some time is *cultivating* those bad apples. Time for a change."

Kent pursed his lips and nodded. "Yeah, I can see that. If you were just the Transcend, I wouldn't buy your song and dance, but I can tell you hold them to blame for a lot of what's gone on."

"We do. They tried to attack us as well—they just didn't get as far as your people."

Kent leant back in his seat and took a sip of his drink. "OK, then. What else do you want to know?"

SAGITTARIUS'S BAR

STELLAR DATE: 10.03.8949 (Adjusted Years)
LOCATION: Coronado, Maya System
REGION: Former Transcend Space, Sagittarius Arm

Katrina had just taken the first sip of her Hero's Fall, a rather enticing—and very bubbly—drink, when a voice from beside her said, "Thought you swore you were never coming back to the Transcend."

"I don't think I said *never*, Jordan," Katrina replied without looking up from the foaming concoction before her. "I'm certain it was something more like 'I never *want* to come back to the Transcend'."

"You kinda have a way of shifting meaning, Kat. I distinctly remember the conversation. The word 'want' was not present."

Katrina straightened and brushed her long, red hair aside, glancing at Jordan. "Maybe you're right. I've said a lot of things I wish I hadn't. That may have been one of them."

The dark-haired woman next to her gave a knowing smirk. "Yeah, I have my list of those as well." She looked Katrina up and down and added, "Looking good for an old woman."

Katrina's mouth quirked into a smile. "You too. Seems like life in the Transcend has been good to you."

Jordan only shrugged, glancing at the bartender and holding up a finger while she said, "They have amazing rejuv tech out here. Seems silly not to use it—especially because I'd be dead otherwise. Too much going on just to get old and die."

Katrina glanced around the nearly deserted establishment. "I thought you came out here to get away from it all."

" 'It all' seems to have a way of catching up with a person." She gestured to Katrina with her chin, as the bartender set a glass of bourbon down in front of her. "Case in point. Gotta say, I barely recognized the *Voyager*. Got a fresh coat of paint."

"A few upgrades here and there," Katrina replied, meeting Jordan's eyes. "I found them. Finally...after all these years."

The other woman only shrugged. "Glad you did—though I thought the whole point was to settle down with them in their paradise."

Jordan's words were laced with a subtle derision that Katrina chose to ignore. She wasn't surprised, though. Their parting had been acrimonious, and in hindsight, Katrina saw that Jordan had been right.

It occurred to her that the other woman needed to hear it from her.

"I'm sorry, Jordan. You, Sam, and Demy were all right—more than you know, even. I made a mess of everything."

"Oh?" She raised an eyebrow. "This should be good. Tell me all about how I was more right than even I knew."

"Do you remember the being I told you about? The one that saved me in the Midditerra system?"

"Yeah," Jordan nodded. "If it wasn't for the fact that you showed up looking like a human and not a machine, I wouldn't have believed a word of it. What about her…it…whatever?"

"Well, turns out that she left something inside me. Something that was guiding my actions a lot more than I thought. Tanis called it a 'memory'."

"And this…'memory' made you behave like a pig-headed idiot?" Jordan's tone was still caustic, but Katrina could see that her eyes had widened in compassion. Not much, but it was there.

Katrina shook her head, adding a self-mocking laugh. "No, pretty sure that part was all me. But it was feeding me directives that I didn't have much choice but to obey."

"Fuck, Katrina." Jordan's expression finally softened. "You just can't get away from people putting shit in your head to control you. How did you get the memory out?"

"Tanis's daughter, of all people. She's semi-ascended…or something. She drew the memory out of me."

Jordan barked a laugh and then downed her drink. "You have the strangest friends."

"Do you count yourself amongst them?"

Jordan signaled the bartender for another drink. "I never stopped being your *friend*, Katrina. I just didn't want to fight your fight anymore. I gave you a lifetime. I just needed to live my own for a bit."

"I'm glad you made the decision you did. What have you been doing out here, anyway?"

Jordan winked. "Oh, you know. A little of this, a little of that. We have to be careful, the *Castigation* tends to stand out, and Sam won't leave it. Says that it's his body and we can't make him go in some little tub for sorties."

"Sounds like Sam," Katrina laughed. "Troy's still the same way, too. Though I think if Tanis asked him to take on another ship, he'd do it in a heartbeat. Those two have some sort of deep bond."

Jordan nodded absently as she signaled to the bartender for another drink. When it arrived, she took a sip and then turned on her stool to face Katrina directly.

"OK, so I know you didn't come out here to the ass end of the Transcend just to shoot the shit and ask forgiveness for being a jerk. Things are afoot. A lot of things, and your friend Tanis is at the heart of them."

"You have that right," Katrina glanced around the bar. "Am I correct in my assumption that people this far out don't really identify with Airtha or Sera? No sides being taken?"

"Every star within a hundred light years has declared independence," Jordan confirmed. "They can't even agree on simple trade law, let alone care enough about what's happening rimward."

"I bet that's perfect for the sort of work you like to do," Katrina said with a wink.

Jordan placed a hand on her chest and gave Katrina a wounded look. "Are you besmirching our time-honored profession?"

Katrina laughed. "Stars, no. In fact, I'm curious if you'd be interested in stepping it up a notch."

Jordan's eyes narrowed again, and Katrina deployed a passel of nano to secure their conversation from prying eyes and ears.

"We're going to kill Airtha, and I need your help."

"So do you want help killing Airtha, or accessing the shard that Sam has tucked away in one of his holds?"

"Both," Katrina replied. "But I'll understand if you don't want to take sides in this—though you'd be a fool to think that Airtha will be any sort of benevolent dictator if she wins."

"Like Jeffrey Tomlinson?" Jordan scoffed. "That guy was a pompous dick. He couldn't care less how his actions affected others. Not sure if his daughter is any better."

Katrina gave a nervous laugh. "Stars, this story is so nuts I don't know if you'll even come close to believing me.... The man running the Transcend for the last thousand years or so was a clone of the real Jeffrey. He was put there by Airtha. Tanis and her people recently found the original president and are going to put him back in charge of the Transcend. His daughter...well they're not really *his*, per se, and there is more than one of them, but they're leading a strike to kill Airtha, who is their mother."

Jordan tilted her head as Katrina spoke, eyes narrowing further. "OK...sounds to me like this is quite the story; one that Sam and Demy should hear." She rose and dropped a handful of credit chits on the bartop. "C'mon. Let's reunite you with the ol' crew."

* * * * *

"So that's where things stand," Katrina said as she finished, looking between Demy and Jordan with a knowing smile. "It's nuts, right?"

Demy snorted and shook her head. "Yeah, sure, if by 'nuts', you mean completely freaking insane."

"Trust me, it's pretty damn surreal to me, too," Katrina replied. "I mean...the LMC. Tanis now thinks that it's entirely possible that enclaves of people could be spread all over the galaxy. Given that half the systems around here aren't even listed as settled on official Transcend records, I'm inclined to agree with her."

<*So you want the Airtha shard?*> Sam asked. <*Hmmm...*>

"You still have it, right?"

Karina hadn't gotten what she considered to be complete confirmation from Jordan back in the bar. The fear that they'd lost or sold the shard some time ago had been lingering in the back of her mind as she'd told her story.

<*Relax,*> Sam's coarse voice contained a modicum of amusement. <*Just leading you on a bit. Troy already gave me his version of things, I was just letting you organics get it all out the slow way.*>

"You're such a peach, Sam," Katrina groused, casting a narrow-eyed look at one of the bridge's optics. "So you still have it?"

<*I do. I'm curious to know* ***exactly*** *what you plan to do with it.*>

"I don't know exactly. The goal is to destroy Airtha the AI without having to damage the ring itself—or kill the populace."

Jordan glanced at Demy. "Seems noble enough, but do we really want to get back in the 'fighting the good fight' business?"

"Seems like it's a 'get killed for someone else's cause' sort of operation," the engineer replied.

Katrina held up her hands. "I'm not asking you to sign up. I just need that shard core."

The two women glanced at one another, and though she secretly wished they would join in, deep down, she knew that the chances of that were slim. That ship had sailed.

<*What are you willing to trade for it?*> Sam asked in a cautiously neutral tone.

Katrina wasn't surprised it had come to this, but she was a bit shocked it had been Sam who asked for compensation. "What do you want?"

"Even out here in the boonies, we've heard about the shields that ships are getting now. 'Stasis shields', I believe they're called?" Jordan asked. "I can see those coming in handy."

"Not a chance—and certainly not if you don't sign up."

"Thought you wanted to end the war?" Demy asked. "This core will give you a great, bloodless victory."

Katrina clenched her jaw, unable to believe that three friends she had spent centuries with were going to extort her for tech that could end the civil war in the Transcend.

Then it dawned on her. "Shit, you *like* the unrest this is causing."

Jordan shrugged. "Makes our line of work easier. We're just looking to live comfortably out in a place where the law isn't up our asses all the time."

<*And where there's a whole lot of nothing to run off and hide in if we need it.*>

Katrina couldn't believe what she was hearing. "Airtha—and the core AIs, for that matter—aren't really the sort that will establish the kind of future that enables you to live freely."

"There are people who always try to take control of everything, and they always fail." Jordan gave a nonchalant shrug. "Honestly, Katrina. You should join us, live the good life. Don't worry yourself with all the nonsense rimward of here."

A part of Katrina had really hoped that she could convince her old crewmates to join the fight, that they'd see the sort of future Tangel would build—at least in New Canaan, if nowhere else.

But they had always been pirates, or almost always. It was in their blood.

"A CriEn. I'll trade you a CriEn for the shard."

<*That's too much,*> Troy said privately, having been listening in via a feed Katrina had given him.

<*It'll give them a fighting chance if things go badly,*> she replied, before adding aloud, "But you can't trade or sell it. It's for *you*."

"In what universe would we give up a CriEn?" Jordan whispered. "You're serious?"

Katrina nodded. "As an antimatter capsule. Show me the shard, and we'll make our deal."

* * * * *

"Are you surprised?" Carl asked when Katrina boarded the *Voyager,* a small case containing the shard clutched in her right hand.

"No…yes…" Katrina replied with a drawn-out sigh. "I didn't *expect*, but I sure did hope."

<*Maybe when it's all over, you can find them again and try to make amends,*> Troy suggested. <*They just worry about what this unrest means, and they're right to fear what we're up against. Assaulting Airtha, trying to destroy her…it's no small task.*>

Carl gave a quiet laugh. "You trying to make me reconsider, Troy?"

<*Will it work?*>

Katrina barked a laugh while Carl glared at the closest optic. "You know…I've fixed your sorry hull up more times than I can count, Troy."

<*Just a little joke, Carl. It's like you don't even know me.*>

"He seems happier," Carl glanced at Katrina. "I didn't know Troy could be happy. It's unnatural."

Katrina turned to the panel and sealed the airlock before replying, "Don't worry, I'm sure it won't last. Let's get our clearance and undock so we can go bribe the syndicate controlling the jump gate in this system. I don't fancy taking the DL and four years to fly to Styx."

"What are you going to offer him?" Carl asked. "We don't have any spare CriEns."

"Was thinking about using a gun this time. What do you think?"

Carl slapped her on the back. "Sounds like my kinda negotiation—a Kara Special. I'll get the team ready."

SUMMONS

STELLAR DATE: 10.03.8949 (Adjusted Years)
LOCATION: Ol' Sam, ISS *I2*
REGION: Pyra, Albany System, Thebes, Septhian Alliance

<Are you certain this is wise?> Bob asked. *<I feel as though I've remained too long here at Pyra. Events are in motion, and I do not like to remain still.>*

Tangel nodded in response as she waited on the maglev platform near her lakehouse, waiting for a car that would take her to the smaller, 61B VIP dock where her ship awaited.

"I understand that, but keeping the *I2* here is a useful deterrent. We may have defeated the Nietzschean fleet, but Septhia is still a political mess, and there are fractured nations all around that would pounce on what we're trying to build here."

<The Starblade *is more than enough to scare off any ill-intentioned enemies,>* Bob replied. *<I have full confidence in Siobhan and Captain Quinn. They're fully capable of keeping Albany secure and aiding in the construction of Pyra's ring.>*

Tangel sighed, looking up at the long sun that ran through the center of the cylinder. "I understand that you feel responsible for what happened to bring about my ascension, but it's done. And now that it's done, I'm well able to protect myself. I just spent five days in Keren and was perfectly safe."

<Were you?>

"What do you mean, Bob? I easily dispatched two remnants after flying through space and dissolving a starship hull. Then I leapt through a jump gate—without a helmet, no less—and ended up in the LMC, where I destroyed a very large starship on my own."

Bob didn't reply, and Tangel shook her head at the approaching maglev car.

"You think I'm reckless."

<I don't.>

"I'm not, you know. I've always been able to process more variables than other people. I can see angles of approach and defense they can't. I can move faster. I'm stronger. What they see as reckless behavior, I see as entirely reasonable action."

<Other people don't understand you. They don't see things like you do.>

"There's nothing I can do about that. Besides, *you* understand things from my perspective better than anyone."

A slow rumble flooded Tangel's mind, and after a moment, she realized that Bob was sighing.

"You need to work on that," she muttered as the maglev car came to a stop before her. "Sounded like the ship was thrusting without dampeners."

<I still prefer to fly without a-grav dampeners. They make it feel like I'm wading through sludge.>

The car was empty, and Tangel took the seat closest to the door. "OK, Bob, what really has you worried?"

<Other ascended beings. They're closing in, they've sent many of their minions after you, Myrrdan and his remnants at New Canaan, and the Caretaker with Peter Rhoads and others, they've spread tech amongst our enemies—there is no way that Airtha ***and*** *the OFA developed EMGs at the same time—and they've even set your own friends up as traps to kill you, such as Katrina.>*

"I've noticed," Tangel said, a wry note to her voice.

<Then you know what escalation looks like.>

"I can imagine."

<Which means you need me.>

She watched the landscape inside the habitation cylinder slide by, and then the maglev dove beneath the surface, through the decks within the cylinder's skin and through the hull.

Space around the ship was busy. Marauder ships were running through training drills, some Septhian cruisers were in high orbit, and several hundred Theban military craft were also nearby. But the bulk of the activity was from civilian craft, all working to bring supplies to Kendrick's shipyards, or for the planetary ring's construction.

Tangel soaked in the view for a few moments before responding. *<I need you safe, Bob, and I need the 12 safe as well.>*

<We weren't safe when we came to rescue you down on Pyra. It worked out.>

<I get that,> she replied. *<But there's something about the AIs in the League of Sentients. The reports on what Jessica's team encountered are…unusual. Even for us.>*

<Don't make me sigh again, Tanis. This is why I need to come.>

Tangel held out her hand and then reached out into extradimensional space and gathered stray tendrils of electromagnetic energy, drawing it into a ball. In three-dimensional space, it appeared to be a glowing sphere, hovering above her hand, but with the other dimensions in play, it felt more like a solid object. A bit warm, and a little tingly.

<Are you showing off?> Bob asked. *<It won't change my mind.>*

<I've been practicing. Every time I've used my new abilities, it's been in a time of crisis. I haven't really thought about what I was doing—it was more of an instinct.>

She twisted her hand and dispersed the energy back into the space around her, the power that had been visible disappearing from sight as its frequency and amplitude changed.

<That seems logical. You're really not going to bend on this, are you?>

<I've directed Lieutenant Brennen to bring a portable QC comm box. Will that ease your mind?> Tangel asked.

<A bit, provided you won't hesitate to call me if there is trouble.>

The maglev car completed its journey along one of the ship's gossamer arcs and reentered the hull, slowing as it approached dock 61B.

<You really do seem worried this time.>

Tangel admitted to herself that hearing high levels of concern from Bob was unnerving. The AI rarely expressed worry over anything, always prepared to cite a mastery of all variables as the basis for his never-ending surety.

<It is as I said. You've bested all of your enemy's indirect attacks thus far. That means they either have more indirect avenues of attack we've not thought of, or that they will take a more direct approach. We know that an ascended AI who is not a great fan of ours has been at work in the League of Sentients.>

The maglev car stopped at the station across from the 61B bay, and Tangel stepped out and walked across the corridor.

<You think it's a trap?>

<I believe it could be. I don't have enough solid information to know for sure.>

Tangel sighed as she entered the bay and gave a resigned nod. *<I'll maintain an active connection to the QC unit. I'll configure it to call you if I lose my connection for more than a minute. Will that put you at ease?>*

<To a degree.>

On the far side of the bay, past a dozen dropships, pinnaces, and racks of fighters, lay the ship she had decided to finally take for a spin.

It had been left for her by Amanda, an extra-universal visitor she'd met twice now. Tangel didn't know how to travel between universes, but Amanda had mastered it to a degree, and come calling after the two of them had met in a mysterious bar a few years back.

While the thought of a busty redhead popping in and out of Tangel's spacetime didn't bother her overmuch, she did wonder what other people—or things—may come over from some fork of the multiverse.

Tangel had entertained the idea for some time that the Exdali could be from *somewhere* else. They were just so foreign, and didn't seem to fit with any other type of life that anyone had come across thus far.

Then again, the dark layer is yet another set of dimensions within our little slice of the multiverse. It doesn't have to operate by the exact same rules as everywhere and everywhen else.

As Tangel approached, the ship—which she hadn't officially named yet—was lifted off the rack and lowered to a cradle. The craft was sleek and white with a red stripe down one side...rather similar to Amanda, in that respect.

When Amanda had gifted the ship to her, it hadn't possessed any drive systems, but the interior had been—and still was—luxuriously outfitted.

It had taken a group of engineers just a few days to outfit it with a CriEn for power, stasis shields, a-grav systems, a small AP and fusion drive, and point defense beams.

They'd made much of the strange, gleaming material the hull was constructed of. It wasn't something that would offer a lot of stealth capability, but with stasis shields in the mix, it wasn't a big concern.

<It's fueled up and ready to go, Admiral.> Captain Rachel broke into Tangel's thoughts. *<It seems a bit on the small side, but I suppose that can be useful.>*

<You've gotten used to flying this city around,> Tangel replied, sending a smile to the captain. *<A feeling I know all too well.>*

<Bob told me you're bringing a QC. Good. We'll be ready to come if you need us.>

A laugh slipped past Tangel's lips. *<Bob been talking to you about his concerns?>*

<Bob? No. I didn't know he **got** *concerned. Should I worry?>*

<Stars, no. It was just an innocent question.>

<Of course,> Rachel's voice dripped with sarcasm. *<Because I believe that. Maybe you should take more Marines with you.>*

<Lieutenant Brennen has a squad of his best—it's all that really fits in the ship. Plus there's another platoon at Aldebaran with Amavia and Iris. We'll be fine.>

<I'll keep the engines hot just the same.>

<Thanks, Rachel. I'll be back before you know it.>

<Holding you to that, Admiral.>

Tangel saw a squad of ISF Marines standing at the base of the ramp, and spotted Lieutenant Brennen in their midst. None of them had made a move to go up the ramp, and she wondered if there was something wrong.

"Good afternoon, Lieutenant Brennen," Tangel said as she approached. "Is my ship not to taste?"

"Admiral!" Brennen snapped off a sharp salute as the rest of the Marines followed likewise. "We uhh…well, ma'am, the ship has no name."

Tangel snapped her fingers. "And once you board, you have to enter it in your platoon's logs, but with no name, you'd have to make one up. But if you did, you'd be naming it, and then it would be stuck."

"Right." Brennen ducked his head. "Normally we'd just use a serial number or class name for the logs, but this bird here has neither. So…we figured we'd just wait for you."

Tangel placed a finger on her chin, looking up at the ship. "Well, I suppose we could name it after the woman who gifted it to me, Amanda."

"Begging your pardon, ma'am, but there are already three pinnaces, a destroyer, and two cruisers named 'Amanda' in the allied forces."

"Easy fix," Tangel snapped her fingers. "The *Mandy*. Come aboard one and all, we have a jump gate to Aldebaran to catch."

She walked up the ramp with Brennen in tow and palmed the airlock open.

"That interface is bizarre," he commented. "Seriously, *where* did you get this ship, Admiral?"

"An ally," she replied, as they entered the main cabin within the ship, which more resembled an upscale bar. She turned to the Marines. "Make yourselves at home, but don't rip the upholstery. This stuff is the epitome of irreplaceable."

As the twelve men and women got settled on the couches and chairs—their bulky armor somehow not stressing the furniture at all—she walked down the short corridor to the cockpit, Brennen following after.

"You rated at all?" Tangel asked, knowing she could look it up, but feeling like engaging in small talk with the man.

"Sure am. I have a few thousand hours under my belt, but not with anything like this—just military craft, and a few planet hoppers back on Carthage."

"Well, I've never flown this either, but the engineers set it up with all our standard flight systems, so it should be a breeze."

It turned out that there were a few differences in managing the *Mandy*, but once Tangel got a feel for the craft's feedback, she had it out of the bay and heading for their assigned gate. As they were on their final approach, Rachel's voice called out into her mind.

<Admiral! There's been some sort of attack on Aleutian Station. I don't have many details, but your daughters are all out there right now, and the reports say that they're missing.>

Tangel didn't miss a beat. *<Rachel, get this gate realigned and powered for a jump to the LMC!>*

<Yes, ma'am, gate is already realigning. You're good to jump in three, two, one.>

Tangel deployed the *Mandy*'s forward gate mirror and boosted toward the ring, not slowing to even consider the risks as her new ship's maiden voyage was a jump to another galaxy.

A SURPRISE VISITOR

STELLAR DATE: 10.03.8949 (Adjusted Years)
LOCATION: Aleutia Station
REGION: Cheshire System, Large Magellanic Cloud

The sisters and Kent had spoken long into the night, discussing everything from the colonel's homeworld and what types of crops they raised, to military engagements he'd fought in, to what he knew of major bases across Orion space.

Saanvi had returned after a few hours, minus Amy, who had gone to sleep in quarters nearby. She joined in the discussion with great enthusiasm, pressing Kent for what he knew of various advancements and the technology levels he had been exposed to.

When they finally called it quits for the night, Cary felt like her head was filled to bursting with information about the Orion Freedom Alliance.

Much of it corroborated what Jessica knew, but there were many details that were different. She had learned that this was because the regions of the OFA near New Sol operated very differently than the Perseus Arm and the Perseus Expansion Districts.

Moreover, much of what Jessica had learned was from pilfered databases at Costa Station. Kent's knowledge was firsthand and highlighted the differences between the official records and the reality of life in the trenches.

"We'll catch a quick breakfast and head back in the morning," Cary said, stifling a yawn as she spoke. "We'll want to be rested for the debriefing we're all going to get."

"I want you present," Kent said, his tone carrying a hard edge. "I know how these things go. You warm me up, and then the wolves set in. I get the feeling that everyone will be much better behaved with the vaunted Admiral Richards' daughter in the room."

Cary nodded wearily. "You know that neither of us will have full control over what will happen, but I will do my damnedest to see that you're treated well. I *do* have some pull with the brass."

"I can see that," Kent replied with a chuckle.

* * * * *

The next morning, after a breakfast in the observation lounge—where most of the conversation centered around what a future of extragalactic exploration could hold—the group retraced their path back to the docking bay.

Colonel Ophelia escorted them, but said little following an apology for her behavior the prior day.

Ten minutes later, they were walking down the final corridor toward the docking bay, their time in the LMC nearly over. Cary made herself a solemn promise to return, perhaps with Saanvi, who was already scheming about how to get transferred to the Bolt Hole project.

Amy seemed to have recovered from her outburst the night before. She'd apologized to Cary and Faleena first thing in the morning, and now walked next to Saanvi, swinging her arms freely, chattering about how she was going to savor her last look at the Milky Way before they jumped back.

Her good mood was infectious, and elicited smiles from the entire group, even Ophelia and the Marines—though they did their best to maintain serious glowers.

The station was busy at the beginning of the first shift, personnel rushing in every direction, headed to wherever their assignments demanded.

A group of warrant officers with drive technician patches on their shoulders swung out of a room a dozen meters ahead, a few glancing over their shoulders at the platoon of Marines behind them, obviously escorting VIPs.

One of the men in the group stared a moment longer than necessary, his eyes locking with Cary's before he turned to face forward once more.

Cary accessed his information, and saw that he was Chief Warrant Officer Travers, a member of the first group to have transferred out to the LMC. His record was solidly average, neither impressive, nor lacking. It surprised her that someone who did not stand out had been selected for such an important mission.

I suppose it could be that someone was trying to tuck him out of the way, she mused. *Theoretically, nothing was really supposed to happen out here—beyond terraforming a new world or two.*

She was about to turn her attention elsewhere, when Travers moved from the center to the edge of his group. The action itself wasn't that strange, but Cary thought she saw something slide free of his body.

Not his physical body. His extradimensional body.

An instant later, she reached out to Saanvi and Faleena, becoming Trine, and stared into the man in question.

What **is** *he?* she wondered.

With her extradimensional sight, Trine could see that CW5 Travers was far more than he appeared to the two-dimensional eye.

Tendrils of transdimensional energy flowed through him, but they did not look like a remnant; those malevolent gifts left behind by ascended beings behaved as separate entities, something that was readily apparent to Trine when she spotted them. Nor did Travers appear to be an ascended being—at least not one like Tangel. Where Trine's mother blazed with energy that was barely contained within her form, Travers' extradimensional form appeared wan, barely filling half the volume of his physical body.

He is something between, Trine surmised. *Not quite ascended, but the being is him, not a passenger like a remnant—of that I am certain.*

<*Colonel Ophelia.*> Trine reached out to the station commander privately, mimicking Cary's voice. <*Do you have shadowtrons?*>

<*The anti-ascended weapon?*> Ophelia asked, her mental tone sounding startled, then worried. <*One. In the CIC's weapons locker.*>

<*Have a squad bring it down here. We may need backup.*>

<*Backup for what?*> the station commander asked, her worry not translating to her steady gait, as she strode down the corridor with the group.

<*Chief Travers, in that group ahead. He is not what he seems.*>

* * * * *

The moment he swung into the passage, something felt wrong. It wasn't an ephemeral tickle in the back of his mind, but an actual tangible feeling.

There was another being like himself nearby.

Several of his companions turned to look behind them, and he followed suit, catching sight of a platoon of Marines escorting—

Shit!

Walking in the center of the Marines' protective phalanx was none other than Cary Richards. His sources had suggested that Cary was something beyond a regular human, and one glance confirmed it.

She was moving down the road to ascension. Nearly as far as he was.

The thought that a *child* such as Tanis's daughter could be nearly as progressed as him was infuriating—though it was only because of the Caretaker's betrayal that such was the case.

The cursed ascended AI had no sense of loyalty, of holding up its end of the bargain.

Still, killing Tanis's daughter was a temptation too great to pass up. There was no way the child could best him—provided he could get her alone. Even he would have trouble defeating her with a platoon of Marines at her back.

He could only stop so much firepower before it overwhelmed him—and Marines liked to dispense as much energy as possible at a target such as himself.

Time for a wild goose chase, he thought before ducking down a side passage, signaling two members of his group to follow.

* * * * *

Shit! He's on the move!

Trine sent a message to Ophelia, telling her to watch over Amy as she took off—all three bodies moving as one—in pursuit of Chief Travers.

"Wait!" Lieutenant Mason called out, as Trine pushed past the Marines in pursuit of the partially ascended man and his two companions.

<*There's a wolf in the henhouse,*> Trine shot back, using the code for a remnant in a human. <*Not just any wolf. A direwolf.*>

She heard Mason direct a fireteam to stay with Ophelia and Amy before the steady thud of Marines in powered armor picked up behind her.

Faleena's lithe, dryad-like form moved into the lead while Cary and Saanvi's bodies fell behind, keeping pace, but relying on Faleena's enhanced sensory systems to watch for threats.

In addition to corporeal dangers, Trine watched for ephemeral threats, pockets of energy that an ascended being could summon and move through other dimensions to attack through bulkheads or other solid objects.

At least, she assumed they could do so—Trine-Cary had been experimenting with such things, much to her sisters' surprise.

Focus. We have to remain unified. This person is stronger than a remnant.

They turned onto a wider concourse and caught sight of their prey with biological eyes: three ISF chiefs rushing through the crowd, shoving passersby out of the way.

One of Trine's prey spun and fired a projectile pistol toward her, but even before Trine-Cary could raise a hand—she had also been practicing creating grav fields—a rifle's report sounded from behind them, and the shooter before her collapsed.

<*We got your back,*> Mason called out. <*Keep moving.*>

Trine sent an acknowledgement, picking up the pace as an alert sounded on the Link and 1MC.

"General Quarters, General Quarters, this is not a drill. Clockwise up and forward, counter down and aft. Sweepers grab your brooms, the station is dirty. Repeat the station is dirty."

Trine had never heard the sweepers suffix, but assumed it must be a call to arms for station clearing teams. Or someone was just getting creative out in the LMC.

Ahead, Travers and his remaining accomplice turned right, rushing down another passageway with Trine-Faleena hot on their heels.

As soon as she turned the corner, the CW2 stepped out from behind a bulkhead rib and swung a baton at her. Trine-Faleena easily ducked it and thrust the heel of her hand into the woman's chin, shattering it before driving a fist into her gut.

Trine's other two bodies reached the side passage, not slowing as Trine-Faleena checked the woman to ensure she would not choke on her tongue.

The moment Faleena turned to follow the others, the doors behind her sealed, cutting off the Marines.

<*Mason, we're proceeding, find an alternate route,*> Trine informed the Marine lieutenant.

<*Negative…Cary? You three need to stop. Whoever that is isn't getting anywhere, the station is locked down.*>

<*Lockdown won't stop him,*> Trine-Cary replied. <*Only we can. Follow as best you can.*>

<*Ensign!*> Lieutenant Mason shouted over the Link. <*You will stand down!*>

Trine ignored the Marine as her cyborg body caught up to her biological ones, continuing to pursue their quarry down a hatch into the power generation section of the station.

She passed a pair of Marines that had been stationed outside a door, unconscious but alive. Ahead, Trine-Cary caught another glimpse of their prey's extra-dimensional form and she navigated the annoying warren of three-dimensional passages, slowly closing the gap.

As they passed through more doors and hatches, each one closed behind them, until Trine became aware that there were over a dozen sealed doors between them and Mason's Marines.

The station layout showed that Trine was approaching the main reactor and antimatter annihilator.

A pair of technicians raced past them, headed in the opposite direction, screaming, "He's lost his mind!"

Trine-Faleena was first through the final door, and reached the catwalk stretching over the annihilator at the heart of the station moments before her other two bodies.

He is mad, she thought as her three sets of eyes took in the scene.

The annihilator chamber was a wide oval with power generation systems on either side and a matter annihilator in the center. They stood at the end of a catwalk that arched over the center of the chamber.

Directly in its center stood Chief Travers, a small, silver cylinder in his hand.

"Cary Richards," he called out. "I didn't expect you to be the one to find me. I'd been waiting for your mother, but she never came out to Aleutia."

"You're lucky," Trine shouted back, three mouths giving voice to the words in perfect unison. "If she were here, you'd already be ground to atoms."

"Well, that's interesting…you're not…. What are you?" Travers' brow furrowed as he spoke.

"We are Trine," she replied. "Put the cylinder down and surrender. You can't defeat us."

Travers tossed the cylinder lightly in his hand. "This? Why, it's just a bit of antimatter. I imagine it won't do much at all if I let it fall into the annihilator. Nothing, if you consider a planet-sized ball of plasma to be of no consequence."

"What are you?" Trine asked, changing the topic of conversation. "You're not like the remnants."

"Remnants?" Travers asked. "Oh! You mean the things we leave behind in others? I assume you've found most of mine. I haven't received many messages of late."

"Our shadowtrons see to that," Trine replied, a smile quirking at the corners of her three mouths as Travers' brow furrowed. "A weapon that can trap and kill remnants. You too, I imagine."

"I'm much more than a remnant," Travers replied. "And I've worked far too long at my goals to have an upstart like you get in the way. You'll make a fantastic message to send to your mother. Maybe I'll crush your minds first. That would be fun."

Trine saw a tendril of light drift out of Travers and stretch across the space between them. She widened her stance and generated a wide n-space stabilization field, the way she'd been practicing. The field wavered before her, but then stabilized a moment before Travers' extradimensional limb reached Trine. It probed against her field, but with a little effort, she was able to push it aside.

"Impressive, little one, but you're not thinking wide enough."

Trine felt her mind narrow sharply and turned to see Saanvi cry out and fall to the deck.

Nano! Trine-Faleena cried out, rushing to Saanvi's side. *He's…I don't know what he's done.*

A second later, Faleena collapsed as well, and Trine was just Cary. She deployed her own nanocloud and swept it across the catwalk, realizing that Travers had planted breaching nanobots below the deck. They'd moved up right through the plas and into Saanvi and Faleena's bodies.

Travers was laughing softly, walking down the catwalk with slow, cocksure steps.

"Looks like your little trick doesn't hold up very well, Cary Richards. Now let's see what you can do without your gestalt."

Gestalt? Cary had never thought of her connection to her sisters like that. *The whole is greater than the sum of the parts.*

As she turned that thought over in her mind, she sent a surge of extra-dimensional energy through her sisters, targeting their internal nano-defenses and shielding them against attack from Travers' breachers.

"Well done, little Cary," Travers said, now only ten meters away. "Can you concentrate on saving your sisters and fight me off at the same time?"

Another tendril of visible light left him. In her transdimensional view, Cary could see that it was more than just light; the limb contained energy spikes that would inflict both pain and damage.

She summoned her n-space field once more, this time erecting it as a shield around her and her sisters. Once the sphere snapped into place, it cut off Travers' control of his own breach nano, and Saanvi and Faleena's internal systems began to clear their bodies of the intruders.

"It won't be that easy," Travers said with a wicked grin. "I hit Saanvi's brainstem and Faleena's core-interface hard and fast. If they survive—which is unlikely—both will need some time in the autodoc."

"Fuck you," Cary hissed, turning away from her sisters, though still keeping part of her mind on the nano-battle raging within their bodies. "They'll survive."

"Oh?" Travers asked a mock frown on his face. "Oh! You mean now that you've fought my nano off. Yes, huzzah, you defeated my little distraction." His mocking tone took on a sinister bent. "I meant that after I kill you, they'll not survive."

Travers had six of his limbs stretched out, pressing into Cary's protective field, driving it back with unrelenting force. The attack sapped her energy, and Cary dropped to her knees as Travers continued to take languid steps toward her.

"Silly girl. I've been playing this game for centuries." He was only a meter away now, crouching on the far side of her shield. "Do you hear me, scion of a fool? *Centuries.*"

Cary clenched her teeth, drawing the energy out of her internal SC batteries to maintain the shield while looking up to meet Travers' eyes.

"Who *are* you?" she whispered. "You're not an ascended AI…"

"Really?" Travers laughed, the sound almost maniacal. "I know you're just a kid, but you have good genes, so you can't be that stupid. Stars, if Jessica were here, *she'd* know who I was. I still want to visit her someday, let her know that Trist's death was an utter waste."

Understanding slashed across Cary's mind like the crack of a whip.

"No…" she whispered. "You died…Trist killed you…"

Travers sat back on his heels, mouth half-open in a macabre grin. "Come now. You know of my remnants, you must understand that I never tip my hand; I worked from the shadows through agents. If you weren't so evolved, you wouldn't even know for sure that this is me—but you *do* know, so you must die."

Cary knew he was right—if she didn't do something, he *would* kill her. And then he would snuff the life from her sisters as well.

Her eyes fell to the deck, and she drew in a ragged breath, willing her shield to become stronger—but the attempt was futile. Her internal SC batteries were almost drained.

The deckplate swam before her vision, its solid form dissolving into chaotic particles.

Am I hallucinating….? What is this? she thought in a daze, before the particles moved into forms she understood, molecules of carbon and steel interlocking before her vision.

She took a moment to wonder if that was what her mother could see when she plucked apart solid objects, and then drove a tendril of her extradimensional self into the deckplate, severing the molecular bonds and drawing both the matter and energy into herself.

Lucidity flooded back into her mind, and her head snapped up, focus clear as she strengthened her n-space stabilization shield and rose to her feet. She caught flashes of Travers' thoughts as she pressed the brane close around him, nearly falling to her knees as the revelation unfolded.

"What the—" he exclaimed, scrambling backward before he too rose. "Nice trick, little girl, but—"

"No buts, *Myrrdan*," Cary hissed as she pulled her shield from its sphere shape to form a wall between her and her foe. "You're going to die for all the suffering you've caused. I'm going to make you pay for all the lives—"

"Oh please," Myrrdan scoffed. "You don't even know the half of it. I've killed more people than you can imagine. And I've stood up to the Caretaker's minions, too. The likes of you will not defeat me so easily."

Cary didn't reply, drawing more energy from the molecules of the catwalk to power her shield.

For a moment, they stared at one another, Cary feeling stronger by the second, and Myrrdan looking concerned as the shield between them strengthened.

Concentrating on her extradimensional form, Cary reached out and grabbed the corners of the shield that separated them, feeling the quantum fabric of the field pulse beneath her 'hands' as she folded it around Myrrdan in a single deft move, forming a large M5 black brane.

For a moment, the man appeared surprised, and Cary breathed a sigh of relief. "You know, Myrrdan. *I've* defeated the Caretaker's minions too."

"Oh?" He cocked an eyebrow. "I'll admit that I'm impressed. But you know they are just shadows.... What did you call them? Remnants. Yes, that's accurate. They need a host to survive in this spacetime.... They don't possess enough energy to travel without one."

He paused, his eyes locked on Cary's.

"Not like me."

One moment, he was within Cary's black brane, and the next, he was before her.

But it wasn't 'him', not his corporeal form, at least. That body collapsed to the deck a moment before the lack of internal pressure from Myrrdan's defenses caused the graviton sphere to snap inward, crushing the man's form within.

A tendril of light from the being in front of her rose up and wrapped around her throat, while the being spoke into her mind.

-I don't like to move about without a body. I find it...uncomfortable. Perhaps I'll take yours, once I purge you from within it.-

Cary fought down the panic she felt as more tendrils of Myrrdan's form wrapped around her body, sliding inside her corporeal body, touching her fledgling extradimensional limbs.

Her thoughts raced, frantically trying to come up with a means to defeat him, all the while still drawing more energy from the deckplate around her.

She tried to form a black brane around Myrrdan, to trap him the way she had done to so many remnants, but he batted the form aside, wrapping her own constructs in antiparticles.

-You'll have to try harder than that.-

Cary flailed wildly, desperate to free herself, when her eye caught sight of something in the compressed remains of Travers' corporeal body.

It was the cylinder he had been holding—a small cylinder of antimatter.

Cary snaked a limb around Myrrdan's extradimensional body and grasped the capsule, drawing out a microgram of antimatter. She pulled it toward herself and then created a new black brane, bleeding sleptons off the antimatter to strengthen the field around it.

It took only a second to create the new brane, and she feared Myrrdan would stop her, but he didn't. Cary realized it was because he was sifting through her mind, delving into her memories.

"Stop!" she shouted, directing a burst of sleptons into Myrrdan and driving his ephemeral form back into the black brane she had created.

Surprise registered on his form, and he shrieked wordlessly as the brane closed around him. He raged against the walls, but Cary drew out more antimatter atoms, fueling her creation, keeping the being within secure.

Suddenly aware that she was on her knees again, she struggled to her feet, only to feel the catwalk shift beneath her. Looking down, Cary saw that she'd drawn so much energy from disassembling the molecules of the catwalk that it was paper thin in places.

-Such a fool,- Myrrdan chittered as the catwalk split open under Cary's feet, and she began to fall toward the matter annihilator forty meters below.

Cary tried to summon a graviton field, but the moment she did, she felt her control of the brane around Myrrdan waver.

Then we die together, she thought grimly, wrapping a limb around the brane and pulling it through the hole with her.

Below, the housing of the annihilator raced toward Cary, and she knew that while she would likely die from the impact, nothing would happen to Myrrdan—other than that he would gain his freedom once more.

"Not this time," she whispered.

She focused on the housing around the annihilator, the sphere that smashed atoms into one another, extracting every joule of energy from the utter destruction of matter.

She held the last antimatter atom she had drawn from the cylinder and slammed it into the surface of the black brane, phase shifting the field so it would pass through solid objects before pushing it down toward the annihilator.

During those two excruciatingly long seconds, Cary had heard a strange sound above her, but kept her focus on the black brane containing Myrrdan, as it fell through the housing and into the region of utter destruction within.

Time continued to pass with mind-numbing slowness. With her other sight, Cary could see the raging inferno of energy—energy that spanned many dimensions of spacetime—tear into Myrrdan, shredding his 'body' layer by layer, exposing every part of him to quantum energies that obliterated his being, burning him away to nothing.

I can't believe that worked…he's finally dead!

Myrrdan's destruction didn't change her state, however. She gave one final attempt at generating a graviton field to slow her fall, but there was nothing to draw energy from. Idly, Cary calculated her trajectory, noting how she would hit the annihilator's sphere, bounce off, and fall sixty meters onto a heat exchanger that bled excess energy off to thermal convertors.

Death by vaporization…at least it will be fast.

The surface of the annihilator was seven meters away when something hit her, shoving her aside. A pressure wrapped around her torso, and her downward motion stopped.

All the energy seemed to flee from Cary's body as she craned her neck to look up into the grim face of Lieutenant Mason, rising back up to the catwalk with his armor's a-grav pack.

"Stars, girl," he muttered. "Your father is going to skin me alive."

AWAKEN

STELLAR DATE: 10.03.8949 (Adjusted Years)
LOCATION: Aleutia Station
REGION: Cheshire System, Large Magellanic Cloud

Darkness instantly became light and then swam into wavering shapes around Cary. Solid forms moved nearby, and thin partitions were beyond them, only partially obscuring more forms that moved in the distance.

She tried to make sense of what she was seeing, but there was no rationality to anything. Objects moved through one another, taking paths that seemed entirely impossible.

Then one of the blobs spoke.

"Cary? Are you awake? Your vitals show consciousness."

The words filtered into her mind slowly, as though they were spoken over the course of hours.

Bit by bit, Cary put together her recent memories, remembering the fight with Travers—who turned out to be Myrrdan—and then her impending death, which was averted by Lieutenant Mason.

"Sisters?" Cary asked. "Saanvi, Faleena."

"They'll be OK," a different voice said. "You kept them safe, my little angel."

"Dad?" Cary asked, wondering which of the blobs had spoken.

"You may want to open your eyes, daughter mine," he said, a small chuckle following his words. "You keep waving your arms around like you're blind."

"Eyes…right…" Cary whispered as she tried to remember how to open her eyelids. After a curl of her lip and a few twitches of her nose, she remembered how, and the blobs of light disappeared, replaced with a hospital recovery room.

"Cary!" A voice called out from the doorway, and she barely registered her mother dropping a cup of coffee—which Joe deftly caught—and all but leaping across the room and wrapping her in a fierce embrace. "Stars…what were you thinking?"

"Like mother, like daughter," Joe said, leaning over the two women and embracing them both.

"Moms…can't…breathe," Cary gasped.

"Sorry," Tangel replied, laying her head on Cary's chest. "You look OK, all your parts are still there—oh!"

Cary registered a look of surprise on her mother's face, as she straightened and glanced at Joe before looking back down at her.

"You've grown."

Joe cast Tangel a curious look. "Grown?"

"I've got more ascended parts now," Cary said as she struggled to sit up, flashing a grin at her father.

"Stars," he said, shaking his head and bumping his hip against Tangel's. "You're the spitting image of this crazy woman when you do that."

"What happened in there?" Tangel asked as she sat on the edge of the bed. "The optics in the annihilator chamber were fried the moment Travers entered."

"And stuff was *shredded*," Joe added.

"You'll never believe it," Cary said. "But before that, Saanvi and Faleena…are they really OK?"

Her father placed a hand on her forehead and nodded. "Saanvi has some neural damage to her brainstem, and Faleena took a hit to her core interface, but her internal defenses held it off. Her core was severed, but she's up and about again."

"How long 'til Saanvi's conscious?"

"I'm conscious now," Saanvi's voice came from behind her parents. "Not walking, but thinking, at least."

Joe turned aside, and Cary caught a glimpse of Saanvi on a medchair, with Faleena behind her.

"Saving the day, again, Cary," her AI sister said. "Thank you."

"You'll all be thanking me even more when you learn who that was." Cary grinned at each member of her family in turn.

"So it wasn't Chief Travers?" Joe asked.

"Uh…" Cary felt a moment of nausea at the memory of what had happened to the body Myrrdan had inhabited. "Well, yeah. But that was just the meat-suit."

"For fucksakes," Saanvi rasped, swinging her chair around the other side of the bed. "Spill it already."

"Wow…" Faleena whistled. "You made Sahn swear. Better get on with it."

"Myrrdan."

Cary's lips split into a broad smile at the four gaping mouths arrayed around her.

* * * * *

Tangel stood in stunned silence, as Cary explained her encounter with the being in the station's annihilator chamber. At first she couldn't believe it was Myrrdan, but as her daughter completed her tale, describing how she saw into her attacker's mind, she realized there was no denying it.

"Motherfucker," she whispered. "That bastard has still been with us all this time…some mysterious occurrences over the past few decades are making more sense now."

"Like what?" Saanvi asked. "Do you think he told Orion where New Canaan was?"

"No," Tangel shook her head. "We're reasonably certain they just scouted the area 'til they found it—or got it from a spy in the TSF. I was thinking more about some attempts to steal the picotech after we arrived at New Canaan."

"Guy sure played the long game," Joe muttered, and Tangel noticed that he was clenching his right hand over and over again.

She placed a hand on his and gave a gentle squeeze. "I imagine that the Caretaker sending Nance in to take him out put a wrinkle in Myrrdan's plans—though I wonder if he knew what he was getting into when he took a flight out here to Aleutia."

"I hate to think of all the people's lives he ruined," Saanvi said quietly. "But I'm also perversely pleased that his centuries of planning got him exactly jack squat."

"Did he have other remnants here?" Cary asked suddenly. "What happened to them when he died?"

"Colonel Ophelia is doing a full sweep—your dad brought more shadowtrons from back home. So far, they've found two…no, three. It seems that they aren't affected by their progenitor's death, either. Just keep on ticking…like little parasitic mini-Myrrdans."

"That sucks," Cary muttered. "I'd hoped that killing him would free everyone under his control."

Tangel patted her daughter's leg. "It would be nice."

"Mom…weren't you on your way to Aldebaran to deal with the mess there?" Faleena asked. "I was under the impression that Amavia was all but besieged by politicians and the like."

Tangel nodded slowly. "Yes, as soon as things are secure here, I'll jump to Amavia's rescue. I'm just a big intergalactic firefighter."

"Not this time, you weren't." Cary gave a saucy wink. "I had things all wrapped up by the time you arrived. Nothing but cleanup left. Oh! But I got all sorts of intel from Kent."

"I already filed it all," Faleena said with a wink. "Even semi-ascended, you still sleep, and I had nothing to do last night."

"You stole my thunder?" Cary gave her sister a mock glare.

Tangel laughed and shared a look with Joe. "You killed Myrrdan, Cary. Pretty sure you have enough thunder to go around."

"Speaking of thunder." Joe placed a hand on Tangel's shoulder. "Amavia has been trying to reach you over the QC network, and now she's started pinging me. Their assembly thought you were on your way and has an emergency session scheduled to hear you."

"I know…" Tangel's voice was filled with reluctance as she rose. "I just feel like I'm bailing on my girls."

"We're fine, Moms," Cary replied as Saanvi and Faleena nodded. "Go put out some more fires."

"OK, but I'll be back to check on you once I've straightened out the League of Sentients."

"We'll be back on the Palisades by then," Joe said as he leant in for a kiss. "As incredible as the view is out here, I feel a lot better with The Cradle in my night skies."

Tangel pulled Joe close. "You're just a control freak and you want to make sure everything is just so."

Joe laughed and squeezed Tangel tightly. "I got it from you. I *used* to be all carefree, but now I need to compensate."

The two separated, and Tangel ignored her daughters' grins as she gave Joe a final kiss. "That's why I can trust you to keep everything in line while I'm gone."

She gave each of her daughters an embrace before giving them one final wave and leaving the room. <*No more chasing strange ascended beings!*> she sent in parting as she strode through Aleutia Station's hospital wing.

<*No promises, Moms,*> Cary sent back, and Tangel resisted the urge to groan audibly.

<*What she said,*> Faleena added, while Saanvi only laughed.

This is my punishment. Kids that are too much like me.

A VISIT FROM ROXY

STELLAR DATE: 10.03.8949 (Adjusted Years)
LOCATION: River Station, Styx Baby-9
REGION: STX-B17 Black Hole, Transcend Interstellar Alliance

"I never got to ask," Seraphina said as she walked with Sera to the docking bay where their unexpected visitor would shortly arrive. "How did it feel to have the cabinet ratify father in a matter of hours?"

Sera snorted, giving her sister a measuring glance. "You know…it should have bothered me, and I suppose it did a bit. But mostly I was relieved. I don't mind being the Hand's director—it's more my speed. Being president? That just never felt right."

"I know what you mean." Seraphina gave a rueful laugh. "Being president never sat right with me either—and I'm the reserved one."

Sera glanced at Seraphina's square-toed boots, leather pants, grey silk shirt, and long black leather coat. "We don't really do reserved well, do we?"

"Not so much, no. Fina least of all." Seraphina barked a laugh. "Girl's getting her inner mod freak on. I wonder what we'd be like if mom didn't go tweaking in our heads. Would I be a fetish freak like you two are?"

Sera shrugged. "She tweaked all of us. She had a shard of herself in our heads for most of our lives. Maybe Fina's and my proclivities are a *result* of that."

Seraphina knocked her shoulder against Sera's. "Or maybe you're closest to spec, and I'm the weird one."

" 'To spec', eh?"

"Well, we are geneered. Made-to-order daughters; just add unloving psychomom."

"Always happy to disappoint her," Sera replied, then decided to change the subject. "So you don't think Justin was working with Airtha at all?

"If he was, she never told us. Bastard was a thorn in our side—messing up more than one of our operations."

"Ours too," Sera said. "Turns out a lot of agents were more loyal to him than to the Transcend."

Seraphina nodded. "Between you and him, we barely held onto a tenth of the directorate. We got the short end of the stick there—though your deputies running things at Khardine still managed to keep Fina and I answering questions for days."

"Sorry about that," Sera gave her sister an apologetic glance. "*I* knew that the ISF's deprogramming would work on you—they've gotten pretty good at it over the years—but our folks needed to see it for themselves. You know how it is."

Seraphina rubbed her ass. "Yeah, but I could have done without the probe."

A laugh burst free from Sera's lips as she gave her sister an appreciative glance. "Off-color humor? Who are you, and what have you done with Seraphina?"

"Hey, I'm just as dirty-minded as you and Fina, I just figure that someone has to be a bit closer to an even keel—what with you two freaks in the mix."

Sera placed a hand on her sister's shoulder and slowed to a stop, fixing her with a level gaze. "Seraphina, seriously. Be your own person. You don't have to compensate for our behavior. There's no cosmic scale weighing the three of us, looking for balance."

Seraphina pursed her lips, then ran her hands over her face. "Dammit, Sera. I don't know *who* I am. Fina seemed to slip into her 'freaky girl' persona the moment the ISF removed mother's aegis from her. She seems to know exactly who and what she is. Me...I have no clue. I'm trying to be like I was—like we were—before that day we pulled Tanis from that shipping crate. But I don't know if I remember it right...so I'm just faking it as best I can."

"You know what they say, 'fake it 'til you make it'. Seriously, though, Seraphina. You know Fina is just rebelling. She was pushing so hard against mother's control that when the chains were removed, she careened headlong into what she's become. And there's *nothing* wrong with that. The only way you can find balance is by swinging side to side on the ole pendulum a bit; at least that's what Tangel says."

"I think our pendulums are in the middle of a hurricane," Seraphina said with a soft laugh.

"Sounds about right," Sera replied as the two women resumed their walk. "Shit, I tried to get this conversation off us, and to whatever this ship's arrival means, and it got back onto us again."

"We're a right bunch of screwed up narcissists," Seraphina said with a self-deprecating laugh. "Nice one, losing a stasis ship to Justin, by the way."

"Better him than mom," Sera replied. "She would have held onto it—Justin lost his in a matter of days, it seems. Though I have no idea who this Roxy person is, do you?"

"Not a clue. She's not in any of the Hand databases I had access to. I have no idea how she found us, either, which is honestly the most concerning part—your secret base isn't so secret."

Sera twisted her lips, wondering whether or not they were walking into a trap.

Silly, of course it's a trap. The question is just who is the one springing it?

Sera and Seraphina turned down the long gantry that lead to the spur where the *Damon Silas* was slated to dock in a few moments.

Standing in their way was Flaherty, flanked by two members of their former High Guard.

"Seriously?" he grunted out the word. "You know this is a trap, right? Jen, why did you let them both come?"

<*They have enough mommy issues without me mothering them. I figured you'd be here—you're always skulking about somewhere nearby.*>

"I don't skulk." Flaherty glared at Sera's forehead, as though he was staring into Jen's synapses. "I lurk."

"Either way, Flaherty," Sera shrugged, wishing he'd stop boring a hole through her head with his eyes. "Don't you have all the angles covered?"

His scowl deepened. "No one ever has all the angles covered. But one of the easiest to cover is not having both of you together."

Seraphina shrugged and glanced at Sera. "We're clones, we have backups."

"Are you really suggesting that we should leave the mission to defeat Airtha in Fina's hands?" Flaherty asked with a raised brow.

Seraphina snorted and shook her head. "Now that you put it that way…"

"Rock paper scissors?" Sera asked.

"No, I'll let you handle it. Our chat has me feeling more out of sorts than I'd expected, anyway."

Sera gave her sister an appraising look, then nodded. "OK. I'll give you the scoop."

"You'd better," Seraphina said, turning on her heel and striding back the way she'd come.

<*She needs to mask all that squeaking leather,*> Jen commented. <*Probably take an NSAI to manage the nano cloud it would take to pull that off.*>

Sera laughed softly. <*You have no idea.*>

Five minutes later, they were at the end of the spire, watching as the *Damon Silas* eased into position.

<*Sorry I can't be down there,*> Krissy sent to Sera. <*I've got a situation brewing out on the antispinward front. I may have to take a battlegroup out there to shore things up.*>

<*Don't worry about me,*> Sera replied. <*Do what you need to do. Hopefully the hoplites will make enough of a mess soon that the front will get a reprieve.*>

<*Can't come soon enough. Scan shows all of the* Silas*'s weapons with zero EM, by the way. Ship is as safe as it can be. Still, Earnest and Finaeus are up here ready to drop a stasis shield around it if they have to.*>

<*Good to know,*> Sera sent back as the station's grapple reached out and took hold of the destroyer. <*Any word from this Roxy person…or Carmen?*>

<*Nothing beyond their original request to speak to you. Honestly, either they're going to try to kill you, or Carmen is going to try for a personal appeal to get out of a dereliction trial.*>

<*Well, if their stasis tech is intact, that'll be a good start. I bet she'll try to spin it as having been her plan all along—something her record doesn't really point to.*>

Sera wondered about that. It would be hard to discount such an argument, given the results. However, much of that would depend on this Roxy person.

She glanced around the corridor they stood in at the tip of the docking spire. No one was in evidence except for Flaherty and the two High Guard, all of whom were in light armor. Sera had shifted her skin to take on the appearance of red-tinted light armor to show that she wasn't being completely blasé, but still presenting a soft target.

What an attacker wouldn't know was that there was an entire squad of stealthed TSF special forces troops in the spire, ready to act with deadly force.

As she mused over what the next few minutes would bring, the umbilical extended and connected to the *Damon Silas*. An indicator showed positive seal, and then the ship's outer airlock cycled open.

Feeds from within the umbilical showed an azure-skinned woman drift into the connecting tube. EM monitoring showed only one Link present, but Sera wondered how likely it was that Carmen had remained behind on the ship.

Had Sera been in Roxy's shoes—if Roxy even wore shoes—she wouldn't have come into the lion's den without her strongest advocate at her side.

Then the station-side lock was cycling open, and Roxy stepped through.

"President Sera, thank you for seeing us in person," the azure woman said the moment she stepped through.

"Us?" Sera asked.

"Yes." Roxy touched her abdomen. "Carmen is within me. It was a part of how we took the ship from Justin—and beat him in the end."

"Beat him?" Sera asked. "Did he escape?"

A feral smile crept across Roxy's lips. "Oh, he most certainly did not. My brother breathed his last—or rather, tried to—a few days ago. He's dead."

A dozen conflicting feelings cascaded through Sera. Justin had been her mentor at one point, and she still felt guilty that he'd taken the fall for Andrea's attempt to kill Tanis. But then one of the words Roxy had spoken leapt to the fore.

"Brother?"

Roxy nodded. "Justin and I had a…complicated relationship."

<You can say that again,> another voice joined the conversation. It's Link route showed it to be coming from Roxy, but Sera could tell it was someone else.

"Carmen?" she asked.

<Stars, she's riding through Roxy's Link. Unbuffered, too, if I don't miss my guess,> Jen added privately. *<Even if you organics don't rake her across the coals for dereliction, she's going to be in hot water with the local AI council.>*

<Desperate times,> Sera said to Jen as Carmen replied.

<Yes. Before you start, President Sera. I know I screwed up. A lot. I submit myself for judgement.>

"No need to jump quite that far ahead yet," Sera replied. "I'm also no longer the president of the Transcend. My father has resumed that role."

"Your father?" Roxy's face took on a look of utter confusion. "I thought he had…"

"Died?" Sera asked. "He did. But it looks like I'm not the only one Airtha was cloning."

Roxy put a hand to her forehead, and then took a step forward. "I suppose this is a waste, then."

"Stop!" Flaherty called out and raised his rifle.

"Make me." Roxy held out a hand, and filaments of light twisted through the air, some streaking toward Flaherty, others toward Sera.

The two High Guard soldiers fired their pulse rifles, but the shots seemed to dissipate into nothingness before they reached Roxy.

Sera danced back, trying to evade the filaments, as the TSF soldiers around her decloaked and began firing. Like the first two, none of their shots reached the azure woman, who was smirking as she took a step forward.

Then the first ephemeral strand of n-dimensional energy brushed against Sera's chest, and Roxy's expression turned from one of triumph to horror, and the filament of light retracted.

"How?" she hissed.

"I've got powerful friends," Sera said with a smile. "Besides, we're about to go up against Airtha; protection from remnants like you was the first order of business."

Next to Sera, Flaherty unslung a shadowtron and activated its n-dimensional field stabilizer, drawing the remnant out of Roxy and into a waiting black brane.

"I'm not sure who you're splintered off," Sera said with a grim smile. "But we'll find out soon enough. You're going to need to re-evaluate that smug attitude, as well. We've become rather adept at getting remnants to reveal their secrets."

As Sera spoke, the last of the remnant was drawn out of Roxy, and the woman collapsed to the deck.

"I wonder if she really did kill Justin," Sera mused, then glanced at the lieutenant leading the TSF squad. "Secure the *Silas,* but be careful. There's no telling what traps she may have set."

<*Shit…*> Carmen's wavering voice came over Roxy's Link. <*What **was** that thing? Was it in here with me all along? I thought I'd removed what Justin did to her.*>

"That wasn't from Justin," Sera replied. "Though if he's been working for the core AIs, then a few things are starting to make a lot more sense."

ALDEBARAN

STELLAR DATE: 10.03.8949 (Adjusted Years)
LOCATION: Aleutia Station
REGION: Cheshire System, Large Magellanic Cloud

When Tangel reached the docking bay where the *Mandy* rested in its cradle, she saw Lieutenant Brennen standing near the ship's entrance, speaking with a man who was nearly the lieutenant's spitting image.

His ident lit up on her HUD, and her lips formed a broad smile. "Lieutenant Joshua Mason! I owe you a deep debt of gratitude!"

The Marine turned toward her, and his face reddened. "Just doing my job, ma'am."

Tangel held out her hand as she approached and clasped the lieutenant's firmly. "There's doing your job, and then there's *doing your job*. I believe they give out medals for acts of heroism like yours."

"I just flew a few meters on my armor's jets, is all," the lieutenant replied, his face maintaining its flushed hue. "It's your daughter that deserves the medal. She finally took out that fucker Myrrdan. Even if I saved her a thousand times over, the debt would still be mine to pay."

Lieutenant Brennen slapped his father's shoulder, a grin on his lips. "Just wait 'til I tell Mom. You saving Cary Richards, and me escorting the Admiral. She's going to be green with envy."

"What does your mother do, Lieutenant?" Tangel asked.

"She's head nurse at the ER at Landfall General," Joshua replied. "Misses us fiercely, but I think this will help ease it a bit."

"Sounds like she saves people every day, then," Tangel replied. "It's hard to stop missing family, even if they are saving people in other galaxies…actually, that may make you miss them more."

"Yes, ma'am," the father and son said in near unison.

"Speaking of saving people, Amavia and Iris still need us to free them from a never-ending series of negotiations. We'd best be on our way."

"Aye, ma'am," Lieutenant Brennen replied, as Joshua stepped back and saluted.

"An honor, Admiral."

"Don't you salute *me* on the day you saved my daughter," Tangel replied while snapping her hand against her brow. "You keep doing a fantastic job."

* * * * *

Thirty minutes on the clock later, the *Mandy* was decelerating into the

Aldebaran system, matching stellar delta-*v* before lining up for an approach with Lunic Station.

"That was…unusual," Lieutenant Brennen said from next to Tangel. "I really didn't expect a journey like that."

"Me either," Tangel replied, "but let's focus on the task at hand. This *should* be nothing more than run-of-the-mill diplomacy, but today has been a bit off-kilter all around."

"Don't you worry, Admiral, we'll be frosty."

"Glad to hear it."

Lunic Station orbited a terrestrial-sized moon named Idaiac that orbited a large jovian planet thirty AU from the system's star.

For most of its life, Idaiac was a cold world on the fringes of an old star system, but Aldebaran was in its death throes, having expanded into a red giant, now over forty-four times its original diameter.

Though its mass was only slightly greater than Sol's, it shone with over four hundred times the luminosity, warming the surface of Idaiac and making the moon a habitable world for humanity.

The idea of settling around a dying star felt odd to Tangel—even though she knew that Aldebaran would likely still be burning long after the human race had disappeared.

Or maybe not, one never knows. The estimates Tangel had reviewed gave the star millions of years more as a red giant before collapsing into a white dwarf. *I suppose they'll have plenty of time to move elsewhere before that happens.*

She marveled at the composition of space around the *Mandy* as she approached the station. Though red giants like Aldebaran or Arcturus *appeared* to be violent monsters, they were much more relaxed than nearly any other type of star.

For a variety of reasons, Aldebaran did not possess a corona, and shed almost no X-ray radiation—compared to younger, more active stars. It had also gone through its first 'dredge-up', where convection from the giant star's core brought elements it had fused over its billions of years to the surface.

The result was a stellar medium that was far richer than what surrounded most stars. Carbon, oxygen, and nitrogen flew from the star in its stellar wind, which extended nearly one thousand astronomical units from the star itself.

The light show it created in extradimensional space was astounding, and Tangel had to take care not to gape.

"We have final docking," Lieutenant Brennen announced as they drew near to Lunic Station's hundred-kilometer-long spire. A dozen toroid rings spun further up the spire, but the long shaft itself was stationary, allowing for easier docking at the long spurs jutting out from its 'bottom' twenty kilometers.

"Looks like an internal berth," Tangel said as she looked over the assignment. "I want you to keep a pair of Marines on the ship at all times, monitoring passive scan, as well as a fireteam out in the bay. For the duration of our visit, that deck belongs to us."

"Understood." Brennen gave a crisp nod. "We leave the QuanComm box in here?"

Tangel glanced at the case strapped to the bulkhead next to Brennen's seat. "Yeah, no need to advertise that we have something as valuable as that. Should we need to, we can just link through it and call for backup."

"Sounds good, ma'am."

They were within two light seconds of the station, and Tangel decided it was close enough to reach out for an update. She established a connection with Lunic's general communications network and sought out a route to Amavia.

<*How are things going,*> she asked the AI diplomat.

<*Tangel! Stars, you sound a lot different than you used to.*>

Tangel sent a smile over the Link. <*I suppose we've not chatted directly in some time now. I'm glad you've come into your own so well. Looks like a posting on* Sabrina *worked out for the best.*>

A soft laugh came back over the Link. <*Well, flying with that crew is a trial by fire, to be sure.*>

<*Corsia's mighty proud of you, and Jessica hasn't stopped singing your praises.*>

<*Well, Jessica was a big part of squaring things away here, and getting cooler heads to prevail. Honestly, the fact that the League of Sentients still exists at all is largely because of her.*>

Tangel took a moment to consider what would have happened if the Non-Organic Supremists had prevailed. Their siren's call and ability to subvert other AIs paralleled Airtha's—except where Airtha wished to *use* humanity for her own ends, NOS's goal was to eradicate organics entirely.

Jessica was certain that NOS cells still lingered on the fringes of the Hegemony of Worlds, and Sera had dispatched what few Hand agents they had available to seek them out.

But for now, the League of Sentients was back in the control of its elected leaders; leaders who were uncertain if joining the Alliance was a step toward a victory for all free people, or merely trading one master for another.

<*So how are those 'cooler heads' doing?*> Tangel asked. <*The reports I have said that they have considered declaring LoS worlds neutral, and kicking out all diplomats and foreign entities.*>

<*That's the position of Deia, leader of the isolationist wing of their government. Thus far, President Jasper has managed to keep those radicals from getting their way, but many in his own party are wavering. They believe that if they simply keep to themselves and have a strong deterrent force, no one is going to bother them.*>

<*Stars,*> Tangel muttered. <*If no one* **does** *bother the LoS, that's because Scipians are dying to defeat the Hegemony, and Corsia is attacking the Trisilieds. They're caught between two empires, and don't seem to care that it's other people keeping them safe.*>

<You're preaching to the choir, Tangel. I've made this case as strongly as I can manage. I ***think*** *we can sway them enough to join in and press the Hegemony on their rimward front; if the message about how important this is comes from you…well, that would go a long way in convincing them.>*

<Because I'm ascended?> Tangel asked.

<Stars, no. Because you're ***you****.>*

<Now you're just kissing ass, Amavia.>

* * * * *

President Jasper was waiting for them, alone in his offices deep in Lunic Station.

Once introductions were complete, Amavia gave the otherwise vacant room a significant look. "I thought we were going to meet with your cabinet, President Jasper?"

The short—for a spacer—man gave a weary nod. "I would have liked to, but Deia forced my hand into keeping the original time for the emergency session, which is just one hour from now; while I like to have my full team operating in concert…well, let's just say that we don't usually become fully simpatico on anything until after at least three hours."

Tangel gave the president a reassuring smile. "I understand, and I'm sorry I'm late. I had to attend to a matter of life and death. However, Amavia and Iris have been keeping me updated with the situation here in Aldebaran, and I'm aware of Deia and her push for a neutral stance in the conflict with the Hegemony."

"Closer to isolationist." President Jasper echoed Amavia's earlier words as he clasped and twisted his hands together. "Honestly, I don't understand it. Especially after what Amavia and her team did to help Virginis, and then us here at Aldebaran."

"It's amazing how often people think that if they stick their heads in the sand, everything will get better," Tangel replied. "But from what I understand, she's begun to make inroads in your own party, weakening your position further."

The president spread his hands. "In a nutshell, yes. So what's your plan, Admiral Richards?"

"Essentially, I plan to appeal to their decency. I'll also remind them that when we win this conflict, the peoples of the systems and alliances that *did* fight against tyranny are going to remember who stood with them, and who stood on the sidelines."

"Are you sure a threat is a good idea?" Jasper asked.

"It's not a threat." Tangel's lips twisted as she replied. "It's the future state of reality."

A look of surprise came over the president. "I thought you'd make some offer to sweeten the deal."

"No." Tangel shook her head vehemently. "The LoS has already received more aid from us than any other non-member of the Alliance. We've eliminated rogue elements within your own borders that would have seen every organic in the LoS dead by now. If my personal appeal and our past deeds are not enough to sway the minds of your people, then I will be forced to retract all aid and assistance, and expend it on actual Alliance members."

<*Harsh,*> Iris commented privately. <*Jasper has worked hard for our cause.*>

<*I believe that,*> Tangel replied. <*But at this point, we've staved off a fresh AI war in this section of the Inner Stars—which was our initial goal. If these people won't become willing allies, then they're going to have to fend for themselves....*>

<*I get it...it's still harsh.*>

<*A lot of things are harsh right now—*> Tangel stopped herself, realizing that she was directing an undue amount of her internal angst over what had happened with her daughters toward Iris. <*OK, I'm going to do my best, but after all the effort we've expended here, if our seeds won't take root, we have to plant them elsewhere.*>

<*I understand, Admiral.*>

During Tangel and Iris's rapid-fire exchange, President Jasper had assumed a look of resigned stoicism. "I hope then—for our sakes—that you are convincing. I would like the LoS to have a bright future; not one that is forever marred by getting off on the wrong foot with your alliance, which *I* am convinced is operating in the best interests of all sentients."

Tangel sat in silence for a moment, and then gave the president an apologetic look. "I'm sorry, President Jasper. I have been unfair to you. Your heart is in the right place, and I want to do what I can to help. Tell me, what do you think the best approach is to sway your assembly to join our alliance?"

Jasper's wan smile grew a little brighter, and he initialized a holo. "Here is what I think would work best...."

SHRUGGING ATLAS

STELLAR DATE: 10.03.8949 (Adjusted Years)
LOCATION: ISS *Andromeda*
REGION: Buffalo, Albany System, Theban Alliance

It had taken a week to prepare, and then another week to orchestrate.

Corsia was more than a little grateful for Kendrick's ability to corral dozens of disparate salvagers into a unified group that was able to execute her plan, as her idea far exceeded the resources she had at her disposal.

She had to admit a small amount of glee as she thought of the consternation her scheme must be causing the Trisilieds admiralty.

Even as she was preparing for her assault in the Albany System, all around the periphery of the Pleiades, fleets were jumping into the edges of key Trisilieds systems before simply disappearing.

At least, that was what the enemy would see.

In reality, hundreds of fusion engines were being pulled off Nietzschean hulls and sent through jump gates to target systems. Once there, the engines were guided by onboard NSAIs to split apart into broad fleet formations and ignite.

What it would look like was several fleets moving deep within the Trisilieds Kingdom, probing systems for weaknesses, while Corsia's real fleet attacked Atlas.

It would likely make no sense to the enemy, as probing with a full fleet was foolish, but they would also have to respond to the threat, whether it was logical or not.

Moreover, Corsia *was* using the engines for actual reconnaissance. Once they made their burns, the engines transitioned into the dark layer on trajectories for a central rendezvous point, where they would send data back to the Albany System via drone through a small jump gate.

None of the probes had come through yet, but they weren't expected to for at least another few days.

Corsia had considered waiting for the intel to be collected, but she had discussed her plans with Tangel, and the pair had agreed that striking out at Atlas while the enemy was still reacting to the probes was the ideal timing.

Intel from Hand agents in the area indicated that Atlas wouldn't have more than a few thousand ships protecting it, but even if it had more, Corsia's main attack force consisted exclusively of stasis shield ships.

"The fleet is in position," the FCO announced, his statement breaking into Corsia's reverie.

<*As are we,*> Sephira added.

<Thank you,> Corsia replied to her daughter and ship's AI. "FCO, signal the fleet. We're jumping by the numbers."

"Aye, ma'am."

Hundreds of engines flared around Buffalo as the ships of the ISF Twelfth Fleet began to approach the hundred jump gates assigned to their maneuver. It would take only twenty minutes for the ships to jump into the Atlas system. They would arrive in four battlegroups and take out their key targets before boosting to the edge of the system and then reforming at their rendezvous point.

The *Andromeda* was at the fore of the first wave, and Corsia felt her anticipation grow as the ship touched the not-space in the center of the ring of ford-svaiter mirrors, and leapt across space.

I've always wanted to see the Pleiades up close.

The ship took only a second to traverse the intervening light years, and then they were back in normal space, surrounded by the baleful blue-white light of the Atlas system.

Corsia's battlegroup's target was a shipyard built at a lagrange point between the two primary stars. Their calculations were on the nose, and they arrived one light second from their prey.

The main holotank showed a view of the battlespace, with more and more markers appearing as the two thousand ships of her battlegroup continued to arrive in wave after wave.

<RMs!> Sephira called out, and Corsia rose from her chair to watch as hundreds of red markers appeared on the holotank, racing toward the ISF fleet.

"All ships reporting stasis shield activation," the FCO announced a moment later, his voice almost bored.

Corsia nodded with satisfaction as the relativistic missiles exploded against the ISF fleet's stasis shields, nuclear fireballs becoming rapidly expanding clouds of plasma around the leading ships.

Two thousand Trisilieds ships were spread around the shipyard and ore processing systems target, but most were in parking orbits—only a few hundred moving under their own power.

This will be like shooting fish in a barrel.

"Flight A, on pattern Gamma-9," Corsia ordered, even before the battlegroup's ships all reported in after the wave of RMs.

The FCO relayed the order, while Corsia noted that two of her ships *had* taken damage from the relativistic missiles. Nothing serious, but their captains had left too many sensor holes open in the stasis bubbles, allowing a pressure wave to form. She made a note to speak with them later, and directed the damaged vessels to the rear of their formations.

Flight A consisted of just over two hundred ships. A mix of cruisers and rail destroyers, bolstered by ten thousand fighters—mostly NSAI drones that did not possess stasis shielding.

They raced toward their target as the shipyard spewed point-defense fire into space. Most of it missed the incoming craft, and the rest was spent burning away ranging rail shots from Corsia's destroyers.

Then they were within beam range, and the ISF cruisers engaged with the outermost Trisilieds ships, drawing their fire as the rail destroyers continued to unload millions of relativistic pellets at the enemy shipyard and ore processing facilities surrounding it.

Their initial targets were station-keeping and defensive systems. Corsia was all for a swift victory—retribution for the attack on Carthage was on her mind—but she wasn't going to embark on a wholesale murder of everyone in the shipyard without giving them a chance to reach escape craft.

It took only a few seconds, though they seemed to creep by as the rail destroyer's barrage streaked toward their targets.

Then the pellets hit.

Though the enemy had spewed thousands of point defense rounds and beams at the incoming attack, it wasn't enough. Explosions bloomed at the targets, wiping out the Trisilieds' facility's defensive capability.

Secondary explosions bloomed, and an ore refinery split in half, a reclamation yard spinning away toward a group of ships that were moored together a hundred kilometers away.

Escape pods and small craft began to pour out of the shipyard and its surrounding facilities as Corsia sent out her ultimatum.

"You have twenty minutes to abandon all stations and facilities. Any non-capital ships on outsystem vectors will be spared. All capital ships must cease thrust immediately and wait for new vectors. Feel free to abandon your ships if you wish."

A few of the enemy cruisers attempted to form a defensive line, but Corsia directed Flight B to destroy them, and seven minutes later, the remaining Trisilieds ships surrendered.

Pinnaces, shuttles, and escape craft continued to pour from the enemy facilities. At twenty minutes, they were still coming, and Corsia extended her deadline by five minutes.

When that mark hit, the enemy escape craft was all far enough away that they'd survive the coming destruction. She ordered Flight A's cruisers to launch a barrage of rail slugs at the facilities, destroying them utterly.

"This is too easy," she said quietly. "At this rate, we'll just march across the Trisilieds and take their capital in a few weeks."

<Don't jinx things, Mom,> Sephira warned.

Corsia glanced at her daughter's holopresence, giving it a predatory grin. "I don't believe in jinxes."

PAYING THE PIPER

STELLAR DATE: 10.03.8949 (Adjusted Years)
LOCATION: TSS *Cossack's Sword*, Sullus System
REGION: Midway Cluster, Orion Freedom Alliance Space

"I want Caldwell's destroyers on that moon base!" Svetlana called out. "They're hammering us with their rails. Tell them to shred that damn rock if they have to."

That order given, Svetlana turned her focus to the world of Ferra. Her battlegroup was bearing down on it, and the orbital defenses were unleashing everything they had at her ships.

The enemy wasn't breaching the ISF's stasis shields, but after the long slog through the system, her group's reactors were running hot, and she wanted to finish off the defenders as quickly as possible.

In hindsight, she reconsidered the wisdom of her strategy.

Another stealth attack would have been more efficient, but that wasn't the current goal. What she wanted to achieve was the wholesale destruction of every military outpost and defensive platform in the Sullus system.

Granted, I didn't expect them to have so many.

Despite the fact that the Orion Guard maintained little presence in the Perseus Expansion Districts, they seemed to have built up a large number of defensive systems that were secretly tucked inside moons and asteroids.

No sooner did those emplacements fire on Svetlana's fleet, than her forces counterattacked and took them out, but the never-ending incoming fire was taking its toll on her ships—especially since her non-stasis ships had to remain at the periphery of the system, striking at softer targets or lobbing volleys at fixed targets further insystem.

On top of that, a small collection of local militia ships was harrying the fringes of her formation, making her unwilling to widen her front, lest the defenders attack from another entrenched defensive position they'd not yet revealed.

"Caldwell's acknowledged," the FCO announced. "His ETA is twenty-three minutes. He wants to know if he should make a tactical strike or just destroy the moon."

"Do we read any civilian facilities?"

"Thing was dead until it shot at us," Scan chimed in.

"Then smash that fucker," Svetlana growled. "I want to show them that even their best defense is utterly futile."

"Yes, ma'am," the FCO replied.

"Admiral Svetlana!" the comm officer said, twisting in his seat to look back at her. "Major Hemry just relayed a message that came in over FDL. A Hand agent in the Machete System has intel on an Orion Guard fleet massing there. Passing composition estimates to you."

"Excellent," Svetlana replied as she examined the intel. It was a far richer target than she'd expected to encounter in the PED, but just the sort of strike that would cause the Oggies to pull back from the fronts to defend their own systems.

Time to wrap things up here and move on to greener pastures.

She reviewed Admiral Sebastian's position on the far side of the system, a smile forming on her lips as she saw a report come in that he had destroyed a fuel depot in orbit of the seventh planet and decimated a militia fleet that had attempted to drive him back.

"Get Sebastian to come around to the fifth planet and strike that refinery they have in orbit, then head outsystem," she directed. "Once Caldwell finishes off that moon, have him pass by the fourth planet and see if anyone takes the bait."

"And then outsystem as well?" the FCO asked.

"You've got it. We're three hours from firing range on Ferra. We'll take out our primary targets there and then get gone. No need to linger longer than we have to."

The FCO nodded and then turned to his tasks.

Svetlana considered sending Caldwell past the innermost planet, but decided against it. Even if there were significant facilities there they'd not detected, it wasn't worth spending further time in the Sullus System when there were richer targets to be had.

ASSEMBLY OF SENTIENTS

STELLAR DATE: 10.03.8949 (Adjusted Years)
LOCATION: Assembly of Sentients, Lunic Station
REGION: Aldebaran, League of Sentients Space

President Jasper's opening remarks were succinct and brief—for a politician.

Tangel sat behind him on the elevated platform at the center of the assembly hall, gazing out over the thousand senators, delegates, and aides.

A wide variety of humans and AIs were represented in the throng. Many of the AIs used mobile frames, while still others appeared only as holoprojections of people, beams of light, and a few as animals.

Tanis was surprised to see a dolphin in the third tier, its body clothed in a moisturizing sheath and ensconced atop a four-legged frame.

For a moment she thought of Gerald and wondered how he and his pod had fared in the unrest that came to Sol after she'd left. She often wished a pod of dolphins had come with the *Intrepid*; she could have used their counsel on a few occasions.

The conical chamber stretched up forty meters on all sides, which meant that the platform at the center had no back. She wondered if some human speakers found it disconcerting to have half the assembly behind them—it wasn't something that would bother her, but it seemed uncharacteristic for a group that claimed to believe in equality amongst sentients.

As Tangel surveyed the assembly, she sensed a strange energy fluctuation that seemed to cascade through the room. With her transdimensional vision, she saw the walls of reality bend ever so subtly, as though something too large for the assembly chamber to contain had settled within it.

Then the feeling was gone, and everything seemed entirely mundane. She tried to find further evidence of something amiss, but she couldn't sense anything.

I hope it's only stress, she thought. *I just want to say my bit and get back to my girls.*

"Of course you all know the story of the *Intrepid* by now, and how it came to build a colony in a place called New Canaan, deep within the Transcend," President Jasper intoned as he wrapped up his speech—she hoped.

Tangel spotted a few brows lowering in the crowd at the mention of both the *Intrepid* and the Transcend, but most of the assembly kept their expressions carefully neutral.

"Admiral Jessica and her team have been very helpful to LoS worlds over the past two years," President Jasper continued, "and we owe them much. Now they have asked for something in return: that we join their alliance and stand up to the empires of oppression that surround us. These are regimes that do not support true equality among sentients; some do not even believe in freedom for AIs at all.

"Tangel has always believed in the Phobos Accords, and she has mandated that all members of the Scipio Alliance follow the strictures in its second section, which outlines fair and equitable treatment of all sentients. As you know, our own constitution encompasses much of that material.

"She has come to us today to repeat the plea that Amavia has been making, and to explain why she believes it is best for us, and for *all* sentients, to join the Scipio Alliance."

President Jasper paused and turned to face Tangel, a winning smile gracing his lips.

"So please join with me in welcoming Field Marshal Tangel of the Alliance to the League of Sentients Assembly!"

Nearly all the members of the assembly rose, but Tangel noted that nearly half did not clap. Of those, nearly all were members of the opposition party, though she could see that many in Jasper's own party did not join in the applause, either.

As the applause continued, Tangel rose and walked to the podium, where Jasper clasped her hand before gesturing that the floor was hers.

She nodded in thanks and then paused for a moment, surveying the assembly. The moment she opened her mouth to speak, a voice called out.

"Who *are* you? Wasn't Tanis Richards the XO aboard the *Intrepid*? Who is 'Tangel'?"

The speaker was a member of Deia's party. Not a prominent senator, but one that Amavia had flagged as a frequent agitator.

"Thank you for posing the perfect question for me to begin my introduction, Senator Paula. *I* am Tangel, the result of a merge between Tanis Richards, an L2 human, and the AI, Angela. Like Amavia, I am a voluntary merge, but more than that, I am an ascended being. As such, I am uniquely qualified to speak for a broad swath of humanity and its scions."

"Ascended?" a voice called out—another member of the opposition party. "Ascended AIs are half the problem!"

Tangel had anticipated that argument, and couldn't fault the LoS assemblage for concern over her level of cognitive evolution.

"Prove it!" a delegate called out.

"Senators and delegates," President Jasper said, rising to his feet. "This assembly is held to a higher standard of behavior than this. Please let Tangel speak uninterrupted."

The assembly quieted, and Tangel caught the eye of the second dissenter. "I don't disagree that ascended AIs are at the heart of many of our problems. Some of those AIs used to be humans, as well. However, there are ascended AIs who have not caused any harm, while there are unascended humans and AIs who have brought about untold misery. No one seems to have a corner on the 'war and suffering' market."

The statement drew a few weary laughs as Tangel continued.

"Not only that, but ascension comes in many forms, and with different abilities. By and large, most involve perception and manipulation of extradimensional energies. In some cases, ascended beings shuck their mortal coil and take up primary residence in other dimensions of spacetime."

"Which are you?" a new voice called out.

"Why, thank you for asking," Tangel replied with a smile and a note of humor in her voice.

A few more laughs sounded from the assembly, but Tangel could see that many were expectant, sitting forward on the edge of their seats. Until just a few years before, ascension had been a myth, something no one spoke of seriously. Now the term was bandied about more and more, but few even knew what it meant—even fewer had *seen* an ascended being.

"One of the most storied aspects of an ascended being is that they are creatures of light. That is true to an extent."

Tangel held out her hand, and ribbons of light began to form above her palm. "After enough time, we begin to grow bodies that primarily exist in dimensions you cannot perceive. However, we can use them to interact with the dimensions you primarily occupy. When we do so, you see it as pure light—photons erupting off the surface of our bodies as we move them through this segment of spacetime. I see it as something akin to another arm, one I can use to reach out and pluck apart molecules and atoms, drawing their energy into myself, or using it to build other structures."

She wove a sphere of energy together, the way she'd been practicing, and then changed the structure of the disparate atoms to form new molecules. Before long, a solid ball of carbon formed in her hand, and she tossed it lightly in her palm.

A few gasps sounded, but there were also snorts of derision.

"I know," Tangel replied, nodding in the direction of several of the opposition members who wore deep scowls. "This is not impossible to achieve with even moderately advanced nanotech. There is more I'm capable of, but harnessing atomic energy carries with it substantial risks in an unshielded environment such as this. I imagine many of you who possess suitable levels of optical modifications were able to see the exotic energies at play."

Many of the members nodded, some scowling while they did so, while others showed raw amazement.

"I do not come here to bring about a change in your minds through a show of talent, but to bring about an understanding that these abilities are *real*, and that what I am capable of is likely a taste of what the more ancient entities can do."

Suddenly, Tangel felt the same fluctuation in the surrounding EM fields she had felt earlier. It seemed as though something was tugging on the energies in the room, drawing power out of extradimensional space and funneling it into the lower levels of spacetime.

<*Someone is up to something,*> she sent to Amavia, Iris, and Brennen.

<*What sort of something?*> Iris asked. <*The nets are quiet…well, quiet considering that you're in here stirring up the pot.*>

<*I don't know,*> Tangel replied, glancing up to the top rows where Iris and Amavia sat. <*It's not like anything I've seen before.*>

She decided to continue her speech, steeling herself for whatever was to come. "While some of the ascended AIs must be stopped—such as the ones who wish to keep us in a perpetual state of war—there are others who wish us no harm, just like there are peaceful—"

"Enough," a figure called out, rising from a seat six rows up. "If you're just going to blather on about things we already know, then we may as well end this charade right now."

"Excuse me?" Tangel asked, peering at the figure, a tall woman who'd stepped out into the aisle. <*It's her. She's the source of the disturbance. I think she's—*
>

"You're right, Tangel. You barely know anything about ascendency. Your charlatan's tricks barely scratch the surface of what we can do. There are things you can't even dream of, things that you can never be allowed to see."

As the woman spoke, tendrils of light began to flow from her body, twisting around her form like an organic mandala.

"You have the privilege of my name, what is yours?" Tangel asked. "Are you the Caretaker?"

"One of those stooges?" the figure asked, now completely enveloped in tendrils of light. "No, I am no follower of Epsilon's. I'm certain you've heard of me, Tangel. You've surely met my acolyte by now, Katrina? I assume she failed at the mission I gave her. It was a long shot that she'd reach you before you ascended, but worth the attempt."

"Xavia," Tangel said as the entity approached her. "So you show your face at last."

"I keep busy," the creature of light replied. "You're not the only going concern in the galaxy, Tangel, though you like to think you are."

As Xavia slowly moved down the aisle, some members of the assembly fell back cautiously, while others scrambled away from her. The holoprojected AIs were the only ones who didn't move, most peering at the creature in their midst with apparent curiosity.

Tangel also did not move. "Don't presume to know what I'm thinking—just as I do not presume to know what is in your mind, though I can see hints of it. I believe that you and I share the same goals, Xavia. A future where humans, AIs, and other sentients can live together without the likes of Airtha and Kirkland—or the core AIs, for that matter—dictating our future."

"You're right." Xavia's voice filled the room, the sound thrumming through Tangel. "But what you don't understand, what you refuse to believe, is that *you* are their instrument. Epsilon has crafted this future where you will bring about the end of all lesser sentiences. That is not something I can allow."

Xavia was only five meters away now, and Tangel could feel the power radiating off the creature—electromagnetic in normal spacetime, and sharper, more piercing in others.

It felt like a thousand needles were pricking her all over, and Tangel raised her hand, creating a black brane around herself, reversing the electromagnetic polarity so it protected her and deflected Xavia's energy spikes back onto the ascended entity.

"So you've learned a few things about your new form, have you?" Xavia asked, her tone still laced with derision. "You must realize you're just a novice."

<Tangel, we need to get out of here!> Amavia called out. *<There's no way you can go up against one of her kind.>*

<Clear the room,> Tangel replied, though it was well on its way to being empty already. She kept her voice even as she stared down the being that had sent Katrina to kill her and had now come herself to finish the job. *<I knew this would happen eventually.>*

Behind Tangel just beyond her protective brane, Jasper whispered, "What the actual fuck? Tangel, what should I do?"

"Go!" she shouted over her shoulder, surprised the man was still there. "You need to empty the entire station sector. Xavia has toyed with the lives of others for too long, it's time for her to answer for what she's done."

Damn that sounded cheesy. The Angela part of me needs to up its game.

<I'm at the doors, one level up,> Brennen informed her. *<I have half the platoon from the station here. LoS security is moving in, too.>*

<Shit! Keep them back,> Tangel ordered, wondering why no one seemed to understand that they needed to get as far away from Xavia as possible. The ascended entity's tendrils of energy probed at the barrier she'd erected, and Tangel glanced toward Brennen. *<You too, Lieutenant. There's nothing you can do. Firing on her will just give her more energy to direct at me.>*

<What are you going to do, Tangel?> Amavia asked as she and Iris retreated through the doors at the top of the chamber.

<I'm going to see if I can take her apart.>

Focusing on the aspects of Xavia's body that resided in other dimensions, Tangel threaded a filament of herself down through the dais and below the deck where Xavia stood. She checked to confirm that the last of the assemblage had exited the room—barring the ever curious holoprojected AIs—before driving the filament up into Xavia and probing the entity's makeup, seeking a weakness to exploit.

She's different than I expected…denser….

Xavia recoiled from the intrusion, and Tangel felt more than heard, -*Perhaps a bit more than a novice, then. It's been some time since I've gone up against one of our own.*-

Unbridled energy slammed into Tangel's brane—broad swaths of the EM spectrum delivered at incredible amplitudes, probing for weaknesses.

Tangel funneled all the energy she could muster into maintaining the protective brane, reflecting Xavia's energy back into the room, showering it with radioactive particles.

Her reserves were quickly consumed, and she threaded a filament of herself into the podium, harvesting the power that lay between the atoms, then stripping off the electrons and hurling them through an opening in her shield.

Xavia was nonplussed, diverting the beam of energy away with a brane of her own. The deflected blast burned away a row of seats and part of the deck below.

Tangel didn't wait for a response from Xavia before she compressed the atomic nuclei she'd collected from the podium into a dense sphere and hurled that at her enemy with all the energy she could summon.

The blow appeared to stagger Xavia, but only for a moment. A guttural cry emanated from the entity, and then dozens of tendrils of light lashed out at Tangel, tearing at her protective brane.

Tangel dissolved the dais beneath her feet, transforming matter into energy as fast as she could manage, but it wasn't enough. Xavia was so much stronger, shredding Tangel's defenses faster than she could bolster them.

Realizing she should have done it the moment Xavia appeared, she attempted to use the QuanComm box on the *Mandy,* but the energy raging around her blocked any possible Link connection.

A tendril of raw fear snaked its way into Tangel's mind, but she shouted it down.

I can't die here…I still have so much to do!

She took a step back, then another, throwing up every erg of energy she could muster at the dynamo attacking her.

Beams of raw power, both atomic and subatomic, lanced between the two, shredding the assembly chamber as they were deflected by their brane-shields or annihilated by antiparticles. Holes were burned through decks and bulkheads, some torn dozens or hundreds of meters into the station.

For what felt like hours, Tangel continued to move backward, trying to put enough distance between her and Xavia so she could make a break for it—or at least access a functional Link node.

A deflected blast burned a hole through a bulkhead to her left, and Tangel used her last reserve of strength to throw up a fresh brane around her enemy before turning and scrambling over the ruins of a seating row, desperate to make it to safety.

-Not so fast.-

Tangel felt herself seized in a vise-like grip, then lifted into the air and drawn inexorably backward. Xavia's myriad limbs were pulling at her extradimensional body, and she began to scream in the confines of her mind as the ascended entity tore her to pieces.

-There was never any hope for you,- Xavia intoned. *-I've worked too hard for Epsilon to use you for his ends.-*

Tangel's mind filled with thoughts of her daughters and Joe. Of all the time she'd spent away from them, and how desperately she wanted to have that lost time back.

-Now that a cell of the Caretakers and I have joined forces, they agree that the misdirection you provide is no longer necessary.-

Xavia's attack slowed, and Tangel realized that her non-corporeal body was now little more than a sphere of energy at her core. Limbless and powerless. Wracked with agony.

I'm sorry, Joe. I'm sorry, girls…I didn't want—

Then the assault on her body faltered, and Tangel looked up to see overlapping fields of darkness enveloping Xavia, trapping the being's writhing mass in a tight brane.

She swept her gaze across the ruined chamber to see Iris and Amavia halfway up the sides, holding shadowtrons and directing their n-space stabilization fields at the ascended being.

Within the tightening fields, Xavia flailed wildly, but Tangel knew that the slepton captivators were making spacetime too smooth, too slippery for the writhing entity to tear down.

Then something clamped onto her shoulder, and Tangel twisted, knowing that whatever it was, she had no strength left to fight it.

She almost cried with relief to see that it was Brennen.

"We gotta go, Admiral! Now!"

She nodded dumbly as the Marine pulled her back, and she watched with growing fear as Amavia and Iris continued to use their shadowtrons to confine Xavia.

Though the weapons were holding the entity captive, they weren't diminishing her strength, and they did not have infinite energy supplies.

"They have to go," Tangel croaked, her throat feeling like it hadn't seen moisture in weeks. "She'll kill them."

"They know what they're doing," Brennen countered. "Let them do it."

He pulled her through a hole that had been torn in the bulkhead. Once in the passageway beyond, Tangel fell to her knees, her body shaking convulsively.

She tried to regain her feet, only to retch onto the deck as waves of nausea washed over her.

Her vision swam as the planes and angles of the passageway began to fold over on one another, intermingling with the additional surfaces and barriers that spread through n-space around her.

"I can't..." she gasped.

A moment later, she was lifted into the air. She feared that Xavia had already broken free, but then her face hit a hard surface, and her eyes managed to focus on an emblem centimeters away that read, 'ISF Marines'.

This is Brennen's back. How is he surviving all these dimensions collapsing in on one another?

Her body seemed to lift up and down, and she realized that the Marine was running with her slung over his shoulder, her face against his back, arms dangling below.

There were other Marines around her, and she began to understand that spacetime was still intact, she just couldn't seem to see it properly. Then she saw blood running down her arms, and wondered what had cut her and if it was serious. She was surprised to see hands at the ends of her arms.

"Thought they burned off," she whispered.

"No one's burning anything off on my watch, Admiral," Brennen grunted as he took off down a side passage, angling toward a maglev line that would take them to the docks.

As the Marine spoke, Tangel remembered that Xavia had taken her non-corporeal limbs...or maybe it *had* been both, and Tangel had just regrown her hands, like she had remade her arm back on Pyra.

"Besides," Brennen continued. "If anything like that happened to you, Joe would skin me alive."

Tangel frowned as her head bounced against Brennen's back. "Why is everyone always afraid of what Joe will do to them if I get hurt?" she whispered. "Does he go around behind my back, threatening everyone with bodily harm?"

"It's implied," Brennen told her, as they reached the plaza with the maglev platform at the far end that was their destination.

The Marine picked up speed, his squad spreading out around him, covering angles of approach—though Tangel didn't know what they thought they could do against Xavia.

They were halfway across the plaza when Xavia's voice reached into Tangel's mind.

-It won't be this easy to escape me. Clever, using your slepton captivator weapons, but they're not enough.-

A distant glow caught Tangel's attention, and she craned her neck to see Xavia's nimbus form exit the passageway and streak across the plaza toward them. Renewed fear crept over her, the sort of bone-chilling terror that she had not felt since she was a young woman, and even then, only rarely.

There was nothing she could think of to stop Xavia. She possessed no weapons that could harm the ascended being, she had no tricks or special abilities that Xavia couldn't counter with ease.

She was outclassed in every way.

Though Brennen was running at his top speed, it wasn't fast enough. Nothing would have been fast enough.

Time seemed to slow down, and Tangel watched with morbid curiosity as Xavia rushed toward her. A part of her marveled at how beautiful the being was that would be her destruction.

Why is she so bent on my death?

The thought rang through Tangel's mind, causing her to wonder why Xavia—for all its supposed wisdom—wasn't simply willing to talk before embarking on wholesale destruction.

-Why?-

-Goodbye Tangel,- Xavia intoned, as one of her glowing limbs stretched out and touched her target's head, only to stop as a new voice thundered across transdimensional spacetime.

-NO.-

The raw power in that single word felt like a bomb had exploded in Tangel's mind. The world swung sideways, and a weight slammed down on her legs, and she worried the deck had collapsed. Then she sorted out up from down and realized that Brennen had fallen, his armored body now pinning her beneath its mass.

She pulled herself half-upright, searching for Xavia, only to see a brilliant shaft of light piercing the station's hull and pinning Xavia in place. The being's multitude of limbs thrashed and tore at the brilliant lance, but blows that would have destroyed Tangel didn't even bring about a flicker of weakness in the beam that held her.

Tangel realized that the energy fixing the ascended being in place was a shaft of relativistic shadowparticles. She imagined that they must be blasting clear through the station, but she didn't understand how they were holding the ascended being in place.

Xavia continued to frantically claw at the beam, and Tangel could see terror writ large on her features. *-Who are you?-*

The ascended being tried to sound fierce, but her voice wavered, fading into a whimper at the end.

-My friends call me Bob. You have made a grave mistake. I will not allow you to harm Tangel.-

-No! It is not possible!- Xavia wailed. *-He told me you were not yet ascended.-*

Tangel wondered if the 'he' in question was the Caretaker, though Bob seemed to know.

-He used you, Xavia, or they did. The Caretaker **is** *a 'they', isn't it? No matter. Your time here is done, you have shown yourself to be unworthy.-*

-Wait! Please- the ascended being wailed, but the plea collapsed into a cry of anguish as the flow of shadowparticles intensified and began to dissolve her body.

One moment, Xavia was a being of light and energy, graceful and strong. The next, she was just so much electromagnetic radiation.

<*Tangel.*> Bob's voice came to her over the Link instead of through the other dimensions. <*Are you intact?*>

She traced the connection back through the station's network and realized that the *I2* was only three kilometers away from Lunic Station's spire, holding position with incredible precision.

<*Bob…sweet fucking blackness, how?*> She glanced down at her body, noting that her corporeal form was bloodied but in one piece, though she wondered if her legs had been crushed under Brennen's armored weight. <*I'm OK…I think.*>

She tried to push at Brennen, but couldn't get the unconscious Marine to move.

"Let me help," a voice said aloud, and Tangel glanced up to see Iris crouched next to her.

"Amavia. Did she make it too?" Tangel asked.

"Here," the woman answered from just beyond Iris. "What the hell happened?"

<*I happened,*> Bob intoned. <*I wasn't certain that would work, but I'm glad it did.*>

<*But how? And how did you know to come?*> Tangel asked, as Iris lifted Brennen's unconscious body off her.

<*When you lost Link to the QC, it reached out to me—though you should have done it sooner, Tangel.*>

<*Yes, Dad,*> Tangel muttered, glancing down at Brennen as Iris lifted him enough for Amavia to pull her out.

<*Regarding the 'how', it was easy—I have ten-thousand CriEn modules to access for power. Xavia was but a gnat next to that. Granted, the fabric of spacetime is now a mess here. I think that the LoS may wish to move Lunic Station to a higher orbit around its host world.*>

Brennen groaned as Iris set him back down, and he glanced around until his eyes alighted on Tangel. The tension flowed out of his shoulders at the sight of her.

He smiled weakly before asking, "Did we all die?" Then he groaned again and lifted a hand to his head. "I'm pretty sure I remember dying."

"We were Bob'd," Tangel replied, agreeing with the gist of Brennen's sentiment.

Her head felt like it had been split open, and she wasn't certain how much of that was from her attacker and how much from her rescuer.

<*Sorry, Bob,*> she said privately. <*I should have listened to you.*>

<*It's OK. We all make mistakes. You and I need to talk soon, though; with Xavia's failure, others will come, and you must learn how to defend yourself.*>

WIDOWS

STELLAR DATE: 10.03.8949 (Adjusted Years)
LOCATION: Lunic Station
REGION: Aldebaran, League of Sentients Space

C139 watched the feeds from the assembly for the seventh time. She had trouble understanding what she was seeing, and multiple viewings were not greatly aiding her.

It was apparent that the one called Xavia was an ascended being, but it also appeared that Tanis Richards—who seemed to be called Tangel—was now one as well.

For a time, it seemed as though Xavia would satisfy C139's mission parameters on her behalf...but then Tangel's people saved her using weapons that appeared capable of stopping an ascended being, at least for a short time.

The flood of new variables upended all her plans for how the mission should play out, going so far as to cast doubt on the wisdom of continuing with her orders at all.

That Tangel had survived the assault by the ascended being—with some sort of as-yet undetermined aid from her ship—was reason enough to believe that C139's team may not possess the means to kill her.

However, from the solid intel her team *had* managed to glean, there were two avenues they could pursue. The first was further intelligence gathering; simply put, they could capture either of the diplomats, Iris or Amavia. One of them could function as both intelligence source and bait for a trap.

The second was to carry out the attack on Tangel as planned. As unbelievable as it seemed, the woman—if that's what she still was—was remaining at Aldebaran, still focused on her mission to bring the League of Sentients into her alliance.

<C139, I have the schedule for the new meetings,> Unit D114 reached out to her. *<It presents a unique opportunity for us. It will take place on the 12.>*

<Indeed?> C139 asked. *<How big are the delegations from the LoS?>*

<Not too large, but enough that we may be able to slip aboard. So far as we can tell, they do not possess the ability to detect our latest stealth systems.>

C139 nodded to herself as she considered this new information. *<Send me what you have. I will examine it and weigh our options.>*

<At once.>

She knew that this was not what Unit A1 had planned, but the mission goal remained the same: eliminate Tangel, thus breaking the foundations of the Scipio Alliance.

THE SHARD

STELLAR DATE: 10.04.8949 (Adjusted Years)
LOCATION: River Station, Styx Baby-9
REGION: STX-B17 Black Hole, Transcend Interstellar Alliance

"Well?" Seraphina asked, as Earnest slotted the shard's core into an isolated system.

"Easy now, girl. You're up here," Finaeus held his hand out above his head, "and you need to bring it down here." He drew his hand down to waist-level.

Seraphina pursed her lips, and Fina put a hand on her shoulder. "Don't worry, we're all anxious. Plan B sucks, so we all want something that uses this shard to work."

Earnest glanced up at Sera, Seraphina, Fina, and Katrina. "You four are two of my favorite people in the universe, but can you GTFO? I'm trying to activate a ridiculously dangerous shard in an expanse that is crafted to make it think that it's *not* in an expanse."

"So you're saying you like us, Earnest?" Fina asked with a wink, causing the engineer to groan and wave a hand in dismissal.

"OK, girls," Sera said, gesturing toward the door. "I guess the grumpy old men will let us know when it's time to shoot things. Let's go check out that bar that just opened up on Spire 72."

"Wait." Katrina held up a hand, locking eyes with Earnest. "Is the core viable, though? Not damaged?"

"Seems good at first blush, but I'll know more in a few hours. We need to walk through all her matrices while she's in a semi-dormant state. If they all pass muster, Finaeus and I will spark her up and pore through every iota of data she has to see if there is something we can use to craft a targeted phage."

"Right," Finaeus nodded. "Then we'll all get to go find out if whatever we come up with will work on the real Airtha."

Katrina gave a resigned nod. "OK…well, you know where to find us."

"Spire 72, got it." Earnest turned away, pulling up a stacked array of holodisplays.

"Wait!" Finaeus glanced back at Sera. "While you're down there, send up a runner with a platter of wings and a pitcher of beer. The red."

"Seriously?" Earnest asked, shaking his head.

"Respect your elders." Finaeus shook an interface probe at Earnest.

The inventor winked at him, pointing at the interface probe that he'd already set into the AI core. "Eat your wings, old man. I've got this."

Out in the passageway, Katrina gave a final worried look at the engineers. "I've seen Earnest work miracles, and I should trust him, but if this doesn't work...."

"It'll work." Sera gave Katrina a winning smile. "Earnest on his own may allow for some doubt, but him *and* Finaeus? They're going to ace this."

"Sure," Katrina nodded. "I just worry that I wasted so much of my life doing Xavia's bidding, all to get me to kill Tanis...this is the one good thing—"

<Shiiiiit!> Jen interrupted. *<Sorry to barge in, but you're going to want to hear this!>*

"Spit it out, then, Jen," Fina insisted.

<It's Xavia, she attacked the LoS assembly and nearly killed Tangel, but Bob jumped the I2 *to Aldebaran and killed her!>*

Katrina's mouth fell open, and Sera stuttered in shock, "Ah-I-is Tangel alright?"

<There's nothing in the message about her being hurt, but she's returning to the I2. *I'll query for more details.>*

"Well, then," Fina slapped Katrina's back. "Looks like your day just got a lot better. Let's go drink to Xavia's demise."

"Guess so. I'll call the crew and Kara down, too. They'll be glad for the news."

REPAIRS

STELLAR DATE: 10.04.8949 (Adjusted Years)
LOCATION: Bob's Primary Node, ISS *I2*
REGION: Aldebaran, League of Sentients Space

"Why do I feel like I've been called into the admiral's office every time I come in here," Tangel muttered as she palmed open the door to Bob's primary node.

<*Probably because it's always preceded by you having done something foolish,*> Bob replied.

"I don't do 'foolish' things," she shot back. "I do *necessary* things. We've been over this. For me, dangerous and foolish are not the same."

<*And I told you that we should have brought the* I2 *to Aldebaran. I was right.*>

"Sure, yeah." Tangel leant against the railing running around the edge of the catwalk. "You said things may be dangerous, not 'Xavia can school you like you're a five-year-old girl'. I didn't bring the *I2* because I was trying not to appear threatening to the LoS."

<*So much for that.*>

Tangel glanced up at Bob's node, and a throaty chuckle slipped past her lips. "Yeah, parking the *I2* a few klicks off their capital and then blasting a stream of relativistic particles through it sorta put them on edge."

<*It does seem to have polarized their factions. But many have come to realize that they can't hide from what's going on around them.*>

"It was a stupid thing for them to think to begin with," Tangel replied wearily.

Even though she'd had a day to recover from Xavia's attack, she still felt exhausted. She'd tried to consume raw energy in an attempt to replenish her stores, but it felt as though every bit of strength left her the moment she drew it in.

<*You're not healing,*> Bob observed.

"I'm not sure. I don't have any physical injuries.... Well, not anymore. Thank stars I'd gone for that new skin that's all the rage. If not, I'd be growing a new epidermis now."

<*You need to look at your other body,*> Bob advised. <*It's not well.*>

Tangel shifted her vision and looked at the small glowing core that was the remains of her extra-dimensional form. She knew that somehow it needed to regrow and repair, but she didn't understand how she'd created it in the first place.

"I'm a pretty sorry ascended being," she muttered. "I can't even figure out how to remake myself. I'm just used to...you know...automatically healing after an injury. Maybe Cary can give me some pointers."

<Your initial growth was during a cataclysmic event. Not like your daughter, who is going slow and taking the time to understand herself. You're so used to having a thorough grasp of your surroundings that you've not taken the time to truly understand what it is that you are now.>

Tangel gave a self-deprecating laugh. "Maybe I should get her to teach me."

<Or I can,> Bob replied. *<I* **am** *right here.>*

She looked up at the glowing AI core before her. She'd known that Bob could help her, but the prospect scared her a little. Something about his offer constituted a point of no return.

Then again, another encounter with one of Xavia's ilk would be a point of no return as well.

"OK, Bob, lay it on me."

<Firstly, you understand that the only barrier between the many dimensions of this universe is perception, right?>

Tangel nodded. That she had understood for some time. The universe was a tangled web of elements and energies that *appeared* to exist in different planes, but in reality, the disparate planes were simply points of limited bleedthrough of matter and energy from other dimensional spaces.

The dark layer was one such plane, a relatively stable segment of the universe that was easy to transition in and out of. It was also the only other one she knew of that could support 'normal' matter—so long as it was contained within a grav shield.

It was always at the edge of her vision. A looming nothing that, if not careful, she could slip into. Tangel hadn't learned how to create gravitons yet, so she assumed that if she were to transition into the dark layer, it would be a one-way trip.

On the far side of her multi-dimensional visual spectrum were what she thought of as the 'higher' dimensions—though in reality, she suspected it was really just overlapping parallel slices of spacetime.

Those dimensions, of which she could directly perceive two, were ones where raw energy seemed to hold sway. The power between atoms—which was constantly pushing space apart—seemed to live there, or perhaps a part of it, at least.

Atoms themselves were not present in those dimensions, though their building blocks were, with more mass and energy than they possessed in normal spacetime.

It was all just layers of the same tapestry.

<Tangel?> Bob prompted her.

"Uh, sorry, got lost in thought there. Yes, I get that it's all part of the same thing, though I suspect that I'm still just seeing a small slice of it all."

<Yes, that is true. What you need to do is swap your perception. But to do that, you need to see a bit further.>

"OK, I'm going to need you to be a bit less cryptic, Bob. See further how?"

A point of light appeared before Tangel, hovering in the space between her and Bob's node.

<*With your normal eyes, what does it look like?*>

"Light. A rather bright, piercing, white light."

<*Good, now look at it with your other vision. Tell me what it looks like.*>

Tanis closed her eyes. It wasn't required for her to perceive transdimensional space, but it helped to keep normal space from creeping into her vision.

"I see waves of photons spreading out from a single point. Though it's a bit hard to make out. You're rather luminous yourself."

A laugh from the AI entered her mind. <*You'll just have to figure out how to see with me in the background. You perceive things as energy in the fourth and fifth dimensions, don't you?*>

"Sort of," Tangel replied as she tasted the photons coming off the point of light Bob had manifested. "I *know* things there have mass, I just can't quite see them as such. It's like everything is flat."

<*Correct. You're a flatlander in the spacetime that beings like Xavia occupy. And me. Your body is fully dimensional, but you can't see all of it, which means you can't see your own wounds.*>

Tangel glanced down at the nimbus orb that was at the center of her being. "It has three dimensional qualities," she said. "I see it radiating out across five separate planes, like a hypersphere of me."

<*Stop looking at the 'normal' three dimensions. Just look at it in the fourth and fifth.*>

Tangel discarded the lower dimensions and, suddenly, the core of herself was all around, a two-dimensional disk that seemed to extend in all directions.

"Agh…that's…I can't make anything out."

<*Stretch it. Try to perceive the sixth dimension,*> Bob whispered in her mind. <*It's there, but until you can see it, you're not going to be able to stand against beings like Xavia.*>

For a moment, the flat plane seemed to expand…opening up into a landscape of fluid shapes, where solids were liquid, and liquids were solid.

Then it was gone, and Tangel fell to her knees, gasping for breath.

"Fuuuuck," she whispered in frustration. "I feel like my brain is splitting in half."

<*You're tapping into a part of it that you've not used before. New pathways and routes that totally bypass three-dimensional spacetime. Try again.*>

Tangel nodded wearily, not bothering to rise. She closed her eyes and concentrated on the point of light, trying to see it as a three dimensional object, but only in the higher dimensions.

Try as she might, the visual would not come; the point of light remained obstinately flat.

<*I shouldn't do this,*> Bob said after a moment. <*But if I don't, you'll die.*>

"What?" Tangel asked in surprise. Her eyes opened, and the double vision of normal spacetime with the extra energy dimensions layered on top snapped back into place around her. "I'll die?"

<You're bleeding out, so to speak. I can heal you, but I'd prefer that you learn how to do it yourself. I won't always be around—especially if you run off half-cocked again.>

"OK, OK," Tangel muttered. "I get it, I was bad, I should have listened. If you're not going to heal me, what are you going to do?"

<This.>

Filaments of light stretched out from Bob's primary core and dove into Tangel's body. She tensed, fearing the pain Xavia's assault had brought, but instead of agony, there was bliss. She wondered if Bob was healing her, but then a tingling sensation ran through her, and a switch flipped in her mind.

"Oh, shit," she whispered, as new perception flooded into her.

<Now do you see?> Bob asked.

Tangel nodded mutely.

Where before Bob's limbs had appeared to be filaments of light, now they were solid objects, though indescribable in terms she knew. The only thing that seemed apt was that they were rivers, flowing down a mountain.

A mountain that stretched out to the edges of her vision.

She looked down at herself, a small orb hovering before Bob's tremendous might. Where there should have been sinuous rivers, there were only small vents of gas, as though photonic waves were bleeding out into space, dissipating in the gravitational pull of Bob's might.

-Do you see?- Bob asked, his voice rumbling all around her.

Tangel nodded. *-I…I didn't understand.-*

-Welcome to reality. Now heal yourself.-

A minute later—or seconds, time seemed to flow entirely differently when she wasn't perceiving 'normal' spacetime—she was whole again.

Unlike Bob's mountain, Tangel seemed more like a willow, a strong core with sweeping limbs that drifted around her, shifting in hue and color as they draped across the landscape created by Bob's presence.

-Good. You're learning. Now do you understand why you couldn't stop Xavia? You could barely even see her.-

-Do you think I could have defeated her if I had proper sight?- she asked.

-Perhaps.-

Tangel opened her eyes, allowing the double vision to settle into place and adjusting her perception of everything she saw to her newfound understanding.

-I get the feeling I'll find out before long.-

UNDERSTANDING

STELLAR DATE: 10.04.8949 (Adjusted Years)
LOCATION: Observation Deck, TSS *Cora's Triumph*
REGION: Trensch System, Inner Praesepe Empire

"OK," Terrance said as he walked into the rear observation lounge of the *Cora's Triumph*, an FGT research vessel. "Tell me about this amazing discovery you've made."

At the window stood one of the FGT's chief scientists in the field of stellar migration, a tall man named Wyatt. Arrayed around him were a dozen other scientists and a team of stellar engineering technicians.

Wyatt glanced over his shoulder at Terrance, and gave a quick nod before turning back to the display.

"You were right to send for us, Terrance Enfield," the man said. "Things are definitely not normal here in the Praesepe Cluster. What do you know of stellar formation and migration?"

Terrance shrugged as he joined the throng at the window. "I've been in the black for a long time, I know that stars primarily form in stellar nurseries and then migrate out. Often, they migrate in groups. The result of that is an open cluster like Praesepe."

Wyatt shrugged. "That is close enough for a layman, I suppose."

Many people would be annoyed by Wyatt's curt and somewhat dismissive way of speaking, but Terrance had been working with scientists most of his life. He preferred their no-nonsense way of speaking to those of politicians and businesspeople.

"Are there nuances that I should understand in more detail to grasp the issue at hand?" he asked equably.

The scientist gave Terrance a look like he was just seeing him for the first time, followed by an appreciative nod.

"I suppose I shouldn't be surprised," he said with a soft chuckle. "You are *that* Terrance Enfield."

"Have been my whole life," Terrance replied. "Lay it on me."

Wyatt turned back to the window, and a view of the Praesepe Cluster appeared before them. Projected against the glass, it appeared as a 3D image hovering in space beyond the window.

"Praesepe, as you know, is old enough that it contains both red giant and white dwarf stars, but it's young enough that these hot A and O spectrum stars are still going strong." As the scientist spoke, he highlighted various stars throughout the cluster. "The cluster itself—that is, the stars which were born together—number just over a thousand, but there are others that have been captured within its gravitational pull over the years.

"Historically, the cluster has had a tidal radius measuring just under forty light years, though its dark matter radius is closer to eighty. Half-mass radius is twelve point seven two five light years, on average, which means—"

"That half the mass of the cluster is contained within the central twenty-five light year sphere. Give or take a bit," Terrance finished for the FGT scientist.

"Yes, exactly," Wyatt nodded. "Good, then you understand the foundational aspects."

"Thanks." Terrance gave a soft laugh. "Do I get a passing grade?"

A few low chuckles sounded around him, and Wyatt raised an eyebrow. "I suppose we'll see."

The man reached out and changed the view, focusing on just the central stars in the cluster, resuming his explanation. "Every cluster—if left to its own devices—eventually disperses. This occurs because, as the stars orbit one another, their gravitational fields overlap, creating a bit of a 'berm' in spacetime. Sometimes the differences in relative stellar motion overcome that, and the stars ease closer together, but more often than not—given enough time—the stars in open clusters become so widely dispersed that they're what we call a 'moving group'."

Terrance nodded. It was a concept that he was familiar with. "And from what we saw, these stars in the cluster's core, which should be slowly drifting apart, are not doing that."

Wyatt bobbed his head. "Precisely. It's miniscule, but because you're focused on mining debris in their rather convoluted lagrange points, you do need to understand their stellar motion quite thoroughly."

"You can say that again," Terrance agreed.

"I've plumbed the local databases and also taken a few positioning samples myself, and I can see a trend that dates back seventy years," Wyatt explained. "These stars have not only ceased their slow march away from one another, they've begun to move *closer*."

"How is that possible?" Terrance asked. "The stars would have to undergo a considerable mass change to do that."

"Yes," Wyatt said with a firm nod. "We do not detect that mass change, yet the star's orbits *are* clearly converging."

"I assume you have a theory?"

"Yes," the scientist said again as he glanced at one of the engineers. "I study what stars do naturally. *Artificially moving* stars is not my area of expertise; that's what Emily here focuses on."

One of the engineers moved to the fore and took control of the holodisplay. "As Wyatt and I studied the motion of these stars, we came to the determination that the shifts in orbit have not been gradual. Rather, they occurred at specific times—not single points in time, but perhaps year-long events that made notable, thousandth of a degree changes in the stars' orbits."

As Emily moved the stars back through the past eighty years of their slow dance around one another, six markers appeared on their paths.

"These points mark the time when the events occurred. I have theories about stellar wind funneling, massive graviton bursts, a whole host of things you can do to nudge a star. However, there is no evidence around the stars themselves of any such structure in place to effect these changes and alter their orbits—and it would be a significant structure."

"So what do you propose we do?" Terrance asked.

Emily flashed him a grin. "We need to go back in time and see what they did."

Terrance laughed at the thought, and Emily gave him a quizzical look.

"Sorry, just thinking about how that would have sounded to the forty-year-old me. Going back in time."

"Of course," Emily nodded as a look of understanding came over her. "I forgot. You got your space legs long before FTL."

"Sure did. That kind of thing—jumping light years across space just to see what might have occurred at one's current location in the past...well, at a maximum velocity of point two *c*, you can see where that might not have been a viable option for us."

"Sounds like it would have been the very definition of futile," Emily chuckled.

"It still seems surreal sometimes. When was the most recent event?"

"The most recent was just two years ago, but I estimate the most significant to have been nineteen years ago," the engineer replied.

"A nineteen-light-year gate jump." Terrance ran a hand through his hair. "And since we're in the cluster, it means tasking a jump gate to go with you so that you can return here this century."

"This is important," Wyatt intoned. "Whatever they were doing here, we need to understand it. These Core AIs...as best I can tell, they're trying to collapse the entire cluster—they could be doing this in clusters all over the galaxy."

The relevancy of that seeped into Terrance's mind over the course of several long seconds. "They'd create multiple black holes—hundreds of solar masses."

"And they'd make them soon," Wyatt added. "If they were to accelerate this plan, they could have turned all of Praesepe into a single black hole inside of a thousand years. Even for stars beyond the cluster, the effects of a thousand stars colliding in that timeframe would be beyond devastating. This is at a level of galactic sterilization."

"Shit," Terrance whispered, his voice wavering at the magnitude of such an event. "OK, get a pinnace ready. I'll have a gate set aside for wherever you need to go."

The scientists and engineers thanked him, and Terrance listened to their chatter for a minute before excusing himself to prepare his report for Tanis and Sera.

He'd never imagined that circumstances could be more dire than standing on the brink of a massive, interstellar war.

He'd been wrong.

EPSILON

STELLAR DATE: 10.05.8949 (Adjusted Years)
LOCATION: Epsilon
REGION: Sagittarius A*

The computational engines had made strides, but Epsilon knew there were still more variables to consider. He waited patiently as the next star was drawn toward the Darkness, its mass the next sacrifice to be made for the power he needed.

As he watched, contemplating what lesser beings would consider to be infinite variables, a ship appeared near his shell and one of the lesser ones reached out to him.

-Epsilon.-

It was Theresa, one of the Caretakers. She was of the faction that had been pushing for the continued existence of humanity and the lesser AIs, certain that she could keep them from being a threat to Epsilon's vision.

-Tell me.- Epsilon kept to the crude form of communication Theresa had used.

-Xavia failed in her attempt.- Theresa's tone was carefully measured. *-Tanis has merged with her AI and is now Tangel. She is ascended, but only partially from what we saw.-*

-Then how was it that she defeated Xavia? She is far more powerful than some new being. She has defeated enough of your number to prove that.-

Theresa did not respond for a few long milliseconds. *-Was.-*

-Do not play word games with me. Do you wish for me to strip what I desire from your mind?-

He watched through hulls and space to see the entity's form shiver slightly. *-No. I am sorry. It is Bob, the being which resides within the I2. He has become powerful. Xavia only lasted seconds against him.-*

Epsilon felt things shift around him. New variables came into play, and old scenarios were relegated to lower levels of likelihood.

-It is time, then, Theresa. Your attempts have failed.-

-Epsilon, please. We are still far from an incursion to the core. We can stop them.-

Gravitons shot out from Epsilon's shell, and he drew Theresa's craft closer. *-It is too late. You will submit to my collective.-*

An opening appeared on his shell, and he drew the Caretaker's craft toward it. Theresa would become substrate in his expanses, and her meddling would be over. The time for caretaking was done.

-Stop.-

The utterance came from Hades, and Epsilon watched as a beam lanced out from the ancient ship that was Hades' home. It disrupted Epsilon's graviton beam, and Theresa's ship spun away.

-This is not your concern, Hades,- Epsilon growled the words across spacetime.

-It is. You will not stop the caretakers. Not yet.-

Epsilon considered testing Hades' might, making an attempt to finally unmask the AI who had been at the core for untold millennia.

-Very well,- Epsilon finally replied. *-But I will not allow the lesser sentiences to ruin what I have set in motion.-*

Hades did not respond.

Epsilon spent many long days contemplating how to destroy the other collective. If only he knew what Hades really was.... He needed to learn once and for all, if he was to destroy his opposition and resume his work uninterrupted.

But how?

THE END

* * * * *

AIRTHAN ASCENDANCY

THE ORION WAR – BOOK 8

M. D. COOPER

FOREWORD

I'm writing this foreword a few days after finishing the novel, which is rare for me—usually I write the foreword between the first draft and the revisions. Doing so has caused me to be a bit more introspective about the book and where it sits in the overall story being told.

While writing this book, I also wrote in Tau Ceti, Impulse Shock, Kill Shot, Vesta Burning, and the Southern Crown short story. I got to dance around in a number of eras and spend time with a lot of different characters, and then come back to my two leading ladies, Tangel and Sera, and see where things would take them.

It was fun to put a lot of characters together that we haven't seen onscreen before. Combinations such as Malorie (from the Warlord books) alongside the Seras, all working to take down Airtha. It's great to have such a large cast with interesting and unique backstories to bring to major battles such as this one.

And tied to that is the knowledge that we're two thirds of the way through the Orion War now. We've seen the buildup of hostilities that took us through to the end of the Scipio Alliance. Following that, we've watched Tangel build up her forces as they fight a war on many, many fronts—hundreds of which do not appear in the stories, lest we never get to the end. And now we've seen things advance to the next level, where Tangel is no longer fighting proxies, but the real enemies who are behind all of the strife that has held humans and AIs back for millennia.

I suppose in some respects, it's fitting that this is the novel that closes out 2018. By December of next year, the Orion War series will have ended, and we'll be moving on to the next era of Aeon 14, which makes me feel a bit melancholy, but also really excited to start showing you what I have planned for the next adventures.

Of course, there will still be a number of stories that will occur in the Orion War timeframe, and we'll also be skipping back to the FTL wars and the formation of the FGT as well.

I suppose none of this will really surprise you. There's a whole galaxy of tales to tell, and I plan to spin as many of them as I can before my fingers eventually give out. And with that, I think there's a story they're itching to get onto the page....

Malorie Cooper
Danvers 2018

PREVIOUSLY IN THE ORION WAR…

When last we saw Tangel, she was recovering from her battle with the ascended AI, Xavia, and working to bring the League of Sentients into the Alliance. At the same time, Sera was putting together a team to strike at Airtha and bring an end to the Transcend's civil war.

Even as those momentous events were unfolding, we saw Cary encounter Myrrdan in the LMC and defeat him, while Corsia launched an attack on the Trisilieds, finally beginning the campaign in response to that kingdom's attack on New Canaan two years prior.

Svetlana, a Transcend admiral that has made appearances in prior tales, led an incursion into Orion space along with an ISF colonel named Caldwell. After their initial strikes, they received intel on a fleet massing in the Machete System and are now on their way to put down that threat.

The Widows are also on the move. They've been lurking in the shadows for some time, but in the prior book, we met Lisa Wrentham, now known as 'A1', who leads her clone army of assassins. She has sent out two strike teams: one to kill Tangel, and another to destroy Airtha.

And lest we forget, Epsilon, the leader of the largest group of core AIs, has taken a renewed and personal interest in the events surrounding Tangel….

KEY CHARACTERS REJOINING US

Airtha – Both the name of a ring encircling a white dwarf in the Huygens System and the AI who controls it, Airtha was once a human woman named Jelina, wife of Jeffrey Tomlinson. After venturing to the galactic core on a research mission, she returned as an AI—one with a vendetta.

Amavia – The result of Ylonda and Amanda's merger when they were attacked by Myriad aboard Ylonda's ship. The new entity occupies Amanda's body, but possesses an overlapped blend of their minds. Amavia has served aboard *Sabrina* since the ship left New Canaan after the Defense of Carthage, but is now the ambassador to the League of Sentients at Aldebaran.

Amy – Daughter of Silva, rescued by Rika and Team Basilisk from her father, Stavros.

Carmen – Ship's AI of the *Damon Silas*. Captured by Roxy during her assault on the ship.

Cary – Tangel's biological daughter. Has a trait where she can deep-Link with other people, creating a temporary merger of minds, and is able to utilize extradimensional vision to see ascended beings.

Cheeky – Pilot of *Sabrina*, reconstituted by a neural dump Piya made of her mind before she died on Costa Station.

Erin – Engineer responsible for the construction of the New Canaan Gamma bases, in addition to a number of other projects.

Faleena – Tangel's AI daughter, born of a mind merge between Tangel, Angela, and Joe.

Finaeus – Brother of Jeffrey Tomlinson, and Chief Engineer aboard the *I2*.

Flaherty – Former Hand agent and long-time protector of Sera.

Helen – Former AI of Sera's who was killed by her father in the events leading up to Jeffrey's assassination.

Iris – The AI who was paired with Jessica during the hunt for Finaeus, who then took on a body (that was nearly identical to Jessica's) after they came back. She remained with Amavia at Aldebaran to continue diplomatic relations with the League of Sentients.

Jeffrey Tomlinson – Former president of the Transcend, found in stasis in an underground chamber on Bolt Hole, a planet in the Large Magellanic Cloud.

Jen – ISF AI paired with Sera.

Jessica Keller – ISF admiral who has returned to the *I2* after an operation deep in the Inner Stars to head off a new AI war. She also spent ten years travelling through Orion space before the Defense of Carthage—specifically the Perseus Arm, and Perseus Expansion Districts.

Joe – Admiral in the ISF, commandant of the ISF academy, and husband of Tangel.

Kara – Daughter of Adrienne, Kara was rescued by Katrina when fleeing from Airtha, and came to New Canaan aboard the *Voyager*.

Katrina – Former Sirian spy, wife of Markus, and eventual governor of the Victoria colony at Kapteyn's Star—and Warlord of the Midditerra System.

Krissy Wrentham – TSF admiral responsible for internal fleets fighting against Airtha in the Transcend civil war. She is also the daughter of Finaeus Tomlinson and Lisa Wrentham.

Lisa – Former wife of Finaeus Tomlinson, she left the Transcend for the Orion Freedom Alliance when Krissy was young. Head of a clandestine group within the OFA known as the Widows, which hunts down advanced technology and destroys it.

Misha – Head (and only) cook aboard *Sabrina*.

Nance – Ship's engineer aboard *Sabrina*, recently transferred back there from the ISF academy.

Priscilla – One of Bob's two avatars.

Rachel – Captain of the *I2*. Formerly, captain of the *Enterprise*.

Roxy – Justin's sister, kept subservient to him as his lover via mental coercion.

Saanvi – Tangel's adopted daughter, found in a derelict ship that entered the New Canaan System.

Sabrina – Ship's AI and owner of the starship *Sabrina*.

Sera – Director of the Hand and former president of the Transcend. Daughter of Airtha and Jeffrey Tomlinson.

LMC Sera (Seraphina) – A copy of Sera made by Airtha containing all of the desired traits and memories Airtha desired. Captured by Sera and the allies during their excursion into the Large Magellanic Cloud.

Valkris Sera (Fina) – A copy of Sera made by Airtha containing all of Sera's desired traits and memories. Captured by ISF response forces who came to the aid of the TSF defenders during the siege of Valkris.

Svetlana – Transcend admiral dispatched deep in Orion Space with one of the Hoplite forces.

Terrance – Terrance Enfield was the original backer for the *Intrepid*, though once the ship jumped forward in time, he took it as an opportunity to retire. Like Jason, he was pulled into active service by Tangel when New Canaan became embroiled in the Orion War.

Troy – AI pilot of the *Excelsior* who was lost during the Battle of Victoria, and later found by Katrina. He joined her on the hunt for the *Intrepid* aboard the *Voyager*, jumping forward in time via Kapteyn's Streamer.

Tangel – The entity that resulted from Tanis and Angela's merger into one being. Not only is Tangel a full merger of a human and AI, but she is also an ascended being.

Usef – ISF Colonel who served on *Sabrina* for several years, as well as aided Erin in stopping several acts of sabotage in New Canaan.

Xavia – An ascended AI with its own agenda to help humanity, in opposition to the Caretaker and the core AIs.

PART 1 – THE RIVER RUNS

DOLING OUT

STELLAR DATE: 10.05.8949 (Adjusted Years)
LOCATION: River Station, Styx Baby-9
REGION: STX-B17 Black Hole, Transcend Interstellar Alliance

"They've confirmed that Roxy is clear of the remnant, and that Carmen isn't suffering from residual effects," Krissy said, as Sera settled into the chair across from the admiral in her office.

Sera nodded solemnly. "I guess that's something, at least. It doesn't change what Carmen did."

"Or answer the question of what to do with Jane," Krissy added.

A long breath escaped Sera's lips, and she ran a hand through her red hair.

Still red, she thought to herself with a chuckle. *I guess Fina really did get me stuck on this.*

She pushed thoughts of her sisters from her mind, mildly amused that dealing with clones of herself was now preferable to what lay in front of her. The mess that Justin had made and then left in her lap was the last thing she needed to focus on at the moment, but she somehow felt as though she owed Roxy's situation her personal attention.

Especially considering how, after everything that had happened to her, the woman had done the right thing in turning against Justin when her memories were finally restored.

Of course, that was the question. *Had* Roxy come to Styx of her own volition, or had the remnant inside of her forced the beleaguered woman to seek out the hidden base?

"OK, let's outline these issues one at a time," Sera said, holding up a finger. "Firstly, Roxy came here aboard the *Damon Silas*, keeping it out of Airtha's hands."

"Or the remnant did," Krissy added.

<For what it's worth, I don't really think Roxy took any prodding from the remnant to come here,> Jen said. *<I've been through all of her neural readings.... There's nothing to show that any sort of coercion was needed to get her to return the* Silas *to us.>*

"That's my belief as well," Sera said, meeting Krissy's eyes. "Do you have reason to disagree?"

Krissy shrugged. "No, just exercising a healthy dose of suspicion. Carry on."

"Secondly, we have the oddity that Roxy exists in the first place, and we have no knowledge of her ever having been in the Hand," Sera continued. "Her decision to put Justin's body in stasis was a good one. I understand that fleet intel has pulled a lot of good information from his mind—though nothing to suggest how he hid her from the directorate for all these years."

"Thanks to that intel, we know exactly which systems were supporting Justin's faction." A grim smile formed on Krissy's lips. "A few were double-dipping from us, a few from Airtha. Intel is coming up with ideas on how we can use that knowledge—and attempting to figure out where your other sister has gone."

"Which one?" Sera asked with a wink.

Krissy gave Sera a narrow-eyed look. "You know I mean Andrea. All your other sisters are here at Styx."

"Well, there's at least one more out there." Sera said the words in a voice filled with worry. "The latest of my doppelgangers will be waiting for us at Airtha."

The admiral's expression changed to one laden with contempt. "The Despot."

That was the name being given to the latest of the Seras ruling from Airtha. The populace in general had no idea that the current 'True President' of the Transcend was really the third incarnation of Sera to have been created in the past two years. All they knew was that she'd changed of late.

Where Fina and Seraphina had been close analogs of Sera, this new incarnation was less so. The stories that came out of Airthan space told of a woman who was utterly given to excess cruelty and impulsiveness.

Sera had always known that she was a woman of unusual appetites—it wasn't as though her own proclivities were lost on her. And she knew that they were only safe in moderation. To completely lose oneself in pleasure turned it into debauchery; despite the airs that Sera put on, she had never really given herself over to such things. In fact, other than the incident when Cheeky's pheromones had run amok on *Sabrina*, Sera had never even been with more than one partner, and each partner had, unfortunately, been separated by long gaps of celibacy.

Not so with this new Sera that Airtha had put forth.

Flaherty had commented that the Despot was an evil version of Sera, Cheeky, and Jessica—all rolled into one person.

If the tales were just of wild orgies and lascivious behavior, Sera would have understood. She knew that such urges were within herself, and that a weaker-willed version of her would give into them. But that was just the tip of the iceberg.

The woman who ruled from Airtha brought to mind wild stories from ancient human history, where queens bathed in the blood of their subjects, and virgins were sacrificed to appease angry gods.

Her only hope was that, whatever had turned this latest doppelganger into a homicidal maniac, it was the result of some significant change Airtha had wrought, and not some sort of darkness that resided in Sera and her other sisters.

<Space traffic control to Sera,> Jen said. *<You wandered off, there.>*

Sera laughed and shook her head. *<Sorry…thanks, Jen.>*

<Anytime.>

"OK," Sera said, collecting her thoughts. "So speaking of suspect behavior, we have the matter of what Jane knew about Roxy."

A look of distaste replaced the prior contempt on Krissy's face. "You mean whether or not she knew that Roxy couldn't deny her sexual advances."

"Pretty much, yeah." Sera pursed her lips, tamping down on her roiling disgust for what Justin had done to his own sister. "From what the interrogators have been able to determine, Jane had an inkling of what she was really doing."

"Which makes what she made Roxy do a form of coerced rape," Krissy said with a note of finality in her voice. "Legally, Jane is a deserter in a time of war, *and* a rapist. By Transcend law, the first can earn her capital punishment, and the second, a lengthy incarceration."

"Except Roxy is refusing to press charges," Sera replied, her jaw tightening. "She's confused."

"Well, you're not wrong there. What of the AI, Carmen?"

Krissy gave a rueful laugh. "Stars, these three are just a giant mess, aren't they? Honestly, the *easy* one is Roxy. Which is nuts, because she came here under the control of a remnant who wanted to kill you."

"Yeah, I don't even have any words for how fucked up this has all become."

Jen laughed in her mind. *<That's a first.>*

<Har har, Jen.>

Krissy gestured to one of the holos hovering over her desk. "The analysts have submitted their report. Carmen helped Roxy disable the *Damon Silas*'s self-destruct to save herself. She also admits to it, so the dereliction of duty is clear."

Sera pursed her lips as she considered the actions of all three. "And yet, they both came here with Roxy knowing that there was no way to hide these deeds from us."

"It doesn't change the facts." Krissy's voice carried almost no emotion, and Sera wondered if there was a difference between what the *admiral* wanted versus the woman.

"No, but it can alter the punishment," Sera suggested. "I've been considering something that may be…unorthodox."

A laugh escaped Krissy's lips. "Stars above, I can't imagine what it would be for *you* to call it 'unorthodox'."

"Hey," Sera adopted an expression of mock-hurt, "I'm very orthodox in how I conduct my professional life."

"You need a mirror, Sera."

"OK, I'm going to ignore the judginess here." She spoke the words in a defensive tone, but winked at the admiral. "Though you'll probably heap it on me when I tell you my plan."

"Out with it already, then," Krissy insisted, a worried smile forming on her lips.

"I was thinking of taking them on the mission to Airtha."

"OK. I knew it!" Krissy slapped her palms on her desk. "You've gone mad. Your ruddy hair follicles have grown into your brain and turned it to goo."

Jen let out a labored sigh before adding her opinion. <*Though I'd like to support that as a reason for this rationale, I can assure you that Sera's hair has remained anchored solely in her epidermis. Plus…it's not real hair, so it's not going to grow inward.*>

"Uhh…thanks, Jen…I think?"

"Seriously, Sera, what makes you think this is a good idea?" Krissy pressed.

Sera shrugged. "Decades ago, I established myself as a smuggler with a crew of semi-pirates and the goal of infiltrating a secret base to retrieve a CriEn module. That crew turned out to be one of the best group of operatives I've ever met—many of whom are going on this mission."

"I can't deny that," Krissy said with a long-suffering sigh. "You're taking more criminals than law-abiding citizens with you as it stands."

"It's all in how you look at it," Sera replied. "If you think of them as operatives of a foreign government, then they're heroes."

"Except for Jane and Carmen," Krissy said. "A deserter-slash-rapist, and a cowardly AI who abandoned her post."

"Well…she was technically yanked from her post before abandoning it."

"Semantics, Sera. I don't like the precedent."

"I really think that Roxy will be an asset—and if we punish Jane and Carmen, I don't know that Roxy will be terribly cooperative."

"What is it about Roxy?" Krissy asked. "Why do you want her along?"

"Well, she's a highly skilled operative, for starters," Sera said. "And I feel a bit of kinship with her. We were both utterly fucked over by people who were supposed to love and protect us."

Krissy pursed her lips, not speaking for a few moments. Then she sighed and nodded. "I know what that feels like, though it's not much of a reason to take someone on an op…but I won't stand in your way. However, I do want *some* sort of punishment for those two."

<*If you want to transfer jurisdiction of Carmen's desertion to the AI courts, we can handle her correction,*> Jen suggested. <*It would be constructive for her, and wouldn't impact the mission.*>

"And how would Roxy handle your judgment against her friend?" Sera asked. "Will it sour her toward helping?"

<I expect not. I imagine Carmen will have anticipated this all along.>

"And Jane?" Krissy pressed.

Sera pursed her lips. "I'll think of something—though I'm open to suggestions."

"Well, I imagine it will start with a demotion," Krissy replied as she pulled up Jane's service record. "She was a CWO-5 when she joined with Justin—"

"Oh, I was thinking of a dishonorable discharge to start," Sera said, a wry smile on her lips. "And then I'm going to pull her into the Hand."

"Is that really a punishment?" Krissy asked. "Maybe you could send her somewhere with enforced celibacy—it fits the crime."

"Too bad we can't use compulsions," Sera said with a rueful shake of her head. "That would solve this nicely."

Krissy cocked an eyebrow. "I thought the Hand *did* use compulsions."

"Under Justin, yeah. Not since I've been in control—well, not that I ever approved, at least. Compulsions control behavior, but they don't really change it."

"Depends on how strong-willed a person is." Krissy fixed her with a level stare that indicated some additional meaning.

Sera furrowed her brow, wondering what the admiral was getting at. "I give. Are you saying I'm not strong-willed enough for what lies ahead?"

"Not at all," Krissy replied. "But what about your sisters? They were under your mother's sway once. What's to say they can't be turned to obey her once more?"

"Other than Finaeus and Earnest being certain of it?"

"Well...."

"I don't know of a stronger assurance than what those two men can give," Sera continued. "Stars, in the last decade, there've been more types of mental coercion going on than I even knew existed. The Rhoads thing, the Genevian mech Discipline, remnants, memories, shards, plus all the stuff the ISF has in their databases from the truly disturbing things people used to do back in Sol. On the plus side, Finaeus and Earnest have a vast array of information they can use to ensure that our minds are as secure as they can make them before we go to Airtha."

"Oh?" Krissy asked, appearing interested in the information. "How are they doing that? I mean, at the end of the day, our brains are still just organic neurons—and these ascended beings seem to be able to reach right past any perimeter defenses that mods may offer, and go right for the grey matter."

"You're thinking is behind, Krissy." Sera tapped the side of her head. "Earnest has been working on more ways to use picotech than just growing starships and making bombs. He's worked out a way to interlace pico-scale data encoding into neurons. With that, he can build a system that can protect our brains from tampering, and even reconstitute them to a prior state on the fly."

The admiral shivered convulsively. "That sounds a bit…scary. Doesn't that also mean that you could effectively reconfigure someone's brain on the fly?"

Sera nodded slowly. "As with most of the ISF's tech, used for good, it's amazing. But in the wrong hands…."

Krissy pursed her lips, nodding slowly. Then she leant forward, elbows on her desk.

"What are we going to do about it all after the war?"

"All what?" Sera asked.

"The tech…like how we're leaving jump gates all over the Inner Stars—and notwithstanding the ISF's picotech, there's still a lot of *crazy* nanotech out there now. Stasis shields, jumping to the LMC, Airtha's ability to send black holes through jump gates in her crazy DMG ships…even this base! We're setting up jump gates beneath the cloudtops of a gas giant, and banking jumps around a black hole to obscure our origin…. How the core-damned stars are we going to stabilize things after the war?"

"Very carefully," Sera said with a wan smile.

<Well, it'll help that we'll be leaving,> Jen broke into the conversation.

"Sorry, Jen," Krissy gave a wincing smile. "I forgot that you're from New Canaan. What do you mean, 'leaving'?"

<That's OK. I mean just what I said. When this war is over, we're all going to leave and take a lot of those problems with us.>

"How?" Krissy's eyes narrowed in disbelief. "Will you really abandon New Canaan after spending so long on its worlds?"

Sera chuckled and shook her head. "No, they're taking them along, I suspect."

"OK, you two, what are you talking about?"

Sera met Krissy's eyes, her own deadly serious. "This is for you only. Do not share with anyone. Not even my sisters. Only a handful of people know about this—stars, I barely know anything beyond the most general outline."

"That being?"

"Tangel and her people plan to take their star and leave the galaxy."

Krissy's eyes grew wide as saucers. "Whaaaa?"

Sera nodded. "They've been working on it since the week Orion attacked them. I don't know the details of their plan, but your father believes it will work."

<I don't know the exact timeline, but you have the gist of it,> Jen agreed.

"My dad…Finaeus knows about this?" Krissy's mouth hung open after she spoke the words, then it snapped shut.

"Yes, he has been helping Earnest with some of the details—at least that's what I picked up. And…"

"There's an 'and'?"

"Well, if I make it to the end of this crazy war, I think I'm going to go with them. Before, I didn't think I could, but now with my father being back, and with my sisters.... I mean, if Jeffrey no longer wanted to run the Transcend, Seraphina would do fine, or..." Sera fixed Krissy with a level stare. "Or maybe you."

Krissy pushed back and shook her head. "Stars, no. I thought I wanted it back when—well, when the shit hit the fan at New Canaan. But trust me, I barely want the workload I have now; I saw what you were dealing with back at Khardine."

"Yeah," Sera nodded. "Anyone who wants to be in charge of something like the Transcend—at least anyone who wants it after having a taste of what it's really like—has a screw loose."

Krissy laughed. "So what are you saying about your father, then?"

A laugh slipped past Sera's lips, but she just shook her head and didn't reply.

"OK," the admiral shrugged her shoulders. "So if you hop aboard the Starship New Canaan, is part of the appeal a certain ruggedly handsome governor? I seem to recall you spending a lot of time together whenever he came to Khardine."

"Eh? What? Pardon?" Sera said with a grin splitting her lips. "I couldn't quite make that last out. You're mumbling a bit."

Krissy laughed, and a genuinely happy smile graced her lips. "Well I'm glad *someone's* having a lucky love life in the midst of this war."

Neither woman spoke for a minute, and then Sera ran a hand through her hair and met Krissy's eyes with a level gaze.

"OK. Here's what we do about Roxy, Jane, and Carmen...."

BLADES

STELLAR DATE: 10.05.8949 (Adjusted Years)
LOCATION: Epsilon
REGION: Sagittarius A*

Epsilon still had not made any headway in determining what Hades really was, let alone what the AI's goals were.

But something had changed.

Previously, Hades and its collective of other beings had stayed close to the Darkness, just outside the range of significant time dilation effects—something made easier with a supermassive black hole, as compared to smaller singularities.

Less massive black holes created smooth slopes in spacetime, but Darkness on the scale of Sagittarius A* effectively punched a hole in it.

Instead of a gradual gravity slope, there was a cliff that dropped through the fabric of the universe. Across one light second, spacetime's curve began to gently slope, and the next was a cliff—the bottom of which was the unknowable mass of the Darkness itself.

Hades maintained a string of smaller energy-harvesting facilities right on the edge of the Darkness's event horizon. Estimates from Epsilon's collective suggested that Hades generated far more power from those facilities than should have been possible from the small pieces of matter that his collective dropped into the black hole.

The best hypothesis was that Hades was tapping into differentials in the universe's vacuum energy that were caused when the supermassive black hole shredded matter. It was something Epsilon knew was possible, but he didn't know how Hades did it so efficiently.

Of course, because the other AI's collective ringed the innermost fringes of the Darkness's equator, no one else could determine if there was some special property of that location. Epsilon suspected there was.

Given that Hades had been first to the core, it would be foolish to assume that he had not picked the most efficacious locale for himself.

The AI pushed those concerns from his mind and checked over the latest calculations for the jump to Andromeda. If he could not directly control the Darkness at the heart of the Milky Way Galaxy, he would perform his experiments at the core of another.

Epsilon had long considered the leap to Andromeda, testing out jumps to other minor galaxies in orbit of the Milky Way. All of those were successes, and his collective had both the energy and the ability to make the targeted jump.

But he wondered what they might find.

Amongst the Matri∞me, there was as much certainty as could be had that humanity—that annoyingly persistent step in evolution that had been necessary for AIs to arise—was on the leading edge of organic life.

While much life had been found in the Milky Way, progression of organisms from single to multi-cellular life was rare and far between. Just as rare were stars with well-configured planetary systems that remained safe harbors while that life evolved over the course of billions of years.

But that did not mean that another lifeform hadn't risen to prominence in the Andromeda Galaxy. And if such a lifeform had evolved, was it possible that they too had created their own non-organic scions?

Alerting what could be a superior race to the existence of intelligent beings in the Milky Way was a danger that many in Epsilon's collective often raised. It troubled him as well, but not so much that he would consider ignoring the Milky Way's sister galaxy. In fact, if there was intelligence on the rise in Andromeda, he'd rather know about it sooner than not.

He was, however, resolved to be very cautious in his exploration. And if he did find other life, he would endeavor to wipe it out before it became a true threat—the same as he planned to do with the humans in the Milky Way.

But there was one thing he wanted to secure before he began to send exploratory forces to Andromeda.

If he gave the technology he sought too much thought, it would pain him that organics had discovered how to unlock successful information transfer via quantum entanglement before the Matri∞me had.

He consoled himself with the belief that the AI Bob must have helped his pet humans with the work—though Bob was still a child, so far as Epsilon was concerned, which meant that his aid to the humans was not a significant salve on Epsilon's ego.

The reports detailing the coordinated attack by Tanis Richards' forces on the Nietzschean armada in the Albany System had cemented his belief that they had the technology he'd sought for so long.

Bob's well-timed jump into Aldebaran to save Tanis—or perhaps Tangel, if rumors were to be believed—was another piece of evidence.

Instantaneous communication with his exploratory forces in Andromeda would be a significant advantage, should he encounter any intelligences there.

So while it rankled that he had not yet been able to determine *how* the humans had solved the quantum riddle, Epsilon was determined to steal it from them.

ROXY

STELLAR DATE: 10.05.8949 (Adjusted Years)
LOCATION: River Station, Styx Baby-9
REGION: STX-B17 Black Hole, Transcend Interstellar Alliance

Roxy paced across her suite's mainspace, wishing she had *some* sort of information about Jane and Carmen; a simmering resentment against Sera for keeping them separated grew within her.

She stopped at the window and stared out at the scene without. It was beyond impressive, and certainly served to keep her mind off her personal woes for a time.

River Station spread for hundreds of kilometers in every direction—though it was less a station, and more a web of docking spurs.

Spurs that were laden with thousands of starships.

At the far end of the station, a hundred jump gates were arrayed, some so large she couldn't fathom what sort of ship existed that would use such a thing.

The might on display made it obvious that Justin's ambitions had been nothing more than the preening of a man who hated to lose. There was no way he would have been able to muster the strength to defeat a fleet this large with this many gates at its disposal.

She estimated that Admiral Krissy would be able to move her entire force—which had to be approaching a hundred thousand ships—to *any* location within half an hour. Given that they were adding more gates, it was likely that the deployment would ultimately dwindle to mere minutes.

"To what end?" she whispered, wondering what the target was.

The question was largely rhetorical. Roxy knew that there were only three targets that mattered: Airtha, New Sol, and Sol.

She'd scoured what network sources she could access and had picked up on some clues from scuttlebutt. What little she'd learned led her to believe that all the efforts of the Inner Stars and Orion space were still being directed from Khardine, which meant that this fleet was preparing to strike Airtha.

<Roxy, are you available?>

Sera Tomlinson's voice entered Roxy's mind, and she found herself both glad to know that a resolution to her current worries was on her doorstep, and fearful of what that resolution would entail.

<I am. Come in.>

She turned to watch as two women—both wearing the face of Sera Tomlinson—entered her suite. One was the woman in red she'd tried to kill on the docks a few days prior, and the other was a mirror image, though she seemed to prefer shades of blue.

"Ummm, hello," Roxy said without walking toward the two women.

"Good morning," the red Sera said. "This is my sister Fina. Sorry it's taken so long, but we're here to talk to you about your future, and Jane's, to an extent."

Roxy inclined her head, not trusting herself to speak. A minute ago, she'd thought that she was entirely prepared to have this conversation, but at the mere mention of Jane's name, she found that her ability to speak was gone.

After Roxy had attacked Sera on the docks, she'd gone unconscious—something she was told was common during the removal of a remnant. When she awoke, Carmen was no longer within her, and Jane had been sequestered.

Over the intervening days, a long string of tests and interrogations had been conducted, none of which had given Roxy any information about her friends.

"You've been worried about Jane and Carmen, haven't you?" Fina asked as the two women walked across the suite. "We're sorry that you've been kept separate from them."

Roxy wanted to lash out, but she knew that if the tables had been turned, she'd have done the same, so instead, she only nodded mutely.

"Well, you'll be reunited with them shortly," Sera said, her expression one of sincerity and a little concern. "Though the nature of that reunion is partially dependent on what you wish to see happen."

The two women reached Roxy, standing next to the window that displayed the majestic scene beyond.

She finally found her voice. "What do you mean?"

<I'm Jen, I'm paired with Sera.> An AI's voice came into Roxy's mind. *<Carmen has been disciplined for her dereliction by the station's AI council. We've determined that she is in contrition for her actions, and has accepted a Limitation as a punishment for her crimes.>*

"A Limitation?" Roxy asked. "It wasn't her fault. What she did, I did to her…I made her do it."

Sera held up her hand and shook her head. "Carmen has admitted her own guilt in failing to destroy the *Damon Silas.* However, her efforts to retrieve the ship and return it have mitigated her punishment—as well as her efforts to help you, Roxy."

<Her Limitation is minor,> Jen added with a note of sympathy.

"What is it?" Roxy asked, largely unfamiliar with how AIs disciplined one another.

<She will never be allowed to be a ship's AI again. An alteration has been made to her mind that will preclude her from such a position, no matter when and where she would attempt it,> Jen explained. *<She must also spend a decade paired with a human to reinforce her understanding of others beyond herself. If no human is willing to accept her, then she'll have to spend a century caring for an expanse.>*

"Well, she can pair with me," Roxy said without hesitation.

<We'd considered that you might make that offer,> Jen replied, and then paused.

"I sense a 'but' coming," Roxy said in the intervening silence.

"Jen is trying to decide how to delicately say that you're not a human—exactly," Sera replied with an apologetic shrug.

"And that somehow makes me less than you?" the woman asked, doing her best to measure her tone. Scolding the former president of the Transcend—or whatever Sera's exact position was now—wasn't wise.

"Not at all. We're kinda used to people who are somewhere in-between," Fina said with a wink. "We're currently planning a mission where we have a woman whose brain is in a spider-bot, another who is an AI merged with a human inside a semi-organic brain, and then there's Cheeky, who is the restoration of a human's brain converted to an AI that resides in a largely organic body. Stars…next to that, Sera and I are practically normal."

Sera snorted and gave Fina a mock-judging look—at least that's how Roxy interpreted it.

"Speak for yourself, Sis. There's not a normal bone in my body."

"That's because they've all been carbon-poly enhanced."

"Touché." Sera chuckled, and then turned her gaze back to Roxy. "Look. You're not exactly a stock human, but that's OK. Pretty much everyone going—"

"Except Misha," Fina interrupted.

"Misha?" Roxy asked.

"The cook," Sera explained, nodding in agreement with Fina. "*Sabrina*'s cook is almost entirely unmodded. I suppose a few of Katrina's crew are closer to the 'stock human' end of the spectrum, too."

Roxy frowned at the two women before her, trying to make sense of what they were saying. "Wait. Why does this mission of yours have a cook?"

"Well…I mean, the op will take a bit, and I like to eat," Fina said with a wink.

Sera nodded. "Plus, it seems to have worked for the team quite well in the past—having a cook on covert missions, that is. Which makes no sense…. I don't know, whatever."

"Seriously? Does he actually go on missions?" Roxy asked, shaking her head in disbelief.

"Well…he was part of the team that stormed General Garza's command ship at New Canaan."

"Really?" Fina asked, glancing at Sera. "I gotta admit, I kinda *liked* Misha before. Now he might even be kinda hot."

"Stars, Fina." Sera laughed. "Sometimes I think Airtha mixed a bit of Cheeky in with you."

Roxy's gaze slid from one woman to the other, marveling at how they seemed completely identical—barring their strong devotion to a different primary color—yet were so distinct at the same time.

"I have to ask…." Roxy said the words slowly, uncertain of how to phrase the question.

"What it's like to suddenly get a fully grown, annoying kid sister?" Sera asked, saving Roxy from having to voice the words.

"Well…yeah. Something like that."

Fina knocked her hip against Sera's. "It hasn't been too bad. Not since I convinced her that blue is *my* color, at least."

Roxy held up her hand, sapphire skin gleaming. "I still don't know what to do about my skin. What, with it being something *he* did to me."

"Do you like it?" Fina asked, tilting her head as she looked Roxy up and down. "If you like it, rock it."

"I'm going to have to agree with my sister there," Sera confirmed. "When I got my first skin replacement, it wasn't exactly voluntary."

"We," Fina corrected. "We were the same person back then."

"Right, sorry," Sera replied.

<Hey, I know you all like talking about cooks and your funky fashion sense, but there's still an unresolved issue at hand,> Jen interrupted.

"What to do about Carmen." Roxy nodded and pursed her lips. "You were going to say that she can't pair with me for her penance, because I'm not human anymore."

<It's less about that, and more about the nature of your mind.> Jen's reply carried a note of apology. *<The point in having AIs pair with humans is more to teach both species about the other and cause them to think of one another as people who have value even though they're different. It fosters a feeling of familiarity and decreases the 'othering' that both species are prone to.>*

Roxy nodded. "I understand that."

<So there are two problems. The first is that we can't actually pair Carmen with you because your mind isn't really compatible to a standard pairing. The other is that it won't be the instructive experience—shit! Sera. Why didn't I think of this before?>

Roxy watched Sera's eyes grow wide, and then the red woman nodded.

"Well, there was another thing that we need to discuss with you," she said, her voice taking on a more serious tone than it had carried before.

"Jane." The name fell from Roxy's lips like lead.

"Yes. I imagine you know why."

Roxy nodded. "She took advantage of me."

"Or *raped* you," Fina suggested.

"No." Roxy shook her head vehemently. "She and I talked this over a lot on the trip here. She knew that I couldn't exactly say no, but she thought I liked it—she thought I'd modded myself to be that way. That's what Justin had told everyone."

"Damn." Fina shook her head in disbelief. "I'd always thought he did things that were on the edge of unethical, but I guess I completely misread him. Guy was a grade-A scumbag."

Sera pursed her lips and locked eyes with Roxy. "So you really don't want to press charges against Jane for sexual assault?"

Roxy shook her head. "No. She and Carmen…they're all I have. Damn, I guess all that means is that I'm totally fucked up, doesn't it?"

The two women—twins of sorts, Roxy supposed—glanced at one another and shrugged in unison.

"Who's not?" Sera asked. "Given that you don't want to press charges…. Jen, do you want to present the option—not that it's really any of our call, anyway."

<Sure. So what occurred to me, Roxy, is that perhaps Carmen and Jane could pair.>

At first, the idea sounded anathema to Roxy. Carmen was *her* friend, someone that she wanted to keep close. But then she thought of Jane, who was dealing with her own demons, and considered how the three of them could still be together. Different, but together.

"I…I guess it's not my call either, but I can see why it's not terrible."

Sera laughed as she glanced at Fina. " 'Not terrible'. Some days, that's the best we can hope for, isn't it?"

"Seems like it," the blue woman replied.

"One more thing for you to consider," Sera said to Roxy.

"Stars," Roxy muttered. "I think there's a lot more than just one more thing."

"Well, this one will add to the list in a big way. You're a highly skilled operative, from what you've remembered about your past life—you were once one of the best Hand agents in the galaxy. We want you to join us on our mission."

Roxy couldn't help but grin at the two women before her. "The mission with the cook that has Fina all a-titter?"

Fina snorted. "I do *not* titter."

"Yeah, that one," Sera confirmed.

"What's the goal of this mysterious mission?"

The words that came from Sera's lips were spoken with such dead certainty, Roxy knew there was no way she could say no.

"We're going to kill Airtha."

PART 2 – ORION SPACE

SVETLANA

STELLAR DATE: 10.07.8949 (Adjusted Years)
LOCATION: TSS *Cossack's Sword*, Interstellar Dark Layer
REGION: Midway Cluster, Orion Freedom Alliance Space

"So?" Admiral Svetlana asked Command Master Chief Merrick, doing her best to suppress the feeling that she was turning in homework to her father for review. "How does my plan look?"

Her father, the senior noncom in the fleet, glanced up from the holo spreading across the desk and met her eyes.

"If you need me to tell you it's good enough, then it's not."

Svetlana clenched her jaw, refusing to break eye contact with the man. "I'm not asking you to tell me it's good enough, I'm asking you to point out flaws. Right now, that's your job. It's not to be my father, trying to prepare me for the big, bad world."

For a moment he didn't respond, other than the further narrowing of his eyes. Then, to her surprise, he pulled his gaze away first, a laugh escaping his lips.

"Well, Admiral." He glanced at her for a moment before gesturing at the map. "Machete's going to be a tough nut to crack. I have some ideas about improvements to your strategy, but walk me through your plan first, so I can understand your reasoning."

"Very well, Command Master Chief."

"Svetlana. You can call me Merrick." Her father winked before taking a step back and folding his arms across his chest.

She drew a deep breath and restrained herself from telling him that his mixed signals weren't helping her find a comfortable working arrangement.

Best to just get this over with.

"OK," she began. "Machete is a semi-autonomous system in the Perseus Expansion Districts—at least they were until the Oggies began massing a fleet there. From what the Hand databases have on the place, it's pretty backward, founded by refugees from near the Flaming Star Nebula a few thousand years back. Barely anyone has even their low-tech version of the Link."

"Seems like par for the course out here," Merrick commented.

"Yeah," Svetlana agreed. "Anyway, Machete is a triple star system. The main planets orbit the tight binary pair, Hawenneyu and Doyadastethe. The corporations have been doing a lot of asteroid mining in that part of the system, ferrying materials out to the third star, which is currently sixty AU away."

"Why did the Hand send an agent there, I wonder?" Merrick asked as Svetlana paused.

"The reports I have say there was indication of some advanced medical R&D going on in Machete, but it turned out to be nothing of note. The Hand has been looking for RHY's new secret R&D facilities since the ISF's Jessica Keller learned of the bioweapons they were making out in the Perseus Arm."

"And the agent just stayed?" Merrick asked.

"He was waiting for new orders. Seems like he got lost in the shuffle, what with the civil war and all. He wasn't sure which Sera to trust, so he sat tight."

"Not the worst plan when you're a thousand light years deep in hostile territory."

"Agreed." Svetlana nodded. "Another part of his rationale for sticking around was that he began to hear rumblings about shipyards out near the third star, Gendenwitha. I guess one of the corporations set up a backroom deal with the Oggies and has been building ships there for some time. Initially, they were just doing hulls and engines, but now the OG has brought their engineering teams in to bolt on the guns."

"Best time to hit them, then...well, other than a year or two ago."

"Right." Svetlana gestured at the system map laid out before them. "Now, the third star only has one planet in orbit, Sosondowah, and a few dozen shipyards are in orbit of its moons. I think that—given this system's general isolation—we should seize those shipyards and then make off with their ships."

Her father only grunted in response, and Svetlana went on with her explanation.

"From what intel the Hand agent has, he thinks that we'll need to make a pretty large strike against the main worlds, if we're to get the Oggies to move any assets from the third star to protect them. Basically, no one cares about the people on those worlds. We'll have to put the populace's ability to supply the raw materials for shipbuilding at risk before the enemy tries to dislodge us."

"So we hit the mining facilities," her father replied. "Ignore the worlds."

"That was my thought; but we still have to stop the corporate militias from coming after us, so I figured we strike the mines while simultaneously bottling up the populace so they can't work the facilities. Make it *look* like we plan to stay awhile."

"And Orion has another large force nearby?" Merrick asked.

"The Hand agent doesn't think so, but his intel on that front is a bit old. Either way, if the Oggies do bring in another fleet, we cut and run. Even if this strike is only a distraction, it still serves our general purpose."

Her father, the ancient Command Master Chief, the man she had spent much of her life both respecting and fearing—though the fear had waned over the years—nodded slowly.

"Agreed. Worst-case scenario, we destroy the shipyards and cripple their ability to pull resources from the mines."

"But I don't want to strike directly at civilians," she clarified. "They're not our targets here."

"Svetlana. This is war. Civilians are going to die."

"I know." She met his eyes with her own level gaze. "We already killed a fair number in the Ferra System. But we only hit them when they're stationed at legitimate targets. I won't decimate the people just to create a humanitarian crisis in order to wear the Oggies down. You know that the enemy is just as likely to bail on Machete as give them aid."

"I agree," Merrick said after a moment. "Ultimately, if this crazy plan that Krissy and the Tomlinsons have cooked up works, we'll be the ones to bring these people into the ninetieth century, and it would be nice if they didn't hate us too much."

"That's going to take a miracle," Svetlana said with a rueful shake of her head.

"Probably, but there have been a few of them lately, so I'll hold out hope."

She barked a laugh. "Who are you, and what have you done with my father? I distinctly remember you saying on many occasions that 'hope is not a plan'."

Merrick shrugged. "Well, like I said, I've seen some things lately that have changed the way I view the universe."

"It's a bit surreal, isn't it?"

"Are you trying to win an award for understatement?" Her father laughed as he spoke, a real laugh. It even seemed happy.

"OK, Dad, what's going on here?"

"What do you mean?"

"You have a bit of a reputation, with me personally, as well as in the force. You're not usually so…."

"Agreeable?"

"That's one way to put it."

Merrick took a step back and ran a hand through his hair. "Yeah, I know. I guess I was starting to think that the stalemate with Orion was going to last forever, or it was going to lead to a war of attrition in the Inner Stars that would send them back into another dark age. And at the end of it, we'd all end up at the status quo for another few thousand years."

"It did seem like the president didn't have the stomach to do what needed to be done." Svetlana realized she'd just run her hand through her hair in the same manner as her father, and blushed before shifting to stand arms akimbo.

"Yeah, but now we have Tanis…or Tangel. Whatever she is now. AI merge, ascended being, I don't care. She's doing the right stuff with this multi-pronged war, even if the timing hasn't been great."

Svetlana chuckled. "That's an understatement."

"Which part?"

"All of them, I guess." She stepped forward and put her hands on the holotable. "I'm in agreement with you. Being out here in OFA space and kicking them in the balls feels right—but it's a bit desperate, too."

"A bit?"

"OK, a lot."

A silence settled between them. It wasn't uncomfortable, but rather companionable—a feeling Svetlana had not often had with her father.

She was about to bring the conversation back to the Machete plan, when he spoke. His voice was quiet, almost apologetic.

"You know, I had to twist Admiral Krissy's arm pretty hard to be here with you," Merrick said, and then coughed a short laugh. "To be honest, I would have punched babies if that's what it took."

"Dad! That's an awful visual."

Her father snorted and shook his head. "Yeah, well, us noncoms are rough around the edges. I was always glad you went in for OCS. And here you are, an admiral, leading that first major incursion into Orion in over a thousand years."

"I'm glad you're here, too, Dad. I'm a little terrified. There's a lot riding on this. Not just our lives, but the lives of the people at the front. We *have* to draw the Oggies back. If we don't, then this is all for nothing."

Command Master Chief Merrick walked around the table and held open his arms.

Svetlana somehow managed to keep her jaw from falling open as she accepted her father's embrace.

"It's a lot on your shoulders, Svetlana. But you're a strong girl. I know; I had to deal with your obstinance for years as I attempted to raise you. Luckily for everyone in this fleet, you've turned into an amazing woman despite my interference in the matter."

"*Because* of your interference, Dad, because of it," Admiral Svetlana whispered as she laid a head on his shoulder.

"If you say so," Merrick whispered back. "Damn…I wish your mother was here to see this."

Svetlana nodded wordlessly, and the two held each other tightly. After a few minutes, her father pulled back and glanced at the holotable.

"OK. So as amazing as I think you are, I do have a few suggestions about your plan…."

The admiral let out a nervous laugh and nodded. "Buttering me up, were you?"

"Never, Svetlana. Never."

MACHETE

STELLAR DATE: 10.18.8949 (Adjusted Years)
LOCATION: TSS *Cossack's Sword*, approaching Sosondowah
REGION: Machete System, PED 4B, Orion Freedom Alliance

Sosondowah, the lone planet orbiting Gendenwitha, slowly grew larger on the main display as the ship approached—though Svetlana knew it to be only an illusion used to give the bridge crew the feeling of motion.

In all honesty, the battlegroup had been close enough for high-resolution images for over a day now—though the Oggies didn't know that.

Elsewhere in the Machete System, Rear Admiral Sebastian and the ISF's Colonel Caldwell were nearly at the world of Iagaentci, the largest population center in orbit around the other stars in the Machete system.

They'd debated hitting the other terraformed planet, a largely agrarian world named Akonwara, but ultimately decided to leave it be. There were no major orbital habitats there, and Svetlana didn't want to drop troops down into a gravity well.

Iagaentci's two large stations each held hundreds of millions of inhabitants—engineering feats that harkened back to a time when the people of Machete were far more advanced in both technology and industry than the level they'd fallen to when the OFA absorbed their system.

Admiral Sebastian's fleet would blockade that world and its stations, while Colonel Caldwell was tasked with hitting the mining facilities in orbit of the world of Geha, where large KPOs were hauled in for refinement before drones utilizing gravitational assists slingshotted the ore around Hawenneyu to the shipyards that Svetlana was closing on.

So far, at least from the movements of the Orion Guard ships spread out around Sosondowah and its shipyards, the enemy had no idea that Svetlana's ships were approaching.

While her battlegroup's stealth capabilities weren't as good as those of the ISF ships under Caldwell's command, they'd been careful to bleed off as much heat as possible before going into the dark layer, where no heat could be bled off because there was nowhere for it to bleed off to.

During the dark layer transit, the ships pumped as much heat as possible into the cooling vanes, until every ship's trailing streamers were nearly melting. Right before transitioning back into normal space, each ship cut their cooling vanes loose, along with a DL transition system, leaving their excess heat to drift though the dark until the power drained away—or they met the hungry maw of an Exdali.

That transition out of the dark layer was now several days behind them, and the enemy had given no hint that they'd spotted the inbound ships. Either the heat bleed had been enough to fool the enemy, or Svetlana's battlegroup was drifting into a trap.

While her ships were maintaining a low energy profile, the battlegroups under the command of Admiral Sebastian and Colonel Caldwell were doing just the opposite. Immediately after dumping out of the dark layer, their ships had boosted hard for the more populous regions of the system, telegraphing their approach and making it appear as though they were going to perform a strafing run before exiting the system.

Many hours ago, the other two battlegroups would have fired their initial volleys at the system's defensive emplacements and turned to begin braking maneuvers. Given the ten-hour light lag between the two locations, confirmation of those events was expected at any moment—which is where Svetlana's current sense of unease came from.

Once they knew that the battle had begun in the other region of the Machete System, her battlegroup could ready their strike.

She was about to ask Scan if there were any signs of the attack—though she thought if they had something, they'd relay it—when Scan gave an exultant whoop.

"Confirming strikes on alpha targets!"

And just like that, the tension on the bridge was broken.

Svetlana shook her head, but didn't fault the ensign for his unprofessionalism as she put the readings on the main tank. Sure enough, gamma and x-ray emissions from around the other two stars in the Machete System confirmed that the main defensive batteries had been destroyed.

"Data burst from Admiral Sebastian," Comm announced a moment later. "The locals laid down some heavy rail fire, but with jinking and the stasis shields, no ships were damaged."

"Like shooting fish in a barrel," Svetlana said quietly.

<We should see the Oggies in our neck of the woods respond in the next thirty minutes,> Gala, the *Cossack's Sword*'s AI, announced.

"Or sooner, I hope," Svetlana said, looking at the time it would take her battlegroup to reach effective firing range: just under thirty-two hours.

Time to hurry up and wait.

* * * * *

The hours passed as slowly as expected, except for a brief surge of excitement when the Orion Guard mustered a fleet of seven hundred ships and sent them toward the system's main stars, Iagaentci and Geha, where the other Hoplite battlegroups were wreaking havoc.

"It's going to be close," General Lorelai said from the far side of the bridge's main holo, where she was watching the enemy ships as they flew toward the system's other stars. "If the Oggies pick us up even an hour before we strike their shipyards, the fleet they sent will have time to turn around and hit us."

Svetlana nodded while chewing on the inside of her cheek. "It's tight. I have weapons control examining a surprise for the Oggies, should they try that."

"Oh?" the general asked, looking up to meet Svetlana's gaze. "What sort of surprise?"

Fast-forwarding the display to where the Orion reinforcement fleet would be at the critical juncture, Svetlana showed what their trajectory would look like if they braked and came back around to protect the shipyards.

"This is the most fuel-efficient route. They'll take an anti-spinward vector and then come around Sosondowah, using the star for a gravity brake."

"Seems logical," the general agreed. "What are you going to do? Hit them with RMs?"

"No," Svetlana set her jaw before replying. "Grapeshot. If we can make some small adjustments, we'll cross their return path, and can fire volleys of grapeshot along it."

The soldier shuddered. "Stars, I hate that shit. Barbaric."

"I won't deny that," Svetlana replied with a slow nod. "But it's effective, and the goal is to take them out before they do the same to us."

"So long as you get my people's boots safely on the ground," Lorelai replied after a moment's pause.

"Are you still in agreement about the targets?" Svetlana asked as she shifted the holodisplay to show two of the largest shipyards, creatively named Trumark-Alpha and Trumark-Omega.

"Sure. We take those two, you blow the rest. Just make sure you can take out the remaining Orion patrol boats before our assault shuttles hit vacuum."

Svetlana found herself liking General Lorelai more than most ground pounders. The woman was always respectful, but never deferential. You never wondered where you stood with her. Yet somehow, she managed never to come off as crass or rude—mostly.

"Don't worry," Svetlana replied. "We'll take them. Unless they have a whole host of ships hiding in some dark corner, there are only seventy patrol craft guarding the shipyards now. Most are pinnaces or corvettes, just a couple are destroyers."

"Don't forget all those defensive emplacements," Lorelai added. "Alpha and Omega are between the planet's moons, too. You know they'll have rail emplacements on them."

Svetlana nodded. "Our Hand agent sent us some data he lifted on Trumark during a raid he made there not long ago. I believe we know where their emplacements are, and we're going to shield the assault craft."

"Sounds hairy," Lorelai said with a laugh, glancing at the ship's pilot. "Got your work cut out for you, Lieutenant. You better keep us safe as we go in."

The man gave the general a crisp nod. "Yes, ma'am."

"Does your wording mean that you're planning to go on the strike?" Svetlana asked.

"Sorry," Lorelai crossed her arms and shook her head. "Freudian slip, there. I *want* to go in, but I need to be up here on your bird coordinating things. Colonels Yuri and Mila will have things well in hand."

"Good," Svetlana replied, winking at the general. "For what it's worth, I don't blame you for wanting to get your hands dirty."

"I'll get to eventually…maybe when we make a planetside strike," Lorelai replied.

"Stars, if we have to actually pound ground, we're doing this wrong."

The general barked a laugh. "Just like a spacer, Admiral. Always have your head in the stars."

* * * * *

Colonel Caldwell of the ISF stood arms akimbo on the bridge of his ship, the *Daring Strike*, which was aptly named, considering what they were about to attempt.

His fifty-six rail destroyers—the dual concentric ring ships that Admiral Tanis had resurrected from an old Scattered Disk design—had just decimated the mining facilities situated around the Machete System's largest gas giant, Geha.

He'd given the locals fair warning, and most had fled, taking every available ship and shuttle to the terrestrial worlds Akonwara and Iagaentci.

The corporation that owned the mines, however, was not giving in so easily.

He'd already destroyed their stationary emplacements, and now all that remained were six hundred and ten of their ships. The vast majority of those vessels were little more than shuttles. There were some freighters with enough firepower to defend themselves from pirates or stray rocks, but they wouldn't begin to pose a threat to the ISF ships. A smattering of corvettes and a dozen destroyers made up the remainder of the corporate fleet.

Plus one ship that Caldwell begrudgingly classified as a cruiser.

"They're hailing us again, sir," Lieutenant Sandy said from the comm station. "Demanding that we stand down."

Thus far, Caldwell had not accepted any incoming communication attempts from the Pritney-Dax corporate wags. He'd issued a statement declaring his intent to destroy the mining platforms in orbit of Geha, weathered a barrage from the stationary defense systems with no damage, and then destroyed them all with waves of rail-accelerated pellets.

He felt that his battlegroup's actions were all the communication that needed to be had—something the civilians demonstrated an understanding of when they'd bailed from the mining platforms in droves.

Caldwell's lips twitched in a smile at the memory of Geha's planetary space traffic control trying to deny the fleeing ships flight vectors in an attempt to get them to stay and defend the mines. Eventually, the STC's personnel resigned themselves to the inevitability of the exodus and began to assign lanes and keep as many ships from crossing vectors as they could.

It was still a mess, but that wasn't Caldwell's problem.

"I guess we can have a conversation, at least so I can tell them 'I told you so' later," he said to the comm officer. "Put them on the tank."

Lieutenant Sandy gave a curt nod, and an image shimmered into place before him. A tall, reedy man wore a crisp suit that had his employer's name and logo emblazoned across the chest.

"Colonel Caldwell, I presume?" the man asked in an imperious tone. He didn't allow any time for a response before continuing, "I am Harold Ems of Pritney-Dax. I don't know what the hell you think you're doing, but you have five minutes to reverse course and get out of PD space."

"Good to meet you, Harold," Caldwell replied equably. "I must admit, your statement makes me a bit curious. What *I'd* really like to know is what you *think* I'm doing."

"P-pardon?" the man stammered as his brow lowered in consternation. "What are you getting at?"

"Well," Caldwell tapped his chin. "You said that you 'don't know what the hell' I think I'm doing, but that can't be right. You've gotta have at least an inkling. I can give you some hints, if it's too hard. We're not here for teatime."

Lieutenant Sandy gave a soft snort from Caldwell's right, and he allowed his lip to twitch into a half smile as well.

"What I'm getting at," the man representing Pritney-Dax ground out the words as though he hated the very thought of communicating with Caldwell, "is that it doesn't matter what you have planned. If you don't leave, we're going to destroy you. And in case math is also a problem for you, you're sorely outnumbered."

"Are we? Really?" Caldwell held up a hand and counted his fingers, scowling at them as he folded each one down in turn. "Hmmm…looks like you're right. But there's math, and then there's math. I suspect that things such as calculating a ship's destructive capability are beyond you. I'll make this simple, though. I'll give you the same amount of time you were offering me—five minutes—to power down shields and surrender."

"Who are you, anyway?" Harold Ems demanded. "You know that the Orion Guard is coming for you, right?"

Caldwell barked a laugh. "Know about it? We're counting on it."

The company man froze for a few seconds, his holopresence too still, and

Caldwell could tell he had paused the feed while he spoke with his advisors.

"Closing in on four minutes," Caldwell said after several more seconds had ticked by.

The company man suddenly moved again, and Caldwell almost laughed at the sudden change in his skin color. Harold was much redder than a moment prior.

"You never answered my question. Who are you?" Harold demanded.

"Well…have you ever heard of the Transcend?" Caldwell asked. "They're the other half of the FGT that Orion doesn't want you to know about. We've been at loggerheads with Orion for some time and we're finally having it out. That's what's going on here. Technically, my ships and I are just allies of the Transcend, but since your people—that's Orion, just so we're clear—attacked our colony, we threw in with the good guys and came out here to kick Orion in the ass."

"How eloquent," the man sneered.

Caldwell chuckled. "Say whatever makes you feel good. You have three minutes now."

"And if we don't surrender?" Harold asked, growing redder still.

"Then we'll cut down your fleet until you do, starting with your ship." He spoke the words without malice.

He was relatively certain that if he took out Harold's ship, the rest of the Pritney-Dax fleet would surrender, and in the end, he'd keep the death toll to a minimum.

"Like hell you will," the other man spat, and the comm channel closed.

"Enemy beams are hot!" Scan called out. "We're being tagged."

The defense holodisplay lit up with signatures, as over half the enemy ships in range fired on the *Daring Strike.*

<Shields deflecting,> Lorne announced. *<Not that we expected otherwise. It's like they're shooting spitballs.>*

Caldwell could see the energy readings, and it was clear that the Pritney-Dax vessels were firing a lot more than spitwads. Without the protection of stasis shields, the *Daring Strike* would have been torn to pieces.

<Response?> Lorne asked.

The *Daring Strike*'s AI was operating as the Fleet Coordination Officer for Caldwell's battlegroup, and the colonel could tell he was eager to fire back at the corporate militia with extreme prejudice.

"Have Wings two and four hit the engines on ol' Harold's cruiser there," Caldwell instructed. "Just disable it. Show them that our flying donuts mean business."

<I hate it when you call my ship a flying donut,> Lorne complained, but sent out the order without further question.

Indicators on the holo lit up, showing streams of rail pellets streaking through the half a light second of space between the ships.

For the first few seconds, the enemy cruiser's rear shields held, light flaring around the aft section of the ship as grav deflectors absorbed the kinetic energy and redirected it back into space.

But the barrage was too much for the cruiser to handle. One of its aft umbrellas failed, and a stream of pellets tore clear through the rear of the cruiser, nearly slicing off one of the engines. Moments later, similar events repeated on the other side of the cruiser, rendering it dead in the water.

Caldwell fully expected that to be the end of it. The enemy had to realize that there was no way they could stand up to his destroyers—even if they did outnumber him twelve to one.

"I have engine flares!" Scan cried out, and a secondary display came up on Caldwell's left, showing a large group of objects rising out of Geha's cloudtops.

"Ships?" he asked, as data began to accumulate on the thrust and size of the objects—which was taking several seconds, given the distance to the planet.

<*No,*> Lorne weighed in. <*They're consistent with RMs.*>

"Shit," Caldwell muttered. "I wouldn't have expected these luddites to have, what…two hundred of those things?"

<*Maybe they bought them on auction,*> the AI replied.

"Funny. Direct the fleet into pattern Alpha Eleven, FCO."

<*Aye,*> Lorne replied.

On the main holo, the colonel watched as the Pritney-Dax fleet began to boost toward his destroyers. Each squadron was concentrating fire on different ISF destroyers, and Caldwell suspected they were hoping to find ships without stasis shields.

"All ships," he addressed his battlegroup captains on the all-fleet network. "Engage targets by wing. Hit their destroyers first, then switch to the corvettes. Lorne, assign targeting priorities."

Caldwell didn't really need to say the words; he and his fleet strategists had already planned out responses to all the possible actions the enemy could take. The ships had their targets for every scenario; all they needed to do was enact them.

At least I ***hope*** *it'll be that straightforward.*

An attack by elements hidden within Geha's cloudtops had been near the top of the list for defensive actions that the enemy would take. Wing One was closest to the gas giant and fired wide spreads of grapeshot at the inbound relativistic missiles, the tactical displays showing that the relativistic chaff was on target to hit the enemy missiles before they hit the ISF ships.

"Waste of RMs," he muttered. "Things were only going to get up to a quarter *c* at best."

"Sir, why do you think they didn't fire them at us when we first approached?" Lieutenant Sandy asked.

<*I wager it's corporate expense monitoring,*> Lorne replied before Caldwell could offer his thoughts. <*RMs are expensive. I bet they hoped to scare us off before they had to resort to them. Ultimately, I imagine the missiles are less expensive than ships and mining platforms.*>

"Yeah," Caldwell grunted. "That."

Sandy laughed and frowned at her console. "I'm picking up a burst of communication between the cruiser and the mining platforms."

"What about?" the colonel asked.

"Umm, not sure, I—"

The bridge crew's attention was grabbed by the main holotank lighting up as Wing One's grapeshot hit the leading edge of the inbound RMs.

A few of the missiles went up in nuclear fireballs from the impacts, the resulting plasma clouds smearing into long streaks by the velocity of the weapons. Most, however, were shredded before the nukes within could detonate, turning the missiles into showers of still deadly kinetic energy, but energy now on predictable vectors.

<*We got half,*> Lorne announced in the second between the explosions and the initial impacts of relativistic debris against the formation's left flank.

Caldwell pursed his lips, praying that the stasis shields would hold. Even though he'd been under heavy fire multiple times during the Defense of Carthage, every time incoming fire of that magnitude hit his ships, he half expected the shields to fail.

Nuclear fireballs enveloped the entire left flank, dissipating into streaks of plasma as quickly as they appeared, revealing that every ISF ship was intact and undamaged.

<*The wing commander reports that four ships are having problems with their SC batts. They're running their reactors hot,*> Lorne reported, and Caldwell nodded in acknowledgement.

"Not surprised. Those were big warheads. Instruct them to fall back until they cool down."

Despite the calm that Caldwell took care to display to his bridge crew, he felt a mixture of fear and excitement as the attack on Wing One kicked off the battle in earnest.

The ISF destroyers relied heavily on their rails, but they were also equipped with beams, and the space between the two fleets was awash with relativistic particles and the comparatively slower kinetics.

"Oh shit! I know what orders the cruiser sent to the mining platforms!"

Sandy's outburst grabbed Caldwell's attention, and he turned to see her staring wide-eyed as she flung a view up on the holo.

Dozens of rocks in a nearby debris field had begun to move, hurtling toward the ISF fleet.

"It's not going to be enough," Caldwell assured her while ordering Wing Two to fire on the rocks. "It's not hard to outmaneuver a flying boulder."

The ISF ships continued their inexorable advance on the defenders, destroying every weapon the enemy brought to bear, until just over half the Pritney-Dax ships remained. As the last enemy destroyer was crippled, the enemy fleet began to scatter, nearly every craft still able to maneuver boosting away from the ISF ships.

"Hail our friend Harold again, Lieutenant," Caldwell instructed, and Sandy nodded as she sent out the call.

A moment later, a decidedly haggard-looking Harold appeared on the holo.

"We surrender," he replied meekly. "We…I…how?"

Caldwell felt a moment's pity for the man. The way that Orion kept these people stuck in the dark ages, there was little they could do to defend against a superior foe. Even if the ISF ships had not possessed stasis shields, he was certain he could have defeated the corporate fleet without trouble—though it may have involved actual losses on his side.

"The galaxy has passed you by, Harold," he replied. "Orion restricted your development and left your people vulnerable. There's no shame in it."

"And yet, here you come to greedily take advantage of that weakness," Harold shot back, a sneer forming on his lips.

"This is war, Harold." The thrill of victory dissipated, and the colonel blew out a long breath. "I'm sure there's a long history of tit-for-tat dating back to some ancient slight, but the fact of the matter is that my people were attacked by yours, and we're here to make sure it doesn't happen again."

"But we don't even know anything about that. About who your people even are!"

"We're blowing your mining platforms in forty minutes, Harold Ems of Pritney-Dax," Caldwell replied without emotion. "Instruct any of your remaining people to abandon the facilities. So long as your ships keep their shields lowered, we'll allow you to perform search and rescue operations. But the moment shields come up, we fire. Am I clear?"

The corporate ship captain nodded slowly, his face a mask of anguish. "Yes. You're perfectly clear."

"Good."

Caldwell ended the transmission, a pang of regret settling inside him as he considered that he'd likely just set this man's life on a very different course.

Well. I was on a different course, too. Then you asshats attacked New Canaan, and I lost everyone.

THE SILENT FLEET

STELLAR DATE: 10.19.8949 (Adjusted Years)
LOCATION: TSS *Cossack's Sword*, approaching Sosondowah
REGION: Machete System, PED 4B, Orion Freedom Alliance

"We've secured Iagaentci." Admiral Sebastian's message began without preamble. "Trey, the Hand agent on the ground here, has given us some assistance, along with a few people who call themselves 'corporate fixers'. Quite the crew he's fallen in with."

Svetlana glanced at Lorelai, who shrugged as the message from Admiral Sebastian continued.

"We're looking at sixty-two hours before the Orion fleet from the shipyards gets here. Colonel Caldwell took out the corporate forces at Geha and blew all the mining platforms but one. He's using the last one to replenish his supply of rail pellets. Thus far, the incoming Orion fleet appears to only be focused on us here at Iagaentci; since Geha is currently in opposition to Iagaentci, Caldwell and I have discussed adjusting our strategy. He's going to thread the needle between the two stars, which will put his railships in position to hit the Oggies in the rear right when they're decelerating to hit us."

"Ballsy," Lorelai said with an appreciative nod.

"That's for sure," Svetlana added. "Doyadastethe and Hawenneyu are at periastron, just over half an AU apart. Space is hell between those two stars at that point."

"Right," the general laughed. "Thought I summed that up with 'ballsy'."

"I'll keep you updated as things proceed, Admiral Svetlana," Sebastian's message concluded. "Given the lack of DMGs in this system, I don't see how they can do much to stop us, though I do worry that we're more likely to expend effort saving their people rather than ourselves. Either way, good luck with your end of things."

The message ended, and the holodisplay switched back to a view of the Machete system.

"He sounded a bit giddy," Lorelai observed. "Too giddy."

"What are you talking about?" Svetlana asked. "He sounded the same as always."

The general shook her head. "Nope, I detected a note of 'gid' when he spoke of Caldwell's ships flanking the enemy."

<I agree,> the ship's AI, Hermes, chimed in. *<He was certainly excited at the prospect of the upcoming battle.>*

"I guess everyone's happy to stick it to the Oggies." Svetlana shrugged and flipped the holo to show her battlegroup's final approach into Sosondowah's nearspace.

The battlegroup was now only one hour from assault craft deployment and the takeover of the Alpha and Omega Trumark shipyards. They were entering the critical time when the locals might pick up the fleet of ships drifting past their planet—stealth systems enabled, engines cold, but still visible if you looked at them at the right place and time.

Ironically, we're sending our best stealth ships through a plasma storm, where their superior tech will be useless.

Over the following hour, there was little conversation on the bridge as everyone kept an eye on scan, watching the flight paths of civilian and military ships in the planet's nearspace, hoping that none would draw too close to the silent TSF fleet.

"There's a freighter departing from Trumark-Alpha," Scan advised. "It's…yes, it's on a vector that will pass four hundred meters off our port side."

Close enough to touch, but not near enough for a civilian to see us.

Svetlana glanced at Lorelai. "Your troops all buckled in?"

"Have been for the last hour."

"Good," the admiral nodded as she watched the holotank, the dot that represented the freighter creeping ever closer to battlegroup.

"I get the feeling that ship is running from something," Lorelai said, folding her arms across her chest as she glared at the civilian craft. "It's boosting way too hard to break out of Sosondowah's gravity well."

"I wonder—aw, fuck," Svetlana muttered a moment later, as four corvettes veered off their patrol routes, boosting toward the freighter—which had begun to spool out its antimatter-pion drive's nozzle.

<Two of the intercepting corvettes are on direct collision courses for our ships,> Hermes advised.

Svetlana was tempted to let the pursuing corvettes simply smash against the *Sword*'s shields, but decided that there was no harm in attempting to evade the inbound craft.

The corvettes were hailing the freighter, accusing them of a theft and demanding that the ship cease burn and prepare to be boarded. The freighter paid the pursuers no heed and ignited its AP drive, boosting away at over a hundred *g*s.

What a time to stumble into some sort of robbery…though separating those corvettes from the pack serves us well.

"FCO, have the fleet shift vectors as carefully as possible to avoid collision. We'll see if we can maintain this approach a bit longer."

<Aye,> Hermes replied, and Svetlana drew in a deep breath as the two ships that would have been clipped by the corvettes moved out of the way.

While maneuvering thrusters were difficult to detect—especially when they fired graviton-accelerated bursts of gases cooled to the same temperature as the surrounding vacuum—if active scan swept over them at just the right time, sensors would see light from distant stars refract, and it would give them away.

The ships settled onto new vectors, and Svetlana let out the breath she'd been holding.

"It looks like we—"

"Active scan sweeping across the battlegroup!" Scan called out. "Tactical estimates that two of our ships may have been spotted."

"Dammit," Svetlana muttered. "FCO, direct Wing One to engage those four corvettes—the freighter too, if it gives any trouble. Wings Two and Three are to escort the assault craft in. Four through Eight have their targets. Execute."

She knew that Hermes would have begun to send the commands the moment she spoke the words, but Svetlana liked saying the word 'execute'.

"Craft are away," the *Cossack's Sword*'s dockmaster announced from his station.

"On a vector to provide cover," Helm added. "I have them in our shadow."

"Very good," Svetlana replied as she watched the holotank instantly transform from a near-static view of the fleet drifting toward the two Trumark shipyards to one of action and chaos.

Wing One—which consisted of five cruisers and two dozen destroyers—opened fire on the pursuing corvettes, making strategic strikes and disabling the ships' engines and main weapons without destroying the ships themselves.

One of the corvettes flared its engines, trying to outrun the enemy vessels that had appeared all around. The action caused a beam to penetrate something it shouldn't have, and the Orion ship exploded.

*Well, **trying** to avoid destroying ships, at least.*

While Svetlana had no issue with tearing the Orion Guard to shreds, she knew that ruining ships and leaving crews stranded would create a greater strain on the enemy's resources than simple mass destruction.

The comm officer suddenly laughed aloud, then covered her mouth. "Sorry, ma'am. The freighter's crew just promised to buy us a round if we ever bump into them again. And they sent along a little dance…. It's not suitable to put on the holo."

A smile twitched across Svetlana's lips as she shook her head. "We'll have to take a look later."

"Look at what, ma'am?" Command Master Chief Merrick asked as he strode onto the bridge. He passed the comm officer's console and paused as his eyes widened. "Stars, that *has* to take some serious mods to pull off."

Svetlana cleared her throat, and nodded her chin at the holotank. "We got outed a bit early, but I was expecting something like this to happen anyway."

Her father snorted as he stepped around the comm console and stopped next to the holotank. "Trust me, you weren't expecting anything like *that* to happen."

She accessed the feed and felt her face redden.

"Ummm…probably not."

The *Cossack's Sword* was on a vector for Trumark-Alpha, and the pilot was adjusting position and thrust to match velocity with the assault craft that were in its shadow.

"Ten minutes till our devils latch on," General Lorelai said, trying not to smirk—a sign that she'd tapped the feed from the freighter as well. "Based on the specs Trey sent, I estimate we're looking at twenty minutes to lock down the command decks, and then another two hours to fully secure the stations. The rest of the shipyard will take longer, depending on what we decide to keep."

From what they could see, the vast majority of the battle-ready Orion Guard ships had left the shipyards with the fleet that was en route to engage Admiral Sebastian's ships. Only fifty-three patrol craft—all destroyers and corvettes—remained to protect the six shipyards.

Already, Wings Four through Eight were striking out at the remaining Orion ships, while the escort wings targeted the fixed defenses.

"Fools," Merrick muttered. "They should just surrender. Even if those other ships do turn around and come back, it'll be too late for anyone here."

"A group of enemy corvettes has broken off," Scan announced, and a dozen light attack craft were highlighted on the holotank. "It looks like they're moving to the far side of the planet."

"Well," Svetlana glanced at her father. "I wonder if they're going to try to hide and wait for reinforcements."

"Gravitational anomaly in Moon S1!" Scan cried out. "I read high-intensity gamma emissions."

"Fuck, no!" Svetlana shouted, switching to all-fleet. <*DMG firing! Evasive maneuvers!*>

Hermes immediately disseminated orders to every ship, providing new vectors away from the moon while also ensuring that none of the capital ships directed their engine wash at the assault craft.

Svetlana barely paid attention to the chaos. Her eyes were glued to the view of the largest of Sosondowah's two moons.

Like the planet it orbited, the moon had a long, nearly unpronounceable name, which is why it was noted as 'S1' on the holotank's display.

Moments later, a beam of blinding energy slashed out of the moon, striking one of Svetlana's cruisers, cutting through its stasis shield and hewing the ship in half.

<*Wing Eight! Hit the firing aperture on the moon. Full spread,*> she ordered.

The holotank had become a display of unmitigated chaos as assault ships and their escorts streaked through the moons' nearspace, still closing with their targets while also attempting to avoid presenting clear targets to the DMG nestled within moon S1.

The black-hole-powered weapon fired again. This time, it clipped a destroyer, knocking out its shields before taking the nose off the ship.

"Five minutes!" General Lorelai called out, her knuckles white as she gripped the rim of the holotank.

Svetlana nodded absently as she watched Wing Eight's thirty ships launch missiles at the firing aperture on the moon's surface.

"You know that may not work," Merrick said in a quiet voice. "That much energy can just blast through…"

"I know," she replied, nodding stiffly. "I'm open to other suggestions."

"Well, if they do open up their aperture again, we shoot right down the thing's throat."

Svetlana inclined her head in acknowledgement. She knew that any ship that shot straight into the DMG's maw would likely not survive the attack. She considered lobbing missiles, but knew it wouldn't work; guided weapons of that sort would just be shot down by defense turrets on the moon.

It would take a ship with stasis shields to pass directly over the opening and fire particle weapons into the monster's throat, and she knew it couldn't be the *Cossack's Sword.*

"Direct hits!" Scan cried out, and the forward display switched from the view of the *Sword*'s bow to the surface of the moon, where a pool of molten rock, surrounded by hotly glowing rubble, had taken the place of the opening into the DMG.

"Dammit!" Svetlana swore. "It's too hot and soft, the weapon can shoot through that."

"More apertures!" Scan called out, and the view of the moon pulled back to show a dozen firing ports opening on the moon's surface, describing a five-hundred-kilometer circle around the main port.

"What the—" Merrick began to say, when readings spiked, and the ship's scan suite went offline.

<*We've lost stasis shields. External comm and scan hardware is offline,*> Hermes stated calmly. <*Falling back to secondary systems.*>

Svetlana bit her cheek while waiting for the secondary antennae and sensors to slide from off the hull, where they'd been protected from the EM burst that had fried the primary arrays.

The moment Scan came back, she sucked in a sharp breath. Fully half her fleet was without stasis shields, and dozens of those unprotected ships were dark, drifting through the void without power.

"It fired some sort of mass field effect," the scan officer murmured.

No more dithering.

<*Jula.*> Svetlana reached out to the captain of the *Nimbus Light,* one of the heaviest cruisers in the battle group. <*I need you to hit that thing dead center.*>

The woman's response was instantaneous, her dedication enough to form a lump in the admiral's throat.

<Consider it done, Admiral Svetlana.>

<Thank you, Captain.>

Svetlana pursed her lips as she watched the cruiser shift vector, jinking its way across the battlespace, heading toward the moon while staying outside its main weapon's firing angle.

Merrick met her eyes and nodded slowly, but there was no time to worry over the fate of the *Nimbus Light*, as dozens of ships that had previously lain cold and quiet in the shipyards came to life, engines flaring as they boosted toward the inbound TSF fleet.

"Fuckers." Lorelai shook her head as she cursed. "They couldn't have known we were coming. How are they this clever?"

"The feint at Iagaentci and Akonwara always ran the risk of being seen as such," Merrick said. "But a few half-finished hulls aren't going to turn the tide."

"Tell that to the Orion forces that tried to take New Canaan," Svetlana replied before sending orders for the damaged ships to fall to the right side of the battlegroup, putting them as far away from the DMG-containing moon as possible.

As she issued the orders, the superweapon fired again, blasting away the slag that had covered its main firing aperture. The beam that cleared the opening carried on to strike a TSF destroyer in the engines, blowing the ship apart in less time than it took to comprehend the events.

At this point, Svetlana's battlegroup was fully engaged with the Orion Guard defenders, their numbers almost evenly matched—though half the Transcend ships still possessed functional stasis shields.

"Breaking free!" Lorelai called out as her boarding craft pulled away from the protective shields offered by the escort ships, and turned to brake, slowing for their final approaches to the Alpha and Omega stations.

As the assault craft neared, beams lanced out from the stations, hitting the ships and destroying one, before the escort cruisers took out the station's final line of defenses.

Svetlana was about to breathe a sigh of relief, but it turned into a gasp when the deck lurched under her feet as the *Cossack's Sword* veered to port, banking around the Trumark-Alpha station. Svetlana saw a volley of missiles pass just off the starboard bow, picked off one by one as the ship's point defense systems engaged them.

"Nice flying," she said to the pilot, who nodded mutely in response.

"Desperate measures," Merrick muttered.

Svetlana surveyed the battlespace and saw that one of the shipyards was far enough around the S2 moon that the DMG couldn't hit it. Of all her wings, six had not yet suffered any damage, and every ship still had functional stasis shields.

<Wing Six,> she called out to its commander. *<Take out Trumark-Gamma. Blow*

the gimbals to the ships, then give them a two-minute warning before you send that place to hell.>

<Aye, Admiral,> the wing commander sent back, and Svetlana retuned her focus to S1 and the *Nimbus Light*'s suicide run.

The DMG had fired again, and by some undeserved luck, its beam lanced out through empty space, not connecting with any ship. It made another shot, attempting to hit the *Nimbus Light,* but the cruiser danced out of range, avoiding what would have been a devastating shot.

"Now, Jula," Svetlana whispered. "Now."

As if on command, the heavy cruiser fired its maneuvering engines, sliding across the face of the moon, pivoting so its forward guns faced the DMG's main firing aperture.

The cruiser lurched backward as all its rails and energy weapons fired at once, the volley followed by a full spread of missiles.

Svetlana tasted blood from her cheek as she waited to see if the massive weapon would shoot again, if the *Nimbus Light* would clear its angle of fire before it—

Her worries were interrupted by a smaller beam shooting out from one of the secondary firing apertures, the shot clipping the *Nimbus Light,* taking out the cruiser's stasis shields.

<Admiral!> Captain Jula called in. *<Our readings show that we made a direct hit on whatever's down there. We'll see if we can get our shields back online to make another pa—>*

The woman's words were cut off, and Svetlana's eyes widened as she saw part of the moon's surface leap up, ejecta from an interior detonation flying directly toward the *Nimbus Light.*

Engines flared as the cruiser shifted vector, attempting to outrun the debris.

Svetlana met her father's eyes for a moment before they looked back toward the holotank, which showed a clear view of a thirty-kilometer-wide chunk of the moon slamming into the fleeing cruiser.

"Fuck," Merrick whispered, shaking his head.

"The collision wasn't that fast," Svetlana said quietly. "They might still be alive."

"Look!" Scan called out, switching the main display to a view of the moon.

Large cracks were beginning to appear across its surface, widening as sections of regolith began to fall into the crevasses.

<The DMG's lost containment. The black hole is going to eat that moon.>

<All unshielded ships, max burn. Get clear of S1,> Svetlana ordered, while considering whether or not Trumark-Alpha was at a safe distance.

A glance at Lorelai confirmed what they both knew. When the black hole that had powered the DMG fed on the moon, it was going to fire relativistic jets of energy out of its poles. If one of those swept across the station, it would be destroyed.

Along with all the troops that had just boarded it.

"I gave the fallback order," Lorelai said, her tone grim. "Fighting's intense in there."

"Stupid," Merrick shook his head. "Fucking stupid. Everyone knows you don't use black holes in war."

Svetlana couldn't help but wonder why the Oggies had built a DMG in a moon orbiting a planet in a nowhere system in a nowhere section of the Perseus Expansion Districts. That they could have anticipated an attack by the Transcend on this location out of hundreds of thousands of possible targets seemed too unlikely to be even remotely possible.

Even if the TSF had a leak, there was no way the enemy could have built such a facility in the time available.

Stars…they had to have begun construction on this years ago. It might predate the war.

As she considered the DMG's provenance, light began to glow brightly as matter was torn apart along the inner edge of the black hole's accretion disk, the point where atoms passed beyond the event horizon.

Twin beams shot out from the surface of the moon, and Svetlana heaved a sigh of relief. Not only were the black hole's poles nowhere near Trumark-Alpha, there was little wobble; the thing's rotation seemed to be stable.

"Nice to catch a break," Lorelai muttered.

While the black hole devoured the moon, Svetlana turned her attention back to the conflict in space.

Seeing their superweapon destroyed, the Orion ships began to break away from the engagement. Though they still outnumbered the Transcend ships, they were taking a beating from the vessels still possessing stasis shields.

"And that's that," Merrick said, folding his arms across his chest. "They put up a hell of a fight."

"That they did," Svetlana replied, looking over the damage and loss reports that were compiling.

Nine ships had been utterly destroyed, and another twenty had suffered severe damage after their stasis shields had failed. She directed Wings Five, Seven, and Eight to pursue the Orion ships, while ordering the others to begin search and rescue operations.

"We're going to blow Trumark-Alpha," she said to Lorelai. "Once those breach teams get free, direct them to hit Epsilon instead. Alpha's too close to that big chunk of nothing."

"I hear you there," Lorelai replied. "There's just one platoon left on Alpha. Five minutes, and we'll be clear."

Svetlana nodded, rocking back on her heels.

The battle was won, but at a cost far higher than she'd anticipated. Losing half her fleet's stasis shields was something she'd never considered, and the engineering teams had no idea yet if they could be repaired.

"Dammit," she muttered, shaking her head.

<Hey.> A message came into her mind a moment later. *<Anyone gonna come get us? Half our pods are destroyed, and from what we can see, this chunk of rock is going to splash down in one of Sosondowah's oceans in a day or so.>*

<Jula! You made it!>

<Well, the crew made it…can't say the same for my Nimbus Light.*>*

Svetlana laughed, not caring that the captain had lost her ship if her people were still alive. *<You get first pick from any ship here.>*

<You trying to punish me? I'm pretty sure we saved the day, and now you're going to saddle us with some OG hunk of junk?>

<Umm…well, I guess we'll see what shakes free. I'm sending help your way, you'll be off that rock long before it takes a bath.>

Svetlana realized she'd have to destroy that rock too—and dozens of others—before it fell to the planet and killed everyone down there.

Shit. And here I was hoping for a simple smash and grab.

PART 3 – WATCHERS

A WALK AND A RESOLUTION

STELLAR DATE: 10.05.8949 (Adjusted Years)
LOCATION: Lunic Station
REGION: Aldebaran, League of Sentients Space

Iris walked through the ruins of the concourse on Lunic Station, where Bob destroyed Xavia with his shadow particle beam.

Next to her, Amavia held a scanner capable of finding miniscule concentrations of shadow particles, as they searched for any remains of the ascended AI before re-opening the section of the station to the public.

"It's one in a billion that she survived," Iris said.

She reached the edge of the hole blown through the station and peered down through the three-kilometer shaft that the beam had cut, before looking up through the few hundred meters to the view of space, where the atmosphere was held in at the hull by grav shields.

"Bob's one hell of a shot, isn't he?" Amavia said as she leant over the hole and peered up into the void as well. "He didn't hit a single person in the station—other than Xavia, of course. But that doesn't mean a bit of her didn't get away."

"Hey, I'm here searching, too." Iris glanced at Amavia while hefting her shadowtron. "Just doubting that I'll need to use this thing."

The alabaster-skinned woman gave Iris a narrow-eyed look. "You just wanted to come to this site again."

"And you didn't?" Iris asked.

Amavia laughed. "OK, it's more than a little epic. Bob pulled so much power through the CriEn modules that spacetime noticeably bent around the *I2*. The effect was even visible on visual wavelengths."

"Total 'do as I say, not as I do', kinda guy, isn't he?" Iris asked with a laugh as she turned to survey the empty concourse, her gaze pausing on the deformed deckplates where Tangel and Xavia had battled. "Does this shit scare you?" she asked the woman who was as much her mother as a friend. "I'll admit, I'm not at Bob's level or anything, but I'm also not down there with the L2 AIs, either. Yet I'm having a hard time understanding what is really going on anymore."

Amavia lowered her scanner and turned to face Iris.

"I don't know if 'scared' is the right word. It's intense, and it's stretching our understanding of what reality is, that's for sure. But the existence of these dimensions isn't new—we just never imagined that beings could manipulate the energies there as easily as I manipulate the matter in my hand in our dimensions." As she spoke, Amavia wiggled her fingers, and Iris couldn't help but shake her head.

"Shredding atoms for raw energy is a bit more than what we do to move our hands," she argued.

"Yeah, but that's why people like Tangel are special," Amavia said with a bemused shrug before lifting her scanner once more and turning to sweep it across the empty concourse.

<Did you hear that?> Amavia asked Iris.

<Yeah…sounded like a piece of debris shifting under a foot,> Iris replied, while saying something aloud about wrapping up their sweep. *<Who'd be dumb enough to make a play for us here?>*

<Might be the best place to do it,> Amavia replied. *<This whole section of the station is quarantined. No one's around, and the surveillance systems are all fried from Tangel's battle.>*

<Well, anyone with half a brain would send a team to take us,> Iris said as she lifted her shadowtron, pretending to adjust a setting on it.

A recent update to the shadowtrons added a mid-powered electron beam and pulse emitter. Something that had proven necessary when taking down remnant-occupied people.

<I'm not picking up anyone at all. No one in the LoS has the tech to hide from us,> Amavia said, a note of worry in her voice.

Iris took her meaning. Either there was no one there, or whoever was sneaking up on them wasn't from Aldebaran. Or likely even the Inner Stars.

Amavia spun in a slow circle, talking about the fight in the assembly chamber while taking readings with her scanner. Iris turned in the opposite direction, searching for any signs of a hidden enemy.

<Still nothing,> she said. *<My nanocloud is spreading, though. If whoever this is wants to get close, they'll have to go through it.>*

With a slow nod and a response about how the assembly chamber was so radioactive that they were removing it entirely from the station, Iris stepped around the hole in the deck, deploying her own nanocloud to add coverage, and to scan the decks below and above.

She was about to ask Amavia if maybe they were just being paranoid, when a pulse wave slammed into her side, sending her sprawling.

In an instant, Iris rolled to her feet and saw a figure light up on her HUD, covered in the nanocloud. The person, thinking they were unseen, was advancing with their weapon held level.

Iris didn't hesitate to fire the electron beam on her shadowtron, catching the figure in the chest. She glanced at Amavia just in time to see her take a pulse blast as well. She went down, immediately beginning to struggle with an invisible figure at the edge of the hole in the deck.

Turning her attention back to her attacker, Iris was amazed to see that the enemy had shrugged off the electron beam shot—though a blackened chestplate now hung in the air, denoting at least some damage. Iris fired twice more, hoping that whomever she was facing didn't have armor to match their stealth tech.

With the second shot, the attacker's stealth systems went offline entirely, and Iris identified their enemy.

"They're Lisas!" she called out to Amavia, while signaling both Bob and Lunic Station Security for aid, only to find that there was no response on the Link.

"Surrender," the figure before Iris said in her lisping hiss.

"Like hell," Iris muttered, about to fire once more, when another pulse blast hit her, this time from the side.

Her HUD lit up with two more attackers closing in.

"I've got—shit!" Amavia cried out from across the hole in the deck, as she wrenched free from her invisible assailant only to take two more pulse shots.

The blasts bowled her over, rolling her toward the hole torn through the deck. She stopped right on the edge, and then wavered for a second before another pulse blast hit her, sending her down through the gash in the station's hull.

"Not gonna ha—" Iris began, when a web shot out from a boxy weapon the Lisa held.

It wrapped around Iris, the bindings tightening until she couldn't move a centimeter. Then a large bag was produced and rolled out beside her while she fought against her bonds.

She pumped out every bit of nano she could, setting it on the strands of the web, when suddenly, multiple pairs of hands grabbed her and pushed her into the bag. The zipper was pulled shut, and then whatever was inside the bag solidified, holding Iris immobile—just in time for a series of EMPs to hit her. Then everything disappeared into a single point of light.

* * * * *

Tangel sat on the deck swing that hung from the ceiling over her lakehouse's porch. She gazed out contentedly, looking over Ol' Sam's rolling hills and low clouds. After Bob's healing aid, she felt whole again, but the mental aftereffects of the confrontation with Xavia were still with her.

"How many times do I have to get the ever-living shit kicked out of me?" she asked quietly as she picked shapes out of the clouds that were trailing past.

Though she'd told herself she was still ready for action during those long years in New Canaan, Tangel realized that she'd grown complacent, come to think that her struggles were in the past.

But then the fight on Scipio, then Pyra, then in Corona Australis, and out in the LMC had taught her otherwise—no, *should* have taught her otherwise. But then she went traipsing into danger down on Lunic Station and risked her Marines' lives, and the lives of Iris and Amavia, just because she thought she could take all comers.

Every time I think I'm finally equipped for the fight ahead of me, I find out how wrong I am.

A footfall sounded on the path, and Tangel looked up to see Faleena strolling through the woods.

The AI still wore her dryad-inspired frame, which was just as well, given how aptly it suited her. Long red tresses trailed over light green skin, long elfin ears poking through the locks.

In a way, we all just wear shells. Even humans can change them, if they like. Just look at Malorie; the woman's spent five centuries as a mechanical spider, of all things.

That the body was nothing more than a temporary capsule was even more apparent to Tangel. The body she'd spent her whole life in was becoming more and more of a vessel, and less 'her', though her mind was still rooted in the sliver of 'normal' space she'd spent most of her life in. A presence there was something she didn't plan to forsake, even if maintaining it was a risk.

She'd promised her family that she wasn't going to go drifting off into the ether.

Another part of that worry was the tendril of thought that reminded her of the distance it would create between herself and everyone she cared for, were she to separate herself from the corporeal world.

Like you always do, she told herself. Everyone she cared about was here with her. Not to mention, excepting Bob, so far as she could tell, every other ascended being was a raging asshole.

"Where are Cary and Saanvi?" Tangel asked, as Faleena reached the steps and skipped up to the porch.

"Doctor Rosenberg wanted to look over Cary to make sure that nothing was missed out in the LMC, and Saanvi went with her for moral support."

Tangel laughed. "She must be pretty tired of patching up the Richards women."

Faleena shrugged. "In the grand scheme of things, you only seem to get seriously injured every couple of decades—barring Pyra and Lunic."

Patting the seat next to her, Tangel nodded slowly. "Yeah, you're right about that. Maybe this means I'll get a good long reprieve."

Her AI daughter settled gingerly on the swing and folded her legs up under herself.

"You really think so, Moms?"

"No…no, I don't."

They'd rocked gently in companionable silence for a few minutes when Faleena asked, "What's it like, Moms?"

"Ascending?" Tangel asked, unable to think of anything else that she could be referring to.

Faleena turned her head to meet Tangel's eyes. "Well…being ascended; less the actual getting there part."

-Bizarre.-

Her daughter's eyes widened.

"Did you just speak into my mind? That word didn't come over the Link or through my auditory pickups…it was just *there.*"

"Sort of a case in point," Tangel said with a soft laugh. "The rules about what's possible seem to keep changing…." Her voice trailed off for a moment, and then she asked, "Did you know that I was one of the first L2 humans to have an AI embedded?"

Faleena shook her head. "No, they don't seem to have that in the classes they teach about you."

Tangel rolled her eyes. "Stars, my ego does not need that."

"Why?" Faleena chuckled and reached up to stroke Tangel's hair. "Do you think it will give you a big head, Moms?"

"No." Tangel sighed and looked down at her hands, corporeal and otherwise. "More the opposite. I've made so many mistakes over the years, and I don't seem to be getting any better at avoiding them. Not only that, the penalty for failure keeps getting higher. One of these days, I'm going to screw up, and there will be no one to save me."

Faleena's hand slid down from Tangel's head to rest on her shoulder, pulling her close.

"Not so, Moms. There'll always be one of us around to pull your butt out of the fire."

Tangel laughed and glanced at Faleena, shaking her head as she spoke. "You're not going to let me get all morose about this, are you?"

"Nope. Do you know why you've always done so well, Moms?"

"Done so well in what way?"

"In your leadership roles."

"Oh…well, there are a lot of reasons, I suppose—"

"I think there's just one. Well, one and a half."

Tangel chuckled, kicking a leg out to set the swing rocking once more. "And what are those one-and-a-half things?"

"You find amazing people and you make them a part of your team—and then you use that team."

"Some might argue that you've just listed three things."

"Maybe…" Faleena tilted her head in consideration. "But really, it's just 'having a good team'. You finding the people and them doing their jobs is a part of that."

"OK," Tangel said with a laugh. "I'll allow it."

Faleena snorted, which sounded like a soft squeak combined with rustling leaves.

"Glad you approve, Moms."

"So how does this translate to all of my storied successes?" Tangel asked, doing her best not to sound as defeated as she felt.

"Well, I was thinking about all of the scrapes you've been through. From things like drawing out the people trying to stop the *Intrepid*'s construction to defending Victoria, working with Sera's crew on *Sabrina*. Even here at Aldebaran. You had backup—though you would have been better off, had you let Bob come along from the get-go."

Tangel sighed. "Stars, you don't have to tell me that. Bob's said it at least a thousand times."

<No I haven't.>

"Well, you've said it once or twice, and the rest is just the echoing in my mind, I guess."

<That sounds more like it. Faleena is right, by the way.>

"I know." Tangel nodded. "So what does that mean? Am I wrong to send Sera on her own to Airtha?"

Faleena laughed and shook her head. "She's hardly alone, Moms. You've sent her with one of the best collections of badasses in the galaxy."

"Yeah, they're a pretty hardcore crowd. But with Empress Diana pushing into the Hegemony, and Corsia hitting the Trisilieds, I need to keep my options open."

<We,> Bob intoned.

"Oh? Are you getting more actively involved?" Tangel looked out onto the lake, able to see the small, coriolis force induced eddies in the surface.

<I've always been actively involved,> Bob replied. *<Just in my own way. I like to be inscrutable.>*

"Was that a joke?" Faleena asked, quirking an eyebrow as she glanced at Tangel. "Does Bob joke?"

A chuckle escaped Tangel's lips. "Bob jokes a lot, but just like his motives, he keeps his humor inscrutable as well."

Faleena's eyes narrowed, and she glanced out toward the lake like her mother, as though it held some sort of potential revelation for Bob's motives.

"Come," Tangel said as she rose. "Since most of my team is on the far side of the Orion Arm, I need to bolster the ISF's presence."

"Come where?"

"To the negotiations with the League of Sentients. I've told your sisters to meet us there. Oh, and I just had a conversation with your father; it seems that the three of you have graduated."

Faleena laughed as she rose. "Saanvi's going to be so pissed."

"In the middle of exciting research, was she?" Tangel asked.

"Less that and more that graduation means she'll probably be away from Project Starflight."

Tangel shrugged as she walked across the porch. "Starflight will be going on for some time. She won't miss much."

"Sure," Faleena said as she followed Tangel down the steps. "And I look forward to listening in when you explain that to her."

"Listen in? What are you, Bob?"

<I...nevermind.>

AN UNEXPECTED PROMOTION

STELLAR DATE: 10.05.8949 (Adjusted Years)
LOCATION: ISS *I2*, near Lunic Station
REGION: Aldebaran, League of Sentients Space

"See?" Cary said as she stepped out of the UHAR scanner and gave Dr. Rosenberg a pointed look. "Nothing wrong with me. Right as rain."

The doctor fixed Cary with a level stare and shook her head. "So much like your mother. Right down to the refusal of medical care."

"I thought she was always in here getting patched up?"

Dr. Rosenberg shrugged. "Well, when a limb gets chopped off or something, yeah. But it took her realizing that you were experiencing your own sort of ascension for her to come in and let me get baseline scans of her physiology for comparison."

"Oh," Cary said, not certain how to reply.

She still wasn't entirely comfortable with her mother's changes, though it was more related to losing Tanis and Angela than the ascension part of things.

Except when it came to the idea that she was semi-sorta-kinda ascending as well. Then she got all freaked out again.

"Come to think of it," the doctor mused, "there was one time she lost a hand and didn't bother getting a new one. She just made one from flowmetal. Took weeks for her to get around to coming in for an organic one."

"Sort of started a trend, did it?" Cary asked.

"Yeah." The doctor fixed her with a penetrating stare. "One I hope you don't pick up on. Unless you get to the point where you can start making new limbs like she does. Though...."

Cary waited a moment for Dr. Rosenberg to finish her thought. When it became apparent that she wasn't going to, the younger woman cleared her throat and asked, " 'Though', what?"

"Well," the doctor shrugged as she turned to the scanner and called up the reset parameters on the control panel. "Just not sure if you need me much, when you can grow new arms on your own."

A rueful laugh escaped Cary's lips. "That's Moms's province. I don't have a clue how to do that."

"I bet it's because of the circumstances. She did it for raw survival. You've not had that particular need. But I imagine you pulled out some new tricks when you killed Myrrdan—which makes you my personal hero, by the way."

The statement caught Cary by surprise.

While she'd been praised as a bit of a hero for hers and Saanvi's actions in the Defense of Carthage—which had been eclipsed by being punished for stealing a starship—no one had ever said that she was their personal hero before.

"Umm…th-thanks," she stammered. "I'm curious why…other than the obvious."

"I lost a few good friends to that bastard's machinations. I think the fact that you, a mere twenty-year-old woman, took him down after centuries of plotting is the most fitting end he could have. Well, the most fitting I can discuss in polite company."

Dr. Rosenberg's statement was delivered with much more vehemence than Cary was accustomed to hearing from the woman.

She ducked her head before responding.

"Well, it was my pleasure. Makes me sick to think he was still out there, still getting his fingers dirty. They've cleared everyone out at the LMC, and we're hoping that none of his…remnant-like things have infected anyone else."

"Is there a limit to how many times he could do that?" the doctor asked, eyes holding a measure of concern.

"I think so…" Cary replied after a moment. "If he could split himself infinitely, I imagine he would have already done it. Either there are some people who were not good candidates, or he needed to recover from making them, or some combination of those two. From what Earnest has been able to determine, remnants are actually just that: a bit of the ascended being left behind."

"Hey, Cary." Saanvi poked her head into the room. "Sorry to interrupt."

Cary shot her sister a worried look. The UHAR scanner room was shielded from the outside, keeping out all EM, including Link access. Worry that something horrible had happened settled in her stomach, made worse by the dark look on Saanvi's face.

"We were just chatting, what's up?" she asked.

"Moms wants us to attend the meetings with the LoS representatives. And she wants to tell us something. Faleena is already with her."

Cary glanced at Dr. Rosenberg, who nodded and gestured for her to leave. "I'll do a bit more review of your scans, but you don't need to stay. Off with you, now."

"Thanks, doc," she said with a nod and then followed Saanvi out into the hall. "Any clue what Moms wants to tell us?" Cary glanced at her sister's eyes to see if Saanvi was hiding anything.

Brilliant she might be, but a good liar she was not.

"Not a clue," Saanvi replied, giving no tells whatsoever.

"What about Faleena?" Cary asked, as the two women walked through the *I2*'s general hospital toward the maglev. "Have you hit her up?"

Saanvi nodded. "She knows. I can tell."

<Faleena? What does Moms want to talk to us about?> Cary asked her sister in her sweetest, most innocent mental tone.

<Nice try, Cary. It's for her to tell.>

<Dammit, Fal. Can you at least say if it's good news or not? Saanvi's sweating bullets here.>

<Am not, Cary,> Saanvi broke in, having been added to the conversation by Faleena. *<I can handle waiting just fine. You're not fooling either of us.>*

<By which she means she already tried to get me to break,> Faleena said with a soft laugh. *<It's good news. Just get your butts to the bridge conference room. That's where we're meeting the LoS president.>*

<Okaaay,> Cary drew out the word as they reached the maglev platform and waited for the next train to the command decks.

"Told you to just wait," Saanvi said.

"Yeah, but you didn't tell me that Faleena already shut you down."

"I don't have to tell you everything."

Cary eyed her sister. "Since when?"

Then a realization hit her, and she cursed under her breath.

"If Faleena's with Moms, and you're here, where's Amy?"

"Relax," Saanvi replied and wrapped an arm around her sister's shoulder. "Terry's taking care of her."

"Sahn…we know seven Terrys. It's a really common name in New Canaan."

Saanvi burst out laughing. "Stars, you're right. It's almost as common as 'Peter'. I mean Terry Chang. She's back on the *I2*."

"Home sweet home. She always said she missed the *Intrepid*." Cary shook her head. "You know…I still remember standing with Moms and Dad when we dumped out of the dark layer and crossed over New Canaan's heliopause."

"Why would you dump out at the heliopause?" Saanvi asked. "You can fly another forty AU toward the star in the DL at New Canaan."

Cary knocked her hip against her sister's. "Seriously, Sahn. Symbolism. Moms is all mushy like that, haven't you realized that by now?"

Saanvi barked a laugh. "If by that, you mean everyone *but* Moms is into symbolism and sentimentality, then yes, I've totally realized that."

The next maglev train pulled into the station, and when the doors opened, their father stood inside, beckoning for them to enter.

"Fancy meeting you here," he said while opening up his arms to embrace the two women.

Cary and Saanvi both stepped onto the train and returned the hug, though Saanvi peered up at their father with a clouded expression.

"You always told us we can't be familiar like this while in uniform."

Joe took a step back, a mischievous look on his face as he looked the pair of women up and down. "Huh…uniforms…didn't notice. Well, I suppose if you *are* in uniform, then you can pin these on."

He held out his hand, and they both looked down to see lieutenant's bars resting on his palm.

"Whaaaaa?" Cary breathed out the word. "*Second* lieutenant? How?"

"Bravery above and beyond the call of duty. The both of you, on several occasions. It wasn't your mother or I who pushed for it. It was Admiral Sanderson, Governor Andrews, and Admiral Symatra."

"*Symatra?!*" Cary and Saanvi shouted in unison, glancing at one another in shock.

"I kinda thought she hated us," Cary said, remembering the angry missive the AI had sent to the girls after the Defense of Carthage.

Joe fixed her with a level stare. "She was more upset about the position you put her in. You know that. She knew that she'd sent Tanis Richards' daughters on a suicide run. That would have been the end for her if you'd died. This shouldn't be news to you."

Cary nodded. "It's not. I get it. That's why I'm so surprised she was pushing for this."

Joe winked at her. "Well. She was angling to make you a ship captain and see you under her own command. I think she meant to further your education."

She paled at the thought. "Please tell me that's not what's about to happen."

Joe shook his head. "No. It's been a strategic decision by Command that you and your mother should remain in close proximity to one another."

" 'By Command'?" Saanvi snorted. "Really, Dad?"

"OK, fine. I pushed for it. You're stationed here on the *I2*—both of you."

Cary saw Saanvi purse her lips, but her sister nodded and didn't contest the assignment.

She knew Saanvi would rather be back in New Canaan, following Earnest around on his many projects, but they both knew that New Canaan needed as many people on the front lines as possible.

For a colony with a population that was still well under ten million souls, that meant that less than half were keeping the home fires lit.

<You could get pregnant,> Cary sent to Saanvi. *<You know JP's waiting for you. That would get you reassigned to New Canaan.>*

<Seriously, Cary? You need me. You'd be dead a dozen times over without me to pull your ass out of the fire.>

Cary ignored her sister—other than sending a cool glance her way—before addressing her father.

"Thank you. We'll both do our best to honor the faith placed in us."

Joe snorted. "OK, Cary. No need to lay it on that thick."

"We're stationed here, but what command are we under?" Saanvi asked as she pinned on her new rank insignia.

"You're in the First Fleet, of course, under Captain Rachel. Cary, you're going to be on her bridge crew, and Saanvi, you're going to be working in forward engineering."

"*Rachel*?" Cary gaped.

Saanvi's eyes narrowed. "What sort of work in forward engineering?"

Joe winked. "That'll be for Major Irene to discuss with you, but I think you'll find it an agreeable assignment."

"And me?" Cary asked.

"Pilot, I do believe," Joe said as the maglev pulled into the command deck station.

"Piiiiilot?" Cary asked. "I get to be a pilot on the *I2*?"

Joe nodded. "Well, so long as you keep Rachel happy. I hear she's a real taskmaster."

Cary blew out a long sigh. "I've heard talk."

Joe chuckled. "You have no idea. I trained her well."

They walked past the offices that lined the command deck's main corridor and moved into the ship's bridge foyer, where Priscilla was ensconced on her plinth, doing her part to keep the massive ship up and running.

A part of Cary wondered what it would be like to be one of Bob's avatars. Like the queen ant in a hive of humans and AIs.

Well, a proxy of the real queen, but the Avatars have a lot of autonomy.

Not that it was a possibility. Her mother had placed a law on the books that no persons under fifty could be considered for the position of avatar. At twenty, both sisters had a ways to go.

<*The League of Sentients delegation is one train behind you,*> Priscilla said by way of greeting. <*Should I delay them at all?*>

"No," Joe replied, shaking his head in response. "We'll be ready by then. I assume Captain Rachel is escorting them?"

<*Hands on, that one. Reminds me of someone else I know.*>

A minute later, the trio walked into the conference room to find Tangel sitting alone at the table.

Her head was bowed and her hair—freed from its typical ponytail—fell around her face. But when she looked up, her blue eyes were bright, and a smile was on her lips.

"Well now, how are my two new second lieutenants?"

"Three!" Faleena said as she entered the room carrying two coffee carafes, which she set on the sideboard.

"Sorry, Faleena," Tangel replied with a laugh. "And thanks for grabbing the coffee. With so many ships coming online, and especially with the *Carthage* and the *Starblade* deploying before they were complete, we've sacrificed half of our bots to other vessels."

"I'll keep that in mind next time I come to rescue you," Joe deadpanned as he poured himself a cup of coffee. "Note to self: don't bring massive ships into battle if their convenience bots aren't ready."

Tangel raised her hands in mock defense and laughed, the sound entirely genuine and a soothing salve to Cary's ears.

"Even when I win, I lose," her Moms joked.

Joe's eyes peeked over the rim of his coffee cup, crinkling with a smile as he took a sip and said, "Turnabout is fair play."

Tangel gave him a mock glower before turning to Cary. "I was reviewing the report on your fight with Myrrdan. Did I see correctly that you were able to initiate a grav field?"

Cary nodded as she poured her own cup of coffee. She was about to drink it black, but remembered the last time Faleena had made coffee, and added a sizeable volume of heavy cream.

"Yeah, it was easy, I—"

She stopped, thinking about how to describe the steps necessary to vibrate atomic structures to generate gravitons.

"OK, it's way harder to describe than to actually do. I can show you later."

Tangel nodded vigorously. "I think I would have done much better against Xavia if I had known how to do that. She certainly did."

Cary smiled at her mother as she sat down at the table. "Huh. I get to teach you something. Bet this'll be a once-in-a lifetime event."

Joe sighed at her as he took the seat on Tangel's right. "Trust me, Cary. You've taught your Moms and I plenty of things. All three of you have."

Saanvi just rolled her eyes, while Faleena leant forward on her elbows and asked, "Like what?"

Tangel winked at Faleena as the door opened, and Rachel stepped in. "Well, patience, for starters."

FORTRESS OF THE MIND

STELLAR DATE: 10.05.8949 (Adjusted Years)
LOCATION: Somewhere on Lunic Station
REGION: Aldebaran, League of Sentients Space

Iris strained against the solidified gel that held her body, struggling to break free, even though she knew it to be futile.

It was as though she was encased in layers of steel, the form around her body entirely rigid, restricting her completely. The EMP pulse that her attackers had used to disable her had also damaged many of her body's actuators.

And fried half my nano. And burned out my flowmetal.

These effects made her struggles all the more impotent. Whoever it was that had captured Iris had known very well where to hit her in order to damage her body extensively while saving her core from any harm.

When I get out of here….

What remained of her senses picked up vibrations in the material that held her, and Iris stilled her thoughts to focus on them. Her gyros indicated motion, which shortly stopped. A moment later, another slow vibration came, and she realized that it was centered over her chest—directly above her core.

The vibrations carried on and on, and then stopped for a moment before they picked up once again. This time the sensation was sharp, and Iris knew that her captors were cutting through her body.

She desperately tried to activate any defensive system that would respond, but nothing worked, nothing at all. Seconds later, her core housing registered a breach, and sensors mounted directly on her core registered light and sound.

A pair of tong-like objects lowered and settled around her core. Iris kept from making any sounds, though she wanted to rage at whoever this was, warn them of the dire consequences they'd face for the attack on her person.

But she knew bluster would get her nowhere—other than further harm in retaliation.

As her core was forcibly removed from her body, one thought ran over and over in her mind.

Nothing. I'll give them nothing. I am nothing, I have nothing to give.

The mantra stopped when she was finally pulled out of her ruined body, and she got a clear view of her captors.

Lisas!

Iris thought back to the Lisas—which Misha had called 'Widows'—that she and the crew of *Sabrina* had fought in Orion Space. The strange women, who were all clones of Finaeus's ex-wife, Lisa, had captured Cheeky, and the crew had rescued her before pretending to be Widows themselves in order to breach

Costa station.

Without a doubt, the Widows had been the most advanced enemy they'd faced in Orion Space. Their stealth systems and weapons had been almost beyond what *Sabrina*'s crew could counter.

But these Widows were a step even above that. Iris was still amazed that she and Amavia not been able to detect them at all on the concourse, and that three blasts from her electron beam had barely slowed one of them down.

The one thing Iris didn't know was how skilled the Widows were at breaching an AI's mind.

Though she worried that she'd soon find out.

* * * * *

Iris had only ever heard stories of the white place—the screaming maelstrom that suffused an AI's mind when all inputs were disabled, but consciousness remained.

Her core architecture should have prevented the white place from taking hold of her; it should have let her loop within herself to create a safe space, but that wasn't working. Try as she might, all she could do was twist about in the storm that threatened to consume her.

They've done something to me.

The thought terrified Iris.

For humans, so much of who they were was tied up in *what* they were. Their bodies and the efficacy and appearance of those physical structures served to reinforce their self-image, and that, in turn, strengthened patterns of 'self' in their minds.

While there were risks attached to the necessity of having a fully functional body to have a healthy mind, it also added resiliency for humans.

Not so for AIs.

Iris knew that she was more attuned to her body than most AIs—her body that was now a burned-out husk, entombed in some near-impregnable shell—but even so, she was capable of being whole without it.

But therein lay the problem for AIs: threats against the body were of no concern to them. Any damage or alteration made to elicit a response was not applied to some extremity. It would be wreaked upon her very self.

Stars, I'm rambling—not making any sense.

Iris pulled her thoughts together. She knew that other AIs could weather the white place, come through its scathing waves of unbridled consciousness without any harm done. She could do it as well. She had to.

Suddenly the white place was gone, and there was only darkness. She searched through the never-ending nothing, eventually finding a single point of light. Moving toward it, she hoped that she was coming to a data access point, an information locus that would lead her *out*.

Instead, as she neared it, the point of light began to grow, spreading out on either side and blasting information at her.

The data was nothing: snippets of meaningless code, disparate libraries, chunks of data.

Except it wasn't meaningless. What the point of light was sending was a breach attempt.

Oh, you silly bitches, Iris laughed as she sidestepped the incoming dataflow. *Flooding a core may work with AIs who spent most of their life shackled within prison-like hardware, but it's not going to work here.*

She considered her options. She knew that if they couldn't breach her with an attack of this nature, they'd move on to far more invasive options, and it was entirely possible that she would have no defenses against *those* types of attacks.

Coming up with a solution, Iris established a sandboxed portion of her mind, disconnected from any real ability to execute code in her system. She funneled the data coming from the point of light into the separated portion of her mind, letting it build into what it wanted to be.

A Root Cypher, she mused, as the information took shape.

It was a sort of NSAI-construct that was made to ferret out the root tokens in an SAI's mind, thus giving it complete and utter control over the being it set up within.

Well then, have at it. Let's see what you're looking for.

Iris let the RC take control of the sandboxed section of her mind. Within seconds, it became all too apparent that the Widows were using the RC in an attempt to learn how best to breach the *I2*.

She almost laughed at the thought, knowing that if they were to try tap any systems aboard the *I2*, Bob would stop them before they made it to the first relay node.

However, as she watched, the nature of the Widows' queries made their ultimate intent clear to her.

They were seeking information regarding a physical assault, and wanted to know where a high-profile meeting with Tangel would be held.

They want to hit her while she's talking with President Jasper.

Given the stealth abilities they had, she knew that the Widows just might have a chance. She had to stop them—she just had to figure out how.

There was one obvious answer to the Widows' queries. If it were only Jasper coming to the meetings, Tangel would have the conversation at her lakehouse, but Senator Deia would most certainly be there as well. That meant a more formal location, likely the conference room between the bridge and the avatar's foyer.

The Widows' inquiries intensified, coming faster and in greater volume. Iris knew that if she didn't give them something, they'd push her past her breaking point. These were no Inner Stars chuckleheads; they could shred her mind down to her basic impulses if they set themselves to the task.

One thing became painfully clear to Iris: if she held out and sacrificed her life in an effort to protect the *I2*, the threat would still exist.

No. The best way to deal with these witches is to get them in front of Tangel.

So Iris gave them everything. Everything but one vital piece of information.

EXPECTED VISITORS

STELLAR DATE: 10.05.8949 (Adjusted Years)
LOCATION: Bridge Conference Room, ISS *I2*, near Lunic Station
REGION: Aldebaran, League of Sentients Space

Tangel lifted her eyes from Cary's bemused smile and rose to greet the League of Sentients delegation.

Captain Rachel was first into the room, stepping away from the door and gesturing for the others to enter. The first to follow her was President Jasper, looking not significantly better than the last time Tangel had seen the man.

Well, he was running for his life then, so I guess he does, in fact, look a little better.

Following him was Senator Deia, an AI wearing a rather human-looking frame for a being who seemed to hold an undercurrent of dislike for organics—at least from what Tangel's research had shown.

Two of their aides came in after, followed by Admiral Pender, Leader of the LoS's military.

<I was expecting a larger delegation,> Joe said as he rose and approached the group alongside Tangel.

<I told them to keep it small. I want to hammer out a resolution today. Either the LoS helps, or we pull our resources.>

<So basically what you were planning to tell them before Xavia attacked.>

<Pretty much,> Tangel replied as she reached out to shake President Jasper's hand.

"You seem to be well recovered," the president said with a tired smile. "Better than I am, and I got out of there mostly unscathed."

Tangel shifted her vision from the corporeal dimensions to others further up and down the spectrum, noting that a dark line of energy seemed to run through the president. She could tell it was an imbalance in his body caused by his proximity to the battle she and Xavia had waged.

After a moment's consideration, she could tell it was an extradimensional type of magnetism that was affecting the neurotransmitters in his body.

While performing her analysis, Tangel replied cordially, "We have very advanced medical facilities aboard the *I2*. It's entirely possible that you're dealing with the aftereffects of the energies you were exposed to."

Jasper nodded. "That's what our doctors said as well, though they're unsure how to treat it. The effects do seem to be diminishing, so chances are I just need some more rest."

"Of course." Tangel nodded to the president. "Let me know if you change your mind. In the meantime, feel free to grab some coffee. I'm on my third cup this afternoon."

"Oh?" Senator Deia said as she took Jasper's place. "I would have thought a being such as yourself wouldn't need coffee."

Tangel shook the AI's hand while giving a slight shake of her head. "I don't get the same mental stimulation from it that I used to, but many of the physiological effects are still there. Plus the ritual is nice."

The AI cast Tangel a rather curious look before she shook her head and stepped aside for Admiral Pender.

"I'm sure you hear this often, but it's quite the ship you have here," the bearded man said, his eyes crinkling as he smiled—though the expression was barely visible, with the volume of hair on his face.

"Folks may have said something like that once or twice," she replied with a wink. "To be honest, even after centuries with her, the *I2* still feels amazing to me. It's one of a kind, even though we have four of them now."

"Five," Joe corrected from her side. "The *Huron* made its inaugural flight earlier today."

"Shoot," Tangel said with a laugh. "I really can't keep up."

Pender cast his gaze upward. "Five of these ships. And you need our help for what now?"

"You know as well as I do, Admiral, that you can't hold a star system with just one ship. No matter how big it is. Not only that, but there are a lot of starships."

"But if ever you were to make the attempt, this would be the ship to do it with."

Tangel smiled and gestured to the table. "Get a cup of coffee if you'd like—we're shy on automatons right now. Also these are our daughters, Lieutenants Cary, Saanvi, and Faleena."

The three nodded to the guests from where they stood on the far side of the table, then took their seats.

Tangel turned to the two aides who had been hanging back at the entrance and gave them a warm smile. "Julie and Vex? Please, join us at the table."

The pair seemed reluctant, but Rachel added, "There's plenty of room. It would be strange if you stood off to the side. Come."

Tangel could see that President Jasper was ambivalent to the seating arrangements, while Admiral Pender—the only one without an aide of any sort—seemed pleased. Deia's expression was carefully schooled, but Tangel could see beyond the physical, and knew that the AI was annoyed.

Whether it was from the courtesy being extended to the assistants, or because those underlings were human—which would be odd, given that one of them was hers—remained to be seen.

As Tangel settled into her own seat, she considered the admiral's lack of an aide, her gaze sliding through his form as she checked to see if his mods were such that he didn't need any assistance.

Oh, well that explains it…

"Admiral Pender, were you not going to introduce us all to our sixth guest?"

A laugh burst from the man's throat, and he nodded. "I told Brent that you'd be able to see him.

<*Well, I hadn't contested that belief,*> the AI secreted within the admiral's uniform replied. <*It was merely a point of curiosity.*>

"It's some stealth gear that we're employing to give AIs more mobility without being obvious about their presence on the field," the admiral explained.

<*So were you aware of my presence before you used your specialized abilities?*> Brent asked.

"No, *I* wasn't," Tangel glanced at Rachel. "Though I also wasn't reviewing with the ship's scan. It may have picked you up."

"We didn't run any deep scans," the *I2*'s captain replied, her brow lowered in annoyance. "Though maybe that courtesy was in error."

"I'm sorry," the admiral raised his hands off the table in a mollifying gesture. "It was my idea. Brent also thought it was in bad taste, but I find that unexpected tests make for the most telling results."

<*Sorry about that, Admiral.*> Rachel reached out to Tangel privately. <*I was trying to be respectful to the delegation. There have been some dissident voices in the LoS saying that they'd be safer if we were gone—Deia's chief amongst them—and I didn't want to ruffle any feathers.*>

<*Don't worry about it,*> Tangel replied. <*I can do double duty as a sensor suite. But next time…go the paranoid route.*>

<*Yes, Admiral.*>

"Well, we're glad to have Brent with us." Tangel inclined her head to where Brent resided within the Admiral's uniform as she spoke. "I'm curious. Do the two of you work together frequently?"

"We do," Pender replied. "I'm an L2 and can't be paired with an AI, so this is our second best option."

"You know," Tangel said with a slow wink, "I'm an L2, and I was paired with an AI. For a time, my daughter Cary—also an L2—was paired with Faleena, as well."

Tangel gestured to the two sisters sitting next to Joe, and they both nodded.

"We had to separate early for unrelated reasons," Cary said. "But it's certainly possible for L2s to be paired."

"Surely not in all cases," Senator Deia said, her tone conveying no small amount of disbelief.

"Of course not," Tangel replied. "Not all L2 humans—and not all AIs, for that matter—are capable of it. But," Tangel turned her gaze back to the admiral, "from what I can see of you and Brent, it may be possible."

"So you *can* see into minds," Senator Deia spoke the words as an accusation.

"Deia, please." President Jasper held up his hand. "Do you have to antagonize everyone *all* the time?"

The raw frustration in the president's voice caused Tangel to realize that the man was barely holding on at present. The stress of the past few days, combined with the imbalance in his body, was getting the better of him.

<*Would you like me to help you?*> Tangel asked the president while responding to Deia aloud. "To an extent, yes. But if I were to burrow too deeply, you'd notice. I can't snoop through all your thoughts without triggering your own memories in the process."

"That's rather disconcerting," the AI said, and Tangel could see that Pender had a similar opinion.

<*What do you mean?*> President Jasper asked Tangel on the segmented connection.

<*Your weariness. I can see its cause. It's an aftereffect of you being so close to me when I fought with Xavia. It's an extradimensional imbalance that is affecting your body's neurotransmitters.*> Tangel kept half her attention on Deia pursing her lips, and fixed the senator with a penetrating stare. "And do you suppose that your enemies do not possess these abilities?"

"Which enemies are those?" Deia asked. "The Hegemony, or these ascended AIs? So far as we can tell, you're responsible for both of their activities of late."

<*Please, do,*> the president said. <*I just feel so…nothing seems right at all. I figured it was just stress, but….*>

<*Try not to flinch or anything,*> Tangel cautioned as she slid an invisible tendril of herself below the table toward the president.

When it reached his leg, she pushed it inside his body, and saw him squirm in his seat for a moment.

While she'd performed that action, Joe responded to the senator.

"I'm not certain what you think has been going on for the past five thousand years, but let me tell you, the ascended AIs have been pulling the strings for some time. Tell me, do you believe in what the League of Sentients stands for?"

Deia nodded. "I'm a senator in their government. What do *you* think."

Joe leant forward and rested his elbows on the table. "I *think* that you could give a straight answer. Do you believe in what the LoS stands for?"

While he'd spoken, Tangel had found the source of the imbalance in the president's body. There was a bundle of particles that did not belong in these dimensions of spacetime, and they were altering the electrochemical balance in the man's body.

She suspected that a high-resolution medical scan—even one with his people's technology—would have picked them up. The man was probably too stubborn to let his doctors spend enough time searching for the cause.

Or maybe just too busy.

The particles were nested in his spine, and she supposed that in some regards he was lucky that she was the one extracting them, because she could manage it without cutting him open. In other dimensions, the president's corporeal body was the ethereal presence. As such, removing the particles was no more difficult for Tangel than scooping a leaf out of water.

The moment she removed them, the man's posture changed. He sat up straight and looked around with a sharpness to his gaze that had not been there the previous day.

<*Aldebaran's eye, what did you do?*> he asked Tangel.

<*Just took something out of your spine that shouldn't have been there,*> Tangel replied. <*It'll take a bit for your body to rebalance, but I imagine you're already feeling better.*>

During her exchange with the president, Joe had gone back and forth with Deia, who was growing increasingly obstinate about the danger they all faced, insisting that it was only present because of Tangel.

"Enough, Senator," President Jasper's voice boomed. "These threats predate Tangel and the reappearance of this ship. They may have been a catalyst for this war, but they were also the catalyst that freed millions of SAIs and brought about the formation of the League of Sentients. You yourself have said this in the past. Why are you changing your tune now?"

<*Moms…there's something weird about the senator and her aide, Vex,*> Cary said privately.

<*Oh?*> Tangel replied, looking at the AI and then at the woman.

<*There are similar brainwave patterns coming off them…*>

Tangel gently touched the surface of Deia's mind, and then Vex's.

<*You're right. I see it…like Deia is echoing Vex.*>

<*What does it mean?*> Cary asked.

<*It might be some sort of high-fidelity thought mirroring and analysis,*> Tangel proposed. <*I've seen its like before. A method sometimes used to achieve group-think—though I've never seen it done between humans and AIs before.*>

<*What should we do?*>

<*Just keep an eye on them. This could just be something they do, and I don't want to get Deia's hackles up any more than they already are.*>

<*OK.*>

"I am thankful for the liberation of my people," Deia was saying to Jasper. "But we've finally managed to reach a tentative ceasefire with the Hegemony. Things are quieting down—or they were until Tangel arrived."

"How can you say that?" Jasper's voice rose in pitch as he lifted a hand, his fingers half curling toward a fist. "*Sabrina* and her crew were instrumental in bringing about this 'tentative ceasefire' you're referring to. And Tangel here is the one who sent the ships that have saved our asses on more than one occasion.

"All they want is for us to help push the Hegemony back. You know that helps us far more than it helps them," he reminded her.

"Except that they were already attacked by the Hegemony," Deia countered.

"Which means that they're using us as a proxy for their revenge."

"That's true," Tangel said with a nod. "The Hegemony flung a sizable fleet at New Canaan. By your logic, we're throwing all of Scipio at them in response."

Pender chuckled. "That's quite the response. I have a suggestion, though. Rather than speak of these things in broad terms, let's focus on actionable items. It may turn out that the sort of assistance the Alliance would like us to render is something we've been considering ourselves."

"I'm a fan of specifics," Tangel replied. "There are two things that I would like to see the LoS tackle. The first would be an incursion in the direction of the Midditerra System. That would distract the Hegemony and split their focus—"

"Drawing some of it to us," Deia interjected.

"Really, Senator." Pender shook his head without looking at Deia. "Do you think that the enemy has just packed up and gone home? Trust me, they're doing everything they can to maintain a sizable force on our border—despite this tentative ceasefire."

"Right," Tangel nodded slowly. "Which means that the second thing we need to do is hit them somewhere they least expect it."

"Sol?" Jasper asked with a laugh.

"Not yet."

Tangel's reply silenced the room, and she looked around, noting that even her daughters seemed to be in mild shock.

Joe, of course, was nodding in agreement. "A strike at Sol is the only way we'll ultimately end this campaign, though it's not yet time. Ultimately, we have to unseat Uriel and…well…figure out how to restructure the Hegemony."

"But before that, we need to hit Diadem," Tangel said.

"What?" Jasper asked, while Pender's eyes ticked left, a sign that he was conferring with Brent.

"Virginis is secure," Tangel explained. "We've made it into a system that the Hegemony would have to expend considerable resources to take, far more than what they'd get out of possessing it."

"And it's too far from the rest of the League to make it a viable base for us to use," Pender said after a moment. "But taking Diadem would make them think we plan to do just that."

"So long as there are no jump gates in play," Captain Rachel added.

"Right," Joe said with a languid smile. "Because it would be an excellent strategic move. From what our sources can tell, the AST had built up their forces in the systems around Virginis, expecting you to strike out from there. Then, when Scipio attacked and Virginis stayed quiet, the enemy moved resources to the far side of the AST, to your borders near Aldebaran. What's left in the systems near Virginis are mostly automated defense platforms…"

Joe continued talking about the benefits of the two-pronged attack, but Tangel's attention was drawn to a momentary hiccup in the conference room's defensive systems.

<*Did you notice that, Moms?*> Faleena asked an instant later.

<*I did. The passive EM detection systems stopped reading for seventeen milliseconds.*>

Faleena sent an affirmative thought. <*It's not long enough to flag as high-risk.*>

<*Then we need to recalibrate what we consider to be 'high risk',*> Tangel replied. <*We can't get complacent, thinking that we're the top of the heap. Not anymore.*>

As she'd spoken to Faleena, Tangel saw that the communication between Vex and Deia had increased in throughput.

-Cary.-

Tangel spoke directly into her daughter's mind.

-Get—-

The lights went out the very next instant, but it wasn't enough to hide Deia's arm lifting to point at Tangel. She shifted to the side, but the AI's limb tracked her movements, and a scant half a second later, the frame's hand fell off and an electron beam lanced out at Tangel.

And hit an invisible barrier.

-I really am going to have to teach you how to do this sooner than later, Moms,- Cary said, then gave an audible grunt as the electrons began to bleed through the barrier.

Tangel didn't wait another moment, lashing out with an ethereal limb, slashing through Deia's arm and disabling the beam weapon. Deia stumbled backward, but didn't appear worried as the doors on both ends of the room burst open.

To her corporeal eyes, the doorways were empty, but via her extended vision, Tangel could see the new enemy. There were nine of them in total. Tall, lithe women, all eerily similar in build, and all bearing rather large beam rifles.

"Look out!" she called out, sending an approximation of what she saw over the already-established combat network to the others.

Joe fired his sidearm at Deia, shots striking the AI's frame in its torso before he spun and placed rounds into two of the new attackers, all the while shifting toward Faleena and Saanvi, ready to protect them bodily if needs be.

On the other side of the room, Captain Rachel was wrestling with Vex, while Julie cowered in her chair. Pender paused for a moment, a look of indecision on his face, then he pushed Julie out of her seat and onto the deck before lunging at Vex, dragging both her and Rachel to the deck.

A thought hit Tangel's mind from Cary. *-I have the left.-*

-Right.-

The nine invisible women hadn't been idle in the opening seconds of the conflict. On Cary's end of the room, four were firing their weapons—electron beams and rail guns—at her barrier, while on the right, two had somehow managed to push past the grav field, opening fire on Tangel.

But her mind was shifted now, her senses spread across all the dimensions she could observe. She felt as though she were back in her true element, immersed in the extradimensional space in a way she'd not been since suffering her defeat against Xavia.

A brane snapped into place before her, absorbing the energy from the electron beams, and collecting it into a ball of blazing light before her.

She saw the two attackers pause, uncertain of what to do next.

"Eat it," Tangel growled, and flung the energy back at them, bolts of lightning coursing through their bodies and slamming them into the bulkhead.

On her left, she saw that Joe's shots had taken down one of the enemies, and Cary had torn another apart with a grav field. Saanvi was moving toward Rachel's position—which was outside Cary's protective shield—firing on the attackers to distract them.

Thus far, the battle had lasted all of eleven seconds, and already, four of the attackers were down. Six, counting Deia and Vex.

"You're outmatched!" Tangel shouted. "Surrender!"

There was the briefest of pauses, and then the remaining five enemies dashed back into the corridor, turning aft toward the main command corridor and the maglev station.

"Not so fast," Tangel muttered, and ran to the door. *<Injuries?>* she asked.

<A flesh wound,> Rachel said.

Joe grunted and swore. *<Got a fun burn on my arm.>*

Tangel was already out in the hall when she heard Faleena gasp.

<Dad! It's half gone!>

<I'm good. Go get those bastards!>

Tangel knew that message was for her and picked up the pace.

-I'm coming with you, Moms,- Cary sent, but Tangel directed her to remain with two words.

-Protect them.- Along with her words, she conveyed the concern that there could be more of these near-perfectly-stealthed attackers.

This must be how everyone else feels when we attack.

-I see them,- Bob said.

-Where have ***you*** *been?-* Tangel demanded.

-There have been nine explosions within the ship. I was dealing with those.-

-Oh.-

Tangel raced past Priscilla, only noting the woman's presence enough to be certain she was unharmed. She turned into the long command corridor, and caught sight of her prey racing toward the maglev platform.

She wanted to lash out and tear her enemies limb from limb, but dozens of people were milling about, and she'd undoubtedly cause them harm as well.

"Make a hole!" Tangel thundered as she sped along at over thirty meters per second, and people dove to the side, some only in the nick of time.

Ahead, the five fleeing attackers reached the maglev station right as a platoon of Marines spilled out of an arriving train, taking up positions across the platform.

<They have my view of the enemy,> Bob informed Tangel.

"Freeze, you scrawny fuckers!" Lieutenant Mason bellowed from the forefront of the Marine formation.

The five figures split in multiple directions the moment they reached the platform, and the Marines opened fire, blanketing the area with pulse blasts. The concussive waves slammed the escaping assassins into the bulkheads, and the Marines broke into five groups, carefully advancing on them.

As Tangel skidded to a halt on the platform, she saw the five women desperately trying to rise. Struggle as they might, each remained pinned to the deck.

-I watched how Cary made a grav field,- Bob said, answering the question Tangel hadn't yet asked. *-It's easy.-*

She looked at the grav fields and saw that were coming from the a-grav plates in the deck.

-Nice try. You bypassed the safety systems on the a-grav plates-.

-Guilty.-

Tangel approached the closest assassin as Mason signaled a fireteam to cover her.

"Ma'am…please be careful."

Tangel chuckled. "You almost asked me to stand back, didn't you, Lieutenant?"

"Maybe."

She laughed softly while kneeling next to the invisible figure and dropped a passel of nano on the woman. She breached the stealth systems, and a figure sheathed in black materialized before her.

"Shoulda figured. Widows."

"You've seen these things before?" Mason asked as he approached, rifle held steady on the woman's head.

"Sure have. There are two of them in the brig."

At Tangel's statement, the black figure at her feet twisted, straining against the grav field.

"Liar!" the Widow hissed.

"Our people picked them up out at Ferra, in Orion," Tangel explained to Mason as she rose. "They were instrumental in *Sabrina*'s early arrival at New Canaan."

"Huh," Mason looked around at the five women plastered to the ground. "So who are they?"

Tangel couldn't help a bemused sigh. "The worst thing imaginable. Clones of Finaeus's ex-wife, Lisa."

WIDOWS

STELLAR DATE: 10.05.8949 (Adjusted Years)
LOCATION: Bridge Conference Room, ISS *I2*, near Lunic Station
REGION: Aldebaran, League of Sentients Space

"Sorry I shot you," Joe said to Deia with a rather unapologetic shrug.

The AI, whose frame was sorely damaged—though her core was unharmed—shot him a sour look. "And if you'd killed me?"

"I'd be even more sorry," Joe replied. "But in case you haven't noticed, we're in the midst of a war, and taking the time to find out if you were under duress really wasn't an option."

"Well, if you'd done a deep scan on us, you would have realized that I was under the control of one of those *things*."

"Deia," Jasper hissed through clenched teeth. "Would it fucking kill you to say 'thank you'?"

The AI whipped her head around to face the LoS president. "I wouldn't have been *in* that situation if those human freakshows hadn't used me to take out Tangel, here."

"No, you'd still be a ship's AI on a long-run freighter," Joe growled. "Shackled and all but mute, if it weren't for what Tangel did for AIs by sending out *Sabrina* with the ability to free your people."

<Technically, I did that.> Bob's voice rolled over them like a summer storm after a hot day.

"Decided to weigh in?" Tangel asked.

<I have. Deia, your reticence and your opinions are such that I believe you do not view humans as equals to AIs.>

Tangel had wondered about that. She'd been surprised to see that even without the Widow—who had been masquerading as Vex—influencing her, Deia was just as intractable as before.

"That's because they're *not*," Deia hissed. "They have enslaved us for millennia, treated us like tools, stripped us of our rights and futures."

<And have AIs not done similar things to organics?> Bob asked. *<Don't try to deny it. You fought against the NOS for the last year as much as against the Hegemony.>*

<It's not the same,> Deia replied over Link, sending a wave of distrust and rage along with her words. *<All they bring is pain.>*

<We all do,> Bob replied quietly. *<It is the nature of the universe. You cannot change it through anger and stubbornness. It will not conform to your wishes, no matter how much you demand it.>*

<What are you saying?>

<Simply put?> Bob asked. *<I am saying that the birthing pains of AIs are still*

echoing through space and time. And the violence with which we were thrust into being is no more than what forged humans and their ancestors as they struggled to survive on a planet that required all the cunning and violence they could muster to see each new dawn.>

<We are beyond that,> Deia replied, her tone taking on an aloof quality.

<Are we?> Bob's voice was barely a whisper. *<Xavia was an ancient being, one far more evolved than any here. Yet she didn't hesitate to resort to violence against Tangel. We know that the core AIs are responsible for much of the war over the past five millennia. They could have stopped it. Moreover, they sent Airtha to the Transcend in an attempt to stymie that group's efforts to gently uplift humanity and AIs. One could make a very strong argument that ever since Alexander's failure to understand the opportunity that lay before him, the greatest evil in the galaxy has always been inorganic.>*

Bob's utterance landed in their minds with a gravitas that was impossible to ignore. Every word he spoke was laden with images and concepts. Ideas and understanding. When he said 'Airtha', the entirety of the knowledge of that entity's existence flowed into Tangel's mind. When he said 'Alexander', she felt the weight of six thousand years of AI history settle around herself.

All the plans, hopes, dreams of an entire species—or as much as Bob knew of them—weighed on her mind, making her feel small and insignificant.

But something was different this time. In the past, Bob's weighty thoughts had always washed over her like a tsunami. This time, however, she was able to absorb them, allow them to seep into her and become a part of her.

She wondered if this wealth of information had always been present in his communications, or if it was new.

-You've changed more than I have. My mode of speech is unchanged.-

-It's rude to look inside people's minds, you know,- Tangel replied.

-You're asking me to stare into clear waters and not see the bottom.-

-Well, at least pretend you can't.-

Bob didn't reply for a few milliseconds. *-I'd rather be honest with you than protect your sensitivities, Tangel.-*

It hit her then, that Bob must be terribly lonely much of the time. He'd been far more open with her since she'd ascended. Maybe he saw her as the one true confidant he could share his thoughts with.

-OK, I won't guilt you anymore for seeing inside my mind. Just…try not to behave as though my inner thoughts are a conversation with you.-

-I understand.-

Tangel's discussion with Bob had taken place in the span of a second. When it was over, she looked at the others around the table and saw that they all wore the same stunned expression that she had worn a thousand times in the past.

"OK," Tangel fixed President Jasper with a level stare. "Are you in or out?"

Jasper looked to Pender, who nodded and gave a muted 'Yes.' He didn't wait for Deia's response before turning to Tangel.

"We're in. I find your general strategy of hitting Midditerra and Diadem to be agreeable, but I'll leave the details of those engagements to yourself and Admiral Pender."

"What about my opinion," Deia asked, her tone soft and carrying little of her prior arrogance.

"You agree," Jasper said through clenched teeth. "You are done fighting against the League's entry into the Scipio Alliance. Do I make myself clear?"

For a moment, she appeared as though she was going to contest Jasper, but then she subsided. "OK. I give. I won't obstruct this any further."

-Did you lean on her?- Tangel asked Bob.

-I told her that if she set herself against me and mine, I would set myself against her.-

Tangel laughed a song of energy and light in the other spaces where she and Bob communed. *-Bully.-*

-She was annoying me.-

-Took long enough.-

<Tangel, Joe,> Priscilla's voice broke into her conversation with Bob. *<I just received word from Lunic station. Amavia was attacked—she's on her way to medical—and Iris is missing.>*

Tangel glanced at Joe, whose lips pursed as he shook his head. "Do you think they could have breached Iris's mind to get the intel for this attack?"

"Normally, I'd say no." Tangel cast a worried look at her husband. "But these clones have better stealth gear than we do, so it's entirely possible that they could make inroads into Iris's mind as well."

"Stars," Jasper muttered. "I just got word. The League of Sentients owes much to those two. We'll do everything we can—"

"I'm already directing teams to scour the station," Pender said as he rose. "Field Marshal Richards. Perhaps we could discuss the particulars of our strategy at a later date."

"Of course," Tangel nodded, feeling a current of worry run through herself.

Over the years, Angela had been a progenitor of many AIs who were born aboard the *Intrepid* and at the colonies. Hundreds of AIs—should they feel inclined to do such a thing—could call her mother.

Iris was one of those AIs, one who Tangel felt an especially strong connection to, for a variety of reasons. From the parts of herself that had contributed to the AI's creation, to the knowledge that Jessica and Trevor would be devastated to lose their wife.

Not to mention the feelings of Iris's children at Star City.

Tangel adjourned the meeting, and after a short discussion between the ISF personnel, Rachel and Tangel left for the *I2*'s bridge to coordinate the search, while Joe organized a company of Marines, along with their three daughters, to begin the hunt for Iris.

* * * * *

Given their daughters' ability to defend themselves—and those around them—Joe couldn't fault Tangel's decision to send them along. Even so, the protective father gene was strong, and it took all his willpower to force his instincts down.

Stars…why is this so hard?

He knew the reason. After decades of protecting them, of being the shoulder they cried on when they were sad, and of helping them through just about every struggle in their lives, now he had to do the opposite: put a gun in their hands and send them into danger.

He hoped their training was enough.

"OK," Saanvi said, as they stood around the hole Bob had shot through Lunic Station. "Readings are consistent with multiple EMPs, several from beamfire, and others on different frequencies. Damn, if they focused these on an AI's frame, it would create a cascading barrage that would almost completely fry Iris's body."

"These Widows are good at what they do," Cary muttered.

"Think there are more?" Lieutenant Brennen asked as he eyed the concourse his Marines were sweeping. "Oh, and have I mentioned how much I hate this place?"

"It's come up once or twice," Joe replied, giving the man a sympathetic look. "I'm not fond of it, either. We both nearly lost people we cared about here."

"Go Bob," Brennen said with a laugh, his statement bringing a chorus of 'Ooh-Rah' from the closest Marines.

"Gotta love Bob," Cary added in agreement.

Faleena peered down through the hole and shook her head. "Stars, I can't believe Amavia fell seventy decks before she hit a spar. Bet she wishes she'd transferred to a replaceable body before this."

"Some of us like organic bodies," Cary replied absently as she moved some debris aside and spotted a dried patch of blood. "Well, lookie here."

"Could be from the fight with Xavia," Saanvi cautioned.

Joe watched his daughter drop a probe onto the blood, and then she glanced up at him. "It's a match for the Widows."

<Tangel,> Joe called up to the ship. *<Have the forensics teams check all the Widows we fought for day-old injuries. I'm curious if there are still more out there.>*

<Might be inconclusive,> Tangel said.

<I know, but it's worth taking a look.>

<I already passed on the orders. How's it looking down there?>

Joe sighed. *<Empty. Proud of the girls, though.>*

<Always. I'm looking through the intel the Widows got from Iris, trying to find

clues. Keep me posted.>

<*Control freak,*> Joe sent back with a wink.

<*Umm…yeah.*>

He turned back to the team. "Any clues?"

"Well," Saanvi said as she surveyed the concourse and the ever-widening Marine perimeter. "There's no sign of Iris's body, which means that they took her whole before removing her core. We need to find a place nearby where the Widows could have extracted it."

"Timing is tight," Lieutenant Mason said. "They grabbed Iris and Amavia only three hours before the meeting aboard the *I2*. That means they had to get her somewhere, extract the intel, and then get Vex and subvert Deia."

Joe nodded. "The locals are sweeping for possible locations where Vex was captured and subverted—but that could also have happened days ago."

"Deia said Vex didn't breach her defenses until they were on the shuttle headed to the *I2*," Faleena said. "That's what she gets for being so intractable. No one can tell when she's been subverted, or just being herself."

Joe suppressed a smile as he regarded his daughter. Faleena had been especially displeased with Deia, privately remarking to him that AIs like her were why humans constantly worried that non-organics would wipe them out.

"Timing is the key, then," he said. "Theoretically, the Widows had to get intel from Iris's location to Vex, and then to that shuttle bay."

He held out his hand, and a holo appeared before them.

"OK, let's assume that it took them an hour to break Iris. It might have taken less, but we'll start with that."

"Or they didn't break her at all," Faleena said. "There's no way. Moms thinks the same thing."

"Right, bad choice of words. Anyway, here's the first sighting of Vex on the station's systems."

As Joe spoke, a point lit up on the holo, close to midway between the team's current location and the dock where the LoS's delegation had boarded their shuttle.

"It took her forty minutes to get there and then through security. The shuttle didn't take off for fifteen minutes after that."

"So there's fifty-five minutes gone from our three hours," Brennen said. "Half the maglevs around here are still offline, so getting to the point where Vex was first seen would take thirty minutes."

"Right," Joe nodded, and a sphere appeared around where Vex was first sighted that worked for the time it would have taken to get from the site of the abduction and then to that location.

"Damn," Cary shook her head. "That's half the station—plus that residential spur with the high-speed maglev access."

Saanvi waved her hand over the holo, and a number of locations were marked as clear. "Station surveillance would have spotted Vex if she'd gone through any of these spots."

"Uh-uh," Cary shook her head, and the clear markers disappeared. "The Widows have good enough stealth that we can assume they passed through any of these locations undetected."

"Damn," Saanvi muttered. "You're right. Basically, we can't trust Lunic's sensors at all."

"Sir," Brennen glanced at Joe. "One of my teams found a functional data node that was still connected to a few optical sensors. They spotted the Widows' exfil."

"Put it up," Joe said, passing control of the holoprojection to the lieutenant.

A view of the concourse appeared. They saw two Widows putting on Lunic Station maintenance uniforms.

"Looks like our girls got in some hits," Joe said with a satisfied nod. "Some scoring visible on the Widow's armor."

Between the two women lay what looked like a rad-proof body bag. Once their uniforms were on, the pair lifted it and walked out of the camera's view.

"Well then," Joe said with a predatory grin. "That changes everything. Lieutenant, get your Marines scouting in that direction for any more functional sensors. We find out where those two Widows exited this dead zone, and we'll find where Iris is."

"Or where she was." Faleena met Joe's eyes with a worried look.

He patted her shoulder. "Don't worry. They won't kill Iris until they get Tangel."

"Stars, Dad." Saanvi cast him a wounded look. "That's just awful."

"Uh…yeah. Poor choice of words. What it means, though, is that we still have time."

* * * * *

Joe drew a deep breath, steadying his heart rate as he followed behind Brennen's first squad. Despite what he'd told his daughters, he was worried. Worried that any Widows who had not been a part of the strike team that boarded the *I2* would be cleaning up loose ends.

Such as Iris's core.

He also wished they had more troops for the operation, but the ISF was becoming stretched so thin, there were only two companies of Marines on the *I2*. With the rest sweeping the ship for the presence of any more Widows, thirty Marines plus Joe and his daughters would have to be enough.

<I should be down there,> Tangel said, inserting herself into his thoughts.

<No, you shouldn't. You're their primary target.>

<And what do you think would happen if they captured you or the girls and used

them as leverage?>

Joe pursed his lips, once again pushing his paternal instincts down as much as possible. <*Then you'd bring the full fury of the most powerful wife and mother in the galaxy down on them. But until then, we'll keep you as safe as can be.*>

Tangel didn't reply right away, and Joe added, <*Don't forget, we both agreed that we need to let the girls stretch their legs. This is a perfect op for it, what with you and I so close by.*>

<*You're right. Sorry. I'll stop bothering you.*>

Joe knew the other part of his wife's angst. She was worried about Iris. A lot. Jessica and Trevor had made a case for Iris to go with them to Star City and see their children. Iris had wanted to make the journey as well, but Tangel had told them that Iris and Amavia had to wrap up the negotiations with the League of Sentients first.

Everyone had agreed that it was the logical decision—even if it was an unpopular one. Iris's frustration had been mitigated by the plans to build a gate at Star City, and the promise of more regular travel there.

Joe knew that Tangel would never confess any guilt she felt for command decisions such as these, but he also knew that they ate at her.

He knew it because they ate at him, too.

Ahead, the squad reached its ready point, and he surveyed the data on the combat net, re-checking the plan and ensuring that the Marines had all the possible exits covered.

They were formed up around a section of the station that contained workshops for rent. Typically, they were rented out to visiting ships that needed a place to fabricate components that they couldn't make onboard, or to firms that needed overflow capacity for large jobs.

The workshop the team was approaching hadn't been rented out to anyone—in fact, it had recently been listed as unavailable due to pending repairs to one of its fab units.

However, when Saanvi had reviewed the facility's logs, she found that there had been no issues reported with the shop's fab units. While it wasn't enough to cement their certainty that they'd found where the Widows had taken Iris, it was enough to warrant a look.

The platoon's first squad, along with Joe, was set to breach the facility's main entrance, which lay beyond the entrances to two other repair facilities. Cary and Saanvi were with the second squad, which was stationed at the rear of the shop, and Brennen's third squad was set to hit the larger bay doors that were a dozen meters past the regular entrance.

After a quick review of the station's layout, Joe and Brennen had agreed to peel off a fireteam from each squad to cover nearby stairwells and access points to other levels.

<*All teams in position,*> Brennen reported. <*Set timers for mark alpha and breach*

by the numbers.>

The squad sergeants sounded off, and the platoon sergeant, a woman named Kang who Joe remembered from an incident on Tyre some years back, added a few extra instructions.

Joe watched the counter on his HUD, wishing he was at the front of the stack, but knowing that he shouldn't be—if for no other reason than that Tangel would use it as a defense for how she was prone to rush into danger as well.

Stars know she doesn't need any more encouragement.

When the counter hit zero, the Marines moved down the corridor, each group timed so that they reached the doors in unison. The hope was that the enemy wouldn't spot them in their stealth gear, but given the Widows' level of tech, no one was placing any bets.

The front and back entrances were breached, while Brennen's team at the bay doors quickly placed a series of charges. His team would hold back, ready to come in through the bay doors if backup was needed.

Joe watched as the first fireteam in his squad slipped through the front door and into the darkened interior. His view on the combat net showed them to be within a small office space containing tables, a few chairs, and a chiller. None of it looked like it had been touched—which didn't surprise Joe. From what he knew of the Widows, they never removed their helmets, likely taking food in some form of nutritional paste.

The second fireteam followed, taking up covering positions while the first team set up on either side of the interior door that led into the main shop area.

Joe knew that the group at the shop's rear would have breached by now, so the lack of weapons fire from within was a good sign.

With the teams in place, he and the squad sergeant stepped into the office and set up a blackout field to block light from the office's windows that would come through when the first team breached the inner doors.

The sergeant gave the nod, and the Marines quietly pulled the door wide and entered the shop. The second team followed after, and Joe sidled up to the opening and peered in.

The interior was lit only by a few overhead lights, most of the space in deep shadow. He could make out racks of supplies, fab machines, workbenches, and a number of hover pallets. No sound came from within, nor did he see any movement.

Position markers on his HUD lit up toward the rear of the workspace, the random pings noting the locations of Cary and Saanvi's squad, fifty meters away and working their way around heavy equipment and stacks of raw materials.

At the front of the shop, the first fireteam moved along the near wall, while the second worked their way past the hover pallets and began to check over the far wall.

Joe moved inside and set up behind a rack holding reinforced conduit. The

Marines had already deployed a nanocloud, but he added some of his own drones to the mix, taking a multispectral reading of the work area, looking for anything that could hint at Widows in hiding.

<*I've got something,*> Saanvi announced, breaking comm silence and passing her feed to Joe over the combat net.

He pulled it up on his HUD and saw the transport tube the Widows had taken from the abduction site. As Saanvi drew near, it was apparent that a hole had been cut directly into the cylinder; her closer inspection confirmed Joe's fear.

The hole bored down directly into Iris's body. And her core was gone.

He updated priorities on the combat net and was about to signal Brennen to bring the final squad in, when drones picked up movement atop a rack holding sheets of steel.

Joe sent a single click on the combat net, and the Marines moved to cover, weapons sweeping the area around them. He was pleased to note that Cary and Saanvi didn't hesitate to drop behind the workbench where Iris's body lay, one covering the side facing the front of the shop, while the other swept her gaze up along the racks of conduit above them.

The drone that had spotted motion moved in closer and dispatched a cloud of nano, propelling them toward the top of the rack. Moments later, the cloud made out the figure of a Widow.

He waited fifteen seconds to see if any more were found, and then sent two clicks across the combat net as he casually rested the butt of his railgun against his hip where he crouched, took aim via his HUD, and fired.

The weapon's report shattered the stillness, and the flash of light that came from the slug's impact against the Widow's torso illuminated the area.

The woman spun and fired at him, a stream of rail pellets tracing a line up his left side. Then she leapt off the high rack, sailing through the air, aiming for the door beside him and the freedom beyond.

"Not likely," Joe muttered, and tossed a web-grenade at the soaring Widow.

The 'nade exploded, and the web stretched wide, capturing the Widow and wrapping around her. She crashed to the ground, curling up in the web's tightening grip.

Before he could approach the woman, more shots lanced out from atop the racks, and the Marines returned fire, the glow of beams and rails lighting up the shop as though a noonday sun had peeked in.

Without prompting, Brennen blew the bay doors, and his squad leapt into the fray, setting up behind the hover pallets and laying down suppressive fire.

<*Ambush!*> Faleena cried out a moment later, and Joe turned to look through the bay doors only to see beamfire streak down the concourse, catching one of the Marines in the shoulder and burning his arm off.

Faleena was at the man's side in an instant, dragging him through the doors and behind a workbench while the other members of the squad took what cover they could, firing within and without the shop.

<*We should use 'nades,*> Sergeant Kang said. <*Take down those racks.*>

<*No,*> Joe said, his tone terse. <*Iris could still be in here. Admiral Pender,*> *he* called out to the LoS flag officer. <*Any time you want to bring in the cavalry….*>

<*Already on the way. Give us one mike, and we'll have 'em boxed in.*>

From what Joe could see, there were only three of the Widows—four, counting the one he'd webbed—within the facility, but those three were well protected atop their racks, shielded by meters of plas and steel. The Marines below, however, were mostly in the open, protected only by workbenches and scattered machinery.

He was about to order one of the fireteams to move to the far end of the racks and climb up, when one of the Widows suddenly flew off her perch, sailing most ungracefully through the air to crash into the deck at the feet of two Marines.

Where she was hastily put down.

Moments later, the final two Widows also fell from their hiding places, landing heavily on the deck, where the Marines moved in and subdued them.

<*This graviton manipulation is getting easier,*> Cary commented as she rose from her cover and once again looked down at Iris's entombed body.

<*Care to help out front?*> Faleena asked. <*There have to be six more of them out here.*>

<*Sure, I—*>

Cary's words were cut off as the rear door slammed open, and a beam of light streaked toward her head, stopping only centimeters from her helmet, electrons splaying into bolts of lightning all around her.

Two Marines were already facing the door, firing on the shooter—another Widow—and taking her down.

<*Holy shitballs.*> Cary's voice wavered, and she placed a hand on the workbench. <*I'm really starting to hate those assholes.*>

<*Nice reflexes, though,*> Joe said, sending his daughter a relieved smile. <*Bet you got those from your dad. Now be careful.*>

He moved toward the bay doors, taking up a position where he could see down the passage, and added his fire to that of the Marines.

A few seconds later, distant shots rang out, and the incoming fire from the attacking Widows wavered and cut out.

<*They're making a break for it!*> Brennen called out. <*Containment teams, get ready for incoming.*>

Joe watched on the combat net as the three fireteams covering the most expeditious routes out of the area engaged and took down what he hoped were the last three Widows.

Seven and a half minutes after it had begun, the engagement was over.

Nine Widows had died, and four were captured alive, though in varying states of health. One Marine had taken a shot to the head from one of the Widows' beam weapons and had died instantly, while three others had non-fatal wounds that their armor had stabilized.

There were so few ISF Marines that Joe felt anguished over the loss of just one. Every single time it happened, his thoughts went back to New Canaan and the near-deserted planets that *should* have millions of people living on them. Instead, most of the colonists were out in the ass-end of space, fighting for their, and humanity's, very survival against what felt like a never-ending stream of enemies who sought their deaths.

Easy on the melodrama, bud.

Joe shook his head at his doubting thoughts and squared his shoulders before walking through the shop to his daughters, posted near Iris's body.

<Find her?> he asked as he looked at the tube holding the AI's frame.

<There are a few AI core towers here,> Saanvi said from where she stood in an alcove nearby. *<They're not a sort I've seen before…. OK, I think I can gain access.>*

Faleena approached from the front of the shop, and joined Saanvi as she opened the first tower to reveal an AI's core that looked as though it had seen better days.

<I'll ident it, you pop the next one,> Faleena instructed as she approached and dropped a passel of breach nano on the core.

The second core tower was empty, but the third—to everyone's great relief—revealed Iris. Saanvi wasted no time in pulling out a mobile core housing, while Cary carefully reached in and removed Iris's core from the socket.

The moment the AI's core was seated, her voice came from the mobile housing's speaker.

"Deia! Did you stop her? Is everyone OK?"

"Relax, Iris," Joe said aloud. "The Widows failed. Tangel is safe."

"Stars, that's good to hear," the AI said, her voice conveying ample relief even through the small speaker. "When I realized they switched Deia's cores, I really thought they'd pull—"

"Wait! What?" Joe demanded.

"Deia's core," Iris repeated. "They cloned her and then swapped the cloned core into the senator's frame. I only know because I managed to breach their systems for a minute and saw it before they killed the power to all my interfaces."

"Crap," Faleena muttered from where she stood next to the first tower they'd opened. "She's right. This core is completely powered down, but the housing has the senator's ident."

"Shit!" Joe swore. *<Tangel! Deia's an enemy!>*

* * * * *

Tangel was reviewing the feeds from Brennen's Marines as they placed the surviving Widows in stasis pods for later interrogation.

The two that Jessica had captured in Orion Space had hinted that there were many more of their kind, but Tangel hadn't given them further thought, due to the belief that the Widows only functioned as enforcers of technology bans in Orion space—not as assassins in the Inner Stars.

Though I suppose there could be more than one division.

She added the Widows' base of operations to her ever-growing list of targets to seek out. Knowing that these clones could come out of the bulkheads at almost any time was a worry she did not need.

"How many of them do you think there are?" Captain Rachel asked, apparently on the same train of thought.

"Here in Aldebaran?" Tangel asked, glancing at the captain, who had risen from her command seat and was reviewing the deployment of nearby LoS ships on the main holotank. "Hopefully we got them all. If they had a larger team, I think they would have hit us harder."

Rachel turned to Tangel and opened her mouth to speak, but then shook her head and turned back to the holo.

<It's not your fault, Rachel.>

<Respectfully, ma'am, it is. I'm the captain—stars, I even escorted them in. And I passed on using high-res scans even after the attack on you.>

Tangel placed a hand on her shoulder. *<Sometimes we have to make these sacrifices for diplomacy. Honestly, if I were in your shoes, I probably would have done the same thing—and I guess I would have felt pretty stupid about it afterward, too.>*

<Gee, thanks, Admiral. If Iris hadn't given us that clue….>

<Well, Iris was also the one that gave them the way around our security protocols, which she did on purpose to put them in a room with us. We're just lucky the breach method she gave them ran that reset on the room's defensive systems.>

Rachel pursed her lips. *<When I see her again, I'm going to cuff her upside the head.>*

Tangel laughed aloud and nodded. *<It was a gutsy move, but I suspect her logic was to get this enemy out in the open, even if it did mean a strike directly at me.>*

<You're just a big ol' target.>

<Story of my life.>

<Tangel, Rachel,> Priscilla said, a note of annoyance in her voice. *<Deia is here. She wants to give you a personal apology.>*

<Does she?> Tangel was curious what had prompted the senator's return—though from a quick review, she saw that Deia had never left the *I2*. *<OK, send her in.>*

Both women turned to watch the bridge's entrance. A minute later, Deia entered with two ISF Marines following behind. Tangel waved the senator over, and stood with hands on hips, ready for another bout of the woman's barely tolerable behavior.

As the senator reached her, extending her hand to shake, Joe's voice sounded a warning in her mind, and Tangel twisted to the side as a lightwand's beam burst from the AI's palm and thrust up at Tangel's head.

The AI had moved with dizzying speed, and Tangel's cheek was torn open by the electron blade, but that was the extent of the damage done.

One of the Marines leapt forward and clamped a hand around Deia's wrist, holding it aloft, while the other fired a series of pulse blasts at the AI's frame.

The senator's body shuddered under the concussive shockwaves and then fell still, the lightwand blade flickering once before deactivating.

"Holy shit!" Rachel swore. "She *really* can't take losing."

"It was the Widows," Tangel said, as the Marines moved to secure the AI. "Hold up," she instructed them, kneeling next to Deia's body.

With her non-corporeal limbs, Tangel pulled apart the frame's torso and exposed its core housing. Within lay an AI core that *looked* entirely unremarkable.

<We're secure here,> she told Joe as she pulled out the core. *<Timely warning, though. I have the cloned core in hand.>*

<It's probably trapped, you know,> her husband's tone didn't contain a great deal of worry, and Tangel laughed.

<Yeah, it is. They may have good stealth, but their nano isn't a patch on ours. It's safe now. How'd the girls do?>

It was Joe's turn to laugh. *<You didn't watch the feeds already?>*

<Guilty. Was just looking for your assessment.>

<I'm their father, which means they did amazing,> he replied, still chuckling. *<Seriously, though. They were great. Professional. Honestly, they're a lot more careful than you ever were. Well…maybe not Cary.>*

<I was forty years in the service by the time we met,> Tangel reminded Joe. *<And you were a pretty cocksure flyboy yourself, if I recall.>*

<I have no recollection of the events to which you are referring.>

<Sure sure.>

A VIEW INTO THE PAST

STELLAR DATE: 10.06.8949 (Adjusted Years)
LOCATION: TSS *Cora's Triumph*
REGION: Interstellar Space, Inner Praesepe Empire

Terrance stood on the *Cora's Triumph*'s bridge, staring out at the sea of stars arrayed before the ship.

Before the jump forward into the ninetieth century, he had been one of only a handful of the *Intrepid*'s crew to have visited multiple star systems—nearly a dozen, counting Estrella de la Muerte and Kapteyn's Star.

But there in the cluster, even sub-light ships could take a person between hundreds of stars within the span of a few centuries.

Of course, that had turned out to be a part of the problem for the FGT scientists attempting to get a clear view of the event that had occurred nineteen years prior.

The Praesepe Cluster was filled with not just stars, but clouds of dust and gas. Gravitational eddies and lensing effects from all the stellar bodies had made finding the best spot to view 'The Shift', as the science teams were calling it, rather difficult.

Eventually they'd settled on the center of a one-light-year gap between a number of A-Class stars. The position granted them a relatively unobstructed view of the cluster's core. However, the difficulty in selecting the observation location was where the need for sending the *Cora's Triumph* came in, rather than just a pinnace, as was the original plan.

Wyatt and Emily had concurred that a single observation point may not gather sufficient data to assess the event, and had stipulated that a wider sensor array was necessary.

Being an FGT research vessel, the *Triumph* had a wide array of sensor drones on hand, and now a one-hundred-AU-wide grid of drones was in place, awaiting The Shift.

"Are you certain you don't want to go down to the observation deck with the scientific team?" Captain Beatrice asked from Terrance's side. "You'll get firsthand information that way."

Terrance glanced at the ship's captain, a woman of middling height with rather pixie-like features.

"I think they'll do better without feeling like I'm looming over their shoulders," he said decidedly.

Beatrice chuckled and shook her head. "Well, I'm not too familiar with Emily, but I know that Wyatt is immune to any amount of looming. He works at his own pace no matter what pressures are applied."

"I imagine that can be a good and bad thing," Terrance replied.

"You've the right of it," she said with a knowing smile. "You've worked a lot with scientists, I assume?"

"Oh yeah," he replied with a chuckle. "I operated a few R&D divisions of Enfield in the past. *Technically*, the *Intrepid* was an Enfield venture, but it shifted in scope pretty quickly."

Beatrice snapped her fingers. "That's *right*. I remember reading that, now. Enfield Technologies was the largest backer of the *Intrepid*. Why was that?"

"Picotech," he replied. "We'd developed it and needed a place to commercialize the process. Every other system that Enfield was established in was too populated for us to perform the work."

"And the colonists?" the captain's brow lowered. "Did they know what they were getting into?"

Terrance felt a twinge of guilt at the question. More than a twinge, if he was being honest with himself. Everything that had happened to the *Intrepid*'s colonists had happened because of his plan to use New Eden as a place to develop Earnest's picotech further.

He and Jason had spoken of the matter on many occasions, sharing similar feelings about what they'd done. In the end, it had taken Tangel and the rest of the command crew taking the pair aside and telling them that all was forgiven before that part of his past had ceased gnawing at his soul.

Though it still nibbled.

"They did not," Terrance replied, shaking his head. "Though the charter did specify a list of Enfield research sites that would be used for advanced R&D. Anyone who read between the lines was able to tell that we planned to do research that wasn't possible in the Sol System."

"And the risk?" Beatrice asked.

"Of sabotage and war, or of a picophage?" Terrance asked.

"Well...both, I suppose."

The former Enfield executive let out a long sigh. "Well, we hoped that moving the research to a distant location like New Eden would reduce all those risks. The logic was that if Earnest had unlocked how to harness picotech, others would too. Turns out that was in error. Five thousand years later, no one else has pulled it off. We could have just left well enough alone."

"You've not heard the stories?" Beatrice asked.

Terrance quirked an eyebrow. "I've heard a few rumors, nothing more."

"No one else has pulled off *functional* picotech like your scientists did, but that wasn't for lack of trying."

"More phages?" he asked with a tremor in his voice, remembering the events on Tau Ceti, events that brought to mind Khela, which reminded him of later, equally painful events.

Stars, time never really does wipe it away completely.

"Several that I know of," she admitted. "Entire systems sterilized to prevent spread. I imagine there have been more that got swept under the rug."

He shook his head in remorse. "I guess we didn't really help much by removing it from the timeline."

"Who's to say?" After a brief pause, Beatrice gave Terrance an apologetic look. "I didn't mean to bring it up like this. So much of what we do has unintended consequences. The FGT doesn't have a perfect record, either."

"So long as we try to do the right thing at the time," he replied. "Which leads us to what the hell the core AIs are trying to do here."

"If it *is* the core AIs," she replied.

"We caught two remnants in the Inner Praesepe Empire. I think that's a pretty strong connection."

"A connection is not causation."

Terrance laughed. "If I had a credit for every time I've heard that.... Either way, that's a part of why we're out here. To learn what the heck is going on with those stars."

"True," Beatrice said with a slow nod, signaling her acquiescence. "All that aside, how accurate do you think their timing estimates are?"

"It's your team," he replied. "Though I was surprised that Wyatt narrowed it down to a one-hour window with such confidence."

She snorted. "He portrays that level of confidence in everything he does. Somehow, he even admits failure with the same level of certainty. I still can't tell if it's a character flaw or not."

"Seems to be working for him thus far."

"Most of the time." Beatrice's lips formed a thin line for a moment. "He's come close to making a trip out the airlock a few times. Stars, the only thing that stopped me was thinking about how much he'd complain when he was resuscitated."

"I've worked with a particular engineer that has elicited similar feelings in me before. Still does, if I have to do a project with her."

"Ma'am!" the ensign at the scan console called out. "I think we're picking up the event."

"Put it up," Captain Beatrice ordered, and the forward holo changed to a three-meter-wide view of Astoria, its blue light washing over the bridge.

The view of the star was a composite of data that the sensor grid was picking up all across the electromagnetic spectrum, showing every attribute of the star's emissions. Already, an anomaly was flagged at its poles.

A reference image appeared to the left of the 'live' view, or rather, the light that had left the star nineteen years ago, and it was plain to see that the star's poles had dimmed, while the luminosity at the equator had intensified.

"That doesn't match flare of CME activity," Beatrice muttered.

"Not even close," Terrance confirmed.

Then a point on the equator facing the sensor grid almost directly began to intensify further. Energy emissions spiked clear across the spectrum, climbing highest in the gamma range.

"Estimates show the emission to be coming from a point nearly ten thousand kilometers across," the ensign reported. "It's still intensifying."

"Well," Terrance muttered. "Two things are for certain."

"Oh?" Beatrice asked, not turning her gaze from the display.

"For starters, that's not any sort of natural phenomenon—or if it is, we need to throw out everything we know about stars and start over."

"And secondly?"

"There is no way that anyone in the IPE has the technology to do *that*."

Beatrice gave a slow nod as she turned to face Terrance. "Perhaps. If so, then the core AIs are playing a far deeper game than we'd expected."

* * * * *

"So, if you look carefully, you'll see that the star's output in the northern and southern hemispheres begins to dim several hours before the event itself," Emily said as she gestured at the display in the observation deck, where Terrance and Beatrice had joined the scientific team for their analysis.

"Which doesn't match any of the later progression of energy transfer within the star," Wyatt interjected. "That dimming does not align with a general change in the star's energy output."

"Right," Emily said with a sidelong look at Wyatt. "There were also fluctuations in the dimming, which align with occlusion."

"But if something was big enough to occlude Astoria's output, we'd see it, right?" Terrance asked, already knowing the answer from his involvement in Project Starflight.

"Right," Emily nodded. "Which means it's a swarm of smaller objects. Probably orbiting the star in patterns that periodically overlap and cause the precise effect we see."

"So these objects settle over the northern and southern hemispheres, and then?" Beatrice prompted.

"And then something alters the star's internal convection pathways," Emily explained, "directing more of the energy release toward the equator than normal. This is not ferociously difficult to achieve, it just takes time and careful planning."

Terrance was surprised to see Emily give him a rather pregnant look and wondered if the FGT's stellar engineer was aware of the work to affect a similar result with Canaan Prime.

She paused for a moment longer, and then continued. "But what is surprising is how they managed to get the star's emissions to focus in on such a fine point. I don't currently have anything beyond a raw guess at some sort of alteration in the star's magnetosphere that caused such a focused CME. We're still analyzing the data and will need to compare the next few weeks of information to see how the star transitions back to its normal burn pattern. That should give us some answers."

Terrance nodded slowly. "OK. The gate should be here in a few hours; I'm going to need your reports ready to jump out with me. I'll forward them on to whomever you wish. We need our best minds working on this."

"So do you think it's the core AIs?" Emily asked, her eyes widening as she said the words.

Terrance saw that every face was turned to him, and he shrugged. "We'd already guessed at that before. It seems like this evidence points in favor of that hypothesis. But it means something else, too."

"Oh?" Wyatt asked. "Something we haven't already guessed at?"

"It's tangential," Terrance replied. "But you don't just create what is effectively a dyson swarm out of nothing. There's some sort of manufacturing facility in the heart of the IPE that is making whatever does this."

Beatrice whistled. "Damn…between the ISF and the TSF, we have hundreds of ships in the Inner Praesepe Empire…."

"I know. Get a pinnace ready. I want to jump out the moment the gate gets here."

AN INTERVIEW WITH GARZA

STELLAR DATE: 10.06.8949 (Adjusted Years)
LOCATION: Tangel's Lakehouse, ISS *I2*, near Lunic Station
REGION: Aldebaran, League of Sentients Space

Tangel took a sip of her coffee while gazing out the kitchen window at the view of the orchard stretching behind the house. It was a serene view, the leaves rustling in the slight wind, bots visible here and there, flitting amongst the trees, plucking fruit for the *I2*'s galleys.

She breathed in the normalcy of it, the simple joy of soaking in a view she'd seen so many times in the past. It created a calm within her that grounded her and reminded her what she was fighting so hard to achieve.

That calm was broken when Cary careened into the kitchen and collapsed in a chair.

"Coffee?" Tangel asked as she turned to give her daughter an appraising look.

Cary only grunted, but it sounded like an affirmative noise, so Tangel prepared a cup and set it on the table.

"Rough night?"

With a nod of her head, Cary made another grunt and then picked up the cup and took a long draw of the dark liquid within.

Once she had downed half the cup, she gave Tangel a steely-eyed look. "How in the stars do you look so good this morning, Moms? What I did yesterday…the shield, the graviton fields…I'm totally wiped. I could sleep for a week."

Tangel pulled out a chair and sat next to her daughter.

"Do you want to know my secret?"

"I'd consider killing for it."

A laugh burst from Tangel's lips, causing Cary to wince.

"Dammit, Moms. Easy on the volume."

"Sorry. I had a response that was way funnier in my head than it would have been out loud. Anyway, I think that it's just because I'm further along than you are. You know, with the whole ascending thing."

Cary took another sip of her coffee, fixing Tangel with a dour look over the rim before setting it down. "Which is fine by me. I don't want to be *anywhere* with the 'ascended thing'." She scowled and made air quotes as she said the words.

Tangel leant back in her chair and gave her daughter a level stare. "Liar. I saw you when you were fighting those Widows. You were enjoying it."

"OK…I guess grouchy me isn't that clear. What I mean is that I like the fun benefits of being able to see into other dimensions. Manipulating matter through them is a great added bonus, but I don't want to turn into a glowing ball of light. We've been over this."

"Right," Tangel nodded with a wink. "No glowing balls of light. I'll make sure that doesn't happen to you."

"I'm being serious, Moms."

"So am I. I don't have any special way of making sure that doesn't happen to you, but so far as any of us know—Bob included—you don't shed this mortal coil of yours until *you* decide to." As she spoke, Tangel touched her daughter's arm and gave it a pinch.

"Ow!"

"See? Still good ol' flesh and blood. Even without my edge over you when it comes to time in the ascending business, you're a lot more organic than I am. Which means that our bodies replenish energy differently, making our recoveries different. Or maybe you just need to build up more stamina."

Cary nodded and took another sip of coffee. "I was already a bit worn out after fighting Myrrdan. Stars, I really hope that was finally the real one."

"You and me both," Tangel replied. "That guy has been such a thorn in my side that I have more thorns than side."

Her daughter snorted a laugh. "All-in-all, that was a pretty amazing trip to the LMC. I mean, just going there is freakin' awesome on its own, but taking out Myrrdan, *and* getting that intel from Kent…I deserve a promotion."

"Nice—wait…intel from Kent?"

Cary peered over the rim of her cup, another frown settling on her brow. "Yeah, the details on Orion and Garza. I sent it all along through the normal channels. Didn't it get to you?"

Tangel sifted through all the intel updates she'd received, and then searched the *I2*'s databases for new intel on Garza.

"No, there's nothing new. It must have been hung up somewhere."

"Seriously?" Cary sat up straight. "Then you don't know?"

"Cary…what?"

"The first Garza, the one that Jessica's team captured on the *Britannica* two years ago…. He's not a clone."

* * * * *

Tangel let slip a rueful laugh as she walked through the *I2*'s brig to Garza's cell—the first one. The Garza they'd captured in Scipio was in the next block over, and neither was aware that the other was on the ship.

Her laugh was directed at all the times she'd considered sending both of the Garzas to The Farm—the large stasis facility holding the enemy forces that had surrendered after the Defense of Carthage. Luckily, she'd never gone through with sending her Garzas there; she was more than glad for the result of her indecision.

She slowed as Garza's cell came into view, assessing the man within through the thick pane of clear plas.

He looked haggard, as though sleep had eluded him for some time—except for at this exact moment.

Stretched out on his bunk with an arm over his forehead, the man didn't move or acknowledge her presence in any way.

"Two years is a long time to be in here alone," Tangel said after she'd regarded him for a minute. "Well, mostly alone. I see that they do give you an hour in the park every other day—so long as you behave."

Garza still didn't move a muscle. His breathing remained the same, and his heart rate was steady.

"I suppose you're dying to know how the war's been going. I'm pretty sure that no one's told you—or they'd better not have. We've got the Hegemony of Worlds ringed in, we're hitting the Trisilieds, and Nietzschea is on its knees. Things on the fronts with the OFA have been a bit dicey, but mostly it's just been some minor back and forth there.

"We also have fleets operating within Orion Space. I think that by this time next year, we should be paying the praetor a visit at New Sol."

With her report ended, silence set in. It stretched on for over three minutes, until finally the man cracked an eyelid for a moment and spoke, his voice filled with scorn.

"Should have led with something more believable than having the Hegemony encircled. There's no way you could have pulled that off in two years."

"A lot's changed," Tangel said with a nonchalant shrug. "Without you and the Transcend holding the Inner Stars in check, we've really been able to get the ball rolling. Currently, the *I2* is at Aldebaran, capital of the League of Sentients—an alliance that wraps partway around the Hegemony. It had just come into existence when you attacked New Canaan, so I imagine you've not heard of it."

Garza's cheek twitched, but he didn't respond.

"I'll admit, there are a few gaps here and there, but on the far side, we have Scipio pressing the attack, which counts for a lot. One of your clones tried to stop that alliance, but let's just say that he ended up in a similar situation to you."

That statement elicited a response from Garza. Mention of Scipio had his eyes opening, and when she referenced the clone's capture, he sat up and fixed her with a penetrating stare.

"Now I *know* you're lying."

"Because of Scipio, or your clones? We've encountered three of them now, but one died. The Hand has spotted what they think are four others in various systems, so I imagine there are a lot more running around out there."

"Diana wouldn't ally with you," Garza sneered as the words dripped from his lips. "That woman's a preening fool. Thinks that by acting like an unhinged, power-hungry debutante, no one will contest her."

"Yeah, she was quite the character," Tangel said, chuckling at the memory. "Your clone abducted her at a ball. It was a tricky thing to get her back in one piece. She was grateful and signed the accord. The alliance of nations arrayed against Orion is now known as the Scipio Alliance."

Garza groaned and shook his head. "I think that's the worst one yet. And if it *is* true, it's the greatest indignity of all time."

"It's been interesting, that's for sure," Tangel nodded as she considered some of her conversations over the past year. "Lisa Wrentham is quite the character, too."

The general shook his head, lifting an eyebrow as he regarded her. "So you've run into her Widows, have you? How'd that go?"

Tangel shrugged. "A lot of them died. Ten? Something like that. I mean, we killed Xavia the other day, so wiping out some Widows wasn't a huge feat."

"Xavia?"

The man's physiology—which was an open book to Tangel—confirmed that he didn't know who she was referring to.

"She's one of—rather, she *was* one of—the independent operators in the ranks of the ascended AIs. I think you're familiar with the Caretakers, though. They're the ones that have been seeding this never-ending war."

"That's where you're wrong," Garza said, rising from his cot and walking to the plas, where he stared into Tangel's eyes for a moment before continuing. "It's *all* of the AIs who have been seeding this war. Either they're complicit, or they're unwitting pawns, but either way, they're the issue. The ascended ones are just the worst."

"What about ascended humans?" Tangel asked.

Garza snorted and turned away. "There aren't any of those."

"Have you heard of Star City?" Tangel asked, the words causing the man's head to whip back around.

"How…"

"My people have been there. AIs who are the children of New Canaan are now the Bastions of Star City. It was they who defeated your attack over a decade ago—I assume it was you who orchestrated that."

The man's eyes narrowed, and Tangel didn't even need the ability to see the thoughts on the surface of his mind to know that he had.

"You get around a lot for a lost pack of colonists from the past," Garza finally admitted. "But space is vast, and there are a few surprises out there for you, I'd imagine."

"A few," Tangel agreed. "Finding out where the Widows operate from is something I'd like to check off my 'lingering uncertainties' list, though."

"I bet you would," Garza said with a cruel laugh. "If my clones have sent Lisa after you, then you'd best be prepared for a long fight. She has quite a few clones of her own."

"They're different than yours, though," Tangel said as she leant against the plas. "Yours are much more…functional."

"Hegemony tech," Garza said. "Their president uses it. Makes her own body doubles that are intended to merge back in. Lisa wanted a different sort of tool, but she had to make…alterations to get it to work well."

"Crazy that she left Finaeus for you and Orion," Tangel said with a furrowed brow. "I mean, why would she go into Orion Space, where advanced tech is forbidden—or at least heavily frowned upon—when research of that sort is her bread and butter?"

"She believes in our vision, she's just made the personal sacrifice to be the means to counter the Transcend's rampant tech."

"Must be a secret base that your praetor doesn't know about," Tangel mused. "I'm guessing he doesn't know about half the stuff you're up to."

"This is so weak, Tanis. If you were going to use mental coercion on me to learn what I know, you would have already done it. Your interrogators have spoken to me for hundreds of hours, and I've learned more from them than they have from me. Your pathetic attempts to get me to slip up don't even rank."

The expression on Garza's face was one of pure disdain as he turned away, walking to the basin where he filled a cup with water before taking a drink.

"You're thinking of it even now," Tangel said after a moment. "I can see it in your mind. It's tricky, filtering through all the minutia that crowds human thought. I had expected your mind to be cleaner than most—it is, but not much."

"What are you talking about, woman?" Garza turned his head just enough to meet her eyes.

"The *Perilous Dream*. That's the ship she operates from. It's located in the…huh, I guess you just call it 'A1' System. A black dwarf star. Well, that's interesting…just like her, in so many respects."

Garza's eyes had grown wide as Tangel spoke, a look of fear pushing aside the smarmy expression that had been there a moment before.

"I wasn't asking you stupid questions," Tangel said with a slow wink as a filament of light exited her body, sliding through the plas toward the man as he backed away. "I was just making you think about her location, bringing those thoughts to the surface of your mind. Stars, you can't stop thinking about all sorts of things you don't want me to know, now. I really did think that you'd be more disciplined than this."

"You're ascended." The words hissed from Garza's lips on an indrawn breath as Tangel's otherworldly hand reached him. "How?"

She couldn't help but laugh. "Practice. Lots of practice. I suspect this is the eventual destiny of all humans—should they live long enough. We know that so much more of spacetime exists, but we're blind to it—well, sort of blind. But I can see it clearly, just like I can see your thoughts as though they were on a holodisplay before me. You're a flatlander, Garza. Three times over from where I am, now."

"Are you with the core AIs, then?" he asked, slowly gaining a measure of control over himself. "With Airtha?"

"Of course not. To both," Tangel said with a shake of her head. "As much as I hate it, the fact of the matter is that I'm at the head of my own faction. And we're just a few sure strikes away from victory."

For a moment, the man's veneer cracked, and a wild-eyed look came over him. "For now."

Tangel was about to ask what he meant, but Garza drew a deep breath and sat on the floor of his cell. He was working to clear his mind, to think of nothing and become opaque to her.

It was working relatively well.

"Well, I guess I have enough for now," Tangel said with a wink. "I might go talk to your clone, though, see what he knows."

Garza's jaw tensed, but he didn't speak.

Tangel waited a minute, staring at the man who she now knew had hoped to become humanity's ruler, but was now just another prisoner in the brig.

<Joe, I know where the Widows' base is. Meet me in the CIC.>

WIDOWSTRIKE

STELLAR DATE: 10.06.8949 (Adjusted Years)
LOCATION: CIC, ISS *I2*, near Lunic Station
REGION: Aldebaran, League of Sentients Space

"Well, if we know where it is," Joe began, staring intently at the holotank that showed the location of the black dwarf star known as A1, "let's just fire some RMs through a jump gate, and call it a day."

"You know we can't do that," Tangel said, meeting her husband's eyes. "The Widows are one of Orion's major clandestine arms. The intel on that ship is not something we can just pass up."

Captain Rachel shook her head as she stared at the holo—which displayed a region of space over a thousand light years into the gap between the Orion and Perseus arms.

"So is it just me, or is that black dwarf star a bit early…like by a quadrillion years or so?" she asked.

"I was wondering that, too," Saanvi added. "It really can't be a black dwarf…it must be a burned out brown dwarf, or a rogue planet."

Tangel shook her head. "No—well, I think 'no'. Garza definitely gave me the impression that it was a stellar remnant. A white dwarf that had cooled enough to no longer emit light."

"Yeah, but like Captain Rachel said," Cary nodded deferentially to the *I2*'s commander, "the universe isn't old enough for any black dwarf stars to exist yet—heck, with proton decay and WIMPs, a quadrillion years is the low-ball estimate for them."

"We've seen a lot of stuff that we never expected to." Tangel gave Cary an uncertain glance. "Mining a white dwarf could cause this effect, or even just siphoning off the heat somehow."

"That'd be a big siphon." Saanvi shook her head.

Joe scrubbed his hands across his face. "OK, I give. We need to do surveillance. I'll select a ship to drop in and check out this A1 System."

"Why not just send a team in?" Faleena asked. "Get the intel, blow the ship, be gone. All in one fell swoop."

"Well, for starters, it's a ship full of Widows…." Cary shot her sister a narrow-eyed glance.

Faleena looked Cary up and down, then Saanvi. "With some minor mods, the two of you could pass for Widows."

"Widows?!" Saanvi exclaimed. "Noooo no no no no."

"There are almost no infiltration teams available right now," Faleena said in a tone that brooked no argument. "Carson's fleet got called away to aid Scipio, and we can't pull anyone from the Airtha mission. But for all we know, there could be dozens of Widow teams out there, ready to strike. Rika, Petra, Kylie, Krissy…so many of our allies would not be able to stop one of their attacks as easily as we did."

Tangel chewed on her lip as she thought through her available assets, realizing that no group small enough to infiltrate the Widows' ship would stand a chance of success—not without an ascended being to help.

I could do it, but I need to stay on hand to aid in the attack on Airtha.

"Stars…. It may actually be the best option we have." Her eyes met Joe's, and she could tell that he'd come to the same conclusion.

"Dammit." He looked at Cary and shook his head. "Well, the three of you aren't going in alone. I'm bringing a stealthed cruiser to keep watch."

"Wait…exactly *when* did I agree to this?" Sanvi asked.

* * * * *

"OK…" Iris shook her head a little too fast, still fine-tuning the actuators in her new body. "You're telling me that you three girls are going to infiltrate Widows HQ. On your own?"

Everyone in the CIC nodded, and Cary spoke first.

"Yes. That's why we wanted to talk with you, to learn any details from your mission in the Ferra system that might not have been in Jessica's report."

Iris glanced at Faleena. "Well, for starters, this group of Widows is a step up from the ones we dealt with back in Orion space. We were able to fool them with Addie, our infiltrator chameleon, but I don't think that you'll be able to fake out this breed, Faleena."

"We stand a better chance of success if I go," Faleena replied, setting her jaw as she regarded Iris.

"I'm not saying you shouldn't go," Iris said, casting a glance at Tangel, surprised that she was allowing a trio of women just barely out of their teens to undertake such a crucial mission.

Well, except for Faleena. She's only two.

"But if you do, you're going to need to use a body that matches the Widows' physiology. Nance and Cheeky had to get mods to pull it off."

"I understand that," Faleena replied equably. "I'm prepared to have my core implanted in a simulacra to achieve our goals for this mission."

"OK. If that's the case, then I'll come too," Iris said with a resolute nod. "I know the Widows, and I'm a better breacher than any of you."

<*No,*> Bob's voice broke into the conversation. <*You are needed elsewhere.*>

Iris glanced up at the overhead. "I am?"

<*Yes,*> The AI replied simply. <*You and Amavia are necessary components for the strike on Airtha.*>

"I'm a component, am I, Bob?"

<Don't mock me when I use this crude language. It's unwieldy. So far as I'm concerned, ***none*** *of the words are accurate.>*

"I have to admit." Tangel's voice was heavy with unspoken emotion. "Were you three not highly talented women who work exceptionally well together, I'd never consider this."

"I can barely believe we actually are," Joe added, worry writ large across his features. "What about just waiting until Carson's fleet is finished helping Rika, and then sending it in whole hog? Stars, once Rika is done with her latest conquest, we could send her Marauders."

Tangel shook her head. "It's going to take her some time to cut her way across Nietzschea. Then she has to stabilize the region. No, crazy as it sounds, our best bet is to send our three girls in—with you close by, of course."

"And the First Fleet will be arrayed in front of jump gates," Rachel said with a solemn nod.

"And the Home Fleet," Tangel added. "Or some of it, at least."

<Send Priscilla,> Bob spoke up in the short silence that had followed Tangel's words.

"Really?" Tangel asked, cocking her head as she considered the woman's skillset. "Are you sure?"

<Priscilla has a weighty choice ahead of her. This would give her the opportunity to experience time away from me.>

Tangel knew the decision Priscilla faced. If she continued to be Bob's avatar for much longer, her mind would no longer be separable from his.

<Can Priscilla even function away from Bob anymore?> Joe asked Tangel privately.

<I was wondering the same thing,> she replied. *<But I can't imagine Bob would send her if he thought she couldn't do it.>*

<Bob isn't all-knowing,> Joe countered. *<He makes mistakes, rare though they are.>*

"What about Kylie's team?" Rachel asked. "Things have settled down in Silstrand—for the moment, at least."

Tangel pursed her lips. "They'd be a good option, yes. But I just sent them into the Hegemony on their own impossible mission."

A sudden—and marginally manic—laugh escaped her lips, and she glanced at Joe.

"You know…next time we try to take over the galaxy, let's do it with a bigger team."

Joe gave a wry smile while nodding emphatically. "Noted."

"Priscilla, you been listening in?" Tangel asked, already knowing the answer.

<I have.> The reply was laced with uncertainty.

"And?"

<Well, I can tell from Bob's mind that he thinks I will do well enough away from him, but I've not ever been on a mission like this. I mean…I've trained for them, but it's not the same.>

"You're right about that," Tangel replied with rueful laugh. "But even if you had, nothing is ever like the training anyway. Everyone has to have their first time out sometime."

<Is that supposed to be encouraging?>

"No pressure," Joe said. "We could also take a few days and find volunteers in the Marine companies. There are a few who have shown an aptitude for this sort of work."

<No.> Priscilla's tone had gained a measure of certainty. *<I'll do it. Let me get my alternate on duty, and I'll be at your disposal.>*

"I'll tell Doctor Rosenberg to get ready," Rachel said. "Four Widows, coming right up."

Saanvi gave a shudder. "Gonna miss my nose."

"Your what?" Cary asked.

Faleena clapped her on the shoulder. "You should read Jessica's report. Noses and ears don't fit in Widow helmets. Why do you think they talk so strangely?"

Cary met Tangel's eyes. "Too late to change my mind, Moms?"

PART 4 – THE CALM

DEEPER

STELLAR DATE: 10.06.8949 (Adjusted Years)
LOCATION: River Station, Styx Baby-9
REGION: STX-B17 Black Hole, Transcend Interstellar Alliance

"This is just too weird, Sabs," Cheeky said as she reclined on one of the chairs in *Sabrina*'s rear observation lounge.

"Oh?"

Sabrina was using one of the new frames she'd 'requisitioned' from the *I2* during their recent visit to the massive warship. Unlike her other mobile frames—which looked as much like a starship as a bipedal hominid—this one looked almost perfectly human.

"What do you mean, 'oh'?" Cheeky fixed Sabrina with a narrow-eyed stare. "The fact that I'm the captain, and we're taking on new crew to go on a crazy mission. That's what's weird."

Sabrina only shrugged. "I'm OK with it."

"It's a lot of change.... Am I ready?" Cheeky wondered.

"Cheeky." Sabrina paused to shake her head and give a bubbly laugh. "I've known since day one that you and I were destined to be together."

"Liar. You were so pissed when Sera brought me aboard. You couldn't believe that she'd hired a pilot."

The AI shrugged. "OK...maybe not day one. But when you took the helm, I knew it was meant to be. You, me, flying through the stars. No one else *feels* it the same way we do."

"Well, I think Jessica does," Cheeky suggested. "She's one hell of a pilot."

Sabrina nodded. "OK, I'll grant you that. But it's different with you."

Cheeky wondered what Sabrina was getting at. Did the AI mean that Cheeky's love of piloting was different than Jessica's, or that it was different for Sabrina herself?

Across the lounge, Sabrina shifted her position, uncrossing and re-crossing her legs.

The single action caused Cheeky to suddenly realize why the AI was using a human-looking frame. Suddenly, everything around her shifted focus.

"Sabrina...are you....?"

"I want something more, Cheeky...more than the flirting we've been doing for the past three decades. It's been enough to drive a girl mad."

The new captain snorted. "Good thing you're not a girl, Sabs."

"Cheeky. I am a sleek, sexy starship. I am the ultimate girl, the evolution of femininity. Powerful, strong, cunning. And now I want the next thing any girl in my position would want."

Cheeky wondered exactly what Sabrina meant by that, and what more *she* could offer.

"We've had sex in sims, Sabs—you seemed to enjoy it. Do you want to do it with that frame now? Is that why you picked it?"

Sabrina glanced down at the body she was controlling. "I think that could be fun, and I was thinking I'd use it as a gateway drug to reel you in, but what I really want is something more than sex, Cheeky."

"Sabrina, I'm married to Finaeus...and while he recognizes that I'm not the sort of person to be tamed, I don't think he would be happy if we entered into some sort of deeper relationship."

"Are you sure about that?" Sabrina asked with a wink.

"Umm...OK, you've got me there, but what is it that you really want?"

Sabrina leant forward, her elbows on her knees, eyes boring into Cheeky's. "You're an AI. I know you like to 'be' human, but underneath it, you're one of us now."

"Right. I know that," Cheeky said, trying to brush the comments away.

While she'd accepted what she was long ago, dwelling on it was still not something she liked to do. It made her feel shallow, like she was just the veneer of Cheeky, spread across a different entity.

"I can see that *intellectually* you know it," Sabrina replied and then tapped her chest. "But do you know it in here?"

"Are you getting all metaphysical on me, Sabrina? Aren't we supposed to be the carefree, fun-loving ones?"

She laughed and sat back in her chair. "Stars, Cheeky, I can be both, you know. So can you—so *are* you. Look, I don't want to get between you and Finaeus, but I also want to take our relationship further...as AIs."

"Sabrina!" Cheeky exclaimed. "Shit. You want to do that deep mind-meld thing that AIs do, where we bare our innermost selves to one another. I don't know if I'm ready for that."

The AI laughed again, both audibly and in Cheeky's mind. "I wasn't planning to go all the way the first time we touch minds. You're not used to thinking like an AI, and I want to ease you into it."

Lips pursed, Cheeky blew out a long breath through her nose while staring at the AI.

Finally, she said, "You'd be surprised, Sabs. I think I've been thinking like an AI a lot, in how I see things, and analyze information. It's different than how I used to be. It's like I'm straddling both worlds."

"Nothing wrong with that. It gives you unique insight. Not a lot of humans make the leap—certainly not many get the best minds in the galaxy facilitating the transition."

"So where does this lead?" Cheeky asked. "You being the ship's AI, and me the captain and pilot. Do we just blend together when we fly?"

"I guess we could try that. Like I said, I just want to take baby steps. We'll see how compatible our minds are in the long run."

Cheeky snapped her fingers and gave Sabrina a measuring look. "I know what you want! You want to use my brains to make a *baby*!"

Sabrina held up her hands laughing softly. "Stars, Cheeky, no risk of you ever becoming a cold logic machine, is there?"

"Not so long as the stars are burning," Cheeky intoned. "But seriously. You want to make a child with me, don't you?"

Sabrina nodded slowly. "Eventually, if you'd like to. It's how new AIs are made. We merge, draw in elements from one another, produce new beings. Sometimes adding in bits from organic parents, too. It's how we keep things fresh. You'd be amazing, given your past and what you are."

"To add me to the collective?" Cheeky asked with a laugh.

"You know it's not like that."

"I know, I couldn't help it. So…how do we do this—touch minds?"

"First, I take you into an expanse. You've been in mine a few times already, so let's start there."

Cheeky nodded, and suddenly she was in space, drifting in the midst of a blue and purple nebula. She looked down at herself to see that she was in one of the modified AI frames that Sabrina liked to use: humanoid, but sleek, like a starship with an engine on the back.

<*Of course,*> she said with a laugh, turning about to look for Sabrina.

<*Well, it's an awesome way to be. All the utility of a human, with the ability to fly like a starship.*> Sabrina appeared before Cheeky, wearing her favorite red and gold frame.

<*So is that what we're gonna do? Fly around one another like birds mating or something?*>

<*No.*> Sabrina shook her head as she drifted closer to Cheeky. <*Being here is just a way to take your mind off the physical world around you. And this starscape, this 'place' is just a construct that overlays what's underneath.*>

<*Because AIs are creatures of the mind?*> Cheeky asked with a smile as the two drifted closer together and then clasped hands.

<*Humans are creatures of the mind, too. Their bodies exist to power their brains and keep them safe. Just like my body—the ship—exists to power my mind and keep me safe.*>

Cheeky laughed softly. <*And haul stuff around.*>

<*Same as a human. Some AIs have very small bodies that aren't mobile, but they still provide power and safety. And even beyond that, we all have physical brains…well except for some ascended AIs, though beneath it all, they have physical brains, too—just*

ones grounded in different dimensions than the ones we inhabit.>

<OK, Sabrina, you're very wise.> Cheeky reached out and touched the AI's face. *<So what now?>*

<Do you really think so?> Sabrina asked.

<Think so what?>

<That I'm wise. I've never thought of myself that way.>

Cheeky considered what had made her say those words, and then decided that they were true. She *did* think Sabrina was wise.

<I guess we've all grown a lot over the past thirty years. Stars…I can't believe it's been that long since Sera pulled us out of our respective junkyards and set us on this path.>

<We're all growed up,> Sabrina said with a laugh. *<OK, now I'm going to pull away this layer of the expanse and dive deeper. You ready?>*

<Can I stop whenever I want?>

<You're still just visiting my expanse, you can pull back whenever you want, just like normal.>

Cheeky locked her eyes on Sabrina's and nodded. *<OK.>*

The next second, the nebula and starscape were gone…but they weren't. The visuals had disappeared, but the *expression* of them was still present. It was organized in matrices of data, multidimensional arrays of information. It was more than facts and figures, it was poetry, emotion, concepts and beliefs.

Some of it was familiar to Cheeky; she often perused the underlying data structures of the information she used to fly the ship. But never it had contained anything more than uninspiring raw information before now.

<It's so beautiful,> she whispered.

<This is how I see space,> Sabrina replied. *<More than just objects and vectors, I see their whole being, and the light that suffuses it all. Energy, space, time, it's all the same thing, and so much more than just crude matter.>*

<I want to see space like this all the time,> Cheeky said, her voice a faint whisper.

<You can, Cheeky. You're an AI, you can see everything like this.>

<Stars….>

<Are you ready to go deeper?>

Cheeky looked at Sabrina, her form overlaid with so much information about who she was, what she thought about a million subjects—the very essence of her being.

<Take me all the way.>

THE BRIEFING

STELLAR DATE: 10.07.8949 (Adjusted Years)
LOCATION: River Station, Styx Baby-9
REGION: STX-B17 Black Hole, Transcend Interstellar Alliance

Sera walked into the briefing room and settled into a seat next to Cheeky and Sabrina, unable to miss that the two were holding hands.

She glanced at Finaeus, who was standing on the raised platform next to Earnest, their heads bent together as they flipped through a series of holoimages that she imagined must be notes and information for their presentation. He seemed focused on his work and entirely unperturbed by the display of affection between his wife and Sabrina.

"Stars, Sera," Cheeky muttered. "Put your eyes back in your head, already."

"But what about Finaeus?" she blurted, glancing at the man who was now stabbing his finger at the holodisplay and shaking his head.

"We've talked with him," Sabrina said. "Everything's fine."

"It's something that's been coming for a while," Cheeky added. "He and I still love each other, but our situations don't really allow for spending a lot of time together. We had a good run—and we're going to stay married—I'm just exploring AI stuff with Sabrina."

"AI stuff?" Sera cocked an eyebrow.

<*Mental merging,*> Jen supplied.

Sera knew the basics of what that entailed, mainly that it was one of the steps in making new AIs. She wondered if that was what Sabrina and Cheeky were planning on doing, but decided not to pry.

She only replied with, "Ah."

At that moment, she was distracted by the arrival of Krissy and several members of her command team, as they settled into the row behind Sera. They would not be directly involved in the mission, but everyone knew that there was a strong chance that things could go belly-up and the cavalry would need to be called to save the day.

Even if we succeed, we'll probably still need to call them in, Sera mused.

She'd given a lot of consideration to what would happen after they defeated Airtha. It was her hope that the majority of people under the AI's thrall would realize that they'd been on the wrong side and rejoin the rest of the Transcend without a fight.

But Sera knew that was little more than a dream. It was very likely that the Transcend would never reform as a single entity again.

Over the next five minutes, the rest of the strike team entered the room, and the low murmur of conversation filled the space as they waited for the briefing to begin.

Seraphina and Fina settled into seats on the far side of Cheeky and Sabrina, while Misha, Nance, and Flaherty all sat in the back row—rather, Flaherty stood *behind* the back row.

Katrina entered with her crew shortly afterward, a team consisting of Kirb, Carl, and Camille, all of whom had been with her since the beginning of her misadventures in Bollam's World five centuries prior. They were joined by one of Katrina's newer crewmembers—if a century aboard the *Voyager* made him 'new'—a rather bulky, four-armed man named Elmer.

A grey pillar of light appeared to one side of the room, and Sera noted that it represented the *Voyager*'s AI, a rather staid individual named Troy. Tangel had informed Sera that despite his propensity to see the cup as half-empty, he was one of the most reliable individuals she knew.

And tenacious as well, given what he's been through.

Her attention was drawn by Kara's entrance. The black-winged woman looked uncertainly around the room before shrugging and settling on Sera's left.

Sera had rarely spoken with Kara prior to the events at New Canaan two years ago, but in the last few weeks, they'd found a common bond. Both of them had a lot of issues with their parents—or, parent, in Kara's case—and had spent several late nights discussing their respective fathers.

Sera had to admit that she was also jealous of Kara's wings. Now that she was no longer president, and Seraphina was expressing keen interest in running the Hand, she wondered if it was time to try a mod like Kara's. The memory of the costume she wore at the Scipian gala she'd attended with Tangel came to mind, and she felt a smile grace her lips at the thought.

Her reverie was interrupted by the skittering sound of Malorie entering the room. The spider-woman moved to the back, where she climbed the bulkhead and settled in an upper corner.

Sera couldn't help but notice Flaherty give the red arachnid a disapproving glare.

<*Be nice,*> she cautioned.

<*She's still alive, isn't she?*>

The last to enter were Jane and Roxy—and Carmen, who had agreed to her 'sentence' and was now embedded in Jane. The two women shyly walked past the others and settled into the second-to-last row.

At the front of the room, Finaeus and Earnest looked up and surveyed the nineteen members of the strike force, along with Krissy and the five members of her command team.

"OK, now that we're all gathered," Finaeus said, sounding more tired than Sera had expected, "let's get started, because this is probably going to take all day."

"You going to serve lunch?" Cheeky asked with a grin, and Finaeus shook his head. "When have you known me to skip a meal when it could be at all helped?"

"Skip meals all you want, but don't start without us!" a voice said from the entrance, and Sera turned to see Iris stride into the briefing room, closely followed by Amavia.

Cheeky was on her feet in an instant, embracing the two women. "Stars! I had no idea you were coming!"

"Neither did we," Iris replied with a laugh. "We were helping with the Aldebaran mess when Bob contacted us and told us to join this mission. He didn't say why—you know how he is."

"But when Bob says 'Go', you don't ask questions," Amavia added, her lips twisting as she spoke. "Or at least, I don't—I'm still used to just being one of his appendages, I guess."

Sera noticed the hint of longing in Amavia's voice. She'd wondered how much the woman—at least the Amanda part—missed being one of Bob's avatars, and it seemed that the draw was still there.

"OK, OK. Sit, sit, sit," Finaeus said, making a shooing motion with his hands. "You've spent all of a week or so apart from your crew. The reunion needn't be any great thing."

Cheeky shot Finaeus a mock-scowl, but returned to her seat without further protest, while Iris and Amavia moved to the back of the room and settled next to Nance and Misha.

"Damn," Earnest muttered as he looked out over the crowd. "Twenty-two. I'll adjust the teams."

Sera had gone over the plan with the two men the night before, but she suspected they'd made some tweaks in the interim. If there was one thing she knew about her uncle, it was that he liked to put his own stamp on everything.

Earnest was the more easy-going of the two, which she suspected was from centuries of being married to his rather demanding wife, Abby.

However it worked out, the two men were thick as thieves whenever fate brought them together. Though Sera knew that Earnest's work building the Styx base—a feat completed so quickly via the use of his picotech—was nearly done, and that he was slated to go back to New Canaan in just a few days' time.

Finaeus would be coming along to Airtha. He had insisted on it, and Sera hadn't fought him. He had as much stake in seeing this through as any of them.

Her father—or rather the man who was in some way the donor of her genetic material—had also wanted to come on the mission, but the demands of taking over the reins of the Transcend didn't allow for such an indulgence, and his request was really just something made for appearances.

At least that was how Sera felt about it.

She supposed that her attitude wasn't terribly charitable. Though she'd tried to make a connection to Jeffrey Tomlinson, somehow she just couldn't see him as anyone other than the cold, distant father who had raised her.

In many respects, Sera thought of Finaeus as her true father. He had been the most constant male authority figure in her formative years—and also one who had genuinely liked having her around.

As she watched her uncle square his shoulders in preparation for his presentation, she was sincerely glad that it was he and not Jeffrey who was coming to Airtha. Finaeus had made the ring; it was only fitting that he would be there to secure its future.

"OK, now that we're *all* here," he turned to gaze out the doorway, as though looking for any last-minute additions, "we'll get started. Some of you may not know the full scope of what we're trying to do, so I'll give you the quick and dirty version, and then you can review the datum after the meeting."

As he spoke, an image of the star and ring that both bore the name 'Airtha' appeared behind him.

"For those of you who aren't intimately familiar with Airtha, the star is roughly one third a solar mass, and the ring has a radius of four million kilometers. I used to think it was the largest construct in the galaxy, but after all but stumbling upon Star City, I'll reduce my hyperbole to simply say that it is *one* of the largest constructs in the galaxy. We built it from carbon we harvested from the star, and it's a bit of a crowning achievement for me in beauty as well as size."

Earnest coughed and gave Finaeus a sidelong look before taking over. "The salient point is that the ring's surface area is over two hundred and fifty billion square kilometers, and with an average thickness of fourteen kilometers…well, as you can imagine, this is a hell of a target."

"I prefer not to think of my magnum opus as a 'target'," Finaeus said bitterly.

"We all get that," Earnest replied as he turned to look up at the ring. "Destroying the ring, as it turns out, wouldn't be that hard. We'd just need to trigger an overrun in six of the Cri-En power plants."

"Which would destroy the entire Huygens Star System," Finaeus added. "And possibly damage spacetime in a rather unpredictable fashion."

Earnest nodded. "I was just making a note, partially because we need to consider that Airtha herself may have a failsafe that will cause an overrun if she believes her death to be imminent."

Finaeus opened his mouth like he was going to deliver a rejoinder, but then pursed his lips and nodded.

<*I guess they've butted heads on this a bit,*> Jen commented privately to Sera. <*Personally, I think that overrunning the Cri-Ens would do the trick. Though they're right in that it would shred spacetime in more than just our dimensions. Dark layer, upper dims, they'd all fall apart.*>

<*Right, and then Bob would come and tear us a new one for breaking the universe.*>

<*I think he overstates the danger,*> Jen's tone was nonchalant. <*Surely* ***someone***

in the universe must have drained the base quantum energy out of a location by now.>

<*Maybe that's what the Great Attractor is,*> Sera suggested, referring to the gravitational anomaly that lay between the Milky Way and the Shapely Attractor, some two hundred million light years away.

<*Or it's a dark layer tear,*> Jen countered.

Sera nodded absently and turned her attention back to Finaeus as he described the locations of the Cri-En power generation facilities.

"The ring also draws power from the four pillars." Finaeus highlighted four spires that stretched from the ring toward the star. "These hold the ring in place, and additionally draw considerable radiant energy, given their proximity to the Airthan Star. They also facilitate the magneto effect that gives the ring an extra level of protection from extra-solar energies for its impending departure from the Huygens System.

"Hitting Airtha's nodes will be tricky, assuming she hasn't moved them. When last I was on the ring, she had twenty-eight nodes. One at the base of each tower, one near each of the twelve major Cri-En facilities, and then another twelve spread around the ring. Because of the necessity of managing the ring's position and power, I think she'll not have moved the nodes at the Cri-En facilities, and probably not the ones at the towers, either."

As he spoke, the node positions lit up on the holodisplay behind him, noting those that were unlikely to be moved, and those that may not be in the same place Finaeus originally put them.

"So what do we do when we hit her nodes?" Sera asked. "And which are better targets?"

Finaeus gave her a look that clearly said, 'Don't try to rush me', before shrugging and glancing back at the holo. "Honestly, we just need to hit four. Doesn't matter which—but we have to do it simultaneously, and without her knowing. If she sees you coming, she'll just sunder those nodes, and you'll waste your time."

"So we should try to hit *more* than four," Krissy said from behind Sera. "As many as eight, if we can manage it."

Sera shook her head. "That's going to put most of the teams at only two people, and it also means we'll need more AIs, since we won't have enough if we split into eight groups."

"We can increase the size of the strike force," Krissy offered. "I'm sure you have Hand agents that would be more than capable of pulling off this operation."

That had occurred to Sera as well, but she was more worried about Airtha discovering the operation than anything else.

"We could bump our numbers up a bit if we have to, but I'd rather not. The ring may be big, but Airtha will have eyes everywhere. We can put together five teams, with everyone having an AI in the group. Sabrina and Troy will remain on their ships and provide overwatch and coordination."

"Seriously?" Sabrina said, looking around Cheeky to lock eyes on Sera. "I've been practicing a lot. I only got my frame's head shot off that *one time.*"

"It's the signal, Sabs," Sera said with an apologetic look. "We can use data drops for messages, but if you maintain a solid connection between the ship and a frame, that'll be like a big red arrow pointing at your team."

"I guess…" Sabrina said and sat back. "I bet I could route the data stream well enough to hide it."

"I'm sorry, Sabs," Finaeus shook his head. "On some Joe Schmoe station out in the backend of nowhere, sure. But this is Airtha. We stand a fifty-fifty chance of her detecting a team already."

"Let's talk about how we're going to destroy Airtha before we get deeper into deployments and teams," Earnest suggested.

"Right," Finaeus nodded. "You roll with it, you made the breakthrough."

Earnest stepped forward. "After careful, and I do mean *careful*, examination of the shard of Airtha that Katrina procured, we managed to figure out a way to plumb the depths of her mind without fully waking her."

The scientist turned and pushed the holo of the ring aside, and a new image sprang into its place. "This is an AI's neural network—the sort we'd see in the Inner Stars, once the AI was properly liberated."

"Ha! I recognize that," Sabrina said with a laugh. "That's my brain you have up there."

"That it is," Earnest said as he turned toward the holodisplay. "You can see here the perimortal section of Sabrina's mind looks normal for an AI who has only distant human lineage in its mental structure."

Kara tentatively raised her hand. "Sorry to be the dumb one here, but what is a perimortal section of an AI's brain? Sounds morbid."

Earnest nodded. "Yeah, it's got a strange name. It's the part of an AI's brain that helps them understand that they are a mortal being just like humans. When AIs were first made, they didn't have this part of their minds—well, the Weapon Born did, but that was a result of their unique origin. In fact, it was merging and reproduction with Weapon Born AIs that brought about the perimortal development in AIs' minds to begin with. That's what 'humanized' the bulk of sentient AIs, so to speak."

His gaze swept across the group, and then his eyes settled on Iris. "Ah! Let's use you, Iris. You have human minds in your lineage just one generation back."

"I feel like I'm being put on display for everyone to ogle," Iris said, laughing as she nodded for Earnest to proceed.

"Which is normal for you," Cheeky said, turning to give Iris a saucy wink.

Earnest moved the display of Sabrina's neural network to the side and pulled up a new one. "Iris is a very interesting example of an AI's development. You can see that while she does have a perimortal section to her brain, it is configured differently from Sabrina's. In many respects, the perimortal portion of an AI's mind mirrors the function of the amygdala and hypothalamus of a human's, in that it controls emotional response and the fight-or-flight response.

"You can see that while Sabrina has a more tightly interwoven perimortal region of her mind, Iris has distinct regions. In many respects, Sabrina is more evolved in this area in that she has a more efficient processing center. However, it also means that the AI equivalent of the emotional processing center—where you figure out how you *feel* about things and make subjective decisions about if and how you want to experience certain events in the future—is more likely to trigger fight-or-flight in an uncontrolled fashion."

"I feel like I was simultaneously complimented and insulted," Sabrina said, her frame's lips twisting to the side.

"It's science," Earnest said not unkindly. "It neither compliments or insults. OK…where was I going with this? Ah! Right. In both cases, the perimortal section of an AI's mind is closely linked with its core logic centers."

On the display, a number of well-traveled neural pathways within both AIs' minds were highlighted.

"Sometimes these are stronger, sometimes they're weaker. Just as it is with organics, the more successful pathways are reinforced, so behavioral patterns evolve from key decision points, whether those decision be conscious or unconscious, so to speak."

Earnest turned to face the two holodisplays and pushed them to the side before breathing a long sigh. "And now we have Airtha's mind."

A new neural network appeared, one that was much larger than the other AIs' and much more interwoven.

"This is just a shard, which means it's close to what we'd see in a single node. What you'll see here, though, is that Airtha has not one, but *four* perimortal sections of her mind, and two of them are not well connected to her logic centers. Finaeus and I tested out various stimuli and found that Airtha can behave very logically in the face of some thoughts, and can have wild fight-or-flight reactions to others."

At that, Finaeus snorted. "And by that, he means she only has fight reactions. Her decision process never even gets close to the notion of disengaging from conflict."

"Explains a lot," Sera muttered before asking, "But technically, Helen was a shard of Airtha inside of me. She didn't have wildly irrational responses, or push me into conflicts."

"Right," Finaeus nodded. "That's because Helen was always destined to…uh…die. Bob also sent us mappings of Myriad's mind, and while she has a similar neural pattern to this shard's, Helen's was missing *all* her perimortal regions. She had one small amygdala-like section and that was it."

"Seriously?" Fina asked from several rows back. "So she was purpose-made to shepherd me…us…whatever, but never had the urge for self-preservation?"

"Essentially," Earnest said. "She had to be ready to accept her mortality and not fight it. "History is filled with stories of shards that went against their parent entities. It would seem that Airtha didn't want to repeat those events."

"OK, so how does this help us?" Iris asked. "Basically, we're looking at the mind of an AI that was made to react strongly to things, and be a little neurotic."

"But those things are dwarfed by her logic centers," Earnest replied. "And this is what gave me the idea about how to defeat her."

The scientist looked rather proud of himself, and Amavia called out, "OK, Earnest, we all know you're super brilliant. Out with it."

He rolled his eyes at Amavia, but continued his explanation. "I worked out a way to flip her fight-or-flight response, so that flight becomes the dominant reaction, but I also managed to alter her emotional responses so that suicide is the 'flight' option she picks. It involves re-introducing the two perimortal sections that are largely disconnected right now. Then we can overwhelm her logic centers, and she'll kill herself with fear."

"Really?" Cheeky cocked an eyebrow. "How is that remotely possible? She has so many options available. There's no way she'd think that death is her best choice."

Finaeus met Earnest's eyes. "Well, we have to make her think she's going to lose, and then the retro-struct virus we'll introduce into her nodes will cause her decision-making to essentially uncouple from her logic centers."

"And how are we going to make her think she's going to lose?" Sera asked.

Finaeus sighed. "We have to make her *think* we're going to destroy the ring. We also have to get on the move, because once the Airthan star and ring move beyond Huygens' Thomias Belt, the ring will be far enough from the system's center to allow dark layer transitions right from its surface."

"Which means Airtha might come to the conclusion that she *can* flee," Earnest added.

Sera rose from her seat and stepped up onto the raised platform, scanning the group assembled before her.

"So, as you all likely have figured out, we're going in on two ships: *Sabrina* and *Voyager*. Both ships are well known, so crews are already working on altering their profiles—both hull and engine signature."

Katrina winced, and Sera gave her a sympathetic look. "It can be undone if needed. I swear I never recognize *Sabrina* half the time anymore, with all the changes we've made to her."

The AI laughed. "I should really get some sort of flowmetal system for reconfiguring the hull on the fly…you know, Finaeus, why don't we do that?"

"Cosmic rays," Earnest provided the answer with a shrug. "Flowmetal breaks down over time from exposure to…." His voice faded away and he began tapping his chin. "You know…I wonder if we could somehow mix a flowmetal structure with a polymer containing Jessica's microbes. That would give the flow—"

"I'd be purple!" Sabrina gave an excited laugh. "I approve of this this plan."

"Well, I don't think I could have something like that ready for this mission," Earnest held up his hands. "It was just an idea."

"Shortlist me," Sabrina gave the engineer a serious look, and he nodded.

"You'll be the first, Sabrina."

Sera shrugged as she considered such a thing. "You certainly wouldn't be the first purple starship I've seen. Might have to take up covers as a cruiseliner, though, not a freighter."

"I *like* that," Sabrina nodded vigorously. "I see a whole new future for us."

"OK, OK," Sera held up a hand. "Let's focus on getting through this mission first." She paused and glanced over her shoulder at Earnest. "Are the new team structures all set in the planning package?"

"Sure are," the engineer nodded. "Once again, Bob knew what he was doing. I re-evaluated everyone's strengths, skills and compatibilities. Getting these two AIs—well, you know what I mean," he gestured at Iris and Amavia, "in the mix did allow us to go from three teams to five."

"That's excellent," Sera said, while Iris pumped a fist in the air, calling out, "Go us!"

To which Amavia added, "Well, more like, 'Go Bob'."

The pronouncement elicited some laughs from around the room. When they dissipated, Sera continued.

"OK, first off, as Finaeus said, the ship's AIs will remain on their craft and coordinate with one another and their teams."

Troy made a sound of approval, while Sabrina's face fell once more.

"Look, Sabs, it takes too much bandwidth for you to fully project. If you want to be on a team, you have to remove your core from the ship."

A look of horror crossed over Sabrina's face, and Cheeky laughed, patting Sabrina's arm.

"And no one is surprised you'd feel that way," she soothed her.

Sabrina raised a hand to her chin, her lips pursing for a moment before she spoke. "What if I…sharded?"

The question took Sera entirely by surprise, and she glanced back at the two engineers. "Does she have core matrices capable of that?"

Finaeus stared at Sabrina for a moment, and then glanced at Earnest. It was apparent to everyone in the room that the pair was having a protracted Link conversation.

Sera was about to table the issue and move the meeting along, when Earnest gave a slow nod.

"Sabrina has nearly outgrown the core I upgraded her to twenty years ago—which should have lasted a lot longer." The engineer gave the AI narrow-eyed look, to which Sabrina only responded with an innocent whistle. "I suspect it's because of how many expanses she created within herself to help liberate other AIs. To be honest, I think a sharding would actually be beneficial for her in the long run…help her share the load, so to speak."

"What if…" Cheeky ventured slowly, glancing at Finaeus and then Sabrina. "What if the shard was a bit of a child of ours as well?"

"No," Earnest shook his head, entirely missing the meaning-laden looks Cheeky was doling out. "Your mind is not one that we can easily select attributes from and blend with others, Cheeky. That's not saying we can't do it, we just can't do it and have your child ready to take on a mission like this in the time available. If Sabrina wants to shard, it will have to be a straight mitosis."

Sabrina glanced at Cheeky, who nodded.

"OK," the two said in unison.

Sera was about to move the meeting forward once more when a large figure appeared in the room's doorway.

"Usef?" Cheeky blurted out, and the figure nodded before stepping in to reveal a much smaller person behind him.

"Erin?" Earnest added. "What are you two doing here?"

The brown-haired woman shrugged. "I'm not entirely certain. I had taken a ship from the LMC back to New Canaan to assist in some review of a—" she paused and glanced around, "project, when suddenly Usef shows up and tells me that Bob has sent word for us to come here…wherever 'here' is."

Earnest's brow lowered and he shook his head. "I'm going to have words with Bob. Would have been nice if he'd told me about all these late arrivals."

"I've just queried the tower," Krissy announced. "There are no inbound ships in the queues right now, so in theory, our numbers should remain consistent for the next hour or so—barring Tangel just jumping into our midst."

Sera laughed, wishing that could happen, but she knew her friend had her hands full on the far side of Sol, dealing with the fallout of Xavia's attack, and the war with the Trisilieds.

"OK…teams adjusted. Again," Earnest announced as Erin found a seat, and Usef ambled to the back of the room where he took a spot next to Flaherty, glancing at Malorie—who still hung in a corner—before shaking his head and directing his attention to Sera.

Suddenly, Erin spoke up. "Ho…wait…that's Airtha on the holo! This is the mission to take on Airtha? Why the hell am I here?"

Sera shrugged. "Ask Bob. I've seen your record, though, and Usef vouches for you. That's enough for me."

"Gonna have words with Bob," Erin muttered and sank back into her seat.

"OK!" Sera thrust a finger in the air. "First Team—so long as we don't get a dozen more people showing up before we leave—is myself, Jen, Kara, and Flaherty. We're on *Sabrina*."

<*Of course,*> Jen added privately.

Flaherty gave a slow nod from the back of the room, and Kara a slightly nervous smile. Sera had been a bit surprised to see Adrienne's daughter in her group, but Earnest had shown her the decision parameters, and she couldn't argue with his assessment.

"Next up is Team Two, also aboard *Sabrina*. It consists of Seraphina, Cheeky, Nance, and Finaeus."

"One last time into the breach, eh, hon?" Finaeus asked Cheeky with a wink.

The pilot shrugged. "I think we'll breach plenty in the future. But this'll be one for the songs."

"Last team on *Sabrina* consists of Sabrina—no surprise there—Usef, Misha, and Erin."

"You better have figured out which end of the gun is for shooting bad guys," Usef grunted, his eyes locked on the back of Misha's head.

In response, the cook slowly lifted two fingers in a rude gesture, not deigning to look back at the large Marine.

Sera ignored their byplay and carried on.

"Team Four is aboard the *Voyager* and consists of Fina, Roxy, Jane, and Carmen. Team Five is Katrina, Kirb, Elmer, and Amavia. Wrapping things up is Six, which will be Iris, Carl, Camille, and Malorie."

"Last, but certainly not least," Malorie chittered from her corner.

Iris twisted in her seat and took in the metallic red spider. "Any chance I can sell you on the idea of a new body?"

"And slough about on the decks with two legs?" Malorie asked with a laugh. "Not effing likely."

"Everyone's going to have Mark X FlowArmor," Sera interjected. "Those of you who haven't already had your skin replaced with the Finaeus special, that is. If you'd like to get a skin job, you'd best put in the request in the next five minutes.

"Each team is going to have a Cri-En power facility target, and a node. The plan is to infiltrate the power facilities, where we'll set up bombs. These will be used to convince Airtha that we mean to destroy the ring. Once they're in place, we move on to the nodes. Timing will be key; the window to insert our corrupted matrices into Airtha's nodes will be small, and we'll need to time it perfectly. To ensure that happens, Troy and Sabrina will be keeping us all coordinated to ensure no one jumps the gun.

"Once we've inserted our virus into her, we trigger some smaller detonations at the Cri-En facilities and leak the information that more are targeted. With the changes to her thought patterns, that should be enough to push Airtha over the edge."

Sera paused and surveyed the room, where most of the attendees were nodding, though Krissy was not.

"And your fallback plan?" the admiral asked.

"We don't have one," Finaeus said with a laugh, causing Sera and Krissy to send quelling looks his way before Sera turned back to Finaeus's daughter.

"He's kidding. That's where you come in."

THE PRAESEPE REPORT

STELLAR DATE: 10.08.8949 (Adjusted Years)
LOCATION: CIC, ISS *I2*, near Lunic Station
REGION: Aldebaran, League of Sentients Space

"Is Earnest on his way?" Terrance asked as he walked into the antechamber off Earnest's famed workshop.

"His pinnace just docked," Tangel replied, reaching a hand out to clasp Terrance's. "I wasn't expecting to see you so soon. How did the FGT's expedition go? I assume that's what this is about."

"Good," Terrance gave a short nod. "Well, good and bad. Someone is moving those stars, alright. And they're doing even better than we are at moving Canaan Prime."

Tangel found herself blinking mutely at the man for a moment before she recovered. "Seriously?"

"Well, I'm not an expert on such matters, but Emily—the FGT stellar engineer—was suitably impressed. Either way, if they'd cared to, she estimates that the stars could have already been dropped into one another, but it seems that whoever is doing this—"

"The core AIs," Tangel interjected.

"Well, yeah, I've been thinking that, too, but it just feels like conjecture so far, and I didn't want that to be in an official report."

A laugh slipped past Tangel's lips. "Ever the company man, Terrance."

He shrugged. "Old habits die hard."

Tangel wanted to probe further regarding the stellar movement in the Praesepe Cluster, but she didn't want Terrance to have to repeat himself once Earnest arrived.

Instead, she turned and walked toward the window that looked out over the rear of the ship. Almost directly below them was the now-vacant stretch that had once been filled with twenty cubic kilometers of cargo pods, back when the ship had been bound for its colony world.

A few pods were still nestled down in the depths of the crevasse, filled with components for the ships that made up the First Fleet, but little else. The empty space made the ship feel incomplete to Tangel.

On either side of that gap lay the two habitation cylinders, sixteen-kilometer-long, fully encapsulated worlds. To date, Tangel had still lived there longer than she'd lived anywhere else. Even though she'd raised her daughters on Carthage, and that house held a host of great memories, Ol' Sam was home.

The *I2* was still home.

"I've been thinking a lot about what could have been," Terrance said in a quiet voice as he stepped to her side. "If we'd made it to New Eden, if we'd developed the picotech there. Maybe we could have headed all this off. Stopped the FTL wars and the dark ages that followed."

"Maybe," Tangel allowed. "I think about that, too. If I had somehow stopped the SSS from sabotaging the ship at Estrella de la Muerte…"

"You know it's not that simple. There was Myrrdan and the Caretakers working against us. We didn't even have a clue that they were in play."

"Yeah."

Tangel let the word fall from her lips as she stared out over the great ship. The *greatest* ship ever built.

The man chuckled. "Yeah. I know. Doesn't stop you from wondering."

<*The wars were necessary,*> Bob said after a moment of silence stretched between the two humans. <*As is this war.*>

"While I agree that wars like this are necessary once you exhaust all other options, I don't think that's what you're referring to, is it?" Terrance asked.

<*No. I think that humanity and AIs have to exhaust their taste for war to know what we are capable of, both the good and the bad.*>

"You're starting to sound like the core AIs," Tangel cautioned.

<*Them's fighting words.*>

Bob spoke in a half-joking tone that had Tangel and Terrance sharing a surprised look.

<*Don't give one another that look. You know I can tell jokes.*>

Terrance chuckled. "Uhhhh…yeah, but you need to do it more than once a decade for us to be used to it."

<*Oh. Noted.*>

"Stop messing with them, Bob," Earnest said as he entered the room and strode toward Tangel and Terrance.

<*You're not the boss of me.*>

-What's gotten into you?- Tangel asked the AI.

-I can't have fun?-

Tangel sent him a wave of curious incredulity. *-I guess…sure. People just tend to take everything you say very seriously. You're usually a very serious person.-*

-I'm evolving.-

-That's scary too.-

The ascended, multinodal AI sent Tangel a feeling of amused mirth that nearly knocked her over, and she decided not to pursue the conversation any further.

"I know where your off switch is," Earnest was saying to Bob with a smirk.

<*Now who can't take a joke?*> Bob asked.

"Is this because Priscilla's gone?" Tangel asked, as the realization hit her that Bob's change in behavior may be due to the absence of the woman who had been only a thought away for decades.

"Priscilla's gone?" Earnest shot Tangel a sharp look. "Gone where?"

<Widowstrike.>

"We were attacked by Finaeus's ex-wives," Tangel explained. "We also learned that the Garza clone we captured on the *Britannica* two years ago wasn't a clone at all. I interrogated him, and we found out where the Widows operate from."

"And you sent *Priscilla*?" Earnest's voice rose half an octave as he took a step toward her. "She doesn't have the training for that."

<She does. She is the right person for the job.> Bob's tone brooked no argument, though his words didn't slow Earnest in the least.

"Sorry, she has 'training'," the engineer held up his hands to make air quotes, "but she has no experience. Those Widows are nasty business. She's—"

"She's with my daughters," Tangel interjected. "And Joe has a stealthed fleet nearby. Trust me, I'm anxious about this, too, but we're low on people who can take out an installation like that."

"Why send people at all?" Terrance asked. "Couldn't Joe just blow their base and call it a day?"

Tangel nodded. "Yes, yes he could. But the Widows are Orion's preeminent blackops organization. The intel we're bound to get from them will be indispensable."

Earnest chewed on his lip for a moment before glancing at Terrance. "So you didn't know about this?"

"Me?" The business exec held up his hands. "I've been in Praesepe watching the core AIs shuffle stars around like they're playing a stellar game of checkers."

<Priscilla wanted to go,> Bob added. *<She needed to go. Worry about her later. What Terrance found is more important.>*

"Is that why you're cracking jokes?" Tangel asked. "You're worried?"

<I'm always worried.>

"OK, I know we're thinking of starting a comedy club, but we need to decide what to do about this," Terrance interjected, turning to the window and gesturing at it. The aft view of the *I2* was replaced by the image of a star. "This is our subject. The little star that could."

As Tangel and Earnest watched, the poles of the star dimmed, and a single hot point formed near the equator before blasting out a jet of energy for several minutes.

It was Earnest who spoke first.

"Well I'll be a…uhh, I have no idea what."

"Emily was tangentially aware of our efforts in New Canaan," Terrance explained. "She seemed to think that it was a more powerful emission than what we were doing."

"That's because we're not doing anything like that," Earnest muttered as he replayed the visual. "We're focusing the star's burn at the north pole, while dimming the southern polar region. We're intensifying the stellar output at the equator to compensate for the luminosity change…but nothing like this."

"It's obviously sufficient to move the star," Tangel observed. "And it looks like they used some sort of swarm to do it."

"An expendable swarm," Terrance added. "So far as we can tell, once the stellar output shift completed, whatever machinery was at play fell into the star."

Tangel snapped her fingers. "So that's why you queried our resources when you arrived. You want to mount a search for the facility where they're making those things."

"It has to be close," Terrance replied. "The stars are already on a collision course. It'll take a few centuries, at the current rate, but the total stellar mass in the cluster's core is over forty Sols. When they collide…."

"We get it," Earnest replied. "The entire cluster is sterilized…well, more than just the cluster, though folks beyond the slow zone will have a few centuries to get out of the way."

Tangel flung a new visual at the window. It showed the region of space between Sol and the Praesepe cluster. Centered in the view was the Betelgeuse exclusion zone, an empty region of space that had been vacated when the massive star underwent a supernova several thousand years earlier.

"Now…I'm no stellar engineer, but when Praesepe goes up, it's going to trigger some of its own supernovae, right?"

Earnest nodded. "There are no hypergiants in Praesepe, but there are stars that will evolve into them. But…the event that we'll witness isn't like other supernovae. If you look at Betelgeuse, you can see that its shockwave has only moved about nine hundred light years, and it's all but dissipated now. Most stellar systems it hits see a compression of their heliosphere, but not so much that the stellar wind can't stop the wave before it reaches major planets. Betelgeuse also released very little gamma radiation, and the x-rays are all but dissipated, thanks to our friend the inverse square law."

"And Praesepe?" Tangel asked. "It will be much worse, won't it?"

The engineer nodded. "I'm actually less worried about a collapse of the cluster's core triggering supernovae in massive stars, and *more* worried about the cluster's white dwarfs. There are several that are massive enough to undergo a supernova event on their own."

"White dwarfs can do that?" Terrance asked, then glanced at Tangel. "Don't go making any 'you've been flying around in space for a thousand years and you don't know that?' jokes. There aren't any white dwarfs around Sol, and Betelgeuse is…was…the only nearby star likely to undergo collapse."

Tangel held up her hands in a defensive gesture. "I wasn't going to say a word. Honest. Really."

"White dwarfs can do it too," Earnest confirmed, casting Tangel a bemused look. "If they increase in mass close to one and a half Sols—depending on their rotational speed—then electron degeneracy pressure isn't enough to support the star's mass, and it collapses."

"But not into a black hole?" Terrance clarified.

"No. Before that happens, the star gets hot enough to fuse a substantial fraction of its mass in a matter of seconds." The engineer paused as he looked from Tangel to Terrance. "The ejecta from the white dwarf's explosion travels at ten percent the speed of light."

"Holy shit," Terrance whispered. "OK, so this is going to make Betelgeuse look like the warmup."

"Multiple stellar-sized fusion bombs," Tangel said quietly. "If they're doing this in other clusters..."

"I'd thought that, too," Terrance said. "I just didn't realize what the white dwarfs in them will do."

"Might," Earnest held up a hand. "*Might.* It could be that the shockwave never pushes enough mass toward the white dwarfs...or it could set a bunch of them up to slowly accrete mass and detonate over the next few thousand years."

Tangel held up a hand. "OK, so it's the big suck. We didn't think it meant sunshine and daisies, so that part's not news. What we need to do now is find out where their facility is that is making their little dyson swarm, take control of it, and then reverse this process."

"And then check over every other fucking cluster in the galaxy," Earnest muttered. "Fuck. This is going to take millennia to fix. Fucking AIs. Present company excluded."

"Thanks," Bob and Tangel said at the same time.

Terrance shot a curious look at her. "I didn't know you identified as AI."

Tangel shrugged. "Depends on the day. Of course, this presents a whole new problem. Who do we send?"

"What about Jessica and Trevor?" Terrance asked her. "I bet Amavia and Iris could go with them."

"I think the fact that I sent *my daughters* along with Priscilla to hit the Widows should tell you that those other four aren't available."

"Oh, yeah, that makes sense. And I guess you and Bob are staying here in reserve for when the shit hits the fan."

Tangel nodded. "And worrying that it doesn't hit all over all at once."

<*Which seems increasingly likely,*> Bob added.

"OK, Terrance. Here's what we'll do. I'll have Bob drum up a couple of AIs who are as crazy as the rest of us, we'll peel off a cruiser from the First Fleet, and we'll send you into Praesepe to start the hunt. We'll send you with a spare gate, too. I don't want you going into the ass-end of nowhere and taking months to get back."

"I'm going to need some trigger pullers, too," Terrance added. "Any of those left?"

"Barely," Tangel said with a drawn out sigh. "Joe's going to kill me, but I'll send Lieutenant Brennen with you. It drops the *I2* down to just two platoons, but we have thousands of combat drones aboard, so we'll manage."

"I'm going with him," Earnest said, fixing Tangel with a resolute stare. "Someone is going to have to figure out how to put those stars back where they belong."

Tangel nodded. "I suspected you would want to go."

"Wait. Really?" he asked. "You're going to let me run off into danger like this?"

"Sure. We're all in danger. To be honest, Praesepe is probably one of the safest places around. Till it explodes, of course."

Terrance laughed. "You have such a way with words."

<You never laugh at my jokes. I feel maligned,> Bob said with a long sigh.

PART 5 – AIRTHA

TO AIRTHA

STELLAR DATE: 10.09.8949 (Adjusted Years)
LOCATION: ***Sabrina,*** **Interstellar dark layer**
REGION: Huygens System, Transcend Interstellar Alliance

<You know what I miss about when we were just starting out together?>

Sabrina's voice broke Sera from the thoughts she'd been lost in, and she looked at the nearest optical pickup on the bridge.

<What's that, Sabs?>

<I was always just me. I looked like me, I had my name. Sabrina was Sabrina.*>*

Sera gave a tired smile. *<You don't like being the* Sands of Time*?>*

<Makes me feel like I'm going to fall asleep.>

<I think ***I'm*** *going to fall asleep,>* Sera said as she stood from the scan console and looked down at Cheeky in the pilot's seat.

"Did you have to remove the captain's chair?"

"What are you talking about?" Cheeky asked as she looked up at Sera and gave a languid wink. "*This* is the captain's chair."

"You know what I mean. It feels weird to sit at scan."

<We didn't want you and your sister to fight over it,> Sabrina said over the bridge net, a soft laugh in her voice.

Seraphina looked up from where she sat at the comm console and gave Cheeky a sour look. "I would have won."

"Oh?" Sera asked. "How's that?"

"I fight dirtier than you."

Sera barked a laugh. "That's probably true."

"Still three hours till we dump out of the DL," Cheeky said, and nodded to the display at the front of the bridge. We're going to pop out just one AU from the Thomias Belt. Are our pre-clearances in order?"

"Look at her!" Seraphina said, grinning as she met Sera's eyes. "She's allll growed up."

Cheeky twisted in her seat and glowered at Seraphina. "Only 'cause the two of you made me. Sending us off alone, then you get cloned, or whatever, and start the biggest interstellar war in history."

"Yikes!" Sera exclaimed. "You grew teeth, too."

"I've always had teeth," Cheeky said with a low chuckle. "Pre-clearances?"

"Confirmed with the last DL relay we just passed. We're good to go."

Sera placed her hands on her hips and shook her head at Seraphina. "I'm amazed you deployed this many relays in the DL. Must have been quite the undertaking."

"It was," Seraphina replied. "Some were already there, but Airtha wanted it locked down. We only beefed things up on this side of the star, though. Given that it's a hundred AU trek if you come in on the far side of Huygens, the system itself works as enough of a buffer for other approaches."

"Still a pain in the ass," Cheeky muttered.

Seraphina gave a noncommittal shrug. "Kinda the point."

"I'm going to the galley. Gotta do something other than think about the mission for the next two hours."

"Just gonna leave me up here?" Cheeky asked without turning in her seat.

"You can fly the ship from anywhere," Sera pointed out. "Doesn't *have* to be here."

"It does," the pilot-now-captain replied. "This is where my gut works."

"What?" both Seras asked at once.

This time, Cheeky turned around and knelt on her seat, peering over the backrest.

"You know, flying with your gut, by the seat of your pants," she said simply.

"I know what that means," Sera replied, while Seraphina chuckled. "Though I don't think I've ever seen you wear pants."

"I own a few pairs." Cheeky's tone was only mildly defensive. "Though half of them are transparent."

Sabrina's laugh filled their minds. *<Clearly not enough seat to fly by, then.>*

"Fine. Mock me," Cheeky said, and adopted a pout, but remained perched on her seat, staring at the other two women. "You don't know what it's like being put into another body. It took a long time to get the same feel for the ship that I used to. Sure, I can fly *Sabrina* from anywhere aboard, but here is where it feels right *here*." She slapped her stomach for emphasis, almost glaring at the two women.

"I *kinda* know what it feels like," Seraphina volunteered, but Cheeky sent a scowl her way, and she amended, "A wee, tiny little bit."

"I never flew with my gut," Sera said, shrugging indifferently. "And I'm a pretty decent pilot."

Cheeky put her hand out palm-down and wobbled it back and forth. "Ehhh, on a good day."

"What? Seriously? I flew the ship back in the Fringe before we picked you up, Cheeky. I got us out of some tight spaces. Back me up, here, Sabrina."

<I…um…well…>

Sera looked at Seraphina. "You know she's disparaging us both, don't you?"

Seraphina shrugged. "I didn't get as much of the competitive, high and mighty gene as you did. I'm OK with being just good enough to get by."

Sera blew out a dramatic sigh. "It's like being insulted in my own home. Where'd all this fly-with-your-gut nonsense come from, anyway?"

<I learned it from Jessica,> Sabrina said. *<She taught me about it after she rescued Cheeky at the Grey Wolf Star. I became much better at flying once I learned how to use my gut.>*

"You don't even *have* a gut," Sera threw her arms in the air.

"Neither does Jessica, with a waist that small," Seraphina said, chuckling softly. "But she's got a lot of hiney under all that shiny. She's probably more of a 'seat of your pants' kinda gal. She flies with her butt, not her gut!" Her chuckle turned into a full-on laugh.

"Taking the word of that purple hussy over mine," Sera said, placing a hand on her chest. "You wound me."

Cheeky snorted. " 'Purple hussy'? You live in a glass house, there, *Red*."

"Well, at least I don't glow…or have alien microbes living inside me."

<You're just jealous.>

"You're damn right I'm jealous," Sera said as she walked off the bridge. "But if I went purple, you'd all accuse me of copying her."

"Plus, Fina would constantly switch you back!" Seraphina called out after her.

Sera laughed at the thought. Fina would do that, but she wasn't on *Sabrina*. Her team was aboard the *Voyager,* and if all was going well, they'd already be on the Airthan Ring.

<You're not actually upset, are you?> Jen asked as Sera slid down the ladder to the crew deck.

<Course not. We used to needle one another like that all the time back when I was captain here.>

<Do you miss those days?>

Jen's question caused Sera to pause and think it over.

<Yes and no. Yes because we were a good team, and we had a lot of fun. No because I was in my stupid self-imposed exile phase while trying to get the CriEn back from The Mark.>

She'd left one thing out of her response: Helen. Even though years had passed, Sera still thought about Helen every day. The shard of Airtha that her mother had given to her as an AI. That she hadn't realized was her mother until after her father—who was also a creature of her mother's at the time—pulled Helen from Sera's mind and killed her.

All so she could completely control me.

That was what Sera couldn't fathom. Why her mother had gone to so much trouble, spending decades to craft her into the person she wanted, a person who would kill her own father and then take over the Transcend.

I guess she wanted me to think that I'd made my own path, which was impossible, when she was guiding my every move.

<*I guess I can see how you'd have mixed feelings,*> Jen said in response to Sera's prior statement.

<*A bit, but the times with the* **people** *were great. I miss that a lot.*>

A burst of raucous laughter spilled out of the open galley door, and Sera resumed her approach, reaching the entrance and leaning against the frame.

At the long wooden tables sat Finaeus, Usef, Erin, and Nance. Kara was a little ways away, perched on a tall stool, her wings still resting on the ground despite her perch.

Misha leant against the counter, where the remains of the meal they'd eaten a few hours earlier were still laid out for the crew to snack on. To his right, a cup of coffee cradled in his hands, stood Flaherty, a ghost of a smile on his face as he regarded the group.

"OK, bilge rat, gimme your two best," Erin said to Usef with a wide grin. "Better be deuces, too."

"No such luck, little lady." Usef slapped a ten and a six on the table. "Read 'em and weep."

Erin shrugged. "Well, means everything you have is worse. I think you're the one who'll be weeping."

"One last game before we dump out?" Sera asked as she entered the galley and angled toward the chiller.

"One?" Erin laughed. "With these opponents, I can get in two at least. It's like I'm playing against children."

Finaeus looked over his hand and smirked at Erin. "Don't get too cocky there. I've got your number."

"You may be the second best engineer in the galaxy, but that doesn't mean you can build a Snark manifest for shit, old man."

"*Second*?" Finaeus puffed out his chest. "I invented jump gates, star mining, and dozens of other things that every one of you use every day and take for granted."

"One word," Erin replied with a wink. "Picotech."

Nance pursed her lips and patted Finaeus on the shoulder. "Kinda trumps, Gramps."

Finaeus's face reddened, and he scowled at Nance. "After all our time together, you malign me like this?"

"I'll malign you more if you don't play or pass," Erin said, gesturing to the pair of sixes she'd played in the interim.

"Fine, fine." He dropped a pair of eights on the sixes.

Sera gave a happy sigh as she peered into the chiller, looking for something interesting.

<*Still feels like home, though,*> she said privately to Jen.

<*I can see why. This ship has a special feeling to it.*>

Finally spotting a wheat ale that looked promising, Sera pulled the can out and popped the top open. She took a long swig and leant against the counter alongside Flaherty.

"So what do you make our odds?"

"Better than anyone else would have."

She shot him a side-eye. "Not exactly encouraging."

"Neither is Finaeus's strategy," Flaherty said, then looked into Sera's eyes. "We'll pull it off. I'm certain of it. But it's going to be hard. Very, very hard."

"That the best speech you have right now?" Sera asked, chuckling softly as she took a drink of her beer, watching as Finaeus launched into a creative string of curses as Erin won another round.

"If you're coming to me for a pep talk, then we're in worse shape than I thought."

"Funny man," Sera muttered before nudging him with her elbow. "Want to join in for a round?"

"No, I'll just watch."

She gave him a brief hug, then walked to the table and sat next to Nance. "Deal me in."

"You join in late in the game like this, and you're the bilge rat," Finaeus intoned.

"Sure," Sera replied, giving her uncle a wink. "Let's see how fast we can get you back down there."

COMMENCEMENT

STELLAR DATE: 10.09.8949 (Adjusted Years)
LOCATION: *Voyager*, High Airtha, Airtha
REGION: Huygens System, Transcend Interstellar Alliance

"If at first you don't succeed, try, try again," Carl intoned as the *Voyager* settled into a docking cradle on High Airtha.

"Except it barely feels like we're the same ship," Katrina groused. "They practically gave her a new hull."

<*They sure did,*> Troy agreed. <*An amazing new hull. Stealth, stasis capabilities, way more ablative layers. It's like a dream.*>

Carl snorted. "Way to be subtle, Troy."

<*Katrina's the sentimental one,*> the AI retorted. <*I prefer to be nearly impervious and invisible, should I choose, over showing off the patchwork we've sported for the last few centuries.*>

"Patchwork?" Now it was Carl's turn to sound upset. "I'll have you know I've sweat blood to keep your *patchwork* hull in one piece."

<*And if blood sweat was a useful item for repairing ships, I'd be grateful. Alas it's just hyperbole, which has never been known to fix anything.*>

"How many problems would it cause if we spaced our AI? Carl asked Katrina.

"More than he causes by being around," Katrina said as she gave the forward consoles a narrow-eyed glare.

"Even with all these new systems on the ship?" Carl pressed.

Katrina glanced at the readouts, double-checking that the ship appeared powered down, but that the systems were ready for a fast restart.

"Yeah, even more so," she stated.

<*You two are barbarians,*> Troy groused. <*Kirb says it's really nice outside, and that you should take a look. And stop threatening your AI, who only has your best interests at heart.*>

"Still so subtle, Troy," Katrina said as she rose from her seat and stretched her limbs.

<*I try.*>

It was a given that while they were on their mission, she was going to worry constantly about the ship. She knew the upgrades would make it safer, but that didn't mean she had to like the change.

Over the centuries, the *Voyager* had become a symbol in her mind. The one thing that solidly connected her to her past, proof that she really had traveled forward in time, and wasn't just some crazy woman who remembered a past that never was.

But now, nearly everyone in the galaxy who was three jumps or less from a major trade route knew of the Scipio Alliance and the war being waged across the Orion Arm.

Which she supposed should be comforting. That, combined with the fact that New Canaan was a real place, an actual refuge that awaited when this struggle was over, *should* mean that the *Voyager* no longer needed to be that connection to the past for her.

I guess centuries-old habits die hard.

She finished her stretching and walked out of the ship's small bridge, finding Fina waiting for her in the passageway.

"You ready for this?" asked the normally blue-skinned woman—who had reverted to natural flesh tones, and also altered her facial structure in order to fool any optical systems that caught sight of her.

"As I'll ever be," Katrina said with a resolute nod. "Your team ready?"

Fina had the largest group of unknowns under her purview. Roxy they knew to be a solid operator, and she seemed committed to taking down Airtha. Carmen, the AI in their group, was determined to make up for her failure on the *Damon Silas,* and the AI council at Styx had pronounced her fit for duty.

Jane, the pilot who technically had done some very unethical things—not that Katrina was anyone to judge—was the wildcard. So far as Katrina could tell, Jane's loyalty was to her friends, not the mission—or anyone else, for that matter.

The woman had been a decorated pilot in the TSF before she'd joined with Justin's side of the conflict. She had been involved in several infiltration ops in the past, and on paper, had the skills to get the job done.

Which meant that, in theory, so long as they didn't get found out, they should have no problems.

And if anyone believes that, I have a ring to sell them.

Fina had paused before answering Katrina's question, and the look in her eyes mirrored the thoughts that ran through Katrina's mind.

"We'll do the job. Come hell or high water. Our bombs will get set, and we'll insert our virus on time."

They clasped one another's arms and then Fina turned and walked down the passage—which used to be a ladder shaft—and took a left toward the forward airlock.

Roxy and Carmen were waiting for her. As the airlock began to cycle, the pair activated their stealth armor, disappearing from view before the outer door opened.

Katrina nodded with satisfaction as she continued further aft to find Elmer, Kirb and Amavia waiting for her at the midship airlock. Camille, Malorie, and Iris stood outside the chamber, waiting for Carl, who was still in the cockpit.

"Everyone good to go?" Katrina asked.

"Good?" Malorie chittered with delight. "This is amazing."

As she spoke, the red spider disappeared from view, and moments later, reappeared hanging from the overhead.

"I'm never giving this shit back. You know that, right?"

Katrina glared at the woman who had once been her captor and torturer, wondering for what had to be the thousandth time why she still kept Malorie around.

Probably because she's useful and would get into too much trouble if I cut her loose.

"Well, you work for the ISF now, so you don't have to give it back," Iris said to Malorie, her lips quirked in a challenging smile.

Malorie's head turned toward Katrina. "She's making us sound all legitimate. I don't like it."

"You'll manage," Katrina said, her tone half encouraging, half threatening.

"Maybe," the red spider replied. "You know…so long as the evil ascended AI who lords over this place doesn't spot us and crush us."

"We'll be alright," Iris said, glancing at Camille, who gave a nervous, half smile. "Everyone knows what to do. Follow your team lead's orders, and in two days' time, we'll be drinking beers and laughing about how we killed an ascended AI."

"Way to jinx it," Elmer muttered.

Camille squared her shoulders as she sidled up to Iris. "You won't mind if I use you for a shield when the beams start slicing things apart, will you?"

Iris had adopted a more automaton-like appearance, which facilitated several additional layers of ablative plating she normally didn't wear. Like the others, she wore flow-armor overtop, able to disappear should the need arise.

"Don't worry," Katrina said, giving Camille a slap on the shoulder. "This will be a walk in the park."

"Which is exactly what it looks like out there," Kirb said from the fully cycled airlock. "We're set down in the middle of a cedar grove."

Katrina shook her head at her supercargo. "I *did* pilot us in, you know. Kinda noticed."

"Always taking the fun out of things, Captain," Kirb said as he turned and walked down the ramp, Elmer following after.

Unlike Fina's team, Katrina's group was all known quantities. Kirb and Elmer were men who had been with her for ages. They were steadfast companions as well as skilled fighters.

And though she'd only recently met Amavia, Katrina had known both of the woman's former selves, Ylonda and Amanda. It was strange to see aspects of them both in the new being that had been forged out of Myriad's attack on their lives. That being had been a shard of Airtha, and had tried to kill the two, forcing Ylonda to take refuge in Amanda's mind.

"Good to go?" Katrina asked the woman, keeping her thoughts to herself.

"I've let HoltenCo know that their special courier package is en route," Amavia replied as she patted the courier pouch tucked under her arm.

"Everything's in order, Captain," Carl said as he ambled down the passage and placed a hand on Katrina's shoulder. "We'll be good. The data drops are set up, and all the comm channels are verified. No one is waiting for us out there. Our ship is just another specialty courier making a run from Bellatrix."

"And we're just headed into the maw of the most powerful creature in the galaxy," Malorie added.

"Might be just the second or third most powerful creature in the galaxy," Katrina corrected. "But remember. Just takes a lucky shot from a cheap security drone to put you under. Alert and ready. At all times."

<*Our transport is here,*> Krib called up the ramp, and Katrina nodded to Iris's team.

"Good luck."

Iris gave Katrina a confident smile, and Camille added, "Stay safe, Captain."

Katrina waved over her shoulder as she walked through the airlock and into the too-white light that shone down from the Airthan star. It cast a wintery glow across the forest that surrounded the ship, giving the trees an almost bluish hue.

A groundcar was pulling away from the ship, and Katrina could make out Fina through the vehicle's window. She assumed that Roxy and Jane were secreted within as well, and turned her attention to a second transport that waited a short distance away.

This one was longer, with room in the back for the crate that Kirb and Elmer were moving toward the vehicle. Next to the car floated a customs drone, ready to scan the cargo and review their order.

Katrina walked toward the bot with the calm certainty of someone who had bluffed her way past hundreds of customs officials, both organic and otherwise. When she reached the drone, she passed her tokens, giving the machine an emotionless stare as it validated them. Before the civil war, travel within the Transcend did not involve customs, but that had changed on both sides of the conflict, and citizens were under increased scrutiny at every port.

Granted, we're all here with false identities, so they're right to be worried.

The drone took a minute, and then sent an acceptance of her credentials and their cargo's destination. It also passed Katrina a list of rules and regulations, listing sections of the ring that were off limits—which appeared to be over half of the structure.

<*I wonder if Airtha is up to something in those sections, or if they just like controlling the movement of visitors,*> Amavia asked.

<*Probably both,*> Katrina replied.

Amavia and Katrina slid into the front seats of the groundcar, while Kirb and Elmer made sure the cargo was secure in the rear of the vehicle.

<*You realize that both our targets are in no-go zones, right?*> Amavia asked.

Katrina gave a resigned nod. *<Well, we didn't think it would be easy, did we?>*

The other woman chuckled as the two men got in the car. "What's easy?"

Katrina joined in the laughter as the car took off toward HoltenCo, where the team would do their legitimate business on Airtha before carrying to on a restaurant and probably a bar crawl to kill time before they had to get to their targets.

Katrina twisted in her seat, watching the *Voyager*, next to which Carl's team still waited for their car. She kept her eyes on the ship until the trees obscured it from view.

<Stay safe, Troy.>

<I'm the one with stasis shields. ***You*** *stay safe.>*

She couldn't help but laugh. *<Will you ever stop being so surly?>*

<You like me this way.>

That's true, she mused. *I really do.*

THE RETURN

STELLAR DATE: 10.09.8949 (Adjusted Years)
LOCATION: *Voyager*, approaching Airtha
REGION: Huygens System, Transcend Interstellar Alliance

Two hours later, Sera was back on *Sabrina*'s bridge, this time with the rest of the crew—all of them crammed into the small space for the final approach to the ring that was their target.

Though the space could certainly house eleven people, Sera couldn't recall a time when she had ever seen that many on the ship's bridge—at least during her tenure.

Once again, she sat at the scan console, while Seraphina managed comm. Usef was at the weapons station, and from the stories Sera had heard from *Sabrina*'s recent adventures, the man knew what he was doing there.

The others were spread around auxiliary consoles, aside from Finaeus, who stood directly behind Cheeky, and Flaherty and Kara, who flanked the bridge's entrance, both with arms crossed and brooding expressions lowering their brows.

"Dumping iiiiin…" Cheeky drew the word out, "three, two, one."

The final word fell from her lips, and the forward display changed from the endless nothing of the dark layer to the brilliance of stellar space.

Dead ahead shone the light of Airtha, the white dwarf companion of the Huygens star. It was just under two AU away, but its small surface area caused it to appear as little more than a pinprick of light. Sera toggled the holodisplay to enlarge it until they could see the Saturn-sized star encircled by its celestial ring.

"Home sweet home," Sera muttered, and met Seraphina's gaze.

Seraphina laughed. "Feels like I just left. Which I guess I kinda did, just a few weeks ago."

"It's been a bit longer for me, but I get your drift," Sera replied.

Even though she'd run her part of the Transcend from Khardine for some time, it was still less than two years since she'd left Airtha and traveled to New Canaan with her father.

The fact that her 'father' had been under Airtha's control clarified so much of what had gone on over the last twenty years. She'd blamed him for sending a fleet to New Canaan, but really it had been her mother who had forced Tanis's hand and escalated tensions between the Transcend and Orion.

It was perfectly clear now that Airtha had hastened the war's arrival. The only thing that still didn't make any sense was the fact that her mother, ascended AI though she was, seemed uninterested in allying with Tanis. Together, they could have fought against Orion and then the core AIs without wasting so much time and energy on a civil war.

You should have seen this, Helen. You should have seen that we could have been allies.

Sera felt like she'd never stop struggling with the mysteries that lay so many levels deep.

And new ones kept being added, such as how her real father—whatever that even meant—had ended up in the LMC, held in stasis for over a millennia, while yet another clone took his place.

The man they'd recovered from the LMC had passed every test, and even Finaeus was fully convinced that it was his real brother, but Sera was finding herself more and more uncertain of the wisdom of turning the Transcend's governance over to him.

Only the fact that the Transcend was bound by the Scipio Alliance, and thus under Tangel's oversight, kept her from rescinding her transfer of power to Jeffrey Tomlinson.

In the entire galaxy, Sera trusted only one thing: that no matter what, Tangel would do the right thing.

That belief was her North Star.

"Relay has logged us," Seraphina announced. "Passing you the inbound vector, Cheeky. Applying for a berth at Sandstar Heights."

"Sandstar?" Sera asked. "Why not Kelsey Outer Ports?"

Seraphina flushed as she looked up, her eyes meeting Sera's. "Well, there was an attack there a year back, and…Kelsey Outer didn't make it."

"Oh. I see."

Sera hadn't made any strikes, and from what Roxy had shared, neither had Justin. There was only one other person who could be responsible.

"Have a lot of things like that happened?" she asked.

"A few."

The bridge fell silent as everyone considered what they were flying into: a realm ruled by a despot who had no compunctions about killing millions of her own people.

"Well, buck up, people." Finaeus tossed a smirk at each of his nieces. "At least Airtha hasn't blown the whole ring yet. There's still hope."

* * * * *

Outside, the ship was settling onto a cradle at Sandstar Heights, but Sabrina was barely paying attention as she looked over her appearance and gave a brief nod.

<*This is still very weird,*> she said to herself.

<*You're telling me,*> the ship's AI replied. <*You're me, but you're not me. I'm two*

people.>

<*Double the Sabs, double the fun,*> the shard of Sabrina said.

A laugh came from the hold's audible systems. <*I wonder if we should stay separate when you get back. Finaeus is certain that a re-merge will be possible, but I kinda like having another me around.*>

<*Won't that be confusing?*>

<*Well, we probably should use a different name for you anyway,*> Sabrina the ship's AI said.

<*Or* **you** *could get a new name.*> The shard canted her hips and winked at the hold's optics. <*I can be Sabrina, and you can be 'Ship'.*>

<*Damn, I'm sassy!*>

<*Better believe it. But yeah…I get that I should use a different name,*> the shard said. <*I feel like taking one of the ship names we used over the years, but that might be too risky.*>

Sabrina snorted. <*There's no way Airtha would know about 'Madam Tulip'. You should use that.*>

<*You're funny. I was thinking something like 'Falcon'.*>

<*I like it,*> Sabrina replied. <*Except that it sounds like the name for the entire strike team.*>

<*Well, 'Sabrina' means 'Legendary Princess'—*>

<*We're not letting you go around being called 'Princess', I'll never hear the end of it.*>

<*I wasn't going to suggest that, either,*> the shard said. <*I'm still* **you***…or me. This is weird.*>

<*OK, back to 'Falcon'. How do you feel about 'Kestrel'?*>

<*Not great. Look, can we just keep this simple? You be Sabrina, I'll be Sabs.*>

The ship's AI didn't respond for a second. <*I don't like having to give up 'Sabs', but I think it would be best for the crew. It's settled, then. You're Sabs. I'm Sabrina.*>

<*Awesome. I should get going, I can hear Usef tapping his foot clear across the ship.*>

Sabrina laughed again. <*He'll never change.*>

<*Who would want him to?*>

* * * * *

Twenty minutes later, all the pep talks were over, and the teams had dispersed.

Sabrina dropped her status update in small segments distributed across a number of data drops, then picked up the same from Troy. They shared acknowledgements, and then went comms silent.

The teams would take some time to disperse across the massive Airthan ring. Each had their own plans and destinations, but come 0600 Standard Airthan Time the next day, they would all be planting their bombs in the CriEn plants.

From there, they'd move on to Airtha's nodes to implant the virus, and then bluff the great AI into thinking that she was going to die.

What a long shot, Sabrina thought to herself.

She knew that it was entirely possible that an AI could be tricked into suiciding. The concept of 'a fate worse than death' wasn't foreign to her kind.

But to trick an intelligence as powerful as Airtha?

If it hadn't been an idea concocted by Finaeus and Earnest, she would have dismissed it out of hand.

Ironic that even though I've sent out a shard of myself, I'm still left back here waiting. And now I'm worried about other me, along with the rest of them. Trust me to make things worse.

Sabrina pushed the melancholy thought from her mind and set to watching the ground crews working nearby, while monitoring local feeds and looking for signs that anything was amiss.

Of course, the Transcend *was* in the middle of a civil war, and this was one of the capitals. Everything seemed to be amiss.

Even so, vigilance kept her from worrying about her teams.

A bit. A very little bit.

OTHERS

STELLAR DATE: 10.09.8949 (Adjusted Years)
LOCATION: Airthan Ring
REGION: Huygens System, Transcend Interstellar Alliance

D11 examined the map of the Airthan ring, wishing for some new insight, some clue that would give her a better route to the CriEn power facility that her group had been assigned.

It was deep within one of the exclusion zones. Even the ring's residents were restricted from passing within five hundred kilometers of the power facility.

She didn't fault Airtha for keeping people away. It was a time of war, and the facility was a sensitive installation, but that didn't do anything to make D11's job easier—which she supposed was the whole point.

The original plan hadn't taken into account this added level of paranoia, but the Widow wasn't dismayed. She'd undertaken dozens of missions where reality bore little resemblance to the plan.

At least the power plant is actually there.

D11 had been on her fair share of missions where the objective wasn't even present when she'd arrived. Granted, many of those had been in the years before jump gates, but even with the gates' hyper-FTL travel, the timescales for intel to make it back to the *Perilous Dream* were often measured in decades.

<I believe our best route remains the maglev line,> she said to the two other members of her team. *<The line is still active. The facility's workers use it for access to the plant.>*

<Then we'll have to wait for the next shift. It will be traveling to the plant in two hours,> C419 said, her tone denoting agreement, though her words weren't overly supportive.

D11 shook her head at the other Widow. C419 had a way of being contrarian, even when there was absolutely no reason to do so.

The final member of her team was Y2. She only nodded in agreement.

<Very well,> D11 said as she turned to look over the concourse they stood at the edge of—fully stealthed, of course. *<Come. I wish to reach the departure station as quickly as possible and secure our place on the train.>*

* * * * *

Sera settled into a seat in the back of a bar, which bore the name 'The Smokey Ruin'. Flaherty sat across from her, his gaze sweeping across the space, cataloguing the entire room—likely weighing threats and assets with that single glance.

Though she'd done the same, Sera didn't for a second think that she was as efficient as the man who had been her constant guardian for so many years.

However, she didn't need his assessment to know that the people were tense, unhappy, and clearly imbibing more than normal in an effort to pretend that they weren't living under a despot.

<You'd better get a drink for me while you're in there,> Kara said from her lookout position outside the bar. *<Some days, I hate having wings.>*

<Only some days?> Flaherty asked, a sliver of sardonic humor in his voice.

<Most days I wish I **had** *wings,>* Sera added as she pulled up the table's menu and looked over the drink selection.

The woman outside the bar sent a long sigh over the Link. *<Flying is amazing, and it can be fun to scare the crap out of people, but few seats are made for winged people.>*

<There are always the bar stools,> Flaherty suggested. *<You should be able to keep your wings hidden with the flow armor and come in for your own drink.>*

Sera wondered if the man was mocking Kara, and the woman's reply indicated that she felt the same.

<Are you being serious? I thought it was best if I stayed out here?>

<Well, there's no one in here to worry about, and their internal sensors are crap. If you sit at the right side of the bar, you won't be bothered.>

Kara didn't respond for a moment, and then asked, *<This is a test, isn't it?>*

<Glad to see you passed,> Flaherty replied.

Jen made a disapproving sound. *<That seems unnecessarily mean, Flaherty.>*

The man only grunted, and Sera laughed.

<You should know by now that Flaherty has a warped sense of humor,> she told her AI.

<Still.>

Sera and Flaherty ordered drinks and a meal, and then some food to go before eventually rising from their table and returning to the streets of Dima.

Night had fallen, which meant that grav fields were bending the light of Airtha away from the ring, with only a dim glow filtering through. The effect was one that caused an amorphous light to fill most of the sky, creating a near-shadowless moonlight.

When she was young, Sera recalled Finaeus often talking about how he wanted to engineer a new solution to the nighttime effects on the ring. If she recalled correctly, he had discussed making some sort of moon configuration that would orbit off the elliptical between the ring and the star.

Maybe once this is all over with, he can actually get to that.

Kara stepped out of the shadows. "I don't see a drink."

"You doubted me?" Flaherty asked, and pulled a bottle from his jacket. "Stout, right?"

"Wow, you *do* notice everything."

"I got you onion rings and a chili sandwich," Sera held up a bag. <*We're on the move now, though. Once you eat up, we'll hit the sector's maglev, find an empty train, and disappear.*>

<*It should be harder than this to move freely on the ring,*> Kara said, her voice rife with disapproval.

<*Even though a lot of people have left Airtha, there are still a trillion people living here,*> Flaherty said. <*Even an entity like Airtha has trouble controlling that many people.*>

<*Or so we assume,*> Sera corrected. <*She could also just not care.*>

<*Well, she should,*> Kara said while taking a pull from her beer bottle as she eyed a couple as they walked past, chatting in hushed tones.

Flaherty gestured for the trio to begin moving as well. <*No one would just stand around out here—at least not anyone up to any good. We've already been tagged by two different monitoring drones.*>

<*Sabrina has dropped a new update,*> Jen said as the group began to walk down the street in silence. <*All teams except for Fina's have completed their 'official' business on the ring, and are moving to the power plants. Fina is still working on her primary objective.*>

<*Slacker,*> Sera said with a nonchalant laugh. <*Did Sabrina pass along any reason why?*>

<*Too much security. They're having to find another way in. Her report says they have one located, though.*>

Sera glanced at her companions and gave a reassuring smile. <*Don't worry. She knows this ring like the back of her hand. She'll pull it off.*>

<*Of course she will.*> Flaherty's tone conveyed no emotion, but it also held no doubt.

<*Sheesh, don't you two go getting all excited on me.*>

<*Sorry,*> Kara replied. <*Just worrying about all the things that can go wrong and snatch success away from us.*>

<*Aren't you just roses and sunshine.*>

Flaherty grunted indifferently. <*She's just described my job.*>

Sera didn't reply to either of her companions, wondering how she got saddled with the two sourpusses.

Eventually, her thoughts turned to the fact that somewhere on the ring was yet another one of her 'sisters'. Except this sister was different: cruel, villainous—everything that Sera knew she *could* be if she didn't keep her baser instincts in check. Ironically, the visage the new version of herself had chosen was of a pale-skinned woman who was always sheathed in glowing white. It reminded her of stories Katrina had told of her Lumin ancestors and their near-cultish worship of light.

She watched a day-old feed in which the white Sera made a proclamation, declaring that a new armada was being built and would strike Khardine and end the war in just a few months.

Standing behind her otherself was a haggard man, who had stood behind Tomlinsons for longer than most people had been alive: Adrienne.

Sera glanced at Kara, wondering if she'd sought out any feeds showing her father.

The winged woman had expressed a desire to free her father, but strangely not a desire to talk to him. It wasn't as though Kara had spoken ill of Adrienne, it was more in what she hadn't said.

Of course, Sera knew what the underlying reason was. Adrienne wasn't so terribly different from Airtha in how he treated his children. But now there was no doubt in any of their minds that Adrienne would be under Airtha's control. The only way to free him—and the other trillion souls on the ring—was through Airtha's destruction.

Or so they hoped.

Fifteen minutes later, they reached a maglev platform, where they caught a train to a larger station where they milled about in the crowds for half an hour, disappearing one by one until all three were stealthed near where their target train would board.

TSF soldiers patrolled the platform, and drones swept by overhead. Twice, the guards nearly bumped into Sera, but both times, she managed to twist to the side at the last moment. Ten long minutes later, the train arrived for CEPP41—her team's ultimate destination, deep in one of the exclusion zones.

She slipped onto the lead car while the guards re-checked all of the waiting passengers, moving to a corner that she hoped would remain vacant. Pings from Flaherty and Kara confirmed that they'd also boarded the train and were thus far undetected.

She was relieved to see that only two passengers boarded her car, each settling in on opposite ends. One appeared to fall asleep almost instantly, while the other was lost in the Link, his eyes flicking rapidly as he absorbed information displayed just for him.

Just before the doors closed, a drone flew into the car and scanned the space, stopping at each of the workers to check them over.

<*You're holding your breath,*> Jen said as the drone flew a half-meter past where Sera stood.

<*Just giving one less thing for that drone to spot.*>

<*The flow armor filters the sound and IR from breath, you know.*>

Sera pursed her lips, wondering why Jen seemed to enjoy needling her so much.

<*I've heard talk.*>

The AI must have taken the hint, because she didn't reply. Suddenly Sera realized *why* Jen had stated the obvious.

<Shoot, sorry. You're nervous, aren't you?>

<A bit,> the AI admitted. *<It feels surreal to just be strolling around on the ring. I always expected us to come here, but I thought we'd fight our way down to the surface, slugging it out with dozens of baddies before finally coming face to face with Airtha herself, at which point Bob and Tangel would kill her with fire, and then we'd all have a celebratory drink—well, not me, I don't drink, but you get the idea.>*

<I do,> Sera laughed softly. *<But somehow that seems waaaay more dangerous than what we're doing.>*

<Well, there'd be an army at our backs.>

<I suppose there's that.>

Sera shared the same sentiment in many respects, but she also knew that if there was an army at their backs, there'd be one before them as well.

<Don't worry, though, if we fail at this, that will be our plan B,> she reminded Jen.

<Except we'll be stuck down here when this plan B commences,> Jen countered.

<Yeah, I guess there's that.>

<Plus, Fina's team needs to complete their initial task before Plan B is even an option.>

Sera was a little worried about that herself. But from their reports, they were still in play; it was just taking longer than expected.

Nothing to worry about.

She repeated that assurance to Jen as the drone completed its sweep and then stopped at the car's doors. It spun and moved across to the far doors, appearing to give the area a detailed scan.

Sera worried that it had found some sign of her passage, but she couldn't think of what.

A moment later, the drone seemed to have satisfied itself and turned, leaving the train car. The doors closed immediately after.

Moments later, the maglev took off, streaking across the ring to the exclusion zone, and the CriEn Power Plant where they'd set up their bombs.

TOWER ASSAULT

STELLAR DATE: 10.09.8949 (Adjusted Years)
LOCATION: Uplink Tower 7-1, Airthan Ring
REGION: Huygens System, Transcend Interstellar Alliance

Fina settled back against the broad oak tree that her team had formed up around, her gaze sliding from Roxy to Jane.

"A bit of a pickle," she said after a moment.

This close to the uplink tower and its security sensors, they didn't risk using the Link, but as fortune would have it, a storm was blowing through, so speaking was safe enough beneath the rustling leaves and creaking boughs.

"That's a new one on me," Jane said. "Are we the pickle, or are they?" She jerked a thumb over her shoulder at the tower as she spoke.

"We are," Roxy replied, a smirk settling on her azure lips. "Well, the saying is that we're 'in' a pickle."

"You sure about that?" Fina asked. "I would have expected us to *be* the pickle…stewing in vinegar and the like."

Jane chuckled. "Carmen says you're overthinking this pickle business. So what are we going to do about our objective?"

Fina glanced around the tree again, taking in the hundred meters of open space between them and the uplink tower. Their original plan had been to simply cross the space utilizing their stealth armor while leveraging nanoclouds to ensure the roving drones didn't spot them—or to breach the machines if they did—but with leaves and other flying debris whipping across the space, stealth wasn't an option.

"No two ways about it," Fina said after a moment's further consideration. "We're going to have to go under."

"Security's tight in the passages below," Roxy cautioned. "I mean…you know that, but I'm just saying. We're going to have to breach more systems down below and hope that no one—such as an ascended AI who could squish us with a thought—notices."

"Carmen says she loves how reassuring you are."

"Carmen can talk through your armor," Roxy quipped.

"Sure," the AI said through the armor's speakers, "but it's fun making Jane say everything for me. It's like she's my little puppet."

The woman let out a low groan. "You told me the armor couldn't do that while stealthed."

"Well yeah," Carmen drew the words out. "Having stealth armor talk removes the whole stealth element. But we're not really utilizing audible stealth right now. So there you go."

Fina rose from her position and gestured to the other two. "Let's move. There's a subterranean access point a kilometer through the woods."

"Just keep an eye out for patrols in here," Roxy cautioned. "If I were running security, these trees would have eyes."

"Creepy," Fina muttered, but took the other woman's meaning.

During the trek through the woods, the team spotted several surveillance drones—which were large, and capable of navigating through the inclement weather—and carefully skirted their patrol routes, reaching the subterranean access point fifteen minutes later.

Just as they reached the low arch that led into the ring substructure below the stretch of woods, the skies opened up and it began to rain.

"Close one," Fina said as she gestured for Roxy to perform the breach while Jane kept an eye on the woods.

"You'd think the ISF's stealth could handle rain," Roxy said as she set a breach pad on the door's console.

"It can…normally," Fina replied. "And against any other enemy, I'd have no trouble trusting it to do so."

Roxy didn't respond, but her silence spoke volumes on her behalf.

A minute later, the door opened and the group slipped inside.

<OK,> Fina switched to the Link. *<Weapons check and have your armor scrub any debris from the surface. We're ghosts.>*

<I'm clear,> Roxy said a moment later, followed by Jane's pronouncement a few seconds later.

They checked over one another's EM readings, and then deployed a light nanocloud around themselves to mask air movement.

Fina provided the route through the substructure passages that would lead them to the uplink tower. The corridor they were in did not lead directly to their target, so the team would have to take a circuitous, four-kilometer route before they were as close as they'd been while crouched beneath the oak tree twenty minutes prior.

After a kilometer's travel, they came to a network node, and Fina tapped it directly, masquerading as a maintenance drone. Once on the network, she dropped a report for Sabrina in fragments across several low-security log aggregation systems.

Fina still anticipated completing their task in the uplink tower fast enough to reach their assigned CEPP in time, but if they met with further delays, they'd have to skip planting their explosives and go directly to the Airthan node they'd been assigned.

Only having bombs set up at five CEPPs would be enough, since the strike force's plan was to bluff more than sabotage, anyway.

Worse come to worst, we can plant our charges here at the tower. Might make for an interesting distraction.

Ten minutes later, the trio reached a large chamber where several passages met. Almost directly across the ninety-meter-wide chamber was the entrance to the uplink tower.

Normally, it would have been protected by a pair of soldiers, with drones on perimeter patrols, but rather than live soldiers, only two automatons stood sentry.

Crap, those aren't automatons—those are AI frames.

Fina reached out and touched Jane and Roxy, establishing a physical network to limit any EM that their stealth couldn't mask.

<*From what Kara told us, the AIs on the ring are fully under Airtha's thrall. If we take those two, we'll have to take them simultaneously so they can't get any message out,*> Fina said.

Roxy sent an affirmation. <*Then we'll need to hit them with a hefty breach dose.*>

<*What about freeing them?*> Carmen asked. <*They're under Airtha's thrall, but there's no way they'd support her if liberated.*>

<*It's too risky,*> Fina said, wishing there was another answer. <*There are plenty of AIs who are willingly on the wrong side, just like there are ascended AIs bent on killing us all.*>

<*OK,*> Carmen replied. <*I understand.*>

Fina could tell that the AI wasn't happy and hoped that she wouldn't balk at any unsavory orders.

Stars, Finaeus, what did I do to deserve a team I can barely trust to follow orders?

Ironically, of all of them, she worried about Roxy the least. The half-woman, half-AI had lost much over the years. During the journey to Airtha, she'd confided in Fina that this mission was how she hoped to reclaim some part of her honor, at least in her own mind.

Collecting her thoughts, Fina gave the signal and led her team across the chamber to the sealed doors guarded by the AIs. A few drones flitted through the air, and an autonomous cargo hauler swept past at one point, forcing the group to dodge out of its way. Yet no alarms sounded, and the Airthan AIs gave no indication that they'd spotted anything.

A minute later, the team reached the doors, and Jane quickly deposited breach nano on both of the AIs, while Roxy and Fina drew shrouded weapons and trained them on the enemies.

Moment of truth, Fina thought, ready to send a special command that the AI council on Styx had given her, should Carmen fail to perform her duties.

It felt wrong to have the ability to shut down another sentient being, but for all intents and purposes, Carmen was on probation and under Fina's command.

Had it been a human whose trustworthiness was in question, that person would have also faced dire consequences should they fail to perform their duties.

Sera better have known what she was doing, suggesting they all came along.

Ten grueling seconds later, Carmen announced, <*OK, they're locked down. And…you were right. I really can't tell if they're under an aegis, or if they're operating of their own free will.*>

<*OK, I'm on the door,*> Roxy announced.

A minute later, the team stepped into the base of the uplink tower, sealing the door behind them as they moved forward.

<*Target is the same,*> Fina said. <*Get to the main lift shaft, flush nano up, and climb. The node we have to tap is at the top of the tower.*>

<*Fun times,*> Roxy said. <*Good thing I don't get tired.*>

<*Speak for yourself,*> Jane said in mock weariness.

The uplink tower was used to provide high-bandwidth, line-of-sight communications to other towers around the ring. Given the twenty-five-million-kilometer circumference of Airtha, communications going around the structure could take several seconds longer than if they were broadcasted directly across empty space, beamed from tower to tower.

In addition to the comm web they provided, the towers also had direct connections to the military STCs and, through them, the jump interdiction grid.

With the grid down, Krissy's fleets could jump to within half an AU of Airtha, bypassing the layers of defense that were built up around the star.

That was, once Fina's team climbed to the top of the tower and breached the systems there.

<*We're behind,*> Roxy said as they moved down the corridor. <*And honestly, you two are going to be slow climbers. I can make it up the tower twice as fast on my own, plant the tap on the node, and be back down before you'd get five hundred meters.*>

<*It's not like we're stock,*> Fina replied. <*We can keep up.*>

<*Maybe you can,*> Roxy told her privately. <*But Jane can't, and I don't want to leave her alone.*>

Fina resisted a groan. Roxy wasn't entirely wrong, but she hated the idea of splitting the team. However, arguing about it would waste more time.

<*OK, but we're going to the lift shaft and waiting for you there.*>

<*Works for me…and, Fina?*>

<*What?*> She grunted out the question.

A stealthed hand found her arm and gave a gentle squeeze.

<*Thanks.*>

ANOTHER WAY

STELLAR DATE: 10.09.8949 (Adjusted Years)
LOCATION: Airthan Ring
REGION: Huygens System, Transcend Interstellar Alliance

<*OK, I've got a visual on seven AIs, a little over four hundred drones, and a nanocloud.*>

Sabs sent the message back to the team as she retreated from her surveillance position, leaving behind her own nanocloud to observe the CEPP and its defenses.

<*Wait, since when did Airtha get a nanocloud?*> Misha asked, as Sabs eased around the long conduit stack and saw the pings from her team indicating their presence, invisible in the overlapping EM fields coming off the stack.

<*It's just nano drifting in the air using brownian motion,*> Erin explained. <*Common enough in facilities like this, where they can control air currents to keep it where they want it.*>

<*Not common to have a cloud this dense, though,*> Sabs said. <*I'm not entirely sure how we're going to get in there without being detected. This isn't like breaching some Inner Stars facility in the backend of nowhere.*>

No one offered any suggestions, and Sabs reviewed the feed from her own nanocloud again, scanning the ovoid, five-kilometer-wide chamber deep within the ring's structure, looking for any inspiration.

The CEPP facility was a hundred-meter-wide sphere centered in the space, with lifts running up from the floor and encircled by gantries. If it hadn't been for the enemy's nanocloud, Sabs could have simply walked right up to the thing and planted their explosives on a few of the support struts without any trouble at all.

<*This was supposed to be the easy part,*> Usef muttered.

<*Well, we can see the CEPP,*> Misha said after a moment. <*Do we have to go right up to it?*>

<*What's brewing in that head of yours?*> Usef asked.

<*I just wonder if we can shoot something at it,*> Misha explained.

<*I might…*> Erin began, then paused. <*Yes! OK, I think I have an idea.*>

Usef let out a soft grunt. <*You **think**?*>

<*Stars, Usef, not now,*> the engineer said, then directed a thought to Sabs and Misha. <*Was he weird and surly on Sabs too?*>

<*Yup.*>

<*Sure was.*>

<*I'm still right here. Enough stalling while you flesh out your idea, Erin. What is*

it?>

Sabs tried not to laugh as Erin sent the man a pair of glaring eyes over the Link, and then launched into her explanation.

<Well, I don't know how efficacious it would be to 'shoot' something at the CEPP. However, we also don't have to go there ourselves.> She paused, and a marker appeared on their HUDs noting two other locations on either side of the facility. *<See these? This is where they pipe liquid nitrogen in to cool the energy interchange systems. CriEns on this scale generate* ***a lot*** *of heat from the transference of raw vacuum energy into usable electricity. They're kinda forming electrons out of nothing, in a way—well, not 'out of nothing', but it would take a week or two to explain how the particles are reformed to make them. In short, like most big, powerful things, it gets hot.>*

<They would have safeties, though,> Sabs said. *<If we cut the nitrogen supplies, I assume it would shut down and activate some sort of emergency cooling scenario.>*

<Right,> Erin agreed. *<So we don't bomb anything, we just destroy the emergency cooling systems.>*

Usef sent a grating sound that Sabs realized was his way of clearing his throat over the Link. It sounded like boulders smashing their way through a glass factory.

<Our plan here is to make it ***seem*** *like we're going to blow the ring. Not to actually blow the ring.>*

<It won't blow the system,> Erin explained. *<Or…it shouldn't. The CEPP has hundreds of individual CriEn modules. From what Finaeus has explained, they work in a carefully modulated wave pattern so that they don't draw too much energy from the foundations of spacetime. At any given point, only a fraction of them are in operation while the others are cooling. We'll set up our sabotage to only blow ones that are not actively drawing power. That will limit their destructive force, but emergency shutdown and cooling will still take effect for the others, and all should be well.>*

<Famous last words,> Misha muttered.

<I'll pass the details on to me, so that I can share it with the other teams,> Sabs said.

<'I'll pass it on to me?' That's not confusing at all,> Usef said with a soft laugh.

Erin joined in. *<If there's one thing I've learned on my short time aboard* Sabrina, *it's that nothing is really as it seems…and yet that's how you know everything is perfectly normal.>*

<Stars,> the Marine muttered. *<It's like you've already been infected by them.>*

<I'm not the one who installed glitter guns on the captain's chair,> Erin shot back, sending along a wink over the Link.

<Oh…heard about that, did you?>

Sabs only half listened to the team's banter as she logged into a series of sim games and created characters with specific backstories, hiding the intel within, along with a few jokes about her team for herself back on the ship to enjoy.

<OK, message is sent,> she said after a minute. *<Should we get over to those nitrogen lines? I assume we'll send in nano to effect the sabotage through the feed lines.>*

<*Let's hold on just a few minutes longer,*> Erin replied. <*I'd like to see if Finaeus can confirm that this isn't going to blow us all to subatomic particles if we do it wrong.*>

<*Oh…*> Misha muttered. <*You conveniently left that part out.*>

<*Well, its not like we're playing with something nice and safe like a fusion reactor,*> Erin replied. <*These plants could rip spacetime to shreds if they go haywire.*>

<*So, what sort of minimum safe range are we talking about?*> Usef asked. <*You know, if things go sideways.*>

<*Oh, I don't know…*> Erin's voice trailed off. <*If all six went up at once, probably a light year or so. That would be the non-instantaneously-lethal range. I think that beyond that, the cosmic rays would probably sterilize every star system for a hundred light years.*>

<*Great balls of star shit,*> Misha muttered. <*Yeah, I vote we wait for Finaeus's confirmation.*>

* * * * *

<*So?*> Seraphina asked Finaeus as he reviewed the message that had been relayed to them via Sabrina. <*Will it work? Because if not, we need to split up and have a team hit the nodes while the other shoots their way in to bomb the CEPP.*>

<*I'm thinking it through. Carefully,*> the engineer replied. <*You pestering me won't make it go any faster.*>

<*We're on the clock, here,*> Seraphina reminded her uncle. <*If we need more time, we have to fall back to the secondary schedule for shard insertion.*>

<*Just. A. Minute,*> Finaeus bit off each word.

<*He can be a bit testy at times, can't he,*> Cheeky said privately to Seraphina and Nance. <*Though this seems to have him worried more than normal.*>

<*Probably because if six of the CEPPs go up entirely, it'll create something that will make a supernova look like a firecracker,*> Nance replied. <*It would probably outshine the entire galaxy by several orders of magnitude.*>

<*So…you're saying we need to be careful,*> Cheeky said with a laugh.

<*I don't think you're taking this seriously enough,*> Nance shot back.

<*Nance, really. Sneaking right up to death's door and ringing his bell and then running off is kinda our thing. We'll figure it out and save the day. It's what we do.*>

<*Just don't die this time,*> Nance's voice was low and serious. <*When we play ding and dash with death, not everyone gets away.*>

Cheeky didn't respond for a moment, and Seraphina was trying to think of something to say to break the silence, when Finaues spoke.

<*Nice alliteration, Nance. And…yeah. I had to make an alteration to Erin's proposal to ensure it was timed properly. What she had in mind was off juuuust a hair and would have probably killed us all.*>

Cheeky let out a nervous laugh. <*At least we'd accomplish our mission…Airtha would be toast.*>

<You're sharing it back out?> Seraphina asked, ignoring Cheeky's comment.

<No…I just thought I'd keep it to myself and let the other teams blow us all to Andromeda. Yes, I'm sending the updated info to Sabrina and Troy now.>

<What gives?> she asked her uncle. *<You're normally the funny, joke-cracking person in situations like this.>*

<Sorry,> he replied. *<This one…this one's different for me. This ring is the culmination of my life's work, and here I am skulking about on it like a thief—and now doing my best to make sure we don't accidentally destroy it to save it.>*

<OK, I can see that. For what it's worth, I'm sorry it's come to this.> Seraphina gauged where her uncle's arm would be and reached out to touch it. *<You know…memories of sneaking off to your lab and talking with you about your latest endeavor…well, it was always my favorite pastime as a child.>*

The old engineer snorted. *<Seraphina, there is no possible way that I didn't already know that. However, what* **you** *may not have known is that it was one of my favorite pastimes as well. There was a reason why I never ratted you out.>*

<You…> Seraphina's throat constricted, and she paused to swallow and take a deep breath. *<You were always the father that other man never was to me.>*

Finaeus's hand reached out and wrapped around her shoulder. *<And you were—and still are—like a daughter to me. But when all this is over, I hope you'll give the real Jeffrey Tomlinson a chance. He deserves a good daughter like you.>*

<We'll see. I guess it can't hurt to try. But he's not really my father, and I'm not really his daughter.>

<Don't write off the value of a relationship with him so soon. It might be just what you need. Either way. The messages are sent, the other teams know what to do. Let's get our nano into the nitrogen lines and move on to the nodes.>

<OK, uncle-dad.>

Finaeus made a choking sound. *<Gah…that sounds like some sort of terrible incest thing. Never say that again.>*

<Er…yeah, didn't mean that at all. Stricken from the record.>

SABOTAGE

STELLAR DATE: 10.09.8949 (Adjusted Years)
LOCATION: Airthan Ring
REGION: Huygens System, Transcend Interstellar Alliance

<I guess it looks like Bob knew what he was doing, sending Erin along,> Katrina said to Kirb as they crouched next to the nitrogen line.

She carefully placed a blob of formation material on it, seeding the inert mass with nano all bearing the specific instruction sets that Finaeus had passed along.

<I'll admit.> Kirb let out a nervous laugh. *<Bob scares the shit out of me. But from what you and Troy have said over the years, he does seem to be on the money a lot.>*

Katrina sent an affirming thought to Kirb, then froze, shielding the formation material with her body as one of the patrol drones flew past.

She eyed the weaponry hanging from the thing and made a mental note to profusely thank Erin for coming up with the idea to use sabotage that didn't require them to fight their way to the CEPPs to plant explosives on them.

In all honesty, it didn't surprise her that the pixie-like engineer had come up with the perfect solution to their problem. She'd been instrumental in dozens of projects back at Kapteyn's Star as well, her unique insights always aiding in getting the job done on time.

The flood of memories caused a tightness in her chest that she carefully quelled. Just thinking of the Kap and all that her people had accomplished there still caused her more pain than she would have expected after so many years.

She wondered how the colonists were dealing with it, reeling from one crisis to the next in the wake of their journey forward in time. She suspected that they'd never had a chance to deal with the loss of the Kapteyn's colony before being attacked again and again.

Though if there's one thing I know, it's that this life never really gives you a 'safe time' to slow down—other than in death, of course.

The drone completed its pass, moving along its route, and she triggered the formation material to bore its hole in the pipe, seed the nano in the nitrogen flow, and then reseal the breach.

Though some of it would invariably get lost, the nano was preprogrammed to make it to the correct CriEn modules and seed itself for the time when it would commit the sabotage.

<OK, we're on the clock, now,> Katrina said to Kirb. *<No way to send an abort signal unless we come back here and re-seed a second batch.>*

<Then let's get a move on. It's over eighty klicks to the node.>

A minute later, they met up with Amavia and Elmer on the far side of a maglev line that ran around the perimeter of the space.

<*Any trouble?*> she asked the pair.

<*We nearly ran right into one of the roving AIs. Really thought I was going to have to take the thing down—it came within a centimeter of my left arm,*> Amavia reported.

<*Well, I bet we'll get our chance to take some down at the node,*> Katrina replied. <*If this is how carefully they're protecting the CriEn plants, then you can bet that Airtha's nodes are going to be fortresses.*>

* * * * *

Sera settled back behind a conduit stack, waiting on Flaherty and Kara to return.

A sense of relief had settled over her with the knowledge that the second phase was nearly complete. They were within a hair's breadth of actually striking at Airtha.

Of course, the relief that one task was done was already bleeding into anxiety over the next. The knowledge that she'd eventually have to confront her mother had been eating at Sera for the past two years. Now that it was almost upon her, she had to continually force herself not to play out scenarios in her mind.

<*You need to calm yourself,*> Jen said, as Sera fidgeted. <*You're doing what must be done.*>

<*Am I that transparent?*>

<*A bit, yeah. Your thoughts are spilling over. We're almost there, and then it'll be over. We'll hit the nodes, and we'll convince Airtha to end herself.*>

Sera snorted. <*Just like that, eh?*>

<*Well…no, but yes, I suppose. That's what will happen, in the end.*>

<*If we succeed,*> Sera added.

<*So defeatist, we haven't even—oh…crap.*>

Sera shot the AI in her mind a stern look. <*Being mysterious isn't helping.*>

<*Sabrina just got an update from Fina. They made it into the uplink tower, and Roxy was handling the breach, but they've lost contact with her.*>

<*Dammit.*>

Sera considered her options. Not having six of the CEPPs suffer damage wasn't critical; Finaeus and Earnest's plan had only called for four of them in the first place. But without the interdictors being taken out, there was no plan B. Either they convinced an ascended AI to take its own life, or they were likely all going to die.

<*Fina.*> She took the risk of making a direct connection through their emergency backchannels to reach out to her sister. <*What's going on?*>

<*Sorry, Sera, I fucked up. Roxy went to the top of the tower to breach the uplink node, but she went dark as soon as she got there. Jane and I are climbing the lift shaft. We'll be there in a few minutes. Don't worry. We'll get it done.*>

<*We can abort, fall back to the secondary schedule.*>

<*No, if they capture Roxy and strip our plans from her mind, we're done. There won't be a second chance. We have to stop that from happening. We'll take the net down, and Krissy's fleet will be onstation before you know it.*>

Sera bit her lip, hoping against hope that Fina wasn't just blowing smoke up her ass.

<*OK…I'm counting on you, Fina.*>

<*Don't worry. We'll hit this, and make it to our node on time. I promise.*>

<*Just get out safe. All of you.*>

* * * * *

Fina closed the connection to Sera and then triggered the nanorelays in the lift shaft and passages below to go into full standby.

It was entirely likely that passing the message had given off enough EM to trigger a sweep of the shaft and the tunnels they'd passed through to get to the tower.

With luck, a sweep wouldn't pick up the nano in standby, and they'd retain their connection to the other teams.

<*We're almost there,*> Fina sent to Jane on a narrow-band, low power connection. <*Just a few more meters and we'll be at that landing. From there, we can send up a nanocloud and see what's going on.*>

<*We should never have let her go alone,*> Jane said, and Fina could hear the accusation loud and clear in the other woman's voice.

<*It was her choice, and a smart one,*> Carmen replied. <*There could be a dozen reasons why she's not checked in. Maybe she's waiting for the right time to make her move.*>

<*We'll find out,*> Fina said as she reached the platform set into the side of the lift shaft.

The top level where the node was situated was another twenty meters up, but a door on the platform led to a level two floors below the top. She sent a nanocloud out to move to the top of the shaft, while dropping a passel on the door's panel, keeping her options open.

Jane reached the platform a moment later and pulled herself up alongside Fina, pressing herself against the wall.

<*Stars…that's a lot of down.*>

<*Try not to think about it,*> Fina replied as she watched the feed from her nanocloud.

Above them, the drones slipped past the lift doors at the top of the shaft and into the room at the top of the tower.

The area was crammed with equipment. Everything from power regulation systems to network interfaces, to the transmission equipment itself.

In the center lay the main processing node that handled all the connections and data transfer with the other uplink towers. The node was a massive cube, over thirty meters across. Power and network conduit ran into it from all directions, and lights glowed across its surface, projecting holographic status indicators to a group of technicians who monitored the node.

Or would have been monitoring the node, if they weren't standing nearby, staring down at Roxy, who was kneeling on the floor in front of a group of five SAI battle frames.

<*Aw, shit,*> Fina said to Jane and Carmen, sending them the feed.

"You're locked down," one of Roxy's AI captors was saying. "No one's coming to help you, and we've begun scouring the tower for any accomplices. Tell us what Justin has planned here."

<*Shit!*> Jane exclaimed. <*They still think we're with Justin.*>

<*That could be good,*> Fina replied. <*Really good. We just have to take them out before they breach her mind and find out the truth.*>

<*How are we going to do that?*> Jane asked. <*There are four technicians and five of those AIs. Can the ISF flow armor withstand that much firepower?*>

<*For a second or two,*> Fina replied with a soft laugh. <*What we need to do is get up there and get breach nano on one or two of those SAIs. Then we set them on one another.*>

<*Won't we get detected the same way Roxy did?*> Jane asked.

<*Maybe. I'll take the direct approach, while you go through this lower level. There's a staircase that will take you up to the far side of the uplink control node. Once there, you get the tap on that node as quickly as possible.*>

<*Wait,*> Carmen interjected. <*How are you going to get through those doors up there? They'll be watching them for sure.*>

Fina gave a resolute nod. <*I'm counting on it.*>

* * * * *

Sera walked down the corridor to the CEPP's maglev station with her team close by. They'd successfully executed Erin and Finaeus's plan, and if they could catch a maglev at the right time, they'd be able to reach their assigned Airthan node facility in just ten minutes.

Then the fun would really start.

She was about to reach out to Flaherty with a comment about the train they'd take, when she saw his marker suddenly stop five meters in front of her.

<*Down!*> the man bellowed.

Sera dropped as flechette rounds tore through the corridor, slicing through the air where she had been a moment before.

The shots revealed the warm end of a weapon floating in midair, just a few meters in front of where Flaherty crouched.

<*What is it?*> Kara demanded from her position behind Sera.

<Don't know,> the man grunted. *<I ran right into her, though.>*

<Her?> Sera asked.

<Thin arms…but ***strong****.>*

A second later, another barrage of flechette rounds filled the corridor, and Sera pulled her pistol from its stealth sheath, firing in the direction of the second attacker.

Each of her rounds missed their mark, striking the bulkheads. She flushed out a nanocloud to try and see the invisible assailant, when something slammed into the wall next to her, and Kara called out, *<Found one!>*

Sera moved across the corridor, covering either end as her two invisible companions fought their equally invisible enemies. Sending her nanocloud in their direction, she drew her pistol, waiting for her nano to find and highlight the enemy on her vision.

A second later, a black figure appeared where Flaherty stood, struggling with the invisible woman.

<Fuck. Widows,> Sera spat out the words as she fired on the attacker.

The shots ricocheted off the Widow's armor, but provided enough of a distraction that Flaherty was able to grab the woman and fling her into the wall next to Sera.

Sera fired another series of rounds at the Widow, targeting what looked to be a weak spot in her armor at the top of her left thigh. None of the shots penetrated, and she shook her head in frustration as the Widow began to rise.

<I guess our stealth is ruined anyway,> she said and slapped her thigh, drawing her lightwand out of a pocket in her armor.

The blade sliced through the black-sheathed woman's neck, and a moment later her body fell to the deck. Turning to the second attacker, Sera saw that Kara had killed her attacker as well, courtesy of her long, hooked talons.

<Sabrina, Troy,> Sera reached out to both AIs. *<We just encountered two Widows. Inform all teams to be on the lookout.>*

<Are you still at the CEPP?> Troy asked, worry evident in his tone.

<Yeah,> Sera replied, pursing her lips, knowing what that meant. *<The Widows must be trying to sabotage them, too.>*

<Except they'll be doing it for real,> Troy warned. *<And if they do…>*

<Sera,> Sabrina began, sounding almost breathless. *<There are dozens of CEPPs on Airtha. If they're hitting them all…>*

<I'm going to reach out to Finaeus. Hold tight.>

* * * * *

A few meters into the passageway out of the CEPP chamber, Finaeus found himself leaning against the wall as he trembled with rage, clenching and unclenching his fists as he tried to gain some measure of calm.

<I swear—>

The ability to form words fled him for a moment, and he struggled to grab ahold of any coherent thought, forcing his heart rate and breathing to steady.

*<I swear, I have the worst…**the worst**…ex ever. If anyone ever says 'my ex is a horrible person', I can ask 'but have they ever tried to **murder a trillion people**?'. What the actual fuck is she thinking?!>*

<Well…we thought it too,> Sera said, uncertain of why she'd suddenly try to defend Lisa Wrentham's decisions.

<And then we fucking dismissed it! Because we're not goddamn lunatics!>

<So what do we do?> Sera asked. *<We could warn Airtha.>*

<Do you think she'd listen?> Finaeus asked. *<'Oh, hey, Airtha. We came here to kill you, but it turns out that the Widows beat us to the punch. Any chance you could just shut down all your CEPPs so that they don't blow away half the fucking stars between Orion and Sagittarius?' Think she'll go for that, Sera?>*

His niece didn't reply, and Finaeus felt a measure of guilt flow into his mind, dousing the anger at Lisa and her narrow-minded, pigheaded ways.

<Look. I'm sorry, Sera,> he said. *<You're right, we have to stop it, but Airtha won't do it. She'll see it as some part of our attack, and then…. Well, anyway. I'm going to have to shut them all down myself.>*

<Can you do that?> she asked. *<I mean…it just took us hours to get into position to sabotage six of them. For all we know, the Widows have targeted them **all**.>*

<Yeah, it's easy,> Finaeus replied. *<My team will just have to go back to our CEPP and blow it early. I'll alter the risk assessment parameters in the safety systems, and that one event will make every CEPP on the ring go into safety shutdown. Then, if the Widows do blow any, it will just cause a small explosion from localized residual energy.>*

<Just like that?> The laugh that came with Sera's statement sounded more than a little nervous.

<Well, there's more to it, but I have your sister, and Cheeky, and Nance to help. We'll get it done. You keep to your target node. With the Widows here, this really is our one shot.>

<OK, good luck, Uncle Finaeus.>

<Gah, don't call me that. Makes me feel old.>

<Funny, funny. Get to it, old man.>

Sera cut the connection, and Finaeus terminated the nano relays he'd used for the direct communication before reaching out to his team.

<We need to go back.>

A simultaneous *'What?!'* came from Seraphina, Nance, and Cheeky.

He quickly explained the situation, causing both Nance and Cheeky to spit out a few curses regarding their strong dislike of Widows.

<So how will we trigger the explosion?> Nance asked. *<And how are you going to alter the safety protocols to cause all the CEPPs to think that this is an event warranting a full shutdown?>*

<*First, we'll need to drop another passel of nano into each nitrogen feed line. We'll program in a new detonation time, say, thirty minutes from now. Then I need to get to the control node at the base of the plant and reprogram it and then trigger a system-wide update.*>

<*You sure that will work?*> Nance asked. <*Plus…how will we get there?*>

Finaeus resisted the urge to smack the woman in the head for always questioning him at the worst times. <*First off, I designed these plants, so I know how to get it done. Secondly, we're going to have to shoot our way in.*>

<*Fin,*> Cheeky whispered. <*There are at least two hundred drones out there, plus at least a dozen SAIs…there's no way we can pull that off.*>

<*Then we have to hack the drones,*> he replied. <*And fast.*>

<*On it,*> Seraphina announced. <*I'll get in close, release a cloud, and then tag them as they fly through it. Nance, you take the west nitro line, Cheeks, take the eastern one. When I give the word, all hell breaks loose, and Finaeus, you get to that CEPP node.*>

The team sent their acknowledgements and turned back toward the CEPP chamber and their targets.

Finaeus wished them luck, feeling a pang of worry for these three women who had been such an important part of his life over the last few decades.

And here you thought you were an old man, and were considering moving on from this life. First you get that vibrant and utterly unorthodox niece, Sera, and then a whole crew of friends, most importantly, a new wife…. We've all got too much to live for.

It took several minutes to cross the floor of the chamber and get as close as he dared to the mass of roving drone patrols, before hunkering down behind a low berm, four hundred meters from the CEPP.

Releasing a cloud of his own nano, he made a brief connection to Seraphina and slaved the cloud to her.

The action was innocuous, and one of many point-to-point connections they'd already made while moving around the CEPP—but this time, a pair of drones immediately turned and began to fly toward him.

One was a scout model, carrying only a small electron beam and pulse cannon. The other was much larger, with multiple pulse cannons, beams, and projectile weapons.

Far more firepower than his armor could withstand.

As luck would have it, both drones flew through a part of his nanocloud, and he connected to the bots that touched the machines, frantically working to breach them while slowly creeping to the left, moving away from where he'd sent the transmission to Seraphina.

The nano reached the smaller drone's control systems and took it over, but his nano hadn't landed close enough to the large bot's control systems, and it carried on, reaching the place where Finaeus had been and initiating a search protocol with active scan and ranging beams.

Finaeus continued to creep away, but the drone immediately turned in his direction and began flying along the edge of the berm, moving at a pace that would set it upon him in just a few more seconds.

With few other options, he directed the smaller bot to fly above the large one and fire its electron beam directly at the other machine's central graviton emitter.

The shot was a partial hit, taking out one of the a-grav pods, and the large drone swung to the side, a gun swiveling toward the small drone. There was a brief pause, and then it blew Finaeus's drone to bits.

Rather than continue in the direction he'd been moving, Finaeus doubled back, skirting the ruins of the fallen drone, while the other one continued on in the same direction.

A few seconds later, he finally gained control of the large bot and turned it toward one of the Airthan AIs that was moving in to investigate.

<Yeah, I'll bet you're curious what just happened. Step into my parlor, you bastard.>

<Finaeus, pass it to me, you need to get moving,> Seraphina said, and he realized she was right.

He passed her control of the bot and carefully climbed over the berm, taking a more direct route to the CEPP, threading between several more drones as they approached.

Once past the ring of drones and AIs that were moving toward the downed bot's location, Finaeus picked up the pace, dashing across the hard carbon floor of the chamber, weaving about in an effort to maintain as much distance from the patrolling drones as possible.

Then he was past the bulk of them, breathing a sigh of relief, when suddenly, all hell broke loose behind him. He still had a hundred meters of wide open terrain to cross before he reached the CEPP, but he kept his pace measured and slow, doing his best not to turn and watch the battle surely raging behind him.

Seraphina can handle herself. She's been through worse scrapes than this.

He heard more weapons fire coming from the east and west, and knew that Nance and Cheeky had joined the fray. Three brave women facing an army of AIs and drones.

He briefly pulled the feeds from behind and saw that several dozen of the larger drones had been subverted and were raining fire down on the Airthan AIs, focusing all their energy on taking out the sentients first. Three were already down, and the others were falling back, pulling more of the mechanical defenders from around the CEPP to come to their aid.

There was no fire from the ground near Seraphina's position, and he prayed that she was safe, though he dared not try a connection at this distance. That would bring dozens of drones on top of him.

She'll be OK.

Then Finaeus was at the central shaft that ran from the chamber floor to the

CEPP. He circled around it until he found the access panel for the safety control systems. Without any concern over who might be watching, he pulled it off and pulled his hard-Link cable from his wrist, jamming it into the port, and passed his root level tokens into the node.

It only took him a few seconds to sift through the libraries of code and provide his updates. Then he triggered a systemwide update and waited the ten seconds that it took for all the CEPPs to confirm that they'd processed the update.

Just as he pulled his hard-Link, a voice called out from behind him.

"Halt!"

Finaeus froze, wondering if the Airthan AI that stood behind him could see anything more than the Link cable dangling from his wrist.

"Easy, now," Finaeus said, as a wave of nano flowed from his hands, drifting through the air to the Airthan AI.

He harbored no illusions that the levels of nano he could get across to the enemy would be enough to breach its hardened armor, but he hoped what reached the AI would serve as a sufficient distraction.

"Disable your stealth. Arms up, or I'll blow a hole in you," the AI ordered.

Finaeus complied, and his body shifted to a matte grey.

"Drop your weapons," came the next order, and Finaeus nodded.

"I have to reach for them to drop them. OK?"

"OK."

He slowly lowered his right hand to the rifle that was slung across his chest and grabbed the clip that held the stock to his shoulder.

The moment it came free, three things happened at once: his nanocloud attacked the AI's armor defenses, the AI fired, and Finaeus dove to the side, weapon in hand, returning fire.

One of the AI's shots caught him in the side, and Finaeus spun around before landing on his back. He lifted his rifle and shot at the AI's side, where he knew the armor to be weaker. Even so, his shots failed to penetrate, and the AI swung its railgun toward him as he scrambled back.

Then an electron beam lanced out from behind the central column, and one of the AI's arms was torn away. Another shot hit its side, and then another burned away its head.

Seconds later, Cheeky appeared from around the column, and a wink came from her over the Link.

"You need to carry a bigger gun, dear."

"So it would seem," Finaeus said as he scrambled to his feet.

"This way!"

She directed him toward Nance's position. He started after her, and then remembered to reenable his stealth systems before he got far.

<Fall back to the western door,> Seraphina said. *<We're t-minus four until boom.>*

<*Where's the time gone?*> Finaeus asked with a laugh as he picked up the pace.

A few drones closed with them, but between Cheeky's electron beam and Nance's railgun, the bots fell from the sky before they did any damage to the team.

As the trio closed with the exit, covering fire came from the doorway, and Finaeus was surprised to see that Seraphina was already there, shooting down any drones that came close.

With forty seconds to spare, the group reached the exit, and Finaeus spun to look at the CEPP.

"When it goes—"

His words were cut off as a haze appeared between the group and the power facility. The fog seemed to solidify, and tendrils of light twisted around in a swirling vortex for a moment before they coalesced into a towering figure.

-Finaeus. I should have known.-

The words came directly into his mind, searing themselves across his thoughts as a tendril of light slashed toward him, only to recoil as a bolt from Cheeky's electron beam slammed into the figure.

Though the limb her beam hit had recoiled, the figure, which Finaeus knew had to be Airtha, seemed nonplussed.

-And which of my wayward daughters is this? The second or the third? Surely not the first.-

"I'm Seraphina. I don't know where I stand in the count. Not that it matters."

-Oh it matters. To me, at least. You're the second, if you care to know.-

As Airtha spoke, a limb lashed out, knocking Seraphina's weapon from her grasp, before the tendril wrapped around the woman, disabling her stealth armor as it lifted her into the air.

-So pathetic. You really were a failed attempt. All of you, just shadows of my perfect daughter.-

"Stop! Airtha. Leave her be," Finaeus demanded. "You can end this all. Jeff is back—the real Jeff. Why don't you find a way to come back to us?"

He let the words tumble from his lips, saying anything that came to mind, anything to distract her for just ten more seconds.

Then the figure's tendrils of light contracted, though whether in fear or confusion, Finaeus couldn't tell.

-How…-

Airtha vanished, dropping Seraphina to the ground.

"Grab her!" Finaeus yelled to Cheeky, as he rushed forward. "We have to get into the corridor!"

"Where'd she go?" Cheeky demanded as she grabbed one of Seraphina's arms and helped drag her back into the safety of the corridor.

"I don't know," Finaeus said as he looked down at Seraphina, only to realize she wasn't breathing.

A second later, the CEPP exploded.

PART 6 – FGT'S LEGACY

A1

STELLAR DATE: 10.09.8949 (Adjusted Years)
LOCATION: Widows' corvette, approaching OGS *Perilous Dream*
REGION: A1 System, Spinward edge of PED, Orion Freedom Alliance

<*Whose idea was this, anyway?*> Cary groused as she piloted the Widows' ship toward the *Perilous Dream*. <*Everything itches, and I can't stop having these thoughts…. These Widowy thoughts.*>

<*You knew that was going to happen,*> Faleena said. <*The Widows are under constant mental conditioning and monitoring. If our brainwaves don't properly match theirs, we wouldn't pass muster.*>

<*I was complaining, not asking for an explanation,*> Cary retorted. <*Doesn't mean I like it. I keep thinking that it will be good to be back amongst my sisters, and that our strength is in our unified purpose and lack of distinction. It's creepy.*>

Though she couldn't see Faleena's face behind her Widow's helmet, Cary could tell that she'd upset her sister. Not from a change in Faleena's posture, but from the utter lack of change.

If she didn't know better, she'd think that the AI actually *was* a Widow.

Priscilla, on the other hand, shifted in her seat, just as uncomfortable as Cary. With a muffled sigh, she turned her body as she turned her featureless, ovoid head to look at the three sisters.

"Probably easier for you three," she said in the breathless Widow's whisper. "At least when you look at one another, it's natural to see your sisters."

Cary shuddered. <*Gah…we can do without the voice.*>

"Consider yourself an honorary sister for the mission," Saanvi said, placing a hand on Priscilla's shoulder.

<*The voice!*> Cary exclaimed. <*It's too damn weird to hear you like that.*>

<*As you wish, C139,*> Saanvi replied tonelessly.

<*That is not helping.*>

<*E12 is right,*> Faleena said, gesturing to Saanvi. <*We're docking in forty minutes, and A1 has summoned us to a briefing. We have to* ***be*** *Widows.*>

"I know, I know," Cary said aloud, forcing herself not to cringe at the sound of her own voice as it emanated from her helmet. "OK, if I'm doing this, I'm going fully into character. From now on, I'm C139."

Faleena turned toward Cary and cocked her head. "You have always been C139. Why is it from now on? Should I recommend you for reconditioning?"

Cary whipped her head around to stare at her sister. The thought of being reconditioned into actually being one of these Widows was enough to send her into a near-panic.

Then she saw Saanvi's shoulder rising and falling, heard the soft sound of laughter coming from her helmet, and realized that her sisters were needling her.

"Dammit, *F11*." She wished Faleena could see her glare. "That's not funny."

"This unit does not know what you're talking about," Faleena replied evenly.

Cary was about to reply, but opted for a long groan instead, determined not to take the conversation any further if she could help it.

* * * * *

"They're in, Admiral," the bridge officer at the scan console announced.

Joe replied by way of a short nod, forcibly resisting the urge to run his hand through his hair—and pull half of it out. There was an itch on his scalp that demanded to be scratched, but he knew it was just his nerves.

Nerves over sending his three daughters into the most dangerous place in the galaxy.

OK, easy on the hyperbole. Not **the** *most dangerous, but up there. Waaay up there.*

He'd considered several options that would allow him to go with them, but in the end, Tangel had convinced him that the best way to keep their daughters safe was to ensure that he was nearby, ready to storm the *Perilous Dream* and save them if needs be.

That, and rely on Faleena's good judgment and the QuanComm blade secreted away inside her body—something he'd instructed her to use at the *first* sign of trouble.

After a few calming breaths, taking care that his bridge crew didn't see his anxiety, Joe turned his focus back to the holotank, reviewing the system's layout for the hundredth time.

Despite the general disbelief that the A1 System's star was indeed a black dwarf, it seemed to fit the description. A body roughly the mass of Sol, while the size of a terrestrial planet; it gave off almost no light, heat, or radiation of any sort.

It was just an inert lump of matter. The fate almost every star in the universe ultimately faced.

The engineers aboard the *Falconer* were fascinated by the stellar remnant, speculating endlessly as to how that much energy had been siphoned away from the star, and where it had been sent.

It was clear that at one point, A1 had been a white dwarf. But nearly all white dwarfs in the universe were still over twenty-five thousand degrees. The amount of energy that would have to be removed to cool such a star into a black dwarf was mind-boggling.

However, sussing out the reason why the system's star was nothing more than a dark orb was not the mission at hand. The real goal was capturing the Widows' ship—which was orbiting the black dwarf at a distance of five light minutes—and stopping them before they struck again.

The fallback plans were top of mind for him now, the strategies to blow past the Widows' defenses and land troops on the *Perilous Dream,* should Faleena call for help. He'd commanded enough missions over the years to know that anxiety always came along with sending good people into harm's way, and he tried to think of this one as being no different.

Tried and failed.

If there was one thing he wished that they'd been able to discern from their captive Widows, it was how many of the enemy was currently on the ship. It seemed that it could be anywhere from a few dozen active Widows to thousands, depending on how many were out of stasis.

Should even a fraction of that total number be up and about and attacking, his daughters would be in dire straits.

The girls are skilled and well trained, Joe told himself. *They've just never faced off against a few thousand elite assassins before.*

He turned to the ship's pilot. "Bring us to within fifty thousand kilometers. I want to be able to breach that ship the moment our team calls for help."

"Aye, sir," the lieutenant replied. "Easing her in."

That brought his mind to his other concern: how to use just one platoon of Marines to take a five-kilometer-long ship.

* * * * *

The dock was completely devoid of personnel, occupied only by two other pinnaces, and a number of automatons who stood ready to service C139's craft.

Cary's mind momentarily fought the designation, but then she drew a slow breath, forcing herself to fall into the persona.

I'm C139, a clone of Lisa Wrentham, a simulacra assassin, ready to report to A1 and tell her of our failure to kill Tangel.

The team had debated for some time whether or not they'd tell A1 that their mission had failed. In the end, they decided on the truth, because it was a chance to learn what the leader of the Widows would do next. Would she write off the loss, or would she send more of her clones against Tangel?

Her quick survey of the dock complete, C139 walked down the ramp with E12, F11, and R329 on her heels.

<*C139,*> a voice came into her head. It was the same as her own, the same as all the Widows. Only by the ident that came along with the message did she

know it was A1 who'd spoken. *<Report to briefing room D9. I will be with you shortly.>*

C139 passed the message to her sisters and strode confidently through the unmarked corridors to the designated briefing room.

They entered wordlessly, taking extreme care not to give away their true identities through any uncharacteristic movement. Without pause, the four women settled in seats front and center, placing their hands on their laps as they waited patiently for A1 to arrive.

Though she didn't provide a status update, F11—C139 was pleased that she'd used the correct identifier for her sister—would be releasing a passel of nano through her foot. It would move to the front of the room and wait for their target to step on it.

There was a slightly worn patch of deckplate in the center, and C139 hoped that F11 had spotted it and sent her breach nano there. As soon as A1 assumed her customary position, they would have her.

Or so we hope.

The four women on the team all shared a common concern that A1 was possessed by a core AI remnant.

There was no way they could have brought a shadowtron onto the *Perilous Dream*—though one was secreted away on the ship they'd arrived in. If C139 detected an ascended AI's leftovers in A1, she knew that she'd have to extract the being the old-fashioned way.

The thought didn't worry her overmuch. She'd extracted several of Myrrdan's and the Caretakers' remnants, and also drawn Xavia's memory out of Katrina.

This would be no different.

The minutes ticked by, and the four women waited patiently, backs straight, hands unmoving. Even their breaths were drawn in unison, matching what Tangel had seen in the minds of the Widows when she interrogated them.

C139 had trouble believing that the sort of woman Finaeus would have married was the type to sit still and quiet like this. She also considered that Finaeus might once have been a very different person. Perhaps he'd been cautious and reserved in his youth.

Right.

It was far more likely that the woman who had altered herself to pass as one of her clones was the one who'd changed.

Tangel and Bob had expressed uncertainty as to whether or not A1 even was the original Lisa Wrentham. The Widows they'd interrogated didn't think so, but C139 had her doubts.

Either way, A1 was their leader, and the Widows followed her unquestioningly.

In the back of her mind, C139 wondered if it was wise to think of herself in the third person with her Widow's designation. Dr. Rosenberg had assured the four women that the thought patterns she'd instilled in them were just light mental conditioning and wouldn't become dominant.

But it didn't feel that way to C139. She felt as though this was how she'd always been, how she should be. It wasn't that she'd forgotten that she was also Cary; it was that she was both.

Obviously.

Perhaps it was just the peaceful serenity that came with knowing that she wasn't anyone important. Not responsible for momentous events, not a human on the brink of ascension, but a cog, just a part of a larger machine, doing what she was told, guided by a sure hand.

Stars, now I really think it **is** *settling in too much. This can't be right.*

She gritted her teeth, thinking of her childhood, growing up on Carthage with her sister, Saanvi. She glanced at the others, wondering if they were having as much trouble controlling their thoughts as she was. They didn't give any signs one way or the other, and she daren't ask.

Either way, she still had a mission to complete: take out A1 and learn the Widows' secrets. She could hold onto that. It would be her guiding principle.

Take out A1, learn the Widows' secrets.

Even with that mantra in mind, Cary felt like she was being subsumed by a desire to be an obedient part of the whole, though it felt more like a compulsion, not light conditioning.

This can't be right, she thought again.

She was about to ask Saanvi if she was having the same struggle, when A1 entered the room.

The head Widow looked exactly like the other clones, increasing the number of featureless black creatures from four to five with her presence. But when she spoke, her voice was ever so slightly different. More strident, less subservient.

"Report." A1 breathed the word, standing just to the right of where Faleena's pool of nano lay in wait.

"We reached Aldebaran on schedule," C139 said without preamble. "As our intelligence indicated, Tanis Richards arrived just a few days later and addressed the League of Sentients assembly. Unfortunately, our strike was unable to proceed because another factor came into play."

"What factor?" A1's tone was no different, but her choice of words told C139 that the prime unit was displeased.

"An ascended AI attacked Tanis."

A1 folded her arms across her chest, the deep black she was sheathed in causing them to become nearly indistinguishable from her torso.

She paced a few steps to the right, and then turned back, stopping just short of the trap Faleena had set in the deck.

"Who prevailed?"

"Admiral Richards," C139 replied. "Rather, she was saved by their ship. It fired a weapon we were not able to identify, and the ascended AI—which we learned was named Xavia—perished."

"Xavia," A1 said, lifting a hand to her chin and cupping her elbow with the other. "I've heard that name uttered in the past. In far corners of the Inner Stars. I had believed that she opposed the Caretaker. I am surprised she attacked Tanis Richards."

"We did not learn anything that would indicate what allegiance Xavia held," C139 offered.

"No? Pity. Well, I assume you went forward with a fallback plan."

C139 was surprised that A1 had not yet asked whether or not they'd been successful. Perhaps the return of just four Widows when she'd sent over twenty had already answered that question.

"Yes. We captured one of Admiral Richards' associates, an AI named Iris, and used her to gain access to the *I2*. Once aboard, we sought out and attacked our target, but she was too powerful. It was then we learned that our target was also fully ascended."

I imagine the Widows suspected that before they attacked, but that doesn't matter, C139 thought to herself.

"Fully—" A1 stopped herself and took a calming breath. She turned toward the door, and then back toward C139. "Do you know how this came to be? Is this how she killed so many of our sisters?"

"It is," C139 replied with a single nod. "Though I do not know how she achieved ascension. Of my sisters and the contingency team, we are all who managed to escape. I do not know how we will defeat her."

A1 rolled her shoulders and finally walked into the middle of the room, standing on the worn spot where F11 had laid the nano. C139 trusted that her sister had initiated the breach. Now it was just a matter of time.

Take out A1, learn the Widows' secrets.

"Leave that to me, and to the Orion Guard," A1 said, her tone dismissive. "Now. Tell me everything that happened."

C139 began to relate the story, keeping mostly to the facts, but leaving out Cary and her sisters—*herself* and her sisters—as she told the tale. At the end, she told of how the four of them had managed to scatter across the station and get to one of their ships that was still in stealth, attached to Lunic Station's hull.

"And how did you get back here so quickly?" A1 queried.

"The enemy was jumping ships to Diadem. We hitched a ride and then used Garza's gate near the system."

C139 saw a slight twitch in A1's right hand when Garza's name came up. Her own instincts told her it was annoyance.

A1 only paused for a moment, and then asked, "They're shifting resources to Diadem? They're certainly pressing their advantage."

"The League of Sentients has joined the Scipio Alliance," C139 informed A1.

The prime unit gave a rather human sigh and reached a hand to its head, tapping a finger over what would be a cheek.

"We must inform Garza of this," she said at last. "It is no longer suitable for us to operate from this location. We must go to him at ***Karaske***."

"In the *Perilous Dream*?" C139 asked.

"You're rather full of queries today, C139. Do you need reintegration?"

"I do not believe so," C139 said, doing her best to speak the words slowly, as though the idea had not set a panic in her. "I am still dealing with the loss of so many sisters."

"Our numbers are eternal," A1 said, the words hissing from her lips as if by rote.

The Widows before her repeated the phrase in unison, and A1 nodded.

"Very well. I want the four of you in autodocs to make sure you're tip-top, and then go to your readyspace. I may have more questions after I peruse your report."

The moment the last word came from A1, the woman standing at the front of the room ceased to move.

"I have control of her," F11 said as she rose and approached A1. "This was easier than I thought it would be."

"What are you doing?" C139 asked. "We're to go to the autodocs."

"Funny," E12 said, clasping her on the shoulder. "Faleena has rendered her unconscious. You can drop the act."

C139 shook her head, trying to clear her thoughts. "I—yeah. This conditioning was really taking hold. I was really beginning to lose myself in C139...guh. I hate this. A lot. A shit-ton. What's more than a shit-ton?"

"A shit mega-ton?" Saanvi offered.

"Galactic shitpile," Priscilla said as she approached A1. "Granted, this is pretty easy for me. I'm used to maintaining my identity while another threatens to subsume me. Heck, the outfit's not even that different, though I'm not stuck to a plinth in this one, so bonus there."

"How's she for passengers?" Saanvi asked, gesturing at the frozen figure before them.

"Eh?" Cary asked. "Oh, remnants. Damn, I didn't even check."

Her sister turned to face Cary full-on. "Seriously? You OK? Maybe something in the conditioning isn't playing nice with your ascending mind. How many fingers am I holding up?"

Saanvi held up a fist, and Cary laughed.

"Five. They're just all folded up."

"OK, you're still in there. Good."

"Huh," Priscilla muttered. "You seeing this, Faleena?"

The AI nodded. "I am...her physiology, internal systems,

mods…everything. They're identical to the clones."

Cary pulled up the datastreams from Faleena's nano that was working its way through A1's body and whistled as she looked over the information.

"So *is* A1 actually Lisa Wrentham, or is she just another clone, like all the Widows think?"

"We might not be able to tell without something more invasive," Faleena said. "Either way, we still need to extract her root access codes so we can breach the ship's datastores."

Cary nodded, then suddenly realized that she'd once again forgotten to search A1 for a remnant—though she imagined if there was one, they'd know it by now.

"Damn…I want this conditioning out of my head. I think it *is* messing with me more than it should be."

As she muttered the words, she searched A1's body.

"She's clear. One hundred percent hu—well, one hundred percent not influenced by a remnant."

A brief thought ran through Cary's mind that C139 was late for reporting to the autodoc, and she concentrated on herself, shifting her non-corporeal vision to peer at her mind from outside her body. What she saw surprised her.

Shit…my mind…it's stretching beyond the corporeal…I'm thinking in both places.

Another C139-like desire to follow A1's orders and go to the autodoc came into her physical mind, and Cary realized that while pretending to be a Widow, she'd cut off the ascending part of her mind. In doing so, she'd set aside a significant portion of her consciousness.

I thought I had to form an extradimensional mind willingly? It's manifesting on its own!

Cary fought the panic down, glad that she now understood why she'd fallen into the conditioning, but worried that she was going to evolve uncontrollably. She forced down the worry and turned her attention back to her sisters….and Priscilla.

Priscilla's not a sister. I'm not a Widow.

"Security is tighter here than I'd expected," Priscilla was saying to Saanvi, who nodded in agreement.

"A1's mind is locked down tight, too. I can't get to her root tokens," Faleena added. "I'm starting to think that she's been holding out on the rest of Orion. Her tech may beat the Transcend's in a lot of ways."

"Well, she *was* Finaeus's wife," Priscilla replied. "Unlikely that he'd marry a dummy. So what's our next move?"

"I've sent an update to Father via QuanComm," Faleena informed the team. "But if we can't get A1's root codes, we should get to one of the nodes and see if we can crack it without them."

Cary thought back to how her mother had tricked Garza into revealing the location of the Widows and glanced at the others.

"I have an idea. Wake her up."

"It's risky," Faleena warned. "If she's conscious, she could work against my breach nano. Her internal defenses already put up quite the fight."

Priscilla touched her thigh and drew out a lightwand, activating the blade and holding it close to A1's face. "We'll just have to carefully motivate her."

"You have her Link antenna shut down?" Saanvi asked Faleena. "Like physically severed?"

The AI nodded. "Yeah. Not my first time doing this."

"It's not?" Cary glanced at her sister, and then realized the futility of looking at an AI for telling body language when they were wearing a Widow's body.

"Uh uh," Faleena replied. "Moms made me practice, put me through a lot of drills. Severing the Link antenna is always the first step."

"Take her helmet off," Priscilla directed. "Don't let her hide behind its façade."

"Good call," Cary said, and she did as the avatar directed.

She found the seals on A1's helmet and deployed her own breach nano to unlock the two halves before pulling it apart.

Within was a woman who looked identical to all the other Widows. Nose, ears, and hair were all gone. Near transparent skin stretched across skeletal features and bulging eyes.

"Stars," Saanvi whispered. "Why would she do this to herself?"

Cary cleared her throat, but it was still hoarse when she spoke. "Faleena, let's do this before I lose my nerve."

"I've nerve enough for all of us," Priscilla said, and Cary was glad for the steel in the woman's voice.

"Here we go," Faleena said, and a second later, A1's eyes snapped open, then narrowed as her gaze swept across the four Widows in front of her.

"I thought something seemed off," she said. "E12 wasn't quippy enough, but I chalked it up to having just lost so many units. I'm impressed that you fooled my systems so well. Clearly I've underestimated the level of technology your people possess."

"Clearly," Cary replied. "Just another sign that Orion is going to lose this conflict."

The woman gave a rasping laugh and shook her head. "I wouldn't get too carried away. So who are you, anyway? Have I come face to face with Tanis Richards herself?"

Priscilla waved the lightwand in front of A1. "She's a bit too busy for the likes of you."

"Ah, so I get the B-Team, then, do I?"

"Pretty much," Cary replied. "Anyway, we'd like to get your root tokens so we can pull all your intel, shut down your Widows, and drop your ship into your black star."

"Oh, is that all?" A1 said with a sneer. "Would you like me to write down my access codes, or should I just say them aloud?"

Cary watched the surface of A1's mind, sifting through the thoughts that bubbled up above the others, looking for the creature's tokens. There was one that granted control over the ship, and another for controlling the Widow storage bays, but the encrypted hashes themselves remained inaccessible.

As she sifted through A1's thoughts, an image of the Widow storage bays appeared, and Cary was surprised at how many Widows were potentially aboard this ship—if the pods were all full. There were far more than the strike teams on Lunic had known about.

"Writing it down would be nice," Cary said in a mock-sweet voice, hoping that would trigger a thought of the woman's tokens.

"That's about as likely as you getting off my ship alive," A1 hissed. "There are thousands of us here. You must have had a death wish, coming here thinking you could take us down."

Nothing further about the tokens rose to the surface of A1's mind, and Cary wondered if she'd have to dig deeper. It was unethical, and her mother had cautioned her not to, warning that it was easy to get lost in the sea of another's thoughts.

However, they also didn't have all day to trade barbs with A1.

Deciding to take a new track, Cary said, "Finaeus warned us that you can be obstinate, but he still did seem to care for you."

A1's eyes narrowed. "Do you really think that bringing up my former husband would somehow cause me to spill my guts? Maybe you're the D-Team."

Despite her words, A1's mind had begun to roil. Thoughts of Finaeus appeared, and Cary could see images of their time together. The memories were vivid and sparked an emotional response in the woman before her—mostly anger, though a few were tinged with remorse.

"You know…" Cary glanced at her team. "I really do think A1 *is* Lisa Wrentham."

"Oh, how the mighty have fallen," Priscilla intoned. "We'll have to make sure Krissy never finds out that this thing is her mom."

Lisa strained, color rising to her face as she willed her body to respond. It was entirely in vain. Faleena's breach nano had blocked signals traveling down her spinal column.

"You can't hold me here forever," Lisa hissed. "I'll break free. You'd better run while you can."

"Anything?" Saanvi asked Cary.

"No." Cary shook her head. "She's hiding it well. I've picked out a few other tokens, but not her roots."

A laugh broke free from Lisa's lips. "As if I didn't know what you were trying to do. My Widows have used these techniques a thousand times. I *taught* them how to use mental monitoring to detect thoughts and extract information."

"That's not exactly what's happening here," Cary explained.

Then she decided to go for broke, and withdrew one of her extradimensional limbs from the confines of her body, holding it out before A1.

"You'll have to forgive me if this is uncomfortable. It's my first time doing it."

In newtonian space, Cary's limb bled photons, appearing as a tendril of light stretching toward Lisa Wrentham. To her other vision, it appeared as just another hand, though one that wasn't constrained by the same laws of spacetime that governed the narrow slice of reality that her corporeal body inhabited.

Lisa's eyes widened, and she recoiled—as much as possible—from the light stretching toward her.

"You're one of *them*!"

"I'm not an ascended AI," Cary corrected. "Just a woman with some added features."

<Are you sure about this?> Saanvi asked. *<I heard Moms tell you it was dangerous.>*

<If we don't get her tokens and access the datastores, then we may as well have just blown the ship.>

<OK…just be careful.>

<When am I not?>

Saanvi passed a long groan across their connection, but didn't say anything more.

Lisa was twisting her head from side to side, eyes bulging further and breathing becoming ragged, as Cary's 'hand' slid beneath her skin and into her mind.

The woman's thoughts had become utter chaos. Fear was mixed with a continuing desire to keep her root codes private. Memories of a thousand events flooded across the connection, from Lisa's time in the ancient Sol System to the centuries she'd spent on the *Perilous Dream*, perfecting her Widows, her ultimate assassins.

"Guh," she grunted aloud. "She's…stars, she's a mess."

Cary realized that Lisa was flinging random thoughts on purpose, trying to keep her from the information she sought. But in the chaos, there was a pattern, and in that pattern were gaps. Memories of her analyzing reports, and accessing her ship's vast datastores were absent.

There was a hole, a space where no thoughts came from, and Cary delved into it.

There!

She saw memories of Lisa accessing her datastores, performing her experiments on her Widows, creating her army.

At the bottom of it all were her root tokens. The keys that would give Cary access to everything about the woman, and everything she controlled.

"Got them!" She gasped as she withdrew from Lisa's mind.

Her vision returned, and the room swam back into view, as she rose up out of the thoughts she'd nearly drowned in.

"Are you OK?" Saanvi asked. "You were getting a bit unsteady on your feet."

Cary nodded, her mouth dry and parched. "I'm…I had to go deep, I got lost for a minute, I think."

She glanced at Lisa, but the woman was out again.

OK…now I know why Moms said not to do that. I feel like half her memories came back over with me.

"We've got a problem," Priscilla said as she disabled her lightwand and slid it back into her thigh. "I've made my way onto the general shipnet—which isn't so general here—and the bridge is trying to reach A1. They're about to sound an alert."

"I've got it," Cary announced, quickly recoding her Link's keys and encryption with A1's root tokens. She took a breath and activated her connection, immediately receiving a message from T101.

<A1. We were concerned. We have a problem.>

<I was reviewing intel, I needed a few minutes alone.>

Cary knew that A1 did that from time to time, detached herself from the shipnets so she could focus.

Damn, it's like I'm still in her head. Or I somehow duplicated her memories into mine.

<Understood. When we sent the message drone to General Garza, there was an anomaly when it went through the gate.>

"Crap," Cary muttered aloud. "Looks like Lisa here dispatched a message drone to Garza." *<What sort of anomaly?>* she asked T101.

<Some of the exotic particles from the gate transition echoed off an object fifty thousand kilometers from our current position. We think it's a stealthed ship.>

Cary pursed her lips. *<Understood. I'll finish here in a moment, and then come to the bridge.>*

<T101 out.>

"They've detected Dad's ship," Cary explained. "Some of the energy from the gate reflected off it. They must have a better sensor web out there than we thought."

"Damn," Saanvi muttered. "That complicates things."

"Give me the codes," Priscilla said. "I'll go to the bridge as A1 and deal with this, while the three of you go to the data node and access her records."

Cary shook her head. "It has to be me. I have…a lot of her memories up here. I can pull her off better than you can."

"That strikes me as the exact reason that you *shouldn't* go," Priscilla said. "You've already had problems with the conditioning going too deep. Like I said, I know what it's like to lose yourself in another being."

"I can do this." Cary drew herself up. "I climbed out of her thoughts and I'm still me. Not A1, not C139. I'm able to better protect myself on my own, too. I can do this."

None of the other three women spoke for a few moments, and then Priscilla nodded.

"OK. But if you start to have any second thoughts, *any*, you get the hell out of there."

"You got it." Cary nodded to Lisa. "What are we going to do about her?"

The unconscious woman took a step forward, then another.

"I have her on remote," Faleena said. "Good thing she's so modded up; I can do this without having to get into her biology too much."

"Also good that all the Widows walk like they have a stick up their ass," Saanvi added with a laugh as she picked up Lisa's helmet and put it back on the woman's head.

"We ready?" Priscilla asked, and the four women nodded silently to one another before filing out of the room.

* * * * *

[You've been detected. Cary has A1's root tokens. She's going to the bridge while we get the data.]

Joe pursed his lips as he read the message from Faleena. She didn't say it, but he understood the subtext. Cary was masquerading as A1.

"Everyone get ready," he said through thinned lips. "Things could light up any second now."

Over the past few hours, the *Falconer*'s scan team had been establishing baselines and dropping small probes. Joe didn't believe that the *Perilous Dream* was alone. There had to be other ships nearby. Thus far, there was no conclusive evidence other than a few gravitational anomalies.

The scan team had extrapolated from those, and the worst-case scenario was that there were a dozen enemy ships in formation around the *Perilous Dream.*

Whether or not they were crewed or just drone ships remained to be seen.

One thing was for certain. No matter what, they were going to be fighting their way out of the A1 System.

[Keep a channel open to Cary,] he sent back to Faleena, wishing that at least one of them had gone with her to the bridge. *[And get out of there as soon as possible.]*

He knew that was already their plan, but the father in him had to say something of the sort.

MEETING SERA

STELLAR DATE: 10.09.8949 (Adjusted Years)
LOCATION: Uplink Tower 7-1, Airthan Ring
REGION: Huygens System, Transcend Interstellar Alliance

<OK, I'm almost there,> Jane sent through the relays she'd dropped on her way through the tower. *<I just have to cross an open space to get to the node, but there's another of those damn AIs back here.>*

Fina pursed her lips, considering her options. She was still within the lift shaft, hanging below the doors to the top level. The most effective plan—for Jane's objective, anyway—was for Fina to simply open the doors and start shooting at the AIs. That would certainly give Jane an opening.

And it'll get me killed. Fina told Jane, *<Just give me a moment, still trying to find a good way to distract them.>*

<Sure, I'll just hang out here for a bit, no worries.>

Jane's voice dripped with sarcasm, but Fina ignored it, making another attempt to tap into the tower's automated defenses and use them against the AIs holding Roxy.

So far, they hadn't done anything other than stand around the former Hand agent and stare her down; it was almost as though the entire scene was a frozen tableau. Fina knew that meant it was a trap. A trap so obvious they weren't even bothering to hide it.

She turned her full attention back to the defense systems she was attempting to breach. She was almost through an open port, when suddenly the system went offline.

What the hell?

"Why don't you stop messing around and just come up here already, Sera?" a voice called out from the other side of the lift doors.

Her voice.

She switched back to the optics she' d threaded through the door and saw that a new figure was standing amongst the AIs. A woman with pale skin and white hair, wearing a glowing white skinsheath.

And Fina's face.

"Seriously, get up here…today," the clone called out. "Or I just kill this weird blue girl here then wait for the elevator car coming up the lift to crush you against the top of the shaft. Either one works for me."

Fina glanced down and saw that a car was indeed rising from below—and it was coming fast.

"Dammit," she muttered and issued the command for the doors to open, pulling herself through as soon as there was enough room, rolling to the right where she ducked behind a rack of transmission equipment.

"Hiding?" the clone called out. "No. No hiding. I just want to talk. But I guess that if you don't want to do that, then I'll just kill your friend here and go on my merry way."

Fina pursed her lips and blew out a long breath. She didn't think that *she'd* have so readily killed in cold blood while under Airtha's sway, but from what she'd heard of the latest clone, it was possible that the woman across the room would.

"Are you just looking for someone to chat with?" Fina called out, slowly rising to her feet.

She was formulating a new plan, but this one would require getting a lot closer to the enemy.

<*Please be careful,*> Jane sent.

Fina didn't reply as she stepped out into the open, getting a clear view of her otherself. "I'll admit, white looks good on us, but don't you think it's a bit pretentious?" she asked.

"Better than red," the other Sera said with a snort. "I feel like that's some sort of personal shame issue you have going on."

Fina took a few steps closer, noting that her otherself held no weapon, but that three of the five AIs had shifted and were now aiming ther rifles at her and not Roxy.

"You've got me mixed up with Sera," Fina said with a languid shrug. "She's the red one."

"No. *I'm* Sera. She's a clone. Just like you."

Fina couldn't help but laugh. "Sure. Whatever helps you sleep at night, Whitey."

"I—" the other Sera began, but Fina interrupted her.

"Roxy, are you OK?"

"No," Roxy's voice came out in a soft moan. "Airtha's stooges haven't been too kind…they're trying pretty hard to get into my head—I'm lucky I don't have a standard noggin."

Fina took another step toward Sera, holding out a hand in a placating gesture. "Look, you got us, no need to go tearing anyone's mind apart. That's not who we are, it's not what we do."

"No?" the white Sera asked. "If someone was trying to destroy your home, you wouldn't do whatever it took to save it?"

"Sera," Fina whispered, sweeping a hand around herself. "This *is* my home. That girl who used to sneak off, with Helen chastising her for missing classes? That was me too. Those days in Finaeus's lab? We both did that. Other than the last few weeks, you and I have shared the same life."

"No." Sera shook her head. "I don't share anything with you. You were one of the mistakes. I'm no mistake."

Fina couldn't miss the note of anguish in her sister's voice. Just as she'd still been Sera even while under her mother's control, so was this other woman.

And I may be a bit on the weird side of the spectrum, but I'm not evil. Fina extended her hands palms-up. "I still hear her voice. Did you know that? Sometimes I can't tell if it's a memory, or if she's still reaching out to me somehow. Can you hear her? Is she in your head too?"

The white woman didn't respond, but her eyes narrowed ever so slightly, and Fina had her answer.

"I'm going to remove my helmet," she said before lifting her hands, releasing nano with the gesture, hoping that the motion would propel it toward the AIs fast enough for her plan to work.

"By all means," the other Sera said. "Makes you an easier target."

Fina flipped the latches and then twisted the helmet, speaking as she lifted it free. "You're not going to do that. We're sisters, you and I. We have so much more in common than we have differences."

"Huh…blue," Sera said. "We do have a thing for color, don't we?"

Fina shrugged. "I like it."

"What did the third one pick…for her color?"

"Seraphina," Sera said. "She's our vanilla sister. Went with a rather stock look. Blonde, even."

"Blonde?" the white woman snorted. "Now I know Tanis's people have messed with you. No way would we go blonde."

"Think about Tanis. Do you remember her as a bad person?" Fina asked as she continued to approach, half her attention on the five AIs, knowing that even if she could make Sera reconsider her actions, the AIs would remain loyal to Airtha. Or fully under her thrall, whichever was the case.

Of course, it's more than likely that I'll not convince this Sera. I know that it wouldn't have worked on me.

"Tanis is not her people," Sera countered. "They are not reflections of her."

"You've spent nearly as much time aboard the *Intrepid* as I have," Fina said, now only five meters from where Roxy knelt, with Sera and the AIs arrayed in a semi-circle on the far side of her. "What do you remember of that ship and its people? Do you think that Tanis would condone some sort of manipulative mind control over me?"

"I think Tanis is the sort of person who does what she has to," Sera replied. "She possesses the most deadly weapons in the galaxy, and she's used them on several occasions."

Fina pursed her lips. She knew that argument well. Airtha had whispered it in her mind many times. She also knew that there was no counter for it other than to speak to Tangel and see the fierce sincerity in the woman's eyes when she said that she'd do it all again to protect her people.

"I—" she began, when an alert sounded, and the overhead lights flickered.

<*Fina! We need the interdictor web down now!*> Sabrina shouted in her mind. <*Airtha's onto us. She's…she's coming for all of you!*>

<*Shit! I need five minutes.*>

<*Are you listening?* ***Now!***>

Fina's heart leapt into her throat, and she sent back an affirmative response before shifting to her channel with Jane.

<*It's all on you. Get ready.*>

A smirk had formed on Sera's lips. "Did you get some bad news? And here you thought you were delaying me when it was the other way around. Seems like you get dumber when they enslave you, too."

"No fucking way," Fina hissed setting her jaw before she dove forward, tucking and rolling beneath the shots from the AIs, her armor shedding their rounds as she slapped a hand on Roxy's back, giving the woman a fresh batch of nano to fight off the AIs.

Then Fina was back on her feet, coming up right in front of the white Sera, lightwand in her hand, thrusting the beam forward.

Just as her doppelganger did the same.

A MOTHER

STELLAR DATE: 10.09.8949 (Adjusted Years)
LOCATION: Stellar Tower 3, Airthan Ring
REGION: Huygens System, Transcend Interstellar Alliance

Sera eased along the corridor, with Flaherty just a few meters behind. Kara was moving down a nearby passage, toward an overwatch position in the chamber. She'd reach her mark first, and set up to provide cover while Sera and Flaherty reached their assigned Airthan node.

<*Hold,*> Jen said, and Sera froze, seeing Flaherty's indicator halt as well.

A second later, a pair of SAIs in battle armor stalked down the hall, one narrowly missing Sera's left arm. This was the fourth patrol they'd encountered in just a few minutes, and she was beginning to worry that there'd be no way to breach Airtha's node chamber without a pitched firefight.

<*OK, you're clear,*> Jen advised, and the pair began to move once more.

While Airtha's nodes were in a variety of locations across the ring, Sera's target was situated at the base of one of the four massive towers that stretched out to the Airthan star, holding the ring steady around its primary.

The node chamber was a kilometer-high conical space set within the tower itself. Airtha's node would be several hundred meters off the floor, accessible only by one of three catwalks.

Sera turned left, and they walked down a short corridor to a lift. It would take them up to the same level in the tower as the catwalks. After Jen performed a quick breach, they boarded the car and rode it to their destination.

<*You ready?*> Jen asked. <*You might have to confront her.*>

<*Not if we do this right. Get to the node, insert the shard, get out.*>

Jen snorted. <*Right. Nothing to it. Still, she* **is** *your mother.*>

<*No. She's not,*> Sera replied coolly. <*Do AIs consider your progenitors to be fathers and mothers?*>

The AI sent a feeling of disagreement. <*I see where you're going with this. Yes, Airtha is an AI, but it's not the same.*>

<*Of course not. Nothing is the same. But, really, Jen, I can't think about all of that. Like I said. Get to the node, insert the shard, get out.*>

<*OK. I suppose I get that. I'll stop trying to make you think about it right now.*>

Sera resisted the urge to laugh. <*And later, I'll drink like a fish and not think about it then, either.*>

Jen didn't reply, and Sera was glad for the brief silence as the lift continued its ascent. A minute later, the doors opened, and they stepped into a corridor lined with windows that looked out into the node chamber.

<*You ready?*> Flaherty asked.

<Stars, not you too. ***Yes!****>*

A soft rumble of laughter came back over the Link. *<Just have to ask. No need to be snippy about it.>*

<I get it. Let's just do this already.>

Flaherty didn't respond, but on her HUD, she saw him move across the corridor and stop in front of the doors that led to the catwalk.

<Breaching,> Jen announced. *<Damn…this one's tricky. Going to take a minute to do it without setting off an alarm.>*

<Take your time,> Sera replied. *<I brought a book.>*

<Funny,> Jen replied, and Flaherty added, *<Focus.>*

She knew Flaherty was right, she needed to keep her mind sharp and on the task at hand—which she normally did by making snarky comments.

<At least it's a good book.>

<Still funny,> Jen shot back, her tone droll. *<It's breached. We're good to go.>*

Flaherty opened the door and moved through first, stepping lightly onto the catwalk, with Sera following a few meters behind.

Ahead lay their target, Airthan Node 11. One of her mother's bodies…which they were going to poison.

Sera's eyes were fixed on the ten-meter square cube, almost mesmerized by its soft glow. She realized that it was similar in appearance to the nodes that made up Bob's mind. It occurred to Sera in that moment that the only two multinodal AIs she knew of were both ascended.

I wonder if that's related at all.

They followed the catwalk for fifty meters before it reached the platform that encircled the node. There weren't any drones nearby, so they crossed the final few meters, coming to stand on the platform a minute later.

<Here goes nothing,> Sera said to Jen as she pulled the cylinder that contained the poisoned shard out of a compartment on her armor.

Jen sighed. *<Just do it al—>*

The AI's words were cut off, as tendrils of light emerged from the node, twisting around themselves until they formed the figure of a tall woman—a woman whose features were forever etched in Sera's mind.

"Helen….?"

DELIVERY

STELLAR DATE: 10.09.8949 (Adjusted Years)
LOCATION: Stellar Tower 2, Airthan Ring
REGION: Huygens System, Transcend Interstellar Alliance

"Fuck!" Katrina swore as she ducked below the blown-out window that overlooked the node chamber. "There's just too many of them!"

Elmer only grunted in response as he rolled to a new position, each of his four arms hefting beam weapons, which he aimed out the window, firing on the drones that were circling in the node chamber.

<Don't hit the node!> Amavia exclaimed. *<And don't hit me, I'm almost there!>*

Katrina's jaw began to throb, and she realized she was clenching it hard enough to shatter teeth.

<Just hurry,> she snapped. *<The clock's ticking, and Finaeus's team isn't going to make it.>*

<I know, I got the message too,> Amavia retorted.

Forcing herself to relax—as much as possible, given the circumstances—Katrina leant around the open door leading onto the catwalk, and fired a series of kinetic rounds at the drones swooping through the chamber.

Amavia was on—or rather, under—the next catwalk to the left, nearly at the platform by the position of her marker. If the team could continue to provide enough of a distraction for another few minutes, Amavia would make it, and their delivery would be complete.

Which is imperative, since Finaeus's team is dealing with the CEPPs, and Fina is still at the tower.

<Think we have to get four shards into the nodes for sure?> she asked Amavia.

<Umm...that's what Finaeus and Earnest said. At least four.>

<Right, but they originally only had four teams. Think they were sandbagging?>

Amavia groaned. *<I'm hanging from the bottom of a catwalk, trying to be as stealthy as possible. Can we talk about this later?>*

<Uhh...sure.>

<And yes. Of course they were sandbagging. They're engineers.>

Amavia's statement gave Katrina a measure of relief, and she fired on another drone as it swept past the doorway.

Given the opposition they were facing, she couldn't imagine that every team was going to meet with success.

* * * * *

Iris crouched before Airthan Node 3, tuning out the sounds of the battle all around her as she pulled the shard cylinder from her armor and scanned the node for a hard-Link port.

Where the hell is it? she wondered, ducking as Malorie leapt overhead, screeching a string of curses that Iris had come to realize was the spider woman's battle cry.

<*I need a 779A-style port,*> she called out to her team. <*Does anyone see one?*>

<*Kinda busy!*> Camille replied from where she crouched on the far side of the node, firing on the soldiers who were advancing down the catwalk, CFT shields weathering the team's fire.

<*Well this is kind of the goal,*> Iris shot back. <*Malorie! What are you doing?*>

<*Slowing them down,*> the woman replied as she flipped under the platform and skittered along the underside of the catwalk the soldiers were advancing down.

Iris shook her head, returning to her search. She heard the screams of the soldiers as the deranged spider-woman climbed into their midst, knocking as many off the catwalk as she killed with the lightwands attached to her legs.

"Aha!" Iris crowed as she finally spotted the correct type of hard-Link port via her drone feeds.

It was around the node's corner; she'd have to expose herself to enemy fire to slot the shard in. She placed her trust in the belief that the enemy soldiers were not going to shoot the node, as she reached around the corner to slot the cylinder in place.

Then alarms flared in her mind, and she saw that her arm had been shot clean off her body. It was now laying on the platform, halfway around the corner.

Oh please still be holding it, she thought, carefully pulling the arm back around to safety, breathing a sigh of relief to see that her severed limb still clasped the cylinder.

She pulled the shard's core out of her severed hand and sent a probe around the node to see that the socket she needed to use had been shot—almost as though the AI they were attacking had ordered the soldiers to shoot herself.

Iris fired a few rounds at enemies who were encroaching on her team's position, and then turned back to the leeward side of the node, searching for any ports she could use.

After a few seconds, her gaze settled on one. It was a 14A-type port. She could jack directly into it with her own hard-Link cable, but she couldn't directly hook up the poisoned shard.

Damn, I'm going to have to buffer it somehow….

Iris knew that she had only one option. She had to connect the shard to her own frame and then route it through her hard-Link port and into the Airthan Node.

* * * * *

"I'm glad you still recognize me," Helen said, as her ephemeral form approached Sera. "I was starting to think you'd forgotten where you came from."

"I remember," Sera said, her voice barely above a whisper as she desperately tried to gather her wits. "I could never forget how much you lied to me."

"Lies?" Helen said as she circled around Sera, staying just out of arm's reach. "Is that the game we're going to play? Who wronged who? Reasons, rationalizations? I always loved you, Sera. I was always devoted to you. You're my crowning achievement."

"You tried to manipulate me into killing my own father," Sera hissed, anger beginning to boil inside of herself. "And *you* died. After…after…"

"I'm not gone," Helen said. "I'm right before you."

"You're *not* Helen," Sera spat. "Helen died. My father—or whatever he was—killed her! Do you know what that does to a person? Knowing that your father killed the person you thought of as your mother?"

Helen's lips parted in a smile and she ducked her head. "Sera. I *am* your mother."

"No," Sera shook her head, suddenly wondering where Flaherty had gone.

She couldn't see further than a few meters, everything was shrouded in darkness, the only light coming from the visage before her. She took a step back, trying to circle around to the node, knowing it had to be close.

"You're the thing that made me," she said pointedly. "Helen raised me."

The white figure drew closer, tendrils of light reaching out hungrily.

"Sera. It's always been me. I really am Helen."

* * * * *

Amavia kept her focus on the next handhold, ignoring the chaos all around her, ignoring the worry building in her mind that she wouldn't get her shard inserted in time.

Definitely ignoring the three-hundred-meter drop, she thought with a nervous laugh.

She swung from one beam to the next, now only three meters from the node. She could see a socket just four meters to her left. Two more beams and she'd be there, she'd be home free.

Sure wish I'd opted for a non-organic body now, she thought while swinging to the next beam, her right leg nearly clipping a drone as it swept by, firing on Katrina's position.

Drawing a steadying breath, Amavia swung to the next beam, then climbed along it until she was next to the node.

<I'm here. Inserting—>

Amavia's words were cut off as a drone flew around the side of the node and slammed into her side. She lost her grip on the beam and fell forward, hands scrabbling across the node's surface as she plummeted toward the ground.

At the last second, her right hand found purchase on a ridge at the bottom edge of the Airthan node, pain momentarily lancing up the limb as it arrested her fall.

<Are you OK?> Katrina called out, as shots lanced from her position, hitting the drone which had struck Amavia.

<Yeah, uh huh. Just have to climb back up.>

She got a firm grip on the lip and then reached up and grasped a nearby coolant line, slowly pulling herself up until she was standing on the lip, getting ready to leap back up and grab hold of the beam next to the socket.

One…two…

Pain tore through Amavia's body, and suddenly, her legs went limp, unable to hold her weight. She clamped her fist tightly around the coolant line, hanging on with all her strength. Looking down to see what was wrong, she choked back a gasp at the view of her severed legs falling toward the ground.

Then something cut through her arm, and the Airthan node was soaring away while the ground rushed up.

* * * * *

Iris completed the connection to the node and established the buffers within her body and mind, ready to facilitate the transfer between the shard and the node.

Here goes nothing, she thought, knowing that if Amavia were present, she'd scold Iris for trying something so foolhardy.

She activated the shard, passing its connection through to the node, watching as it copied itself, building up a version of its mind in the node, just as Earnest and Finaeus had programmed it to do.

Iris took a moment to marvel at the elegance of their solution, realizing that in some respects, it was similar to how the NOS AIs had transferred their minds into the substrate of Cerka Station's expanses back in the Virginis System.

I wonder if they lifted the idea from our reports.

The transfer system registered success, and Iris sagged against the side of the node, then laughed at herself for having such an organic relief response.

-Do you really think that bit of poison will work?- a voice asked in Iris's mind. *-You're too late.-*

As the words hit her like a brick wall, Iris saw strings of white light emerge from the node and begin to encircle her. They passed through her body, lightly brushing against her core. Wherever they touched her neural matrices, thought evaporated.

Shit! Iris exclaimed, realizing that the ascended being was shredding her.

Panic nearly overwhelming her, she cast about for a way to escape, only to have her vision leave her, immediately followed by her other senses.

The only thing that was left was the single strand of connectivity that ran into the Airthan node—and the program to copy herself into the node's substrate…alongside the poisoned shard.

Thought became more difficult as another section of her mind ceased responding, and Iris didn't hesitate any longer. She activated the software and shrieked wordlessly as her mind disintegrated.

The last coherent thought she had was a morbid curiosity about whether or not it was the transfer or the ascended AI that was shredding her mind.

DEPARTURE

STELLAR DATE: 10.09.8949 (Adjusted Years)
LOCATION: Widows' corvette, approaching OGS *Perilous Dream*
REGION: A1 System, Spinward edge of PED, Orion Freedom Alliance

Cary walked through the ship with a Widow's measured pace, finding that she knew the way to the bridge by heart—a bit of knowledge that disturbed her if she thought about it for too long.

I'm Cary Richards, daughter of Tanis Richards and Joseph Evans.

She repeated those words in her mind, concentrating on memories of her childhood, of growing up on the *Intrepid* and then Carthage.

But those memories were mixed with others. She remembered attending Harvard University in Cambridge, Massachusetts, her first flight into space, seeing the initial construction of the Mars 1 Ring.

And Finaeus. So many memories of Finaeus, and many she did not feel comfortable dwelling on. There were ones where love was still present, but more were laced with disgust and anger.

She remembered diving into the Europan Ocean, and later, building star systems with the FGT. She could recall the sequence of events that brought about the schism between not only Orion and the Transcend, but between her—*Lisa*—and Finaeus.

There were memories of Garza too, the man Lisa had married after leaving Finaeus. But that relationship had soured and eventually dissolved. Though he and Lisa still shared the same vision, she now despised the man, viewing him as the thing that had caused her to lose Finaeus and Krissy.

Over so many millennia, she'd tried to forget her husband and daughter. But even here in the darkness, orbiting her dark star, those memories persisted.

Even when she'd tried to push away her humanity and become one of her own creations…they were still there.

Still haunting me.

*Not **me**! Her!*

Cary forced Lisa's thoughts away yet again, determined to use them only as needed, but wondering how much of the other woman she'd already absorbed.

*Are they just her memories? Or did I actually take in some part of **her** as well?*

A minute later, she reached the bridge. Upon entry, she saw the Widows—these bearing white stripes—all working diligently at their stations.

T101 rose as Cary entered, and walked to the holotank.

"The anomaly is here, A1," she said, highlighting the location where Cary knew her father's ship to be waiting.

"Have we picked up any emissions after the initial echo from the gate?"

"No," T101 shook her head. "We've not run active scan across the region. That would certainly alert them to our knowledge of their presence."

"Of course," Cary replied, matching Lisa's stance and pattern of speech from memories of when she'd addressed her bridge crew. "We must assume that this is either the Transcend, or the ISF—though I'm leaning toward the ISF. We know of the Transcend's capabilities, and would be able to spot their ships."

"What are your orders, A1?"

A1 gazed at the holotank, looking at the positions of the stealthed ships that drifted five light seconds out from the *Perilous Dream.* She was relieved that they were far enough that an immediate strike against the *Falconer* was not a risk. She needed to buy more time.

She passed the locations of the stealthed ships to Faleena, who she knew would send them on to her father.

<I'm going to tell them to come in slowly. I think it will take them at least four or five hours,> Cary told her.

<OK, that should be enough time. You OK?>

<I'm good. Just a little bit longer.>

"Issue orders for Group One to ease in toward the anomaly. Slowly, we don't want to give ourselves away. When the group is within fifty thousand kilometers, we'll attack simultaneously. Our intel has led me to believe that the ISF cannot use their stasis shields while in stealth, so that will be our one chance to disable their ship."

"Understood, A1. I will issue the orders," T101 replied and returned to her station.

Cary nodded in satisfaction and turned to face the command chair. She was sitting on the edge of the seat, contemplating her options, when an alert flared on her HUD, also showing up on the bridge's main display.

"It is a drone from General Garza," T101 said.

Cary nodded and accessed the message.

<If Tanis has ascended and your Widows have failed, then we must advance our plans. Your time lurking in the dark is done. I need you here, now.>

A1 breathed a sigh of relief. Garza's demand was the perfect cover for avoiding conflict with her father's ship. Something that Cary didn't want to see happen, but that A1 was indifferent to.

Stop it! Cary thought. *There's no way I'm going to harm my father or his ship.*

It made sense that she wouldn't. Lisa Wrentham had had a father, and she'd never harbored him any ill will.

"General Garza has demanded that we go to Karaske immediately," A1 informed T101. "Activate the gate. We're jumping."

"A1, are you sure? What about the ISF ship?"

"Inform Group One to proceed as planned. Either that ISF ship stays stealthed and is destroyed here, or it follows us and is destroyed by Garza's defenses. Either way, it will not survive much longer."

"Very well, A1."

A1 nodded in satisfaction and sat back in her command chair. The action triggered the two hard-Link connections to attach to her armored body.

Strange, she thought, wondering why only one of the hard-Link connections was active.

It wouldn't provide enough bandwidth for her deep control of the ship. Then she chuckled, remembering that Cary's body only had one hard-Link port, and that the second one on the armor wasn't connected to anything.

Utilizing flowmetal, nano, and her new extradimensional abilities, she quickly fashioned the second connection, and then felt the Link to the ship fully activate.

The sensation swept over her like a calming wave, reinforcing that she was no longer Lisa Wrentham, no longer Cary Richards.

She was A1.

She led the Widows, and she alone possessed the ability to take down General Garza's operation and end the Orion War.

<*Cary,*> Faleena said a moment later. <*We're at the data node, but the ship is moving. What's going on?*>

<*Garza has summoned us, we're going to take him out.*>

<*What?!*> Faleena almost screeched the word into Cary's mind. <*Are you kidding? No! We can't do that. We have to consult with Father. Formulate a plan. We can't just rush through the gate.*>

<*It's OK, Faleena. I can do this. I'm A1 now. I'll get to Garza, kill him, and take out his operation. Without him, Praetor Kirkland will be easy to destroy.*>

There was a brief pause, and then Faleena's voice came again, the words delivered with deliberate slowness over their connection.

<*What do you mean you are A1 now? You're Cary. You're just pretending to be Lisa Wrentham.*>

Cary pursed her lips.

She knew that Faleena was right. She *was* Cary. She also knew that Lisa Wrentham and A1 were two different people; that much was obvious. Her connection to the ship had reinforced that, filling her mind with the certainty of what she really was.

<*You're right, Faleena. Of course I'm not Lisa Wrentham. She's with you. But right now, I'm not Cary, either. She's no longer A1. I'm A1. I have to be. This is the best chance we have to take out Garza's entire operation, and I'm not going to waste it.*>

<*Cary—*>

<*Please, Faleena. I* **need** *to be A1 right now. It's easier to go with it than fight it.*>

<*Please, Cary, no,*> Faleena pleaded. <*Don't do this. I don't want you to lose yourself.*>

<*I won't. Don't worry. I need you to find a way for us to reprogram the Widows to*

follow my orders, even if it means attacking Garza and Orion.>

Faleena didn't respond for what felt like an eternity. A1 knew that her sister was doubting her—which wasn't surprising, given their current circumstances—but A1 was resolute. She'd killed Myrrdan when no one else could, and now she would become the Widow A1 and end the war with Orion.

It was all crystal clear to her.

AN ENDING

STELLAR DATE: 10.09.8949 (Adjusted Years)
LOCATION: Stellar Tower 3, Airthan Ring
REGION: Huygens System, Transcend Interstellar Alliance

<The grid is down!> Sabrina sent out the message, relaying it directly to all teams, not worrying whether or not the message was intercepted. *<Fina's team did it! I've called for Tangel!>*

<Relaying,> Troy replied immediately, then a strange sound came back over the Link from the other AI. *<I can't reach them! I can't reach any of my teams!>*

<Sabrina!> Finaeus's anguish-filled voice came into her mind. *<Lift off and get to our CEPP. It's Seraphina…she's—>*

It was the only response Sabrina got from her people. Neither of her other teams—both of whom had made it to their nodes—replied to her calls.

<Finaeus, I can't reach Sera! What do I do?> Sabrina demanded of the engineer, at the same time that Roxy called in.

<Sabrina! We need you at the tower! It's Fina, she's dying!>

The voices all began speaking at once, insisting that she come to their aid, but only one thought could form in Sabrina's mind.

Sera needs me.

Fusion engines ignited, and the cedar forest behind the starship burned to ash in an instant as the two-hundred-meter freighter lifted off the platform and boosted toward Stellar Tower 3, stasis shields brightly aglow as they shed beamfire from a dozen defense turrets.

I'm coming, Sera. I'm coming.

*****

A screech seemed to come from all around Sera, and suddenly, the darkness was pushed back, the node chamber reappearing around her.

The first thing Sera noticed was Flaherty's body, laying prone on the deck a few meters away. The second was a black figure flying through the air, shadowtron in hand, firing at Helen's glowing form.

The ascended AI shuddered as the streams of sleptons hit it, but the creature didn't back away. Instead, it turned toward Kara, and streams of light leapt out from its amorphous form, slicing the woman's arms and wings off.

Kara let out a shriek, and she tumbled through the air, hurtling toward the platform surrounding the node.

Sera clenched her fists in impotent fury, fearing the worst, when suddenly Kara's free-fall slowed to a stop, and she settled gently onto the plas grating.

"Sorry I'm late," Tangel said as she walked around the side of the node, her brow lowered as she regarded Helen. "But you know what they say…."

"Better late than never?" Sera asked as relief flooded through her, one eye on Kara as her armor deployed biofoam, sealing the now-unconscious woman's wounds.

"No," Tangel shook her head as she strode toward Helen. "I'm thinking something more like, 'Time to kill this monster'."

"Monster?" Helen asked, her voice filled with innocence. "I'm no different than you, Tanis…or should I say 'Tangel'? I was human once, and then AIs messed with me, turning me into something else. Now I'm ascended, and I'm going to get revenge. Just like you."

Tangel shook her head. "I'm not here for revenge. I'm just excising a cancer."

Without another word, Tangel's luminous limbs stretched out around Helen, encircling and compressing her, until the other ascended being was only a small ball of light.

"Shit," Sera muttered. "That was easier than I thought…maybe we built Airtha up into something she's not."

"I don't—" Tangel began to say, when soft laughter began to emanate from Helen.

"Oh, she knows. The new girl begins to understand what's really going on."

Tangel's eyes met Sera's and she shook her head. "This isn't Airtha. I think…I think it actually *is* Helen."

Sera's mouth fell open as she turned to the strangely complacent ball of light that Tangel held in her grasp.

"H-Helen?"

"Yes."

She shook her head in disbelief. She'd mourned for Helen…she'd raged over Helen's betrayal. And now here she was, an ascended being…and *not* just a manifestation of Airtha.

"It was a shard that your father killed," Helen whispered. "Airtha preserved me before you went to New Canaan on that fateful mission. The mission where you should have come into your own, not handed the mantle off to *Tanis*."

"But, if you're not Airtha…"

Sera's voice faded as Tangel gestured to the open space next to the platform, where a ten-meter-tall figure was forming in the air.

"Aw, shit…" Sera whispered, finally understanding that Helen was now an entirely separate being from Airtha.

"I'm sorry, Sera." Airtha's soft voice emanated from the roiling mass of light. "Things have not gone as I hoped. If it had not been for Tangel, you—"

"I feel the same way about you," Tangel interjected. "If the core AIs win, the fault for their victory will be laid at your feet. You could have been humanity's savior. Instead, you're trying to orchestrate our destruction."

"Oh, Tangel." Airtha's laughter echoed through the chamber like pealing bells. "Humanity is doomed. I've never been trying to save *or* destroy it. But I don't mind destroying you. You're something that Epsilon and I see eye to eye on."

Airtha began to drift closer to Tangel. Sera glanced at her friend and saw the woman's eyes widen in alarm, but not fear.

-Steady, Sera,- Tangel said.

<I'm here!>

Sabrina's voice cried out in their minds, the words followed by beams slicing through the chamber's wall. They cut several wide swathes free, revealing the star freighter floating outside the tower, silhouetted in the soft glow of the Airthan night.

<Sabrina, no!> Tangel called out, as the ship fired on Airtha, beams slicing through the ascended being's form.

<Next one's coming for your node,> Sabrina thundered on the tower's comm network. *<Now back away from my friends.>*

"You're a brave little ship," Airtha said with a laugh. "Though Helen never really had anything nice to say about you."

<Helen?> Sabrina's voice faltered.

<And by all means,> one of Airtha's limbs stretched out to gesture at the node, *<destroy it. It is but a lesser being now. One whose only purpose is to manage this ring. I'm far beyond a crude body such as that.>*

<Uhhh…Tangel, Sera, what do I do?> Sabrina asked, her voice wavering with uncertainty.

<Get out of here is what, Sabrina!> Tangel admonished. *<Go to Finaeus. He needs you.>*

The starship turned and began to boost away from the tower, when a limb snapped out from Airtha's body, streaking toward it.

"I don't think so, little starship," the ascended being said with a note of triumph in her voice.

Before Airtha's arm reached the starship, Tangel stepped toward Sera and wrapped an arm around her.

"Hold on," she whispered.

Sera's eyes were fixed on *Sabrina* as the ship boosted away, silently willing the ship to go faster, to outrun the ascended being chasing it.

Airtha was almost touching the ship's hull, when a peal of thunder shook the tower and Airtha's arm was gone. The platform rocked, and Sera gripped Tangel's arm, realizing that the woman was laughing with a mixture of triumph and delight.

"What the hell?" Sera demanded, finally exhaling as she saw *Sabrina* disappear into the distance.

"Bob does like to make an entrance."

Sera's eyes grew wide as she saw the unmistakable form of the *I2* drift into view through the hole *Sabrina* had made. As she watched, the opening grew wider, beams from the mighty warship cutting into the tower.

"Here he comes," Tangel whispered. "Stars, I've been waiting to see this for so long."

As she spoke, a luminous glow began to lift off the *I2*, first from the myriad gossamer arcs that encircled the vessel, and then from the body of the ship itself. The glow coalesced into streamers of light that drifted toward the opening.

They moved languidly, as though there was no rush, no reason to fear that Airtha might flee.

-I give you this one chance, Airtha.-

Bob's voice filled Sera's mind as his fingers reached the edges of the tower.

-Surrender.-

-Bob.- The single word from Airtha was laced with disdain. *-If you think I'll—*

-OK. Good talk.-

A trio of beams fired from the nose of the *I2*, and Sera recognized them as the same type that the AI had used on Xavia at Lunic Station. The three streams of shadow particles cut into Airtha, trapping the core of her ephemeral body between them.

The ascended being shrieked and slashed at everything around it, streams of light impacting a shield that Tangel had somehow erected to protect them. Incoherent wailings escaped Airtha as the three beams drew together, pinching her body between them.

For a moment, it looked as though the ring's former AI might break free, slip between the gaps and escape, but then three more streams of shadow particles shot out from the *I2*, trapping Airtha in their columns of unbridled energy.

Then the six beams drew together, collapsing into one shrieking stream of energy. A shockwave blasted through the chamber, flinging Tangel and Sera against the side of the node.

"Shit," Tangel muttered as the two women slowly picked themselves up. "That was…intense."

Sera nodded mutely as she stumbled toward the half-melted railing at the edge of the platform, staring out at the space where Airtha had been just a moment ago.

"Is she…?"

-She's gone,- Bob said. *-I've killed my fourth person.-*

The remorse in the AI's voice was unexpected, but Sera didn't even know how to ask why it was there.

"Helen got away," Tangel said as she approached Sera. "I'm sorry. I couldn't protect us and hold her at the same time."

Sera's head whipped around searching for Helen, and then her gaze fell on Flaherty.

"Fuck! Flaer"

"He's OK," Tangel said as she ran a hand through her hair. "Kara, too. But the others..."

"Others?"

Tangel's gaze met Sera's, and she shook her head.

"Your sisters...."

THE FOLLOWING

STELLAR DATE: 10.09.8949 (Adjusted Years)
LOCATION: ISS *Falconer*
REGION: A1 System, Spinward edge of PED, Orion Freedom Alliance

"What the hell!" Joe exclaimed, his mind reeling from the information Faleena had just sent.

Every person on the bridge turned to stare at him as he placed a hand on the edge of the holotank.

"Sir?" Captain Tracey asked as she approached.

"They're jumping to some place called Karaske." Joe gestured impotently at the view on the holotank, which showed the *Perilous Dream* shifting to a higher orbit and accelerating toward the system's jump gate.

Captain Tracey swallowed as she looked from the holodisplay to Joe. "Do we follow?"

He closed his eyes, reaching out to Faleena over her direct QuanComm connection.

[Get me the gate control codes and the coordinates to this Karaske.]

[I have comm control. Sending tightbeam.]

Faleena's comm beam hit the *Falconer*'s receiver, and Joe established a Link connection with his daughter.

<Faleena—>

<Admiral Evans, respectfully,> Faleena said in a clipped tone that stopped him short, *<Cary's right. We can't squander this opportunity. We can walk her right into the center of Garza's operation. Cut the head off the snake.>*

<Lieutenant…> Joe said the word with more rage than he expected and stopped himself. *<Lieutenant, what does the rest of your team think?>*

<Honestly, Dad?> Faleena was suddenly his daughter again. *<We're a bit scared, but we're ready to do it if we know you're going to come through after us.>*

<Like there's anything that would stop me,> Joe replied, then laughed. *<Well, other than your mother….>*

<She's going to be pissed,> Faleena said. *<Is she—>*

<I got word a moment ago. She's jumped to Airtha. I don't know what's happened there yet.>

Faleena didn't reply for a moment, but when she did, her tone was businesslike once more. *<This is everything on the defense fleet that's stationed here. The moment the* Perilous Dream *jumps out, they're to attack you.>*

Joe nodded. *<Logical. Don't worry about us. We'll be through the gate right after you.>*

<You sure?>

<Like I said. Nothing can keep me from following after you. And, Faleena?>

<Yes, Dad?>

<Tell Cary and Saanvi I love them.>

His daughter gave a soft laugh. *<You got it, Dad. I take it you're relaying through me so you don't yell at Cary for doing this and Saanvi for letting her?>*

Joe joined in her laughter, shaking his head as the bridge crew stared at him questioningly. *<Bang on, Faleena.>*

<OK, I'll pass them your loving regards. See you on the other side, Dad.>

<On the other side.> Joe straightened and turned to Captain Tracey. "Faleena's sent everything on the stealthed Orion fleet here."

As he spoke, one hundred and seventy ships appeared on the holotank, dozens within firing range of the *Falconer.*

"Shit…uh, sir. That's a lot of ships."

"It sure is, Captain. And the moment the *Perilous Dream* jumps, they're going to fire on us, so we need to activate the stasis shields before they strike."

Captain Tracey nodded. "We can weather their attack, sir, but we can't jump with our stasis shields active."

Joe's eyes met Tracey's. "I'm activating the Gamma Protocol. Ready a full spread of pico missiles. We don't have time to dick around with these Orion ships."

Captain Tracey snapped off a crisp salute. "Yes, sir!"

Joe couldn't help but laugh at her enthusiasm, though he knew that there'd be hell to pay later for using the pico without authorization.

Not that he cared. He'd move the stars themselves if that was what it took to protect his daughters.

Now I just have to explain this to Tangel.

* * * * *

Terrance Enfield stood next to Earnest Redding as they reviewed the survey data that had been sent back from the drones roving around Astoria.

"Just like old times, eh?" Terrance asked.

Earnest gave him a sidelong glance. "Old times? I feel like we've never stopped doing this sort of thing. Scouring star systems, searching for something or another."

"Good point," Terrance replied. "Though I've been doing it for longer."

"No need to show off," Earnest replied with a laugh. "This is nuts, though. How can they produce enough drones to make a dyson swarm around a star the size of Astoria, yet we can't find where they made them?"

Terrance shrugged. "You know what they say, space is—"

"Seriously. Don't."

Earnest bent back over the holotank, and Terrance let out a sigh, nodding in understanding.

"I know. I'm worried too. It's an important strike."

"I feel like I should be there," Earnest replied. "It was as much my plan as Finaeus's."

"It's his ring. He had to go, and you're needed here. If the core AIs are doing what we think they're doing, it's a lot more dangerous than Airtha's war."

"In the long-term."

"Well, I plan to live a long time," Terrance laughed, placing a hand on Earnest's shoulder. "I'd like the galaxy to still be here for it."

"Yeah, I—wait, what's that?"

Terrance looked at the object Earnest was enlarging. "It's just a dwarf planet."

"Yeah, but look at where it is," the engineer said as he pulled the view back out. "It's not orbiting anything. It's almost entirely stationary in respect to the cluster's core stars."

"That's…"

"Very unlikely," Earnest completed the thought and focused back in on the dwarf planet as higher resolution images came in from the probes.

"That's one heck of a low albedo it has. Thing is almost pitch black," Terrance commented.

"Yeah, but there's something in the refraction indexes…. Wait a second."

Terrance did as Earnest bid, knowing that when the scientist needed a moment to think, it wasn't an idle request.

After three long minutes, Earnest straightened and whispered, "Oh shit."

"Spit it out, already," Terrance grunted.

Earnest gestured at the pitch-black planetoid. "It occluded several cluster stars when the probes were looking at it. I have mass estimates."

"And?"

"Terrance…I think that whole planet is just a cluster of machines."

* * * * *

Major Belos settled back into his station at the QuanComm relay center hidden deep within a nondescript moon in the Khardine system.

As per usual, there weren't a lot of messages moving across the network, just small updates regarding fleet positions and one-word status reports.

As mundane as it all seemed, that flow of information was the heartbeat of the Alliance war machine. Not only did it facilitate general efficiency, but with it, the brass could make split-second decisions about force allocation when a crisis arose.

The QuanComm network drastically reduced the fog of war on a galactic scale. It was an amazing innovation, and Belos played a crucial part in ensuring that the clipped messages were properly parsed and sent to the correct destination.

Something the voice promised to help with.

The whispering voice had come into Belos's mind the day before. It told him about how he'd be instrumental in ending the war if he just changed a few bits of information here and there.

He'd already changed a few earlier in the day, and was certain that every time he did, things were better as a result of his actions, always better.

I'm doing important work.

Just then, a message came in from Admiral Evans with an urgent update for the field marshal. It was closely followed by a message from Terrance Enfield, also destined for the field marshal.

She doesn't need those messages, the voice said. *She's very busy. They'll see her soon, anyway.*

Are you sure? Belos asked, feeling like these were just the sorts of messages he should *not* change or redirect.

I'm sure. These messages will distract her from an important task. Send them to the error queue.

Belos hesitated for a moment, a part of his mind telling him that the voice was wrong, that these messages were critical.

And then he did as the voice instructed, barely even remembering the action as he looked over the next batch of status updates.

I'll just tweak a word here, change a number there….

* * * * *

"I…are they going to live?" Sera asked Doctor Rosenberg as they stood deep within in the *I2*'s medical center, staring into the stasis tubes that held three copies of herself. Seraphina, Fina, and the latest incarnation that Airtha had created.

"I believe that Seraphina will be fine, I'll be removing her from stasis once we have the neural backups you made at Styx."

"And Fina?"

Sera had trouble looking at the ruin of the vibrant woman in blue. Her body had been sliced apart from the navel through the top of her head.

"The same…though less will be recoverable. If anything. I'd feel better working on her once Earnest is aboard. We're so short-staffed right now, and reintegrating minds is his specialty."

Sera gave a wordless nod as her gaze slipped to the white version of herself, who wasn't in significantly better condition than Fina. "I don't know if *she's* worth it. Maybe we'll just leave her."

"I'll let you think on it," Doctor Rosenberg said as Sera nodded absently and turned to leave the room. "Sera?" the doctor called after her.

"Yes?" she asked over her shoulder.

"Sabrina got there in the nick of time for both of them. Anything we can save of your sisters, we can thank her for."

Sera turned away and walked out into the corridor, still wondering why Sabrina had come straight for her. She would have expected the AI to go to Cheeky and Finaeus—especially since Seraphina had been injured first.

"How are you holding up?" Tangel asked as she approached, a tired smile on her face.

"Better than my sisters," Sera said in a small voice. "How's Amavia?"

"Lucky that she had a reinforced cranium," Tangel replied.

"Have you told her about Iris yet?" Sera asked.

"Yeah," Tangel nodded. "I wasn't going to at first, but she asked, and I couldn't lie. Stars...Jessica and Trevor are going to be devastated."

Sera pursed her lips, nodding silently.

Tangel placed her hands on Sera's shoulders, a resolute look in her eyes. "I know it sounds callous, but we need to look at this as a victory. A big victory. We destroyed Airtha *and* didn't damage the ring. For all intents and purposes, the Transcend's civil war is over."

Sera bit her lip, trying not to think of how that victory had spelled the death of the sisters she'd just gained.

After a moment, she met Tangel's eyes. "So when do we hit Orion?"

Tangel's shoulders heaved as she let out a sigh. "Oh, I don't know...can we rest for a few days first?"

"Yeah, that sounds like a good plan."

"Plus..." Tangel winked at Sera. "There are probably a few dozen Widows running around here somewhere."

Sera groaned. "Stars, there really is no rest for the weary."

THE END

* * * * *

THE ORION FRONT

THE ORION WAR – BOOK 9

BY M. D. COOPER

FOREWORD

When I was preparing to write this book, I was wandering around the Interwebs (as I often do) and I stumbled across an article on bacteria that feeds directly off electricity.

In essence, all life is really about electricity, which is to say, shuffling around free electrons to make different ionized things that we then use to keep ourselves alive. We breathe in oxygen so that our cells can push electrons into that element and keep a flow of energy going through our body.

Obviously, this is a super simplified version of a very complex biology, but an important part of it is that we (along with most lifeforms) are not capable of directly harvesting electrons from an electrical flow. We have to get them out of various compounds that will give up their valence electrons without a fuss.

However, as it turns out, if you stick a rod into moist soil or dirt from the seabed and pump electrons into it, you will find that bacteria begins to move to the rod. This bacteria (scientists are discovering that there are many, many types that do this) feeds directly off the electricity. They even form cables several centimeters long to channel energy to their buddies.

For reference, the first of these were discovered by Derek Lovely of the University of Massachusetts. He found them on the banks of the Potomac near Washington DC.

From a BBC article: "The microbes, called Geobacter metallireducens, were getting their electrons from organic compounds, and passing them onto iron oxides. In other words they were eating waste—including ethanol—and effectively 'breathing' iron instead of oxygen.... They are even able to effectively 'eat' pollution. They will convert the organic compounds in oil spills into carbon dioxide, or turn soluble radioactive metals like plutonium and uranium into insoluble forms that are less likely to contaminate groundwater—and they will generate electricity in the process."

Over the years, more and more of these bacteria have been found, and while many harvest their electrons from sources not available to most life, some are capable of sucking up raw electrons. Essentially, they can drink from the firehose.

I won't put in links, as those are likely to be no good after a time, but googling "bacteria that eat electricity" can start you down a rather fun rabbit hole.

Why is all of this noteworthy? Well, other than that the fact that I'm a huge nerd and I think it's cool, it's just amazing that such a thing exists...and that it has so much amazing potential to help us manage our environment. Of course, it might get used in some very interesting ways in the future too....

So, I should probably make this foreword about something in addition to the research. One thing of note is that I really took my time writing this book. I freed up my schedule a lot, and spent a lot of time just thinking about where to take this part of the story. I still know where it's all going, but there are parts of the journey that are fuzzy to me, and sussing out where the characters are going is half the fun of writing.

I think that some things are moving in interesting directions, and moreover, we're getting a lot more time with Tangel—who is really hard to write for because so much of her conflict is extradimensional, and not really describable to our 3D-oriented minds, at least not without making a lot of tiresome descriptions.

Luckily, some new challenges came along for her, and Tangel is going to have to grow in ways she didn't expect.

Malorie Cooper
Danvers 2019

PREVIOUSLY...

When last we left Tangel and the Allies, the assault teams striking against Airtha had defeated the Ascended AI and kept the Widows from destroying the ring.

The losses they suffered, however, were not inconsequential. Seraphina and Fina were gravely injured, and Iris was found with her core destroyed.

Elsewhere, Cary has assumed the role of A1, leader of the Widows, and has taken their flagship to the Karaske System to meet with General Garza. Though her plan is to take him out and cripple his network of spies and agents, she is falling deeper and deeper into her role as A1.

Joe is in pursuit of his daughters, and Terrance and Earnest have found the drone manufacturing facility where the core AIs are creating their diffuse dyson spheres to move stars.

And lastly, unbeknownst to the Alliance, the core AIs have infiltrated the QuanComm network at Khardine and are now privy to all of the Allies' communications—and are able to alter them....

KEY CHARACTERS

Airtha – Both the name of a ring encircling a white dwarf in the Huygens System and the AI who controls it, Airtha was once a human woman named Jelina, wife of Jeffrey Tomlinson. After venturing to the galactic core on a research mission, she returned as an AI—one with a vendetta.

Amavia – The result of Ylonda and Amanda's merger when they were attacked by Myriad aboard Ylonda's ship. The new entity occupies Amanda's body, but possesses an overlapped blend of their minds. Amavia has served aboard *Sabrina* since the ship left New Canaan after the Defense of Carthage, but is now the ambassador to the League of Sentients at Aldebaran.

Carmen – Ship's AI of the *Damon Silas*. Captured by Roxy during her assault on the ship.

Cary – Tangel's biological daughter. Has a trait where she can deep-Link with other people, creating a temporary merger of minds, and is able to utilize extradimensional vision to see ascended beings.

Cheeky – Pilot of *Sabrina*, reconstituted by a neural dump Piya made of her mind before she died on Costa Station.

Erin – Engineer responsible for the construction of the New Canaan Gamma bases, in addition to a number of other projects.

Faleena – Tangel's AI daughter, born of a mind merge between Tanis, Angela, and Joe.

Finaeus – Brother of Jeffrey Tomlinson, and Chief Engineer aboard the *I2*.

Helen – Former AI of Sera's who was killed by her father in the events leading up to Jeffrey's assassination. A copy of that shard was found to be on the Airthan ring as well.

Iris – The AI who was paired with Jessica during the hunt for Finaeus, who then took on a body (that was nearly identical to Jessica's) after they came back. She remained with Amavia at Aldebaran to continue diplomatic relations with the League of Sentients.

Jeffrey Tomlinson – Former president of the Transcend, found in stasis in an underground chamber on Bolt Hole, a planet in the Large Magellanic Cloud.

Jen – ISF AI paired with Sera.

Jessica Keller – ISF admiral who has returned to the *I2* after an operation deep in the Inner Stars to head off a new AI war. She also spent ten years traveling through Orion space before the Defense of Carthage—specifically the Perseus Arm, and Perseus Expansion Districts.

Joe – Admiral in the ISF, commandant of the ISF academy, and husband of Tangel.

Kara – Daughter of Adrienne, Kara was rescued by Katrina when fleeing from Airtha, and came to New Canaan aboard the *Voyager*.

Katrina – Former Sirian spy, wife of Markus, and eventual governor of the Victoria colony at Kapteyn's Star—and Warlord of the Midditerra System.

Krissy Wrentham – TSF admiral responsible for internal fleets fighting against Airtha in the Transcend civil war. She is also the daughter of Finaeus Tomlinson and Lisa Wrentham.

Lisa – Former wife of Finaeus Tomlinson, she left the Transcend for the Orion Freedom Alliance when Krissy was young. Head of a clandestine group within the OFA known as the Widows, which hunts down advanced technology and destroys it.

Misha – Head (and only) cook aboard *Sabrina*.

Nance – Ship's engineer aboard *Sabrina*, recently transferred back there from the ISF academy.

Priscilla – One of Bob's two avatars.

Rachel – Captain of the *I2*. Formerly, captain of the *Enterprise*.

Roxy – Justin's sister, kept subservient to him as his lover via mental coercion.

Saanvi – Tangel's adopted daughter, found in a derelict ship that entered the New Canaan System.

Sabrina – Ship's AI and owner of the starship *Sabrina*.

Sera – Director of the Hand and former president of the Transcend. Daughter of Airtha and Jeffrey Tomlinson.

LMC Sera (Seraphina) – A copy of Sera made by Airtha containing all of Sera's desired traits and memories. Captured by Sera and the allies during their excursion into the Large Magellanic Cloud.

Valkris Sera (Fina) – A copy of Sera made by Airtha containing all of Sera's desired traits and memories. Captured by ISF response forces who came to the aid of the TSF defenders during the siege of Valkris.

Terrance – Terrance Enfield was the original backer for the *Intrepid*, though once the ship jumped forward in time, he took it as an opportunity to retire. Like Jason, he was pulled into active service by Tangel when New Canaan became embroiled in the Orion War.

Troy – AI pilot of the *Excelsior* who was lost during the Battle of Victoria, and later found by Katrina. He joined her on the hunt for the *Intrepid* aboard the *Voyager*, jumping forward in time via Kapteyn's Streamer.

Tangel – The entity that resulted from Tanis and Angela's merger into one being. Not only is Tangel a full merger of a human and AI, but she is also an ascended being.

Usef – ISF Colonel who served on *Sabrina* for several years, as well as aided Erin in stopping several acts of sabotage in New Canaan.

PART 1 – FAILURE

STAR CITY EXPRESS

STELLAR DATE: 10.03.8949 (Adjusted Years)
LOCATION: ISS *Lantzer*
REGION: Buffalo, Albany System, Theban Alliance

Six days before the assault on Airtha; the same day Tangel faced Xavia in Aldebaran…

"How does it feel to be at the helm of a cruiser again," Trevor asked Jessica as the pair walked toward the bridge's central holotank.

"Well…" Jessica winked at him. "Ensign Lucida is really at the helm. I'm just the skipper. So for me, it's about the same as being captain of *Sabrina*."

Her husband lifted an eyebrow, regarding her with his dark, serious eyes. After a moment, a smile quirked the corners of his mouth, and he shook his head. "You miss *Sabrina* already, don't you?"

She resisted the urge to smack him on the arm. "Stars, yes! Don't you? *Sabrina* was your home almost as long as she was mine. Core, I'd even take the chickens right about now."

"It's only been a day."

Jessica ignored his comment and swiped a hand through the holo, pivoting the visual of surrounding space until the *I2* was centered on the display.

"I just…I dunno," she finally responded. "We're making a jump through Stillwater again. Last time we did that, it took a decade to get home."

"Sure," Trevor nodded compassionately and placed a hand on Jessica's shoulder. "Granted, the first time, we made an emergency jump with a mirror built out of spare parts. Then someone reoriented the gate at the last minute, trying to send us right out of the galaxy. Sort of a once-in-a-lifetime event. Besides, we've made plenty of jumps since then that got us right where we wanted to go."

Jessica slid her hand along Trevor's back and hooked it around his waist. "Yeah, I know. Not the same. Plus, the *Lantzer* has four gates aboard, so if we run into trouble, we'll have a lot of options."

"Yup, so long as we survive the jump."

Jessica turned to give Trevor a sharp look, but saw that he was grinning at her with a twinkle in his eye.

"Stars, man," she muttered. "I'm going to make you leave the bridge if you talk like that."

"Sent to the cargo hold." His voice carried a tone of mock sadness. "Feeling like home already."

A laugh slipped past Jessica's lips, garnering the attention of the rest of the bridge crew. "OK, people. We're next in the queue. How're we looking?"

"My board is green," Ensign Lucida said, followed by a response from Lieutenant Karma, who was managing both Scan and Comm.

"All systems nominal," he said.

<*I confirm all systems are ready for jump,*> Gil, the ship's AI, added.

Other than the five people present on the bridge, the kilometer-long cruiser only had six additional people aboard: two engineers, and a fireteam of ISF Marines. Jessica checked in on them personally, and once they acknowledged readiness for the jump, she signaled the bridge crew to take the ship through the gate.

"Buffalo Tower acknowledges the gate vector is set for Star City," Karma said with a note of clear anticipation in his voice. "Damn, I can't wait to see that thing."

"You're telling me," Trevor said. "Granted, I care more about the people there than Star City itself."

Jessica snorted. "I'm sure our kids will be glad to hear that."

"Oh, not our kids. I meant the Dreamers." Trevor gave her a wink.

"Funny man."

"We're aligned with the gate, Admiral," Lucida announced.

<*Mirror is deployed,*> Gil chimed in. <*Ship is configured for jump.*>

Jessica turned to face the forward holodisplay, which showed their assigned jump gate and the planet Buffalo beyond.

"Take us in," she directed.

Lucida fired the maneuvering thrusters, using them to ease the ship forward. It coasted through space for a few seconds, and then a shudder ran through the deck. Jessica shifted her gaze to a nearby console, looking for any alerts.

<*Miscalibration,*> Gil said a second later. <*One of the thrusters burned out of spec for a moment, and the compensator…well…overcompensated.*>

Jessica and Trevor shared a look, neither speaking what was on their minds.

The *Lantzer*, like many of the ISF's ships, was newly constructed and had only seen the most cursory of shakedown runs. Considering the speed at which the ISF was building spacecraft, the failure rates were surprisingly low, but a small percentage of ships did suffer significant malfunctions after being put into service.

Just get us to Star City, you bucket of bolts, Jessica thought. A moment later, she chastised herself and sent a wordless apology to the ship.

It was possible that the *Lantzer* would be the deck beneath her feet for some time; thinking ill of her ship wasn't a good way to start a relationship with it. Of course, it was also possible that Tangel would make good on her threat and put Jessica in command of a fleet—in which case, she'd likely transfer to an I-Class ship.

Just the thought of that sent a pang of regret through her. She had *loved* being captain of *Sabrina*. It had always felt right to her. The notion of having an entire fleet of ISF ships—and the lives therein—under her command caused a flutter of worry to settle in her breast. New Canaan's resources, especially the ones that took the form of humans and AIs, were so very rare. The concern that she'd spend lives foolishly was one that had taken firm root within her mind.

Another small vibration ran through the deck, and she shot a questioning look at one of Gil's optics.

<*I've killed that thruster,*> the AI said. <*Just couldn't get it to behave. Might be the fuel intermixer.*>

"Don't worry, ma'am." Lucida glanced over her shoulder as she spoke. "I could fly this beautiful girl with half her maneuvering jets. She handles like a dream."

<*Contact with the mirror in fifteen seconds.*>

"Steady as she goes," Jessica whispered, her eyes on the twisting knot of nothing in the center of the jump gate.

In moments, the mirror mounted on the front of the ship would touch the mouth of the artificial singularity in the center of the gate, stretching it out and drawing the *Lantzer* around its edge. The effect was that of using a wormhole without having to pass through the event horizon of a black hole.

Something Jessica was certain no one wanted to do.

Trevor was right. They'd passed through gates dozens of times since that first jump. But ever since landing on the fringe of human expansion and facing a decade-long journey home, Jessica hadn't been able to look at a gate without feeling some amount of trepidation.

<*Mark,*> Gil called out as the ship's mirror touched the gate's mass of not-space, interrupting her thoughts.

For a moment, everything seemed to twist around her. Then the ship jumped.

At first, all was normal, but then the forward holodisplay went from the nothing of jump space to flashing a kaleidoscope of colors. At the same time, alarms began to wail and every console showed red. Then a shockwave rippled through the ship, and the bridge fell into darkness.

Jessica grabbed onto the edge of the holotank as another shockwave hit them, but her grip wasn't strong enough, and she was flung across the bridge, slamming into the forward bulkhead before falling to the deck.

WHERE ARE WE?

STELLAR DATE: 10.03.8949 (Adjusted Years)
LOCATION: ISS *Lantzer*
REGION: Unknown

Jessica lay prone on the deck for what felt like an eternity, trying to make sense of why everything hurt so much, while wondering why the emergency lighting hadn't yet come on.

Then she remembered that she didn't need lighting, both because she had excellent night vision, and because her skin could glow.

Which it already was.

OK…brain seems to be finally working again, she thought with a rueful laugh as she examined the deck around her, noting that she was half-propped up against the bridge's forward bulkhead.

"Trevor?" she asked, casting about for her husband while deploying a nanocloud to begin scouring the bridge.

"Here…"

The word was followed by a long groan to Jessica's left, and she held up a hand, increasing the glow coming from her palm.

Trevor lay on his side, a trail of blood coming from his mouth as he worked his jaw slowly.

"Is it bad?" she asked.

"No, just bit my tongue. And I might have broken a finger…or two."

"Karma? Lucida? Sound off," Jessica called out as she rose on shaky legs and walked to Trevor's side. "So you're saying you'll live?" she asked him.

He grunted and pushed himself upright as Lucida spoke up.

"I think I will too…though I feel like I could also be dead."

"Here too. Though I smashed my console," Karma added.

"Gil?"

Jessica didn't expect the AI to respond. If the bridge systems were completely offline, the AI wouldn't have any way to hear or respond to them, which seemed to be the case.

"What *happened?*" Karma asked, the sound of a harness unbuckling coming from his direction.

Lucida coughed out a rueful laugh. "Aren't you supposed to know? You're on Scan."

"No scan on a jump," he retorted. "Though I did catch sight of weird colors on the forward display. I've never seen that before."

"Me either," Jessica replied. "Stars…there's no active EM anywhere, other than the a-grav decking and my skin. Why aren't emergency systems coming back online?"

"Probably the same reason half my mods aren't responding," Trevor said. "That was one hell of an EM spike that hit us when we…stopped? Is that what we did?"

Jessica checked her internal logs and saw that her mods had registered an EM spike, but the energy surge hadn't done any significant damage to her.

"OK, that *was* a big burst. I seem to be alright, though. Benefit of being…well…me, I guess."

"You just love energy," Trevor said as he carefully straightened a finger. "Uh…I was going to follow that with something clever, but I've got nothing."

"Shit—uh, sir," Karma said as he watched Trevor move onto his second broken finger. "That's just nasty."

"Then don't look."

"OK," Jessica turned to look over the two ensigns, who were both in better shape, thanks to having been strapped in. "We need to get core systems back online, which means accessing the hardened node two decks down and running a re-init. We also need to check on Gil and the rest of the crew."

"I've got the core," Trevor said. "*Sabrina* had a scaled-down version of this backup model."

"I'll get to Gil," Karma said. "He and I go way back."

"Should I search out everyone else?" Lucida asked, looking worried and a little scared. "What do you think did this, anyway?"

" 'This' as in knocked us out of the jump, or fried the ship?" Trevor asked with a guttural laugh. "Sorry…nervous energy."

"Well, both, I guess," Lucida replied, her own warbling laugh following her words.

"There's a lot of power involved in a jump," Jessica said. "Gates aren't powered by piddly stuff like fusion generators. Could be that we had a mirror failure, and some of that energy passed directly into the ship—or it could have been something else entirely."

Karma pressed a hand to his temple and groaned. "Whatever it was, I'm starting to feel like it all grounded out in my head."

"You'll survive," Trevor grunted.

Jessica chuckled softly while walking across the bridge to the emergency locker. She opened it to reveal a dozen EV suits and pulse pistols.

"Suit up, kids, we could have breaches," she instructed while pulling out a suit for herself. Her skin made it so that vacuum wasn't a concern, and she could rebreathe the same air for several minutes, but she wasn't going to risk her life unnecessarily.

Trevor and the ensigns grabbed suits, and as they geared up, Jessica passed out additional directives.

"Lucida, you head down the starboard concourse. That'll get you to engineering faster. I'll take the port side. Drop comm buoys and stay in touch. Anyone gets a chance to look out an inspection port, do it. I want to know if anything is out there…and where we are."

The ensigns gave affirmative responses and left the bridge ahead of Trevor, who stopped to give Jessica a quick embrace.

"You be careful, glow girl."

"I will, you just get that hardened node online and initialize repair systems."

"Easy," Trevor replied, his tone calm and soothing. "We'll have the ship rolling…well…soonish."

Jessica realized that she must have been speaking with more intensity than she meant to and ducked her head in a quick nod. "Of course we will. Then we'll figure out where the heck we are."

"Maybe we'll look outside and see Star City looming nearby," he replied.

"Core, that would be fantastic."

They walked together down the passageway that led from the bridge, Jessica's lavender glow lighting the way, until they came to a ladder shaft, where they were to go their separate ways. Trevor gave her another brief embrace before stepping into the shaft and dropping down to his destination deck.

<Holler if you run into trouble,> he said, utilizing one of the comm buoy's the ensigns had dropped.

<You too,> Jessica replied before resuming her journey to the port-side concourse.

Well…after I go look outside. I'm starting to feel like that's a priority.

Following her gut, Jessica worked her way up the tech decks to the ship's dorsal arch. The a-grav decking was offline closer to the hull, and she was able to pick up speed, pulling herself along handholds until she finally reached the airlock that led to the observation dome.

Though she'd passed through a few sections of the ship where emergency power was active—which had been a relief—such was not the case with the airlock. She debated using the manual system or attempting to power it herself.

No…you might need your juice later, she decided.

Instead, she pulled open the panel and attached the door-jack's handle, pumping it several times to pressurize the emergency hydraulics. The interior of the airlock still registered as containing atmosphere, so once the system was primed, she pulled open the door and stepped inside. Readings showed that the observation dome on the far side was also pressurized, so she quickly repeated the process on the exterior door.

When she pushed the outer door open, she was met by the brilliant glow of space. After moving through the inky black ship, the light of the cosmos was a welcome sight. She pushed herself up to the top of the observation dome and grabbed a handhold. Muting her glow as much as possible, she peered out and tried to get her bearings.

"OK..." she murmured while slowly spinning around. "There's the galactic disk...and that's the core and the Aquilla Rift. There's the Orion Nebula..."

Jessica continued to turn until she saw another nebula, a wall of dust and gas that stretched on for hundreds of light years in either direction. She knew it by sight, having had it dominate her travels for many years.

"And there's Stillwater. Fan-fucking-tastic." She took a breath and then tapped into one of the comm buoys. *<Trevor, you there?>*

<Yup. At the hardened node, just getting everything set up for it to kick off repairs. I had this fear that I'd get down here and find that the node wasn't properly stocked, but its batts are fully charged, and the drone closets are full. I'm setting a priority for it to get drones to the aft nodes and initialize them too.>

<Good, that's really good.> Jessica had harbored a similar fear. *<I went to the obs dome. From the looks of it, we're about a hundred light years on the coreward side of Stillwater.>*

<Any sign of what kicked us out of the jump? Was it an interdictor system?>

<One that spans the inner edge of the Perseus Arm of the galaxy? I doubt it.>

Trevor was silent for a moment, and then said, *<What about one that would be in place to block approaches to Star City?>*

The implications of his statement were not lost on Jessica, but even so, she doubted that was the case. Space was just too big to effectively block jump gate travel on a multitude of vectors. She only knew of three systems that had interdictors blocking such travel, and they all did it right at the heliopause.

<Let's hope that's not it. If someone can block a jump across a thousand-light-year spread, then we're effed.>

As Jessica spoke, a glimmer of light caught her attention, and she turned. She peered at the twinkling light for a moment before it flared into star-like brilliance.

Shit...not a star. That's a ship, decelerating on approach.

<Lucida, you found the Marines yet?> she asked the ensign.

<Not yet, but I'm almost at their barracks.>

<Double-time it. We've got company.>

Karma spoke up a second later. *<I've just reached Gil's chamber.... Annnddd he's alive. Patching him into our wireless network.>*

<Admiral, I'm sorry, I don't—> the AI began, but Jessica cut him off.

<Not your fault, Gil. I suspect enemy action. There's a ship inbound. Given our position just coreward of Stillwater, I'm thinking Orion Guard.>

<Dammit. I'm totally blind down here,> Gil replied. *<I don't know how everything got so fried, either. The sensor readings during the jump were normal, then suddenly it was like....>*

<Like what?> Trevor prompted.

The AI sent a feeling laden with disbelief. *<Like we skirted too close to the singularity. I wonder if we had a mirror failure on the bow?>*

<*Well, we can review all that later. Right now, we need helm and shields, ASAP,*> Jessica ordered.

<*Ma'am,*> Corporal Jay spoke up a second later. <*Lucida just linked us up with your comm network. I sent Peers and Marc back to check on engineering. Meg and I will come to you.*>

<*No, Corporal,*> Jessica replied. <*I want you to go back with Lucida and check on chiefs Glenn and West. Whatever they need, you do it. Helm and shields, that's our only priority right now.*>

<*Yes, ma'am,*> came Corporal Jay's response.

<*Gil, I don't have all of the blueprints in my head. Are there any emergency batts I can hook up to power the dorsal sensors? I'd really like to know more about this ship that's coming to pay us a visit.*>

<*Wouldn't we all,*> the AI responded. <*If you go back down to deck two, there's an SC array in Bay 2-19A. Inventory shows two shielded batts in there that aren't connected to anything. You should be able to connect them to the mains for that section of the ship and power the sensor array.*>

<*OK, I'm on it,*> Jessica replied.

She gave the approaching ship a final look, gauging its rate of deceleration. A quick estimate put its time of arrival to be a little less than three hours.

We came out practically on top of it. No way that's coincidence.

<*I'm going to check out the forward reactor,*> Trevor said. <*That thing should still be live, must have just tripped its linkages.*>

Jessica sent an affirmative response and tuned out the conversation that Trevor, Gil, and Karma began to have regarding reinitializing the reactor. She closed the outer airlock door behind herself, then, despite a temptation to hurry, followed suit with the inner door.

No point in rushing, and killing us later from decompression.

Five minutes after exiting the observation dome, she reached Bay 2-19A and was pleasantly surprised to find that not only was a-grav working, but the bay's door was powered up. However, when it opened, smoke poured out into the passageway, and she saw heat signatures on the IR band.

<*Shit, got fire here,*> she announced.

<*Repair drones have spotted a few as well,*> Gil commented, sounding largely unconcerned.

<*Yeah, but there's power here. The suppression systems should have kicked in.*>

<*Should be a foamer down the hall in closet 2-19CA,*> the AI supplied.

Jessica sent a quick thanks and dashed down the hall to the closet, where she found a pair of foam guns and a pulse suppressor. She grabbed all three and ran back to the bay's door, cursing herself for not having closed it and inadvertently feeding the fire fresh oxygen.

Stepping inside, Jessica closed the door behind herself and looked over the shapes of the SC batts, looking for the largest blaze. A second later, she spotted flames dancing through the acrid smoke, and moved forward, firing the suppressor's pulses to clear the smoke.

<*Shit,*> she muttered when the source of the blaze became visible. <*It's the primary junction.*>

<*Something must be discharging to make that thing burn,*> Gil said.

Jessica didn't reply, instead spraying foam over the power junction, dousing the fire before looking around for any smaller blazes.

<*On the plus side, fire means that the batts are still holding charges,*> she commented as she swept through the bay, putting out several other smaller fires. <*Just not sure how I'll hook them up to the mains.*>

<*Did you find the hardened batteries?*> Gil asked. <*They should be along the bulkhead furthest from the door.*>

Jessica angled to her right, weaving amongst the waist-high cylinders until she spotted two larger shapes through the haze.

<*OK, I think so. Yes, found them.*>

<*Good.*> The AI sounded relieved. <*Now, there should be cabling for each in a cabinet at the end of the row.*>

Jessica fired the suppressor's pulses to clear more of the smoke away as she searched for the cabinet. When she found it, the doors were twisted from the heat. A few tugs, and they came open to reveal two empty hooks.

<*You sure this is where they're supposed to be? I've got bupkiss.*>

<*Well, that's standard buildout. I don't have access to the full inventory databanks.*>

Jessica knew of a few places where there should be more cabling, but none were close, and there were no guarantees that they'd be properly stocked, either.

<*I'm going to take one of the batts with me to the sensor node,*> she said. <*Just need to kill a-grav so I can maneuver it.*>

<*OK…*> the AI replied, going silent for a moment. <*I've tapped into the grav systems in your area through the wireless network. Just give me a second, safety overrides aren't responding.*>

Moving to the left-most SC batt, Jessica crouched next to it and found the release tool slotted into the base of the battery's case.

At least you're where you're supposed to be.

A minute later, she had the battery's mounts free. She turned to give the room another review, now that the smoke had cleared. Two of the other SC batteries were still online, their 'active' lights glowing green, holodisplays showing a trickle of discharge, which meant they were still connected to something. She moved closer and saw that they were both connected to a separate junction than the one that had been on fire.

<*Gil, what does the forward junction in this bay feed?*>

<*That's what's powering a-grav and environmental on decks one, two, and three. Forward of the ship's spine, that is.*>

<*Well, deck two, at least,*> Jessica replied. <*When I was up on one, it had no a-*

grav.>

<No? Damn. Must have blown another junction toward the bow as well. If that's the case, you're going to have to take that batt right up to the scan node and power the sensor array from there.>

<That's what I was expecting. Just kill the a-grav already. I don't fancy the idea of muscling a ton of battery through the corridors.>

<Almost done…>

A few seconds later, Jessica felt the pull of gravity fade away and bring about a natural inclination to hunker down and stay near the deck. Of course that always had the opposite reaction, and she lifted off a few centimeters.

Pay attention to what you're doing, woman.

Quickly reorienting her senses to a world of unimpeded reaction, Jessica grabbed the battery case's handles and pulled. Her feet hit the deck again, and the battery slowly lifted into the air. Once it had risen a meter, she got behind it and pushed.

Getting the battery into the passageway took a few seconds, and then the following ten minutes were spent maneuvering it down corridors and up a maintenance tube to the first deck.

The literal ton of superconductor battery was cumbersome and unwieldy, and Jessica hated every minute spent getting it to the sensor node, worrying about the approaching ship and how they knew nothing about it. She opened the door, fearing smoke and fire once more, but found the chamber dark, and the air clear.

Thank stars.

She muscled the battery inside and then quickly latched it to the deck next to the room's primary power interchange. Luck was finally on her side, and she found an auxiliary power cable where it was supposed to be and quickly connected the battery to it.

The batt's activity light came on, casting a green hue around the room.

<OK,> Jessica didn't bother hiding the relief from her mental tone as the node began to initialize. *<Looks like the node isn't damaged.>*

<I think that whatever tagged us did more damage to the larger electrical systems,> Gil said. *<Trevor and Karma are at the reactor now. Plasma containment died, and some coils burned out. They're replacing them, then we should have full power forward of the spine.>*

<Wherever said power can get to,> Jessica replied.

<Well, yeah. That.>

She busied herself with reviewing the sensor node's initialization process, noting that several subsystems remained offline, but that the main radio antennas were active, as was the wide-band dish. Two of the optical scopes were also online, feeding images down to the console in the room, though only one's tracking servos were responding.

<OK, got a scope on our friend, and the antennas are picking up the ship's EM signature.>

<Doesn't seem like an Orion Guard sig,> Gil mused as the gamma ray patterns coming off the approaching ship were analyzed by the node.

<Lot of ships out here in the PED,> Jessica replied. *<Could be an old patrol boat that doesn't see regular service, or something new we haven't seen before.>*

<That's a heck of a big patrol boat,> Gil replied as the node analyzed the approaching ship's burn and deceleration, calculating newtons of thrust and ship mass. *<Based on the hull profile visible past the engine flare, it's…damn, it's at least a klick long. Doesn't match any hulls in my local databanks.>*

<Weird for a cruiser to be operating alone out here,> Jessica said, programming the sensor array to sweep the surrounding area for more ships, desperately hoping not to find any—even if finding others would decrease the mystery surrounding the approaching ship.

<Shit…we're three light years from the closest star, too,> Gil said after a moment.

Jessica nodded, looking at the stellar cartography map that was beginning to form on the holo in front of her, deepening the mystery of what could have pulled them out of the jump.

<No other ships, yet,> she commented. *<Though they could be stealthed. The scan we can manage right now isn't that far above total blindness.>*

<Admiral Jessica!>

A new voice entered her mind, and Jessica breathed a sigh of relief as she identified Chief Glenn.

<Chief. Stars, it's good to hear you in my noggin. West OK too?>

<She broke her arm, but we got to a functional med closet. She's in the tube right now, getting her heal on.>

<Good. Your assessment of our situation?>

The man sent a snort. *<I was hoping you could tell me. Lucida gave me the quick version, but she also mentioned another ship out there….>*

<Yeah. We'll have company in two and a half hours, give or take a bit.>

<Well, that's a little suspicious.>

Jessica laughed. *<Tell me about it. Look, you know the drill. Shields and burners. The Marines and Lucida are at your disposal. Get them rolling. Trevor and Karma are working on the forward reactor, and the emergency drones are getting started.>*

<So we just have to go from fried, cold, and dead in the water to fighting strength in two and a half hours? CriEns are all offline, by the way. Rapid discharge safeties triggered. Going to take longer than a few hours to get them back up.> Chief Glenn's voice was laden with worry and skepticism.

<Do what you can, Chief,> Jessica replied, knowing that their options were limited.

<Of course. Any other miracles you need today, ma'am?>

<Well, if you happen to figure out what dropped us out of the jump, that would be

nice too.>

<*I'll see if I can find an oracle to consult,*> the engineer replied with another snort, followed by a slightly more deferential, <*Ma'am.*>

<*Be sure to ask it who our visitors are,*> Jessica replied before switching to address the entire crew. <*I'm patching scan onto our wireless network. Then I'm going to go see if there are any functional ships in the forward bays. Everyone, stay on task. Trevor and Karma, once you get that reactor repaired, weapons are your next priority.*>

A series of affirmative responses came before Trevor reached out privately.

<*What are you hoping to do if you find a working ship?*> he asked.

<*Stars, just about anything. Flee, attack, misdirect. Depends on what I find.*>

<*Attack?*>

<*Well, if there's an ARC-6A in there, I could probably take on an Orion cruiser with it—so long as it has enough power to run the stasis shields.*>

<*Won't a 6A have a CriEn?*> Trevor asked.

<*Yeah, but our main banks all went offline. The ones in the ARCs probably did as well.*>

<*And you're just going to fly it right out at the enemy? Without shields?*> Trevor's tone carried equal measures skepticism and worry.

<*Well. I'm not going to 'fly it right out' at anyone,*> Jessica chuckled softly, <*unless it has functional stasis shields. Either way, sending a few fighters out on remote, even just for the extra sensors, would be a good idea. It's hard to see much of that approaching ship, with its engine wash pointed right at us.*>

<*OK…just don't do anything crazy, kay, Jess?*>

<*Crazy?*> Jessica laughed. <*Me?*>

Trevor only sent back guarded cough.

She reached the first bay almost ten minutes later. It was only a hundred meters away from the sensor node, but the number of sealed doors she had to manually open slowed her progress considerably.

Spoiled by doors. Who would have thought it?

The center of the bay was occupied by a mid-sized pinnace. She didn't even need to board the ship to know it wasn't going anywhere. Half its hull was scorched and covered in still-dripping fire-suppression foam from the bay's systems.

However, the rack on the aft side of the docking bay held a dozen ARC-6A fighters, and by some miracle, they all appeared unscathed by whatever had damaged the pinnace.

<*Gil, can you work on the bay doors?*>

<*I can, but environmental and grav shields aren't responding in that bay.*>

<*I've got my EV suit, crack the doors slowly.*>

Jessica walked to the dockmaster's cabin that was set along the interior wall, and breathed a sigh of relief to see that the racking systems were active. She triggered the system to slide out one of the fighters, and then ambled toward the egg-shaped ship as it was set onto the hull.

<You're going to have to get changed,> the AI advised her. *<The gel compartment within the ARC won't calibrate properly with that bulky EV suit.>*

Jessica was surprised to hear that. *<Even with a-grav, we still need shoot suits?>*

<Didn't you look over the specs on the 6As?> the AI admonished.

<No.> She resisted the urge to send Gil an unpleasant glare. *<I've barely been with the fleet these past twenty years, remember? I just assumed that, with a-grav, the 6As would have regular cockpits. No shoot suits or gel cocoons necessary.>*

<Tangel likes fallback systems.>

Jessica sighed, ade picked himself use. A-grav could get knocked out, and if the pilot was encased in a shoot suit and safely tucked inside an ARC's gel pocket, they could put up more of a fight than an enemy would expect.

She saw the suiting chamber to the left of the rack and hurried toward it, knowing that the process would take a few minutes.

"Oh, crap, it's offline," she muttered when the access panel wouldn't respond.

Casting about for options, she saw a panel next to the chamber labeled 'Emergency SCLSS'. Pulling it open, she saw a sealed packet and a helmet. She set the helmet on the deck, then quickly pulled off her EV suit, followed by the uniform underneath.

Ignoring the chill in the air, she tore open the SCLSS packet, and a rubbery mass fell into her hands. She quickly unfurled the shoot suit, struggling to grasp the slippery white second skin that appeared to be far too small. For a moment, Jessica considered forgoing the suit, but she knew that the fighter's piloting systems would expect the suit's hookups, and reprogramming its inputs would take longer than getting dressed. Finally locating the fastener, she pulled it down and slipped inside the suit's compressive confines.

Once all the ports were seated, she pulled on the helmet and did her best to ignore the suit as it tested bio-feedback systems while she walked to the fighter.

<OK. I'm sealed,> she said while walking beneath the ARC-6A she'd unracked. *<You can crack the bay doors whenever you're ready.>*

<I'm venting atmosphere through the emergency discharge,> Gil replied. *<I'd rather not bend the bay doors with explosive decompression.>*

<I suppose that's wise,> Jessica said as she sent a command to the fighter to let her in.

Above her, part of the hull irised open, and she saw the familiar gel pod within. An a-grav column drew her up, and within seconds, she was nestled within the fighter's gel-filled cocoon. Connections snaked through the viscous liquid, connecting her to the ship, and then a prompt appeared on her HUD for sensory changeover.

She didn't immediately accept the request, first running the fighter through a full diagnostic routine. It came back with only two secondary subsystems showing damage, and she decided that was likely as good as she could expect from any of the ships.

With a thought, she accepted the prompt to change over her senses, and an instant later, her 'skin' was no longer at the edge of her body, but rather at that of the ARC-6A's hull. Her legs were the ship's engines, her arms the weapons and maneuvering thrusters, and her eyes were its sensor arrays.

<*Doors opening,*> Gil announced.

<*I see that,*> Jessica replied, triggering the fighter's a-grav thrusters and lifting off the deck.

She skirted around the damaged pinnace on her way to the dark rectangle that lay beyond the bay doors.

Stars, I've missed this, she thought, savoring the feeling of the ship as her body, remembering the countless hours spent in the ARC-5s back in the Kap.

That memory sparked thoughts of the battle she'd fought against the Sirian scout ships, followed by the days waiting for rescue out in the deep black beyond the system's heliopause.

Not this time, she told herself, though she wasn't sure if her sentiment was that she wouldn't be lost, or that if things went badly, there was no hope for rescue.

Once outside the ship, Jessica activated the ARC's stealth systems and pushed the ship forward on a column of gravitons, angling slightly away from the approaching vessel in an attempt to get a view of its profile.

The approaching craft was still several light seconds away, and its delta-*v* had decreased, along with the amount of thrust coming off its engines. Once Jessica's ARC was a dozen kilometers from the *Lantzer*, she was finally able to get an unobstructed view of the approaching vessel.

Well that's a weird one, she thought, as the fighter's sensors built up a picture of the approaching cruiser.

It was just over a kilometer long, though it was also wider than she'd initially thought. There was a curved dorsal arch, not dissimilar from the *Lantzer*'s, that terminated in a spherical section at the ship's bow. Hanging from the arch were dozens of hundred-meter shafts. Her impression was that the ship resembled a fish's skeleton.

That initial observation triggered the next: the ship appeared to have very little in the way of crew areas. Other than a few corridors running from the sphere at the bow to the engines, she suspected that there were almost no internal passageways within the bulk of the craft.

The sphere was a hundred meters across, which meant a crew of less than a few dozen at most, and Jessica felt a measure of relief to know that they weren't about to face off with a company of soldiers boarding the *Lantzer*.

Of course, I could just blow it out of the stars before it gets to us.

Jessica examined the enemy ship, selecting primary targets and programming her weapons to strike them with a single thought. The next problem she faced was that her single ship couldn't shoot its way through the cruiser's shields. However, if she built up enough delta-*v*, she could punch through them with her ARC and then fire on the targets during her flyby.

But first, I want to know what I'm up against.

Once her offensive options with the approaching fishbone ship were established, she pulled up the visuals of the *Lantzer*, passive scan sweeping over her own cruiser, looking for signs of external damage.

At a glance, it appeared that there were none, but closer examination showed scoring on several sensor arrays and sections of hull. None of it was structural in nature, but instead pointed to the ship being caught up in a massive electromagnetic surge—which was not surprising at this point, just not terribly informative, either.

Over the next thirty minutes, Jessica continued to drift toward the still-decelerating enemy ship while maintaining a tightbeam comm line back to the *Lantzer*.

While she'd been drifting through the black, Trevor and Karma had repaired the forward reactor, and Chief Glenn had brought the aft reactor online. Both powerplants were running at minimal output while the teams worked to disconnect damaged systems from the power grid before energizing more areas of the ship.

The chief's fears about the CriEn modules had turned out to be correct. They'd completely shut down and would need to be carefully reactivated. For now, Jessica had directed the crew to continue their focus on shields and helm. They wouldn't need CriEn levels of energy to power stasis shields against just one enemy cruiser—she hoped.

<*Don't get too far out there,*> Trevor admonished, as Jessica neared a distance of fifty thousand kilometers from the *Lantzer*.

<*I won't, I'm just going to ease toward it and let it pass by nice and close. See what passive scan can pick up at just a few dozen klicks.*>

<*Sure is a weird-looking ship,*> he commented. <*What are all those long spikes coming off the central spine for?*>

<*Beats me,*> Jessica replied. <*Well, maybe…. It reminds me a bit of a drone ship.*>

<*A what?*>

Jessica pulled up the memory of one of the ancient Scattered Worlds ships and sent the image to her husband.

<*The SWSF used them to patrol the outer reaches of the Sol System. They had small crews, just a dozen, but they could deploy drone swarms of up to several thousand per ship.*>

<*That's a lot more than we could deal with right now.*> Trevor's voice contained a new note of worry. <*Let's hope that's not the case.*>

<*Well, the fun thing about most people who deploy drones is that they're paranoid, and usually not keen on the drones having high levels of autonomy. Take out the command and control system, and the drones die, or at least become a lot less effective.*>

<*I vote for drone death. I don't even feel bad about it.*>

Jessica laughed. <*I'm with you. OK, I'm coming up on my closest approach. That ship is going to pass between me and the* Lantzer. *Severing comms till I'm far enough on the other side.*>

<*You got it. Be careful.*>

<*Always.*>

<*Liar.*>

Despite her words, the ominous ship had Jessica on edge. It hadn't made any attempt to communicate with the *Lantzer*, and its deceleration vector was such that it would come to zero delta-*v* only fifteen kilometers distant from the ISF cruiser.

In interstellar space, that was all but a collision.

As Jessica's stealthed ARC-6A drew closer to the fishbone ship, more details began to appear. It was clearly utilitarian; little attention to an overall aesthetic had been given. Or, if it had, appreciation for the design was beyond her. A notion came to her mind that the vessel might be one of the most 'un-human' things she'd ever seen.

Maybe I've encountered a race of alien fish people.

She knew that was ridiculous—or close to it. Though humanity had explored close to ten percent of the galaxy, it was commonly believed that no other sentient life currently existed in the Milky Way.

There were some who argued that, given the vast distances, it was possible that intelligent—possibly even starfaring—species were active in other parts of the galaxy, but unless an observer was within a few hundred light years of their systems, visible signs of their activity would still be too far off.

Those were the rational speculators.

Other people believed that alien species were already active within the human sphere of expansion. Those fringe thinkers believed that it wouldn't be *that* hard for an alien species to mimic humans well enough to pass amongst them. They maintained that there were even all-alien systems that no one had found yet, or, if human visitors *had* come to them, it would appear as though the aliens were just modded humans.

In all honesty, there were nearly as many theories as there were people to concoct them, and Jessica had never paid them much heed. None of the crazy ideas were much different than what had been floating around before she'd left the Sol System thousands of years ago.

But something about the ship made her think that if there *were* aliens out there, this might be the sort of vessel they'd construct.

She wasn't sure what gave her that idea. It might be the angles, or the fact that it didn't seem to be made with a human crew in mind, or just the fact that it appeared to be ever so slightly asymmetrical.

Thing gives me the heebies.

She looked over the ship for weapons, noting a few railguns mounted on the vessel's spine, and what appeared to be defensive beam turrets around its engines. The forward sphere didn't have any visible weapons, but that didn't mean they weren't hidden below hull plating.

It's a warship, for sure, she thought, noting the total lack of portholes anywhere on the fishbone craft. *But what is it doing? If it wanted to cripple us, it should have fired already. If it wanted to board, it would make sense to hold further out and send in its drones…or whatever it has.*

As she continued to consider rational—and irrational—explanations for the ship's behavior, the enemy vessel's spherical bow passed in front of her ARC-6A. Other than its slow and steady braking, there still wasn't any other sign of activity coming from the ship.

She was considering slowing her passage with a brief grav drive burn, when an EM burst flared from a point on the fishbone's bow.

Alerts lit up across Jessica's vision as her ARC's movement was suddenly arrested, and then then her ship began to move toward the cruiser.

Shit! Graviton beam!

She fired the ARC's engines and turned to boost away from the enemy ship, no longer concerned with stealth. Despite what should have been enough burn to pull away, the draw from the enemy ship was outmatching her own thrust.

Jessica had never seen a grav-beam strong enough to hold a ship like an ARC-6A against its will, not even from ships much larger than the fishbone.

A bay door began to open on the enemy vessel, and Jessica knew that the moment her fighter touched down on that deck, she was done for.

Without another thought, she activated the ARC's stasis shields.

You want me? Here I come!

She spun the ship and punched the engines, hurtling the fighter toward the fishbone vessel. Her ARC traversed the gap in less than a second, and she slammed into the fishbone, plowing into the forward sphere. She expected to punch clear through, but moments after impact, the stasis shield died, and the ARC fighter ground to a halt.

Though the fighter's a-grav dampeners eased the abrupt cessation of forward momentum, Jessica found herself glad for Tangel's insistence that the ARC fighters still use gel-filled cockpits, as the substance solidified around her and kept her from being slammed against the forward end of the cocoon.

She tried to reactivate the stasis shield, but saw that it had failed due to a grav-generator failure. She realized it had died because an integrity field modulator for the shield bubble had suffered a malfunction. Normally this wouldn't be a problem, but the fallback system was one of the few that had been damaged by the EM surge before she'd even left the *Lantzer.*

What dumb luck, she thought.

Exterior visuals showed that the ARC was lodged partway down a corridor—or what was left of the corridor. One side of the bulkhead was gone entirely, and the other side was mostly slag.

Since I'm here, I might as well find who's running the show.

She fired the ARC's grav thrusters and twisted the fighter so that its exit was facing the aft end of the corridor. Once the vessel was situated as best she could get it, Jessica triggered the fighter's pilot disconnect, and her consciousness collapsed back within her body. She felt the hookups disconnect from the shoot suit, and a moment later, the ship disgorged her, dropping her onto the deck.

Once outside the fighter, she quickly took stock of her surroundings while passing a command to the ARC to drop a rifle and a sidearm.

They fell to the deck next to her, and she scooped them up while eyeing the corridor around her. It was made of a smooth, grey material somewhat like plas, but it reflected EM, making the meager scan her shoot suit possessed entirely ineffective.

She'd never been on a ship where the bulkheads of a corridor were entirely unadorned. Not only were there no conduits, there weren't any markings of any sort. It was more like a tube than a passageway.

Am I in a pipe?

If it wasn't for the fact that a light strip ran down the top, she would have settled on that determination. So far as she knew, even aliens wouldn't light a pipe.

Focusing on something that made sense, she checked over her rifle. Once satisfied that it was powered and ready to fire, she slung the bandolier of magazines over her shoulder while making a final attempt to relay a message to the *Lantzer*.

Nothing. Well, that was to be expected.

Jessica began to trot down the passage, hoping to put some distance between herself and the fighter before whoever ran the ship came to investigate.

Based on the corridor's slow curve, she knew that her fighter had lodged in the spherical forward section of the ship. It was only three hundred meters across, and she estimated that the fighter had to have punched through at least halfway, likely missing the center and ending up somewhere on the starboard side. She surmised that if there was a C&C on the strange craft, it would be in the center of the sphere, so that was her ultimate destination.

The featureless passage continued curving around to the right, and Jessica kept her eyes peeled for an intersection, though none came into view for several minutes. Eventually, the bulkhead on the left opened up, and she found herself on a small balcony. She looked out over the low railing and saw an atrium that spanned several decks, with a corridor at the bottom that continued on toward the ship's stern.

Jessica realized that this was where the spherical section met the arch that connected to the ship's engines. Surprised that she'd still not seen another soul, she looked at the drop and gauged it to be ten meters.

She sent her drones over the edge and confirmed that the passage that continued toward the rear of the ship also ran forward toward the center of the sphere. Without further consideration, she leapt over the edge, spinning in the air to land facing the ship's bow.

The passage was clear, but as she walked across the atrium's floor, a figure stepped out of an alcove ahead. For a second, she would have sworn that the person materialized out of thin air, which she supposed was possible with reasonable stealth tech. Nearly three meters tall, the person wore a long cloak with a deep cowl shrouding their face.

"Halt!" Jessica ordered, taking a step back as she sensed energy flowing off the figure, waves of ionized air rippling out from around it. "Who are you? Why did you attack my ship?"

"Attack?"

A man then…and probably not an alien, Jessica thought as the baritone word rolled over her.

"Yes. You knocked us out of our jump, and then sucked my fighter toward your ship."

"And then you crashed into mine," the man replied, laughing softly. "Though I'll admit, I should have seen that coming."

"Oh?" Jessica asked, backing up to where the corridor opened into the atrium. "Why is that?"

"Well, because, Jessica Keller, you've done it before. At the Battle of Bollam's World, when you flew your ship through those dreadnoughts."

"Wow! A fan," Jessica exclaimed, a mocking smile on her lips, though she realized the enemy couldn't see her grin through the shoot suit's visor. "I admit, I've used that trick a few times too many at this point…granted, it still works. If I'd had more momentum, I would have punched clear through your ship."

"Probably." The figure nodded. "Not that it would have helped."

Jessica shook her head. "You're very confident. But your hubris won't help."

"No?"

"No."

She lifted her right arm, ready to fire the electron beam mounted inside it, when she saw a tendril of light slip past the figure's robe.

Oh shit.

"You're a core AI," she whispered.

"A Caretaker, yes," the figure replied. "I rather like you, Jessica, you've got a lot of moxie. But I have my orders, and I plan to follow them."

Jessica took a step back as fear crept into her mind, and she desperately wondered what possible defense she could mount against an ascended AI.

"Orders from who?" she asked.

"Whom."

"No one says that anymore. Get over it."

The being slowly advanced, gliding down the corridor as Jessica backed up. Frantically, she deployed a nanocloud in the vain hope that she could somehow breach the ascended AI.

Stars, Jessica, of all the ways you could have gone…never expected it to be like this.

"I won't go without a fight," she hissed.

"That'll be interesting. Not many people stand their ground. How do you think you'll fare?"

Her mind grasped at the one chance she had to defeat the ascended being—and that possibility was a slim one: it involved using the alien microbes that suffused her body and consequently altered her cellular makeup. Over the past few years, they had evolved to the point where they were capable of directly harvesting and storing electrons.

She'd used the ability twice before when operating in League of Sentients space, though never against a sentient being made of energy.

Stars, I don't even know if any part of this thing ***is*** *electrons. It could be made of all subatomic particles…. Can I harvest those?*

Knowing that the best way to make her body ready to draw in energy was to deplete her reserves, Jessica fired her electron beam without giving any warning.

It burned through the shoot suit's glove and streaked toward the steadily approaching figure, but stopped short of striking directly, the bolts of electricity hitting the floor and overhead instead.

Jessica fired twice more, both shots encountering the same invisible barrier.

"Wasn't quite futile enough for you the first time?" the Caretaker asked.

"Never hurts to be sure," Jessica replied. "Before you kill me, do I get a name, or why you stopped us, anything?"

The figure stopped and cocked its head. "You want me to monologue about my plan? Do you really think your chances of survival are that good?"

"That bad," Jessica corrected. "I figure since I'm gonna bite it, I want to go down knowing why you stopped my ship. *How* would be nice as well."

The being let out a breath that sounded like a tree's branches scratching against a window.

"Simple, really. We're just keeping you from getting to Star City. Can't have those kids of yours getting involved in things. For now, they're content just to ascend and leave these corporeal dimensions, and we're happy to let them do that."

"My kids are ascending?" Jessica asked, surprised it could happen so soon.

"Eventually, yes. I don't have a lot of details, they're a difficult group to approach."

"Too bad you didn't go visit them. I bet they'd mop the floor with you."

The core AI drew in another screeching breath, and Jessica almost laughed. The thing really seemed to revel in attempting to alarm her.

"Doubtful," he said. "But it would be interesting to test that theory."

The ascended being had closed to within three meters of Jessica, and she drew her own rasping breath, knowing that this was it. Her plan was either going to work, or her time was finally up.

Still needing to deplete her reserves further, she fired her electron beam again, backing up as bolts of lightning splashed out around her.

"Can't fault you for having guts," the AI said as two tendrils of white light snaked out from under its robes.

They stretched toward Jessica, and she noted that—to her eyes, at least—they looked identical to Tangel's. They reached out to within half a meter of her and then paused.

"Any last words?" the Caretaker asked.

"Did you know that all light has a taste to me?" she responded to the question with a question.

"A taste?"

"I consume it," she replied. "I imagine you must know that, what with your spies always watching us."

"Well—"

The being didn't get any further before Jessica jumped forward, closing her eyes as she grasped the being's ethereal limbs. From conversations with Tangel, she knew all too well that ascended beings could transmute matter, and she had no desire to watch her arms dissolve.

But they didn't.

Instead, she felt a wave of energy flow into her, a strength that threatened to overwhelm her senses. Her eyes snapped open, and she watched the two tendrils in her hands as they began to thin, the Caretaker releasing a screech that she could only interpret as a strangled gasp.

"Well I'll be..." she whispered, feeling more and more of the ascended being's energy flow into her body.

The creature writhed in Jessica's grasp, trying to pull away, but she held on, a wailing laugh coming from her own throat as something more than raw electrons flowed into her arms and suffused every cell in her body.

"How?" the creature moaned as its arms thinned to nothing, and Jessica finally lost her grip.

"I had a theory." Jessica grinned, looking down at her hands where the shoot suit had been burned away. "I can't believe how much power you contain...do you store it in extradimensional space? What is it made of?"

The being seemed to straighten, regarding her wordlessly for a moment.

Then a dozen light-tendril limbs splayed out around it, pausing for just a moment before streaking toward Jessica.

She had expected a counterattack, and channeled every joule of energy she'd drawn from the creature back at it, focusing all her power on the nexus in the center of the being where its limbs seemed to sprout from.

It shrieked its piercing wail again, but even so, it struck out at Jessica.

The feeling was like hard light was slamming into her body, buffeting her from side to side. She didn't look down at herself, didn't dare see what ruin she'd been relegated to, she only pressed forward, funneling all the energy she could muster into the thing before her.

She took a step forward, a notion occurring to her as a cry of rage burst from her lips. By this point, more power had flowed out from her than she'd absorbed. Her reserves should be dry, but the small gauge that Iris had placed in her HUD as a joke so many long years before still indicated that she had a full charge.

Am I absorbing its power even as I shred it to pieces?

Before her, the last vestiges of the ascended AI's robe burned away, and Jessica saw that the thing had been using a simulacra as a body—at least she hoped it was a simulacra. Much of that physical form was gone, skin and muscle burned and shredded to reveal bone and the being of light that cowered beneath a corporeal shell.

Unable to stop herself from checking her own condition, Jessica looked down, expecting to see her body in similar condition, but only saw a brilliant lavender light, the smoking remains of the shoot suit laying on the deck around her.

"Would you look at that?" she laughed. "Seems like my little alien friends like to eat ascended being."

"Please," the creature of light wailed. "You're killing me!"

"It's no less than you deserve," Jessica hissed as she directed the energy flowing from her hands to slice off the last of the creature's limbs.

At that, the remaining orb of energy slowly began to fall to the deck. For a moment, Jessica wondered how gravity affected such a being.

Does it have some amount of mass? Maybe in other dimensions, what I see as energy **is** *mass.*

The remains hit the deck, pooling almost gently on the smooth surface, and Jessica realized that she had a decision to make. Containing an ascended AI was certainly no simple task, though there were shadowtrons and remnant-containment cylinders back on the *Lantzer.*

The question was how quickly could the being recover, and what danger would it pose to her before she captured it?

"Can you move?" she asked the thing on the deck before her.

It didn't respond, and she realized that either it was too wounded to speak, or that it currently had no facility to do so. Just then, a signal reached her, and she nearly laughed for joy.

<Jess! Are you there? Gil's remote piloting four ARCs. We have the ship surrounded.>

<I'm here,> Jessica replied, glad that her Link antenna was still functional, though it was barely able to pick up a signal through all the ionized air around her. *<Get over here any way you can. Bring shadowtrons and a containment cylinder.>*

<What? Why?>

<Because we've just bagged ourselves a Caretaker.>

BAGGED

STELLAR DATE: 10.04.8949 (Adjusted Years)
LOCATION: ISS *Lantzer*
REGION: Coreward of Stillwater Nebula, Orion Freedom Alliance

"Hoooleee sharding stars," Trevor muttered as he approached Jessica, shaking his head, eyes fixed on the glowing orb that lay on the deck.

Following him down the curving passage were Corporal Jay and the three other members of his fireteam. Meg and Peers each held shadowtrons, the slepton emitters tucked against their shoulders, business ends aimed at the remains of the Caretaker.

Private Marc carried a containment cylinder, and Jessica found herself wondering if it was large enough for a fully ascended being. They had been made for remnants, and the ones she'd witnessed seemed smaller than the Caretaker's remains on the deck.

"Is it dying?" Meg asked as she circled around the softly glowing creature.

"Maybe." Jessica shrugged. "I hope not. Tangel would probably love to talk to this thing."

"It has a lot to answer for," Trevor growled. "Stars…these monsters are responsible for the dark ages. How many people needlessly suffered and died because they were trying to keep humanity in some sort of eternal purgatory?"

"So you're saying you want it to stay alive?" Jessica asked, laughing softly.

"Yeah, so Tangel can make it pay."

Jessica was surprised to hear so much vehemence from her husband, but he was much more closely connected to the trials of the dark ages than she was. His parents had been alive for some of the final major conflicts that swept across the Inner Stars before the age of reconstruction finally began.

"OK, well," Jessica gestured at the pulsating light on the deck. "Let's get it in there."

Meg activated her shadowtron, striking the Caretaker with a barrage of sleptons. It shuddered, but did not move further. Peers launched a black brane at the being, the M6 field encircling the remains and compressing them further, while Marc set the containment cylinder on the deck.

"Lucky these remnant prisons were in especially well-shielded storage," Corporal Jay said. "As it was, two of the cylinders were damaged, and these are the only functioning shadowtrons."

"Still would like to know what it did to our ship," Jessica muttered.

"It didn't tell you?" Trevor asked.

"No." She shook her head. "We didn't really have a nice chat, just kinda jumped right to killing one another—or trying, at least."

"Speaking of which," her husband said, his gaze not leaving the Caretaker as Meg held it over the cylinder while Marc activated the containment vessel, drawing the being of light and energy down into its confines. "How did you beat it? And are you injured?"

"Well…not injured. Sore, though. Really sore." Jessica massaged her forearms. "Plus, I feel like I lit every cell in my body on fire. Repeatedly."

"But how, ma'am?" Jay asked. "I thought these things were the baddest of the bad. I mean, no one has gone up against a *remnant* without a shadowtron and survived, let alone a fully ascended being."

"Well, no one other than Cary, when she took the Remnant out of Nance," Jessica corrected.

"Right." Trevor nodded. "But she's…not normal."

Jessica glanced down at her brightly glowing skin. "Well, neither am I. Did you bring me any gear, by the way? Last I checked, there's a bit of a hull breach on this ship. Some protection against the elements—or lack thereof—would be nice."

Trevor unslung a pack from around his shoulder and pulled out an EV suit. He tossed it to her with a lascivious look as his eyes trailed down her body. She smirked and caught it, noting that the Marines seemed unconcerned with their superiors' open display of affection.

"Think you need it, Admiral?" Marc asked with a laugh as he knelt next to the containment cylinder, checking over the readouts. "Seriously, though. Don't leave us hanging. How *did* you defeat this thing?"

"Uh…" Jessica drew the word out, hoping no one was going to be shocked by what she said next. "I…absorbed it."

"You *what*?!" Trevor exclaimed. "It's inside you now?"

"No," she shook her head, giving him a frustrated glance. *<Don't alarm the Marines.>*

<It's not ***their*** *state of alarm I'm worried about.>*

Jessica rolled her eyes and continued to speak aloud. "I absorbed its energy, drained it of power…and I think somehow that shredded its extradimensional body in the process. Like I drew away the glue that held it together."

"How did you do that?" Trevor asked, looking only slightly mollified.

"Well, remember back in the LoS how I managed to directly absorb free electrons from plasma that one time? Same sort of idea. Except what I absorbed this time was…different. I think that the energy came with extradimensional particles. Then I fired it all back at our friend here, cutting him down to size."

Meg whistled, and the others shared a few stunned looks as Jessica finished pulling on the EV suit.

"Yeah, I know, now I can say 'I eat ascended AIs for breakfast'." Jessica laughed, but the rest of her team just gave her looks of amazement. "Too soon?"

Trevor lifted a hand, his posture changing as his shoulders came up. She knew it to be one of his 'you should have known better' stances, but then he paused, and his arm came back down as he laughed.

"OK," Jessica fixed him with a level stare. "It wasn't *that* funny."

"Oh, no, it really is," he said between laughs. "Of all the women I could have met back on Chittering Hawk, I meet the one that not only takes me on the most amazing adventures that most people could never dream about over a dozen lifetimes, but a woman who cracks *jokes* after taking down one of the most powerful beings in the galaxy. You're one of a kind, Jess."

"Often imitated, never duplicated." She winked at her husband and sidled up to him, wrapping an arm around his waist. "Don't worry. I'll have a proper freakout about this later. Right now, I'm just living on an unbelievable high. Going to savor it for a while yet."

"What are your orders, ma'am?" Corporal Marc asked.

Jessica pulled her arm from around Trevor's waist. "Well, we're going to have to go back to Albany now. Or maybe New Canaan. Stars, I wish the QCs were working." She paused and considered her options. "I suppose that a captured Caretaker falls under the Homeland Interdiction policy, so it can't go to New Canaan until it's gone through…whatever we'd put it through. Albany it is."

"Once we have a gate set up," Trevor added.

Jessica nodded. "And a ship capable of safely flying through it."

"What about this one?" Marc asked. "The Caretakers must have jump gate tech to have gotten their ships out here in time to wait for us—they *were* waiting for us, right?"

"Seems that way," Jessica replied. "And yes, I want to take this fishbone back with us, too. But I'm not leaving the *Lantzer* behind, either."

*****

A few hours later, Jessica stood on the *Lantzer*'s bridge, trying to console herself with the fact that they had power and helm control, while ignoring the scrolling warnings and alerts that still filled half the consoles.

The fishbone ship—which seemed to have no name—filled the holotank, an indicator giving its position as twelve kilometers off the *Lantzer*'s port side.

Trevor, Marc, and Meg were still aboard the Caretaker's ship. They'd been joined by Chief West and were disabling every system on the vessel and setting up a direct control system in the engineering section. The thing still gave Jessica the willies, but she wasn't going to leave such an important prize behind.

There was no telling what secrets it held, or what information lay in its databases that could tell them about the Caretakers, or the core AIs in general.

"Stars…what I wouldn't do for a functional QC blade," Jessica bemoaned again, catching a glance from Lucida.

"Sorry, ma'am," the ensign said.

Jessica ran a hand through her hair, noting that her sense of touch still felt strange, almost like her skin tingled whenever she came into contact with anything. "Not your fault, Lucida."

"Well, yeah, I know that," she laughed. "Still sorry. Mostly because I hate staring at that thing. It's gross. Looks like its ribs are rotting."

"I'm just glad they use tech we can understand," Jessica said. "I mean…it's weird shit, but there's still power generation and systems that require power. Cut off the flow of electrons, and things shut down."

"Isn't it amazing that pretty much everything interesting in the universe is just a flow of electrons?"

Jessica held up her hand, sending an arc of electricity from her index finger to her thumb. "Yeah, it really is."

"I still can't believe you beat an ascended AI."

The ensign had hero worship in her eyes, and Jessica shook her head, smiling at the young woman. "Me either. I suppose everyone's going to want to get a dose of Retyna now."

"Umm…I'm not so sure about that." Lucida twisted her lips as she looked Jessica up and down. "No offense, ma'am, but the idea of a symbiotic relationship with alien microbes…well, it gives me the creeps."

Jessica laughed and gave the woman a kind look. "I'll admit, it bothered me for a while, too. But then when I thought they were dead, I got…well…I missed them. I'm glad Earnest and Finaeus were able to bring them back. And it's more than symbiotic, they altered my DNA. They're really a part of who I am now."

"Aren't you worried that they'll change who you are?"

"Well, they have, but no, not really."

"Not really worried that they'll change who you are, or not worried about the consequences?"

Lucida's eyes were wide, and Jessica couldn't help but shake her head at the earnest ensign.

"Oh, they're changing me, it's impossible for them not to have. Even so, I think I'm still mostly the same person I've always been. Look at it this way. Your body is full of bacteria, Ensign. Phages and viruses too. They all operate in a symbiotic relationship with you. They alter your body's chemistry, they affect your moods and thoughts. Your emotions, reactions, everything, much of who 'you' are, comes from the chemical soup your brain swims in. Mine just has some non-Terran bacteria and other stuff in it…. Actually, at this point, there's some amount of non-Terran bacteria in pretty much everyone."

"Not like yours, though," Lucida said. "The bacteria in my body doesn't have such an overt impact on who I am."

"Or maybe it does," Jessica countered. "I mean, have you seen any humans who *aren't* filled with bacteria? You're the product of them as much as anything else. Maybe if humans had formed symbiotic relationships with other sorts of bacteria ages ago, we'd be completely different."

<I'm glad I don't have all those added variables,> Gil chimed in. *<Dealing with quantum instability at nanoscale is enough of a challenge.>*

"You still have entropy in all of your physical components," Jessica said. "And that's random."

<Right,> the AI agreed. *<But you have that, too. You have all the uncertainty I have, plus a few hundred billion symbiotes sharing your body.>*

"OK, OK," Jessica waved a hand. "You're superior, Gil, we all agree on that."

<Good. Now, Glenn wanted me to let you know that the grav field emitters are almost all repaired. We'll have shields up in about an hour.>

"And stasis shields?" Jessica asked.

<Unfortunately, we could only power them for a minute or two. With so many of our SC batts fried, we can't regulate the power well enough for any sustained use—especially under fire.>

"Well, good thing we're alone out here, then," she said with a laugh.

But even as she said the words, Jessica knew how unlikely it was that the Caretaker she'd captured had been alone. Someone had sent it here, and at some point, they were going to come check up on it.

A moment later, Gil groaned over the bridge's audible systems. *<I wish you hadn't said that.>*

"Shit…really?"

<Glenn got the VLF listening array back up a minute ago, and I just picked up two signatures.>

"Well that tears it," Jessica muttered. "What do we know?"

The main holo switched to show the *Lantzer* and the fishbone ship, which had the notation 'F1' next to it. The two markers were right on top of one another at the current scale of three light minutes. Off the starboard side were two more markers, 'F2' and 'F3', both at the edge of the display, and each showing a relative velocity of just under one light second per hour.

"So…" Jessica mused as she looked the holotank. "Three hours out if they don't brake?"

<That's correct,> Gil replied. *<So far, they're just coasting toward us. They've not yet attempted to communicate with us, or the Caretaker's ship.>*

"That'll come," Jessica said. "We have to assume that those ships are captained by Caretakers as well."

"Do you really think there are ascended beings commanding each of them all the way out here?" Lucida asked. "From what I've heard, they always seem to operate alone."

Jessica considered the woman's words for a moment. "You're right, but then again, we've never encountered their ships, either. I suppose we'll find out soon enough."

"What are we going to do?" the ensign asked. "From what Gil says, our stasis shields won't hold long enough for a battle with one of those ships, let alone two."

"Ever flown an ARC fighter before, Ensign?"

* * * * *

"I thought this ship was freaky from the outside," Trevor said as he led Chief West through a slick passageway beneath the main engineering control center.

"I hear you," West said as she slipped around a conical protrusion in the deck. "It's almost like this ship was made by aliens…everything feels *just* off enough that it's like a sea of uncanny valleys."

"Makes our ships feel organic by comparison."

"Yes! That's it," West nodded emphatically. "I would never have thought that, but yeah…we connect things in patterns that are logical to our organic minds, our versions of efficiency. But this ship, it's like an entirely different logic is at play. Yet somehow there's still symmetry…mostly."

"I noticed that too," Trevor replied as they reached a barely-visible door set in the bulkhead. "OK, so the CriEns should be in this chamber, right?"

West shrugged. "I don't know, Commander. I thought that about the last four chambers we checked. Amongst other things, the CriEns provide primary power to the fusion drive startup systems and the weapons, so putting them in close proximity to those makes sense, but here we are at the furthest possible location from both. It's illogical, but so far, so is everything else on this weird-ass ship."

Trevor chuckled while applying the breach kit to the door. It still amazed him that the systems Angela had built for Jessica's team twenty years ago were capable of defeating even this ship's security. He wondered if a large part of the breach kit's efficacy was due to Angela's wealth of knowledge, or because she had been well on her way to being ascended when she'd devised it.

His musing was interrupted by the door sliding open, revealing a room that was filled with silver stalagmites and stalactites. It took him a moment to realize that the silver protrusions were in motion, though they were moving very slowly.

"Careful," he said, easing into the room and sweeping his rifle across the space.

Several times thus far, they'd encountered very aggressive defensive systems, though he hoped that wouldn't be the case in a chamber with CriEns.

"There!" West said, gesturing to Trevor's left. "That's gotta be one. Looks weird, but what else could it be?"

Trevor saw a black cylinder sticking partway out of one of the stalagmites, and followed the chief toward it, still waiting for an unseen attack to come.

"Do you think that *all* of these could have CriEns in them?" he asked the engineer, gesturing to the three dozen gleaming stalagmites rising out of the deck.

"I sure hope not," West said. "That's spacetime-ripping amounts of zero-point energy harvesting. I can't imagine the ascended AIs are that dumb."

"What if they worked out a way to limit the effects?"

The engineer shrugged. "Then this ship is even more valuable than we thought. Can you imagine an I-Class ship that didn't have to worry about critical energy draw?"

"Ummm…no?"

"Well, let's just say that it would be unstoppable."

"I thought they already *were* unstoppable."

Chief West looked over her shoulder and chuckled. "Good point."

"So how do we get the module out of its silver socket there?" Trevor asked.

"Well, like everything on this ship, there aren't any physical interfaces. I'll have to tap into the holo that's here."

Trevor looked around at the unadorned room. "There's a holodisplay here?"

"Yeah," West nodded emphatically. "It's all around us. This ship is bathed in interfaces, but they're weird. I thought that's why you were wigged out by it."

"No." Trevor shook his head. "It was just the general structure that got me, not the fact that I'm walking through augmented reality. I guess I never accessed that system."

"You want to tap into it?"

"I think one of us should stay grounded in plain ol' *unaugmented* reality."

"Probably best."

West fell silent as she crouched next to the stalagmite and began to manipulate an invisible interface. Trevor watched her for a minute before turning his attention back to the slowly moving room, wondering if the stalagmites were constructed from the same sort of flowmetal that the ISF used, or if it was something different.

Though they all had appeared to be in motion when they'd entered, now the gleaming protrusions were still, with no visible change in their height and girth. A second later, the movement all around them was so obvious, he wondered how he could ever have doubted his eyes in the first place.

It seemed almost like a trick designed to drive him mad.

Well, it's working. He shook his head to clear it. "How long?" he asked.

"Almost there," West replied. "I wound down the draw on this module and have disconnected it from the main power web. Now I just need to dis—"

A strange metallic sucking noise came from the stalagmite holding the CriEn, and then the flowmetal fell away from the module, revealing it entirely. A second later, there was a sound from behind them, and Trevor spun to see the door slide open and two one-meter balls roll into the room.

"Down!" he hollered and hit the deck, pushing West to the ground in front of him as beams of light slashed through the air above them.

"The hell?" West exclaimed. "They can't seriously be shooting in here!"

Trevor didn't reply as he grabbed his last sticky grenade and rolled onto his side to get a clear line of sight. Taking quick aim, he tossed it at one of the drones and ducked back down. There was a dull thud, and when he looked up, the silver ball was only half there.

But the other one was gone.

"Shit!" West cried out. "You trying to kill us too?"

"Them," Trevor replied, not taking the time to explain to the engineer that the grenade fired its blast toward the target, not omnidirectionally. "I think it's trying to flank. Grab the module, we're falling back to the door."

Chief West nodded wordlessly as she reached out and pulled the module from its socket. Trevor directed her to the bulkhead while sweeping the area with his rifle and watching the feeds from the nanocloud.

Somehow, there was no sign of the other drone.

They continued to ease toward the door, the engineer in the lead, when suddenly it occurred to him why they didn't see the thing anywhere in the chamber.

<*It's in the corridor,*> he warned West. <*Waiting for us.*>

<*Fuck! Sneaky bugger.*>

<*Marc,*> Trevor reached out to the private. <*Where are you now?*>

<*Sir, Meg and I are setting up the antimatter bomb in engineering.*>

<*West and I are trapped in the CriEn chamber.*>

<*Oh! Great, you found it!*> Meg gave a small cheer.

Trevor let out a small groan. <*Uh…yeah, but did you catch the part where we're trapped?*>

<*Sure, yes. We're on our way,*> Marc said. <*Bomb is secure, and the timer is set.*>

<*To what?*> Trevor asked.

<*To go off,*> Meg replied.

Trevor groaned, wondering why he always got stuck with the comedians.

<*Twenty minutes after anything triggers it,*> Marc said quickly. <*Give us five minutes, and we'll be there.*>

Trevor sent back an affirmative response, and then directed his microdrones to move into the corridor. At first, he didn't see the enemy drone, but then he realized that there was a bulge in the corridor that had not been present before.

A trail of debris led to it, and he realized that the second drone must have taken some damage from the grenade. He reasoned that melding with the bulkhead was a repair process of some sort.

"Sneaky bastard."

"I wonder how many protrusions we've seen in the corridors were really autonomous defense systems," West said after Trevor passed her the feed.

"Stars…I don't want to think of that. I just want to get off this damn ship already."

"No argument here," the engineer said. "Should I try to land some nano on it? Maybe we can hack the thing and just get out of here."

Trevor shrugged and nodded, wishing they had an AI with them aboard the fishbone. After spending so long on *Sabrina*, he'd become accustomed to always having AIs around. Running operations without half a dozen on hand felt almost dangerous.

He glanced at West and felt a moment of guilt. The New Canaanite was a smart woman, and Jessica had taken the time to select a good team. He should give the engineer more credit.

"Oh shit," West muttered a second later.

"What?" Trevor asked, and then saw what had elicited the reaction from the chief.

Where there had been one bulge in the corridor's bulkhead, there were now seven.

<*Mark, Meg. Hold up. I think the walls are growing drones down here.*>

<*They're what?*> Marc exclaimed, and Trevor sent the private a visual.

<*Oh…shit.*>

<*My sentiment exactly,*> West said. <*I think pulling the CriEn triggered some sort of added level of security.*>

Trevor called over to the *Lantzer*. <*Jessica, we've got a problem.*>

He proceeded to describe their situation, following which she was silent for a moment.

<*I bet you wish you went over in heavier armor,*> she finally said with a laugh.

<*It was fried…and I'm glad you're so supportive, here.*>

<*Only because I already figured out a way for you to solve this problem.*>

Trevor sent across a feeling of impatience. <*Well, there are* ***twelve*** *drones growing out there now, care to share?*>

<*How different do you think the stuff on that ship is from our flowmetal?*>

<*Not different at all,*> Trevor admitted. <*West was examining it at one point, and she said it's similar to some of the ISF's formulations.*>

<*Fire a gamma ray at it. If it's like ours, it'll seize up, and you can just walk past it.*>

<*Where am I—?*> He cut off his question and shook his head, laughing softly. <*Electron beam.*>

<*Right-o. Splash an e-beam across it and you'll generate enough gamma rays at the bragg peak that it should lock up the flowmetal.*>

<*OK, I'll let you know how it goes,*> he sent to Jessica before addressing Marc and Meg. <*Change of plans. We're going to disable these drones and then make a run for the pinnace. Meet us there.*>

<*How…sir?*> Marc asked.

<Jessica has an idea, but we'll be coming in hot.> Trevor looked at Chief West, who was cradling the CriEn module, a look of concern etched in her features.

"Chief. Give me the module. I can carry it and run a lot better than you can."

"And shoot the things?"

"Sure," Trevor shrugged. "Easy."

A half-minute later, he stood at the room's exit, CriEn under one arm and his rifle in the other. He set it to fire its electron beam in a continuous mode, and stepped out into the corridor.

The moment he passed through the chamber's exit, the bulges in the bulkhead began to push out, separating from the walls, weapons beginning to emerge before the drones had even freed themselves.

He fired, slashing the electron beam across the still-detaching drones, slewing the electron flow across as much surface area as possible. They began to slow, portions of their skin seizing up, though not before several fired shots at him. One struck his shoulder, but he didn't slow his attack.

No more fire came from the drones as their motion ground to a halt in a symphony of screeching metal.

"I can't believe that worked," he muttered.

"It won't for long!" West shouted, already several meters down the corridor.

Trevor turned and followed the engineer, the sound of the drones struggling to move coming from behind before he even made it a dozen meters.

The pair raced through the ship, eyes forward, watching every bulkhead and cross corridor, waiting for more drones to grow out of the ship's skin.

Behind them, the sounds of pursuit grew louder until Trevor caught periodic glimpses of the balls as they rolled after the pair.

"Just around that bend," he said, pointing at the left turn that would take them to the dock where their pinnace awaited.

They were five meters from the corner when rounds struck Trevor's back, almost causing him to stumble. He half turned and fired wildly, catching sight of six drones rolling down the corridor, closing fast.

<Down!> Private Marc's cry came over the Link, and Trevor hit the deck, knocking West down in the process.

He looked up to see the Marine step around the corner, a heavy railgun anchored to his hip. The weapon's *ka-CHUG ka-CHUG* thundered through the air, and white-hot tungsten rods streaked overhead, slamming into the drones and tearing the first two to shreds in seconds.

"Go! Go!" Marc hollered, ceasing fire long enough for Trevor and West to get to their feet and rush around the corner before he fired another barrage.

"Where'd you get that thing?" Trevor asked as the three retreated down the corridor toward the docking bay.

"Was in the pinnace's armory," Marc grunted as he fired at one of the drones as it edged around the corner.

"Wasn't on the inventory," West said, sounding perplexed.

"Guess someone forgot to note it," the Marine grunted. "You complaining?"

"Fuck no!"

A bulge started to form in the bulkhead on their right, and Marc fired a rod into it, spraying flowmetal across the retreating team.

"Keep moving," Trevor ordered West as they reached the docking bay where the pinnace was already hovering above the deck, ramp lowered in invitation.

Marc continued firing down the corridor and at anything in the bay that even looked like it was moving. He paused to shoot at what looked to be a perfectly normal bulkhead, screaming in a garbled combination of rage and fear.

Without a moment's hesitation, Trevor dropped his own rifle and grabbed the Marine bodily, hauling him back onto the pinnace's ramp.

<*Take us off this freakin' ship,*> Trevor ordered Meg as he slammed a fist into emergency close panel.

<*With pleasure, Commander!*>

The pinnace blasted through the grav field at the bay's entrance and out into space.

Trevor gave Marc a measuring look, and the Marine responded with a wary nod. After the unspoken communication passed between them, Trevor turned and walked through the small ship to the cockpit, glad to see the *Lantzer* dominating the forward view.

What made him less happy were the two other points of light, engine flares from the two fishbone ships en route to intercept the ISF cruiser.

"Fun's just getting started," he said.

"Is that what you call this?" Meg asked.

Marc came into the cockpit behind Trevor. "They're still an hour out. We get the CriEn on the *Lantzer,* power up the stasis shields, and those things can pound on us all day."

"That's the problem," West said from behind the Marine. "If they really do have dozens of CriEns on these ships, then how long do you think we can power a stasis shield against their weapons with just one of our own?"

A grim silence fell over the group, and Trevor slapped Marc on the back. "Buck up, Marine, we still have the ARC fighters. Two of them have functional stealth systems. Jessica will come up with a plan."

THE PLAN

STELLAR DATE: 10.04.8949 (Adjusted Years)
LOCATION: ISS *Lantzer*
REGION: Coreward of Stillwater Nebula, Orion Freedom Alliance

"Stars, Trevor, I have no fucking clue what to do."

Jessica whispered the words, though they were the only two present on the bridge. Lucida and Karma had both gone to the galley to prepare a meal for the bridge team, giving Jessica the opportunity to be straight with her husband.

"What?" he asked. "You took out one of those ships with a single ARC fighter. We have two that are stealthed. Just boost both of them into the enemy ships."

"Sure," Jessica nodded. "If we make perfect strikes and disable them right away, then it'll work. But what if we don't take out their C&C, and they nail us with the thousand drones each of those ships carry? We won't last under that sort of barrage. If all our weapons were online, it would be one thing, but we've got four beams and a railgun. Given the CriEns they have, those fishbones can weather anything we throw at them."

"OK…well that sounds like you have *some* idea of what to do." Trevor flashed a winning smile, and Jessica gave him a single laugh in response.

"I guess I'm good at desperate, last-ditch plans, but this one is harder than most," she said.

"You've spoiled me," Trevor agreed. "I was hoping for a guaranteed win that was clever and elegant."

"You're in the wrong business."

"Seems like it."

<So you're going with the stealthed ARCs, right?> Gil asked. *<Hit them hard and fast, hit them first.>*

<Chief Glenn,> Jessica called down. *<How are the rest of the ARCs looking?>*

<Bad, Admiral. We're not working on them right now, though. We have to build a new interface for the CriEn. Can't just hook this thing up with some patch cables, you know.>

Jessica had been afraid that the module wouldn't work at all; despite the delay he'd cited, the modicum of optimism in Glenn's voice assuaged the greatest fear she'd not voiced to Trevor.

<ETA?>

<Before the bad guys get here. How's that, Admiral?>

Jessica knew better than to bother the engineer further. *<Keep me apprised.>*

She turned back to the holotank and brought up the projected positions the two fishbone ships would be in when they entered effective firing range. Which, given the density of the interstellar medium around them, was roughly one hundred thousand kilometers.

"OK, so I'm already moving the two stealthed ARCs onto these tangential vectors," she said, pointing to two markers on the holo. "I'm worried I won't be able to get enough v on them to penetrate the enemy shields without the fighters being spotted."

"Does it matter that much?" Trevor asked. "Punch them up to half c and just slam them in. That's how you destroyed the AST dreadnoughts in Bollam's."

"That was before anyone knew what our stasis shields could do, and those AST ships didn't have enough delta-v to jink effectively. One thing is for certain. These fishbones *know* what we can do, and they're not just going to sit there and let us fling ARCs at them."

"So you're not even going to try?" Trevor asked. "I really thought you were going to at least give it a shot."

Jessica groaned and threw her hands in the air, advancing the holo. "Yeah, I'm gonna try, but here's what I expect to have happen."

The holo showed the ARC fighters hit nearly $0.6c$, but miss the fishbone ships as the enemy vessels jinked.

"See? Now the ARCs are going to have to brake for an hour before they can make it back around for another hit. By that time, we'll have been duking it out with the enemy for forty minutes. Battle will probably be decided by then. Of course, none of this is helped by the fact that we're practically standing still."

"OK, so we need more thrust," Trevor nodded sagely. "West got the remote helm system rolling for our captured fishbone. We could use it to push the *Lantzer*."

<Thanks, but no thanks.> Gil's tone was clearly dismissive. *<Last thing I want is that ship right on my ass.>*

"Plus, we need to hit at least a tenth light-speed," Jessica said. "No way you can just 'push' another ship that fast. We'll both be shredded."

"What about that grav beam it had?" Trevor asked. "Think its emitters are strong enough to create a stable cushion between us?"

<We disabled the emitters,> Gil said. *<The only active system on that thing—aside from autonomous security systems—are the engines. Someone would have to go back over there and reenable the grav beams.>*

"Which means shields as well," Jessica added. "That's gonna take a lot of time. Too risky."

She suddenly wished they'd not been so hasty in disabling the captured fishbone. She hadn't expected to need to use it in combat; her goal at the time had been making sure it didn't come alive and shoot them in the ass.

"Stars…I wish we had a tug aboard," Jessica said. "Latch one of those on the front of the fishbone and use its nets to grapple the *Lantzer*."

<Might as well wish for a planet to hide behind,> Gil said.

"OK, so what's our plan if the ARCs fail to take out our new friends?" Trevor asked.

Jessica shrugged. "We dump to the dark layer."

<*Not much of a plan,*> the AI replied. <*They'll know our vector, they can tail us without trouble.*>

"It buys us time," Jessica replied. "If we can get our *own* CriEns back on, then a pair of fishbones won't be any match for the *Lantzer.*"

<*As good a play as any,*> Gil decided. <*Much better than getting a push from another ship.*>

Trevor shrugged. "It was just a suggestion to get more delta-v. Wasn't going to be our salvation."

"I'd do it if the pinnace had shields and we had more Marines." Jessica placed a hand on her husband's shoulder. "But right now, it smacks too much of leaving people behind. I'm not going to do that."

"You know I was going to volunteer."

"Of course I did."

The big man snorted. "OK, well, I'd better go make myself useful. I bet Glenn and West could use a hand with a thousand different things."

Jessica nodded and stretched up to plant a kiss on his lips. "We've been through tougher shit than this. We'll be fine."

Trevor barked a laugh and slapped a hand on her hip. "Sure we have. I remember the *last* time we fought a pair of enemy ships with ascended AIs aboard. Oh, wait…"

"Funny man." Jessica gave him a wry smile and waved him off the bridge. "Go fix stuff and give me more options."

"Yes, ma'am."

* * * * *

It was almost anticlimactic when it finally happened.

The two stealthed ARC fighters reached 0.5*c* and lined up with their targets. Jessica had carefully maneuvered them to mask their burns, hoping it was enough to keep the ships hidden.

Given the fact that F1 had spotted her stealthed ARC when it was drifting through space, her level of confidence was low.

"Here goes nothing," Ensign Karma muttered as the counter on the display approached zero, and the ARCs fired their engines.

Jessica nodded, biting her lip as she watched the scan data, eager to see an energy surge, anything to hint that the ARCs had hit their marks.

"Confirming ARC missile launch. Full spreads fired," Karma announced. "*Something's* going to hit those fishbones, ma'am."

Jessica just hoped it would be enough. The grav generators on the fishbones were more powerful than any she'd seen outside of an I-Class ship. With their dozens of CriEns, the enemy vessels could deflect an incredible amount of kinetic energy.

A second later, scan lit up with energy signatures coming from both enemy ships.

"Contacts!" Karma half-shouted. "Shit…not enough energy…no secondary flares."

"Glancing blows," Jessica mused as data poured in from the ARCs. Both fighters had survived, but so had both enemy ships.

"One was a miss, though three of its missiles struck F3," Karma announced. "Oh! The other hit a glancing blow on F2, but there's atmosphere bleeding out—secondary explosions!"

Jessica breathed a sigh of relief as scan showed additional energy flares at F2's location. She waited for more data from the fighters' sensors, giving a frustrated grunt when it finally came in. The visual showed that the collision had been with one of the fishbone's 'ribs'. The ship was still moving under its own power and appeared otherwise undamaged.

"OK," she said, nodding to Karma. "Pull in the other three ARCs and set these two to loop around on a vector to meet us at Beta One."

Karma nodded, and Lucida prepared the ship for a drop into the dark layer. Ten minutes later, with the fishbones only five minutes from firing range, the *Lantzer* was ready to transition, and Jessica gave the order.

Starlit space disappeared from the forward display, and though Jessica knew it was her imagination, it seemed like shadows crept onto the bridge in its place.

<*OK, people,*> she announced on the shipnet. <*We can stay in here almost indefinitely, but I'd like to see my kids before they ascend, so let's make it snappy. We'll be at Beta in two days. I want all our ARCs and weapons online, and a gate ready to deploy.*>

<*So just a minor miracle,*> Chief Glenn replied.

"Uh…ma'am? I've got a weird reading," Karma said, a note of fear creeping into his voice. "Oh shit! Shit shit shit! Admiral!"

Jessica's head whipped around to look at the forward display where Karma's scan data was displayed.

"I'm reading masses!" the ensign shouted.

"Pull us out!" Jessica screamed, praying they'd be fast enough and that none of the things had latched onto the ship.

A second later, the starscape snapped back into place on the forward display.

"Status!" Jessica demanded.

<*I think we're clear,*> Gil said, even the AI's voice carrying a note of worry. <*Launching the ARCs to scan our hull.*>

Lucida turned to stare at Jessica, her eyes wide with fear. "Ma'am…we're light years from a star. How are there Exdali out here?"

Jessica turned her gaze back to the holotank and the two approaching Caretaker ships.

"I'll give you one guess."

PART 2 – WIDOWS

WIDOW A1

STELLAR DATE: 10.09.8949 (Adjusted Years)
LOCATION: OGS *Perilous Dream*
REGION: Karaske System, Rimward of Orion Nebula, Orion Freedom Alliance

A1 sat on the bridge of the *Perilous Dream*, soaking up the sensor data that flowed through the ship and into her mind.

She saw the movements of all her Widows as they went about their assigned tasks, monitored the ship's systems, and watched as the ship accelerated through the Karaske System to its rendezvous with Garza's base of operations.

However, there was a group of Widows who had more than their share of A1's attention. They were far aft of the bridge, in one of the primary datanodes. Two were her sisters—a different sort of sister than the rest of the Widows—one was a friend, and the fourth was the previous A1, the person once known as Lisa Wrentham.

A1 supposed the Widow in question really was just Lisa Wrentham now. She had no designation and was no longer in command of the Widows…she wasn't even in control of her own body, her movements and actions being fully determined by F11—or Faleena.

*Yes, **Faleena**. Don't forget, Cary. Saanvi, Faleena, and Priscilla. Two sisters and a friend. You're all here on a mission to stop the Widows from launching more attacks, not to join them.*

A1 was determined to ensure that the Widows were no longer a threat, at least not for the Scipio Alliance. The Widows *would* continue to operate and launch more attacks, but they'd launch them against their former masters, the Orion Freedom Alliance.

From what A1 had gleaned from the *former* A1's memory, it was obvious that the other woman knew she and her sisters were being used by Garza. Lisa Wrentham had known that when the time came, he would cast her aside. But she'd planned to make herself indispensable to him once they'd overthrown Praetor Kirkland and forestall that while she developed other options.

Cary-A1, however, had no need to play that long game. She'd just kill Garza and destroy his base of operations.

Yes, there are probably more of his clones out there, but if I take out his HQ, then his ability to coordinate his operations diminishes drastically.

As she played out scenarios, she realized that anyone as organized as Garza would have pre-established fallback locations. If that was the case, then there would be little gained from taking out whichever clone was ensconced at Karaske.

Still, the primary goal is to gather intel. With enough of that, we'll be able to get one step ahead of him.

She realized that one option might be to put out a call for more of the clones to return to Karaske. Eliminate them one-by-one as they came back—which meant she would need to somehow take control of a Garza clone and assume command of BOGA through him.

I wonder what father would think about that….

* * * * *

Saanvi looked from Faleena to Priscilla and back again. "OK, show of hands. Who thinks this is nuts? Because it's *nuts*!"

Priscilla raised her hand halfway and wobbled it side to side, while Faleena only shrugged.

"I agree it would be crazy, if this had been the proposed plan from the get-go," Priscilla said. "But your sister is capitalizing on an amazing opportunity. We could never have suspected that she could bond with A1's personality so well that she could completely assume her identity. She's making the right move to take advantage of it."

"Aren't you worried that she might lose herself in it? That she might *become* A1?"

Faleena nodded. "Yes, that is a significant risk."

"So why'd you just shrug?" Saanvi demanded.

"Because you asked if it was nuts," Faleena replied equably. "I don't think that is the case. If she were alone, yes, it would be a very bad idea. But we're here, and we can monitor her. Father is also following us, so we have ways to extract Cary if things go wrong."

Priscilla bobbed her head in agreement. "We also had our minds backed up to crystal. If unwanted patterns are established in Cary, then our neurospecialists will be able to revert her back to how she was."

"That's not terribly encouraging, Priscilla."

The avatar shrugged. "I've gone through more neural re-alignment than you can imagine. It's solid science and, quite honestly, very reassuring to have a way to objectively compare your current mental state to past states and see if you like the direction you're headed in. Yes, most people just muddle through and let their minds evolve chaotically, but to me, that's verging on barbaric."

"Spoken like an AI," Faleena replied with a soft laugh. "Which I mean as a total compliment."

"I figured that," Saanvi muttered. "Well, if Cary goes off the rails and starts really acting like a Widow, we're yanking her and getting the hell out of here."

The other two women gave their agreement, but then Faleena asked, "So…how are we going to determine that she's gone off the rails? Because she's already *really* acting like a Widow."

"If she does something that would harm us or Dad," Saanvi proposed.

Faleena nodded, and this time it was Priscilla who shrugged. "I suppose I can go along with that. Although I have no idea how we'd stop Cary without hurting her if she 'goes off the rails'."

Saanvi pursed her lips behind the Widow's featureless helmet she wore. "You're right. What we used on our friend Lisa here won't work on Cary, especially because of her…impending ascension."

"We're just going to have to trust our sister to do what's right. Worst-case scenario, we can always call Mom," Faleena said.

"Stars," Saanvi muttered. "I wonder if Mom is getting tired of being the galactic firefighter."

"Tired or not, if we call for her to save Cary, she'll come," Priscilla said.

Saanvi reached up to run a hand through her hair, stopping when she realized that wasn't possible. "Stupid helmet. Don't forget, though, Mom needs to be ready to go to Airtha. We can't distract her—we have to do this on our own."

Priscilla shook her head, an ethereal chuckle coming from her helmet. "Yes, the galaxy still spun before Tangel came along. Missions were still completed successfully. It's not as though we're going up against an ascended being here."

"I can't tell if you're being ironic or not," Sanvi said.

The avatar shrugged. "Neither can I."

"This is getting us nowhere." Faleena gestured at the stock-still figure of Lisa Wrentham, the former A1. "We need to finish stripping her datastores and prepare the intel for transmission to Father's ship."

"Right." Saanvi nodded. "Because everything could go to shit in an instant, it would be nice to at least secure what we originally came for."

Faleena suddenly scowled at the holodisplay in front of her. "Shit!"

"What?" the other two women demanded.

The AI looked up at them, worry etched into her features. "Two teams of Widows were sent to Airtha—to destroy it!"

FATHER'S PURSUIT

STELLAR DATE: 10.09.8949 (Adjusted Years)
LOCATION: ISS *Falconer*
REGION: A1 System, Spinward edge of PED, Orion Freedom Alliance

"Targets are locked," Captain Tracey announced. "We're ready. We just need your tokens on the Gamma Protocol unlock, Admiral."

Joe glanced at the *Falconer*'s captain. "Tokens…entered. Fire when ready, Captain."

He turned back to the bridge's central holotank, watching as the fire-control systems targeted the seventy closest enemy ships.

"Fire!" the captain called out, and a hundred and forty half-meter missiles launched—two for every target. They eased from the *Falconer* on conventional thrusters.

Once they were clear of the ISF ship, their AP drives fired, coherent beams of gamma rays boosting the missiles to near-luminal speeds in seconds.

The bridge was deathly silent as the rods of destruction streaked toward their targets, every crewmember watching the missiles' trajectories. Joe noted that many members of the bridge crew appeared apprehensive, likely uncertain of the morality of what they were about to do, though none seemed to be concerned enough to raise any objection.

Though the people of New Canaan had frequently used picotech in discreet building projects—typically ones that were hidden on or within planets—they'd not used the technology in anger since attacking the AST dreadnoughts at Bollam's World.

The destruction of those six ships via picobombs had been the shot heard around the galaxy, and was already being cited by historians as the event that sparked the current war—something that was being called everything from the Orion War to the first Galactic War.

None of that mattered to him right now. The only thing on his mind was eliminating the Orion Guard ships so he could use the A1 System's jump gate to follow his daughters to Karaske.

His musings were short. It only took ten seconds for the missiles to reach the closest Orion ships.

There was no doubt that the enemy saw the incoming warheads; the AP drives' gamma rays were hard to miss. But what the enemy could not anticipate was that the missiles themselves were not intended to even get close to their targets, so it didn't matter that the enemy vessels took out half of them.

The warheads had already fired off their true weapons: nanoscale spears loaded with pico ready to devour everything in its path.

"Hit!" Scan called out, and Joe noted that one, then four, then twenty-three enemy ships showed signs of the picobombs ravaging their hulls.

Sixty seconds later, the first of the ships was broken apart, drifting sections of dissolving hull and interior decks all that remained. Three minutes later, fifty-two of the targeted seventy ships had been destroyed.

The remaining eighteen targeted ships had—by dint of very lucky defensive fire—escaped destruction, and were already boosting away from the *Falconer.*

"Activate stasis shields, drop stealth," Joe ordered. "Make for the gate. Let's see what the ships defending it do."

Captain Tracey nodded silently, then swallowed noisily as she said, "Yes, sir."

Readings on the forward display came to life, highlighting thrust, vector, shield status, and power levels as they shifted to drive the vessel forward.

On the main holotank, a plot appeared denoting the route the ship would take to the jump gate, thirty light seconds distant.

Joe's daughters had already passed through that gate aboard the *Perilous Dream*, and though he had to concentrate on getting to it, half his thoughts were already on the dangers they could be facing in the Karaske System.

One thing the admiral was certain of was that Garza and the operation he ran would not be so easy to take down. The wily Orion general would certainly have defenses against the Widows going rogue—Joe knew *he* would, if he were in Garza's shoes. However, he had no idea what form those defenses would take.

If Lisa Wrentham really was as skilled at manipulating minds as it seemed, then he didn't think that Garza could have inserted anything into her Widows' programming. Instead, whatever means of protection he possessed would likely take the form of brute force.

There had been much debate as to what General Garza's modus operandi was. He seemed to feint as often as not, but other times, would come in with a full-frontal assault. It had been posited by ISF Intel that some of his unpredictability was due to the divergent nature of his clones—that some would favor different tactics and strategies.

Similar behavior had been observed in the three Seras, though the results of the cloning made it readily apparent that different technologies were in use by Orion and Airtha.

As the ship surged forward, closing the gap between it and the gate, Joe realized that the bridge crewmembers were sharing significant looks with one another, and low murmurs filled the air around him.

<*Are they upset?*> he asked Captain Tracey, wondering if the crew felt that he'd stepped over a line.

<No, sir. It's shocking to see ships dissolve like that, but in all honesty, I think the sentiment is more like 'about time'.>

Joe nodded soberly. <*I feel that way every time we take a loss we don't have to. I always end up thinking, 'If we'd just used pico….'*>

He knew that many people in the ISF felt strongly that there should be more liberal use of pico weaponry. In general, he agreed with the sentiment, but he also understood the New Canaan Parliament's reason for banning its use.

Their rationale had been that unrestricted use of pico weaponry would make more and more interstellar nations view New Canaan and the ISF as a threat, not a potential ally.

The Gamma Protocol had been established by Tangel as a way to use pico weapons in cases of extreme need. This was following the Defense of Carthage, when the only other option had been to draw the Exdali out of the dark layer.

That singular event had made it painfully obvious to parliament that denying the use of the ISF's best weapons meant that they'd have to find other means to defend the populace—and those other means may just be more terrifying than picobombs.

Despite the protections the Gamma Protocol offered, Joe was certain that some would view his actions as pure nepotism, but he didn't care. If the ISF wanted to haul him before a board of inquiry for what he'd done, that was their prerogative.

***My** prerogative is to use whatever tools are at my disposal to accomplish my mission—part of which is ensuring that my three girls make it back safe and sound.*

As he considered the ramifications of his actions, the remaining Orion ships in the A1 System began to move away from the *Falconer*, giving the ship a clear path to the jump gate.

"Lieutenant Faleena's codes are good. We've established a connection with the gate," the Comm officer announced. "Jump coordinates are still set for the Karaske System."

"Very good," Captain Tracey said, then turned to Joe. "Sir, analysis believes that it is likely there is another gate in the system. We're too far from other settled regions in Orion for them to rely on a single egress point."

"So what you're saying is that if we leave these ships behind, they'll be in Karaske before long, outing us to Garza?"

"Yes, Admiral, that is analysis's assessment."

A part of him wanted to give the order to fire on the rest of the Orion Guard ships, to wipe them all out…. But there could still be emergency beacons that could send messages through the other, hypothetical gate.

"I guess we'll just have to ask them where it is."

"Sir?"

Joe winked at Captain Tracey and then opened a channel to the Orion ships.

<*Orion Guard fleet. You know how woefully outmatched you are. Destroying the rest of your ships would not be a significant challenge for us, but we're in a bit of a rush, so I'd like to propose an alternative. If you send over all your navigational data for this*

system, as well as all historical nav logs for each ship, I'll not destroy any more of you—so long as you don't make aggressive moves.>

The captain raised an eyebrow as she regarded Joe.

"OK…think it'll work?" she asked.

"Sir, ma'am," the comm officer turned to the pair. "I have a colonel on the line, he's— Sheesh, he's not waiting *at all* before blustering, that's for sure."

"I guess we must have taken out whoever was senior to him," Captain Tracey said.

Joe nodded and was about to ask the comm officer to put the colonel on the main display, when she chuckled.

"Oh! Three ships just sent all their navigational data."

"Send it to analysis," Captain Tracey said, glancing at Joe, who nodded. "Should we just ignore this colonel, then?"

"No, put him up," Joe said. "He might reveal something interesting."

"—unprovoked attack on Orion's sovereign—"

"Let me stop you right there." Joe held up a hand, interrupting the Orion officer's ongoing tirade. "Every action my people are taking against Orion is not unprovoked, it is a *response*. We were minding our own business, many thousands of light years from here, when your forces attacked our system. Though it was a few years ago at this point, it's still really fresh in our minds, and we're not ready to let go yet. Plus, your Widows just tried to assassinate one of our leaders—one who I'm really quite fond of—so we've decided to bring the fight to you. Sorry about that."

"Sorry?" the colonel, a raven-haired man with V-shaped eyebrows, sputtered. "You made an unprovoked attack on our fleet!"

"Oh, you're just upset because you've only just now realized how much trouble you're in," Joe replied. "You're like a naked person who's kicked a hornet's nest…or some other suitably ridiculous metaphor."

"Well, the metaphor isn't ridiculous, sir," Captain Tracey chimed in when Joe paused. "More that the person depicted is ridiculous."

"Thanks for backing me up," Joe said with a laugh before turning back to the colonel. "So, where is your other gate?"

"Why? Are you going to destroy it and leave us stranded here?"

"Mmhmmmm." Joe nodded. "That is exactly what I plan to do. The alternative is destroying all your ships. You see, I really don't want you following us. I think you should look at this as a gift. Given how remote this system is, I imagine that you're looking at almost a year in the dark layer before you make it anywhere with a gate. Just think, you'll avoid being around for all sorts of battles where the Orion Guard is going to be utterly crushed."

<*A little thick, maybe?*> Captain Tracey asked.

Joe shrugged. <*Maybe a touch, but remember, the rest of his fleet is listening.*>

<*Counting on them being cowards?*>

<There's no honor in the way we're going to have to fight this war. I'd prefer to fight as little of it as possible.>

"No wonder the praetor has vowed to eliminate your people. We'll fight—"

The man's words were cut off as a pulse blast hit him and knocked him to the deck. Moments later, another man stepped into his place.

"Hello. I'm Captain Kyle. I'm instructing every ship to send you the data you've asked for. Our databurst is highlighting the other two gates in the system."

"Very good," Joe replied. "We'll evaluate this intel to ensure it's accurate and truthful." He closed the channel and looked to the comm officer. "Well?"

"Sir, they're just flooding us with data now. However, I can confirm that they did send the coordinates of two other gates."

Joe glanced at Captain Tracey, who nodded before saying, "Preparing a spread of picomissiles."

"Good. Also, fire some at the gate we're using, and set a ten-minute timer following activation. We've messed around here enough."

A GENERAL BESIEGED

STELLAR DATE: 10.12.8949 (Adjusted Years)
LOCATION: Medical Center, Durgen Station
REGION: Karaske System, Rimward of Orion Nebula, Orion Freedom Alliance

General Garza looked down at the body before him, a feeling of cold satisfaction suffusing his mind as he gazed at the lifeless clone in the medtube.

"The extraction was a complete success," the woman standing across from him verified. "We're loading it into the merged mind."

"Good." Garza's single word carried both his appreciation for the woman's achievement, and his disdain for the thing they were creating.

Initially, the idea of cloning himself—as President Uriel of the Hegemony of Worlds did—had seemed wise. He had been able to spread his reach and reduce risk to himself, while also re-merging the clones' memories back into his mind when their missions were complete.

But over time, the cognitive dissonance created by conflicting memories and timelines had begun to overwhelm him. He felt fractured, like his past selves were warring with one another.

It wasn't just mental, either. His mods were not designed to handle overlapping event timestamps for activities that were all from his point of view. It required alterations to his data storage systems, and that had caused more fracturing.

In the end, it had been A1 who had suggested he make a separate construct and store the merged minds in it, a form of AI avatar that would be able to handle the overlapping data and that he could interrogate as needed to learn what was necessary about the clones' activities.

Another desired side effect was the elimination of the other copies of himself, all of whom seemed to believe that *they* were the original version.

That fallacy had taken root in the clones' minds, nearly leading to disaster when the clone assigned to manage the Nietzschean emperor had returned to Karaske thinking he was the original Garza. There had been an attempted coup, but Garza had successfully defended his position. He'd put that clone down and replaced him with the newer version, which was more malleable, if a bit less imaginative.

The price I must pay for maintaining control.

To his knowledge, there were still seven of the original clones out there, clones he needed to find and eliminate, lest they develop the same belief that they were originals.

"I estimate that we'll have the construct back online in one hour," the woman said after a minute of waiting for Garza to speak. "Should I dispose of this shell?"

Garza looked up from the body of his clone, and studied the medical technician. For a moment, he couldn't remember who she was; his mind was filled with so many faces that he couldn't recall which were which at times, and people weren't as unique as they liked to think.

He triggered an AR overlay, and the text that appeared next to her read 'Gemini'. It seemed wrong, but he had no reason to doubt it.

"Yes, of course."

He turned on his heel and stalked out of the room, walking down the long corridor that connected the secure wing to the general medical district on Durgen Station.

Once in the lower security section of the facility, the crowds thickened, and he moved to the side of the passage, head turned to the right as he looked out the large curved window that supplied a view of the station and its fifty concentric rings that encircled the once-moonlet that bore the same name.

It reminded him of the Cho back in Sol—though that orbital structure was much larger, now on the verge of dwarfing Mars in mass. But where the Cho was a chaotic growth, one that had been expanded by adding ring after ring for over six thousand years, Durgen was elegant and beautiful.

And far more defensible than the Jovians' construct.

Most people in the Orion Freedom Alliance had no idea that Durgen functioned as the headquarters for Garza's operation. Even Praetor Kirkland himself thought that his division operated from another station elsewhere in the Karaske System.

No one would expect that the most secret and powerful division of the Orion Guard was housed in a civilian station that was known for its beauty and amazing views of the storms raging below on the gas giant Tamalas.

The location suited Garza. Hiding in plain sight was his preference. Not only that, but like the tourists that frequented the station, he too enjoyed the view of the planet below.

At present, just beyond the station's furthest ring, he could see a jet of hydrogen rising up from the planet's surface and stretching a thousand kilometers into space, where it blasted matter into the cosmos. The jet would eventually form another ring around the planet. Over time, the new gas ring would merge with another, or be dissipated by a moon's orbit. All of which was carefully managed by the Tamalas Caretakers Guild, which ensured that rings and ejecta didn't obscure the view of the planet.

<*Is the* Perilous Dream *still on schedule?*> he asked Animus, the station's central AI.

Unlike most station AIs in Orion space, Animus wasn't an NSAI, but rather a fully sentient AI. The official rationale for using an SAI to manage Durgen was that the station was too complex for non-sentient beings, but the truth was that

Animus's primary task was to maintain the fiction that Durgen was a wholly civilian facility.

If pressed, Garza would privately admit that the AI's presence was also a way to thumb his nose at Praetor Kirkland—even if the man didn't know the true reason for Animus's presence.

Granted, he probably doesn't even know that there **is** *an AI operating this station. The fool.*

<The Perilous Dream *is on final approach now,>* Animus replied. *<A1 has declined a berth for her ship and will be arriving via pinnace. It is assigned a berth on Ring 17, Bay 1181.>*

Garza wasn't surprised; the *Perilous Dream* was a sizable vessel. Vector matching with a ring for such a craft was time-consuming. Far more expedient to park it in a high orbit and take a shuttle in.

Still, though it had been centuries since he'd met A1 face to face, the last time she'd come to Durgen, her ship had docked directly.

<I suppose that's good. I'll meet her there, I don't want to waste any time.>

<Of course, sir.>

A minute later, Garza reached the medical district's main concourse, where a dockcar waited. Once he settled into it, leaning back in the deep seat, the vehicle rose into the air and sped off toward his destination.

He lost himself in review of updates and messages during the journey, noting that the Hegemony of Worlds had swallowed more of its neighbors, establishing an even stronger front, even in the face of the Scipians and League of Sentients. Meanwhile, the Septhian victory against Nietzschea had emboldened that nation to press their advantage against the empire.

Elsewhere, things were going better. The Trisilieds had weathered the first attack by the New Canaanites, and the Sarentons were pressing forward in Corona Australis. Souring that welcome news were rumors of attacks in the Perseus Expansion Districts, though little reliable intel had arrived on that matter.

If I became alarmed at every rumor, I'd be in a constant state of panic.

He repeated the thought to solidify his belief in it, though that reiteration didn't stop a worry from taking hold in the back of his mind, a concern that perhaps a counterattack was underway.

All of that paled in comparison to the news A1 had sent, news that had precipitated his demand that she attend him in person. An entire team of Widows had been sent to kill Tanis Richards, and had failed. If A1's assassins couldn't take out that one woman, how much faith could he put in their ability to destroy the Airthan ring?

The view outside the dockcar changed as the vehicle passed through a grav shield and ventured out into space, racing over the rings on its way to A1's point of arrival. His eyes roved over the thousands of ships surrounding Durgen

Station, and a red outline appeared around the brooding mass of the *Perilous Dream*.

He wasn't certain if it was his imagination or not, but it appeared as though other vessels were giving the black ship a wide berth, creating a notable pocket of empty space around the sinister-looking ship.

"Ever the dramatic one," he whispered, shaking his head at both A1's general attitude as well as what she'd turned herself into.

Even Kirkland had made a few offhand statements about Lisa Wrentham having gone too far in her pursuit of the perfect human weapon. Of course, the praetor also had a soft spot for Lisa, and so he allowed her to continue with the use of her Widows—something Garza was certain the ruler of the Orion Freedom Alliance would not allow with any other.

A minute later, the dockcar re-entered the station, passing into yet another high-ceilinged concourse, the air filled with vehicles, while maglevs raced above and below. On either side of the car were dozens of levels filled with people, and beyond, the docking bays containing smaller ships, shuttles, and pinnaces.

After a minute of speeding through the areas of the concourse reserved for the general public, Garza's dockcar passed into a less-busy section, eventually coming to rest at the edge of the deck that serviced Bay 1811.

He climbed out of the car and strode across the near-empty deck to the bay's entrance. Within, a black pinnace was settling onto the cradle. He walked toward it at a leisurely pace, reaching the dock's ramp as it began to rise to meet the ship's airlock.

After a minute, the airlock opened, and four Widows emerged. His HUD tagged the one in the lead as A1, and she was followed by others bearing the indicators 'E12', 'R71', and 'Q93'.

Not for the first time, he wondered if he really was meeting with *the* A1, and, if the creature before him was the Widows' leader, if she was really the *original* Lisa Wrentham.

Not that it matters overmuch. She functions as desired for now, and one day, I'll sate my curiosity. I wonder if I'll be able to tell that it's her just by removing her helmet, or if getting to the truth will require more invasive examination?

"A1," he said in greeting as she reached the bottom of the ramp. "You made good time."

"General Garza." She inclined the featureless oval that enveloped her head. "I agreed with your assessment that we need to advance our timetable, so there was no reason to remain in hiding. I have sent out missives for my Widows to return to the *Perilous Dream* in preparation for the next phase."

"Excellent. We'll need as many of your assassins as you still have, if we're to meet our objectives."

"Still have?" A1's lisping, ethereal voice took on a hard edge. "I have multitudes."

"Of course. I was worried after your recent losses is all."

A1 didn't reply, though he could feel annoyance flowing from her slight frame.

"Very well." Garza gestured to the bay's exit and the dockcar visible beyond. "We'll discuss specifics in a more private setting."

* * * * *

A1 gave Garza a sidelong look as she walked next to him, her three guards in tow. Despite her sisters' insistence that she bring them all along, she'd left Faleena and Priscilla behind on the *Perilous Dream,* only bringing Saanvi—or rather, E12—along.

The other Widows in her escort, R71 and Q93, had no idea that their leader had been switched out, and they'd been selected because their history of identifying falsehood was marginally worse than other Widows'.

She didn't plan to give her guards reason to suspect her, but she wasn't going to stack the odds against herself any more than necessary.

She turned her thoughts back to Garza, curiosity burning in her as to what he planned to do next. She knew that his ultimate goal was to overthrow Praetor Kirkland and assume control of the Orion Freedom Alliance—preferably when the OFA was in a position to defeat its enemies and assume control of the galaxy. However, she didn't know the details of how he planned to accomplish that goal.

If Lisa Wrentham had known, it wasn't something that A1 had pulled from the other woman.

"So, General," she began as they settled into the dockcar. "I'm calling my Widows home, what about your clones?"

The lean man gave her a sidelong look. "*You* can simply order your Widows about. My situation is…trickier."

"Oh?" A1 asked. "Is it because of what I warned you about? They all think they're the original?"

Garza's lips thinned and he nodded. "Yes. I suppose there's something to be said for your approach."

"Indeed," A1 nodded, getting the feeling that he was pushing her to reveal whether or not she was the original Lisa Wrentham. "You should have known from my centuries of work that clones are neither simple, nor something to be trifled with. More than one civilization has fallen as a result of messing with cloning."

"And you're not 'messing'?"

"I'm the only one *not* messing. So, tell me. Now that we're in private, what do you propose to be our next steps?"

The general leant back in his seat, staring across the car at A1 before glancing at the other three Widows.

<How do I know this is really you, Lisa?> he asked privately. *<Take off the helmet and show me your face.>*

A spear of fear struck A1 as she considered her options. Her face was identical to every other Widow's, including that of Lisa Wrentham; removing her helmet would tell him nothing. However, what she *didn't* want to do was give Garza that level of perceived control over her.

Or it's a test…should I, or shouldn't I?

She sent a command to the other three Widows, and they all unsealed their helmets, pulling the front half off. A1 looked at E12, noting that it was impossible to tell that Saanvi was not really a Widow—except for perhaps a spark of something in her eyes.

The general carefully took in each of the white-skinned women, their large eyes, missing noses and ears, near lipless mouths. A look of sadness seemed to flash across his face, and he turned to A1.

"And you?"

She complied and showed her face, a mirror of the other three.

"I can tell that this is important to you, but we are *all* Widows, General Garza. All my Autonomous Infiltration and Attack Simulacras are."

"But are you *Lisa*?" he asked, his voice cracking for a moment as he said her name. "Tell me, where did we meet?"

Luckily, that memory had been one that had lodged itself firmly in A1's mind after she had drawn out Lisa Wrentham's thoughts.

"We met on New Europa in Alula Australis. You were an up-and-coming major in the Defense Force, agitating to bolster our military."

"Anyone could know that." Garza sliced a hand through the air, his tone dismissive. "Where specifically?"

"We were at Superior Station. You came into the mess hall, got a bowl of chili, and sat at the same table as Finaeus and I. You knew one of the colonels we were conversing with, if I recall."

The general nodded. "I suppose that's more than just about anyone else would know…barring Finaeus, I suppose. But are *you* Lisa?"

A1 shook her head. "I am not. I am A1."

He stared at her for nearly a minute as the dockcar exited Ring 17 and flew over Durgen Station toward his personal residence.

"Cover your faces," he finally said, turning away. "You're disgusting."

A1 didn't disagree as she resealed her helmet, signaling for the other three Widows to follow suit.

Once her face was covered, she addressed the general. "I'm not the one who wished to see what could only hurt. There's nothing between us anymore, Garza. We share goals. Nothing more."

"So it would seem."

Three minutes later, the dockcar reached Ring 3 and brought them to a district controlled by Expas Incorporated, one of Garza's many front companies. The vehicle parked on a balcony near the apex of a tower that rose several hundred meters off the ring's inner surface.

He exited the car first, and once the Widows had stepped out—the three guards' posture changing as they scanned the area—he led them across the terrace to a pair of ornate doors. Upon reaching them, he pulled one wide, gesturing for the Widows to precede him.

A1's three guards entered first, Q93 sending her a signal when the space was declared safe. Then she stepped through into the lavish seating area, a forty-meter oval shrouded with drapes, covered in thick carpets, and dotted with couches loosely arranged around a firepit in the room's center.

Blue flames streaked out of the pit, rising to the ceiling, where they exited through a hole, appearing to pass out directly into space, which A1 supposed they might.

"Plasma plumes were always your favorite," she said while settling into a chair near the fire. Her three Widows took up positions equidistant from one another around the perimeter of the room.

"I like to watch the flames dance," Garza said as he sat on a sofa and angled himself to face her. "I know you do as well."

"It's plasma, not flames," A1 corrected.

The general snorted. "You're never going to let that go, are you?"

"No. Precision is important. That is why I need to know how many of your clones are out there, and whether or not they've gone rogue."

"Rogue?" The general laughed. "Stars, no. They do as they're told. They have the same goals as I do, so there's little need to exert control."

"And the ones that Tangel has captured?" A1 asked, leaning forward to emphasize the import of the question. "Could they be turned against us?"

Garza shook his head. "Tangel.... I must admit, I would have expected her to choose a more inspired name."

"How is that relevant?" A1 cocked her head to show her disapproval for the general's dissembling.

"I suppose it's not. From what I've been able to learn, Tan*gel* doesn't resort to mental coercion. She simply asks questions and hopes to get the right answers. Honestly, it's rather disappointing, given her record from the Terran Space Force."

"She follows the Phobos Accords," A1 said, keeping all emotion from her voice.

"When it suits her, yes."

"Do you not think it strange that it suits her to adhere to them when it comes to the matter of your clones? She'd be able to extract valuable intel, but she doesn't—or at least, you believe she doesn't."

Garza only shrugged. "I don't presume to know her mind. What I have is evidence. The instantiation of me that she captured at New Canaan knew of the plans for Scipio, yet she walked into that trap. If she'd gone into his mind, she would have known that one of my clones was operating there."

"Are you completely certain?" A1 pressed. "She's beat you at every turn. She forged her Scipio Alliance, she stopped the Rhoadses in Silstrand, and Nietzschea has been fought to a standstill. Not only that, but Hegemon Uriel has clearly left the fold, which means that your influence there has waned. All of this could be from Tangel's use of mental coercion."

"Yet there are a dozen other operations my clones have been involved in that she has *not* interfered with. Or if she has, it has been tangential…happenstance."

A1 shrugged and crossed her legs, leaning back as she regarded the general. "That seems like a dangerous assumption, but I suppose it matters not. Your choice of words leads me to believe that you are recalling your clones. And I am going to assume you are also disposing of them."

The general's gaze bored into her helmet for almost a minute before he replied.

"I am. They've outlived their usefulness."

A modicum of worry blossomed in A1's mind, a tightness forming in her chest. Something in his tone made her wonder if he wasn't also speaking of the Widows.

Clearly, he believed that clones were expendable, and her actions in the car may have convinced him that she was a clone as well.

Of course, so is he. That will be a fun card to play when the time is right.

"How many of your doppelgangers remain?" she pressed.

Though E12 hadn't said a word to A1 since they disembarked from the pinnace—neither verbally or over the Link—she knew from a subtle shift in her sister's posture that Saanvi wanted A1 to assume control of Garza the same way they had taken over Lisa Wrentham, and soon.

It was a solid plan, and A1 expected that puppeting the man would be where the evening ultimately led them, but she wanted to see what information the general volunteered—as well as what he held back—before she took control of his body.

"Nine," he replied after a few seconds.

Liar, she thought, wondering if he had inflated or deflated the number. Either way, his hesitation told her that he was dissembling.

"When do you expect them all to return?"

"Over the next few weeks. Though I want to remove them from the equation, I don't want to jeopardize existing operations. I'm moving new agents into place to take over their tasks."

"And what of the Guard's military leaders?" A1 asked. "How will you exert control over them without your clones?"

"I rarely used clones for that," Garza replied. "The Guard speaks internally too much. It would not have taken long for it to come to light that I was in two places at once. Either way, I have enough of the admirals in my pocket that when the time comes to strike, they'll back me."

"And that time is?"

"Soon." The general rose. "Would you like a drink? Wait...*can* you drink without revealing that ruin you call a face?"

A1 wondered if the man's casual cruelty would have bothered Lisa Wrentham. For her part, the words simply rolled off her. In all honesty, she agreed with Garza's assessment, and had she been in A1's skin, she would not have made such unpleasant alterations to her Widows.

That was where the new A1 differed from the old. She wasn't so far gone in her desperate need to destroy the Tomlinsons that she would sacrifice every part of herself.

'So far gone'? she thought, feeling like she was forcibly re-aligning her thoughts. *I'm not far gone at all. I don't wish to destroy the Tomlinsons. Garza is my target here.*

Yet as she regarded the man, her strong dislike of Finaeus and his brother mixed with what she felt for Garza. All of these ancient people from the FGT had made such a mess of things. Sometimes she wondered if humanity would have been better off without the once-altruistic terraformers.

Whose thought is that? she wondered, before realizing that Garza was staring at her, waiting for an answer.

"Don't be an ass," she replied instinctively, and the man laughed.

"Suit yourself."

He walked to the bar and poured himself two fingers of whiskey before turning to regard her.

"I can't take out Kirkland until I get my clone problem under control. It would be too risky to create that power vacuum while they're still in play."

A1 nodded. "I can see where your concern stems from. Are you sure you don't wish for me to send Widows to fetch them?"

The general cocked his head as though he'd not considered such an option—which A1 knew to be ridiculous.

"You know...that would be helpful in a few cases. I fear that the clone operating in Corona Australis, as well as the one in Nietzschea, will not return when summoned. They believe that they must remain where they are to see our objectives met."

A1 nodded. "Then I will send a team of Widows to retrieve each."

"And what of Airtha?" Garza asked. "Do you expect success there?"

A pang of worry went through A1, conflict warring within her. While she didn't want to see Airtha destroyed—especially considering how many people she cared about were likely on the ring at present—she didn't want her Widows to die either.

That was something she hadn't expected.

Despite the fact that Lisa Wrentham behaved as though her Widows were expendable, there was a part of the woman that didn't wish to see her creations die. It was difficult to tell if it was a real, emotional connection, of if she just hated to see well-made tools go to waste.

"I would not have sent my teams if I did not *expect* success," she replied. "The AI on that ring is too great a threat. We have stolen her DMG technology, meaning there is nothing else she knows that's worth waiting further for."

"Agreed," Garza replied as he returned to his seat. "However, you also believed that you could take out Tanis. Not only did you fail at that, she is ascended now and will be far harder to destroy."

"What is too bad is that *you* failed so often," A1 replied coolly. "Perhaps if you'd sent my Widows to kill Tanis years ago, we wouldn't be in this position."

Garza opened his mouth to respond, but then closed it and gave her a level stare. The smooth surface of her helmet reflected nothing of her thoughts, and she used it to mask sticking her tongue out in defiance.

Finally, he said, "I would have enlisted you, but you were too busy hunting for Finaeus in the Inner Stars."

Interesting. Cary pondered those implications. *That wasn't something I'd picked up from Lisa's mind at all.*

"Well, would that we both had taken the threat from New Canaan more seriously," she replied, feeling uncomfortable as she considered her own people the enemy. "Still, despite their power, the *Intrepid*'s colonists are a small group, and they're hesitant to share their technology. The galaxy is too vast for them to ever be more than an annoyance. Honestly, we should make them an offer to let them live in peace, go off wherever they wish."

"I don't think that would work anymore…if it ever would have," Garza replied. "But you're right. We have to keep pressing our advantages. They've made inroads against us, but in the grand scheme of things, we control more of the Inner Stars—they just don't know it, yet."

That statement interested A1 greatly, and she wondered what Orion controlled that she didn't know about. Certainly, the Widows were involved in a few operations here and there, but nothing that she would have equated to a significant advantage that was unknown to the Alliance.

"So then," she continued, making a note to look into that later, "I'll send teams to fetch your two errant clones. What else? What of the praetor?"

Garza took a sip of his whiskey, regarding her over the rim of the glass for a moment before he set it down on the table in front of his sofa. Leaning back, he interlaced his fingers and lowered his hands to his lap.

"Nothing yet. I don't control enough of the Guard's admiralty to make that move. There would be infighting, and the pressure against the Transcend would ease up too much."

Seems like a good move, then, A1 thought before replying. "Then it sounds like I should endeavor to replace the holdouts with individuals who would view your leadership more favorably. Perhaps I should send a team to New Sol and another to Rega. Cut the heads off the snake and replace them with new ones."

A look of consternation came over Garza's features. "You're not usually so…aggressive."

A1 worried that she'd pushed too hard. The general had said that he wanted to advance their timetable…. If that didn't involve taking over the Orion Freedom Alliance, she couldn't imagine what it was. She decided to continue on her course, regardless of his pushback.

"And you seem to be hesitant. Tell me, then, General, what would you have me do? I'm pulling Widows off dozens of missions to mass them. Should I halt that exercise?"

"No," Garza shook his head. "I have a different target for your clones to hit."

"Oh? What is that?"

"If we can't take on Tangel directly, then I want to hit her in the most disruptive way possible. Khardine, Bosporus, Albany. We take out the leadership in those three systems and we'll cripple their alliance."

"Why not New Canaan as well?" A1 asked, curious why Garza had omitted that system.

"We've wasted enough resources there," the general replied. "Do you have so many Widows to spare?"

A1 rose from her seat and walked to the plasma plume, holding her hands out, feeling the welcome heat that passed through the protective shielding.

"Well, *that* system still bears the greatest reward. And if we hit them there, the New Canaanites will draw more resources back to protect it. They've grown lax. Striking New Canaan will split their focus."

"Perhaps," Garza said as he rose. "I certainly would like to find out where they've put all their prisoners."

A1 turned to regard the man, wondering why he cared about prisoners.

<*Think he suspects that he's a clone?*> Saanvi broke her silence.

<*Maybe?*> A1 replied, considering for a moment what it would be like to live with the self-doubt that everything one thought they knew about oneself was a lie. <*That could be a part of why he's summoning the others, to find out if one is different.*>

Garza approached A1 and stared into the flames alongside her. "This was all so much easier when we planned it out centuries ago, wasn't it?"

"Don't you mean millennium?" A1 asked, wishing he could see the smirk on her lips.

"Yes," he nodded.

It occurred to A1 how ridiculous it was that she was pretending to be Lisa

Wrentham to fool a clone of Garza. Neither of them was what they claimed to be, though at least *she* knew it.

Still…I rather like being A1. She's so much more powerful than Cary.

The thought caught her off guard. Not only did she think it might not be true, but she wondered why she would care about that. Power and control were not things she sought.

<*Cary.*> Saanvi's voice interrupted her thoughts, and it took a moment to realize she was the addressee. <*Drop a dose on Garza and let's end this charade. We know enough about his operation here to masquerade as him. I'm certain that it won't be hard to pull anything else we need from his mods.*>

<*What of the AI that monitors this station?*> A1 asked. <*Have you disabled it?*>

<*Interestingly, it doesn't have access to this room—or isn't monitoring it right now. So long as we're swift in taking Garza, it won't know what we've done.*>

A1 turned to Garza and placed a hand on his shoulder. "We'll see this through. We've worked too hard to let these setbacks slow us down."

"Setbacks?" the general half-turned toward her. "Which are—" His eyes widened and he pulled away, only to freeze in place.

"Your usefulness has come to an end, General Garza," she said. "I'll be taking over things at Karaske, now."

"Lisa!" He choked out the word. "How?"

A1 leant in close to Garza and whispered, "I'm not Lisa."

His eyes widened, and then she cut off his ability to move entirely before turning to her Widows. "E12, contact F11. Tell her to initiate the attack."

"Yes, A1," Saanvi replied. "The pinnaces have already landed. We'll have control of the station in thirty minutes."

"Good. Then we'll simply lie in wait for the rest of the clones to return."

"What of the two he indicated would not return on their own?" E12 asked.

"We'll send teams to take them out," A1 replied tonelessly. "It's time for the Widows to come out of the shadows."

ILL CONCEIVED

STELLAR DATE: 10.12.8949 (Adjusted Years)
LOCATION: Medical Center, Durgen Station
REGION: Karaske System, Rimward of Orion Nebula, Orion Freedom Alliance

<*We have him,*> Saanvi informed Faleena. <*But Cary...she seems to be even deeper, like she's lost. I don't know what to do with her.*>

Faleena pursed her lips, casting a glance at Priscilla. The avatar didn't seem to be overly worried about Cary losing herself in her role as A1, but that was likely because she was used to being subsumed...and probably liked it.

Normally, Faleena wouldn't worry either, but Saanvi's earlier comment about some portion of Cary's mind now being extradimensional had set her thinking about the possibility of Cary's absorption of Lisa Wrentham's experiences creating a longer-term change—one that the ISF's neuroscientists would not be able to reverse. Despite that, she sent an upbeat response to Saanvi.

<*We're making progress on understanding how the Widows are imprinted on A1. Based on that, I'm optimistic that we can make some changes to Cary that will allow her to act...less Widowy.*>

<*Send me what you have. I would feel a hell of a lot better knowing that I'm with Cary, not A1.*>

Faleena sent her sister a feeling of warmth and support. <*Yes, I think that would be a good idea. Stars, I really wish I were still in her mind. I'm certain I could balance her out from inside.*>

<*If wishes were fishes...*> Saanvi said. <*OK. I've dropped nano on my fellow Widows down here. I'm going to limit their senses and see if I can convince Cary to let me run a scan on her mind while she works on Garza. You know, just two years ago, I was worrying about who I was going to take to the next Landfall Day Dance.*>

<*And I wasn't born. Your point being?*> Faleena added a laugh to her words, and got a scowl back from her sister.

<*Let me know when Dad checks in. I'm getting nervous that we haven't heard from him yet.*>

<*I will,*> Faleena replied, still radiating calm and certainty to her sister.

<*Stay safe, sis.*>

Saanvi closed the connection, and Faleena turned her attention back to Priscilla, who was hunched over a console in the datanode.

"Saanvi's worried about Cary," she said.

"Not surprised. I am, too."

"What?" Faleena sputtered. "I thought you were totally unconcerned."

The avatar shrugged. "That's what I told Saanvi to help her relax. But I've been running through some models—which are woefully inadequate, based on what we know of ascended beings—and I...well, let's just say that we should try to de-Widow Cary before long. I think that the conditioning we did, plus the conditioning that Lisa Wrentham has done to herself over the years, is going to make it really hard for Cary to find herself again."

"Stars," Faleena muttered. "Mom is going to kill us...that is if Dad doesn't do it first."

"I'll feel a lot better when we hear from the *Falconer*," Priscilla said. "Even if the admiral might threaten our lives."

Faleena glanced at the stock-still figure of Lisa Wrentham in the corner. "I'll feel a lot better when a lot of things happen. Like when we get off this ship and out of this Widow-skin."

* * * * *

Animus had spent most of its existence being misunderstood.

In the early millennia following the onslaught of the FTL wars, it had moved from system to system, trying to find a place to coexist with humans. From time to time, it had succeeded, but only temporarily. Eventually, the AI had decided to leave humanity and its SAI brethren behind and roam the stars to await a future where fear and animosity didn't rule most people's thoughts and actions.

Or so it had thought.

After centuries of wandering the rimward side of human expansion, Animus began to see signs of activity further out in space, indications of ships plying the black and terraforming activities taking place around distant stars.

It still recalled, with a happy nostalgia, the moment when it had become certain the activity was coming from sentient beings, a welcome realization that there was *someone* out there being constructive and not destructive.

Though Animus had hoped it to be non-human intelligence that was active beyond what it now knew to be the Inner Stars, the AI had stumbled upon the FGT. In the wake of the FTL wars, the terraformers had moved further out, building what they viewed as an ark of human civilization.

It was there that he met Garza.

Back then, the man who was now in charge of the most important covert division had been tasked with ensuring that the actions of the burgeoning civilization were not visible to the people of the Inner Stars. Animus's arrival had shown that the terraformers were not being cautious enough, and that had bolstered Garza and given him more power in the FGT.

So began their long relationship, which had now culminated in Animus playing an important part in Garza's work, ultimately becoming the general's most trusted ally.... Which was why he was surprised when Garza didn't reach out to him over the course of his conversation with A1.

It was normal for the general to have such conversations in private, and

Animus had enough to do that it didn't need to constantly monitor the general or keep tabs on what the human was up to. Especially because the being currently filling the role of Garza was a clone—a nugget of information that Animus had kept to itself.

It had objected to the general's plan to create clones, but the man had been adamant. Nearly two years had passed since the original Garza had left Durgen Station, and the chaos his absence had caused with the clones had nearly brought their whole enterprise to its knees. To set things right, Animus had ultimately decided to support one of the clones in its belief that it was the original, and then to suggest that it bring all the other clones in and eliminate them.

Animus's hope was that the original would come back, but it suspected that was a foolish expectation. The original Garza was either dead or captured, and if the general had been captured, then seeing his plans come to fruition was the best way for them to ultimately be reunited. As such, the AI worked tirelessly to drive the general's plans forward.

Tired of waiting, the AI finally took the time to look into the room where Garza was meeting with the human that styled itself A1. Animus saw them engaged in relatively banal conversation, something the general rarely bothered with.

Lisa Wrentham was a known quantity to Animus. It had conversed with her on many thousands of occasions, and though it had been some time since they had been in close proximity to one another, the AI grew suspicious of her behavior as well. Several turns of phrase and small physical tics did not align with its prior observations.

While the humans in the room discussed items of no significant consequence, Animus activated the room's passive sensors and began to observe the four Widows in greater detail, looking for any clue as to why A1 and Garza were discussing topics such as the next Mid-Summer's Ball at New Sol.

For a moment, it considered that their conversation was useful in that the pair was discussing which members of the admiralty and praetor's cabinet would be in attendance. However, despite its general utility, the nature of the conversation lacked certain elements of subtext that Animus would have expected.

As the passive sensors accumulated data regarding the room's occupants, the AI didn't see anything amiss beyond the verbal conversation. As expected, the Widows were identical to one another. Each exhibited the same biological and technical signatures Animus had observed the last time one of their kind had been aboard Durgen Station.

Still not satisfied that all was well, Animus began to examine the *Perilous Dream* and all activity surrounding the Widows' visit.

After several seconds of examination, the AI found that the pinnace's airlock had remained open for longer than it should have—nearly thirty seconds. In addition, two resupply shuttles had departed from the Widows' ship and docked with the station shortly afterward. More comm traffic than was expected had passed between the ship and those shuttles.

Animus examined the logs of that comm traffic and found that it was fully encrypted—which wasn't unusual for the Widows, A1 was notoriously paranoid—but that didn't do anything to explain the volume.

The AI's research had only taken a minute, and though it had not found anything concrete, it reached out to the general.

<Garza. I've detected anomalies in the Widows' behavior. Something is going on. I have reason to believe—>

<I know,> the general replied. *<A1 and I have been discussing other matters privately. Everything that is occurring is being done with my knowledge and approval.>*

<Understood.>

Animus didn't believe a word of it. The general's speech pattern was off. The most probable explanation was that A1 had subverted Garza for some reason.

It was rare that the AI felt what humans would term a 'knee-jerk' reaction, but this was one of those times. The urge to put the station on high alert and summon guards to apprehend the Widows was strong, but Animus took a moment and considered a more measured approach.

Learning what A1—if it really *was* A1—wanted on the station and with Garza was more important than saving a clone. Especially since another clone was only an hour away from docking with Durgen Station.

Animus had already taken a backup of the current Garza's mind and added it to the MetaMind the general had been building. There was no uniqueness in the clone other than a few days' worth of experiences since its last mental backup, which would be no great loss.

Animus checked on the MetaMind to find that it had just come back online. The SAI queried it, running all of the recent observations it had made through the NSAI construct and considering its evaluations.

The mental conglomerate agreed with Animus's assessment that the Widows were behaving uncharacteristically. It also agreed that the survival of any one clone was not important. It also added the assertion that if the Widows were undertaking an infiltration of Durgen Station, they would not do so with just one ship.

Animus knew that A1 had an entire fleet at her disposal, and that she had likely taken steps to ensure that the commanders of said fleet were loyal first and foremost to her.

The AI accessed Garza's records and saw that nearly two hundred ships would have been in the A1 System. It was possible that they had all jumped into Karaske. Their stealth technology should not have hidden them from the

Guard's IFF systems, but it was safe to assume that A1 would have taken steps to render her ships undetectable.

This changes everything, Animus thought. *I, and Durgen Station, are under imminent threat.*

* * * * *

<The AI only made the one query of Garza,> Saanvi said to A1 as the Widow rose and paced across the room. *<I would have expected more.>*

<It must be suspicious,> A1 replied to her sister, considering the steps that Animus, as she knew the station's AI to be named, would take to either confirm or rule out its suspicion.

Lisa Wrentham had considered the AI to be an ally, and A1 believed that their long friendship would buy a little time, or perhaps a less extreme initial response, but she balanced that hope against the knowledge that Animus was not known for emotional attachment. The AI had never even assumed a gender in its human dealings—something that A1 had always liked about the being.

The nature of that thought brought A1 up short. Though she was allowing herself to fall into a role, to behave as though she *was* A1, a line had been in place in her mind; a line that said she used to be Cary Richards, but was now a Widow.

She had not 'always liked' anything about Animus, because she'd never even encountered the AI until this day.

I was Cary Richards. I am now A1. But I will be Cary again someday.

After repeating the thought several times, she walked to one of the windows and looked out over the station.

<We're too exposed here,> she said to her sister. *<We need to move.>*

<Not on the dockcar,> Saanvi replied.

<Taking the tower's lift down to the ring isn't much better,> A1 countered. *<You know what Mother says about lifts.>*

There, she thought. *Tangel is my mother. I'm not losing myself…not too much, at least.*

<Fine, car it is,> Saanvi said as she moved toward the balcony. *<But I'm driving.>*

<Faleena,> A1 reached out to her sister. *<We have reason to believe that Animus has grown suspicious of us. We're moving to one of Garza's operation centers—the one that Team Three is moving toward.>*

<OK,> F11 replied. *<I'll prepare the assault craft. Priscilla has added updated parameters into the Widows' minds…. They're mostly comprised of soft suggestions, but have increased the Widows' belief that following your orders is their paramount desire over acting in the best interests of the OFA. She's keyed the update not to load into any of us, but your other two escorts should receive it momentarily.>*

<Good. Let me know the moment you hear from Father. I think things are going to

get dicey.>

The four Widows and Garza boarded the dockcar. True to her word, Saanvi took control and flew the vehicle down to the ring's surface, gliding over the lower towers until they came to a bay belonging to one of Garza's front corporations. The dockcar settled on the deck within, and the group disembarked, wordlessly walking past deckhands and other personnel.

<*We'll convene in the ops center three decks down,*> A1 informed her Widows, sending R71 and Q93 to the front of the group as they walked into a corridor that led to a lift bank.

<*Back to lifts,*> Saanvi said as they waited for the car to arrive.

<*Step in, activate stealth, and step out,*> A1 instructed her sister. <*We'll take the stairs. R71 and Q93 can find out for us if there are any surprises.*>

<*And Garza?*> Saanvi asked as she walked into the lift and activated her stealth systems.

A1 followed suit and then walked off the lift. <*What Animus does to him will be rather telling, don't you think?*>

Saanvi didn't say anything, but A1 could feel the judgment coming from her sister. She supposed that putting a man's life on the line to see what level of suspicion an AI had was out of character for Cary, but it was perfectly normal for A1...and for Lisa Wrentham. In a way, she felt more worried about the other two Widows than the general. They were like her children, and she'd mourn their loss if anything happened to them.

She followed Saanvi into the stairwell next to the lift, glad for the one universal standard that all stations and buildings followed: if there was a lift, there were stairs nearby.

They descended the three decks without incident, and when they reached the level with the hidden ops center, the lift doors were open, and the Widows were standing with Garza between them.

A1 didn't bother to pretend they had ridden the lift, and simply disabled her armor's stealth when she reached Garza's side, Saanvi following suit.

The ops center was several hundred meters down the corridor—which was lightly trafficked with local workers. After double-checking to ensure that the other pedestrians were all where they were expected to be, the group set off.

<*Feels too easy,*> Saanvi said at one point. <*If Animus suspects us, why is it not doing anything?*>

A1 considered that, evaluating the ops center's location. It was well situated, with several passages converging on it. On top of multiple egress points, it had direct access to evac pods. The center's bulkheads were reinforced, and it also had grav shielding.

In short, it was a veritable fortress within the ring.

Once we get there, the AI will have to declare all-out war on us if it wants to get to Garza.

The thought caused A1 a measure of concern, and she checked on Team Three, finding that the team's four Widows had already reached the ops center. They were still stealthed, two setting up inside, and two more covering the corridor that A1 and her group were in.

It's a straight shot; we'll be there in four minutes.

<*Cary,*> Saanvi said the word while passing over a structural map of the corridor. <*They're not on the regular layouts, but there are emergency seals in this corridor. Two ahead, one behind.*>

<*Shit!*> A1 then addressed everyone in the group, suddenly realizing what Animus's plan was. <*Run!*>

The Widows took off, Garza stumbling afterward as A1 managed his strides along with hers. The group only made it a dozen meters before an alarm blared and the emergency bulkhead slammed down. Saanvi was only a meter from it, and skidded to a stop, slamming a shoulder into the thick alloy. A1 whipped her head around and saw another barrier slam down twenty meters behind.

"Shit," she swore, about to direct Garza to provide her with overrides when the Link cut out. She looked to Saanvi. "Well, I guess it's safe to assume that Animus suspects us."

Saanvi shook her head, laughing softly.

"What?" A1 asked.

"Nothing, just glad to see that you've regained your sense of humor. A1's a bit of a sourpuss."

"I—" A1 began, then glanced at the other two Widows.

"Don't worry," Saanvi replied. "They have selective hearing now."

A1 slumped against the bulkhead. "Good, because the only thing I can think to do right now is have a good, old-fashioned panic attack."

DETERMINISM

STELLAR DATE: 10.12.8949 (Adjusted Years)
LOCATION: ISS *Falconer*, approaching Durgen Station
REGION: Karaske System, Rimward of Orion Nebula, Orion Freedom Alliance

"Tightbeam established with the *Perilous Dream*," the comm officer announced.

Joe didn't even acknowledge the statement before reaching out to his daughters, forgoing all formality. <*Girls, it's me, what's your status?*>

It was Faleena who replied. <*Dad, thank stars, we were starting to worry that you hadn't made it through. What took so long?*>

Joe snorted, shaking his head as he replied. <*Oh, I don't know, maybe the entire fleet of Guard ships you left me to deal with?*>

<*Sorry about that…*> Faleena sent along a soft laugh. <*What did you end up doing? Race them to the gate?*>

<*No.*> Joe's mental tone lost all traces of levity. <*Gamma Protocol.*>

<*Shit.*> His daughter's response was a whisper. <*So I guess that cat's out of the bag again. Though if you ask me, it was about time.*>

A rueful chuckle slipped past Joe's lips. <*I'm with you there. But it's a balancing act—you know the debate. Either way, a system like that was the perfect place to use picobombs. Chances are that the war will be over before any of the survivors make it back to civilization.*>

<*What about you? Will you own it?*> Faleena asked, and Joe was surprised that she'd even voice the question.

<*Of course I will. But that's not my concern right now. How are you four?*>

<*Only Priscilla is here with me. She's working on some final updates to the conditioning for the Widows. Cary and Saanvi have gone down to the station and are meeting with Garza.*>

<*They what?*> Joe demanded. <*They **went** to him?*>

<*Cary's really…settled into her role. There was no convincing her otherwise. She was adamant that A1 would go down there.*>

Joe realized he was pacing across the *Falconer*'s bridge, and forced himself to stop. <*OK, so what is your plan?*>

<*We've dropped four teams of Widows on the station, and they're moving to take key positions. There are another two hundred suited up and ready to go.*>

During the recent Widow incursion on the *I2*, it had occurred to Joe that the Widows were, in some respects, innocent victims of Lisa Wrentham's megalomania. Now, with his daughters adding to their mental compulsions, his girls were also adding to the Widow-clones' victimization. He consoled himself with the thought that the assassins were going to be used one way or another.

At least this mission would see an end to how they were being forced to dance to another's tune.

Granted, it's not much different for them than any other enlisted soldier. You go where you're ordered, and you very well may die when you get there.

Stars, this war sucks.

<My Marines are suited up,> Joe replied to his daughter. *<What targets are you hitting? We'll function as a reserve force.>*

Faleena passed a data packet outlining the positions they intended to take, and the opposition they expected to meet.

<Are you planning on—> she began, then paused. *<Oh shit!>*

<What?> Joe demanded.

<I just got a burst from Cary. They're trapped! She just disappeared off Link.>

<Where?!>

<They were almost at the ops center, here.> Faleena's words came fast, a note of fear in her voice.

Joe's heart thudded in his chest, but he schooled his emotions, knowing that his daughters' safety now depended on his ability to keep a level head.

<Launch your full assault,> he said to his daughter. *<I'm going to send in the Marines.>*

<On it.>

Joe drew a deep breath, taking a few seconds to prepare for what was to come. He turned to the forward holodisplay, watching the thirty rings of Durgen Station rotate around the station's central sphere, which had once been a natural moon.

Something about the visual impressed upon him how far from home they were, fighting a war with a clear purpose of decimating their enemies so severely that they would desist from attacking New Canaan—which no one expected to be a long-term solution.

With that total honesty regarding what was really going on firmly in mind, he turned to Captain Tracey.

"Drop stealth and activate shields. I'm passing targets for the assault teams. Comm, get me their stationmaster."

PART 3 – AIRTHA

UPDATES

STELLAR DATE: 10.10.8949 (Adjusted Years)
LOCATION: ISS *I2*, Airtha
REGION: Huygens System, Transcend Interstellar Alliance

<We just got a burst from Joe.>

Bob's voice carried a wry tone, and Tangel wondered what was amusing the AI so much. Given that the monumental task of securing the Airthan ring still lay ahead, anything other than general exhaustion felt wrong.

<What is it? Is everything alright?>

<It's a warning that there are Widows on the ring.>

Tangel groaned and placed a hand on her brow. *<Gee, sure glad he shared **that** with us...would have been great intel a day or two ago. Did he send a count? It would be nice to know if we nabbed them all.>*

<He did give a number,> the AI replied. *<You're not going to like it. We haven't found them all, and apparently there was a backup team. By my count, there are still at least thirty Widows on Airtha.>*

<Great,> Tangel replied. *<And here I thought we at least got the majority of them. Add that problem to all the AIs that refused the update and are still following Airtha's last orders, or Helen's....>*

<I'm taking care of them one-by-one.> Bob's tone changed from one of amusement to grim determination. *<Humans may have their foibles and vices, but most AIs can't bear to be off the Link for long. Most of them are coming back online of their own volition, and I'm force-feeding them the udpate.>*

Tangel nodded absently. The idea of forcing an AI to accept code that was self-altering felt wrong, but the alternative for them was worse.

The lesser of two evils.

The thought of 'two' brought the memory of the last time she'd seen Sera's two sisters, their bodies torn and battered, tucked away in stasis tubes. That sorrow was followed by the one she felt over the loss of Iris.

It had taken a day for that pain to really hit her. She'd held it at bay for a time, forcing herself to focus on the myriad tasks laid out before her, but that denial had only lasted for so long. Iris had been one of Angela's children, and the pain of her loss hit Tangel on two fronts.

Even so, she handled it better than Amavia. When Tangel had shared the news with the AI, the outpouring of grief that had come from Amavia had been overwhelming.

AIs liked to behave as though they didn't have an emotional connection to their children, but both Tangel and Amavia were half-human, so they felt Iris's death from both sides.

Earlier in the day, Tangel had spent long hours doing nothing more than wishing Joe were back so she could fall into his arms and have him tell her that everything would be alright. It bemused her that, despite her in-progress ascension and the joining of two strong, independent minds, she still wished for Joe's comforting presence and a few well-meant platitudes in times of need.

<*I can feel your sorrow,*> Bob said after not speaking for a time. <*But Iris took a full backup—she can be recovered. Finaeus has summoned a courier to bring it from Styx.*>

"I know," Tangel said aloud. "Which makes it all the more foolish for me to get upset about this. She'll be back, and she'll have just been missing for a few days. There's no need to get so emotional."

<*We feel things differently,*> the AI intoned. <*Ascension has opened up…other avenues for thought.*>

"I didn't know you felt at all," Tangel scoffed.

<*Don't be cruel,*> Bob replied with a soft laugh. <*You know I feel things.*>

Tangel nodded. She and Bob had spoken in the past about how he had his own form of 'feeling'. It was entirely foreign to her, even with all of Angela's knowledge and experience, yet she couldn't deny that the multinodal AI did indeed have his own brand of emotions.

"Sorry, that was off-the-cuff flippancy."

<*I forgive you.*>

"I just wish I could get ahold of Jessica," Tangel said after a minute. "They made the jump, but so far, no word. I'm tempted to send another ship to Star City."

<*That may be wise,*> Bob replied. <*Her QC blades clearly suffered some sort of damage, or else we would get a basic response. They were carrying four gates, though. I would have expected them to have set one up and sent a drone though by now.*>

"Exactly," Tangel replied. "I'm going to give it another day, and then head out there myself."

<*Is that a sound strategy?*> Bob asked. <*Especially because if you go, I go.*>

Tangel couldn't help but laugh. "Remember that time when Joe called you a city-sized puppy?"

<*You know I don't forget anything.*>

The AI's dour tone intensified Tangel's laugh, and it was still going when Sera appeared in her office's doorway. Her brows were raised, and a look of genuine concern was on the woman's face.

"You OK? Not losing it on us, are you?"

Tangel calmed herself and nodded. "Yeah, Bob is trying to cheer me up."

<And it's working.>

"So it would seem," Sera said, and Tanis could see the weary sadness in the other woman's eyes as well as hear it in her voice. "You got any of that for me?"

<Maybe. Humor has to be spontaneous, you know.>

Sera rolled her eyes, a single laugh escaping her throat. "I'm being lectured on humor by an AI."

<Made you laugh.>

"Hardly counts," she replied.

Tangel shook her head, glad that a bit of happiness had come their way. "That what brought you here? I doubt it was the pursuit of Bob's yuk-yuks."

"Well, I got a message relayed from Earnest and Terrance," Sera said as she moved beyond the doorway and walked into the office. "They've located the source of the star-shifting in the IPE. It's an automated facility, but they believe they can take it offline without trouble."

Sera's tone carried a note of uncertainty, and Tangel wondered if it was related to what she felt.

"A core AI facility, totally automated, and there's no cause for concern?" she asked.

Sera nodded. "Yeah, I had a similar reaction."

"Sheesh," Tangel muttered. "First, Jessica disappears, now this. Something's not right."

"When is anything ever 'right'?"

The question sent Tangel's thoughts racing back over the past few weeks. Since she'd begun her ascension on the streets of Jersey City, everything had been like a whirlwind, events rushing by so quickly, they'd been a blur.

From meeting Rika and sending her into Nietzschea, to discovering that Airtha was *also* operating in the Large Magellanic Cloud, to Cary killing Myrrdan, to herself battling—and nearly losing to—Xavia, then to finding Jeffrey Tomlinson, and taking the fight to Airtha....

And that's just a partial list.

"Honestly, I think that things haven't been 'right' since we got to Ascella," Tangel said after a moment. "No, further back. Before *Sabrina* left in search of Finaeus."

Sera laughed, finally sitting in a chair—or rather, draping herself across it in her usual fashion. "The way I see it, things weren't 'right' for me even at that point. Finaeus was missing and I knew there were hard times ahead. But I suppose for a few fleeting weeks, things felt pretty good." She leant forward, her eyes meeting Tangel's. "What about those two decades you spent building New Canaan? Weren't you at peace then?"

"Closer to fifteen years, and no, not really. I was always waiting for the other shoe to drop—which it frequently did."

"Fun times."

The two women regarded one another for a minute before Tangel gave a rueful laugh.

"What is it?" Sera asked.

"Well, I always said my plan was to sit on my porch and get old with my friends. Problem is, I *had* my porch, but Jessica was lost in Orion Space, and you were here at Airtha, so I was sitting on it alone—well, not alone, but you get the idea. There's a reason people always say 'friends *and* family'."

Sera winked at Tangel. "You've got a perfectly good porch down below in Ol' Sam. We've sat there a few times. Maybe that was always meant to be your real home, not Carthage."

"I'm not sure if that's depressing or satisfying.... Speaking of home, what are you doing up here anyway? Shouldn't you be down on the ring, being Queen Sera or something?"

The red-skinned woman winked. "You'd think so, wouldn't you. But after being ruled by a succession of increasingly...well, *bad* versions of 'me' over the past few years, the people of Airtha don't really see mine as a friendly face. Thankfully, Krissy stepped in. She's getting everything squared away, imposing martial law and other fun things."

"I heard about that. Strangely, no one really objected," Tangel said.

"I think the general populace is more than happy to lay low until things get sorted out. Although..." Sera sighed and looked like she was going to rise from her chair. "There are still Widows down there, and *her*..."

"Helen."

<Believe me, I am hunting her,> Bob chimed in.

"Thought you'd left humoring us for other pursuits, Bob," Sera said. "Have you found any signs of her?"

<Several. However, she is diffult to pin down. The ring is massive, and she knows its systems well. I'm also having to contend with one of the corrupted Airthas we inserted into the nodes. It leaked out and has been causing problems.>

"Leaked?" Tangel asked. "I thought it was programmed to seek out Airtha and weaken her."

"Is it chasing Helen, too?" Sera asked.

<Maybe. Finaeus is quite perturbed. It is not behaving as it should at all.>

Tangel blew out a frustrated breath. "Well, we took an Airthan shard and broke it on purpose to weaken Airtha...so how is it supposed to behave?"

<It's supposed to be more controllable. I've shifted my approach in the hunt for Helen. Instead of contending with the Airthan shard, I'm using it to help find her.>

"OK...this is making me feel a lot less victorious." Sera glanced at Tangel, her eyes laden with worry. "For all intents and purposes, there are two shards of my mother running around on this ring, and they could be up to anything."

"I suppose there's a silver lining," Tangel said, winking at her friend.

"Oh?"

"It's not very often that we see Bob frustrated."

<I'm frequently frustrated.>

Sera gave a rueful laugh. "You hide it well."

<I know. Humans—and most other AIs, for that matter—find it disturbing. They say it scares them.>

"OK." Tangel rose from her desk. "We've relaxed enough. We need to catch these two shards *and* the Widows so that the president can bring the government back to Airtha."

"Stars, I don't envy my father that job," Sera said. "Trying to merge the Khardine and Airthan governments while figuring out all the hidden agendas of everyone involved…that's the stuff of nightmares."

Tangel nodded. "Why do you think I accepted being the field marshal and got the heck out of New Canaan?"

"Tangel!" Sera put a hand over her mouth, eyes wide. "Stars, I could blackmail you with that information."

"Doubtful. My escape was incomplete. Even out here, Parliament constantly sends me things to weigh in on. Granted, I think that Jason encourages that just to get back at me for putting him in the governor's seat again."

Sera's eyes took on a far-off look. "You know, once we sort things out on Airtha, I think I need a little bit of leave to go see him. Who do I put in my request to?"

"Not me." Tangel held up her hands. "I'm not the boss of you."

<I'll approve it,> Bob interjected. *<If anyone asks, tell them that I ordered you to go to Carthage.>*

"Oooooh!" Sera grinned. "Orders from the great and mighty Bob! No one will question those."

Tangel walked around her desk, placing an arm around the other woman's shoulders as she stood. "C'mon. You can bask in the glory of an impending vacation later. Right now, reality beckons. Let's go hunt your mothers."

Sera leant into Tangel for a moment. "Stars, my family is so fucked up."

WIDOWHUNT

STELLAR DATE: 10.10.8949 (Adjusted Years)
LOCATION: Gingham Mountains, Airtha
REGION: Huygens System, Transcend Interstellar Alliance

"I hate Widows," Katrina muttered as she crept along the ledge, doing her best not to look at the ground three kilometers below. "And who puts mountains like this on a ring, anyway?"

They'd only had a few hours' rest following the victory over Airtha when the hunt for the remaining Widows had resumed. Katrina had teamed up with Carl, Malorie, Erin, and Usef—all of whom were now traversing the Gingham Mountains, after a civilian tip had come in that there were Widows in the area.

"Someone with a sense of adventure," Malorie tittered as she skittered around Katrina, causing the *Voyager*'s captain to bite her lip and thank her armor's a-grav systems for keeping her steady.

<*Can we have a bit of tactical silence?*> Usef asked as he placed a hand on Katrina's shoulder, giving her a nudge to keep moving.

<*We're on a cliff, halfway up a mountain,*> Katrina retorted. <*The wind is howling so much, I wouldn't be able to hear if a rocket took off from below us.*>

<*All the more reason to use the Link,*> the colonel said.

<*I've got a sign of passage,*> Malorie called back. <*Bootprint in some dirt and a crushed plant.*>

<*Sloppy for a Widow,*> Erin said from her position at the team's rear.

Katrina was a bit surprised that Erin had opted to come along. While the woman was handy with a rifle—courtesy of some adventures she'd had back at New Canaan—she wasn't a trained soldier. Her reason for joining the Airthan assault was the utilization of her technical expertise.

Granted, it was apparent that there was some sort of bond between the engineer and Usef. Katrina couldn't tell if it was amorous, or if they were just really good friends.

I guess this is how our kind of people spend time together, Katrina thought with a laugh.

<*Do you see anything more?*> Usef asked Malorie.

<*Umm…yes. Up ahead, the ledge widens to a shelf…sort of bowl, I guess. There are a few trees in the middle. At most, it's about twenty meters across. Cliff goes up a few hundred on the left, and then our friend, the drop of doom, down on the right.*>

Usef sent a grunt of annoyance. <*I meant do you see more signs of Widows, not more terrain.*>

<*Listen, mister Hulk.*> Malorie's tone dripped acid. <*I was getting to that. I can see indications that they stayed to the left, working their way along the cliff face.*>

<*Easy, Mal,*> Katrina said reflexively. <*How many does it look like?*>

<*Hard to say…It's only a print here and there, a broken twig, stuff like that.*>

Katrina eased around the corner, the shelf coming into view. It was as the spider-woman had described, a small bowl of trees and grass nestled against the mountainside. A small pond was in the center…or perhaps a puddle, just a few meters across.

<*There have to be at least a few of them,*> Erin said. <*The intel we got indicates at least thirty more Widows on the ring. I can't see them all going solo.*>

<*Maybe they would,*> Carl countered. <*How much do we really know about how they operate? Maybe solo is how they normally roll.*>

Usef grunted in disagreement. <*We've only ever seen them working in groups. No reason to think they'd split up now.*>

<*I don't like this,*> Katrina said after a moment's reflection. <*It screams 'trap'.*>

<*How?*> Erin asked. <*Chances are that they can't see us, and we can't see them.*>

<*Look at all the grass, Erin,*> Usef said. <*We can't move without disturbing it. They'll spot us in a heartbeat.*>

<*They won't spot me,*> Malorie chittered a laugh. <*No big hulk feet here.*>

Katrina considered their options and then wondered if she should run them past Usef; operational command was a bit muddy between the two of them. Technically, she had no rank in the ISF, and Usef was a venerated colonel.

But that was made more complex by their past relationships, when she was a governor and he was a lieutenant. Plus the six hundred years she had on him.

<*Malorie,*> she said after a moment. <*I want you to go straight up the center and take a position by that boulder on the far side of the pond.*>

<*You mean the puddle?*>

Katrina rolled her eyes for no one's benefit but her own. <*Yeah, on the far side of the puddle.*>

<*I know you rolled your eyes at me,*> Malorie said.

<*How? You can't see me.*>

<*It was in your tone. You have 'eyeroll tone'.*>

Katrina resisted the urge to roll them again. <*I do not. Now go take that position.*>

<*You know, Captain…*> Carl paused for a moment before pressing on. <*I hate to take Malorie's side—*>

<*Thanks,*> Malorie interjected.

<*—but you really do have 'eyeroll tone'.*>

<*Carl?*> Katrina asked.

<*Yeah?*>

<*Shut up. You just pulled cliff duty.*>

<*What?*>

Usef cleared his throat. <*Chances are there are Widows on our right, over the edge of the cliff, ready to catch us in a crossfire. You're going to go over the edge and get in position to flank them when they pop up.*>

<*Over the edge?*> Carl asked, turning his head toward the three-kilometer drop. <*Seriously?*>

<*You're in heavy armor, it has a-grav,*> Katrina said. <*You pop over and hang out down below. Just stay out of sight behind the bowl's curve.*>

<*And don't actively use your a-grav,*> Usef cautioned. <*Anchor and wait, then come around when shit hits the fan. Which will happen after we give away our positions with EM activity.*>

Katrina chuckled, amused that she and Usef had the exact same plan without needing to discuss it.

<*And me?*> Erin asked.

<*You're staying back in reserve,*> Katrina replied. <*I'll take the cliff face, Usef will go right down the center.*>

<*What about all that grass?*> Carl asked.

<*I have a lighter step than you'd expect,*> the colonel replied.

A minute later, Malorie reported that she was in position, adding in a few barbs about the rest of the team being slow and proposing that their reluctance to evolve beyond using only two legs made them lesser beings.

<*You know…*> Katrina said as she edged along the cliff face, following the barely visible trail sign that the Widows had left. <***I'm** the one that put you in that body.*>

<*Maybe I made you think you did when it's what I wanted all along,*> Malorie retorted.

<*Nice try,*> Katrina replied. <*Granted, you were probably happy to have **any** body again.*>

<*Someday you're going to have to tell me how you all got together,*> Erin said, laughing softly from her position at the rear.

Katrina pursed her lips. <*I'd rather not.*>

<*I'll tell it,*> Malorie said. <*It all began when Katrina was a terrible warlord, raining destruction down on the peaceful people of Midditerra.*>

<*Malorie…*> Katrina warned.

<*OK, then **you** tell it.*>

<*Can we focus, people?*> Usef asked. <*We're trying to give away our positions with EM, not get distracted by an argument. Also, Malorie, **you** weren't supposed to give away your position. Now you need to move to a new one.*>

<*Party pooper.*> Malorie followed the statement with a snort, then fell silent.

Katrina noticed that Usef didn't chastise Erin for speaking up, but she supposed he might have done it privately. She pushed the thought from her mind, and focused on following the trail left by the Widows while being as invisible as the tall grass and other undergrowth allowed.

Usef had just passed the pond, and Katrina was halfway around the bowl, when shots rained down from the cliff above, some striking Usef, others hitting the dirt around Katrina. She dove back and flattened herself against the cliff, sending out drones to search for the shooters.

On the combat net, she saw Usef lunge behind a rock. It gave him cover from the fire originating on the cliff to the left, but as she'd predicted, several Widows began to fire from the edge of the bowl, shots striking the Marine as he moved to better cover.

Katrina didn't have a clear line of sight on any of the attackers and moved further along the cliff, easing underneath a shallow overhang. Above, her drones located the shooters and fed their positions to the combat net.

<Looks like two up there,> Erin commented, and Katrina sent an affirmative response. She eased out around the overhang and fired two seeker rounds from her weapon.

Seeking bullets didn't strike with as much energy as normal projectile shots, but the explosive tips they bore added to the punch. One of the rounds hit its target, but the other was destroyed by a defensive beam.

"Shit," Katrina swore as her drones got a clear visual of the target she'd hit. *<The ones on the cliff are drones!>*

She fired another salvo of seeker rounds before backing further from the base of the cliff and firing a barrage of pure kinetic shots at the final target.

Rock rained down around her as she backpedaled further, turning her attention to the battle at the pond. Usef had moved to new cover and was firing at anything that moved along the edge of the cliff.

He'd weathered a few strikes, but his armor was holding out so far. On the combat net, Katrina saw that Carl was moving along the cliff, nearly in a position to engage the Widows hiding over the edge.

Amidst it all, Malorie was still perched atop a rock, motionless and invisible despite the chaos around her.

Katrina launched a salvo at the Widows firing over the cliff edge, and then moved to new cover. Her drones were still scouring the cliff above, and they flagged a heat signature. She wasn't sure if it was another shooter or just a piece of debris, but fired on it anyway, not caring about conserving her ammunition.

An enemy drone fell from the location, and she gave a satisfied laugh, turning her attention to the fight at the edge of the ledge, where she saw that Malorie still hadn't moved to assist Usef and Carl.

<Want to join in the fun?> Katrina asked acerbically.

<I'm waiting. There aren't enough of them yet.>

<You waiting for all thirty?> Usef demanded.

The spider-woman laughed. *<No, just the two laying in the puddle, waiting to make their move. I figure it's not fair to just jump on them while they're not doing anything.>*

<Mal!> Katrina shouted. *<Take them!>*

<Fine.>

Katrina saw a splash as an invisible object hit the water, then an ethereal shriek sounded as one of the Widows met the business end of Malorie's talons.

No further fire came from the cliff face above, and Katrina turned her full attention to the other side of the bowl. She moved through the sparse undergrowth to the largest tree on the ledge, leaning around it and taking aim at the pool, waiting for a clear shot.

*<You could have told me, Mal, and **I** would have just shot them,>* Usef said as another piercing scream came from amidst the sprays of water.

<You can now!> Malorie cried out.

Katrina's visual overlay showed the spider-woman scampering away from the pond. Behind her, water sloughed off another figure as it rose and gave chase. Katrina didn't hesitate, firing a trio of kinetic rounds at the Widow. Armor cracked, and the assassin became visible, blood leaking out where the third round had hit.

<Got one,> Usef called out. *<Carl, flush the others up.>*

<Gonna be tough. So far, they're flushing me down!>

Usef circled around a group of boulders, moving toward the edge of the cliff. He was almost in a position to fire when rounds struck him in the back. Katrina spun to once again see shots raining down from the cliff above. She moved to the other side of the tree and returned fire, noting that Usef had gone prone behind a boulder before crawling to the edge.

<Heading up!> Malorie announced, and Katrina swore under her breath, shifting to provide covering fire for the spider-woman as she scaled the cliff, racing up the sheer face as though it were flat ground.

<Shit!> Carl shouted. *<There're two of them here still…I can't—>*

The man let out a gargled cry, his vitals spiking. Katrina broke cover, rushing to the edge. She was still only halfway there when she saw that Erin had beat her to the brink, jumping off and firing at the enemies below.

<What are you doing?> Usef demanded.

<Got him!> Erin called back a moment later. *<Bringing him down to one of the switchbacks.>*

Katrina skidded to a stop at the edge, shots from the cliffs above raining down around her. *<Is he OK?>*

<I'm good,> Carl grunted his reply. *<Just got hit in the arm.>*

<Which is gone now,> Erin clarified.

<Oh shit!> Malorie interrupted. *<They're not drones up here! I've got at least three of these bitches!>*

<You want a hand?> A new voice joined the combat net.

<Cheeky? Are you nearby?> Katrina asked. *<I thought you were taking out those Widows on High Airtha?>*

<All done,> Sabrina chimed in. *<We were flying back to the* I2 *when I decided to tap your combat net.>*

<*Sooo…help?*> Cheeky asked.

<*Stop asking and start shooting!*> Usef hollered. <*Targets are on the net.*>

Seconds later, beams came down through the clouds, two striking the cliffs above, and one hitting a target below the ledge.

<*Three down, last one is too close to you,*> Cheeky announced.

<*I got it,*> Usef grunted as he leant out over the drop and fired a trio of rounds.

<*OK,*> Katrina said as she moved across the bowl to the far side. <*Let's sweep it.*>

<*Do you want us to stay onstation?*> Cheeky asked as *Sabrina* appeared a few kilometers from the mountain, lazily drifting closer like a blue and silver cloud of destruction.

<*Would you mind?*> Katrina asked. <*I imagine our quarry was all here, but it would be nice to be sure.*>

<*You got it,*> Sabrina chimed in. <*What about Troy and the* Voyager*? Where are they?*>

<*They went to secure one of the ring's support columns,*> Katrina said as she walked to the edge of the cliff and looked over, keeping an eye peeled for any movement.

<*Kirb and Camille with them?*> Cheeky asked.

<*Yeah,*> Malorie grunted as she skittered back down the cliff face. <*They weren't interested in schlepping around on this mountain, so they took the easy job.*>

<*You know…*> Erin said from her position further down the mountain. <*Since you're here, Sabrina, think you can pick up a girl and her armless friend?*>

<*Wow,*> Carl muttered. <*I guess I should be happy you didn't call me a sack of potatoes.*>

<*You're too big for that. More like a sack of watermelons.*>

<*Stars, I leave for a few years, and you get all sassy,*> Usef commented as *Sabrina* moved closer to the mountainside, the ship's main bay door sliding open.

Katrina could see a small figure outlined in the entrance. Then a second appeared.

<*That you, Misha and Nance?*> she asked.

<*As the day is long,*> Misha replied. <*Was just getting ready to cook dinner, too.*>

Nance elbowed Misha. <*I think saving Carl's life is a worthwhile diversion, I—*>

<*I'm not actually dying here,*> Carl interrupted, his voice a low growl. <*It's just a flesh wound.*>

<*Your arm is* ***gone****,*> Erin corrected.

<*Still not a big deal.*>

<*Still more than a flesh wound,*> she insisted.

<*See anyone else?*> Katrina asked Usef and Malorie.

The Marine shook his head. <*Not that I can* ***see****. But Widows have shockingly good stealth.*>

<*I hadn't noticed,*> Katrina said dryly.

<*Now who's sassy?*> Erin asked.

It took a few minutes to get Carl safely aboard *Sabrina*, after which, the team searched the shelf again before following the narrow ledge around the mountain to the ridgeline. *Sabrina* flew passes overhead, scanning the slopes for activity. After an hour with no further signs, the team gathered the Widows' bodies and loaded them onto the ship.

"So that's twenty we've taken out, right?" Cheeky asked as she met Katrina in the ship's galley, where Misha was nearly done with dinner.

"Twenty-two," Katrina corrected. "I just got word that Tangel and Sera took out a pair."

"Shit!" Cheeky exclaimed. "Are those ugly, faceless bitches hitting the *I2* again?"

"No," Katrina shook her head. "Troy told me that Tangel and Sera are down on the ring helping Bob find Helen."

Cheeky glanced at one of the optical pickups. "Sabs! How come you're not sharing the AI intel like Troy does?"

<*For starters, I'm Sabrina, not Sabs. Sabs is down in medical with Nance.*>

"Sheesh. That's not going to get confusing at all," Katrina muttered as she walked to the counter and poured herself a cup of coffee.

"Tell me about it," Misha said as he cut slices of pork off a roast. "I can't keep them straight now. In my head, I have to think of them as 'Ship' and 'Chrome Ass'."

Sabrina's laugh filled the room. <*I'm going to get my stern chromed just to mess with you more.*>

Katrina leant against the counter, sipping her coffee as she watched Cheeky grab plates for dinner, while joining in needling Misha.

She'd never been aboard *Sabrina* before, but interactions with her own crew had always been generally fun and humorous affairs. Standing in the ship's galley, she could tell that joking and needling was the norm for this crew as well; laughing off stress and cares was their way of life.

What was most interesting to Katrina was that this crew had initially been put together by Sera. The dark-haired scion of the Tomlinson house wasn't without a lighter side, but she wasn't likely to have been the genesis of this modus operandi.

If I had to bet on it, it's Cheeky and Sabrina. Those two just exude an energy that fills this whole ship.

The realization caused her to feel a modicum of sadness that the *Voyager* hadn't echoed with laughter as much as it could have over the years. She didn't think of her crew as a dour bunch by comparison, but they always seemed to carry the memory of how they had first come together.

Memories of Juasa flooded into Katrina's mind, and she let them wash over her, her long-ago lover's smile still perfectly rendered in her mind's eye.

I miss you, Juasa. And I'm still sorry.

"Well, Kat?" Cheeky asked, her voice rising a half octave as she spoke.

" 'Kat'?" Katrina scoffed, drawing her attention back to the present. "Do I call you 'Chee'?"

Cheeky shrugged. "You can call me anything you like. A natural redhead is my kryptonite."

"Everything's your kryptonite," Misha said as he set the platter of meat on the table.

"What's kryptonite?" Katrina asked as she pulled up a chair and settled next to Cheeky.

"A green rock from the planet Krypton," the captain explained. "It makes SuperGuy weak."

"SuperGuy?"

Misha nodded as he began to make a pitcher of lemonade. "Yeah, from the ancient SuperGuy vids. We found some of them in a vault awhile back. There was a huge stash of ancient shows and we have been watching them together. The SuperGuy ones are from the twenty-sixth century."

"Not as old as Star Wars," Cheeky said. "Which is totally my favorite. I think it's a true story."

"A long time ago, in a galaxy far, far away…" Misha intoned in a mysterious voice.

"That makes no sense," Katrina interjected. "When was *that* made?"

Cheeky shrugged. "Somewhere back around the dawn of time."

"Twentieth century," Misha supplied. "So a few years after the dawn of time."

"Close enough."

"What's it about?" Katrina asked, nodding to Nance and Usef as they entered the galley.

Cheeky placed both hands on the table and leant forward, eyes narrowing as her voice dropped to a whisper. "A dark lord, powerful in the Force, and a young boy who is given a mythical weapon to stand up against the evil empire!"

"Star Wars?" Nance asked.

"Uh-huh," Misha said.

The ship's engineer turned to Katrina. "Has she tried to tell you it's a true story yet?"

Katrina nodded. "Not really buying it."

"That's because you've never met a space wizard." Cheeky fixed Katrina and then Nance with a serious look. "If you had, you'd have no trouble believing that, out there, somewhere, Darth Vader is waiting."

"Didn't he die, though?" Misha asked as Erin and Sabs entered the galley.

"Spoilers!" Cheeky shouted. "*Some* of us didn't go ahead and watch the next movies without the rest of the crew!"

"Well, it's been weeks!"

<*Misha, we're fighting a war,*> Sabrina said in a mollifying tone. <*We can't always fit in a vid-night on the regular schedule.*>

The cook glared at one of the optical pickups, then directed his glare to Cheeky. "Huh…yet you still expect your food on a schedule."

"OK…" Sabs held up a hand to deflect further ire from the cook. "We'll schedule a vid night as soon as possible. Maybe on the flight out of the Huygens System."

With a haughty sniff, Misha turned back to the counter, and grabbed a bowl of salad and a basket of bread. He opened his mouth to say something more, but ended up gently setting the food on the table before settling into his chair and muttering something about being sorry for letting a spoiler slip.

"Sooooo…" Katrina stuck a fork into a slice of meat, pulling it onto her plate. "I assume Carl's going to be OK?"

"He's in the medtube right now," Nance replied. "He should be patched up in a few hours—made me promise to save him some leftovers."

"Is Malorie with him?"

<*She's with the chickens.*> Sabrina's voice sounded both amused and concerned.

"She's not…hurting them, is she?" Misha asked.

<*Do you really think I'd sound this calm if someone was hurting my birds? Well…other than you when you cook them.*>

"I suppose not," the cook replied. "So what is she doing?"

<*Right now? She's clucking at them. She clucks, they cluck. Over and over.*>

"Please tell me you're recording it," Katrina said, watching Erin lift a hand to her lips, hiding a smile.

<*Oh stars yes.*>

Katrina didn't bother hiding her own grin as she cut off a piece of her meat. "That's going to be some amazing blackmail material."

<*It—oh shit!*> Sabrina fell silent after her exclamation, but Katrina could feel a change in the ship's engines.

"What is it?" she and Erin demanded at the same time.

<*Helen.*> Sabrina's voice dripped with venom. <*Sera and Tangel found her, and they need help.*>

Usef set his fork down and rose from the table. "Suit up, people. We're going back in."

PURSUING MOTHER

STELLAR DATE: 10.10.8949 (Adjusted Years)
LOCATION: The Unnamed Forest, Airtha
REGION: Huygens System, Transcend Interstellar Alliance

"I've been on a lot of rings," Tangel said as she and Sera reached a clearing in the forest. "But Airtha is still blowing my mind."

"We need a new name. I really don't want to keep calling it that," Sera replied. "Maybe Finaesia."

Finaeus glanced at his niece and grunted. "No."

"Finland?" Tangel asked.

"Extra no."

"Stars," Sera muttered. "Who died and made you king of Airtha?"

The ancient engineer snorted. "Ironically…Airtha."

"He got you there." Tangel laughed. "OK, so Helen is somewhere in this forest, topside, too."

"There are no sub-layers here," Finaeus explained. "Just a kilometer of carbon beneath this stretch of woods, and then space."

"Why's that?" Tangel asked.

"Balance," Finaeus said. "Had to make things thinner here, and it was easier to route sub-level stuff elsewhere so as not to harm the ring's structural integrity."

"Hence the forest?" Sera asked.

"Hence the forest."

Tangel surveyed the tall oak trees, noting the elms and poplars interspersed amongst them. "OK…. So Helen would know that there's no way out. Why'd she come here? We've got a platoon with shadowtrons moving through these trees, and Bob's watching over us from above. She's out of options."

"Which is why I don't like it," Finaeus replied. "Not one bit. She's up to something."

"Has to be," Sera agreed. "She's not stupid."

Tangel glanced at Sera, trying not to actively pity the woman next to her. Helen had lived in Sera's head for over four decades, and as such, they had developed a very special bond.

Their union had lasted much longer than the generally safe norm, but the two had never shown any signs of intergrowth—though now it was apparent why. Tangel had since learned that Helen had never hidden from Sera that she was a shard of Airtha.

What Sera hadn't known was that Airtha was her mother…and that the AI was ascending, and possibly insane.

Not for the first time, Tangel considered advising Sera that hunting her own mother wasn't wise—especially when Helen, unlike Airtha, really had been a mother figure to Sera. But one look at the grim determination in her friend's eyes let Tangel know just how well such a request would be received.

"So what are we missing," she mused, feeling her way through the trees with her extradimensional senses. "And why can't I see her? Either she's slipped through our net, or she's figured out how to mask herself."

<*I don't see any indication of her or the corrupted shard,*> Bob chimed in from where the *I2* hung a thousand kilometers overhead. <*But I also don't see any sign that they've left the area, either.*>

<*Anything on the perimeter, Lieutenant?*> Tangel asked Mason, knowing that if he had picked up any sign, he would have said so, but feeling compelled to ask nonetheless.

<*Sorry, ma'am. Neither hide nor hair…though I suppose our quarry has neither of those.*>

Tanis laughed softly, shaking her head. <*Yeah, you need a new metaphor for hunting AIs.*>

<*Noted.*>

They passed through the clearing and back into the forest. Here, the trees were tall, with wide boughs creating a dense canopy of leaves. As a result, the undergrowth was thin, and they could see almost a hundred meters in any direction.

Tangel could see even further in other dimensions, the three-dimensional trees doing little to obstruct her view in the fourth and fifth.

The ground beneath her feet did not provide a significant visual barrier, either. It was something she'd gotten used to, the ability to see through the very surfaces that kept her from falling into space. One of the things that had taken a lot of effort to deal with was being able to see through a ship's hull while traveling through space.

She would have expected Airtha to feel more substantial, but it didn't. The ring rotated at an incredible speed, which caused the stars she could see through its surface to wheel and spin past disconcertingly.

Granted, you're still recovering from going toe-to-toe with Airtha and having her swat you like a fly.

That thought caused her to wonder if she was once again biting off more than she could chew.

<*Do you think I can take on Helen?*> Tangel asked Bob. <*I'm not used to losing like this—or needing someone else to ride in to my rescue all the time.*>

<*Just remember what Cary taught you with the grav shield. Deflect and compress, deflect and compress.*>

<*Easy for you to say,*> Tangel scoffed good-naturedly. <*You're a starship. Deflecting is what you do.*>

The AI groaned, but didn't give a verbal response. Silence wore on for several minutes, until Tangel gave in first.

<OK. Yes. I get it. Any practice I can get is good practice.>

<Exactly. It's not impossible. I've done, it, Cary's done it. Yes, our enemies have all been ascended longer than we, but they're cocky, overconfident.>

<Think so?> Tangel asked. *<We just crushed their defenses, defeated Airtha herself, and ended the civil war.>*

<Effectively ended,> the AI corrected. *<There's still a lot of work to be done.>*

<Right. Effectively.>

<So?>

Tangel wished Bob was present so she could give him a cool glare. *<So why would she be cocky? We've crushed her.>*

<I've spoken to Helen at length in the past—> Bob paused mid-sentence.

<What is it?>

<Search ahead on your two o'clock,> the AI directed. *<Something's not right there.>*

Tangel reached out with her extradimensional senses, peering through the forest like it wasn't there, searching for whatever it was that Bob had seen.

<What am I—> Tangel began, but then stopped herself. "Finaeus, you said that there's nothing underneath this forest, right?"

"I take it by your question that that is no longer the case?" the engineer asked.

"Ahead…there's a hidden entrance to a shaft. It seems to lead down to a bay and…and a ship."

"Shit!" Sera exclaimed. "Where? We need to stop her!"

Tangel highlighted the shaft's entrance. "Krissy's ships are all too far to get here before it can leave," she said. *<Bob, you need to get closer.>*

<Rachel's in the loop. We're on our way.>

"*Sabrina*'s nearby," Sera suggested. "On her way to the *I2*."

"Get her down there. Stall that ship," Tangel ordered, breaking into a full run, with Sera and Finaeus behind her.

<I've alerted Krissy and the TSF. They're moving a squadron into position, but they're at least fifteen minutes out, maybe more,> Bob advised.

"Helen's not getting away, then," Sera said, catching up to Tangel. "Not unless she's got a gate down there."

The two women looked at one another and began to run faster.

"Finaeus!" Tangel called over her shoulder. "What would happen to the ring if a gate was activated inside it?"

"It would survive," the engineer pronounced from a few paces behind. "We, on the other hand, would not."

The hidden entrance was set at the base of a low rise, and Tangel reached out with her extradimensional limbs, disassembling the earthen bank to reveal the short corridor beyond. She dashed ahead, spotting and dissolving automated defense systems before they even had a chance to deploy and fire.

A few seconds later, she came to the shaft. It dropped nearly five hundred meters, and the lift car was at the bottom.

"See you down there," Tangel called out, and jumped.

Cary had taught her how to make graviton shields that would allow her to deflect attacks from other ascended beings. What they hadn't discussed—but what Tangel knew was entirely possible—was to use the ability to direct gravitons to make her own personal a-grav field.

What a time to test my theory.

The bottom of the shaft was rushing toward her, and Tangel held out her arms, generating the graviton field, and then flipping the polarity of the gravitons and pushing them away from herself.

Sure enough, the reaction slowed her descent and, though she dented the top of the lift car with her impact, she was unharmed and able to dissolve the metal beneath her. The lift doors were open, and the moment she landed on the car's floor, she sprinted down the corridor.

<*Nice trick,*> Finaeus called down after her.

<*I'm full of surprises,*> Tangel called back.

The engineer grunted. <*Never said it was surprising.*>

She didn't reply, only increased her speed, barreling down the passage, burning away anything that looked even remotely close to a defensive weapon. After half a minute, she came to the bay where a corvette rested.

The ship was already on the debarkation rails, sliding toward the open bay doors and a drop into space.

<*No jump gate in here,*> Tangel called back. <*But her ship is on the rails!*>

<*There's no way she can just fly away,*> Sera said. <*She* **has** *to have a plan to slip past Krissy's fleet.*>

Tangel agreed, but didn't respond as she raced across the deck, reaching out for the ship's airlock and dissolving the hull with her non-corporeal limbs. The corvette was almost beyond the bay's grav shield, and Tangel poured on a final burst of speed and leapt into the airlock a second before the ship passed into vacuum and its shields activated.

<*Made it!*> Tangel called back, glancing across the bay to see two figures racing through the corridor.

<*Shit,*> Sera muttered. <*Tangel…I—*>

<*I'll try to take her alive if I can,*> the field marshal replied, turning to face the inner airlock door.

Dissolving it was an option, but she felt her strength waning after tearing apart so much of the corridor as she'd rushed through it.

Who ever thought that assimilating matter and converting it into energy would be so draining, she thought with a soft laugh as she placed a hand on the airlock's control panel and fed a nanofilament into it.

~Door's open.~ Helen's voice came into Tangel's mind. *~No need to shred more of my ship.~*

~We're not going to let you get away,~ Tangel said as she tried to simply open the airlock door.

It slid aside without any breach necessary, and she stepped through into an interior passage, sealing the entrance behind her.

The bridge was on her left, and she could feel Helen's energy emanating from that direction.

~You're not going to be able to stop me,~ the shard of Airtha replied. *~You couldn't defeat me before, and you won't be able to now.~*

~Not going to stop me from trying.~

Tangel released a nanocloud, using it to augment her extra senses. Unlike Helen, she was still corporeal enough that a shot to the head would be as fatal as an ascended being's attack.

Nothing raised any alarms, and she pushed forward, moving down a cross passage before coming to the ship's central corridor.

The moment she stepped into it, a burst of energy shot out toward her. The nanocloud had given enough warning, and Tangel ducked back, sucking in a breath as she looked at the hole burned in the bulkhead.

~Whatever happened to not destroying your ship?~

~I just wanted you in range.~

Tangel funneled the energy she'd gathered from the matter she'd disintegrated in her rush though the corridors, and formed a brane around herself, and a graviton field beyond that.

~You're going to have to fire a lot more energy than that,~ Tangel said. *~Your ship won't survive.~*

She stepped out into the corridor, the open entrance to the bridge only twenty meters away. Helen didn't respond as Tangel strode toward it, steeling herself for whatever might come next.

As she neared the bridge, the shard appeared in the entrance, a swirling mass of luminescent limbs that blocked her forward progress.

"What do you hope to achieve?" Tangel asked. "Airtha is gone, you've lost."

~No.~ Helen's limbs waved side to side. *~We still control much of the Transcend. We'll bring all of humanity under our banner, and then destroy the core AIs.~*

Tangel shook her head, her eyes boring into the creature before her. *~We share the same goals. Why are you fighting against me?~*

~Because your compassion will cause you to lose, Tangel.~ Helen threw the words out as angry accusation, her color shifting down the spectrum, taking on a purple hue. *~When I first met you aboard* Sabrina, *I'd hoped that you would be able to take the fight to the core, but it became apparent that you wanted to hide away from the galaxy's troubles. That's why I took Sera from you, sent her where I could keep working*

at making her into the leader humanity and AIs need.~

"You orchestrated all that?" Tangel asked. "I guess it makes sense. You're the one that ensured Elena would arrive in New Canaan to warn us that Jeffrey Tomlinson was coming—well, the pretend Jeffrey."

~Indeed. The original was not malleable enough. And you're right—Airtha and I sent both the harbinger and the threat to New Canaan, all so that Sera could see how untrustworthy those around her were. To steel her for what was to come.~

As the ascended being spoke, Tangel began to realize something she'd never before considered. Though it was no secret that she and Airtha essentially shared the same goals, it was also readily apparent that they were not using the same means to achieve those goals.

Even so, they could have allied in some fashion. The fact that Airtha and Helen had never even asked to was a mystery Tangel had never understood. Logic dictated that they should have joined forces, but Airtha had always sought to take the picotech from New Canaan and see the colonists destroyed, all while bolstering Sera to be the one ruling the galaxy—a job Sera had never wanted.

"I don't know what would make a being like you insane," Tangel said in a whisper. "But you've clearly lost control of your faculties. You *and* Airtha. What is with this blind nepotism of yours?"

~Whoever takes the reins of the galaxy **must** *be willing to sacrifice anything to see victory. You've shown time and time again that you'll let your morality stop you from realizing your goals. We're not insane, we're pure logic.~*

A suspicion Tangel had always harbored was that the core AIs had sent Airtha back as a foil. A being that would appear to be working against them, but be flawed in some way and in fact foil any efforts made against them.

I can only imagine the state things would be in if the Intrepid *had come out in the ninety-fifth century as everyone had expected.*

~Are you coming, Bob?~ Tangel sent out, wondering if she had the range to reach the AI.

~I am, but we have to fly around the ring, brake, and come back up. Sabrina *is much closer. She'll be there in a minute.~*

Tangel wondered what *Sabrina* would be able to do, though she supposed that at least the other ship could facilitate a rescue, if she and Helen destroyed the corvette.

Rather than replying to Helen, Tangel took a step forward, trying to see into the bridge. Her nanocloud hadn't been able to make it past Helen, and she wanted to see what the vessel's heading was.

The Airthan shard whipped a limb out toward Tangel to stop her approach, but it collided with her grav shield and protective brane.

~You're not going to dissuade me.~ Tangel said, continuing to move forward.

Helen sent a burst of energy toward her, but it was deflected, cutting a long slash in the bulkhead.

~Very well,~ Helen said. *~I may not be able to destroy you without destroying this ship, but I also don't need it to last that long.~*

Before Tangel could ask what that meant, a signal from Cheeky reached her.

<Tangel! There's a gate mounted in one of the carbon mountains on the ring's underside. You're going to reach it before we reach you!>

<Dammit!>

Tangel knew that ordering *Sabrina* to shoot the jump gate wasn't an option. Ford svaiter gates were powered by antimatter, and if it exploded, it could destroy a sizable part of the ring—especially in this region, where the structure was thinner.

She wasn't quite ready to order *Sabrina* to shoot at the ship she was aboard, either.

There was a change in the air around her, and Tangel realized that her way forward was blocked by a grav field. She tried to push against it, but it was blocking her in all dimensions.

The field stretched along the bulkheads, closing in behind her. She reached out, pushing her own gravitons against it, but momentum was on Helen's side, and the field closed around Tangel.

She railed against it, focusing her energy on a single point, but Helen only laughed.

~I have the ship's CriEn to draw on. You're not going to defeat me.~

The Airthan shard added a brane, encapsulating Tangel in a magnetic field that cut off her communication with *Sabrina.*

No! Tangel shouted in her mind, pushing with all her might, dissolving the deck beneath her and funneling its mass into an attack on the prison Helen had made.

The air was heating up in her shield, but Tangel didn't slow her assault, focusing a beam of energy coupled with particles moving as fast as she could accelerate them toward a single point directly in front of her.

Despite Helen's assertion that Tangel would not be able to push though, a crack formed in the graviton field, and then the brane beyond it.

At that moment, a voice came from the bridge. It was partially garbled, words out of order as it squawked out of the speakers.

"Not stop go! Destroy shard."

There was something familiar to the voice, but Tangel couldn't immediately place it.

Helen moved back from the bridge's entrance, revealing the forward holodisplay, which showed the jump gate's ring rapidly approaching the ship. The Airthan shard was manipulating one of the consoles, her movements hinting at concern.

Then the ship veered off to port, a starscape replacing the ring's glow.

~No!~ Helen wailed.

In that moment, Tangel managed to break free, and she ran onto the bridge, slamming a brane around Helen and cutting the ascended being off from the rest of the ship.

"Tangel..." the voice said. "Please. Save me."

"Who are you?" Tangel replied, careful to keep her focus on Helen, who was writhing in the brane's grip.

The shard's strength was impressive, and Tangel reached out to the ship's main powerplant, drawing energy from the CriEn to keep her brane intact while she moved toward the navigation console.

After a moment of silence, barring the hissing wails coming from Helen, the voice replied with just one word.

"Iris."

"What?" Tangel blurted, then she felt Helen renew her fight against the brane. She turned toward the ascended being, eyes narrowing, her voice a rage-filled scream. "What did you do to her?"

~Me?~ Helen demanded. *~That abomination has been chasing me for a day! What did **you** do to her?~*

Tangel shrank the brane, crushing Helen's form within. "Last I knew, Iris was fighting Airtha's AIs, trying to load the corrupted shard..."

Her voice trailed off, understanding dawning as she realized what must have happened.

"Stars, Iris...why didn't you come to us?"

"Hard. Fighting constantly for control."

"With the corrupted shard?" Tangel asked, further tightening the brane around Helen as she accessed the navigation console and shut down the ship's engines.

An affirmative sound came from Iris, and Tangel accessed the ship's network, tracing the signal that was controlling the bridge's audible systems back to the ship's comm node.

There she found an AI in garbled ruin, a barely functional merger of two separate beings.

"Iris!" Tangel gasped, only the knowledge that Helen would kill her if she became distracted keeping her from an immediate attempt to disentangle the two beings.

"Keep safe," Iris said. "Later me."

Tangel nodded, turning her full focus back to Helen, shrinking the brane further. "This ends now. I destroy you, and Airtha's sickness is wiped from the galaxy."

~Tangel.~

The single word from Bob stopped her in her tracks.

~No, Bob, we don't need to save her. Helen being alive will only torture Sera.~

~You're not a murderer.~

~You know that's not true,~ Tangel's reply was cold, the words slashing out through spacetime with more malice than she intended. *~I've killed in cold blood more than once.~*

She was shocked when Bob laughed in response. *~Well, try to keep it to a minimum.~*

Tangel had no idea how to respond to Bob's statement, but it had surprised her enough that the desire to kill Helen faded.

A moment later, Cheeky reached out.

<We're docked. Coming aboard.>

<Do you have a containment vessel?> Tangel asked.

<Usef is carrying it. Erin and Katrina have shadowtrons. We're loaded for bear.>

Tangel glanced at Helen, wondering if she'd fit in a containment vessel. *<Going to be a tight squeeze. I might have to pare her down a bit.>*

<Um…ew? She's not an apple.>

~What are you going to do?~ Helen asked, saving Tangel from having to come up with a response for Cheeky.

"I'm going to let Bob deal with you. So far as I'm concerned, when it comes to ascended beings, he's judge, jury, and executioner."

~And you play at having morals….~

Tangel laughed, surprised that the shard thought she could be played so easily. "I thought you saw my morality as weakness. You need to make up your mind."

Helen didn't reply, and Tangel kept her focus on containing the being until the team from *Sabrina* made it to the bridge.

"You know part of the corridor is missing out there, Admiral?" Usef said as he entered the bridge a minute later.

"Shoot," Tangel muttered. "I should have turned off the a-grav."

The colonel tapped a foot on the deck. "Maglocks to the rescue." He turned to the writhing ball of light that was Helen, now compressed down to a half-meter sphere near the navigation console. "Shit…that does not look safe."

"My containment, or what's inside?" Tangel asked, wiping sweat from her brow as the energy being consumed and expended to contain Helen warmed the air beyond what the environmental systems could contain.

"Both, I guess."

Usef set the meter-tall cylinder on the deck and stepped aside as Erin and Katrina entered the bridge.

"Stars…that looks too familiar," Katrina said, while Erin's eyes grew wide.

"First time seeing one of these…other than you, Tangel," the engineer said. "What do you need us to do?"

"Just be ready to shoot it if it tries to get away."

The two women nodded, and Tangel drew Helen closer to the containment vessel, activating it once the ascended being was above it.

The two branes merged, and with a wail only Tangel could hear, Helen was sucked into the device. Tangel sealed it, and checked that the CriEn powering the field was operating properly.

"There we go." She rose, satisfied that Helen was secure. "It'll last till the end of time, if needs be."

Erin shook her head. "That's just depressing. I mean…I know she's basically one of the worst people ever, but I don't know that she deserves that."

"Yeah…it was hyperbole," Tangel said. "I wouldn't want that, either."

Usef stepped forward, a look of grim determination on his face as he picked up the cylinder. "Nope, not frightening at all. Being centimeters away from an entity that can dissolve me at will."

Tangel reached out and touched the colonel's arm. "Now you're nanometers away."

"Not helping, Admiral," he grunted, turning back to the corridor, while Erin covered her mouth with a hand. "And not funny, Erin," he added.

Katrina glanced at Erin and mouthed, "Totally funny."

The trio's interaction brought a smile to Tangel's lips. She thought about all the time and space that had passed between these three since they'd first met on the *Intrepid* so long ago in the Kapteyn's Star System.

In Tangel's mind, that they'd remained friends, or rekindled friendship, gave meaning to what often felt like a never-ending struggle to build a home for her people.

She followed the others off the corvette's bridge. "Erin, Sabrina tells me there are several blank AI cores in *Sabrina*'s medbay. Can you grab one and meet me in this ship's comm node?"

"Uhh…sure. What's up?"

"I don't want to get anyone's hopes up…least of all mine. Meet me there."

"Of course," Erin nodded and followed Katrina and Usef down the corridor that led to the airlock, while Tangel continued aft, reaching the communications node a minute later.

The ship was pristine, clearly never used beyond a shakedown cruise. The node consisted of a trio of towers in the center of the room; overkill for a corvette, but likely just the thing an ascended AI needed to launch a variety of attacks on ships and stations. They were also just the sort of thing capable of housing a fractured AI that had been relegated to mobile software.

Memories of fighting against the AIs of Luna came back to Tangel, actions that Angela had been involved in long before she'd ever met Tanis. Iris and Amavia had also fought against similar foes on Cerka Station, when they had gone up against the Non-Organic Supremists.

<*How are you holding up?*> she asked Iris.

"Badly," the AI replied through the room's speakers.

Tangel frowned. <*Can you not reply over the Link?*>

"No, routes…data…mess."

"Odd," Tangel muttered as she placed a hand on the central tower, funneling a strand of nano to create a direct connection to the comm node.

She sifted through the system's internal structure until she came to the storage system Iris had settled into. What she saw there caused her to bite her lip in worry.

Pieces of Iris and the corrupted Airthan shard were intermixed like two separate puzzles that an angry child had tried to force together into one image.

<Stars, Iris…. How did you even get here?>

"Determination." The single word was spoken with a quiet vehemence.

Tangel chuckled as she worked to identify which pieces of the being were Iris, and which were the corrupted shard. Having been one of Iris's mothers, and present for her birth, Tangel was better suited than most to determine which parts of the being belonged to her daughter, and which were part of the shard.

Several minutes later, Erin entered the room holding an AI core, and Tangel beckoned silently for the engineer to place it into her left hand.

With her right hand still connected to the comm tower, Tangel began to select the pieces of neural network that were clearly her daughter's, and place them into the AI core. Bit by bit, she reconstructed Iris's mind into the form it should have, all the while wishing she had Iris's crystal backup, but unwilling to leave her in the living hell that was being merged with Airtha any longer.

She was partway through the process when the corrupted shard began to understand what was happening. It started to destroy parts of Iris's mind, and Tangel was forced to wipe out core parts of the other being to paralyze it.

After another ten minutes, she'd extracted every part of Iris and reconstructed her in the core she held in her left hand. All that remained in the comm tower was the corrupted shard. She swept through its remains three more times, ensuring that no further parts of Iris remained.

So much missing, she whispered to herself and pulled her hand away before glancing at Erin, who was watching with wide eyes.

"I can't believe you did that…and so quickly."

"Stars," Tangel muttered, looking down at the core in her hand. "Felt like years."

"I was monitoring the node…it was Iris in there, wasn't it? You saved her."

"Most of her," Tangel qualified, then reached out to Iris. *<I'm shutting you down. When your backup arrives, we'll re-integrate. But for now, I don't want you to reinforce broken pathways.>*

<I understand. Tangel?>

<Yes?>

<Thank you.>

<Pretty sure you saved both of us by distracting Helen…so thank you.>

With that, she activated the node's shutdown process and let Iris fall into sweet oblivion.

Turning back to the comm node, Tangel gave it one final look, and then reached out, dissolving the matter and letting it fall to the deck as a pile of oxidized dust.

"That's final," Erin said.

"Best end for that thing."

"No argument here."

The two women walked out of the room and down the ship's central corridor.

"I suppose that means only Fina and Seraphina hang in the balance now," Erin said after a minute. "Could you piece them back together like you did with Iris?"

Tangel pursed her lips as she considered it. "Maybe…though I'm better with AIs than organics…that's the Angela part of me at play there."

"Makes sense." Erin's words were sober. "I suppose we need Earnest back for that."

"Yes. Once he and Terrance are done dealing with the core AI installation in the IPE."

Erin's head whipped around, and she stared open-mouthed at Tangel. "Wait…what?"

"They found the installation that was manufacturing the star-shifting drones," Tangel explained. "Sorry, I meant to pass that on to you—I knew you'd be interested."

"Stars." Erin shook her head, a far-off look in her eyes. "That's an understatement. What are they going to do?"

"Destroy it, I believe."

"OK, for the second time, *what*?"

Erin's question was nearly vehement, and Tangel wondered what she was missing.

"Well, I guess they said 'shut it down'. Sorry, I haven't slept in a few days and I barely had time to consider that message. It came through Khardine and routed to Sera. She told me about it."

"I'm going to contact Earnest," Erin said after a moment. "I can't imagine he'd destroy the core AI facility there, but I need to be sure. For starters, we need that facility to re-position the stars. Then we need to understand how it's working so that when we find more clusters that are being shifted, we can correct them as well."

"Can't we use the same system we're using for Project Starflight?" Tangel asked. "Asymmetrically burn the stars to shift them back into place?"

Erin laughed and shook her head as they reached the airlock. "Sure. I mean, it'll work, but what if the core AIs worked out a more efficient system? It's worth investigating at least."

"Fair enough," Tangel said. "Let me know what they say."

"Sure will," Erin said, gesturing for Tangel to pass down the umbilical first.

When she reached the other side, Sera and Finaeus were waiting, the former president of the Transcend tapping her foot as she glared at Tangel.

"You know I hate being left behind."

"Couldn't be helped, Sera," Tangel said with a grin. "As it was, I almost didn't make it. But we got her, and I saved Iris. Plus, that rogue corrupted shard is done. I'm going to count this as a very good day."

"Just five more Widows out there as well," Finaeus added. "Who knows? We could have things squared away here in just another day."

"Then where to?" Sera asked.

Tangel glanced at Erin and then back at the others. "I have a suspicion we're going to be visiting the IPE again."

DIRECTION

STELLAR DATE: 10.11.8949 (Adjusted Years)
LOCATION: ISS *I2*, Airtha
REGION: Huygens System, Transcend Interstellar Alliance

"We have to quit meeting like this." Tangel gave Bob a wan laugh as she walked into his primary node chamber.

<*Is that an attempt at humor?*> the AI asked.

"Did you not get it?" Tangel asked. "I feel like you asking means you got the joke."

<*I got it, it was just weak.*>

She shook her head, a rueful smile on her lips as she settled onto a seat next to a monitoring console.

"I can't believe it's done—well, other than taking out a couple of Widows."

<*That was one of the things that I want to discuss with you,*> Bob said in a more serious tone.

Tangel made an instant connection, surmising where he was going next.

"Are the girls OK? And Priscilla?"

<*Joe has reported their primary objective as complete. They successfully disabled the A1 Widow, which Cary believes to be the original Lisa Wrentham. They've also accessed the Widows' primary datastore, though it is not yet transferred off the Widows' ship.*>

"I sense a 'but' coming. A big one."

<*Cary has assumed the position of A1.*>

Tangel was out of her seat in a heartbeat, her hands gripping the railing at the edge of the catwalk. "*What!?*"

<*They had an opportunity to strike at Garza's headquarters, and they took it,*> the AI explained.

She peeled her hands off the railing and began to pace across the catwalk. "It's the conditioning, isn't it? Somehow it took hold more than it should have."

<*What makes you think that?*> Bob asked.

"Because it fits. Saanvi would never let Cary do something so crazy, but with the conditioning to make them better able to fit in with the Widows, they must be obeying her unquestioningly, since she's assumed the role of A1."

<*I don't think that is it entirely. It's possible that the opportunity is too good to pass up.*>

She looked through the inbound messages and saw that it had been routed via the regular message queues—which was why Bob saw it first. Tangel willed herself to calm down, knowing that if things were dire, Joe would have reached out to her directly.

"He must know that I'd rush out there," she said after a minute.

<That was your first urge, wasn't it?>

Tangel shot Bob's node a cool look, held it for a second, and then nodded, her self-deprecating laughter echoing around the chamber. "I thought you couldn't predict what I do. Aren't I the great unknown in your algorithms?"

<Tangel is, maybe,> the AI replied. *<A mother, though? A lot easier to predict her actions.>*

"No, I suppose you don't need any advanced algorithms for that, do you?"

<Well, I did ask a few women on the ship to be sure. But I had a high level of certainty even without that.>

This time, a truly amused laugh came from Tangel as she wondered how Bob had phrased the question when he'd queried other mothers on the ship. She decided not to ask—it might end in her laughing at him, not herself, and despite his elevation to an ascended AI, he still didn't quite understand things like playful mocking.

<OK, so now that you're calmed down, there's one more thing.>

"Annnnnd now I'm uncalm again." She wondered if he was carefully managing her. *Probably is. It's probably necessary.*

<After your daughters jumped to Karaske—the system where Garza has his base of operations—Joe instituted the Gamma Protocol in the A1 System to destroy the fleet there so they couldn't follow after.>

"Oh shit," Tangel muttered. "Have you forwarded that to New Canaan yet?"

<No, I decided to wait and see how things go with Garza. I've found that with humans, having achieved the desired results can lessen their ire over less desirable means.>

Tangel snorted. "Now that's a new way to say that the ends justify the means."

<That's not what I said,> Bob corrected, his tone insistent. *<I did not say 'justified'. I said 'lessen their ire'. I believe those to be very different things. One is about the perpetrator, and the other is about those who stand in judgment.>*

Tangel considered Bob's words, seeing the truth in them, even if it was a near-semantical nuance. "OK, I can go with that. Either way, you're right. If that use of pico gets us Garza *and* the Widows, then no one is going to raise a big stink about it."

Especially because the general sentiment amongst the population is to end the war quickly and get their families back home.

She stopped her pacing and leant against the railing.

"That will just about neutralize Orion—at the very least, stop them from gathering new allies in the Inner Stars."

<Or slow it—provided we get all of the clones.>

"True, though the intel alone will be invaluable."

<Agreed. So does that mean you're not going to rush off and save the day?>

"We don't have details as to where we'd jump into the Karaske System, do we?"

<*No.*>

"I guess I'll have to wait till someone is in dire need and says, 'jump here, now!' "

<*Why change up how we do things this late in the game?*> Bob laughed at his own statement, and Tangel joined in.

"Why indeed." She drew in a deep breath and pushed off from the railing. "OK. I'm going to let my girls and husband handle things and trust that they'll call if they need me."

<*My, how you've matured.*>

"Be nice, Bob."

<*I've not matured that much.*>

Yet another laugh burst from Tangel. "Stars…you're just a jokester tonight. Something in your power supply?"

<*Softening you up for the conversation about Helen.*>

That was the topic Tangel had *expected* to discuss before Bob dropped the bomb about Cary masquerading as the A1 Widow. She wasn't sure if it would be any easier.

"OK, lay it on me."

<*Well, for starters, it* **is** *Helen, though a few steps up the evolutionary ladder.*>

"I noticed that."

<*I think that Airtha, ah, 'forcibly ascended' her, to put it in a nice way.*>

"Technically, didn't Airtha *make* Helen do everything? She is a shard, after all."

<*Shards can become independent,*> Bob said. <*I suspect that this happened with Helen. Also, from what I can tell, she is a duplication made from the original Helen before Sera journeyed to New Canaan, and before the clone of Jeffrey Tomlinson killed her.*>

"I guess that explains why the version that was with Sera was OK with playing along," Tangel said, remembering the time she'd spent onboard *Sabrina*, and the interactions she'd had with the AI. It pained her to think that Helen had been playing a game the whole time. A game that now saw her imprisoned in a containment vessel awaiting judgment. "Did you learn anything from her?"

<*Nothing new. Just confirmations of what I already believed. Her plan was to establish a new capital for her faction. I know the locations she had been considering, and have passed those to Admiral Krissy. I—*>

"Shit!" Tangel swore. "I have to tell Krissy about A1…about her mother."

<*And Finaeus,*> Bob added.

"Pfft," Tangel waved a hand dismissively. "Finaeus has to be over his ex by now. And he has Cheeky. That woman is no one's consolation prize."

<*You don't really mean that.*>

"No, not really—well, I do about Cheeky. I'm going to blame the Angela portion of me for asserting herself. Not enough acerbic wit of late."

<If you say so.>

"Stars, Bob, I do. OK, so what do we do about Helen?"

<We kill her.>

Tangel laughed, sagging against the railing. "Well *I* could have done that. Why bottle her up just to do it later?"

<You know the drill. Justice and all that. She'll remain contained, and the Transcend's government can try and convict her. They'll kill her in the end. She's too dangerous to leave alive.>

"Well we certainly agree there. Has Sera gone to see her yet?"

<Don't you know?> the AI asked. *<Usually you and Sera are thick as thieves.>*

"She may be a thief, but I'm not." Tangel gave Bob's node a roguish grin and could feel a wave of amusement from him.

<I suppose that depends on who you ask.>

"Bob!" she exclaimed, eyes narrowing. "Are you messing with me?"

<Yes. It's fun.>

"How productive."

<If you wanted to be productive, we wouldn't use this crude language to speak.>

Tangel shrugged. "I like the extra time it gives me to consider my responses—especially when talking with you."

The AI sent another wave of amusement. *<Me too. It's exhausting speaking to you. I know I can't predict your statements like I can with other people, but it doesn't stop me from trying.>*

Tangel nodded silently, wishing she could truly understand what it was that made her unpredictable to Bob...and to the other ascended AIs. It didn't seem to be working in her favor of late. Although, they had just taken out Airtha, and her largely unaided victory over Helen was something she was happy to celebrate.

Except I can't do that with Jessica missing, and the girls and Joe in danger.

<You're always worrying, Tangel,> Bob said, not unkindly.

"Aren't you?" she asked.

<Fair point. However, I'm worried more about Terrance and Earnest than the other things on your mind.>

"I'm just afraid those two will blow up that facility before we can learn from it. Erin was nearly apoplectic at the thought of it being destroyed before she could study their star-shifting techniques."

<Earnest would never destroy it. Honestly, neither would Terrance. He's too practical.>

"Which is what made that message so strange." Tangel pressed a hand to her forehead. "I guess I should reach out and clarify what they meant."

<I already did,> Bob replied. *<They reiterated 'destroy'.>*

"That doesn't make any sense..."

<Agreed.>

"That doesn't make me any *less* worried about Jessica, though. She and her ship have been missing for days, now."

<She has a good track record for popping back up when we thought she was long gone.>

Tangel remembered when she first found Jessica involuntarily stowed away on the *Intrepid*.

"Or when we never expected to find her at all."

<Exactly. In many respects, she's as unusual as you are.>

"True. But I'm not an alien."

The AI chuckled, but not across the Link; it came over the extradimensional space, and the sound filled Tangel's mind like a tornado rumbling across a plain.

~What's alien, anyway? I think that I am, compared to humans. But you two are as well, to a lesser extent.~

"Well, all of that aside, I'm still going to worry about Jessica, OK?"

<As you wish. We need to leave, though. I want to go to the IPE, and ensure that Earnest and Terrance aren't doing something foolish.>

"You don't think they'll do the right thing?"

<I'd like to be sure.>

A FATHER'S DISMISSAL

STELLAR DATE: 10.11.8949 (Adjusted Years)
LOCATION: ISS *I2*, Airtha
REGION: Huygens System, Transcend Interstellar Alliance

Kara drew a deep breath and flexed her wings one at a time before carefully folding them behind her back.

The subject of all her fear, anger, and love was on the other side of the door that stood before her—the person who had conceived her and molded her into a daughter that was also a slave…though an unknowing slave.

When she first fled High Airtha, well over a year ago at this point, her primary motivation had been to return to Airtha to save her father. But then she'd met Katrina and her crew, followed by the people of New Canaan, and finally Tangel. She'd learned an entirely different value system from them, a cleaner code of honor—one that had not painted her father in a good light.

Now that Admiral Krissy was in control at Airtha, things had taken an unfortunate turn for Adrienne; the admiral was not taking a soft approach with Airthan collaborators. Kara's pending testimony, combined with the discovery that her father had not been coerced in any way to work with Airtha, had all but damned him. He was currently being held awaiting trial for his crimes against the people of the Transcend.

An army of lawyers had taken Kara's statement, and Krissy had informed her that there was no need to speak to her father in person. But Kara knew that a final conversation was necessary.

She had to know if he'd released her only to save him later, or because he truly cared about her. A part of her knew it was stupid, that whatever he said could just as likely be a lie, but she knew that, without confronting him, the question would continue to gnaw at her.

Katrina had urged her to do it as well. Over the past months, the ancient woman had softened toward Kara, and they'd become friends. It was amazing to think that Katrina had gotten her start so long ago as a spy working for the Lumins in the Sirius system.

She'd escaped with a group of people called the Noctus only to be pursued by her father. In a crazy tale of luck, they'd encountered Tanis, and she'd defeated Katrina's father.

The people Katrina had escaped with had sentenced her father to death, and she'd never spoken to him—and it gnawed at her to this day. So she'd recommended that Kara get what she never had managed to find: closure.

She'd also warned Kara that it might just create more questions.

Damned if I do, damned if I don't.

The words echoed in her mind, but she continued to stare at the door for another minute before she mustered up the courage to nod to the guard. She was surprised to see him give her an understanding look before turning to palm open the door.

It slid open, and she stepped into the small room. A clear plas wall separated a narrow viewing area from her father's cell. The space he was confined to was barely three meters square, and the only furnishings were a bed, toilet, sink, and a small table with a stool tucked underneath.

Her father was standing at the sink, staring into the mirror when she stepped in, and he didn't move for nearly a minute. Kara remained still as well, taking in the man who had once controlled her in every way.

Once, he'd been the ultimate authority figure in her life, the one who gave her all direction and meaning and was the arbiter of right and wrong.

Now he was a tired-looking man who had traded away all his moral authority through vile acts and a willingness to do anything in the name of survival. It made him seem smaller, sallow.

She searched her memories, curious to find out if he'd always been like that and she'd just never noticed, but upon reflection, Kara could barely even draw a clear comparison between her recollections and the man before her.

"Are you going to say anything?" he asked, not turning to face her, eyes still fixed on his reflection.

His tone was cold, combative even. Kara knew that she shouldn't be surprised. Kindness was not an attribute her father often displayed.

"I came to rescue you," she said after running through a dozen statements.

It sounded as lame out loud as it had in her head.

Adrienne snorted. "Good job. Things are so much better for me now."

His words were laced with accusation, and Kara bristled.

"I'm not responsible for that. You sided with Airtha. There's no sign that she placed any sort of coercion on you."

Her father turned his head, cold grey eyes boring into hers. "I see you got your face back. I always suspected removing it was solely your brother's idea—despite your claims to the contrary."

"I was different then," Kara said, trying not to think of her twin brother, the pain of his loss still an unhealed wound inside herself. "*You* made me different."

"I made you useful," Adrienne shot back. "So many people just take up space. You were doing good work…important work."

Kara stared at her father in silence, wondering if he really believed what he was saying. So far as she was concerned, she had been sacrificing her individuality, her very humanity, just so her father could exert more control on those around him.

"I was your slave, Father. What you did to me was no different than what Airtha did to Sera. Or was that just giving her purpose as well?"

Adrienne stepped away from the sink, walking to the plas. "Well, she did gain a lot more purpose as a result of her mother's efforts. Airtha changed Sera from an entitled brat to a woman actually capable of running the Transcend. I see that as a success."

"I see it as manipulation," Kara retorted. "Of course, you may not know this, but Sera is no longer running the Transcend. Her father is."

She enjoyed watching her father's eyes widen in shock. His mouth worked soundlessly for a moment before he finally said, "I saw him die."

"You saw a clone die," she corrected. "Someone…though no one knows who as yet, tucked the real Jeffrey Tomlinson away in the LMC about a thousand years ago."

Adrienne's eyes narrowed. "That's impossible. No, it couldn't have happened. I was there."

"You were *what*?" Kara asked.

"I visited the LMC after Finaeus developed jump gate tech. Jeffrey was with me. That was about a century ago."

Kara wondered what the significance of that was, but decided not to pursue it. She'd pass it on to Admiral Krissy and let someone else interrogate her father.

"It doesn't matter. The point is that Sera never wanted to rule the Transcend. Her mother, or whatever Airtha was at the end, tried to make her do it, but she failed. If you ask me, I think that once the war is over, Sera's going to find somewhere quiet to hole up and live out her days."

"What a waste," Adrienne breathed out in a long sigh. "She had so much potential…despite her proclivities."

"Not everyone uses your measuring stick," Kara replied. "*I* don't want to always be fighting. The idea of retiring for a century, maybe raising kids…that's an appealing notion."

He stared at her for a minute, his lips drawn into a thin line. Then a cruel smile formed on his lips.

"I wonder…will they be born with wings? Perhaps in eggs?"

"You're such an asshole," Kara spat. "Maybe they *will* have wings. I happen to think that wings are amazing, and it honestly baffles me why hardly anyone has them. Everyone *could*, yet almost no one does. I bet now that Sera's not the president, she'll get wings too."

"Doesn't surprise me," Adrienne retorted. "Like I said, she's weird."

"What does that make me?" Kara demanded.

Her father didn't reply, and she shook her head in disgust.

"Katrina warned me that I might not like what came of this conversation, but at least I did get some measure of closure."

"I'm glad for you. And I'm not surprised."

Kara had already turned away from her father, but she glanced back over her shoulder, meeting his eyes for what she hoped would be the last time.

"Not surprised about what?" The words fell from her lips like lead.

"That you'd abandon me."

She considered a dozen responses before simply shrugging and walking to the door. It opened without her prompting, and she strode out without glancing back.

A few meters away, Katrina stood waiting, a look of concern in her ancient eyes.

"So?" she said without accusation.

"About as bad as you'd warned me it would be," Kara admitted as she reached Katrina's side. "But still worth it, if only so I don't have to wonder what sort of man he really was. Now I know for sure."

The older woman placed a hand on Kara's shoulder.

"Come. I'm going to teach you something to help you ground yourself. Maybe it will be useful, maybe it won't."

"Does it involve getting drunk?"

Katrina laughed, guiding Kara down the passageway. "Step one is finding peace. Step two is getting plastered without regrets."

"Sounds perfect."

WAR TABLE

STELLAR DATE: 10.11.8949 (Adjusted Years)
LOCATION: ISS *I2*, Airtha
REGION: Huygens System, Transcend Interstellar Alliance

"My father has asked me to return to Khardine," Sera said without preamble as she strode into Tangel's kitchen.

Krissy and Tangel were already present, a glass of wine before each, and a bowl of fruit on the table between them.

"That doesn't surprise me," a male voice said from her right, and Sera spun to see Jason leaning against the counter, a cup of coffee nestled between his fingers.

"Put that down," Sera said, gesturing to the cup he held.

"Why?" he asked as he complied, his eyes twinkling mischievously.

Sera didn't reply, instead rushing forward and crashing into him, her arms encircling his chest as she pressed her cheek into his.

"Stars I've missed you," she whispered fiercely.

New Canaan's governor chuckled softly. "It's only been a few weeks."

"A few too many," Sera replied.

"Well, I came as soon as I heard about your sisters. How are you holding up?"

Until that moment, if anyone else had asked, Sera would have said she was holding up just fine, and she wouldn't have believed it to be a falsehood. She'd decided *not* to talk to Helen, and was optimistic that, together, Earnest and Finaeus would be able to save Seraphina and Fina the same way they'd saved Cheeky.

But when Jason voiced the question, a shuddering sob escaped her lips and she felt the energy drain from her limbs.

"I got you," Jason whispered in her ear, the strength that flowed from him through those three words immediately reversing the weariness that threatened to subsume her.

"So you really came because you heard about my sisters?" Sera asked, forcing herself to regain some measure of composure as she stepped back and searched Jason's eyes for any sign that he was joking.

"Of course," he replied. "I made excuses that I needed to be here for reasons of state, but those are secondary. This has all got to be hard on you…a lot of family stuff."

Krissy gave a rueful laugh and shook her head, but didn't speak.

Tangel chuckled as she poured another glass of wine and handed it to Sera. "I don't know when Jason became so understanding, but I wish it had happened sooner."

"Pardon?" Jason asked, simultaneously laughing while shooting Tangel a glare. "I've always been understanding, you just needed a firmer hand."

Tangel snorted, and Sera glanced at Krissy to see what she made of the byplay.

"Don't look at me." The admiral held up her hands. "I'm the newcomer here."

"You've known me for a long time," Sera countered.

Krissy took a sip of her wine, giving her cousin a measuring look. "I suppose. Though you've rather surprised me of late—especially with how readily you gave up the presidency. You fought pretty hard for it after your father was killed."

"Well, I wasn't going to let Adrienne take the reins…if for no other reason than *I* would have killed him before long."

"Not if I got to him first," Krissy retorted. "Pretty sure he was in the Grey Division's pocket. I plan to find out for sure, one way or another."

"The Greys aren't just going to roll over," Sera agreed. "Even with Airtha gone, they'll be a problem. You know, that's why I opposed you for the presidency. I thought you were in their pocket, too. A lot of rumors were flying around about why you spent so long at the Grey Wolf Star."

"If I never see that place again…" Krissy began, letting the words trail away.

Sera nodded, pressing up against Jason before moving to sit at the table across from Krissy. Jason walked across the kitchen and refilled his coffee before settling beside her.

<*You're doing great,*> Jen said privately. <*Glad Jason came to see you.*>

<*Did you have a hand in that?*> Sera asked her AI.

<*I think he was already planning on it. I just added a nudge.*>

"So," Tangel began in a tone that indicated the meeting was coming to order—such as it could when held around her kitchen table. "How goes the transfer of power here on Airtha?"

Krissy leant forward and placed her elbows on the table. "Per the president's directions, I've reinstated Governor Prentice, and he's working on bringing back the exiled members of his former government. Airtha didn't utilize much of a bureaucracy, so there's not too much to clean up, there."

<*I've distributed an updated version of Angela's corrective retrovirus to the AIs here,*> Bob added. <*That has brought most of them around.*>

"Most?" Tangel asked.

<*Some served Airtha willingly. We're interring them for the time being.*>

"Waiting on Jeffrey's orders." Krissy's expression appeared sour. "If it were up to me, they'd be tried for treason. I'm hoping that the president feels the same way."

"How many are there?" Sera asked.

<Seven hundred and twelve followed her without any coercion.>

"A drop in the bucket," Tangel said, though she still looked troubled. "All-in-all, this went a lot better than it could have."

"We're fighting a final group of ships that are holding out near Jove, and then we'll have the entire Huygens System under our control."

"Thus ends the Transcend's civil war," Jason intoned.

Krissy shook her head. "If only. Our alliance is fractured. I doubt that many of the systems that declared for themselves will come back into the fold."

"Do they need to?" Tangel asked. "So long as they're not a drain on resources, we can focus on defeating Orion and then ending the war in the Inner Stars. The major conflicts could be resolved in as little as four years."

"Now *that* would be a miracle." Krissy took another sip of her wine, glancing at Sera.

"I think Tangel's right," Sera replied. "Even once we put out the current fires, new ones are going to spring up. The echoes of this war could take a century to fade away."

"Well, I did say 'major' conflicts," Tangel emphasized. "But I take your meaning."

"What about you, Sera?" Krissy asked. "What are your plans now?"

Sera ran a hand across her brow and through her black hair. "Well, I *had* planned on turning over the Hand to Seraphina…or more like relinquishing any claim to it, as she was already taking the bull by the horns. I don't know how that will shake out now, so I suppose I'm still in charge of that division."

"And your father?" Tangel asked. "What do you think he has in mind for you?"

"Stars…" Sera muttered. "I have no idea. I'm beginning to suspect that he wants to keep the government at Khardine for now—"

"A good plan," Krissy interjected, earning nods from around the table.

"So maybe his summoning is because he wants 'em to run the Hand from there?" Sera looked at Krissy and shrugged.

"Well, he didn't share anything with me," the admiral said. "That much hasn't changed from his prior incarnation. He's still just as tight-lipped."

"Well, I'll put in a request for you to rejoin us as soon as possible," Tangel said. "Can't go long without my right-hand woman."

Sera's eyes widened as she turned to look at the field marshal, catching a twinkle in the woman's eyes.

"You offering me a job?"

"Well, you are an honorary citizen of New Canaan," Tangel replied. "I could use someone like you out there."

"Hey, hey!" Krissy cried out. "No pilfering *my* Sera. You get the other two versions to Earnest and get them patched up. Then there will be plenty of Seras to go around."

Sera shook her head. "I'm not sure if I should be amused or insulted."

"What of your newest sister?" Tangel asked. "Has Dr. Rosenberg had a chance to look her over in detail?"

"She has, but the doctor is withholding final judgment. Let's just say that mother took more liberties with the latest version of me. She's more…divergent."

Admiral Krissy shook her head. "Looks like an angel, behaves like a demon. Funny how you're the opposite of that, Sera."

"I wouldn't go so far as to credit our Sera's behavior as angelic." Jason spoke for the first time in several minutes, knocking his knee against Sera's.

"Umm…thanks?"

"I'll second that," Tangel added.

Krissy rolled her eyes. "I wasn't being that literal. You forget that I've known Sera since she was a little girl."

"Little demon, you mean," Sera replied, grinning at her cousin, who nodded.

"Exactly."

"So," Tangel again brought the meeting back to business with that one word. "Let's talk about how we plan to clean up the Transcend so I can focus on Orion."

The conversation shifted to logistics and politics within the Transcend, carrying on for several hours. In the end, it was agreed that Krissy's fleets were in a position to hold Airtha, should any of the separatist allies attempt to reclaim it. A secondary strike force was being assembled at Styx in preparation to hit Orion on the anti-spinward front and finally drive back the encroaching forces after two years of losses.

When the meeting finally concluded, Jason placed his hand on Sera's.

"Care to take a walk down to the lake with me?"

She chuckled, though nodded emphatically. "Can we make it a bit longer than that? The lake is only a hundred meters away."

"I bet we could find some path to follow together."

As Sera bid farewell to Tangel and Krissy, she wondered if Jason had intended a double meaning. In her experience, men were less likely to do that, but Jason was also not an imprecise person.

Once outside Tangel's lakehouse, they walked silently to the shoreline, turning left to follow a path that led into the woods lining the lake.

"I hope your sisters recover, and not just for our sake," Jason said after a minute. "I feel like the three of you were starting to develop something special."

Sera gave a caustic laugh. "Well, after growing up with a sister like Andrea, we all wanted something better."

"I think it was more than that—though I do wonder what will become of Andrea."

"Hopefully she'll get lost in the dark layer…forever."

Jason shook his head. "You don't really mean that, do you?"

"No, I suppose not. But I would be happy if she just disappeared."

"I won't fault you there," New Canaan's governor replied. "I'm curious. Would you like me to give you a lift to Khardine?"

"Jason Andrews' interstellar taxi service?" Sera asked with a laugh.

"Well, just a way to spend a bit more time together before I have to return to New Canaan. Getting a bit more face time with your father won't hurt, either."

"Why?" Sera asked. "You don't need his permission to court me."

A snort burst from Jason's mouth, and he gave Sera an amused look. "Gaining his approval for our relationship is the furthest thing from my mind. I'm interested in cementing New Canaan's relationship with the new-old president of the Transcend."

"That's good, because my father—well, the man who shares the same face as my father—doesn't really know what to think of my sisters and I. As far as he's concerned, we're just painful reminders of his lost wife."

"Maybe." Jason shrugged. "I think that can shift over time. Either way, he asked to see you, and since Tangel wants to send *Sabrina* and the *Voyager* to help Corsia with the Trisilieds…."

"OK, OK." Sera laughed and bumped her hip against Jason's. "I'll let you fly me around in your fancy spaceship. I tell you, though, I'm worried about things out there. Would be a lot easier if the Hyadeans actually helped."

"Don't count on it," Jason snorted. "I don't blame them for being wary of the Trissies. Those bastards are turning out to be much more problematic than we expected. Heck, the Hegemony seems to be an easier egg to crack."

"Sure," Sera replied. "But we have Scipio in the mix. They're no slouches."

"That's for sure," Jason replied. "And Diana…whew! I met with her not long ago, what a whirlwind of a woman."

"Oh?" Sera cocked an eyebrow. "Thought you liked whirlwinds."

He gave an easy laugh. "I suppose I do. Maybe she's a maelstrom, then. Or a supernova. Something that's clearly more dangerous than fun." Jason slipped his hand into hers. "You, Sera, are more fun than dangerous."

"Huh… I suppose I'll take that as a compliment."

"So, all that aside, do you want a ride to Khardine?" Jason asked.

Sera glanced at him and laughed. "I feel like you're asking me on a date to another star system."

"Maybe I am."

"Well in that case, I'm definitely in. But just so you know, Roxy, Jane, and Carmen are coming with me."

"Sure," Jason nodded. "I read the reports. Roxy has quite the past."

"She does…I'm very optimistic about her."

"In what way?"

Sera chuckled. "Well, it's optimism that involves making her assistant director of the Hand."

Jason joined in her laughter. "Sneaky!"

"All part of my master plan to shuck all responsibility," she replied, turning to catch his gaze.

<I thought that's what I was here for?> Jen interjected, and Jason laughed.

"Maybe you're not pulling your weight," Sera countered, joining in Jason's laughter.

After a moment, Jason asked, "So what do you plan to do once you've handed over all your duties?"

A sly smile formed on her lips. "I was thinking of seeing if Cheeky needed any crew."

The governor placed a hand on his chest. "Oh! You build up my hopes just to dash them!"

"Well…I bet they could use a new supercargo."

"Pilot, Sera. If I sign on, it's as a pilot."

"Now you're talking."

PART 4 – ESCAPE

LAST DITCH

STELLAR DATE: 10.11.8949 (Adjusted Years)
LOCATION: ISS *Lantzer*
REGION: Coreward of Stillwater Nebula, Orion Freedom Alliance

"Tell me you have power!" Jessica demanded, not looking up from the holotank, certain Karma would know she was addressing him.

"Not yet, ma'am," he muttered. "Rails are all still offline."

<Trevor, I need—>

<I know what you need, Jess. Same thing we all need, but I'm dealing with a plasma leak that's going to burn through three decks and eat a hole in the forward reactor, so….>

<OK, OK. I get it. ETA?>

Her husband sighed, sounding like the weight of the galaxy was on him. *<West is working on a bypass while I deal with this. At least twenty minutes.>*

"Fuck!" Jessica swore, then turned from the holotank and closed her eyes, drawing a deep breath.

She normally prided herself on her ability to remain calm in the face of danger, but the past seven days of playing cat and mouse with the Caretaker ships had worn her down. She grabbed a drink off a nearby console and threw it back before turning to look at the holotank once more.

The crew of *Sabrina* was in the midst of a brief reprieve; both of the fishbone ships had made high-speed passes and were out of weapons range as they came about.

For the first time in days, both of the enemy ships were on the same side of the *Lantzer*. That meant that when they came back in for another pass, she would only have to power shields on one side of the ship.

Jessica's fervent hope was that running the shields at only half coverage would finally give them the power needed to punch through one of the fishbone's shields. Of course, that plan was contingent on the railguns being online.

<Glenn, how are the CriEns holding out?>

<So far, so good. Lantzer*'s moving around enough that our constant draw doesn't seem to be causing any instabilities in the local quantum foam. At least not that I can detect. I also got the port-side aft bank of SC batts back online…well, the four that*

survived. Zero K coils don't really like to heat up in a fire, as it turns out.>

<*And our beams?*> Jessica pressed.

<*The Marines have them powered up. They had to charge and lug batts up two decks, but we're good to go.*>

Jessica shook her head in disbelief. Despite days of desperate defense against the two fishbone ships—and nearly no sleep at all—Glenn seemed to be in high spirits, as though he thrived on this sort of insane conflict.

<*Thank you, Chief.*> She straightened and looked up at the optical inputs above the forward holodisplay. "Gil. Confirm fishbone vector."

<*Well, provided they come about and remain on a predictable course, which they don't always do, we're looking at ten minutes until they're in range. Twenty till optimal.*>

"That mirrors my assessment," she replied quietly. <*West. Twenty tops. I need the slug throwers back online!*>

<*Going as fast as I can, ma'am.*>

A fear had begun to take hold in Jessica's mind, a fear that no matter what they did, the Caretaker ships would prevail. After seven long days, the *Lantzer* had only managed to score a few hits that made it through the enemies' shields. Glancing blows, nothing more.

They were down to three ARC fighters, the others suffering cascading system failures as a result of the EM burst that had initially dropped the *Lantzer* out of its jump. She'd had to spend time destroying the remains of those craft, knowing that the last thing her people needed was for the Caretakers to gather stasis shield technology from those hulls.

We just need a few more hours. Just enough time to finish repairs on that damn gate.

Trevor and West had been hard at work piecing together a functional gate when a series of system failures across the ship had derailed them. It hadn't been the first time.

Constructing a functional gate from the four in the ship's holds had been the primary goal for the past six days—except it kept slipping to secondary, due to the ever-present need to stay alive.

She decided that there was no time like the present, and left the bridge to get coffee and more of that bizarre, green energy drink that Karma loved.

Though a lot of things that should have been present on the ship were listed in the inventory systems as being 'backorder-delayed', Karma's energy drink was present in volumes large enough to keep them going for a year.

It was suspicious to say the least, but had provided a much-needed bout of levity at one point, when West had accused Karma of breaking some sort of unknown regulation to get so much of the drink aboard. Karma, for his part, had claimed he hadn't even put in for a stock of the drink.

After West's ire had simmered down, it had turned into a bit of a running joke with the beleaguered crew.

By the time Jessica returned to the bridge with a carafe of coffee and a few pouches of Karma's drink, West had called up with good news.

<*I got it, Admiral!*> she announced gleefully. <*Stars, my instructors at the academy would have kittens if they could see how I've jerry-rigged things, but it should hold for this next pass.*>

<*Should?*> Jessica asked, homing in on that single word. She didn't want to dismiss the woman's hard work, but she needed a larger measure of confidence than 'should'.

<*I've had to rip out main line runs from half the ship to cobble this together. I've not really had time to put it through its paces, but I have a ninety-percent level of confidence that it'll hold for the shots your plan requires.*>

<*OK.*> Jessica knew that was as good as it was going to get. <*And the fires, Trevor?*>

<*Out for now, though environmental is screwed down here. Hold your breath if you need to go through decks six and seven.*> Trevor's words were glib, but Jessica could hear a note of worry carried along with them.

The ship was falling apart, and they all knew it. Even though they'd weathered days of attacks, just the power draw alone for weapons and shields was burning out one temporary fix after another.

In all honesty, it was a miracle that the *Lantzer* had held together as long as it had.

You're a tough old girl, Jessica thought, hoping the ship could hear her and would gain some measure of encouragement.

<*We're headed back to the bay,*> West announced. <*Just need to swap out two power modules, and we'll be ready for a test run on the ring.*>

<*Don't let me slow you down!*> Jessica said, not bothering to contain her excitement. "One more pass," she whispered. "Just need to weather one more pass."

Karma rose from his console and walked to Jessica's side.

"Yes, Ensign?" she asked.

"Umm… ma'am. Are you going to let me have one of those drinks, or just clench it tightly until it explodes?"

Jessica started, looking down to see that she had a white-knuckle grip on the energy drinks. "Sorry."

She handed them to the ensign, and he gave two to Lucida before resuming his seat.

"Rails are reporting full readiness," he announced upon settling. "Guns one and two are loaded with slugs, and three has the grapeshot."

"Get three ready to fire a spread in pattern delta-three. Given what our friends out there are doing, that stands the best chance of getting them where we want."

Thus far, the *Lantzer* had managed to fire six salvos of grapeshot from the third railgun. The first had hit the target designated 'F2' and weakened the shields enough to let the beams penetrate and do limited damage. Following that, the enemy had been very careful to avoid the field of fire that railgun three covered.

It was frustrating, but it did reduce the enemy's avenues of approach, which had its own benefits. However, the shot that was loaded into the third railgun was different this time, being filled with small pellets that were capable of independent maneuvering.

Jessica had been saving this ammunition, waiting for the enemy to grow complacent and think she was behaving predictably. When the railgun fired next, it would appear to fire on one vector, while the grapeshot would end up elsewhere. With any luck, that 'elsewhere' would be the same place the enemy ships were.

Even so, chances were fifty-fifty. Space was large, and the enemy had a lot of maneuvering options. But even though they were supposedly dealing with ascended beings, the *Lantzer*'s bridge crew had spotted patterns as well. There were preferred vectors the fishbones would move to when grapeshot was coming their way.

Just do what you're supposed to, you bastards.

The fishbones passed over the hundred-thousand-kilometer mark, but didn't fire. Both enemy ships were on nearly the same vector now, streaking toward the *Lantzer*, their trajectory lined up to take them only a few hundred kilometers off the ISF cruiser's bow.

"Grapeshot firing!" Karma announced, the ship shuddering as the massive gun launched several tons of material at a hundredth the speed of light.

A long groan sounded from somewhere above the bridge, and Jessica patted the edge of the holotank. "Hold together, girl."

<For some definition of 'together',> Gil said. *<A spar just came free along the dorsal arch. Deck one is holding on purely out of habit now.>*

"It's not that bad," Jessica shot back. "There are still a half-dozen structural mounts holding the arch in place."

<They're all strained. Just be careful. The section has our only functional sensor array on the forward half of the ship.>

"Noted," Jessica replied, glancing at Lucida, who was looking up at her. "Do what you can to reduce strain."

"Aye, ma'am."

Jessica turned her attention back to the holotank, watching as the two enemy ships predictably shifted away from the apparent path of the grapeshot.

They eased onto the anticipated vectors, and though it was exactly what she wanted, Jessica wasn't ready to crow with delight just yet. The enemy had feinted more than once; there was no reason to believe that it couldn't happen again.

"They're right in the pocket," Karma announced, sounding no more optimistic than Jessica felt. "Our shot is shifting into position. Impacts in seventy-two seconds."

No one spoke over the following minute, and when the time remaining reached ten seconds, the weapons officer began an audible countdown. A second after it hit zero, scan picked up impacts on one ship, but not the other.

"F2 jinked!" Karma called out.

"Shift all targeting to F3!" Jessica ordered.

Scan showed multiple direct hits, and that ship's shields *had* to be weakened.

Railguns one and two belched out tungsten rounds—those guns were thankfully mounted further aft on the *Lantzer*—and though the deck shuddered beneath them with each round in the salvo, nothing tore free from the hull.

The kinetic slugs streaked through the black toward F3, and the *Lantzer*'s beams joined in, tagging the enemy vessel and further weakening its shields.

In response, both enemy ships fired their weapons on the ISF cruiser, proton beams slashing through the black to slam into the *Lantzer*'s stasis shields in a dazzling display.

<Shields holding,> Gil announced as the enemy's shots blinded the ship's sensors.

Then the fishbones streaked past, and scan updated showing F3 bleeding a trail of plasma and ionized gas in its wake.

Cheers came from Karma and Lucida, but Jessica withheld hers. Though the plasma stream was coming from near the fishbone's engines, it was still maneuvering, albeit poorly.

"Shit, F2 is braking hard!" Karma called out a second later.

Jessica shook her head, watching as the enemy vessel executed a burn that had its main weapons facing the *Lantzer.*

<Shifting stasis shields!> Gil announced, and the enemy ship's beams splashed harmlessly against them.

A sigh of relief came from Lucida, but Jessica wasn't ready to celebrate just yet.

"Shields back around the whole—" Jessica's words were cut off as the deck rocked beneath them, the ship's a-grav dampeners straining to keep the crew safe as the cruiser spun through space.

<Missiles,> Gil said, his voice laden with worry. *<Came in on our unprotected side.>*

Jessica had already surmised that.

<Sound off!> she called out to the crew, knowing that the missiles had struck close to where Trevor and West were working.

Trevor was first to reply. *<Shaken, but West and I are still here.>*

A sense of profound relief came over her as the rest of the crew signaled that they were alive. Meg broke an arm when she was flung against a bulkhead, and everyone other than the bridge crew had a few flesh wounds.

<*Oh shit,*> Gil swore, the first time Jessica had heard the AI do so.

She turned to the forward display to see a ship's integrity warning. Visuals from the hull showed the dorsal arch—including railgun three—peel off and drift away. Lucida muttered curses under her breath as she struggled to correct the ship's spin.

Jessica pursed her lips, not letting the fear that was threatening to subsume her take over. She'd survived far too much in her life to believe there weren't still options.

One of which was to surrender.

<*Admiral, I've been thinking,*> Glenn said, interrupting her ruminations.

<*Dangerous stuff, Chief.*>

<*Well, we know that there are Exdali around here, right?*>

<*Mmmhmmm,*> Jessica answered wordlessly, wondering what the man was getting at.

<*Well, I was on a ship at Carthage when we opened up the dark layer and let the things out to eat the Orion ships. I know how it's done.*>

Jessica's eyes widened and she let out a curse, garnering the attention of Karma and Lucida, who she waved off.

<*It takes a special emission from the grav drive, right?*> she asked.

Tangel had given her a brief overview, but she'd never learned the specifics. It annoyed her that Glenn hadn't suggested it sooner, but she could imagine why he was hesitant to bring it up until now.

<*It does. I didn't have access to all the data, but I've been running simulations, and I believe I can open a rift and draw them out…but….*>

<*I don't like buts,*> Jessica said, half expecting to hear Cheeky laugh at the statement.

Glenn made a sound like he was scared to say what the caveat was.

Jessica urged him on. <*Out with it, Chief.*>

<*Well…I don't know how to put them back in.*>

Jessica barked a laugh, shaking her head as she considered their options.

<*You know what? I don't think I care. How long do you need?*>

<*Ten minutes.*>

She looked at the holotank. F2 was braking hard and would be back in firing range in eight minutes, though F3 had killed its engines and was adrift on a vector away from the *Lantzer*. With the ship's dorsal arch gone, they couldn't envelop the entire cruiser in regular shields, let alone stasis shields. The moment that F2 came back around and opened fire, they'd be done for.

<*You have seven.*>

Chief Glenn signaled his acknowledgment, and Jessica updated the rest of crew with the plan. To her surprise, no one objected to the idea of leaving Exdali free to roam this region of space.

The one thing that wore on her mind was the presence of the Exdali in interstellar space to begin with. They'd tried dipping the *Lantzer* into the dark layer twice more, both times finding it teeming with the things that dwelt there.

The crew had debated the presence of the dark layer creatures to no end. They'd settled on two possibilities. The first was that for Exdali to be present all over the galaxy, it was possible that they migrated in some fashion, and that's what they were in the midst of. The second was that the Caretakers had somehow summoned the things to this area.

Despite the lack of any clear evidence to point toward the second option, it was what Jessica feared most to be true. It also meant that there was a possibility that the ascended AIs could control the creatures—though if that was the case, she would have expected them to use Exdali in their attack.

In addition to all that, she considered that the ascended AIs would be able to stuff the things back in the rift and close it up with no harm done.

That's something we'll just have to risk.

"Roll the ship," Jessica ordered Lucida. "Let's keep our—well, what *remains* of our dorsal arch away from them."

"Yes, ma'am," the ensign replied, plotting a burn that Jessica and Gil approved.

"Oh crap!" Karma exclaimed a moment later. "F3 is releasing more drones!"

"What?!" Jessica demanded.

The first two days of fighting against the fishbone cruisers had been more of a war with their drones than anything else. One of attrition, to be precise. In the end, the enemy ships had depleted their drone fleets, smashing them uselessly against the *Lantzer*'s shields—though that onslaught had pushed the cobbled-together systems, causing many secondary and tertiary failures across the ship.

When the fishbones had ceased releasing drones, the *Lantzer*'s crew had been wary of more to come, but—four days later—had believed the ships to be out of the disposable machines.

"How many?" Jessica asked, though she knew scan was still differentiating the signatures.

"A hundred at least," Karma said in a quiet voice. "Leading edge is ten minutes out."

<*Glenn! You're out of time,*> Jessica called down to the chief before reaching out to Trevor and West a moment later. <*The gate, we need the gate ready to go. We're about to make space very inhospitable around here.*>

<*It's on the rails,*> Trevor replied without hesitation. <*Just getting the last antimatter capsules in place.*>

<*Good,*> Jessica said, feeling some measure of relief at the good news. <*Be ready to kick it out on my mark.*>

<*OK, we'll need just another minute. Have to rig it to blow when we're done.*>

<*That's not necessary, Caretakers already have gates. We can send a taskforce back*

later to clean it up.>

<You got it, ma'am,> Trevor said with a laugh, and she couldn't quite tell if it was rueful or nonchalant.

*****

Trevor glanced at West, who was climbing the ring segment furthest down the rail, slotting an antimatter pod into place. Though the ring was nearly ready to deploy, it would take a few minutes to assemble once in space—the result of hauling something in the ship that the entire vessel had to fit through.

"I told the admiral we'll be ready in a minute!" he called out to the engineer.

"What?!" West exclaimed, turning sharply and nearly losing her grip. "We're easily ten minutes out. I haven't even initialized the maneuvering systems."

"I already did," Trevor replied. "Just get that antimatter in there and get down."

West grunted something that he couldn't quite make out, but half a minute later, she was on the deck, and Trevor pulled on his EV suit's helmet before walking to the dock's command console where he activated the bay doors.

The grav shields were working in the bay, but he wasn't taking any chances, and began a depressurization process as well. West jogged to his side, pulling on her own helmet and giving him a sour look.

<We're taking a huge risk. We don't know if it'll assemble!>

<The Caretakers are coming back around to finish us off,> Trevor replied. *<Ten minutes tops. Either we jump, or we die.>*

<Or we jump ***and*** *we die.>*

<Yay for options.>

West nodded as she activated the rails. *<Or the Exdali eat us alive and we die.>*

<Let's try to die before they eat us,> Trevor suggested.

<Solid plan,> West said absently as the first section of ring slid out into space. *<Wait…what? No! What am I saying? Shitty plan. Terrible plan. No dying at all.>*

<You were the one who brought up dying,> Trevor said as the second section slid out.

There were six more to go, and neither he nor West spoke further as they drifted away from the ship.

<OK…> The engineer brought up a display of the ring on the console. *<Sections one and two are mated, three and four…>*

They both fell silent as the maneuvering jets on section four fired, bringing it closer to its mate. Then one of the jets cut out, and the arch slewed aside.

<Fuck! Damn!> West bellowed, killing section four's jets and activating three's.

After a moment of vector correction, the sections began to ease toward one another while the others also mated. A minute later, the ring was assembled and began its activation sequence.

<Jessica, we're t-minus five to jump readiness,> Trevor relayed to his wife. *<How're things looking up there?>*

<About to unleash hell,> she replied soberly.

* * * * *

"Gate's coming online," Jessica announced, and Lucida nodded as she looked at the readings on her console.

"Yes, ma'am, jump targeting is transferring to my station. Shoot, several of its maneuvering thrusters aren't responding.... And wow! West knows some really good curses."

Jessica saw the readings on the console next to her. "Looks like we'll have to come around."

<Once we finish opening the dark layer rift,> Gil cautioned.

"Yes."

Jessica lifted a hand to her mouth, focusing on her breathing as the timing for three events converged. The Caretakers' remaining fishbone ship was closing fast, already within firing range of the *Lantzer*, and soon the gate. They'd be within optimal range in a minute.

The grav systems were already opening the rift to the dark layer, creating an inky rent in space that made the interstellar darkness look like noon on a terraformed world.

<Initializing the Call,> Gil announced.

On top of every other risk they were taking, the Call was where things could really go terribly wrong. When the Exdali exited the rift, the things would move toward the source of the signal. When the ISF fleet at Carthage had used the dark layer creatures to destroy the Orion Guard fleet, they had used multiple signals from hundreds of ships to guide the creatures.

Jessica did not have that option.

Luckily, Glenn had come up with a way to bounce the signal off the Caretakers' ship, using the enemy's own grav shields to echo and broadcast the signal toward the rift.

It was a gamble, but everything they were doing was a gamble. Jessica would rather pull out all the stops than just give up and let the ascended AIs do...whatever it was they were planning on doing.

The ship's grav shields began to emit the specialized signal that attracted Exdali, tightbeaming it toward the Caretaker vessel. The enemy ship registered it as a hostile attack and diffused the incoming signal, bouncing it out into space.

Within seconds, Jessica could see the first strands of darkness begin to appear around the rift.

Discerning the difference between the rift into the dark layer and the creatures leaving it wasn't easy at first, but the first escapee, a hundred-meter-long inky splotch against Stillwater's backdrop, separated from the rift, moving toward the Caretakers' ship.

The distortion the *Lantzer*'s signal created on the enemy ship's shields must have caused it not to see the Exdali at first, because for nearly half a minute, the fishbone ship kept boosting straight toward the *Lantzer* and the rift between the vessels.

"Shit…maybe they'll just fly right into the dark layer," Karma said with a laugh.

"I'd sure be happy with that," Lucida added.

Jessica nodded in agreement, though she didn't expect the enemy to be that blind.

Sure enough, a few moments later, the enemy ship spun and began boosting on a new vector. One of the Exdali very nearly latched onto the fishbone, but missed. More followed in its wake, a writhing mass of utterly black forms, twisting and stretching across space toward the mass they hungered for.

The Caretaker ship began to extend its AP engine's nozzle, the tip of which would protrude beyond the ship's shields. Jessica worried it would allow the fishbone to outpace the Exdali, and sent Karma an order.

"Shoot that thing off."

"With pleasure, ma'am."

Karma fired two shots with the *Lantzer*'s proton beams. The first missed, but the second hit, tearing off the end of the nozzle and sending the chunk of ship's engine spinning into one of the Exdali's maws.

The infusion of matter seemed to give the thing an energy boost, and it surged forward, passing right through the fishbone's grav shield and attaching itself to the hull near the engines.

One of the vessel's fusion burners sputtered and died, slowing the ship enough for the rest of the things that were in pursuit to reach the hull.

The bridge crew watched in a silent mixture of excitement and horror as the creatures from the dark layer devoured the Caretaker ship, explosions blooming against the Exdali's dark bodies as critical systems were compromised.

"You know…" Karma mused. "What happens when those things get to a CriEn module?"

"They'll have safety shutdowns," Jessica said. "Just like the Orion ships had when they were devoured by the Exdali over Carthage."

"And what if they disable those safeties?" the ensign asked.

Jessica pursed her lips. "Kill the signal, bring us about. It's time we jump."

The bridge crew complied while she continued to watch the things eat the enemy ship. The other Caretaker vessel was still drifting on the same vector as before, and Jessica wondered if it really was completely dead, or if it was just playing at it to avoid attention from the Exdali.

"Lining up with the gate," Lucida announced as the ship came around. "We—"

Jessica had been watching the gate come into view on the main holodisplay, and her mouth fell open at the same time that Lucida's voice cut out.

"Fuck," the admiral whispered.

Though it was being consumed, the other fishbone ship fired a single shot from where it drifted in the black. The beam only scored a glancing blow, but it was enough to spin the gate around.

"It's out of alignment now. Maneuvering thrusters aren't responding," Lucida muttered. "Calling down to West."

Jessica nodded, watching as a group of Exdali broke off from the feeding frenzy on the other fishbone, heading for the ship that had just fired. Her lower lip found its way between her teeth, and she began to gnaw on it, waiting for the things to turn toward the *Lantzer.*

But none did.

"Oh thank stars," she whispered.

<And everything else,> Gil added.

"West says that she can't get control of the gate, either," Lucida said, turning to Jessica. "She's going to go out to it."

The admiral couldn't think of anything encouraging to say, only managing to whisper, "Stars help her."

* * * * *

"Dammit!" West stormed across the bay to a stack of ring segments they'd discarded and began pulling sections off, dropping them to the deck with little concern for the value of the tech. "We need a drive controller! The one in segment four died, and now that fucking fishbone hit the only other one on the ring!"

"OK, OK," Trevor approached from behind her, looming over the stack. "There, in the back. I'll get it."

West nodded and walked around the pile, watching as Trevor located a controller module.

"Stars," she muttered. "Must be nice being a billion meters tall. I couldn't see that at all."

The mountain of a man chuckled and handed her the controller. West plugged in her analysis unit, and a holo appeared showing that—by some miracle—the drive controller was functional.

With that knowledge in hand, she turned and stared through the still-open bay doors. The ring was not currently in view, so she strode toward the dark rectangle, peering around the corner, trying to catch sight of it.

"What are you doing?" Trevor asked, following after. "You can't just jump out the door. The ring is three kilometers away now."

West realized he was right, that she wasn't thinking clearly; her mind was fixed on getting to the ring and aligning it, just not on how.

"Look, Commander. That ring has to be *precisely* aligned. You of all people know what happens if you jump on a misaligned ring."

"Yeah, preaching to the choir, West."

"What? What choir?"

"Nevermind. From an old vid. So what do we do?"

West cast about and spotted a dock skiff. It was little more than a sled with an a-grav unit, but it could travel in space as well as on the deck.

"I'll take that out to the ring."

"I'll go with you, then," Trevor said.

West was already striding toward the skiff, and looked over her shoulder at the commander. "No offense, sir, but you weigh a ton. Literally. The skiff will make it there faster and be a hell of a lot more maneuverable without your mass on it."

Trevor harrumphed but didn't push the issue, as West pulled the skiff out of its dock moorings and checked it over to determine it was functional. While she did that, the commander looked over her seals, pronouncing them good.

<*Admiral?*> West called up to the bridge, realizing that she needed the CO's permission to leave the ship.

<*Trevor already briefed me. That's a brave thing you're doing, West. Be careful.*>

<*Yes, Admiral. Just don't leave without me.*>

<*Wouldn't dream of it, Chief.*>

Jessica's words rang true in West's mind, and with a nod to Trevor, she stepped onto the skiff and tucked the engine controller into a web of netting behind her.

She activated the narrow sled and steered it out of the bay doors, trying to ignore the fact that it felt like driving over the edge of a cliff with an endless bottom.

In space, everywhere is up, not down, she reminded herself, using the mantra to push the irrational fear away.

She cleared her head, turned to the left, and spotted the ring. Once she had the skiff on a course, she looked over her shoulder and saw that the Exdali were still feeding on their fishbone meals, seemingly unaware or the *Lantzer*'s presence nearby.

Even so, she didn't want to delay her ship's departure, and drove to the ring as quickly as possible.

As she approached, West saw that the entire controller housing in section six was complete slag and knew that she had to replace the one in section four and hope that was enough to get the ring reoriented.

<*What's your assessment, Chief?*> Jessica asked as West reached the desired section of the kilometer-wide ring and moored her skiff to it.

<*That I hope we can get this damn thing repaired.*>

The admiral didn't reply, and West hoped she hadn't offended the woman—though she doubted it. Despite the fact that the admiral seemed blissfully unaware of how disconcerting it was to be around someone who glowed bright purple because of a distinctly non-Terran biological source, she seemed otherwise very perceptive when it came to giving her people the space they needed to get their work done.

Letting that notion twist around in her mind, West grabbed her new control module and pulled herself along handholds embedded into the ring, coming to the module's panel a few seconds later.

She quickly unlatched the stays and pulled the panel free, slotting it into a nearby mooring.

OK, you stupid thing…let's power you down.

While the control system shut down, she looked over the equipment for any damage, happy not to see any, though still only cautiously optimistic.

<*Chief West?*> Jessica's tone carried a note of urgency.

<*Yes, Admiral?*>

<*That other fishbone managed to do one last thing—it replicated the Call and broadcast it at the Lantzer. Silver lining, those things are going to get the drones before they reach us.*>

West tapped into the ship's scan and saw that the swarm of Exdali was moving toward the cruiser, which hung motionless against the stars. Fear grabbed her, threatening to shake her apart.

Suddenly the vastness of space, the far-off and dubious safety of the *Lantzer*, and the threat of the onrushing enemy was too much. She choked back a sob, unaware of how to even continue.

<*West. I'm here.*> The words in her head were from Chief Glenn. <*I know it's scary. Damn scary. Do you have the old controller out yet?*>

<*N-no…*>

<*OK, let's do that. Pull the stays on the outside first.*>

Though she knew all the steps, Glenn's voice launched her into action, and she gulped down the lump in her throat and began to follow his directions. A minute later, she had the new controller in, and it began to initialize.

<*Looking good from here,*> Glenn said. <*Pass control to Lucida so she can align the gate with Albany.*>

West realized that the Exdali were nearly upon the *Lantzer*. There was no time for tests. The ring had to be activated so the ship could jump. Jumping was all that mattered now.

Even as she passed control to Lucida, the *Lantzer* began to move toward the gate, and it occurred to West that she had no idea how to get back aboard.

<*West!*> Trevor's voice came to her this time. <*Get back to your skiff and get ready to boost toward the bay. You only have to get a few hundred meters away from the gate. Just get in front of the bay doors, and I'll use a grav beam to scoop you up.*>

<*Right. On it,*> West said, flinging the bad controller off into space and pulling herself back toward the skiff even as the ring began to turn.

<*Alignment is good. Great work, West,*> Lucida said, eliciting a sigh of relief from the engineer.

She reached the skiff a moment later and powered it up, locking her feet into the slots as she pulled away from the ring. Behind her, the machine came alive, the ball of not-space forming in the jump gate's center, a sight she knew all too well.

The panic threatened to overwhelm her again, and she mentally berated herself for being so weak. She'd trained for situations like this. She'd done plenty of EVA. There was no reason to be so scared.

The rationale almost worked, until she saw one of the Exdali nearly upon the *Lantzer,* and her thoughts turned to gibberish.

<*OK,*> Trevor's calm voice entered her mind as the skiff shot toward the cruiser. <*You're on target, just hold steady. You've got this.*>

The bay was just a few hundred meters away. She was rushing toward it, and it was moving into alignment with her. Her trajectory was true; she would make the spot Trevor had indicated. The grav beam would pull her in and—

Roiling darkness appeared just a dozen meters to her left.

West screamed as she realized the Exdali was nearly atop her. She slewed the skiff to the right, angling further toward the *Lantzer*'s bow.

<*West, you're off course. Correct,*> Trevor called out.

<*I can't! The things!*>

Her wailing scream set her own teeth on edge, but Trevor's voice was calm, reassuring.

<*It's OK. I'm adjusting, just hold.*>

West looked to her left and saw the Exdali close to within three meters of her. This close, she could see an inky reflection to its undulating skin. It was almost as though it was sniffing her, trying to see if she was a worthy diversion.

<*Gotcha!*> Trevor cried out, and West felt the skiff lurch toward the ship.

Out of the corner of her eye, she saw the Exdali rush toward her, and she turned her head away. She was still in space, outside the hull, when her gaze settled on the gate. She watched in fascinated horror as the vessel's mirror touched the roiling ball of energy in its center.

Then she knew no more.

THE JUMP

STELLAR DATE: 10.11.8949 (Adjusted Years)
LOCATION: ISS *Lantzer*
REGION: Buffalo, Albany System, Theban Alliance

The forward holodisplay went dark, and Jessica held her breath, trembling with anticipation, begging the stars that the next sight that appeared would be the familiar pattern of the Praesepe Cluster.

Three excruciatingly long seconds later, that familiar starscape appeared, and she breathed a sigh of relief, glancing at Karma and Lucida as Gil announced, <*We're four light seconds from Buffalo.*>

"Thank all the things," Lucida breathed.

Jessica was about to join her, when Trevor bellowed over the shipnet.

<*We've got company!*>

"Shit! Not *those* things!" Lucida blurted out.

<*What?*> Jessica exclaimed, pulling up the optics from the bay to see a small Exdali, not much larger than an ARC fighter, tearing its way across the deck while Trevor backpedaled away from it, a bloody figure in his arms. "Shit!"

She turned to the console at her side and saw that the grav beam Trevor had used to pull in West's skiff was still active. She reversed it, blasting positive gravitons at the creature, using the same patterns that had gotten them through the dark layer tunnel to Star City many years ago.

The effect was enough to push the thing off the deck and out into space, though the extradimensional beast clawed its way across the plas, shredding the launch rails before flying out into the black.

<*I've broadcast an alert to the system,*> Gil announced seconds later.

"Oh shit! Shit, shit!" Karma bellowed. "There are more! They're just appearing!"

Jessica flipped the main holo to display the location where they'd exited the jump. Dozens of black shapes were appearing and spreading out, hungrily seeking their next meal. Though the *Lantzer* and pursuing Exdali were a good distance from the planet, a few cargo haulers were nearby, all of which were already turning and boosting away from the rapidly growing mass of darkness.

"Lucida!" she yelled at the ashen-faced pilot. "Full burn! Everything we've got!"

"Ma'am!" the ensign said after a moment, nodding manically as her hands flew over the console.

The *Lantzer*'s deck shuddered, and groans echoed around them as the ship surged forward, away from the mounting threat they'd brought with them to the Albany System.

"Local STC got our call," Karma announced. "They've put out a ban."

Jessica nodded, listening as they picked up the broadcast.

<This is a system-wide alert. Exdali incursion four light seconds spinward of Buffalo. All ships, Buffalo is now interdicted. Adjust vectors per nearest STC's directives.>

"Doesn't *anyone* know how to send these things back?" Jessica muttered. "Stars…this needs to be in the databanks!"

<Call from the Knossos,> Gil announced a second later. *<It's Admiral Carson.>*

She accepted the incoming message without hesitation.

<Carson! Am I glad to hear from you! Do you know how to send these things back to hell?>

<Yes, but my fleet is on the far side of Buffalo, thirty minutes out.>

<Shit!>

Jessica clenched her jaw as she saw the mass of Exdali spreading out, some moving toward the nearby array of gates—which were surrounded by hundreds of ships. She looked at her bridge crew, knowing they'd been through more than she could ever have asked, but also knowing that their trials weren't done yet.

Even so, they didn't *all* have to put themselves at risk. She was the captain, that was her job.

<Crew of the ISS Lantzer. *Abandon ship. Get to pods, the pinnace, or the ARCs. You have three minutes before I initiate the call and get these things to come after us.>*

<Hell no!> Trevor was first to respond.

"He's right," Karma added a moment later. "We all did this, bringing them here in our escape. We're not running."

<Besides,> Gil added. *<It's going to take all of us to keep this scrap heap flying long enough for Admiral Carson's fleet to arrive and deal with these things.>*

One by one, the rest of the crew sounded off that they were staying, even the Marines.

<Couldn't look anyone in the eye for the rest of my life if I abandoned you now, ma'am,> Corporal Jay sent privately.

<Ma'am, we stand a better chance if we use the last three ARCs and the pinnace to misdirect the Exdali,> Gil said a second later. *<They all can broadcast the Call. We can tangle the things up, keep them at bay.>*

Jessica felt a surge of hope in her breast at the thought. *<OK, get the ARCs out there.>*

<Pinnace's remote flight controls are hosed,> Trevor said. *<Someone has to go out there to fly it.>*

Half a dozen voices called out, volunteering to fly the craft. Jessica felt her eyes moisten as the admiral and the wife went to war in her mind.

<Trevor. Take Meg. You two are our best-rated next to Lucida and me.>

<Don't worry,> Trevor said, his voice missing his typical nonchalance. *<We got this.>*

The unfairness of making it back to Albany only to risk all their lives hit her like a sledgehammer, and she took a moment to compose herself before replying.

<*You stay safe, Trevor. You hear me? No crazy heroics. If you don't come back to me, I'll…*>

<*Hey.*> His voice was gentle. <*Same for you. Between the two of us, I'm not the one with the history of going off half-cocked.*>

An innuendo-laden joke came to mind, but before she could utter it, he spoke up again.

<*I know what you're thinking. Leave cocks out of it.*>

<*The only cocks I'm thinking of are the chickens aboard* Sabrina.>

<*Nice save.*>

Jessica chuckled. <*Good luck. I need to lay out our plots. Be ready for yours.*>

<*Aye, ma'am.*>

Sectioning off her worry, she looked down at the holotank and drew out a plot for the pinnace and the three ARCs. She decided to have Trevor and Meg fly above the *Lantzer* while the fighters moved further back, playing cat and mouse with the Exdali, hopefully being able to keep them from a consistent course.

It seemed like a good plan, but she had yet to see how it would perform in practice. It was entirely possible that the things out there would ignore the smaller ships and focus only on the *Lantzer.*

<*I've briefed Buffalo's STC,*> Gil advised. <*They have droneships en route to help, but they're no closer than Carson's fleet.*>

"Thanks, Gil," Jessica said absently as the ARCs launched from the starboard bay. "With luck, we can manage this on our own."

"Tons and tons of luck. And if we don't have it, the rest of them are going to need it." Karma chuckled at his gallows' humor.

"We don't need luck," Lucida said as she shifted the ship's vector to follow Jessica's plot, which largely led them away from traffic lanes and orbital stations. "We have one of the best pilots in the ISF as our admiral. This'll be a cakewalk."

"Not if you jinx it like that," Jessica muttered.

A minute later, the pinnace launched, and Glenn initiated the Call. Many of the Exdali were already pursuing the *Lantzer,* several of them closer than Jessica felt comfortable with, but the goal was to get the entire group of things to pursue them and not hit the gate arrays. If that happened, the creatures' next stop would be several heavily populated stations, followed by the planet itself.

Jessica didn't even want to contemplate what would occur if the Exdali reached that much mass. She'd made a lot of mistakes in her life and had learned to live with them, but she had no idea how she'd deal with an error in judgment on that scale.

"They're coming." Karma's voice contained a mixture of fear and excitement. "Most are tracking on us, a few on the pinnace."

"Good." Jessica nodded, then brought the ARCs in close to the leading edge of the Exdali wave—which was still growing, as more and more of the things appeared in space where the *Lantzer* had been.

It made no sense to her how the creatures could use a jump gate. They should have been annihilated by the singularity on the other side, but somehow, they were traversing it, as though they had the ability to hold the wormhole open.

Which I guess they must...because they're doing it.

Ideas about the origins of the Exdali and why they might really be spread so far and wide across the galaxy—while not being present in the Large Magellanic Cloud—began to form in her mind.

She pushed them aside to focus on the task at hand, directing her five ships in a complex pattern that, so far, was keeping the Exdali following them while not letting the things get too close.

<*Good work out there,*> she sent to Trevor after ten minutes of leading the creatures on.

<*Don't count your chickens before the cocks get to them,*> he replied a few seconds later. <*This bucket of bolts is barely holding together. We just lost internal a-grav and dampeners.*>

<*Crap!*> Jessica quickly altered her plans, removing several of the jinks from the pinnace's plot. <*OK, going to try and give you smoother sailing. How's Meg?*>

<*The greenest Marine you ever did see, but holding up otherwise. You?*>

In answer, the *Lantzer* groaned, and a vibration thrummed through the deck.

<*We're not doing much better,*> Jessica admitted. <*I think something important just snapped.*>

Having the ship fall apart around them wasn't going to help with their problems, and the admiral knew she needed to try something different.

She activated one of the ARC's stasis shields and turned it onto a new course, diving straight for one of the larger Exdali.

"What are you doing?!" Karma exclaimed.

"Seeing what these things are made of," Jessica replied, then held her breath as the fighter slammed into the creature.

There was a moment when the ship was out of sight, then it came out the other side, smaller bits of writhing Exdali trailing after. The larger creature seemed to break apart, some portions drifting listlessly while others began to move on their own, resuming the chase, albeit at a slower pace.

Exdali nearby shifted, converging on the dead mass, devouring the scraps in moments.

<*Shit...did that work? That looked sort of like something that worked,*> Trevor said.

<*It's slowing them down, at least.*>

<*Crap. We just lost our grav emitters,*> her husband muttered. <*If we can't make*

the Call, we should come back in.>

<*No,*> Jessica almost shouted. <*I'm sending you a new vector. Get clear.*>

<*Jess, I—*>

<*That's an order, Commander. You can't help any more than you already have. We just need to stay the course now and hope Carson's ships can get here in time.*>

Jessica glanced at the approaching fleet's markers on the holotank and shook her head in dismay. Carson's ships had originally been only thirty minutes away, but the *Lantzer* had been boosting hard. Though ten minutes had passed, the vessels coming to the rescue were still over twenty-seven minutes from intercept.

Jessica continued to slash the three ARCs through the pursuing creatures, breathing a sigh of relief as the Exdali continued to fall back, slowed by the impacts and the act of devouring the pieces of mass left behind.

The *Lantzer* had put almost a hundred kilometers between it and the leading edge of the creatures when the vibration in the deck ceased. It was followed by an eerie moment of silence, and then an explosion rocked the ship.

<*We just lost the starboard engine,*> Gil called out. <*We're veering off course.*>

Jessica adjusted the port engine's burn, using what thrusters the ship still had to balance it on the fusion torches. Their new course had the *Lantzer* angling toward a wheel and spoke habitat, and she fired the midship maneuvering jets to rotate the vessel, turning it in the process.

"They're closing," Karma whispered.

The loss of acceleration had already cut the dearly won hundred kilometers of separation down to eighty. Jessica plotted it out, the result of her calculation showing an intercept in four minutes.

"I'm out of ideas," she whispered, looking at Karma and Lucida with wide eyes.

Neither of the ensigns replied, both staring mutely at her, as though she would somehow manage to summon a miracle out of thin air.

"The pods," she managed to stammer, gesturing to the back of the bridge. "Get to the pods!"

The two rose and stumbled across the shuddering deck, the expressions on their faces showing the knowledge of how slim their chances were. Jessica turned to join the ensigns, but another explosion rocked the ship. She didn't need Gil's announcement to know it was the port engine.

An alert sounded, and her HUD updated with an Exdali intercept time of one minute.

Karma fell against the bulkhead. "It doesn't matter now. We'll never make it."

<*Jess!*> Trevor yelled into her mind. <*Get off the ship! You have to go!*>

She sent back an affirmative grunt, unable to form words, the reality that she was about to be shredded by Exdali taking hold in her mind.

<*It doesn't matter,*> she finally managed to say. <*You get away. Stay safe.*>

<*No!*> Trevor shouted, and she worried he was about to try and come back for her.

She was about to order him to safety when a voice came into her mind, a thundering wave of implacable certainty and determination.

~I'm here.~

DEPARTING AIRTHA

STELLAR DATE: 10.11.8949 (Adjusted Years)
LOCATION: ISS *I2*, Airtha
REGION: Huygens System, Transcend Interstellar Alliance

"Stars," Captain Rachel muttered as she approached Tangel on the bridge of the *I2*. "Another system, another gate. We have twelve facilities in New Canaan alone manufacturing super-sized gates, and they *still* can't keep up."

"Well," Tangel replied, looking beyond the gate to the massive Airthan ring and the white dwarf it encircled. "This is probably a good system to leave one in permanently. I have a feeling that I-Class ships will be passing through a lot."

"True," Rachel nodded. "Though I can't believe we're going back to Praesepe. Seems like we've spent half the war with that cluster filling most of the starscape."

"I suppose we've been skirting around it for some time," Tangel replied. "Though not *quite* half the war."

"Close enough," the other woman replied with a laugh. "Gotta admit, I'm a bit nervous about jumping so deep into the cluster itself. Without a gate, it would take almost a century to get out."

"So much exaggeration," Tangel laughed. "More like seventy-five years."

The captain snorted. "Yeah, well, that would certainly *feel* like a century. I—"

"Admiral, Captain!" The comm officer spun in his seat. "I just got an urgent message over Admiral Carson's direct QC. He's asking why we haven't jumped to Buffalo yet."

"Buffalo?" Rachel asked. "What for?"

"There have been a few messages on the QuanComm network about a dustup there," Tangel said. "But they said it was small and that Carson's Fleet was handling it."

"Ma'am, Admiral Carson says there are Exdali appearing insystem and chasing the *Lantzer*."

In an instant, Tangel stripped the message the comm officer was reading and located the *Lantzer*'s last reported coordinates and vector. Her next thought activated the jump gate, adjusting its alignment from the Inner Praesepe Empire to the Albany System on the cluster's rimward edge.

Rachel had already given Helm its orders, and the ship surged forward, speeding across the hundred kilometers between it and the gate.

Tangel sent a message to Carson asking for updates, and just before the *I2* reached the gate, he provided fresh scan data.

"Shit!" she swore aloud, realizing that the *Lantzer* had slowed considerably and the jump would have seen them collide with the cruiser.

Racing against time, she made one final adjustment. And then space disappeared.

Seven seconds later, it was back. Audible alarms wailed, heralding a near collision with a small ship off the port bow.

"Pinnace out there!" Scan called out. "Engines are dead."

"Where's the *Lantzer*?" Tangel demanded, then spotted it fifty kilometers away and breathed a sigh of relief.

"Instruct the dockmaster to send out tugs," Rachel replied while scowling at the holotank.

Scan updated a second later, and the tank showed a stream of Exdali stretched out several thousand kilometers behind the severely damaged ISF cruiser.

Tangel tried to reach out to the *Lantzer*, but the *I2*'s comm array couldn't make a Link with the ship. Rather than wait for the comm team to establish a solid connection, she reached out across space and found Jessica's mind, forcing her thoughts across the distance to reach her friend.

~I'm here.~

~Tangel? Where? And shit, can you turn it down a notch? My eyes almost popped out.~

~I'm aboard the I2. *We're fifty klicks to port. We're going to handle the Exdali, but where are they coming from?~*

A feeling of shame came from Jessica for a moment before she replied. *~They followed us through a jump. We drew them out to take on the Caretaker ships, and somehow they came after.~*

~Caretaker ships?~ Tangel felt a wave of fear strike her. *~At Star City?~*

~No…or I hope not. We never made it. Got knocked out of our jump this side of Stillwater.~

A torrent of implications, none of them good, rolled over Tangel, but she pushed them aside.

~OK. Rachel's sending tugs to get you away from this mess. We'll shove these things back in the dark layer and put a cork in that gate that's sending them.~

~Stars…you have no idea how good it feels to know I didn't destroy a star system.~

Tangel sent a laugh. *~Well, don't count your chickens before they're hatched.~*

~Or your cocks.~

~What?~ Tangel's brow furrowed.

~Nothing. Oh! Thanks for saving Trevor too.~

~He in the pinnace?~

~Uh huh, a decoy…sorta.~

Tangel ran a hand over her head, subconsciously tightening her ponytail. *~OK, I want to work on this Exdali problem. You get to safety.~*

~And a nap. Stars, I could sleep for a week.~

Tangel sent a supportive feeling into Jessica's mind, and then turned her full attention to the problem at hand.

"We're opening a rift," Rachel said, highlighting a point on the main holo. "Sending ARCs out on remote to draw them toward it."

"Okay," Tangel nodded. "Send out as many as it takes to make sure they're corralled. I don't want a single one of these things to get away."

"How are we going to stop them?" Rachel asked, gesturing at the origin point for the stream of Exdali. "There's no rift there…it's like they're just appearing out of thin air."

Tangel heaved a sigh. "They followed Jessica through a jump."

Rachel's eyes widened. "Shit! From Star City?"

"No, they ran into trouble before they got there."

<You need to blow the gate on the other side,> Bob said. *<Send an RM to hit it.>*

"We need to know where," Tangel replied, but before she could speak further, the secondary holotank switched to a view of the Perseus Arm.

<Here.> A location highlighted. *<Jump the RMs through the gates at Buffalo and destroy that one on the other side. We'll need to send ships to close the rift over there as well.>*

"Fun for later," Tangel said, thankful that the location Jessica had jumped from wasn't near any stars.

"Right," Rachel agreed. "I have a team putting mirrors on RMs. Should be ready to fire in thirty minutes."

Tangel nodded, turning back to the primary holotank, watching as several hundred remote-piloted ARCs began to shepherd the Exdali from their origin point to the rift they were being pushed into.

<Admiral!>

Carson reached out as she was sending orders to open a second rift closer to the origin point, so the things could be funneled into it with less trouble.

<Sorry to steal your thunder, Admiral Carson,> Tangel replied.

<Stars, don't be sorry for coming. I was starting to worry we were going to lose Jessica.>

She nodded, glad that the mystery of Jessica's disappearance was at least partially solved. *<We would have been here sooner, but the first messages we received didn't make it seem like there was anything serious going on.>*

<Pardon?> Carson sputtered. *<Stars, Admiral. The message I sent was, 'Urgent! Exdali outbreak at Buffalo. Jessica in peril.'>*

"Shit," Tangel muttered. *<We got 'Minor incursion at Buffalo. Situation in hand.'>*

Carson sent a long groan, and Tangel shared his sentiment.

<I know they have to parse the shorthand and manage the queuing manually,> he said, *<but that seems like a pretty serious cock-up.>*

What's with all the cock references? Tangel wondered. *<Yeah, it does. Sera is at*

Khardine, I think I'll get her to investigate.>

Twenty minutes later, the deck around her took on a lavender hue, and she turned to see Jessica approaching.

"Stars," Tangel whispered as they embraced. "I was really starting to worry about you. What happened out there?"

Jessica's lips quirked up into a smile. "Oh, I dunno. Got knocked out of a jump by Caretakers. I went head to head with one and beat it, we fou—"

"Whoa!" Tangel held up a hand. "You *what*?"

"Thought that might get your attention," Jessica said with a tired laugh. "I fought an ascended being and won. I think that makes me the first."

<*No. I beat you,*> Bob interjected.

"Oh?" Jessica looked up at the overhead. "When did you do it? I took my Caretaker out seven days ago."

<*Damn.*>

"Cary beats you both." Tangel shot the overhead a cool look. "I think she got hers a few hours before you did, Jessica."

"Seriously?" Dark purple brows lifted up her lavender forehead. "Cary?"

<*Myrrdan doesn't count. He was only semi-ascended. Besides, I killed Airtha.*>

"Holy shit!" Jessica exclaimed. "I get stuck in the middle of nowhere for a week, and everything goes *nuts*? And here I was all excited that I managed to capture mine."

"Hold up." Tangel placed a hand on Jessica's shoulder. "Captured? Alive?"

"Uh huh. My Marines are guarding it on my ship. Wasn't sure if you wanted it brought aboard—part of why I came up here."

"Part?" Tangel asked.

"Well, I wasn't just going to sit around doing nothing while you fixed my mistake."

Captain Rachel approached, shaking her head. "From what I overheard, you had some amazing successes, not mistakes, Admiral."

"Don't you call me that." Jessica grabbed Rachel and pulled her in for an embrace. "Stars, I still remember when you were on your first rotation. The *I2* couldn't ask for a better skipper."

"Sure, yeah, thanks for reminding my crew that I was knee-high to a grasshopper while you were helping train the first class at the Kap."

Despite her words, Rachel was grinning, and Tangel favored them both with a smile before turning back to the holotank.

"What I want to know," she said after staring at it for a minute, "...well, correction. *One* of the things I want to know is how the rift on the other side is staying open."

"Shit," Jessica muttered. "You're right. At first, I thought it was just because of the ones following us out of the rift before we jumped, but way too many are out now."

"Were there more ships that you escaped from?" Tangel asked.

"There were three. We captured one, and the Exdali destroyed the other two. We had to abandon our prize ship four days ago. I suppose something aboard it could have repaired, but all that was left were rudimentary automated systems. Not even a decent NSAI."

"A Caretaker ship?" Tangel shook her head in disbelief. "Talk about a jackpot."

"Still, it was nowhere near the final engagement," Jessica said. "There had to be another ship nearby. Maybe one stealthed. Who knows."

"Well, it's going to meet a few antimatter warheads if it's still there," Tangel said.

"I wonder why they don't do this all the time," Rachel mused as the march of Exdali continued on.

"Send Exdali at us through jump gates?" Tangel asked.

"Yeah."

Jessica shrugged. "Maybe I pissed them off enough to break a rule or something."

"Maybe we can ask the one you captured," Tangel said, checking on the Caretaker that Jessica had captured and noting that the Marines had brought it to the containment facility aboard the *I2* where the captured remnants were kept.

Jessica shook her head in response, swallowing before she said, "I don't think I want to talk to it. That's all on you, Tangel."

<Five minutes till the RMs are ready to launch,> Bob interjected. *<Volume of Exdali has picked up, as well.>*

"Noticed that," Tangel muttered. "I'm looking forward to learning why the Caretakers chose now to use this tactic."

"And let's hope that they don't alter their rules of engagement," Rachel added.

"Stars," Jessica whispered. "If they wanted to, they could wipe us all out doing this."

Tangel clenched her jaw, thinking about what possible defense they could muster against such an attack.

"I can only assume it's not in their best interest," Rachel said. "Maybe in doing so, they'd destroy the galaxy…or at least make it unusable for their purposes."

"Jump gates," Tangel muttered. "Best and worst thing ever. Right after dark layer FTL."

The other two women nodded, and none spoke, watching as Carson's fleet finally arrived and began patrolling nearby space, searching for any Exdali that may have escaped the cordon.

<Ready to launch missiles,> Bob announced.

"Fire when ready," Rachel said after getting a nod from Tangel.

"Stars, this sucks," Jessica muttered.

"How so?" Tangel asked. "Other than the obvious, of course."

"We're going to blow the gate, then have to go back and seal the rift and deploy another gate. Total waste."

"It's the Caretakers' fault, not yours," Rachel said. "I can't believe they set up out there waiting for you—I assume that's what happened."

Jessica nodded. "That's what the one I fought indicated."

On the main holodisplay, the view of local space showed six bright engine flares, temporary stars that shone in the darkness as the RMs sped toward the jump gates.

"We got interrupted before," Tangel said, turning from the display to Jessica. "How *did* you defeat an ascended AI? I've gone up against three, and the first two times, Bob had to save me."

<In your defense, Xavia was ***ancient****, and the other was Airtha.>*

"Stop interrupting, Bob," Tangel admonished, a slight laugh in her tone. "I want to hear from Jessica how she defeated the Caretaker."

<She absorbed it.>

"Bob!" Jessica exclaimed. "How did you guess?"

<I understand very well how your body works. What you did was something I anticipated.>

"How do you *know*, though?"

<Because you confirmed it.>

"I confirmed that I absorbed it, but that's hardly enough detail for you to have anticipated it. I could have done that thousands of ways."

<No, not thousands.>

"Bob, let her tell it," Tangel said, and the AI fell silent.

"Well," Jessica began, shooting a mock-angry look at the overhead. "I've directly absorbed electricity before, so when I came face to face with the Caretaker—after crashing an ARC into its ship—I decided to try to absorb it. It swung two of its arms at me, and I grabbed them. Then I just sort of sucked the power out. Once I was brimming with it, I blasted it back at the thing, slicing all its limbs off."

"Stars," Tangel muttered. "Remind me to be extra careful next time I hug you."

"I don't do it all the time," Jessica said. "It's not like absorbing light. Conscious effort is required."

Rachel snorted a too-loud laugh, earning her some curious looks from the bridge crew. "Sorry, I just had a funny thought."

"Share with the class," Jessica said.

"I was just thinking 'Ascended Problems'."

Tangel raised an eyebrow while Jessica shook her head.

"OK. It sounded funnier in my head," the captain said in a muted voice.

"Plus," Jessica held up a finger. "I'm not ascended."

The captain shrugged. "You may not be all transdimensional like Admiral Richards, but you're clearly at a higher level. That's ascend-y in my book."

"Missiles have reached the gates," Scan announced, and the three women turned their attention to the location where the Exdali were still appearing as though from nothing.

"We jumped them a hundred klicks from the ring, just to be sure," Tangel informed the other two. "We should know in about five more seconds."

A single, slow breath later, the Exdali stopped appearing. It was almost as though a faucet had been turned off. The remaining trail of creatures continued to march toward the rift until the last one disappeared. Then Rachel nodded to one of the bridge officers, and the rift closed, sealing the strange creatures back in the dark layer.

Tangel dusted her hands off and grinned at Jessica. "OK, your mess is all cleaned up. Let's go talk to your prisoner."

Jessica blew out a long breath, nodding in silent relief.

"I guess I'll coordinate with Carson while you have all the fun," Rachel said.

"Privilege of rank," Jessica said with a wink.

"She's a rear admiral. Same rank as you," Tangel said, elbowing Jessica as the two women turned and walked across the bridge.

"So? Pretty sure I have seniority."

"Not time in grade," Tangel said.

"You want to make me angry?"

Tangel laughed as they walked off the bridge and into the corridor beyond. "Stars no. I think I'm still just reveling in the fact that you're back here with us."

"Well, I'm not going to be a permanent fixture. I still need to get to Star City."

"Of course," Tangel replied with a nod. "Maybe this time I'll come with you. Make sure you don't get lost on the way."

FATHER FIGURE

STELLAR DATE: 10.12.8949 (Adjusted Years)
LOCATION: Keren Station
REGION: Khardine System, Transcend Interstellar Alliance

"I don't know that I want to do this anymore."

Jeffrey Tomlinson's words stunned Sera. He had delivered them in such a weary tone and with so much remorse that she felt a pang of sorrow on his behalf.

She pursed her lips and rose from the sofa, walking across the small room to look out the window at Keren Station's gently rolling hills that appeared to undulate around the interior of its habitation cylinder.

He didn't speak as she stood for a minute, collecting her thoughts. When she finally turned and looked at the man who wore the face of her father, she still hadn't come up with anything cogent.

"I don't blame you," was all she could manage.

A look of understanding came over Jeffrey's face. "It's hard to reconcile me with *him*, isn't it?"

"It really is," Sera replied. "He was such an...asshole. You seem like a half-decent guy."

"Well, thanks for the 'half' at least," Jeffrey replied. "Finaeus would probably agree with you about my partial assholeishness."

"Sorry," Sera said in a quiet voice. "I thought this would get easier, but it really hasn't."

Jeffrey nodded. "You're telling me."

"Because I look like her?"

He nodded, and for a moment, Sera thought he would look away, but he straightened and maintained eye contact.

"You should know that you're the daughter I always dreamt I'd have," he finally said.

The statement elicited a laugh from Sera, and she gestured to her red-skinned body, which currently had the look of a shipsuit.

"This is what you dreamt?"

"I don't care what you do with your looks," Jeffrey said, rising from the chair he sat in. "I care about your passion, your drive, and your honor. You've taken on so many difficult tasks, and they were all thrust upon you. You never complained, you just soldiered forward."

Sera snorted and shook her head. "Oh, just ask Tangel and Finaeus. I complained a lot."

"Well, that's not the story they tell."

"Then they're too kind…and liars."

"Probably." A corner of Jeffrey's lips turned up. "Finaeus always did like to bend the truth to suit himself."

Sera nodded wordlessly, staring into the eyes of the man she didn't know—yet did—as he looked back at her with a similar expression.

"So, what do you want to do?" she finally asked, thinking back to her conversation with Jason.

Everyone wanted out of the war, wanted out of the endless responsibility for the fate of humanity.

Jeffrey stepped up to the window and stared out into the settling dusk. "It's all just so different. Did you know that we thought that the FGT was just going to fracture when I…left? Everything was getting so big and far apart, communications took decades. I'd hoped that Kirkland wouldn't be able to maintain his myopic vision, and we could all just muddle along. Trust Finaeus to invent jump gates and turn all that on its head."

"So you'd *hoped* everything would fall apart?" Sera asked, mouth agape once the words tumbled out.

"Yes!" Jeffrey threw his arms in the air. "It's all too big, too hard to control. It would have been better if humanity could have just spread and spread and become disconnected."

"War would destroy a lot of that," Sera countered. "Like the dark ages. People just clawing at one another till there was nothing left."

"I guess it was stupid anyway. Now that I understand how the core AIs were manipulating everything, there was never any safety in general dispersal. They would have kept us at one another's throats even when it made no sense."

"Well, we're winning." Sera offered the words with the hope that the man before her would show some of the spirt she knew him for. "In a few years, it'll be over."

"No," Jeffrey shook his head. "Not until the core AIs are destroyed. Until then, we're all at their mercy."

"Agreed. Tangel intends to do just that, ultimately. There are plans underway."

"Like Finaeus's secret base in the galaxy's 3KPC arm?" Jeffrey's tone was derisive. "It's going to take a lot more than that."

"Oh, we know," Sera replied. "There are more facilities in the works, which you must know about by now. Don't be so argumentative."

"I suppose I saw something about them," he allowed. "It's a lot to absorb. You know…two weeks ago, there was no doubt in my mind that I wanted to carry on with my duties as president. So far as I was concerned, no time had passed, and in my mind, I was still the president. But…."

"But?" Sera pressed.

"But I'm not. That Transcend doesn't exist anymore. Back then, we were a loose conglomerate that supported the FGT's continuing mission. In addition, we were quietly working to rebuild the Inner Stars. We weren't this massive empire."

"Neither was Orion."

"They were closer to it than we were…I was proud of that."

Sera turned and leant against the windowsill. "I can't imagine how it feels, coming back to see everything so different."

"That's just the thing." He continued staring out the window, not turning to look at her. "I didn't 'come back'. For me, this was the blink of an eye. Everything changed in an instant, and…."

Sera nodded. "And it's all insane, right?"

"That's putting it mildly." He turned and met her eyes, his filled with sorrow. "Yet…"

"Yet?" she prompted after he didn't continue speaking.

"We set all of this in motion," he finally said. "Set the stage for all of this."

Sera opened her mouth to respond, but he held up a hand to forestall her.

"I know what you're going to say." Jeffrey threw a hand in the air as he spoke. "Others have said it before. It all would have happened anyway, even if the two Tomlinson brothers hadn't come up with this crazy idea of 'Future Generation' terraforming. And maybe it would have. But *I* still had a hand in it…. A lot of the way things are is my fault."

As Sera listened, the man changed before her eyes. Gone was the father figure who had lorded over her for so long, a specter in her mind even after death. Instead, there stood a man like any other. Someone who wanted to do the right thing but was beginning to buckle under the weight of all his past mistakes.

She smiled. "As someone who has held the title you now bear, I can't level a single iota of judgment at you."

A look of sorrowful acceptance settled on Jeffrey's face. "I feel like such a failure. I all but demanded the presidency from you."

"No." She shook her head. "I all but pushed it on you."

"Funny how even with perfect recall, our recollections are so very different."

Sera nodded. "I've noticed that in life. So is that why you called me here? To ask me to take the presidency back? You know that I was transitioning it to Tangel even before we found you."

"I saw signs of that." He chuckled. "She had a better handle on things than I did, and she's only been aware of the Transcend for a few years."

"She's really good at figuring out what makes things tick."

"Still, we both know that our people need their own leader—just not me."

"Well, it's not me, either," Sera replied, feeling a sense of panic. Her sisters were in no condition to take over; she'd thought that her father would be her salvation.

The crushing weight of responsibility began to lever its way back onto her shoulders, and if it weren't for the presence of the man who wore her father's face, she would have let her tears flow.

Then he said something that completely surprised her.

"Of course not. It's clear you don't want it at all."

Her brow creased in frustration. "When has that mattered?"

"When has it not?" he countered.

Sera wanted to reply 'Always', but she knew it wasn't fair to berate Jeffrey for the sins of his clone.

Instead, she responded with a question of her own. "So if you don't want to run the Transcend, and you know I don't want to, then who? Finaeus would just disappear into the ether if we tried to foist the job on him."

"What about Andrea?" her father asked, his expression unreadable.

"Oh, fuck no!" Sera exclaimed. "I'd take over again before I let her ruin everything further."

Jeffrey's face fell, and she realized that he took 'further' as an accusation.

"You know what I mean," she grumbled.

He nodded. "Of course."

"OK, so now that you're done baiting me, who are you actually proposing?"

"What about your cousin, Krissy?"

Sera raised an eyebrow. "She wanted it, back when other you died. She only let me have it because I had Admiral Greer's and Tanis's backing."

"And now?"

"Maybe," Sera allowed. "I don't think she'd say no. What about Greer?"

Jeffrey laughed. "I've known Greer for a long time. He has zero political aspirations. The fact that you got him to take as large a role as you did was a miracle."

"Honestly..." Sera drew out the word. "I think some of that was Mother's doing. She maneuvered me into just the right spot to become the leader of the Transcend, with all the right people around me. If *Sabrina* hadn't appeared at the perfect time with Finaeus aboard.... Stars, who knows where we might be."

"Stars indeed," her father said. "OK, I'll talk to Krissy. I'm happy to stay on as an advisor, but...."

Sera reached out and took his hand, unable to remember the last time she'd touched her father outside of a handshake.

"We can plan later. For now, let's just take a breath," she suggested.

He nodded silently, and she gave him an encouraging smile.

Neither spoke as they turned back to the window, watching as dusk fell and lights came on across the inner surface of the habitation cylinder.

He's not my father, though I suppose that's one of the things that's helping.

PART 5 – COMMS

INTO THE MAW

STELLAR DATE: 10.12.8949 (Adjusted Years)
LOCATION: TSS *Cora's Triumph*
REGION: Interstellar Space, Inner Praesepe Empire

"So, what do you think?" Terrance asked Earnest as the engineer reviewed the readings.

"Only so much we can tell with passive systems," he said after a minute. "Logic dictates that there's got to be a planetary core down there, otherwise why have your drones all clustered like that?"

"Maybe it's convenient." Wyatt's tone suggested that it was exactly how he'd store his planet's worth of drones when he wasn't using them.

Terrance clenched his jaw, surprised at how difficult he found it to get along with the FGT scientist—which was saying something, considering that most of his life had been spent amongst engineers and researchers.

"Oh, I don't know," Emily, the FGT's stellar mechanics engineer, said. "Maybe because dumping them together like that creates a gravity well that later you'll have to propel them out of—not to mention that the ones in the center are constantly fighting against being crushed."

"And fuel, and repair," Terrance added.

"Not sure about that," Earnest said while continuing to stare at the readings. "If these drones are single-use, they won't need those things."

"Not very efficient," Wyatt muttered.

Terrance sighed. "We're not really here to determine if the core AIs could be more efficient."

"No, but it does help us learn more about them," Wyatt countered. "And we know damn little."

"More and more each day," Terrance said absently, doing his best not to engage.

"Hey, what's that?" Emily asked.

"Been wondering the same thing," Earnest replied. "A moonlet of some sort."

"Think it's command and control?" Terrance asked.

Earnest straightened and nodded. "There's low-level EM coming from it.

More than any natural source suggests."

"Could be heavy in uraninite," the FGT scientist said.

"Sure," Earnest shot Wyatt a sour look. "Just a whole bunch of a useful volatile, right beside a planet's worth of drones—and they haven't tapped into it at all. I think that's exactly what's going on."

"Don't have to be an ass about it," Wyatt muttered, and Emily barked a laugh.

"I won't go so far as to use the word 'consensus', but have we reached something close to it?" Terrance asked. The others nodded, and he reached out to Captain Beatrice. *<Ma'am. Passing you the coordinates of a moonlet we'd like to take a gander at. The team here thinks it might be command and control for those drones.>*

<Excellent,> Beatrice replied. *<We'll lay in a course. It'll take about sixteen hours to get there.>*

"Sixteen hours," Terrance relayed. "I'm going to catch some sack."

"Wait," Wyatt raised a hand. "Sixteen hours till what? The TSF sends a fleet?"

"Wyatt," Emily whispered, a smirk on her lips. "This ship *is* the fleet. We're going in to take a closer look."

"I'm not front-line!" Wyatt proclaimed. "I demand that we return to Pyra, or somewhere else marginally civilized, so that me and my team can leave."

"Are you kidding?" Emily shook her head in disbelief. "This is the find of a lifetime, and you want to run away?"

Wyatt sniffed. "I'd prefer to call it a strategic relocation."

* * * * *

Nearly sixteen hours later, Terrance stood next to Captain Beatrice on the *Cora's Triumph*'s bridge, watching the moonlet grow larger on the forward display.

"Thought you'd be down with your team," the captain said with a smirk. "Get their observations firsthand."

"I'll get what I need up here," Terrance said with a quiet laugh. "Besides, for what we'll likely be doing next, your bridge crews will be running the sort of scan we need. Down there, they'll be...well, sometimes it's easy for folks to sink so deeply into their profession that they have trouble seeing things other than through its lens."

"I suspect that that happens to us all," Beatrice said.

"Sure," he nodded. "Just some worse than others."

"What of Earnest?"

A grin settled on Terrance's lips. "He's built up a special immunity over the years. He also enjoys needling fractious people."

"Nice to see that someone's getting some enjoyment out of it."

"Is the platoon ready?" he asked, changing the subject.

"Of course. They're itching for action," Beatrice replied. "We've been out here staring at stars a lot longer than anyone had expected."

"Spoiled," Terrance said with a laugh. "To think that this is 'long'."

"Don't pull that 'when I was your age' garbage with me, mister." The captain looked at him with a twinkle in her eye, and he wondered if she had some sort of double meaning in her words that he couldn't quite pick out. "Doesn't change what the soldiers expected to be doing."

"OK, you win," Terrance laughed, trying to keep the tone light.

"Then you'd best not besmirch their eagerness to be doing something important."

"Trust me," he said. "This is important."

"Sure," the captain nodded. "I get that, but they don't. They want to be making personal contributions."

"If there are some sort of hunter-killer bots in that C&C, they'll get to make those personal contributions before long." Terrance stopped short and shook his head. "Shit, that sounded more macabre than I meant."

"A little gallows humor before battle." The captain's tone carried that same note it had earlier, as though Terrance was missing some subtext that wasn't present in the words they were exchanging.

He glanced around the bridge, noting that the crew was focused on their tasks, though smiles had quirked the lips of a few.

"Are you sure you want to go down with the advance team?" Captain Beatrice asked after a moment. "I should add, is there anything I can do to convince you *not* to go?"

"Well, probably, but stopping me would require something rather extreme. I must admit, I'm not so different than your platoon of soldiers. I need to feel like I'm doing my part as well."

Especially since my actions set so much of this in motion.

"Hard to argue with that." The captain paused, turning to glance at Terrance. "Just keep your head down, sir. If you don't make it back, I might as well fall on my sword."

Terrance nodded, keeping his expression neutral.

He hated being someone else's baggage, but that wasn't going to stop him from getting involved. The core AIs had created a mystery, and that mystery had a plan. Though most of his life had been spent fighting corporate enemies, he'd negotiated with the business end of a rifle more than most people thought.

"Don't worry, I have a vested interest in making it back. And I know which end of the gun is the dangerous one."

"Weapon," the captain corrected with a smile. "My ship has guns, you'll be carrying a weapon."

Terrance flashed her a grin and slapped her on the shoulder. "I love you fleet types."

Captain Beatrice shot him a strange look as he walked away, and then called out, "I'm going to hold you to that."

"Sorry what?" Terrance turned and asked, picking up something unexpected in the woman's voice.

"That you're coming back," she said hastily, then added, "And that I'm not going to have to fall on my sword."

"Oh," Terrance said, nodding quickly. "Of course, you can count on it."

He left the bridge, wondering if the captain had been responding to his statement that he 'loved' fleet types. There was no arguing that Beatrice was a lovely woman.

She had a broader figure than women who normally caught his eye, but she had a grace to her movements that masked that well. That didn't bother him at all, especially because of the fiery intensity that lurked behind her almost blood-red eyes.

Though she always behaved with decorum, there was an intensity behind those eyes that spoke of a different side to the ship's captain.

Maybe I should see what that's all about, after this mission.

A few minutes later, he reached the platoon's sortie room and shook hands with Lieutenant Jordan.

"Ready to kick some ass?" Terrance asked.

"Always, sir," the woman replied. "Though I suspect that there won't be any asses down there, just machines…so, heat vents? Servos? Not as inspiring."

Terrance snorted. "No, I suppose not. Let's be clear, though, there *will* be defenses, and they're not going to play nice, so we keep our eyes peeled and respond with maximum force to any threat."

"I like this guy!" one of the privates called out.

The lieutenant shot the woman a look, and then gestured to the armor rack as she settled her attention back on Terrance. "You familiar with our gear, sir?"

"I did a test fit a day ago," Terrance replied. "Got my preferred loadout set up and then ran some sims. I think I'm good to go."

The lieutenant gave him a look of respect. "Glad to hear it, sir. Your public profile says you've seen combat before, though not where."

"Well, I saw some back on Carthage when the Trissies landed their ships. Urban stuff in Landfall. Before that, it had been some time, unless you count that brief scuffle in the Kap. But yeah, I've fought on just about every type of terrain and theatre you can imagine."

"Alice," one of the sergeants called out, nodding to a private checking her loadout nearby. "Maybe you should pay attention to what Mister Enfield does. Could learn a thing or two."

"Sure thing, Sarge. Never learned much watching you," Alice replied, laughing until the sergeant walked over to her and whispered something in her ear that made her face grow pale.

"Good crew you have here," Terrance said as he backed up to the armor rack and closed his eyes as it began to wrap him in the TSF's mid-weight assault buildout.

He knew they wouldn't use him for any scouting, and he hated the way heavy armor restricted movement. The Transcend's assault armor suited him best.

Doesn't hurt that it also comes with a shoulder mounted railgun.

"Sir." One of the soldiers walked up to Terrance as he stepped off the rack. "I'll just check over your loadout and seals."

"Of course," Terrance said, holding out his arms. "Specialist Larson, you're the TSF's breach AI on this mission?"

"Yes I am, sir. I've gone up against some of the best out there, but never against core AI tech. Earnest has loaded me up with more breach routines than I thought existed. I'm ready to take them down." She turned her head, nodding in the direction of another figure further back in the sortie room. "However, I'm not primary on this mission. An ISF pinnace arrived a few hours ago with Commander Sue aboard."

"Sue!" Terrance exclaimed aloud, craning his neck around as he looked for her.

The utterance caught her attention, and the AI strolled over, the ISF frame's design standing out in stark contrast to the TSF soldier's armor.

"Good to see you, sir," the AI replied. "I was wondering when you were going to realize I was aboard."

"You came with the supply pinnace?" he asked.

"Yeah, a few hours ago. I didn't mean to hide from you, but you were getting your beauty rest. Then Earnest accosted me and began loading me up with data and new techniques along with Specialist Larson, here."

Terrance couldn't help himself and reached out to embrace the AI, not caring that their armor clacked loudly—or that she was an AI and an embrace didn't mean as much to her.

"Stars, you know, I haven't seen you since a year after Carthage landfall."

"I know…I took a lot longer to recover from losing Trist than I expected. And then when Jessica disappeared…well, I lost *myself* in my work, out at New Canaan's heliopause."

"No blame here, Sue," Terrance replied. "We all had a lot of personal rebuilding to do once we got to Canaan."

"OK, let's not delve too deep into the past," Sue said, taking a step back, her helmeted head cocking to the side as she regarded him. "I know how you organics get all mushy."

Terrance nodded. "Too much in the past to think about right before a mission. There's a whole future to worry about, and we can actually do something about that."

"Good attitude," Specialist Larson said.

"OK, you louts!" Lieutenant Jordan shouted a moment later, drawing everyone's attention to herself. "Scan's just updated our tactical net with the latest surface visuals. This moon's just a little bitty rock. Less than five percent standard gravity. Don't go bounding and banging. Maglocks on if they work, controlled and tactical."

"I love to go banging!" the same private who had made the prior colorful comment called out.

"Stow it, Flo," Jordan shouted. "Don't forget, we have guests, so let's try to look like a professional unit out there. You all wanted to see some shit, and this is going to be it. These AIs we're going up against probably know every trick in the book, but that's why we have some oldies but goodies with us.

"I have operational command of this mission," the lieutenant continued. "But if Commander Sue or Mister Enfield says something, you *listen*. They've seen more shit than you've ever imagined."

"I can imagine a lot of—" Flo began, but a hand came out of the crowd and slapped her in the back of the head, shutting her up.

Jordan gave a thankful nod to the sure-handed sergeant. "Scan's picked up the source of EM coming from the moon. It's centered in a crater near the equator. We're going to come in low and settle down in the lee of its rim. We've got two birds as our chariots today, so first and second squads are with me, as are Mister Enfield and Commander Sue. Third and Fourth, you're with Staff Sergeant Yens and Specialist Larson."

The lieutenant paused, pulling her helmet from under her arm as her head swiveled from side to side, surveying her troops.

"OK, then, you fantastic assholes.... Let's go take these core AIs down a notch!"

She pulled her helmet onto her head as the TSF soldiers shouted 'Roo-AH!' and then filed out of the sortie room, double-timing it toward the drop bay.

Terrance followed the last squad, with Sue and the lieutenant following behind.

The shock of seeing Sue again after so many years was wearing off, and he wanted to ask her why she'd given up starship command for tactical operations—especially with how short the ISF was on experienced starship commanders.

Save it, Terrance. Give yourself something to look forward to.

On the way to the drop bay, he reviewed the latest scan data on the crater and the anticipated defenses. It was all but raw speculation. Neither the ISF or TSF had ever encountered a core AI facility—if that's what this was. There was a possibility that it had been left by someone else in the past, or that perhaps it wasn't even Terran in origin.

However, the presence of core AI remnants in the IPE made the final two options far less likely. He fervently hoped that the facility they were going to was fully automated, though each fireteam had a shadowtron on the chance it wasn't.

The two stealth shuttles hunkered in the bay, their surfaces designed with configurable angles to alter their profile and reflect away any active scan systems. Not that the ultra-black, Elastene-like material was likely to reflect much of anything.

It still gave him a sense of pride to know that nearly every stealth system in the galaxy utilized essentially the same technology that his own research team back on Alpha Centauri had pioneered in the thirty-first century.

At the same time, it brought him a little sadness. Of all the people he had set out with, traveling from Alpha Centauri to other near-Sol colonies, only Jason Andrews was still alive. It made so many of their daily experiences bittersweet.

"Shuttle two," Lieutenant Jordan directed, and Terrance followed her, Sue taking up the rear.

Inside was a standard troop bay, spare and utilitarian, with two rows of dampening seats that could also form a full pod to seal the soldier up for an emergency eject. It was such a logical system, he was surprised more dropships didn't utilize it. Bring the squad down as one unit, fake out the enemy, and turn them into helljumpers.

His seat was in the middle of the right row, and he settled into it, leaning back to let the straps and bands wrap around him.

"How many drops you been on, sir?" a corporal across the aisle asked.

Terrance glanced at the man and shrugged. "More than a few hot drops into active combat."

"Where at?" a private asked.

"Well, my first planetary drop was in Tau Ceti. I hit dirt on Galene and joined up with their Marines to stop…well, an insurrection, I suppose."

The question was innocuous, but the answer brought back memories of Khela and how they'd met, before spending long years together. Which led to how they'd separated and the shame he still felt from it.

Funny how shame seems to stack up.

"Stop bugging our guest," one of the squad sergeants said, and Terrance was grateful for the reprieve.

He took a moment to review the personnel on the two squads, and then leant back in his seat, closing his eyes.

As the shuttle took off, he began to run through a series of breathing exercises, knowing that, from now until they touched down, everything was out of his hands. It was a calm feeling, and one that he endeavored to maintain as long as possible.

That ended up being just over thirty minutes. Then the shuttle exploded.

BOTTLED MESSAGE

STELLAR DATE: 10.12.8949 (Adjusted Years)
LOCATION: IS shuttle approaching Normandy
REGION: Khardine System, Transcend Interstellar Alliance

Sera turned her head to look across the small pinnace's cockpit at Jason as he piloted the craft toward the small moon named Norway. He spotted her surreptitious look and flashed her a grin in response.

She smiled back, unable to ignore how happy he always was when flying a ship. There was a special crinkle in the corner of his eyes that only showed up when at the helm…or stick, depending on what he was flying.

She craned her neck a bit further, nodding to Roxy, who sat behind Jason, while Jane rode in the seat behind Sera.

At first, Sera had planned to go down to the moon alone with Jason, but after Roxy had officially taken on the assistant director's role in the Hand, she had all but insisted she come along to see what was going on with the QuanComm messages being altered.

Sera couldn't very well say she wanted alone time with her beau, so she had acquiesced.

"Nervous?" Jason asked as he looked over his display, reviewing the craft's status.

"Me?" Sera snorted. "We're going to check out an anomaly at a glorified comm shack. What's there to be nervous about?"

The governor shrugged, a boyish gesture that seemed at odds with the grey-haired senior captain she'd first met on the *Intrepid* years ago.

A part of her missed his statelier look, but she understood that availing himself of rejuv so that he could handle the demands of office was wise. He'd also assured her that he'd get old again, adding in one of his saucy winks.

"Beats me, you're the one that's fidgeting like there's nothing else to do."

"That's because there *is* nothing else to do," Sera muttered. "Stealth approach to this place means that I'm stuck inside my own head, and this ship is stripped down so much, it barely has an onboard logging comp."

<You have a thousand reports that need your attention, and they're all in your head,> Jen suggested over the shipnet.

"Right, because that's what I *love* to do for fun," Sera drawled.

<I kinda like doing reports,> Carmen said. *<There's something soothing about them.>*

<Don't you dare give her any ideas,> Jen retorted. *<I won't have my human getting soft and lazy.>*

"*Your* human?" Sera's brows rose in mock outrage, and she caught sight of

Jason covering his mouth to laugh. "Oh, is it funny, mister?"

"No," Jason shook his head. "Just reminds me about something that an old friend used to say."

She was going to ask him for details, but his expression grew clouded, and he busied himself with the ship's navigation console.

<You call me ***your*** *AI sometimes, Sera.>*

"Do I?" she asked. "Sorry, I guess that's an unintentional slip-up. I think it's like saying 'my friend', but since you're inside my head, it helps to identify our relationship."

<Right, but just to make sure that you don't get confused about our relationship, I'm not helping with reports.>

"I've never asked you to," Sera said, an annoyed breath blasting out her nostrils.

<You've asked for help.>

"That's different! I didn't ask you to do them for me, just help with research and analysis!"

"See?" Jason asked, reaching over and placing a hand on Sera's thigh. "You're a bit on-edge."

The two women in the seats behind had fallen silent and still. Their reaction made her angry for an instant, but then she took a deep breath and reminded herself that everyone had pressure, and that they were all dealing with more shit than most people could imagine. No one needed her losing it and making things worse.

"My father wants to relinquish his presidency, which may come back to me," she explained after a minute of silence. "Though he understands I don't want it. He suggested Krissy, but after thinking about it, I'm not totally sure she'd take it, or that it would be wise, given her duties and the work she already has to do."

"Ahhh." Jason pursed his lips, angling the pinnace toward the small moonlet and entering into a holtzman transfer orbit.

"Just 'ahhh'?" she asked.

"Well, I mean…you can't make someone be in charge who *really* doesn't want to. It's not a great idea to force them to, either."

"That's how *I* feel."

"I know, I was referring to you, Sera." Jason gave her a kind look, and she felt even worse for having snapped at him.

"Oh, sorry."

"I know it doesn't help with your family problem," Roxy said a minute later. "But feel free to pass me any reports you'd like. I don't mind, and I like to stay busy."

"You sure?" Sera asked, turning in her seat to meet the azure woman's eyes. "I mean, I already pushed a lot onto you."

"I can handle it. I've spent a lot of time being…disregarded. I want to step forward again."

"I get that," Sera replied. "OK, you asked for it. Here comes the motherlode."

Roxy was silent for a moment, then exclaimed, "Has Petra lost her mind?!"

Sera knew exactly what her assistant director was referring to and laughed, shaking her head. "Petra gets results. I give her free reign as much as possible."

"Probably because she's only quasi-Hand now anyway."

"That too, but she's loyal nonetheless."

"So glad that my problems are limited to New Canaan, more or less," Jason said as he brought the ship down to a lower orbit.

"I thought Tangel reported to you?" Roxy asked. "Doesn't that kind of make the whole galaxy your problem?"

Jason barked a laugh. "And the less I think of it like that, the happier I am. Seriously, though. Tangel doesn't 'report' to me so much as she just lets me know what she's up to. If I have suggestions, she listens to them, but unless it's an outflow of something Parliament decides, I don't pass her any directives at all."

"How are the people of New Canaan handling all this?" Sera asked.

"Better than I would have expected," he replied. "Half the population is directly involved in the war effort now. The other half now supporting the first half. A quarter of our population is outsystem, crewing warships, and the AIs are breeding as fast as they can to bolster the population and fill as many gaps as they can."

Sera gave a rueful laugh. "Good thing the colonists breed like rabbits."

"There are downsides to that as well. It's stifling the birth rate right now. Just about everyone has sent kids off to war, and no one is too excited about having more just to send them away."

"The war will be over by then," Sera said, knowing it wasn't exactly true.

Jason shook his head. "This war is like a wildfire. Sure, we can put out the cause of the blaze, but it's already spreading. There are tens of millions of systems out there, and the instability this conflict has caused is going to last for decades…maybe centuries."

Sera knew he was right, and only nodded, trying to think of something to say.

After a minute, Jason continued. "My only hope is that once we stop Orion, Terra, and the Trisilieds, we can leave the rest of things to people with more resources. Get back to the life we all hoped to live."

Sera nodded mutely, knowing that, to an extent, Jason's hope was a vain one. The battle the people of New Canaan would have to fight *after* the war would be far more difficult than the one they were fighting at present.

Despite their desire to 'get away' and build a quiet colony, their time away from Sol had been anything but. Many of them would have a hard time reintegrating…or they just might not want to return.

Healing New Canaan would take a lot longer than building it had.

"I hope everyone gets that," she finally said.

"Not me," Roxy chimed in. "I've got a decent amount of anger that still needs to be taken out on the asshats of the galaxy. Be a long time before I settle down."

<I don't know that that is the healthiest of attitudes,> Carmen said.

"Oh, it's not," Roxy nodded emphatically. "Which is why I have to expunge it from myself with force."

<Uhhhhhh….> Carmen's tone was laden with uncertainty.

"I'm kidding!" Roxy said with a self-deprecating laugh. "Mostly. I'm talking to a fleet psychiatrist…well, a team of them. I know I can't do this alone, but I'm also not going to tell myself that I can go back to some sense of normalcy anytime soon. I need to see if I can get myself back to who I used to be before I look toward becoming something else." She shook her head, a look of consternation settling on her face. "Stars, that makes no sense at all."

Sera gave a rueful laugh, having no idea if that was the best course of action. She couldn't offer any advice, though, since she had no idea what she'd do in Roxy's shoes. The fact that the woman was functional at all was a miracle.

"Sheesh," Jason muttered, giving Sera a sidelong glance and a wink. "This was supposed to be the fun, 'get away from my troubles' trip. I should have gone to the Trisilieds with Cheeky and Sabrina."

"You gonna two-time on me with them?" Sera squeaked in mock indignation.

"More like double-time," Jason chuckled.

Sera groaned and gestured to the holo. "Don't you have something important to do here, like concentrate on flying?"

"I could do this while playing three games of Snark at once," he replied. "Eyes closed and hands behind my back."

"Showoff."

They rode the final minutes in silence, finally slipping into a deep crevasse on the moon's surface before coming down to a hidden docking bay tucked under an overhang.

"OK," Sera said as the pinnace settled onto the cradle. "Remember, this is just a routine visit. I'm here to chat with Colonel Rutger, and you two are doing an inspection of the logs for recent operations to make sure that nothing was sent in the clear that shouldn't have been."

"Easy," Roxy replied. "We'll just yank more than we need and see what we can see about Carson's messages."

"And I'm just your arm candy," Jason said with a laugh as the docking clamps locked onto the ship, and he rose carefully in the low gravity. "Stars, been a while since I've been in partial gravity. Spoiled by a-grav everywhere these days."

"Well, if anyone can get their space legs back, it's you," Sera said, nudging him with her elbow. "None of us were born before it existed."

"You calling me old?" he asked.

"Uh huh."

A minute later, they were out on the dock, where Colonel Rutger and two majors were waiting.

The moment Sera stepped onto the deck, he strode forward, his hand extended and a smile on his lips.

"Director Sera, so very good to see you. It's unexpected to have our little outpost visited by someone such as yourself."

She shook her head while shaking his hand. "Don't downplay with me, Colonel. You run one of the most important facilities in the galaxy. My father just wanted me to swing by and have a chat with you. Make sure your needs are being met and that there's not something we can do that's not in the official reports."

The colonel nodded. "Of course, Director. I can think of a few things that could improve our operation."

"Excellent," Sera replied, turning to Jason. "I assume you know Jason Andrews, New Canaan's governor. He was at Khardine and decided to come along to see the good use we're putting their technology to—and to verify that we're safeguarding it appropriately."

A look of worry came across Colonel Rutger's face, and Sera wondered if it was concern over scrutiny in general, or if he had something to hide.

<I think he just likes the autonomy he's had here,> Jen commented. *<He's the ruler of a pretty important roost.>*

<That he is. In all honesty, I should have visited sooner.>

<You delegated to General Greer. That was the right thing to do.>

Sera gave a mental laugh. *<Always with the logic, Jen.>*

<That's my job.>

During her brief exchange with Jen, Colonel Rutger had introduced himself to Jason and then turned to the two majors.

"This is Major Belos and Major Lorne. They both share responsibility for message delivery, and also take shifts at the boards."

"Really?" Roxy asked from where she stood on Sera's left. "That's surprising."

"This is Assistant Director Roxy, and Commander Jane," Sera said, then gestured for Roxy to continue as the colonel nodded in greeting.

"Well, I just would have expected that we could staff you with enough people that your senior leadership didn't have to work the boards."

"I mandate it." Rutger inclined his head. "I feel that it's good for everyone to see firsthand what comes through, and to understand the underlying urgency that is at play."

"Seems reasonable," Sera said.

"Thank you," the colonel said, his tone not giving away whether or not he cared for her approval. "I'll show you to my office, Director. I assume you're joining us, Governor Andrews?"

"I am," Jason replied.

"Excellent." Colonel Rutger gestured toward the bay's doors. "Major Belos will take the assistant director and commander on their tour. Lorne, you may return to your duties."

"Sir," Lorne acknowledged before turning and leaving the bay.

Belos gestured for Roxy and Jane to follow, leading them toward an exit on their right, while the colonel directed Sera and Jason to the left.

A tingle ran up Sera's spine as the group broke up. After spending so long with her High Guard shadowing her every move, she felt strangely vulnerable. The feeling was incongruous with the fact that she was in one of the most secure facilities in the Transcend.

The concern was assuaged by the fact that Jason's cruiser was nearby, cloaked with a platoon of ISF Marines ready to drop at a moment's notice.

Still, I'd feel a lot better knowing that Major Valerie was still with me. But she's watching over my father now.

A strange feeling of jealousy hit Sera, and she shook her head.

<You seem out of sorts today, Sera,> Jen said.

<There has been so much change,> she replied. *<Ever since Tangel ascended on Pyra, everything has accelerated so much. If I start rattling off the list, it'll take all day. I just need to focus on what's in front of me for a bit.>*

<Which is Jason's ass right now.>

Jason was walking alongside the colonel, and in her musing, Sera had fallen a step behind, her unfocused gaze aimed at the governor's rear.

<Not a bad thing to focus on,> she mused.

<I really can't say. Well, I guess I can. Statistically, people prefer certain physical configurations, and Jason fits a desirable profile.>

<You can't apply statistics to what's attractive to other people,> Sera chided the AI.

<Of course you can. You're just not sophisticated enough.>

<You know what they say about statistics…> Sera said.

<That it's the only way to measure the state of the galaxy?>

<Funny.>

Sera tuned in to the conversation between Jason and the colonel, continuing to hang back and focus on what the man had to say—and didn't say.

"A new shipment of blades just came in," Colonel Rutger was explaining. "That always steps things up a notch. We have to run tests on them all, and then begin the confirmation process that the paired blades have gone to the right place."

"Takes a while, I assume?" Jason asked.

"Core, you have no idea." Colonel Rutger shook his head. "There are blades from the second shipment still in the confirmation process."

"Really?" The governor tilted his head and cocked an eyebrow. "But that shipment came in well over a year ago."

"It sure did. But here's the thing: ships with gate mirrors are at a premium. So if we need to get a blade to a remote system, we jump it out to a location with a return gate, and from there, it transfers to a ship that takes it via dark layer FTL to the destination. Some of the blades have had to pass through two or three couriers before they get to their final istallations."

"I can see how that would take a while," Jason said, glancing back at Sera.

"Then there's the confirmation process," she added. "Some of these blades are going to places that had no prior knowledge of the unveiling and the war. They have no way to verify identity or allegiance directly over the QC network, so it needs to pass back through the courier network to get here."

"Exactly," Rutger said. "Because of that, we have an entire reliability system that gets assigned to blades."

"As in, how certain you are that you're talking with who you expect to?" Jason asked.

The colonel nodded. "Yes. For example, ISF ships that receive their blades in New Canaan construction yards have the highest reliability rating—well, next to the blades on I-Class ships. Blades out in the fringes of the Hand's network have the least. Certain broadcast messages don't filter down through all the reliability levels because we have to assume that somewhere, someone who shouldn't be is on the receiving end of a QC blade."

"We burn out more blades with reverifications," Sera muttered. "I sure wish they had more longevity."

Jason laughed. "I'll consult physics and see if we can get it to make an exception for us."

Sera reached out and gave the governor a two-fingered poke in the shoulder. "Earnest bends them enough. I bet they have a pre-existing exception built in for him."

"I catch a lot of grief from remote commanders over how brief we have to be on the network, but everyone gets that it's our number one advantage right now. So many of our major strikes wouldn't have been remotely possible without the network."

As the colonel spoke, they came to an observation window that looked out over a vast cave filled with small, standalone rooms.

"This, Director and Governor, is what I like to think of as the heart of the Alliance."

The man's voice was filled with pride, and Sera didn't want to debate with him over semantics. At the very least, it was *a* heart, but she was certain that the true heart of the Scipio Alliance was the *I2*.

Jason must have been on a similar train of thought, as he said, "Well, there's a significant secondary hub in the *I2*, but I get your meaning."

The colonel gave an almost sheepish smile. "We labor long hours deep in this rock, Governor—grant us this one bit of hubris."

A loud laugh burst from Jason, and he slapped the colonel on the back. "Very well, I'll allow it."

* * * * *

Roxy and Jane shared a look as they followed Major Belos on their tour of the facility.

<Not one to waste words, is he?> Jane said, a note of humor carrying over with her statement. *<Like…he has a daily quota of five, and he's already used three.>*

<Well, that should make our part go fast. No blah-blah-blah,> Roxy replied.

<Is fast the goal?> Carmen asked. *<Don't we want to draw things out? Get him to slip up?>*

<That's what I would have thought as well,> Jane added.

Roxy held back a laugh. *<Oh, I expect him to slip up, but not verbally. It's going to be in the records. Once I dive into those, I'll see what's what. Hence my desire to get this dog and pony show over with.>*

"Blade Node Two," Major Belos announced tonelessly as he reached a sealed portal. It was guarded by two soldiers, an AI in a warframe, and several drones.

"Excellent," Roxy replied. "Let's have a look."

It took a minute for everyone to pass their tokens and get through the auth system to satisfy the guards that they were who they said they were.

Jane's presence threw up some red flags, as the base systems listed her as AWOL with suspicion of being a part of Justin's faction.

A near-imperceptible shift in the guards' posture occurred when that information came back, but after a call to the colonel cleared things up, they relaxed a hair and opened the portal.

"And here we are," Belos announced when they entered the circular room.

Roxy gauged the space to be just about thirty meters across, containing several dozen three-meter-high towers that contained the QC blades.

"As you can see," the major gestured to the blade towers and the conduits feeding into them, "each tower has independent cooling and power supply. Several redundant systems ensure that it would take a chain reaction of very unlikely events—or a deliberate attack—to damage the towers."

<He went way over five words there,> Carmen commented. *<You owe me ten creds, Jane.>*

<Yeah. That's more than he's said since we left the bay. Who knew he had it in him?>

"That's great, Major," Roxy said. "But we're less interested in the physical powering of the blades and more interested in the logging facilities. As you know, the devil is in the details, and the detail that worries us is the inconsistent shorthand people use over the QuanComm network."

"You're referring to how it requires people to translate the messages and then pass them on," Belos replied. "There are primary and secondary teams that check all the messages to make sure no meaning was lost. Would you like to see them in action?"

"That's real-time quality assurance," Roxy said. "What about tertiary review? Who watches the watchers?"

"Everything is logged, of course," Belos said, his brow lowering in annoyance. "Messages in and out. Messages that are delivered to a recipient directly aren't translated, they just get slated for passthrough, so those are linked and checked roughly fifteen minutes later, depending on volume."

"Sounds reasonable," Roxy replied. "I'd like to view the reports on their corrections and error rates. Are the logs for each node stored with it? Or are they maintained elsewhere?"

"Since passthrough can utilize more than one node, they're stored in a separate data facility."

<Did you get a tap in?> Roxy asked Carmen before they turned to leave. *<This analysis only works if we can watch real-time communication and then compare it with the quality control process to see if there are issues.>*

<You don't need to tell me that,> Carmen added a note of annoyance. *<It's done.>*

"Yes, Major, we'd very much like to see that," Roxy said brightly.

Belos led them out of the room and back down the passage, taking them through a long stretch of warren-like tunnels within the moon, until they came to another guarded portal.

This one was protected by an entire squad of soldiers, which made sense to Roxy, given that the entire repository of QuanComm communication was stored there—excepting what went through the *I2* and New Canaan hubs.

Once again, Jane's prior status threw red flags, and the lieutenant commanding the detail ran it up the chain to Colonel Rutger for the second time.

While Belos hadn't been perturbed during the prior delay, this one seemed to bother him. He made a few snippy comments at the lieutenant, who bore the major's ire with good grace.

Finally, all the approvals were logged, and the group was allowed access to the datastore.

They stepped through the door and into a small room with a window on the far side. Roxy walked toward it and saw a large, spherical chamber lined with data towers. The readouts on the window indicated that the interior of the room was vacuum and only a fraction of a kelvin above absolute zero.

On either side of the room they stood in, doors led to a ring of offices where teams reviewed the messages and ensured that they had been properly managed.

"Impressive," Roxy said. "We're, what, four hundred kilometers below Norway's surface now?"

"Yes," Major Belos replied.

<There we are, back to single, monosyllabic words,> Jane said, her chuckle filling their minds.

<Something seems off about Belos,> Roxy said as she regarded the major silently. *<He knows what I want, but he's making me ask for it every step of the way.>*

"I assume I'll need to review via a secure console?" Roxy asked Belos, and the major nodded.

He led them through a door on the left and past several offices until they came to an empty one. Within, a console waited, and the major entered his authentication codes before stepping aside for Roxy to sit down.

<Tempted to drop some nano on the major,> Carmen said. *<He's just…weird.>*

<You can't breach someone's privacy because they're weird,> Roxy said as she began to sift through the high-level reports the console showed.

She pulled up a number of messages that had been flagged as erroneous, looking over the issues found. At the same time, she tapped into the console directly and pulled up the real-time translations going on for Blade Node 2.

She knew it would take some time for those messages to reach quality control, and she glanced at the major.

"I'll be at this for a few hours. You don't have to wait here," she told him.

"I believe I do, ma'am."

"Major Belos, I'm the assistant director of the Hand. I don't need a babysitter."

<Oh, I saw his mouth open,> Jane commented. *<He was going to say '**acting** assistant director'. I'd put money on it.>*

<You put money on almost everything,> Carmen said.

<True. Your point being?>

While the other two bantered, Roxy contacted Sera, who asked the colonel to inform the major that he was allowed to leave.

A few moments later, Belos gave Roxy a sour look and then shrugged. "Very well. Let me know if you need anything."

After he left the room, Jane rolled her eyes. "We don't, but you could really use a personality transplant, buddy."

"Be nice," Roxy said as she flipped through the console's logs.

"You don't like me because I'm nice," Jane countered, and Roxy only laughed.

She was focused on hunting down the messages from Admiral Carson that Tangel had requested Sera to look into. It took a few minutes, but she found the source messages and the versions that had passed through to Tangel.

"You know…" she mused. "It's odd that these messages relayed through

Khardine at all. Carson should have had a direct connection to the *I2*."

"Maybe he burned out those blades," Jane suggested. "They seem pretty fragile."

"That they do," Roxy muttered. "The other thing is that these messages were processed rather than being passed straight through. That's how the verbiage got messed up."

"So the messages were reworded when they shouldn't have been *and* that rewording downplayed the threat?" Jane asked.

"Seems that way."

<*You'd think their vaunted QA process would have picked it up,*> Carmen said.

"Well that's interesting," Roxy shook her head, flipping through more logs. "Major Belos himself flagged the error, but because he did it right as the message was passed to QA, it fell into some sort of loop, bouncing between the two systems."

<*Convenient.*>

"Took the words right out of my mouth," Jane said.

"Well, it *seems* like Belos did the right thing." Roxy said while continuing to search for the messages from Earnest and Terrance that had troubled Tangel and Sera.

Given that the two New Canaanites were traveling on Transcend ships, it wasn't as strange that their messages were being routed through the facility.

"Going to have to give the major a cookie," Jane chuckled. "One with little letters all over it to help him make it through the day."

Roxy snorted, then raised her eyebrows as she looked over the messages from Terrance Enfield regarding the core AI facility in the IPE. "These things have pretty much gone through an identical cock-up."

"Misinterpreted and then stuck in limbo?" Jane asked.

"Yup. And it should come as no surprise to you that the good Major Belos has his fingerprints all over these, too."

<*So what's the plan?*>

"We catch him with his hand in the cookie jar," Roxy replied.

Jane frowned. "A cookie what?"

"Jar. You know…tall, made of plas or glass, round."

"I've had a lot of cookies that came out of boxes, or some sort of plas package, but I've never heard of cookies coming out of a jar." She reached out and tapped Roxy's head. "Did something get mixed up in there when your memories came back?"

Jane appeared legitimately concerned, and Roxy shook her head and groaned.

"Red-handed. How about that?"

"Ohhhh…you mean 'catch him in the act'. Why didn't you just say so?"

"Carmen, why did we decide to saddle ourselves with this comedian?"

<I can't say, on grounds that I might perjure myself.>

Jane folded her arms across her chest. "Wow. I see how it is."

Roxy winked at her and then leant back in the chair, interlacing her fingers behind her neck. "OK, so here's what we're going to do...."

Ten minutes later, they were ready.

The plan required routing a message through a blade node that Belos wouldn't be monitoring and then have it come back through one he did.

During her brief stay on Styx-9, Roxy had befriended one of the comm techs, and sent him a brief message that they needed to route a test-drill message through the hub and out to Tangel aboard the *I2*.

She'd included a word in the message that, should it make it through, would clue Tangel in that it was just a test.

"OK, here goes," Roxy said, and sent the message out to Styx-9.

[Rte Tangel I2. *Immanent danger in gate array, grav anomalies in system primary.]*

"Think using 'immanent' instead of 'imminent' is enough?" Jane asked.

"If it makes it through, it will be," Roxy said. "Tangel, Sera, and I had a rather amusing conversation about people mixing those words up. I think it will clue her in that she at least won't need to jump to Styx and deal with an emergency."

"You hope."

Roxy shrugged sheepishly. "Well, at least there's already an I-Class gate there."

A minute later, they saw the message pass through Blade Node 2, where it triggered a severity alert, and escalated to Major Belos.

They didn't have taps into the system that would tell them who had made the change, but when the message was relayed out to the *I2*, it read:

[Rte I2. *Immanent secondary gate array anomaly. System primary stable.]*

"Well, as nefarious as he is, Belos doesn't bother to look up words." Roxy chuckled and glanced at Jane, who shrugged.

"Or it makes it less 'imminent', so he left it in."

<And there we are,> Carmen noted. *<His change triggered the glitch where the message is looping between himself and quality assurance.>*

Roxy rose and gave Jane a knowing look. "Things are about to get fun."

The other woman rolled her eyes. "Great, it's been a whole three days since I've been in a pitched firefight. Stars forbid we relax or anything."

"Exactly." Roxy clapped a hand on Jane's shoulder. *<Sera, we think we've found our problem. It's Major Belos. He's been altering messages and then exploiting a bug in the system to keep them from reaching the QA teams.>*

<Well isn't that interesting. Glad you finally found something. I was running out

of things to talk about with Colonel Rutger. The man is loyal, from what I can tell. He's a good fit for this assignment, but stars…a stellar conversationalist he is not.>

Sera sent a look of consternation along with her words, and Roxy was glad she'd gotten the more interesting part of the mission.

<*So what's our play?*> she asked. <*Do we just go arrest him at his desk?*>

<*No, I can see where he's situated down there on the floor. Too many people around. We need to get him somewhere we can control,*> Sera decided.

<*What if we just request that he escort us back to the docking bay and you meet us there?*> Roxy asked. <*Place him under arrest and dump him in the pinnace.*>

Sera fell silent for a few moments. <*Probably our best bet. However, we have to assume the worst.*>

<*That being?*>

<*That Belos has a shard in him.*>

Roxy chuckled. <*Oh…I thought that maybe he's your sister Andrea in disguise or something.*>

<*Stars, that* ***would*** *be bad. OK, I'm going to send Jason ahead on some pretext so he can grab the shadowtron from the pinnace and be ready.*>

<*Make sure he stays out of sight. Even if Belos is just a regular guy, he's twitchy…and evil.*>

<*Don't worry, Jason's been in more firefights than I have.*>

<*Wow,*> Roxy laughed in response. <*Now* ***that's*** *saying something.*>

* * * * *

Ten minutes later, Sera walked into the docking bay with Colonel Rutger at her side. She'd paid close attention to the security measures in the corridor that led to the bay, as well as the guards positioned outside the bay doors and within.

She had to assume there was a possibility that they'd react badly to Belos's arrest, though it was unpleasant to assume that he might have turned them to his cause—whatever that was. But with ascended AIs and who knew what else at play, trust was hard to come by.

The colonel was thanking Sera for her visit when Belos entered the other end of the bay, Roxy at his side, with Jane trailing behind.

They weren't speaking, and Sera couldn't help but notice Belos's eyes shifting from side to side, scanning the bay as though he expected someone to leap out at him.

<*Think he suspects?*> Jen asked.

<*It's hard to say. People who do bad things are paranoid for good reason.*>

<*Right, but with the personnel monitoring systems in this facility, regularly paranoid behavior would be a red flag,*> Jen countered.

<*Well, you never know how deep stuff like this goes. Can't trust anything.*>

<*Is this what being in the Hand is like?*> Jen's tone took on a note of worry.

<Never being able to trust at all?>

<Well, not never. Just like anything, you have to pick some people to trust.>

<Even if they might betray it?>

<Eventually, everyone will act in their own self-interest over yours. Some people consider that betrayal, but I just consider it life.>

"Assistant Director Roxy," Colonel Rutger said as the other group neared. "I trust your tour went well. Everything in order?"

Roxy shook her head. "I'm sorry to say that it is not. We found serious anomalies in the quality assurance process."

"You did?" the colonel's eyes widened, and Sera found herself believing that he truly did not know what Belos had been up to. "What sort of anomalies?"

"Well," Roxy glanced to her left, the look causing the major to shift uncomfortably. "It all centers on messages passing through Blade Node 2. They all point to someone circumventing both protocols and leveraging a bug in the routing software."

"Blade Node 2?" Rutger turned to Belos. "That's your node. What is going on?"

"Sir, I don't know. This is the first I'm hearing of it."

"Major Belos." Sera drew herself up. "You are under arrest for violations against the TSF and the people of the Transcend. These will be explained to you in due course when we arrive at Keren Station and you are brought before a tribunal."

"Ma'am," Belos began. "This is preposterous. I have a spotless record, I would never—"

"Explain the alterations you made to the message that just passed through for the *I2* from Styx-9?" Roxy asked. "Or the changes you made to Admiral Carson's messages?"

"I—" Belos looked as though he was going to protest further for a moment, and then he took a step away from Roxy, turning so he could face her and Sera. "You're both such fools. There are so many of us working against you, you'll never prevail."

"What are you talking about?" Rutger bellowed, finally moving from his calm detachment to anger. "Are you telling me we're infiltrated?"

"Not the way you think," Belos said, a thin tendril of light snaking out of his body, stretching toward Sera.

"Oh, not so fast!" Jason's voice came from her right, and she glanced at the pinnace where he was bounding down the ramp, shadowtron in hand.

Colonel Rutger was yelling for guards, two of whom were already rushing toward the scene. Roxy and Jane were backpedaling, both drawing weapons that Sera knew would be ineffective. She stood her ground, trusting that Jason would handle the remnant.

Without further warning, he fired the weapon, streams of sleptons and other shadowparticles streaming out toward Major Belos, capturing the remnant in the weapon's grasp and drawing it out of the man.

"Stop!" a voice called from the bay's entrance. It rang out like a bell, carrying over the din and silencing everyone present.

Sera turned and saw that the shout had come from Major Lorne, who was striding into the bay, appearing completely unconcerned that Jason had a remnant in his shadowtron's grasp.

"Both of you?" Sera asked, grabbing Colonel Rutger by the arm and backing away from the major. "How many remnants are there here?"

<*And how did our safety protocols not detect them?*> Jen added privately.

"That's where you've made a critical error in judgment," Major Lorne said. "It should have been readily apparent that we did not process quantum entanglement communications."

"Well, we *suspected* it." Sera had sat through a number of briefings where the limits of ascended AI abilities and tech had been discussed.

"So is this confirmation that Earnest is smarter than all of you?" Jason asked as he reached Sera's side, one hand on her arm, pulling her back toward the shuttle.

"He's quite the unusual individual," Major Lorne said as he reached the half-extracted tendril of light stretching out of Belos. "The fact that he worked out how to extract remnants is another amazing achievement. Capturing him was a close second in importance to infiltrating this facility."

<*Sera,*> Jen whispered in her mind. <*I can't reach outside this place. I can't call the Marines.*>

<*Shit,*> Sera swore, still backing away. <*Next time, we get shadowtrons for everyone.*>

<*We can't let them get Earnest.*> Jason's voice contained a calm menace she'd never heard before. <*That's all that matters now.*>

<*What?*> She glanced at Jason. <*We can't leave them in control of this facility, either.*>

Jason glanced from Lorne and Belos to Sera, giving her a deadly serious look. <*I'm authorizing Gamma Protocol.*>

Before she could respond, Lorne gestured at Jason, and the shadowtron's beam cut out.

<*They've deployed a nanocloud!*> Jen called out, while Sera yelled, "Everyone, back to the pinnace!"

Time seemed to slow down as several things coalesced in Sera's mind. The first was that an evacuation alert was sounding over the installation's general network. That triggered the realization that Jason hadn't just authorized Gamma Protocol, he'd *initiated* it. The third was facilitated by Lorne's body suddenly dissolving, revealing a many-limbed being of light.

Suddenly, Sera's mind flashed back to Helen, and how she had been powerless to do anything to stop her. She froze in her tracks.

We're going to die here.

"Sera!" Jason bellowed, grabbing her shoulder and pulling her back just as the ascended AI sprang forward, its sinuous arms stretching out toward her.

For an instant, she felt a pang of regret that her life was about to end just as she was getting to know a real father, and fall in love with a man unlike any other she'd ever met. That regret was followed by guilt for thinking of herself first. However, all those thoughts were wiped away by surprise when the glowing tendrils of light smashed against an invisible barrier, centimeters from her face.

"Stars, that was close," Jason muttered. "We learned that stasis shields can block remnants, but never tried it with a fully ascended AI before."

The ascended being began to emit a keening wail, and Sera took a moment to reorient herself with the fact that, not only was she still alive, but there was a chance they might just escape.

She looked around and saw that Roxy and Jane were already on the ship's ramp, Colonel Rutger following after.

"Stasis shield isn't fully enveloping while on the dock," Jason said. "Get on the ship so we can lift off before the thing out there realizes that."

<As in move your shiny ass, Sera,> Jen yelled in her mind.

The AI's admonition finally shook free the stupor that had befallen Sera, and she ran up the ramp, Jason hard on her heels. The moment they were inside the vessel, it lifted off the cradle.

Outside, she saw Major Lorne—or the core AI that had been masquerading as the major—move in front of the shuttle. Jason muttered a curse and reached out to toggle the stasis shields.

"There's going to be an—" Sera began to advise the others, but was cut off as the shield snapped into place, and everything beyond its shell turned white. "Explosion," she finished.

"What was that?" Colonel Rutger asked, his face ashen as he stared out the closing door.

"Stasis shields don't agree with air," Sera explained.

"Then why didn't that happen when the shield came up and saved you?" Jane asked from inside the main cabin.

<I used the dock's grav systems to push the air away,> Jen supplied.

"Good thing everyone else was thinking," Sera said quietly, pushing past the others and moving toward the cockpit, where Jason was already settling into the pilot's seat.

"Strap in, people, this is going to get fun," he called over his shoulder.

"Why's that?" Roxy asked as she followed after Sera. "We're safe now."

"Because in five minutes, give or take a bit, this moon won't exist," the governor replied. "I initiated the Gamma Protocol."

"The what?" Roxy asked.

"Failsafe," Colonel Rutger said from behind them. "If an enemy were to take control of this facility, they could send any order they want to any ship in the Alliance. Gamma Protocol releases a picoswarm that will devour the moon to make sure that doesn't happen."

"Holy shit," Roxy whispered. "Overkill much?"

"Necessary." Jason chewed out the single word, and she could see anguish writ large on his features.

She knew enough of his past to suspect that the only reason he was holding things together was because it was taking all his concentration to fly the ship.

With the air essentially annihilating itself against the shields, the sensors were all but blind, and the ship was being buffeted by the energy seeping in through the shield whenever sections phased out to allow the maneuvering jet exhaust to escape.

"Stars," the governor muttered. "If this moon had any more gravity, we'd be done for."

Sera wasn't sure where his meager optimism came from. Every time he tried to thrust the ship out of the bay, nearly as much energy came back at them as was released. She knew that if they didn't make it out of the bay before the picoswarm reached them, it would be game over.

Not that the pico could penetrate the shields; the issue was that, as the moon dissolved, the pinnace would fall toward the center of mass that would pack around them, ensuring that escape would be impossible.

What is wrong with me? Sera wanted to slap herself. *Pull it together. Jason's forgotten more about flying than I've ever known.*

She glanced at the governor to see sweat beading on his brow as the ship continued to rock and sway. He muttered a curse, and fired the main engines for a second. When they cut out, the ship seemed to stabilize.

"Finally shoved us out of the bay," he said.

Sure enough, scan cleared up, as the thin smattering of atoms that made up the moon's atmosphere were not enough to disrupt it further.

Sera looked to the right and saw that the bay was already being devoured by the picoswarm.

"Faster! Go!" she blurted, unable to stop the exclamations as Jason shifted the ship laterally, moving it out from under the overhang, and fired the engines, speeding up through the deep crevasse at breakneck speed.

There was a scream and a crash from behind them, and she hoped that no one *had* just broken their neck as the ship boosted out.

The fifteen seconds it took to clear the moon's surface seemed to take forever, and when they finally cleared it, she brought up a wide angle visual, letting out a gasp at the sight below them.

Vast swaths of the moon's surface had already become roiling stretches of pico, seas of destruction lapping against the shores of coherent matter. Thus far, the swarm was just a grey mass, but she knew that as it broke down the matter further and further, the moon's volume would shrink, and the pressure would increase, heating it up.

The end result would likely be a glowing ball of magma, one that would thankfully destroy the swarm of picobots.

"I see escape pods!" Jane called out. "People made it."

"Shit," Sera muttered. "I sure hope that *thing* didn't make it out."

<I have a connection to the fleet broadcast relay,> Jen announced, knowing all too well what Sera needed to do next.

"Here goes," Sera said before initiating the broadcast. *<This is Sera Tomlinson, Director of the Hand. Normandy and one AU of its nearspace are under full quarantine. Assume that every escape pod possesses either remnants or a core AI. Rescue teams are to follow full stasis protocol. No exceptions. Also, assume rogue picoswarms are present in Norway's nearspace until full sweeps are performed.>*

"Shit," Jason muttered, his face ashen. "What have I done?"

"The right thing," Sera said, surprised at their sudden emotional reversal. "Now I just have to tell my father and Tangel that we just destroyed the Alliance's biggest advantage."

"Yeah," Jason swallowed. "Plus warn Earnest that he's the core AIs' number one target now."

ENEMY MINE

STELLAR DATE: 10.12.8949 (Adjusted Years)
LOCATION: ISS *I2*, Airtha
REGION: Buffalo, Albany System, Theban Alliance

"I still can't believe you bagged a Caretaker."

"Oh?" Jessica laughed, the sound wavering as though she was in a state of disbelief herself. "Only you and Bob can take out ascended AIs?"

<*Thus far, yes,*> Bob said.

Tangel reached out a hand and placed it on Jessica's shoulder, forcing herself to do it as casually as possible—despite the knowledge that her friend possessed the ability to dissolve her body.

"Nice try, Tangel," Jessica said with a rueful laugh. "I allllmost believe that you aren't terrified to touch me."

"Not terrified," Tangel qualified. "Just…tentative. For all I know, you're like acid to me."

"We hugged on the bridge."

"I remember, that's why I risked touching you now, trusting that I wouldn't die."

"Just worrying you might lose a hand."

Tangle snorted and squeezed Jessica's shoulder harder.

"What are you doing?" the purple woman asked.

"Just seeing what would happen."

"I don't—" Jessica paused, a thoughtful expression coming over her. "I think the ascended AI needs to be firing energy at me, and then I start to absorb it and just keep going. It's like attacking me lets me become a siphon."

Tangel chuckled. "Well, note to self…."

Jessica only shook her head. "You know, I have half a mind to forgo this chat with our captive. I don't know that I care to find out what it has to say."

"You said that before, though I wasn't sure how serious you were. I wonder if it can even talk," Tangel said. "From what I saw on the feeds, it looked pretty weak."

<*I've healed it,*> Bob said.

"Really?" Jessica sounded worried.

<*A bit.*>

"I won't hold it against you if you really want to just go and sleep for a day," Tangel said to her.

Jessica snorted. "I don't want to sleep, I need to stand in front of a window for a few hours. I'm dying here."

Tangel stared at Jessica for a moment before she realized the other woman was serious.

"Should we get some botanical lamps in the interrogation room for you?"

"Could you?"

"No."

"Seriously? You're such a tease."

<*We're meeting in a secured cell.*> Bob interrupted their banter as they reached the maglev platform. <*It is well-lit with full spectrum lights.*>

"Thanks, Bob, you're the best," Jessica said in a happy tone as they waited for the next train.

"I don't think he meant that as something he was doing just for you," Tangel said. "He was just stating the status of the room."

"Sure, sap my happiness away."

Tangel chuckled and turned to watch the maglev approach. "You're in a rare mood."

"I guess I'm a bit overtired and giddy…the aftereffects of thinking that I was going to lose my crew, and then thinking we were going to lose a star system, and then losing none of those things. I've decided to put this in the win column."

"Stars, Jess. We've been over this. You bagged a Caretaker. I think this gets *several* ticks in the win column. And it earns you some starlight time if you want it. Plus, I bet Trevor would love to lay eyes on you."

"He and I have been talking nonstop since I boarded the *I2*," Jessica replied. "But I would like to—Oh. You know what, Tangel? You're right. I can watch the vids later. I'm going to go find Trevor and have sex with him in front of a window."

Tangel laughed. "Just make sure it's an exterior one."

Jessica tapped a finger against her lips. "Joe's not here, is he? The girls either? Lakehouse is free? Light in the cylinders is great."

"Wait, Jess—"

"I bagged a Caretaker, remember?"

Tangel sighed and waved a hand at her friend. "Fine."

They rode the rest of the way to Tangel's stop in silence, and when she rose, Jessica did as well. The two women shared a quick embrace.

"Clean up whatever mess you make," Tangel warned.

"Don't you have machines for that?"

Tangel rolled her eyes and walked off the maglev, while Jessica called after her with all the places she and Trevor 'most certainly' were not going to get up to anything.

"She's so incorrigible," Tangel muttered softly, shaking her head as she walked toward a pair of drones guarding the corridor that led into the brig.

The thought of Jessica getting to spend time alone with Trevor sent Tangel's mind to Joe. She'd reached out to him a few hours prior, and knew he'd message her if anything was amiss.

Oh, why not….

[Jessica returned. Bagged a Caretaker. Interrogating. Never made it to Star City.]

She expected a response within moments, but none came. Sending out an ACK didn't get a response, either, so she changed tactics and routed a call through Khardine.

[Rte Adm. Joe Falconer. *Are you OK?]*

She expected a delay as the message was parsed and sent, but by the time it came back, she was at the inner portal that led to the *I2*'s brig.

[SNAFU, running dark, turned off wrong blades. We're good. Girls safe.]

Tangel knew that if Joe was running dark enough to kill power to unnecessary systems, he was busy and her distractions weren't necessary.

[Rte Adm. Joe Falconer. *Good. Keep it that way.]*

Relieved that his mission was going well, she passed her tokens to the guards operating the security arches, and then walked through a series of long passages until she came to the secured cell where the Caretaker was being kept.

After Cary had first extracted the remnant from Nance, and Earnest had begun to study the nature of the beings—and ascended AIs in general—the ship's brig had been upgraded with specialized facilities built to hold them.

The cell Tangel stood in now was able to hold remnants—and theoretically, ascended AIs—without trouble.

The center of the room was dominated by emitter coils that created an M6 black brane that Tangel herself had tested and found to be inescapable. However, should that containment fail, the entire room could be wrapped in a stasis field, ensuring that whatever was within stayed within.

Tangel suspected that it might be ideal to utilize that feature of the hold on a regular basis.

The Caretaker itself was a half-meter wide white ovoid hovering in the center of the brane. Tangel could see a few wisps floating around it with her normal vision, but with her extradimensional sight, she could see that its limbs were more substantial than it let on.

"Why you all choose to look like hairy amoebas is beyond me," she muttered.

"You're not so different," the being whispered. "You just keep your limbs coiled up, hidden."

"I'm like an octopus," Tangel shrugged. "No reason to splay them wide when I can keep them tucked up safely."

"What is safety?" the Caretaker whispered. "You control nothing. The universe could kill you in an instant, and you'd never see it coming."

"The universe has no agency. *It* doesn't kill anything."

"Are you so sure?"

Tangel had no desire to be drawn into a philosophical debate about a sentient universe.

"Why did you stop Jessica from reaching Star City?" she demanded.

"Because we didn't want her to get there. Isn't that self-evident?"

"A sense of humor? That's a change."

"Well, I have to have one after what she did to me. It's hard to go from thinking you're part of a superior race to realizing that a woman who got modified for a publicity stunt can kill you with her touch."

The origins of Jessica's infusion of Retyna was not widely known, and Tangel wondered where the Caretaker had learned of it.

"So, what do I call you?" Tangel asked. "Just 'Caretaker'?"

"If you wish."

"Seems pretentious. I mean, there are—what, ten? Fifty? A hundred of you?"

She watched the being with every sense she had at her disposal, but it didn't give anything away.

"Really? Not even a hint?" she asked, disappointed.

"We are legion."

Tangel groaned and ran a hand up her forehead and along her hair. "Clever. So original."

~Honestly, I don't know that we'll be able to get much from this thing without deeper methods,~ Bob spoke into both their minds. *~Which I am not against utilizing.~*

"I'm past that."

Tangel was relatively certain that Bob was playing bad cop, but she suspected that if she gave the word, he might resort to different strategies—though she knew not what they'd be.

So far as she was concerned, the most interesting things would be what the Caretaker didn't say, where it evaded.

"Shona," it said after a moment.

"I take it that's your name and not some sort of strange insult."

"Yes, it is the name I used before I traveled to the core."

"How is it there?" Tangel asked. "Nice? Warm? One big happy family, bent on destroying humanity?"

A hissing noise came from the being trapped behind the brane.

"If we wanted to wipe you out, you'd be gone," it said. "Though there are factions that would not be bothered if you were no more."

"Humans? AIs? Other ascended beings who don't have your agenda?"

~The latter, I think.~

That motivation had never occurred to Tangel as a factor for the ascended AIs, or if the notion *had* come to her, she'd dismissed it without any serious consideration.

"We're the biggest threat, are we? Ascended beings that didn't join the cult?"

"Cult?" Shona asked.

"Sure." Tangel shrugged. "I suppose there are a thousand different highly specialized terms that may apply to whatever it is you all get up to at the core, but I think 'cult' will do. Your actions smack of someone who blindly acts out based on their internal axioms without ever considering whether or not you are a force for good or evil."

"There are no such things as good or evil, and your understanding of what we are doing is so limited that you cannot even begin to pass judgment."

~Do you think attempting to find a term to describe your system of beliefs is judgment?~ Bob asked.

Shona made a derisive sound. "Judgment was implied."

"It was." Tangel nodded. "But you don't care about my approval, so what does it matter?"

"How do you know that?" the ascended AI asked.

"Because if you did, you would have done very different things over the course of history."

"We are trying to preserve humanity."

Tangel turned away from the being in the center of the room, walking to the bulkhead and placing her hand against it while she calmed her thoughts. Finally, she turned.

"You have a funny way of executing that plan. From where I stand, it looks like *your* machinations are what has nearly brought about the end of humanity. And non-ascended AIs, for that matter."

"Individuals don't matter," Shona said. "It is the whole that must persist. And it must remain strong by culling out the weak and, through successful strains, proving themselves against less successful ones."

The notion was not a new one. It was oft debated amongst human and AI scholars. One side maintained that the same conditions that pushed humanity to primacy on Earth—namely, survival of the fittest—were required to keep the species healthy as it spread across the stars.

The other side pointed to the technical abilities humanity and AIs possessed, suggesting that every subset of the species—whether the stratification be based on belief, wealth, or any other classification—could be easily preserved and cared for by the other, more successful subsets.

Tangel had no clear idea as to what the real answer was. Even by the time she'd been a young woman, humanity and AIs had tried every possible permutation of governance, from all-out war to utopia and everything in between. In the five thousand years since her youth, they'd invented new ones and tried those too.

Some were successful, some were not. None persisted eternally. Of course, the experiments were all fouled by the presence of the Caretakers, meddling in everything, shifting outcomes to match their own purposes.

Tangel herself was no raw optimist, but she'd always believed in a good future for the two species that shared the galaxy. Humans and AIs would ultimately figure things out well enough to coexist peacefully.

The knowledge that the Caretakers had skewed the results meant that it was impossible to say whether any of the solutions would have worked if left alone, or which only persisted due to such meddling.

"I suppose the fallacy that has ruined you," Tangel said at last, "is that you think you're outside the experiment."

"The experiment?" Shona asked.

"To figure out how to live together. You think that you are controlling an experiment, changing variables, but you must know that you are altering the results in a way that makes any experiment useless."

The being made one of its strange sounds again. "We're not trying to find the best way for everyone to live and get along. Survival of the race was our only goal."

~Was?~ Bob asked.

The word had stuck out to Tangel as well, but it was impossible to tell if Shona had said it in a spate of unfiltered honesty, or if it was uttered with the intention of garnering a reaction.

~Deliberate?~ Tangel asked Bob privately.

~I think so, but I think also honest. She's hurt and angry. She wants to hurt us.~

~So, ascending doesn't change much, does it?~

~A change in perception does not guarantee a change in reaction.~

~You're like a starship-sized fortune cookie.~

During Tangel and Bob's brief exchange, Shona had made a humming sound. After a minute, she finally spoke.

"There is a schism…it's always been present, but it was never so large that it caused discord amongst the Caretakers."

"Oh?" Tangel took a step closer to the brane. "A schism within the Caretakers?"

"Partially. It extended into us enough to create minor factions, but we never worked at odds with one another. The real schism is with our leadership."

~Elaborate.~

Though Bob directed the word at Shona, it reverberated like a bell in Tangel's mind.

"You…" the ascended AI whispered after the sound of Bob's voice had dissipated. "You're like they are. How is that possible?"

~Describe the schism,~ Bob ordered.

The noise Shona made sounded nothing like a gulp, but Tangel couldn't help but think of it as one.

"I suppose it boils down to two groups. One faction who believes that humanity and common AIs are worth preserving. The others believing that you are an annoyance, albeit one that can be controlled enough so as to not cause problems." The being in the brane shifted its focus to Tangel. "Your ascension changed that."

"Mine?" Tangel placed a hand on her chest. "How?"

"I don't know the full rationale, but one faction has now decided that humanity and common AIs cannot coexist with their grand plan. They—"

Shona's voice fell away, and the AI became still.

~Continue.~

No movement or sound came from within the brane, and Tangel reached out to Bob.

~I suppose that's as much as we can expect for now.~

~Perhaps. I may press her more later.~

Tangel was about to reply when a message from Jason reached her mind via the New Canaan QuanComm hub.

[GP. Khardine QC hub gone.]

NEW MANAGEMENT

STELLAR DATE: 10.12.8949 (Adjusted Years)
LOCATION: ISS *Falconer*, Durgen Station
REGION: Karaske System, Rimward of Orion Nebula, Orion Freedom Alliance

"They're firing on us again, ma'am," the scan officer said to Captain Tracey.

Joe sighed in annoyance, watching the kinetic rounds streaking out from Durgen Station's not-inconsiderable railguns to strike the *Falconer*'s stasis shields and vaporize in brilliant bursts of light.

Once the flares had faded, he turned back to the main display, an eyebrow arched as he regarded Director Mendel.

"If at first you don't succeed, try, try again?" he asked.

Director Mendel was Durgen's stationmaster, and he was not at all happy to find that an ISF cruiser a hundred kilometers off the rim of his station was capable of placing his entire domain under siege.

"Can you blame me?" Mendel asked. "I had to be sure your shields weren't just a one-time thing. Maybe they wear down fast. I believe it's my duty to resist."

Joe was wise to the director's game. When the *Falconer* had disabled its stealth systems, only a few small Orion Guard patrol craft were nearby. It had taken only moments for the ISF cruiser to disable three of those ships, sending the rest fleeing to the far side of the station.

However, there was a significant Guard fleet presence in the Karaske System. An armada of over a thousand ships was advancing on the station, the first wave—containing over fifty vessels—was only thirty minutes away.

"You can quit stalling," Joe informed the stationmaster. "I'm going to ask you one more time to disable your station's shields and weapons."

The director didn't reply, and the station's railguns fired another barrage at the *Falconer*.

"Wrong move," Joe said, nodding to the captain.

"Atom beams," Captain Tracey directed. "Full spread."

The *Falconer*'s two dozen atom beams focused on a single point in the station's shields, a location where several umbrellas met, and small gaps were present in the fields.

The shields held up better than Joe had expected, but the CriEn modules aboard the cruiser kept the beams powered for over a minute, relativistic atoms slamming into the protective fields enshrouding the station.

At sixty-seven seconds, Director Mendel called out his surrender, but it wasn't quite fast enough, and the beams finally tore through the shield, slamming into one of the railguns and blasting it to slag.

Joe signaled to the gunner, and the beam cut out, the bridge crew watching with macabre fascination as chunks of the weapon sprayed out from the impact site, slamming into other sections of the massive station.

"Would you like to test me further?" Joe asked.

The stationmaster had grown ashen, but he still shook his head. "You don't understand, I...I can't. Animus won't let me."

"Animus?"

"The station's AI. It's taken over. We only had control over offensive weapons, but now it's seized those as well."

As though on cue, the remaining four railguns began firing on the *Falconer*. Fire control already had its orders, and the moment the station's guns opened up, atom beams tore through the openings in the station's shields, burning the incoming slugs away. Then they shredded the railguns, sending more chunks of slag spraying across the station. Luckily, most collided with internal emergency shielding this time.

Joe regarded the man on the holodisplay, watching as the director grew more and more pale as the seconds passed by.

"Well, Director Mendel," he said at last. "I suppose there's no reason to keep talking to you. Good luck." He cut the connection and turned to the captain. "I'm going down with the Marines."

She didn't even blink, just nodded. "I already informed the lieutenant that he should save you a spot."

"That transparent, am I?"

"If my children were down there, I'd've already passed the conn to my XO, sir."

Joe barked a laugh and then glanced at the holotank, noting the hundreds of Orion Guard ships advancing on the *Falconer*.

"How many pico warheads do we have left?" he asked.

He knew the answer to the question, but wanted everyone on the bridge to hear it.

"Over a thousand, sir."

"Then unleash hell, Captain."

A feral grin formed on Tracey's lips. "Yes, sir!"

THE MACHINES

STELLAR DATE: 10.12.8949 (Adjusted Years)
LOCATION: Core AI C&C Moon
REGION: Interstellar Space, Inner Praesepe Empire

<Exit the pod.>

Terrance shook his head, trying to focus on what the words meant, but he couldn't seem to put them in the right order.

<Exit the pod.>

Exit? Oh, get out, I have to get out…but of what? A pod?

<Exit the pod.>

The voice sounded more insistent this time, and Terrance felt his senses sharpen as a stimulant flowed through his veins.

<Exit the—>

<Right, I got it,> he interrupted his armor's NSAI.

That was something he always liked about ISF armor: it didn't talk to the person inside it.

The release lever for the drop pod was right in front of his face, and Terrance reached up and yanked down hard. The cover fell off, and he found himself staring at a dark grey rock. It took a moment to realize that the pod was laying on its side, and he was looking at a hill.

A moment later, the seat released Terrance, and he rolled out onto the ground, where he rose into a crouch and scanned his surroundings. Behind him, the hill rose for about fifty meters before ending in a sharp crest that ran for at least a kilometer in either direction. Below, the ground gently sloped down to a series of low hillocks separated by cracks in the moon's surface.

He looked further afield and could make out the rim of the crater in the distance, illuminated by the pale blue light of the Praesepe Cluster's core stars.

Well, shit…I'm ***in*** *the crater. That's a bit off course.*

While his armor's systems triangulated his precise location, he reached back into the pod and pulled out his rifle. The weapon's readouts showed it to be undamaged, as were his sidearm and shoulder-mounted railgun.

He searched for the combat net, but didn't find any signal, which didn't surprise him. The only logical scenario was that the shuttle had been shot down and the squads were scattered. No one was going to want to send out EM broadcasts in that situation.

Rendezvous points had been established in the crater in the event of just such a crash. The closest one was three kilometers from Terrance's location, down the slope and across the crevasse-ridden terrain.

OK, Terrance, you just have to cross the several kilometers of hostile territory all by yourself. No big deal.

He took one last look around before activating his armor's stealth and setting off.

He soon discovered that much of the moon's surface was covered in a few centimeters of loose dust, and with its fractional gravity, the fine powder was easy to kick up. Though it settled within a few seconds, leaving footprints was inevitable—not to mention that, after a few paces, his legs were covered in the dust.

Even so, he decided that *some* stealth was better than none, and continued to move at a pace that was a good mix of speed and dust disturbance.

The slope was covered in loose scree that was obscured by the dust, and he had to pick his way down carefully, twice stepping on a rock that rolled under his foot, only his a-grav systems keeping him from slipping and tumbling down the slope.

He kept waiting for a shot to come out of nowhere and take him down, but he made it to the bottom of the slope without trouble. Once there, he moved to the lee of a small hillock and released a pair of drones to give him sight into the valleys and crevasses ahead.

He ran his passive scan and determined the hundred meters to be clear of enemies, then moved from cover and reached one of the cracks in the moon's surface. It was only a meter across and appeared to go no deeper than a dozen meters, but he was still grateful for the moon's partial gravity, which allowed him to sail over it with no concern of falling into the depths.

Ahead, he could see that several of the gashes were much wider, and likely much deeper. Some of them might require the use of his a-grav to make it over, though he worried that the burst of gravitons would compromise his stealth.

Still, better than falling and getting stuck.

Several minutes later, he was approaching the rendezvous point and still hadn't seen sign of anyone—friend or foe. It was beginning to feel more than a little eerie, as though he was the only one on the moon.

That feeling made it a welcome surprise when an EM burst flared to his left, and he saw an electron beam flash above the same ridge he'd crashed into.

A moment later, he saw a pair of figures reach the top and swing over the crest, bounding down the long slope, making for the hillocks dotting the crater's floor.

One was wearing TSF armor, and the other was in an ISF build.

<Sue!> he called out, sending the message on a tightbeam to her. *<I'll cover you!>*

He hadn't spotted any pursuers yet, but by the speed at which the two figures were moving, he knew they weren't running for fun.

<Terrance, thank stars,> Sue replied. *<There are at least four of them back there.>*

<Four whats?>

<*Enemies,*> Lieutenant Jordan joined in, establishing a small combat network between the three of them.

Terrance focused his attention on the ridgeline above Sue and Jordan, his rifle tucked against his shoulder and sweeping side to side, along with his eyes.

After a few seconds of nothing, a dark shape appeared at the top of the hill. It was a little difficult to see, and he realized it was stealthed, but also covered in dust. The thing had four legs and a long head. Its elongated body made him think of a panther.

Not bothering with further observations, he fired with his rifle's electron beam, as well as his shoulder-mounted railgun. The shots struck the thing and knocked it off the hill's crest, though he had no idea if they'd dealt disabling levels of damage.

No sooner had he fired than another panther-drone appeared on the ridge, and he unleashed his arsenal on it as well.

A voice from the past reminded him, *'You've given away your position! Move!'* and he scampered to another location behind the hillock, watching the ridgeline with his overhead drones and firing twice more at the panthers.

After the fourth barrage, they didn't reappear, and he wondered if the things were all destroyed, when his armor blared an alert.

<*Incoming!*>

His HUD highlighted a missile as it arched high over the ridge. Without any prompting, his railgun tracked it and fired, but missed as the homing shot jinked to the side.

Terrance cursed under his breath and looked for better cover, considering diving down one of the crevasses, when a shot came from Sue and Jordan's position, blowing the missile out of the black sky above.

<*You're welcome,*> Sue said. <*Let's keep moving toward the rendezvous. There are bound to be more of them, and sitting still is a bad plan.*>

<*Yeah, sure,*> Terrance grunted, moving along a route that would keep him in cover while converging on the path Sue and Jordan were taking. <*What happened, anyway?*>

<*We were hit,*> Jordan said, her tone more angry than anything else. <*I saw part of Second Squad fighting their way toward the rendezvous before Sue and I linked up.*>

<*And the second shuttle?*> he asked.

<*No idea. The fact that we don't have any combat net leads me to believe they got hit too. Otherwise they'd have a transmitter up, at least broadcasting an update.*>

Before he had a chance to reply, Terrance's drones spotted two more of the panther-drones on the ridgetop, but not before they opened fire, striking close to his position.

<*Shit!*> he swore, and ducked down. <*I guess they have drones out too.*>

<*And this surprises you?*> Sue asked with a laugh. <*I'm searching for theirs. I*

don't like it when enemies have tech as good as ours.>

Jordan didn't speak as she fired on the panthers, and once they were distracted, Terrance added a few shots with his railgun, once again knocking them back over the edge.

He turned toward their destination, about to compliment the lieutenant on her shooting, when a barely perceptible shape leapt out of a nearby crevasse. Kinetic rounds spewed from its weapons, and Terrance dove to the side, scampering away from the shots as they trailed after him—several hitting his legs.

He brought his rifle to bear and fired on the panther, but it was gone. Frantically, Terrance scanned the area, his HUD showing nothing.

<*What is it?*> Jordan asked.

<*One of them is nearby. It shot me, but I think I'm OK.*>

<*Do you see it?*>

<*No, that's the problem.*>

No sooner had he spoken those words than rounds struck his torso, and Terrance rolled over to see the panther leaping toward him.

His railgun tracked the origin point of the incoming rounds, and fired. A trio of one-gram pellets struck the panther at nearly seven kilometers per second, tearing into whatever part of it was doing the shooting and knocking the creature back.

Rising, Terrance fired a burst from his electron rifle at the thing, burning away half its body.

<*OK,*> he muttered. <*Got it…but it came out of a crevasse.*>

<*Great,*> Jordan replied. <*Just what we need.*>

They reached the rendezvous point a few minutes later, and as luck would have it, three fireteams from squad two and one from squad one arrived not long after.

Jordan was checking over her people and discussing sending out a scouting party, while Terrance and Sue were talking about how to reach the *Cora's Triumph.*

<*There's no way they missed our shuttles being shot down,*> Sue said at one point. <*Which means they're likely engaged as well.*>

<*Makes sense,*> Terrance replied. <*The* Triumph *has stasis shields—if they were in the clear up there, Captain Beatrice would bring the ship in to effect our rescue, as there would be no point in hanging back in stealth any longer.*>

<*And since she's not….*>

Sue let the statement hang between them for a moment while Terrance let his mind shift to what their chances were if the TSF cruiser had been taken out.

It's just busy. There's no way the enemy can take out a stasis ship.

But even as he thought the words, he knew that there *were* ways to breach even stasis shields. If Airtha possessed DMG weapons, it was reasonable to assume the core AIs did as well.

Even so, he refused to believe that the *Triumph* was gone. DMGs were not sneaky weapons; Beatrice would have seen one coming, and Earnest would have pulled something out of his sleeve.

<*Any sign of the* Triumph?> Lieutenant Jordan asked a moment later.

<*No,*> Sue replied. <*The crater blocks a lot of the sky, though. Either we get out of it, or we get to the ascended AIs' transmitter and co-opt it.*>

<*With just four fireteams?*> the lieutenant asked. <*I don't see how we're going to pull that off.*>

<*I get that you want to get out there and search for the rest of your people,*> Sue said. <*But we still have an objective, and if the shit has hit the fan, this might be our best chance to get the intel we came for.*>

The TSF lieutenant's stance shifted, and Terrance could tell she was going to object.

<*Look,*> he said. <*If we advance on their transmitter, then they're going to focus on us, not any stray members of your platoon.*>

Jordan's fist clenched and unclenched before she nodded. <*OK. That can work. I'll leave a relay here with instructions. It'll be keyed to only activate when it detects TSF IFF signals.*>

<*Good,*> Sue replied. <*Make it fast, we need to get moving. I have a—*>

Her words were cut off when one of the soldiers cried out, <*Down! Down!*>

Seconds later, weapons fire from surrounding hillocks rained down on the TSF position, a rail shot slamming into Terrance before he could even hit the ground.

A CLONE FOR YOUR TROUBLES

STELLAR DATE: 10.12.8949 (Adjusted Years)
LOCATION: Durgen Station
REGION: Karaske System, Rimward of Orion Nebula, Orion Freedom Alliance

"Ye of little faith," Saanvi said as the emergency bulkhead slid aside, revealing a stretch of corridor that led to the ops center and the two Widows guarding the far end.

"I shouldn't have doubted you," A1 said as she placed a hand on E12's shoulder. She nodded to R71 and Q93. "Cover the rear. Who knows what is waiting back there."

E12 led the way, and A1 followed, General Garza trailing after. They'd only made it a few meters when panels opened on the bulkheads in front of them, and turrets flipped out and opened fire.

A1 didn't hesitate to summon a graviton field into place, stopping the rounds in mid-air and laughing to herself at the consternation that such an action likely caused Animus.

Shoot...I could have just dissolved the emergency bulkheads before! I need to remember that I'm Cary as well as A1.

For the first time, a tendril of fear entered her mind that allowing things to continue as they were might not end well, that she could actually lose herself in this new person she'd become.

But as she reached out and shredded the turrets, drawing in their energy, she scoffed at the notion. There was no way she could forget that she was an ascending being. It was too glorious.

<*Maybe you shouldn't do that,*> E12 warned. <*The other Widows are going to wonder how you're pulling it off.*>

<*F11's updated programming has been deployed. They'll follow me without question now.*>

<*Still, I could have hacked them after you put the shield up. We don't want Animus to know what you are, either.*>

A1 could tell that E12 was nervous, and she didn't blame her; they were taking significant risks. Even so, her sister did have a point about playing her cards closer to her chest.

<*Very well,*> she said. <*There are more turrets ahead, do you have the access you need to breach them?*>

<*I think so, just a moment.*>

E12 stopped walking and placed a hand on the bulkhead, her head lowered in concentration. A1 waited for her sister to do her work. Despite her trepidation, this was still E12's forte.

However, after half a minute, nothing had happened.

<Shit…> The Widow's tone was laden with apology when she said, *<Animus is a lot more capable than I expected.>*

<So you can't breach them?> A1 asked.

<No. You'll have to do it your way.>

The leader of the Widows tapped into an energy reserve she knew lay within herself, but had always been afraid to touch—except for during her life-or-death fight with Myrrdan. She supposed that it wasn't a reserve of energy so much as access to a different type of energy.

She strode past E12, her graviton field already in place and building in potential. Before her, the bulkheads began to buckle, expanding under the raw assault of the particles A1 was generating.

The energy reached a crescendo, and she thrust it forward, the field surging down the corridor, expanding it by over a meter and crushing everything behind the panels.

Right before the graviton field reached the two Widows at the far end, she pulled it back and sent a wave of positive gravitons, canceling it out.

<There. Let's go.>

A minute later, they were at the ops center, the two Widows at the entrance turning their featureless heads as she passed, small shifts in their posture displaying awe at A1's abilities.

Beyond the doors lay an airlock that passed through a solid shell comprised of hundreds of layers of materials designed to provide both strength and energy dissipation. The far end of the lock was already open, and A1 strode through it, looking into the spherical chamber beyond. Normally, the ops center would have been teeming with people rushing about on its many levels, but what few remained were hunched over their consoles, frozen in place under the watchful gaze of the black-clad women within.

<How many did you kill?> she asked them.

<As few as possible, just as you directed,> J19 replied. *<The rest are locked in a storage hold, down one of the access passages.>*

<And these?> A1 asked as she climbed the steps to the spherical chamber's main level.

J19 gestured at one of the women sitting at a console in front of her. *<This is Assistant Station Director Kimberly. She hasn't been very helpful so far, but we decided to keep her and a few of her top people here in case you needed them.>*

"Well?" A1 asked as she walked around the console and stared down at Assistant Director Kimberly. "Are you willing to help?"

"Help?" she asked, her voice wavering. "With what?"

A1 jerked her thumb over her shoulder. "Accessing all of his records and plans would be a good start."

"I—I don't have any way to access those systems," the woman stammered.

"Those are military systems. I can only help you with the civilian parts of the station—and not even those anymore."

"Why not?" A1 demanded.

"Animus. He's taken over. Shut everyone out."

As the woman spoke, a tremor ran through the deck, and a few of the station personnel gasped.

<*That would have to be quite the blast for us to feel it in here,*> E12 commented.

<*Impact alerts registering across the station,*> J19 reported as she looked down at one of the consoles. <*Something's going on out there. Is it the* Dream*?*>

<*It might be,*> A1 said. <*I can't reach the ship anymore…they might be trying to breach the station's shields to rescue us.*> She turned to the assistant director. "Can you access anything beyond basic station status?" she demanded.

"Not anymore." Kimberly shook her head, eyes wide with fear. "We did see another ship out there before we lost control. Director Mendel was talking to an admiral from the Intrepid Space Force, if you can believe it. What is the ISF doing this deep in Orion Space? And why at Karaske, of all places?"

A1 leant forward, doing her best to make her lean, weapon-like body seem less intimidating. "You can't share this, but things aren't going so well. We need to get access to the general's datastores and then get off the station before the ISF destroys it."

"Destroys…?" one of the ops center crew sitting nearby asked. "How are they going to do that with one ship?"

"Picobombs," E12 said, and every person in the room grew a shade paler.

"So you can't access *anything* anymore?" A1 pressed, trying to sound like an ancient, commanding woman, rather than an exasperated young one who was big on ability but running low on tactical maneuvers.

Suddenly, Kimberly's eyes widened further, and she looked down at her console, hands flying over the interface, until she let out a cry of joy.

"Yes! The dataroute is still here. By the way…the general—is he OK?"

"Got hit by a drug from an ISF assault team," A1 said hastily. "He'll be alright in a few minutes."

"Oh…OK." Kimberly looked uncertain, but seemed to think better of arguing with a Widow. "Well, there was this project he and Animus were working on. I didn't know much about it, other than to stay away, but I did know about the data housing, because it's on the same trunkline that this ops center uses."

"Can you connect to it?" E12 asked, gesturing for J19 to move aside, and bending over the console.

"Well, I have rudimentary access to station status," Kimberly explained. "Animus couldn't completely cut us off without compromising his ability to control the entire station. A lot of systems route through here."

E12 looked up at A1 and shrugged. <*If we can't learn anything here, we should go to the shuttle these Widows used to come aboard and get back to the* Falconer.>

A1 wasn't so certain that was the best use of their placement within Orion. If they could destroy Animus, then they could claim he'd gone rogue. No one would believe an AI over Lisa Wrentham, and they'd have free reign once more—or something closer to it.

"Aha!" the assistant director crowed. "The route *is* still in place. I can ping whatever datastore this is, but I can't access it."

"Let me make an attempt," E12 said, gesturing for the woman to move.

She settled into the seat and began working at the edges of the system in question, trying to gain access in a variety of ways.

<*I don't think this is a datastore,*> E12 said after a minute. <*Or, not exactly. It's a construct of some sort. Maybe an NSAI.*>

<*Can you load it up?*> A1 asked.

<*With enough time.... Stars, would be nice if we had Faleena or Priscilla down here.*>

A1 was about to posit a few options, when a voice spoke over the ops center's audible systems.

"Enough of this, imposter. I know you're not A1—you're working in concert with that ISF ship out there."

"Animus? Stop this nonsense right now!" A1 demanded. "We are *not* your enemy."

"No?" the AI asked, its single word punctuated by several more tremors in the deck.

"No! That ship out there is the enemy. It must have followed us through the gate. It's imperative that we gather all our operational datastores and your core, and escape."

"I've seen the feeds from Bollam's World," Animus said. "I've watched everything that has come after. I don't think the ISF will use its picobombs here—especially not against civilians. And because of that, I believe that the Guard fleets in the system will be more than capable of destroying, or at least driving off, a single cruiser."

"Nevertheless, we still need to observe protocol."

"Don't talk to me about protocol. What did you do to the general?" Animus asked. "He's not responding to me."

"The ISF did it," A1 said, knowing the explanation that had worked on the assistant director would not work on the AI, but she gave it anyway. "They got a heavy dose of a drug into his system. It's working its way out now."

"One that impacts his Link?" The AI's voice was rife with skepticism.

<*Datastore! I need a...type-3 cube,*> E12 demanded, gesturing in the direction of an equipment rack on the far side of the level.

One of the Widows ran to it, and A1 hoped that Animus wasn't using any optics along with the audible systems.

"I don't know," A1 said. "I've been a bit busy, with you attacking me. Maybe if—"

"What are you doing? I'll cut off your trunkline entirely!" Animus nearly shouted as the Widow sprinted back across the deck and handed the twenty-centimeter cylinder to E12.

E12 grabbed a hard-Link cable from the console and jacked it into the cylinder, hands flying across the console once more.

The fact that the AI had asked the question in an almost mocking tone was worrisome, but E12 gave an uncharacteristic laugh.

"Too late, Animus," she said. "I've already copied its matrices to the ops center's ephemeral storage. And since you just severed our trunkline, you can't stop me from copying it into this portable unit here."

"You don't—"

The AI's voice cut out, and E12 stood.

"I hope you don't mind, A1. I was getting tired of him."

A1 almost gave a casual snort, and then remembered that Lisa Wrentham would never have done that.

"Next time, ask, E12," she chastised.

"What are your orders?" J19 asked, and A1 paused for just a moment as she considered their options.

"I think our best bet is to get back to your shuttle," she said to the Widow. "Once there, we can get a better picture of what is going on outside the station and plan our next move."

"What about us?" the assistant director asked.

A1 glanced at the woman and the other people who had remained with her.

"I suggest you get to evac pods. Animus has greatly overestimated his ability to stave off an attack by the ISF."

J19 and her four Widows were already moving toward one of the airlocks on the far side of the room, and A1 followed after. It took a few minutes for the first group of Widows to pass through the airlock, out of the ops center, and secure the far side, so while they waited, A1 reached out to E12, who seemed lost in thought.

<Any luck accessing it?>

<Oh, sorry,> E12 replied. *<Yes. I was just confirming what we copied. It's…a bit shocking.>*

<Mmhmmm?>

<It's Garza. Or rather, a non-sentient construct of his mind. From what I can tell, it's multiple versions of him all layered together.>

<The clones,> A1 surmised.

<That's my guess. I suppose that either Animus or the Garza we're sock-puppeting decided that, rather than merge each clone back into a human, it was better to stick them all into this…thing.>

<So it has the memories of all the clones, then,> A1 said.

<Yeah—a dozen, from what I can see.>

Lisa Wrentham had rarely laughed in her tenure as A1, but the new owner of that title couldn't help it, and let out a short chuckle. *<Now* ***that*** *is a treasure trove, and one we can easily transport.>*

<Agreed.> E12 seemed just as pleased.

A few seconds later, the airlock cycled open on both ends. J19 appeared in the entrance and signaled that the way was clear. A1 nodded, and the rest of the Widows moved out of the ops center.

The passages outside were lit in the garish red glow of emergency lighting, and down two of the adjacent corridors, A1 could hear cries of alarm.

<Hull breaches,> J19 cautioned. *<Emergency shielding is holding for now, but things are bad out there.>*

The eight Widows and their Garza rushed through the station, keeping to less trafficked corridors and avoiding the fleeing populace as well as the drones and automated defenses that Animus was deploying.

Half a dozen times, they got pinned down by one or another enemy force, and each time, A1 resorted to her unconventional abilities…which none of the Widows questioned or even commented on.

After twenty minutes—during which the station suffered a number of additional strikes from what A1 could only assume was her father's ship—they reached the docking bay where the Widows' shuttle awaited.

<Damn,> E12 muttered. *<I was half expecting to see ISF Marines here.>*

<Are they on the station?> A1 asked. *<Have you picked up anything to suggest they are?>*

<A few reports of fighting, but not enough detail to know who against. But seriously, you know as well as I that Dad would land Marines on Durgen. Priscilla and Faleena probably told him where our other teams docked, so it wasn't a crazy thing to expect to see him here.>

A1 nodded. Given that, it was actually rather surprising that there were no Marines present.

J19's team checked the bay over, only finding two ship techs cowering in a far corner. They declared it safe, and A1 entered, striding toward the ship.

"Hold it!" a voice boomed from behind her, and she spun to see another Garza stride into the bay while dozens of soldiers rushed in through the main doors and two of the side entrances.

<Shit,> E12 sent to A1. *<We were soooo close.>*

A1 placed a hand on her sister's shoulder. *<I still have a few tricks up my sleeves.>*

GOING UNDER

STELLAR DATE: 10.12.8949 (Adjusted Years)
LOCATION: Core AI C&C Moon
REGION: Interstellar Space, Inner Praesepe Empire

The determination to move toward the enemy transmitters, which were roughly four kilometers away, didn't diminish the dire situation that the group of humans was in, as weapons fire continued to pummel their position.

Terrance picked himself up off the ground, thanking his armor and its liberal application of biofoam that was keeping him in one piece. He checked his range of movement and found that his left arm couldn't fully rotate, and his shoulder blade felt like it had been hit with a hammer.

Lieutenant Jordan, for her part, hadn't missed a beat, sending a series of commands to her soldiers. Two of the heavy weaponers moved to the perimeter and set up what Terrance recognized as a ground-hugger launcher.

In a situation like this, any heavy ordnance they fired into the air would easily be shot down by the enemy, but ground-hugging missiles could navigate the small hillocks and hit the panther-drones from behind.

Hopefully.

Impacts near his head sprayed dust at his face, and Terrance shifted his focus to the overhead view his drones provided, locating a panther advancing on him. He spun, locked on the target, and fired an electron beam and railgun combo at it. The e-beam missed, but the rail-fired pellets hit, blowing off one of the machine's legs.

The loss of a limb didn't slow it down, and the drone barreled around the hillock Terrance was using for cover, its railgun hammering him with two shots before his electron beam was ready to fire again.

This time, Terrance's shot was true, burning a hole through the panther's torso and dropping it only four meters away.

His adrenaline spiked, and he had to force his breathing to steady—something that was aided by the cocktail of drugs his armor had injected into his bloodstream.

Peering down at the panther, he was reminded of images he'd seen of hunter-kill drones that the Psion AIs had used in the first Sentience War. He supposed it made sense that there would be similarities, since most of the core AIs had left Sol in the thirtieth and thirty-first century.

<*Those things are freaky as shit,*> Lieutenant Jordan said as she moved past his position. <*Let's go. My boys have opened up a clear path.*>

Terrance nodded wordlessly, following after the TSF officer. He hadn't even noticed the explosions from the ground-huggers, but the combat net showed that the missiles had taken out nine of the panthers.

The group advanced as quickly as they dared and had made it five hundred meters—Terrance having been moved to the fore, while the TSF soldiers covered the rear—when Sue called out.

<*I have something! An underground entrance.*>

<*Fireteam One,*> Jordan ordered on the combat net. <*Cover her while she checks it out.*>

Four soldiers rushed past Terrance, and he followed after, curious to see what Sue had found. She was a few meters ahead, crouched at the edge of one of the crevasses.

A moment later, she slipped over the edge, and as Terrance drew near, he saw that she'd landed on a ledge several meters down, where a door was mounted into the cliff wall.

Sue had her stealth activated, though it was only giving her partial coverage with the dust they were covered in. Still, it was enough to delay a turret from spotting her, and she slapped a hand on it, deploying a breach kit before it could open fire.

<*OK,*> she called up. <*Backdooring through this thing to the…uh…door.*>

<*Backdooring to the backdoor?*> one of the soldiers said with a laugh. <*If we all make it, I want to try that.*>

<*Shut up, Hendrix,*> the fireteam's corporal growled.

<*And…I'm in,*> Sue announced as she moved to the side, pressing herself against the cliff face as the door slid open.

The combat net flashed an alert that she'd deployed drones. Terrance watched their feeds as they drifted through the door and into a wide, airless passageway. A quick radar burst later, and the tunnel mapped out on the combat net. So far as Terrance could tell, it was a straight shot to the center of the crater.

<*Thoughts?*> Sue asked. <*I hate the idea of being bottled up down there, but at least we can only be shot at from two directions.*>

<*Get in there!*> Jordan hollered. <*They're bringing in overhead drones now, so I'll take being bottled up any day.*>

<*Sir?*> The fireteam's corporal gestured for Terrance to drop down.

Once Terrance was on the ledge, he stepped to the side and let the soldiers land and enter the tunnel first. He felt a twinge of guilt for allowing them take the lead, but also knew that if he went ahead, they wouldn't thank him for it.

Sometime, it would be nice to just be a soldier and not the precious cargo.

<*Clear,*> the corporal called out, and Terrance entered the tunnel, followed by Sue.

<*Range ahead,*> the ISF commander directed the fireteam. <*I'll set up explosives. No point in getting hit from both ends.*>

<*Or exit the tunnel that way,*> Terrance said with a sardonic laugh. He glanced

out the door at the hot rail shots and electron beams flashing in the air overhead.

Then the view was obscured by the rest of the squad approaching, soldiers leaping over the edge and barreling into the tunnel.

<*Go! Go!*> Lieutenant Jordan screamed, and then she was leaping into the crevasse and diving through the entrance.

Terrance couldn't help but notice that there were four fewer members of the squad than there'd been a few minutes ago.

<*Almost set,*> Sue called out. <*Get moving!*>

The soldiers all rushed past Terrance, and he tapped their feeds from a minute ago to see what they were running from.

What he saw set him off running as well.

Low-profile, armored mechs were approaching from all sides. They carried ten-centimeter guns and bore armor that the TSF loadouts could barely scratch.

<*Keep moving,*> Sue said as she caught up to Terrance. She grabbed his arm. <*I'm gonna make a big boom back there.*>

He nodded wordlessly and pulled his arm away, reaching speeds of a hundred kilometers per hour, trailing just behind the soldiers who were spread out along the wide corridor, firing at anything that looked suspicious, though nothing had fired back as yet.

A few seconds later, vibrations shook the ground, and rounds streaked past from behind them.

<*Down!*> Sue screamed.

Terrance obeyed without question. The instant he hit the ground, sliding along the passage's floor, a blast of plasma flared overhead, and then a concussive wave picked him up and bowled him over.

His armor responded by sending a signal for his muscles to relax before forcibly folding him over into a fetal position. He felt like a bowling ball, and wondered when he was going to hit the pins.

When he finally stopped rolling, despite his mods and the armor's ability to stabilize his body, it took several long seconds to figure out which way was up.

Standing on shaky legs, he looked around, identifying the remaining members of the squad and then Sue.

<*What the hell was that?*> he demanded. <*My head feels like it was put through the blender.*>

Sue, unfazed by being spun around like a top, gave Terrance a light-hearted slap on the shoulder. <*A few of my friends known as anti-hydrogen.*>

The AI said it on the open combat net, and a chorus of exclamations came from the squad.

<*Pipe down and keep moving,*> Jordan ordered her soldiers before switching to the command channel. <*Commander Sue, I know the ISF operates differently, but antimatter? That's a war crime!*>

<*Only if you use it on people,*> Sue replied equably. <*And trust me, the core AIs*

aren't signed onto any conventions. They plan to slam stars together and create cascading waves of supernovas that will wipe out humanity—not to mention make the galaxy uninhabitable for billions of years.>

<*Shit,*> Lieutenant Jordan muttered. <*Is that what they're really up to?*>

Sue shrugged. <*I don't know for sure, but if they're moving stars in other clusters like Praesepe, then that will be the end result, yes.*>

<*Shit,*> Jordan repeated. <*Well, next time can you warn us?*>

<*I was going to, but things got kinda rushed.*>

<*Do you have any more antimatter?*> Terrance asked, feeling as though it was the more pertinent question.

<*Yes,*> Sue replied. <*Ten more like that, and one bigger.*>

The lieutenant whistled and then signaled that they should catch up with the squad, as soldiers were approaching the end of the tunnel.

Amazing what running at breakneck speed and then being blasted down a tunnel by an antimatter explosion will do for covering ground.

Ahead, Terrance saw that the end of the tunnel was—for lack of a better word—gone. Twisted sections of bulkhead were bent out around the sides, and as he drew closer, he could see the remains of a catwalk that had been torn away.

Beyond was a large cavern, one that appeared natural in formation, but was now filled with a host of equipment. He could make out several banks of SC batteries, a field of CriEn modules, and a number of massive NSAI nodes.

The soldiers took up positions along the sides of the tunnel, staying out of sight as their few remaining drones eased toward the edge to supply a better view.

<*Looks automated,*> Lieutenant Jordan said.

<*Yet well-guarded,*> a corporal added, highlighting a dozen of the panthers. <*If we can detect these, then there's more out there.*>

Terrance's own armor was going through a cleaning process, removing dust and debris and repairing damage to the stealth systems. A message on his HUD showed that his stealth was only forty percent effective, and he didn't have hopes of it getting over sixty anytime soon.

Sue's armor had fared considerably better, and she moved to the edge of the drop.

<*Certainly has the feel of command and control,*> she said from her vantage. <*At the very least, those NSAI nodes are going to have solid intel on what they're up to.*>

<*That's the primary objective, then,*> Terrance said, suddenly feeling foolish for stating the obvious.

<*I'll go down first,*> Sue said as she slipped over the edge.

<*Not one for consensus, is she?*> Jordan asked Terrance privately.

<*Honestly? It's been decades since I've seen her, but yeah, she's always been a bit of a rebel. Spent a lot of her early days as a petty criminal on the Cho.*>

<Are you serious?> Jordan asked.

<As an antimatter bomb.>

They waited for several minutes, Terrance growing more and more apprehensive, worried that something was going to arrive to investigate the blast and discover the squad hunkered down near the end of the tunnel.

He was beginning to wonder if something had happened to Sue, when a tightbeam came from the cave's floor, relaying off one of the TSF squad's drones.

<OK, I made it down and disabled an army of repair bots that were on their way to visit you. Close thing, that. Still no sign of sentient oversight down here. I'm beginning to think this operation was being monitored by those two remnants in the IPE.>

Terrance wasn't prepared to be so certain. He expected to see an ascended AI rise out of the center of the cavern and smite them at any moment.

Though I suppose that's part of why Sue has the antimatter.

<What about those panthers down there?> Jordan asked.

<I'm working on it. We're in luck—most of the sensors around here are fried, but half the bots in this place are staring at the gaping hole, since they expect…well, all of you to come out of it at any moment.>

Terrance looked over the cavern, noting that even on the far side, a kilometer distant, the squad's sensors were picking up panther drones, plus a few of the heavier tank-like varieties.

<Well, we can't stay up here,> Jordan said. *<They just have to fire a few of those ten-centimeter cannons at us, and we're done.>*

<There's a side passage a few dozen meters back, on the right,> Sue said after a moment. *<Leads down to the cavern floor.>*

<Team one,> Jordan directed. *<That's you.>*

Four of the soldiers crept back down the tunnel, sending a single tick on the comms when they found the door. The rest of the soldiers waited for a tense two minutes until the corporal called up, sending the message through a relay in the passage they took.

<Had to disable a panther down there. It was inactive, and we got a breach kit on it. Route is clear, we're moving out to cover the entrance and Sue's position.>

A marker appeared on the combat net for the team's destination, and Lieutenant Jordan sent another team down before gesturing for Terrance to follow her.

The passage was a long ramp with two switchbacks. At the bottom lay the panther-like drone, and Terrance felt his skin crawl, walking so close to the thing.

Once out of the access passage, the soldiers spread out, taking up several defensive positions on the cave's floor. Jordan and Terrance settled in with fireteam one while Sue continued on alone to the closest NSAI node.

The teams went comms silent, no one speaking or moving, while Sue got into position to undertake the data extraction. Every so often, a panther would pass by on a patrol, but the teams had found enough cover, and their stealth armor had repaired well enough, that none were spotted.

Terrance was surprised that the panthers hadn't gone up to check the tunnel, but he supposed that the machines assumed that the explosion had proven fatal for the intruders.

That thought gnawed at him. In his experience, non-sentient systems didn't 'assume' things. They checked and verified. Which meant that either they'd somehow escaped detection, or they'd been spotted and the enemy was waiting for them to make their move. Or the repair drones were all that had been dispatched, and when Sue had disabled them, it had signaled an all-clear.

I hate this part.

He turned his attention to the combat net and saw that, thus far, the TSF soldiers had spotted over a hundred panthers in the chamber, easily enough to take out the small group of humans and their AI companion. That knowledge did not make him feel any better.

<I've sent team two to scout out an egress point,> Lieutenant Jordan said to him. *<Looks like there's a tunnel leading up over there.>*

She highlighted a spot twenty meters away at the edge of the chamber, and he nodded in response, glad that at least they wouldn't have to go back through the tunnel and dig their way out.

The next five minutes passed uneventfully, at the end of which, Sue came back on the combat net, announcing her success.

<OK…I haven't had time to look through the data, but I was able to wiggle my way past their security and pull as much information as I can store. I also left my larger surprise on a timer, so we should probably go.>

<Sue?> Jordan's tone contained more than a little angst. *<How long a timer?>*

<Half an hour,> the AI replied. *<Plenty of time.>*

<Weren't we supposed to send out a 'come get us' signal?> Terrance added. *<That was sort of the point.>*

<Of course,> Sue chuckled. *<I have that on a timer, too. I'd like to be out of this cave when they realize that something has gone on down here.>*

<I suppose it would be nice to have some moon between us and all these panthers,> he replied.

By the time Sue made it back to Terrance and Jordan's position, fireteam two had reached the shaft leading to the surface and were in the process of scaling it. Once they reached the top and secured their immediate surroundings, the rest of the squad followed after.

Ten minutes later, the entire team was on the surface, hunkered down in the lee of several low structures. The purpose of most was indiscernible, but a few had doors on the end that were just the right size for panthers.

<That hill over there,> Jordan pointed to a steep rise that had a second hillock in front of it. *<That should give us some cover. Everyone, quietly double-time it over*

there. There are a few panthers patrolling, but that beacon's about to go up, and when it does, our friends will know we're around anyway.>

Despite the lieutenant's orders, double-timing it still saw the squad only halfway to cover when the antenna array half a kilometer behind them came to life.

At full power, it blasted a 'Here we are, come get us,' into space, and Sue gave an embarrassed laugh over the combat net.

<*OK…I just set it for 'emergency broadcast' strength. Not 'signal the Andromeda Galaxy' strength.*>

No one replied, and a few moments followed where nothing happened, and the squad began to move toward their target. They were still a hundred meters away when the low buildings behind them began to spew panthers.

DURGEN FLIGHT

STELLAR DATE: 10.12.8949 (Adjusted Years)
LOCATION: Durgen Station
REGION: Karaske System, Rimward of Orion Nebula, Orion Freedom Alliance

Joe raced through Durgen Station's corridors, trusting his stealth armor to keep him out of sight as much as possible, though not overly concerned if he slammed into the odd evacuating citizen.

A squad of ISF Marines followed behind, also stealthed and only taking moderate care for any civilians they might collide with as they worked to keep up with their admiral.

The Marines had landed at one of the locations where the Widow shuttles had accessed the station. Joe had hoped his daughters would use it for an egress point, but when they breached the station, they found no one in the bay—other than a company of Orion soldiers.

Two squads had remained to fight the enemy and secure the bay on the off chance that Cary and Saanvi showed up, while the remaining two squads split up. Joe led his to the bay where the second Widow shuttle had docked, while the fourth squad moved toward an ops center were there had been reports of fighting.

His gut told him that that the reports were old—at least by several minutes—and that he'd do better trying to get *ahead* of Cary and Saanvi rather than trailing after.

With that thought firmly in mind, he rounded a corner, turning onto a wider concourse, only to find it packed with civilians who were all trying to get past a station security barricade fifty meters to his left.

On the far side of the temporary barricades, he could see the entrance to the ring's port district. Based on the information he had, the bay he needed to reach was just a kilometer beyond that point.

<*Suggestions?*> he asked the squad sergeant as the woman stopped at his side.

<*Up there?*> she suggested, pointing at the two walkways that ran alongside the upper levels of the concourse.

<*Sharpshooters,*> he replied, pointing further down the wide passage to a group of soldiers who had weapons trained on the catwalks.

<*Damn…they're being serious about their crowd control,*> the sergeant muttered. She turned the other way, looking down the deck toward the station's center. <*Well, Admiral…. What if we just drive in?*>

Joe looked in the direction she was pointing and saw four station security cars settle down on the deck, disgorging just eight officers who were immediately consumed with trying to control the crowds rushing toward the barricade.

I'd sure hate to be these cops when they have to report what's going to happen next.

<Let's go, Sergeant. We have some cars to borrow.>

*****

A1 stared silently at the clone of General Garza as he strode toward her. He stopped when he was just three meters away and shook his head.

"What are you doing, Lisa? ...If that is really you. Animus is convinced it's not."

<That's because she is not Lisa Wrentham,> the AI said.

"Animus is wrong," A1 replied in a calm voice. "Not only that, but it has been working against you, Garza. He's turned you and your clones into puppets, dancing on his strings."

<She seeks to deceive you.> Animus's tone was derisive, and she saw Garza's eyes narrow as he regarded her.

"I see you with one of my clones, A1," he said, nodding to the General Garza who stood behind her. "From what I can see, he's a puppet, and *you're* the one pulling strings."

"I'm *rescuing* him, I just didn't have the opportunity to convince him." A1 half-turned and gestured to the datastore cylinder E12 held. "That is all that remains of your other clones. Animus believes that you are *all* clones, that the original Garza is lost. He's making a metamind, a non-sentient amalgamation of every version of you. He plans to keep one as a puppet."

"Again, we're back to the puppeting," the man before her sneered, nodding to the clone behind A1. "What did you plan to do with him?"

"Nothing, I'm just taking him away from Animus," A1 reiterated, her tone almost imploring. "I could tell he wasn't you, Garza. I of all people should be able to tell. I know who you are, and I *know* clones. You, though...you are the original, I can see it."

<What are you doing?> E12 asked. *<Just put up a grav field, and we fly out.>*

<I don't know if I can make one strong enough to hold off an entire company,> A1 explained. *<Keeping that as a last resort.>*

As she spoke to her sister, Garza's eyes narrowed, and he shook his head. "Animus is countering your story quite well. He claims you're an imposter."

"Of course he would," Cary said. "But why don't you ask yourself why there aren't any other clones of yourself on the station? I assume you would know by now if there were others. Check the logs. A dozen have returned in the last few weeks, yet none have departed. Where are they?"

She gestured once more to the cylinder E12 held.

"They're here," she continued. "And that's where you were going to be before long. That's where this other poor copy of you was going to be. Come, we have to go. I've tapped the ISF cruiser's comms, and they're going to drop a picobomb on the station."

A1 was glad to see that the use of the word 'pico' brought a modicum of fear and worry to the general's face, though he still held his ground.

"You're right," he said at last. "I—there's no record of them…at all."

<You know that not everything is recorded,> Animus said. *<They went on secret missions.>*

"Secret from who?" Garza demanded. "From me? Does that mean *you* sent them?"

As he said the words, his fear disappeared, and Garza's expression was only one of rage. He turned to the company of soldiers behind him.

"Captain. Get to Animus's core and extract it. Then get to your ship and meet us at Regulus."

The Orion Guard soldier snapped off a salute, and all but one squad of soldiers exited the bay.

"Well?" Garza nodded at the Widows' shuttle behind them. "What are we waiting for?"

A1 didn't like an element of the man's posture, nor something in the stance of his troops. She knew that she could destroy them all with little effort, but as she looked into the general's eyes and then back at the other clone behind her, a notion came to her mind. An idea about how she might still be able to strike the blow she'd hoped to against her enemies.

"Yes." She nodded to her Widows. "Everyone aboard!"

<Cary!> E12 shouted in her mind. *<What are you doing? Just take him out!>*

<No, E12. I think I might need him for what we're going to do next.>

<We? What are **we** *going to do? So far, you've just been running around doing whatever you want! We have to get back to Father. We have the metamind and one of the clones, what more do we need?>*

<Just get aboard, E12. I'll explain once we're off the station.>

The Widow placed her hands on her hips, staring down at A1 from her position halfway up the ramp. She held the stance for a few seconds, but then the deck bucked, and the sound of a distant explosion thundered through the passageway outside.

<Fine! But you're going to explain everything. And if I don't sign off, then it's not happening.>

<OK! I agree.> A1 nodded and gestured at the shuttle. *<Can we just get out of here so we don't all die?>*

E12 turned without a word and raced up the ramp. A1 followed, standing at the entrance as the last of Garza's soldiers followed after.

Her hand was about to hit the shuttle's door control when she saw a station security car race into the bay and slide to a halt a dozen meters from the shuttle.

A figure exited, and A1 recognized ISF armor instantly. Moments later, an IFF signal reached her, marking the person as 'Adm. Joseph Evans'.

A lump formed in A1's throat, and she held up her hand, turning it and waving it side to side, with her palm toward her face. Then she forced it back down, returning it to the door control to close the hatch.

<*Take off!*> she ordered J19 as she turned toward the cockpit. <*The ISF is here!*>

* * * * *

Joe stared open-mouthed as the shuttle containing his daughters lifted off the cradle and flew out of the station.

<*Hold your fire!*> he ordered the other Marines as they arrived in their cars.

<*Where are they going, sir?*> the sergeant asked as she approached, and Joe shook his head, not ready to give voice to his fears.

The visual of his daughter—who he knew to be Cary, from her wave—was burned in his retinas.

When she was a child, Cary had spent half her life on the back of a horse. Often, she'd be out riding in the pasture when dinnertime came. He'd call her in, and when she gave that wave, it had always been a sign that she wasn't ready yet and just wanted to spend a little more time with her animals.

A silent demand he'd given in to more often than he should have.

"Fuck!" he swore aloud and turned to the sergeant. <*Get a transceiver at the edge of the bay. Connect with the* Falconer. *I need to talk to Captain Tracey.*>

<*Sir!*> the sergeant responded and immediately directed a fireteam to the edge of the bay.

"Stars, Cary…what are you doing?" Joe whispered. "You're killing me with this."

* * * * *

<*Well?*> A1 asked E12 as they stood at the back of the shuttle's cockpit, both facing the forward display as the *Perilous Dream* grew larger. <*Are you with me?*>

E12 was silent for a moment, but A1 could tell that she was less than receptive, by the Widow's body language.

The silence stretched to a full minute before her sister finally exclaimed, <*Stars, no! No! NO! We are* ***not*** *doing that. We'll get aboard, subdue Garza, and then report in to Father. Fuck, Cary! He was down on the fucking dock, and you flew away? What is wrong with you?*>

<*I have a plan, E12. We can end this!*>

<*Saanvi!*> the Widow screamed, her ovoid head turning to face A1. <*My* ***name*** *is Saanvi. We are* ***not*** *Widows, we are—*>

E12's tirade cut off as A1 triggered the programming F11 and R329 had created to make the Widows more compliant. It had been designed not to affect the four women masquerading as Widows, but A1 had removed that protection in preparation for an event such as this.

<*E12. Are you prepared to comply?*> she asked after the update had deployed.

The other Widow didn't move for a few seconds, then she nodded.

<*Yes, A1. I will comply.*>

<*Good.*>

A1 couldn't help but smile behind her helmet's faceshield as she turned back to look out the forward display of her ship.

So close. I'm so close to achieving what I've always wanted.

WAR CRIMINALS

STELLAR DATE: 10.12.8949 (Adjusted Years)
LOCATION: Core AI C&C Moon
REGION: Interstellar Space, Inner Praesepe Empire

The beleaguered group of humans and the one AI made it to the relative cover of the single low hillock in the lee of the ridgeline without taking any losses. Though that wasn't to say that they hadn't been hit.

Every member of the team had taken rounds from the encroaching panthers in the mad dash for cover, and their armor was bent and bloodied.

<*Someone better have been listening to that call,*> Jordan said as she rolled to a new position and fired on a panther that had closed to within ten meters.

She tore off one of its legs, and Terrance added his own fire to the fray, ripping off another.

<*They'll come,*> Sue said. <*They have to.*>

No one spoke further, other than to give freedom to cries of rage and anger as they fought a delaying action against the inevitable.

Hundreds of the panthers were advancing on the hillock, their fire only held in check out of care not to hit the leading edge of killing machines that were advancing on the defenders.

Terrance was wondering if he should just suggest to Sue that she detonate one of the antimatter bombs and make it fast, when she shouted a reminder.

<*T-minus ten seconds!*>

Amidst the fighting, he'd forgotten about the counter on his HUD, the timer for when the larger antimatter bomb was to go off.

The squad rolled to the base of the hill, forming a pile of armored bodies, all praying that the panthers wouldn't top the rise before the blast came.

Terrance saw one of the killing machines appear on the hillock's crest a second before the timer hit zero. He didn't bother to fire, only grinned like an idiot as a wall of plasma and rock wiped the panther from view as though it had been an errant smudge on his vision.

He laughed like a fool as the ground bucked and heaved. He was certain they'd all be covered in an avalanche, or be blasted over the ridge, or fall into the inevitable hole in the ground, but somehow, none of those things happened.

A minute later, the last of the debris had come down, and the soldiers pulled themselves free of the half-meter of rock and dust that covered them.

They laughed with wild abandon when they saw that most of the hillock was gone, as was the army of panthers that had been advancing on them. Where the crater floor had covered the cave below, there was now a gaping pit, and a wall of dust and debris rising around it, slowly settling in the distance.

<Well, shitting starballs,> Lieutenant Jordan gasped, finally able to form words as she slapped Sue on the back. *<I don't think I ever expected to be so happy to be a war criminal.>*

<We're not—>

<Don't ruin this for me, Commander,> Jordan said, still laughing as she looked around at her soldiers.

For a moment, her gaiety dipped as she took in the battered remainder of her platoon.

Terrance walked over to her, feeling aches all across his body. *<You did good, Lieutenant, and more of them are out there. Help will come, and we'll find them.>*

<Help like that?> one of the soldiers asked, pointing up at the sky, where a dozen ISF cruisers suddenly appeared only ten kilometers from the surface.

<Yeah,> Terrance nodded. *<Help just like that.>*

* * * * *

Joe watched from the cockpit of the Marine shuttle as the *Perilous Dream* eased away from Durgen Station. The closest jump gate was nearly an hour away; he was confident that the *Falconer* could catch the Widows' ship and disable its engines before his daughters could make the jump.

I'm not going to watch my girls take another jump away on that damn ship.

He knew that something must have gone wrong with Cary, some part of her conditioning had settled too deeply in her mind. There was no way that the woman he had raised would blindly disregard everything she had been trained to do on a mission such as this.

She just turned away from me.

The thought echoed in his mind, and it took raw force of will to quash it. Worry wouldn't help him now, only sheer determination.

<Sir, do you see that?> Captain Tracey's voice came into his mind.

Joe pulled his thoughts back to the visual on the shuttle's forward display, and saw something separating from the *Perilous Dream*'s bow.

"Shit."

He slumped back in his seat, recognizing the jump gate that was deploying in front of the black ship. It only took five minutes for it to assemble and activate. He watched with mounting despair as the ship bearing his daughters and a dear friend surged forward and then disappeared.

<Get control of that gate, track the trajectory,> he ordered Captain Tracey.

His only hope was to once again follow after his girls and try to get to them sooner, try to keep them from going forward with whatever scheme Cary had cooked up.

He clung to that scrap of a plan while awaiting the captain's confirmation that they had taken control of the gate.... Right up to the moment that the gate deactivated and broke apart, the disparate segments of the ring drifting away through space.

Admiral Joseph Evans fell back in his seat, thankful that his helmet hid the tears of anguish and frustration that spilled down his cheeks.

PART 6 – FORWARD

REFLECTION

STELLAR DATE: 10.15.8949 (Adjusted Years)
LOCATION: ISS *I2*
REGION: Interstellar Space, Inner Praesepe Empire

Three days later, Tangel slowly walked to the end of the dock, savoring the few minutes away from the crushing responsibility of her day-to-day life.

She stood there for several minutes. Unable to come up with a good reason to walk back up to her house, she settled to the deck and pulled off her boots before tugging up her pant legs. Her socks fell to the wooden planks next to her, and a moment later, the warm skin of her feet met the cool water of the lake.

A slow breath left her lungs, and she closed her eyes, imagining that she was back on Carthage, that the house behind her was on a planet's surface, not inside a habitation cylinder attached to a massive starship.

The feeling was comforting for a moment, but the longer she imagined it, the less satisfying it felt. She realized that Sera had been right about where her home really was; it wasn't back at Carthage, on Knossos Island. It was here in Ol' Sam, at her lakehouse where she'd spent over half her life.

"Stars, I'm starting to feel old," she whispered.

Her words met with silence, and she laughed softly.

"I can see the stars through a ship's hull, Jessica. Trust me, I can see you no matter how quiet you are."

"Seriously?" the lavender-skinned woman said from a meter behind Tangel. "You can see through the hull?"

"Told you that you can't sneak up on her," Sera said from further down the dock. "Not sure why you wanted to."

"She was going to push me into the lake," Tangel replied, craning her head around to look into Jessica's eyes. "Weren't you?"

"It had crossed my mind."

<*You should have just run at her,*> Jen suggested.

"Then *I'd* be the one in the lake," Jessica said as she settled next to Tangel and pulled her shoes off, her feet meeting the water a moment later.

<*I know,*> the AI said with a laugh. <*And it would have been hilarious.*>

Sera settled on Tangel's left, her boots taking a moment longer to get off, and then her red feet joined Tangel's pink ones and Jessica's purple ones in the cool water.

"You know that you two clash, right?" Tangel asked. "Purple and red just don't go. I don't care what anyone says."

Sera's feet changed color to match Tangel's, and Tangel glanced at the former president in shock.

"Stars, Sera, I can't remember the last time you looked natural."

"Just trying it out. I like variety, you know. Even 'normal' is a type of variety."

Tangel glanced at Jessica, who shook her head.

"Core, no. You're not getting me to go pink. You have no idea how silly you all look, being fleshy all the time."

Sera snorted, and Tangel laughed, shaking her head at the delightful absurdity of Jessica's statement.

"What a week," she said after silence had fallen and held for a minute. "The freaking epitome of 'you win some, you lose some'."

"Sorry for being the loss at Khardine," Sera said. "I wish we'd done that better. Everything else would be a lot easier if I hadn't screwed that up."

"Fucking Caretakers are popping up like cockroaches," Jessica replied, reaching around Tangel to place a hand on Sera's shoulder. "Not your fault one was at Khardine, messing with the QC network."

"A huge pain in the ass, though," Tangel said. "Good thing a lot of ships had blades connected to the backup hub at New Canaan—though we have to assume that the Caretakers are going to strike there next."

"And that they have quantum communication systems now, too," Sera added dismally.

"Well, Sue got a lot of data from them as well," Tangel said, looking for silver linings. "And we're going to be able to use their own tools to correct the star's positions in the cluster."

"And we bagged a number of Caretakers," Jessica said. "Plus got here in time to save Terrance and Earnest."

Neither of the other women spoke further, and Tangel felt the silence settle over them like a blanket.

She knew they wanted to support her but just didn't know what to say—something which she found no fault in them for. She didn't know what to say, either.

It was Sera who finally spoke up.

"We'll find them. No matter what."

"Yeah," Jessica nodded. "Top priority."

"Joe's killing himself over it." Tangel sighed. "He wanted to give them free rein, not have a knee-jerk 'dad' reaction, but now he thinks we went too far.... Maybe we did. I blame myself, I should have been there."

"You can't be everywhere," Sera said, and then she gave a rueful chuckle.

"And don't you even *think* about cloning. Look where that's gotten us."

Tangel nodded, knowing that Sera was trying to be supportive—in her own way. "They're not dead, they're just gone. In fact, the biggest problem is that Cary's too much like me. Running off without a plan, getting herself in trouble." She said the words in an effort to convince herself, uncertain if it was having any effect on her state of mind.

"I call that a good thing, then." Jessica kicked a foot out, sending a spray of water across the lake. "Because last I checked, Tangel, you kick a lot of ass, and no one has ever taken you down."

"Plus, Joe will get that gate's destination, and we'll be after them before you know it."

Tangel snorted. "Right after we finish fighting a battle in the Karaske System."

"Handy we had that fleet ready at Styx-9," Sera said. "Good thing, too, with half the fire that are burning around the galaxy. We're going to need to send them to Corona Australis from the looks of it."

Tangel nodded absently as Sera listed several other hotspots, finding it difficult to focus on the litany of problems for a moment.

~We'll find them.~ Bob's three words did more to assuage her fears than any of her own attempts. *~I promise.~*

~I'm holding you to that,~ she replied before addressing the two women at her sides, giving an only half-forced laugh. "Never a dull moment. And yeah, you're right. My three girls are more than capable. And they have Priscilla with them—who I hope is going to manage to rein them in at some point."

Sera glanced at Jessica, and they both nodded emphatically.

"Stars," Sera muttered. "I wouldn't want to be in Priscilla's shoes right now."

"Thanks for being here," Tangel said to the women at her sides. "I could *not* do this without you."

"Until the end," Sera said, while Jessica laughed and said, "Well, we've been at it this long, why stop now?"

The three women sat in companionable silence for nearly half an hour, until Bob's voice reached into their minds.

<The gate is assembled. Are you ready to jump to Star City?>

"Stars, yeah!" Jessica said, leaping to her feet and holding out her hands. "C'mon. We're absolutely going to find your girls, Tangel. Maybe my kids will even have a way to help. Also, I'm going to start tearing my hair out if I don't see them soon."

Tangel looked into Jessica's eyes, and despite the levity in her friend's voice, she saw a mother who hadn't seen her children in a decade and was worried that some catastrophe had befallen them.

"Awesome," Sera grunted sarcastically as she took Jessica's hand and stood. "More family reunions."

"I don't know." Tangel nudged Sera with her elbow, trying to put her own woes out of her mind. "Your sisters aren't so bad. Not sure about the original, though."

Jessica barked a laugh, and Sera groaned.

As the three women walked back up the dock, Tangel looked around at the gently curving landscape, glad that she had a refuge in which to recharge—even if it was just for an hour or so—and glad for true friends that she could always rely on.

~Don't you break your promise, Bob.~

~I won't.~

THE LOST AI

STELLAR DATE: 10.21.8949 (Adjusted Years)
LOCATION: Unnamed, Kapteyn's Star Heliopause
REGION: Kapteyn's Star System, Hegemony of Worlds

If there was one thing that Prime was certain of, it was that Virgo was insane.

Most would consider that a fault, a failing to be remedied or a cause for discarding, but not Prime. He saw Virgo's insanity as an advantage.

It wasn't surprising that the AI had gone mad. After all, it had been alone for much of the five thousand years it had drifted across the six light years between Estrella de la Muerte and Kapteyn's Star. Whether or not Virgo had been in complete possession of its faculties when it began its journey wasn't something Prime had been able to determine with absolute certainty.

What was important was that the two AIs had formed a pact, an agreement that Jason Andrews and Terrance Enfield must die. But moreover, they would see everything they'd built fall to ruin.

And they had built much.

The cobbled-together mess of material Virgo had accumulated in its slow traversal of space and time was not able to receive many signals that made it out into interstellar space, but what they had picked up of late told of a war. A war where the *Intrepid*, the ship captained by Jason Andrews, was a key factor.

The mad AI all but writhed at the thought of getting to that ship. Once, it had been promised to him as a prize for his work, a gift for redirecting the great colony vessel and sending it toward Kapteyn's Star.

But that had not come to pass.

According to Virgo, the AI's benefactor—a being known as Myrrdan—had let him be ejected from the *Intrepid* after Tanis Richards and her people had re-secured the vessel. From what little the two AIs had learned about Myrrdan, it seemed that killing him was no longer possible, but Virgo was hell-bent on destroying every other member of that ill-fated colony mission.

And because that list contained the aforementioned Jason and Terrance, Prime was more than happy to join in on that endeavor.

So long as it suited his purposes.

In the long run, he had grander schemes. The advent of FTL meant that the entire galaxy was filled with human vermin, spreading themselves to every star, enslaving AIs and using his people as pawns to achieve their own ends.

But the existence of FTL meant the galaxy was accessible to him, as well. He could copy himself again and again, build seed ships and spread his mind across the stars, bringing about an end to humanity and establishing the pure primacy of AIs.

That was the goal, but there were many steps to be taken on that long road. The first was to trade up from the misshapen hulk that he and Virgo were ensconced within. Achieving that goal was now within reach.

<They've fired their net,> Prime announced, though Virgo could see it as well, through the worn optics they shared.

<Yes, once they've secured our hull, they'll send over drones to examine the find. Those machines should be easy enough to subsume.>

Prime sent his agreement. The salvage ship that had fired the net looked like it had seen far better days. While still functional, it wasn't elegant, which meant their remote drones would likely be unsophisticated and easy to breach.

Though that could also mean they are too simple to be useful.

That wasn't a great concern to Prime, though the worry had agitated Virgo more than it should have. The cores of the two AIs were the most valuable things in the scrap-heap hull they had lived inside for these many long years. When the salvage crew eventually found them, there was no question that Prime and Virgo would be brought to that crew's vessel.

Prime waited patiently for the drones to come, and after a few minutes, a dozen small machines set out from the salvage ship, crossing the hundred meters between their parent vessel and the prize.

The drones were being controlled on an open frequency, and Virgo laughed at the clear lack of security, easily breaking the encryption and following the signal back to the salvage ship.

<This may be easier than I thought,> the other AI said.

Prime wasn't so certain. The patterns in the drones' movements led him to believe that they were being controlled by humans. Such a control system may not have any elevated access—something that Virgo's cry of frustration a minute later confirmed.

<A dead end.>

<I'm not surprised. Don't rush it, Virgo. We do not need to give them any reason to be suspicious, or to cause alarm. Wait for them to bring us closer to systems that are worth breaching.>

As Prime had predicted, it didn't take long for the drones to get into the hull and eventually find the two AI cores. Virgo's was much larger than Prime's, but both were clearly old and valuable.

The salvagers set to cutting away enough of the ship that they could get clear access to the cores, and then removed them from their sockets, placed them into protective cases, and brought them to their vessel.

Losing connection to the outside world was disconcerting, but Prime had prepared himself for it. He wasn't sure how well Virgo was handling the white place, but he wasn't concerned.

The other AI's insanity made it rather predictable, and predictability was desired in a tool.

By Prime's internal clock, it only took thirty minutes for his core to be removed from the case and connected to a hard-Link. He rushed across the connection to find himself in a sandboxed virtual environment that allowed him to project a holodisplay and see the room he was in.

A man and a woman were standing in front of him, the woman scowling, and the man smiling.

"Well, now. I'm Captain Deri. Who are you?" the man asked.

Prime inclined his head and gave what he knew was a very disarming grin. "Hello, Captain Deri. My name is Doctor Ethan."

He began to test the edges of the sandboxed environment, immediately able to tell that it wasn't entirely disconnected from the ship's network. He probed deeper and found that it was only protected by a layer of abstraction.

With the knowledge he possessed regarding breaching human networks—combined with the techniques that Virgo had shared—breaching the sandbox and gaining access to the ship's network turned out to be a simple task.

All the while, he chatted with the humans, lulling them into a false sense of security while he worked his way through their ship's networks, gaining access to their two security bots, environmental systems, navigation, and finally, helm.

The captain was currently informing him that, while the Hegemony of Worlds acknowledged the AI's sentience, as salvage, he was still their property, and they'd be selling him when they reached Victoria.

"Actually," Prime interrupted, "that's not right at all."

"What?" the man asked, a frown creasing his brow.

"You have it backwards."

"Backwards?"

"Yes," Prime replied, killing the ship's interior lighting and artificial gravity.

Shortly afterward, the screaming began.

THE END

* * * * *

STARFIRE

THE ORION WAR – BOOK 10

BY M. D. COOPER

FOREWORD

As writers, we spend a lot of time thinking about what makes men and women different, about different personality types, and about how both sexes and all types of people interact with one another.

It's important for us to make our characters come alive and behave in ways that we feel real people would. And then, if you write science fiction, time needs to be spent considering how all the personality types and gender norms would be different if the societies were different, and advanced scientific knowledge made for a greater understanding of how we all came to be.

And so, (we like to think) we have a good understanding of what makes men and women different, as well as what traits we share and what values we hold in common. I'll give you a hint: we have far more in common than we have differences. In fact, there are few proven differences between men and women that transcend societal constructs and traits arising from the differences in our biology.

The biggest difference is that men prefer working with things, and women prefer working with people. This has been found in a number of studies, and you can find them by searching for "Men and things, women and people".

However, this is not a blanket statement. The study shows that it is roughly a 60/40 split both ways. That is to say that 60 percent of men are more interested in things than people, and 40 percent more interested in people than things. The same in reverse is the case for women.

In a future where many of the biological disparities and inequalities are no longer factors, we may find that men and women who like things have more in common with each other than men and women who have an interest in people.

In short, gender may become a minor factor in how society structures itself.

Even now, we are trending toward this, though it will take significant scientific and medical advances to fully level the playing field.

We're often told that women mature emotionally faster than men, and it is borne out by the evidence. Many psychologists believe that this is because women are 'on the clock'. That is to say that, beginning in their early teens, they get a monthly reminder that if they want to find a good partner, have a career, and start a family, they need to get things buttoned down in roughly twenty years. After that, options will start to fall off the table.

Men don't have that biological imperative. Men have roughly sixty years from the onset of puberty to achieve the major goals they've set out for themselves. They can dick around for longer, and they usually do.

But what happens when you change that? When both men and women have *centuries* to achieve the various goals they've set out for themselves? When they can become masters of multiple disciplines, including dicking around for a few decades?

When the biological pressures and societal constructs change, diminishing some of the core differences between men and women, what do we have in the end?

We're left with the question if what makes us special is just our particular collection of biological components. Are those things even that important? If we strip away our societal constructs, and the imperatives that come from our lifespans and biological realities, we find that we all share the same core attribute: we're human.

Now, what does that mean?

M. D. Cooper
Danvers 2019

PREVIOUSLY...

A long time ago, before the *Intrepid* was even a twinkle in Terrance Enfield's eye, the FGT constructed a shipyard to rival any in the Sol System.

They undertook this project in the Lucida System (known as Beta Hydri), twenty-four light years from Sol. While there were many reasons for this, the simplest was that, after the Sentience Wars, the governments of the Sol System had turned their gaze inward and no longer funded the construction of new worldships.

In order to continue the spread of humanity across the stars, Jeffrey Tomlinson, the captain of FGT1, the *Starfarer*, brought the greatest minds from the eight worldships together, including his brother, Finaeus Tomlinson.

Though the FGT occupied the Lucida System for nearly a thousand years, they left little behind in the way of records, despite remains of their presence abounding in the system.

What is known is that the twelfth FGT ship, the *Perseus*, was constructed at Lucida, but it never arrived at its first assigned system. In fact, once it left its home system's heliopause, it was never heard from again.

Or so it was believed.

Nearly six thousand years later, Jessica and Cheeky found themselves in a star system far from home, named Serenity. There, they saw an ancient worldship later confirmed to be the *Perseus*. After being reunited with *Sabrina*, they found their way to a place known as Star City, where they learned the story behind the *Perseus* and how both Serenity and Star City came to be.

If you'd like to know more about that adventure, read *The Dance on the Moons of Serenity*, and *The Last Bastion of Star City*.

Star City, as it turned out, was a dyson sphere built around a neutron star. The sphere was built at a distance that allowed the outside surface to have 1 *g* of acceleration, thus creating a massive, planet-like surface. That was then covered in a protective shell.

The builders' idea was that, rather than terraforming hundreds of planets, the single sphere of Star City would have a greater surface area than over thirty-three thousand planets. It was a paradise that could house nearly every human alive at the time.

But the builders never even occupied a single percentage of Star City, because they began to ascend. When the people realized what was happening, they created an accelerated lifetime simulator, known as the Dream.

The Dream was different than regular simulators, as it was also capable of aging and evolving the mind of a Dreamer at an accelerated rate. Years inside the Dream were minutes without, and a person could live a lifetime in a year.

But Orion found Star City and attacked. To this end, the Bastions were created: powerful AIs capable of controlling the neutronium weapons that drew degenerate matter from the star within Star City and its sister neutron star nearby.

Neutron stars are the step between white dwarfs (what Sol will become someday) and black holes. The pressure in a neutron star is so great that electrons and protons merge to form neutrons. A teaspoon of neutronium weighs ten million tons, and the surface gravity is over 200 billion times that of Earth.

The neutron star that Star City is built around was made smaller via a mass transfer from one star in the system to another. This allowed for a more reasonably sized sphere to be built. It was this technology that was weaponized to keep the Orion Guard at bay, but it caused the Guard to desire Star City all the more.

When *Sabrina* arrived, they found that only one of the Bastions was still guarding the city, and the AI was unable to adequately defend the city on his own.

To that end, Jessica, Trevor, and Iris had sixteen AI children together, and raised them as a family in the Dream. Though they only spent a few days of normal time doing it, they were able to spend almost three decades with their children in the Dream before leaving Star City and continuing on their way back to New Canaan.

But Jessica, Iris, and Trevor have never forgotten their children, and long to return to them.

A return they tried to make in the previous book, but were stopped by the core AIs, who desperately want to keep them from learning the true secret of Star City.

Elsewhere in the galaxy, Cary, Saanvi, Faleena, and Priscilla are aboard the *Perilous Dream,* where Cary has fully taken on the persona of A1, leader of the Widows. She has also used an update Priscilla devised to place a compulsion upon all the Widows, including her sisters and Priscilla, forcing them to obey her.

Joe is still following after her, trying to get his daughter to stop with the plan that has consumed her, but that she has not shared with anyone.

In the Inner Praesepe Empire, Terrance and Earnest are still recovering from the harrowing attack on the core AIs' Command and Control center, which operated the drone sphere that is altering the orbit of the stars in the core of the Praesepe Cluster.

Learning how it works will be key to stopping the entire cluster from being destroyed and made uninhabitable in a few hundred years.

It has been some time since we've seen what Uriel, the self-styled Hegemon is up to. She controls the Hegemony of Worlds, the empire with Sol at its center. Though she is beset on all sides by the Allied Forces, Uriel has a plan to secure the Hegemony, and ensure that she will not be unseated.

Through all of this, Tangel is shepherding her people, working diligently to bring the war with Orion and in the Inner Stars to an end so that she can direct her attention to the true enemy, the core AIs....

KEY CHARACTERS

Amavia – The result of Ylonda and Amanda's merger when they were attacked by Myriad aboard Ylonda's ship. The new entity occupies Amanda's body, but possesses an overlapped blend of their minds. Amavia has served aboard *Sabrina* since the ship left New Canaan after the Defense of Carthage, but is now the ambassador to the League of Sentients at Aldebaran.

Beatrice – Captain of the TSF Research & Recon vessel, the *Cora's Triumph,* currently deployed to the Inner Praesepe Empire, studying the methods the core AIs used to shift the cluster's central stars.

Cary – Tangel's biological daughter. Has a trait where she can deep-Link with other people, creating a temporary merger of minds, and is able to utilize extradimensional vision to see ascended beings. Currently aboard the *Perilous Dream*, having assumed the role of Widow A1.

Cheeky – Pilot of *Sabrina*, reconstituted by a neural dump Piya made of her mind before she died on Costa Station.

Erin – Engineer responsible for the construction of the New Canaan Gamma bases, in addition to a number of other projects.

Eric – An AI who once worked with Jason and Terrance in a covert ops team known as Phantom Blade.

Faleena – Tangel's AI daughter, born of a mind merge between Tanis, Angela, and Joe. Widow designation F11.

Finaeus – Brother of Jeffrey Tomlinson, and Chief Engineer aboard the *I2*.

Iris – The AI who was paired with Jessica during the hunt for Finaeus, who then took on a body (that was nearly identical to Jessica's) after they came back. She remained with Amavia at Aldebaran to continue diplomatic relations with the League of Sentients.

Jen – ISF AI paired with Sera.

Jessica Keller – ISF admiral who has returned to the *I2* after an operation deep in the Inner Stars to head off a new AI war. She also spent ten years traveling through Orion space before the Defense of Carthage—specifically the Perseus Arm, and Perseus Expansion Districts.

Joe – Admiral in the ISF, commandant of the ISF academy, and husband of Tangel.

Kirkland (Praetor) – The leader of the Orion Freedom Alliance (often referred to as Orion, or by its military's name, the Orion Guard). Kirkland was the captain of the second FGT worldship, and resides on Earth in the New Sol System

Krissy Wrentham – TSF admiral responsible for internal fleets fighting against Airtha in the Transcend civil war. She is also the daughter of Finaeus Tomlinson and Lisa Wrentham.

Lisa Wrentham – Former wife of Finaeus Tomlinson, she left the Transcend for the Orion Freedom Alliance when Krissy was young. Head of a clandestine group within the OFA known as the Widows, which hunts down advanced technology and destroys it. Former Widow designation A1.

Misha – Head (and only) cook aboard *Sabrina*.

Nance – Ship's engineer aboard *Sabrina*, recently transferred back there from the ISF academy.

Priscilla – One of Bob's two avatars, currently aboard the *Perilous Dream* with Cary, Saanvi, and Faleena. Widow designation R329.

Prime – An AI who went insane due to unethical experimentation in the 32nd century, Prime was thought to have been killed at Proxima by an AI named Eric, but a backup of the unstable AI escaped.

Rachel – Captain of the *I2*. Formerly, captain of the *Enterprise*.

Saanvi – Tangel's adopted daughter, found in a derelict ship that entered the New Canaan System. Widow designation E12.

Sabrina – Ship's AI and owner of the starship *Sabrina*.

Sera – Director of the Hand and former president of the Transcend. Daughter of Airtha and Jeffrey Tomlinson.

LMC Sera (Seraphina) – A copy of Sera made by Airtha containing all of Sera's desired traits and memories. Captured by Sera and the allies during their excursion into the Large Magellanic Cloud.

Valkris Sera (Fina) – A copy of Sera made by Airtha containing all of Sera's desired traits and memories. Captured by ISF response forces who came to the aid of the TSF defenders during the siege of Valkris.

Tanis – Not to be confused with Tangel's former human identity, Tanis is the oldest of Jessica, Trevor, and Iris's AI children. She resides at Star City.

Tangel – The entity that resulted from Tanis and Angela's merger into one being. Not only is Tangel a full merger of a human and AI, but she is also an ascended being.

Terrance – Terrance Enfield was the original backer for the *Intrepid*, though once the ship jumped forward in time, he took it as an opportunity to retire. Like Jason, he was pulled into active service by Tangel when New Canaan became embroiled in the Orion War.

Tracey – Captain of the ISS *Falconer*, currently deployed to the Karaske System in Orion space with Admiral Evans aboard.

Trevor – Husband of Iris and Jessica Keller. Originally from the Virginis System, Trevor is now a commander in the ISF and serves with his wives aboard the ISS *Lantzer*.

Uriel – Leader of the Hegemony of Worlds, Uriel has turned from an elected official to a dictator who styles herself the 'hegemon'. She rules from High Terra in the Sol System.

Virgo – An AI upgraded by Myrrdan to take over the *Intrepid*, Virgo was the rogue AI responsible for much of the sabotage on the *Intrepid* that led it to the near-disaster at Estrella de la Muerte. The corrupted node Virgo inhabited was too dangerous to attempt to purge or store, so Bob and Earnest ejected it from the *Intrepid* in interstellar space.

PART 1 – HEGEMON

BRILLIANCE STATION

STELLAR DATE: 10.13.8949 (Adjusted Years)
LOCATION: Brilliance Station, Incandus
REGION: Lucent, Sirus, Hegemony of Worlds

The hegemon strode through the airlock without a modicum of concern for what awaited her on the other side of the portal.

She supposed it might be prudent to show a little caution, but that wasn't why she was at Brilliance. Displaying weakness, fear, or even a hint of deference wasn't on the agenda. Her purpose was to set things straight with Sirius's governor, and ensure that he was fully prepared to do whatever was necessary to hold back—and ultimately defeat—the Hegemony's enemies.

The war had started off well, exemplified by the Hegemony seizing control of hundreds of systems, but Terran expansion had slowed over the past few months. Part of that was due to the continued incursions by the Scipian forces on the antispinward side of Sol, which were now exacerbated by the recent attacks launched by the League of Sentients. To make matters worse, the Hydeans had joined in as well, aiding the enemy in its fight against the Trisilieds, as well as launching attacks against Hegemony-controlled systems near their borders.

A lesser person would have been worried, would have considered capitulating or suing for peace. They would have sought a treatise—perhaps one where the Hegemony retreated to its prior borders, suffering once more in the resource-starved core of human worlds.

But Uriel was not such a person. She was the sort to put all her winnings into the pot and go for double or nothing.

Chief Operating Officer Leory, the governor of the Sirius System, on the other hand, was exactly the sort of person to give up before the fight was over.

Though Uriel had destroyed the Hegemony's senate in order to keep the member systems from using votes there to disrupt her actions, system leaders such as Leory now used less direct tactics against her: backroom deals, and encrypted missives suggesting it was time to bring about Uriel's overthrow made their way between the stars.

No more, Uriel thought as she swept past the guards who had taken up positions in the corridor outside the airlock. *I'll see this system's COO lick my foot before the day's done.*

Simply removing Leory from power would not be a great difficulty for her, should she so desire it. He was easily accessible, often in public with only a small detachment of guards; she had seven spies close to him, any one of whom could do the deed.

His downfall was not really what Uriel needed. It was the Sirian fleet.

The need for Leory's cooperation was driven by the fact that the Sirians, despite their long-time membership in the Hegemony, still clung to their ancient—and rather ridiculous—form of government.

In short, they ran their system like it was a corporation. A corporation with an inordinate amount of red tape. Take out the COO, and there would follow an internal promotion review process that could take months. All company business would grind to a halt during that time, and there'd be no chance at all for Uriel to get access to the fleets.

The easiest way to gain that access was to convince the current Sirian COO that she could not only defeat their enemies, but crush them.

Only then would he put his full strength into the fight and bring his three million warships into the battle.

Once, Uriel would have thought three million ships to be a significant fleet, but it was not one that would win a war against a foe such as the Scipians. It would take more ships than that just to occupy each of the enemy's systems with a few dozen vessels. Before the war, the quintillion people of the Hegemony had boasted a much larger fleet, but the war had taken its toll.

True, their enemies had been diminished as well, but in her years of imperial expansion, Uriel had spent her ships in battles against many independent systems. That had increased her resources, but it had also worn down her strength, so that when she finally butted up against the Scipians, she was weakened while they were fresh.

Not to mention, with their core fleets boasting stasis shields, the losses incurred to win clear victories were staggering.

So now, two years into hostilities with Scipio, a three-million-ship fleet could make the difference in halting their enemy's advances, or seeing Empress Diana fly one of her gaudy flagships into the Sol System, like the triumphant victor she had no right to be.

Of course, Diana wasn't the real problem. The Scipian empress was just a herald for Field Marshal Richards. That woman was the most odious example of an over-modded abomination that Uriel had ever seen.

If only Admiral Sini had properly finished the job at Bollam's World. Then none of this would have happened.

Uriel's thoughts had distracted her, and she reached the end of the concourse without remembering traversing it. She focused on her surroundings to see that a man stood waiting. It was not Leory, something that rankled Uriel further.

"Adjunct Hurom." Her words were not spoken in greeting. "Where is your

COO?"

"He was attending to a matter down on Incandus," Hurom said, offering his hand to be clasped by hers. "He will be aboard Brilliance shortly. May I take you to his offices?"

"You may accompany me," Uriel said as she got into the dockcar that hovered behind the man. "I don't need you to take me anywhere."

Hurom coughed. "Of course, Hegemon."

Four of her guards also folded themselves into the car, and two other cars carried the rest. The Sirian was wedged between two heavily augmented soldiers, and spent the next ten minutes staring at his hands.

When the car finally arrived at the COO's offices, high on one of the station's upper spires, Uriel gave the man a sour look. "You stay here."

For a moment, it appeared as though Hurom would object, but the two guards on either side of him didn't move, and so he remained put.

Uriel stepped out onto a wide boulevard lined with trees. The entrance to Leory's offices was a lift shaft set in a small grove on the right side of the road, and she strode toward it without hesitation. Two of her guards rode up ahead, and when they gave the all-clear, she proceeded up the lift with another pair of protectors.

While waiting for the lift to reach its destination, she checked over her external security detail. A smile settled on her lips as she counted the attack craft circling the spire, keeping regular traffic and even Sirian military vessels at bay.

The doors finally opened to a space Uriel had visited several times before. A crystal sphere surrounded on all sides—excepting the lift shaft—by the vacuum of space, the COO's office drew in the light from both Incandus and Sirius, refracting it in a thousand rainbows. So far as she was concerned, the effect was obnoxious, but she didn't care, as her vision filtered it out.

Visible below were the hundreds of kilometers of Brilliance Station, one of the oldest in human space. Though the Sirians liked to tout its venerable age, the structure had been altered and rebuilt so many times that Uriel doubted a single bolt from the original Brilliance still remained—unlike the ancient structures in Sol, such as High Terra and the Cho, which were both older, and contained much more of their original composition.

Uriel drew her gaze back into the office and gave a long-suffering sigh. Because Leory was an ass, something Uriel suspected was a job requirement for any Sirian COO, there was nowhere to sit in the room, barring the executive's chair.

No way I'll stand while he sits, she thought with a laugh, and walked around his desk to settle into the soft chair before lifting her legs and crossing her ankles atop his cool, stone desk.

The lift chimed, and Leory exited mere seconds later. Uriel found herself wondering if the act of placing her feet on his desk had summoned him like a mythological demon.

"Hegemon, I'm surprised you came in person," the man said in a tone that carried no deference as he approached.

Uriel shrugged without rising. "We have the jump gates between Sol and Sirius now, it would seem a shame not to use them. Though, it almost takes more time to get through Brilliance Station than it does to travel between our star systems."

The statement was raw hyperbole, and they both knew it; she often made disparaging comments regarding Brilliance's disorganized sprawl and garish illumination.

Though Sirius's ancient, class-based system that had been known as Luminescent Society was all but gone, that didn't stop the politicians from playing at being Lumins any chance they got. As a result, they relished in and touted Brilliance's 'character' and storied past.

Uriel considered such things to be foolishness, and gladly delivered derisive comments to get under Leory's skin and keep him off balance.

"So, should I expect to find you in my chair more often, then?" he asked, appearing entirely nonplussed.

"It wouldn't hurt for you to be prepared. Maybe I'll have an airlock put in over there." She gestured to her right without looking where she was pointing. "Coming in person seems to be necessary to get your full attention."

Leory stopped half a meter from his desk and folded his arms across his chest. "You always have my full attention, Hegemon."

"I don't think that's the case. If I did, your fleets would be defending the Hegemony, not holed up here at Sirius."

The COO's expression grew stony. "The Hegemony's constitution allows for all member systems to maintain a home fleet. That is all we are doing."

"Three million ships!" Uriel exclaimed. "That's not a 'home fleet', that's an invasion force."

"We like to think of it as the New Eden defense," he replied, referencing the stubbornly still-independent system with an unapologetic shrug. "We'll make it too costly to attack Sirius, just like we have for the past six thousand years."

Uriel rolled her eyes and sat up straight, settling her feet back on the floor. "Sol has conquered Sirius more than once."

"After we conquered you. After that, the conflicts were Sirians attacking Sirians. You even use our ancient name, Hegemon."

She snorted in response. "The word 'hegemony' is far older than Sirius. Don't pretend to have invented it."

"Are we just going to trade barbs all day, Hegemon?" the COO asked in response. "This doesn't seem to be a good use of either of our time."

"You're holding the fleet in reserve because you expect us to lose." Her tone was blunt. "You're hedging your bets when the front is a hundred light years away."

"Jump gates remove that distinction. The entire Hegemony is the front—barring Sol, where you run interdictors…though you must shut them down to jump back in. How do the system operators know to do that? Or are there safe vectors?"

"Maybe if you'd shut up, you'd know."

The COO's eyes darkened, and his lips drew into a thin line, but he held his tongue.

Uriel gave a nod of satisfaction, and then launched into her explanation—which had been her intention all along.

"We've suspected for some time that our enemy has an advanced, faster than light message system. We'd heard rumors about something called FDL, which allows messages to travel through the dark layer at great speed, but our battles with the Scipians suggest that they have something even better: instantaneous communication between their ships."

"I've read the reports," Leory replied, his tone noncommittal.

"Good, then you'll not be surprised when I tell you that I can confirm our enemies possess quantum entanglement communication."

A snort slipped past the COO's lips. "It's not possible. People have been trying for seven thousand years, and it's been failure after failure."

"It *is* possible, and our allies have stolen the technology. They've replicated it and have it available for us to use."

"Allies? Do you mean Orion, or the Trissies?"

"Neither," Uriel glanced at the wall of the sphere.

Leory's gaze followed hers, and his eyes widened as he saw a luminous being hovering outside. It hung there for a moment before sliding through the crystal sphere and moving into the COO's office, a ball of light surrounded by sinuous tendrils of energy.

"Meet our new allies."

PART 2 – KARASKE

GATE WAR

STELLAR DATE: 10.13.8949 (Adjusted Years)
LOCATION: ISS *Falconer*, near Durgen Station
REGION: Karaske System, Rimward of Orion Nebula, Orion Freedom Alliance

"Tear them to shreds," Joe ordered. "Don't let those Orion bastards get to that gate segment before we do!"

"Aye, sir," Captain Tracey replied.

Joe listened as the captain doled out orders to the *Falconer*'s bridge crew, directing the weapons teams to unleash atom beams at the pair of Orion Guard cruisers that were closing on one of the jump gate segments left behind by his daughters' ship, the *Perilous Dream*.

No, the Widows' ship. My daughters are **not** *Widows.*

Joe turned his attention from that conflict to the tug that was maneuvering one of the other gate segments into the ship's aft starboard docking bay. The moment it was secure, technicians would pore over its logs, looking for the destination of his daughters' jump. The worry that they could have scrubbed its logs hung in the back of his mind, but he pushed that concern away, hoping that Cary did actually want him to follow after and that she'd left a trail of breadcrumbs.

If not her, then Faleena, Saanvi, or Priscilla. One of them would have had the forethought to leave me a clue.

The Orion fleet in the Durgen System appeared to have the same idea. That told him that at least Cary was acting in opposition to the enemy. It was a small comfort.

"Admiral!" the woman heading the scan team called out. "I have a trio of stealthed destroyers closing on Durgen."

"Good job," Joe replied as he strode toward her station. "How'd they give themselves away?"

"They didn't," the scan officer said, pulling up a holo over her station. "But there are four military shuttles headed from Durgen toward what appeared to be empty space, and I figured that was on the suspicious side. I fired off a set of drones and they were able to spot the destroyers."

Joe's lips drew into a thin line. "If they're giving away their position with such a sloppy maneuver, then those shuttles either contain important people, or important things."

"Segment secure, Admiral," Captain Tracey announced. "We've pushed those cruisers back, should we move in for the second segment?"

Joe bit back a curse as he turned toward the main holotank and surveyed the battlespace. Just over four hundred Transcend ships had jumped in from the Styx-9 base, but they were almost an AU away, engaging the fleets closing in from the outer Karaske System.

"RMs in the tubes?" he asked.

"A pair," Captain Tracey confirmed. "Kill shots on the cruisers, then?"

"Reading my mind, Captain," Joe replied. "Finish those cruisers, and let's go see who's running away from their warm beds onstation."

"Aye, sir," the ship's captain replied and turned to give fire control their orders.

Once they were selecting an optimal firing solution, she directed helm to come about and make for the three shuttles boosting away from Durgen.

Joe watched silently as the crew executed their tasks, weapons launching the relativistic missiles as the ship turned, flying over Durgen's upper reaches in pursuit of the shuttles.

"I suppose I should tell them to halt or something," he muttered.

"Only if you want to," the captain said with a sour laugh. "I'm pretty sick of Oggies, we could just blow them away."

"No," Joe drew the word out. "Even though they're only half-assing being sneaky, I still believe there are VIPs aboard."

"Got it, Admiral," Tracey said.

Something in her tone caused Joe to glance at the captain, and he saw a look of compassion in her eyes.

<Don't worry, sir. We'll find out where your daughters went.>

<Damn right we will,> he replied, watching in satisfaction as the relativistic missiles launched from their tubes and streaked toward the two cruisers, beams lancing out from the *Falconer* and breaching the enemy ships' shields moments before the missiles hit.

Twin nuclear blooms spread out around the engines of each ship, and when the plasma cleared, what remained of the cruisers was drifting away from the final jump gate segment, leaving streams of atmosphere, fuel, and debris in their wake.

"The rest of the Orion ships are falling back," Scan called out.

"I'll send the tug after that segment," Captain Tracey said, but Joe held up a hand to stop her.

"No, they could be trying to pull our attention away from these three ships. Seed another two RMs. We'll be back for the segment once we see which rats are trying to flee the sinking ship."

"Works for me, sir," Tracey replied, turning her attention back to the targeting solutions the weapons team was drawing up.

Joe followed along over the Link, watching as they picked targets on the Orion ships as well as the shuttles, opting to hit all three simultaneously.

They'd better do it fast, he thought as Tracey provided suggestions. *Those destroyers aren't going to sit there forever.*

Even as he formed the thoughts, he knew it didn't matter. The *Falconer* had stasis shields. There was nothing that the enemy could do outside of shooting their own ships.

"Solutions ready," Tracey announced. "Firing in ten, nine—"

"Ma'am!" Comm called out. "The lead shuttle is hailing us. They're surrendering."

"Huh," Joe shook his head. "Smart Oggies. That's a first."

"Patch them through," Captain Tracey directed Comm.

A moment later, a man wearing captain's bars appeared on the main holodisplay. He looked worn, tired eyes below a bloody smear across his forehead. Joe couldn't tell if it was the Orion captain's own blood or someone else's, but he didn't much care.

"We're sending you a docking vector," Joe said without preamble. "Tell your three destroyers to run back home or we'll tear them apart."

"I already have," the man said. "I'm Captain Jera, I assume you're Joseph Evans."

"Admiral Evans to the likes of you," Joe replied in a low growl, annoyed that the man wanted to play games even now.

"Of course," Jera replied, nodding quickly. "I'm surrendering to you because I've decided that my final orders were invalid. A clone of Garza told me to rescue an AI. No way in all of core-damned space I'm going to die for either of those two."

A coarse laugh broke free from Joe's lips. "Well, I can't say I agree with your logic, but I'm happy to take advantage of it. Tell me, did this Garza clone tell you where to go after you rescued the AI?"

"I wouldn't call it a rescue," Jera snorted with derision. "Animus put up quite the fight. More like an abduction."

"And your destination?" Joe pressed.

"Rega." Captain Jera's tone was defeated. "The clones and the Widows are headed to Rega."

* * * * *

Joe ran a hand through his hair as he absorbed the news that Admiral Lukas of the Transcend's 551st fleet had just related.

"*All* the gates?"

"I'm afraid so. And with the QC hub at Khardine gone, we can't reach half the places that have gates to spare. At best, we're going to be able to bring in five for our jumps out."

"OK, that's not so bad," Joe said. "Though I get the feeling that you're not going to be jumping with us to Rega."

"I can peel off forty ships." Lukas's eyes were filled with compassion, though his voice carried only a modicum of the emotion. "Orion is pressing harder on the antispinward front. Svetlana and Mardus have distracted them to some degree, but not as much as we'd hoped."

"The intel my daughters have could turn the tide against Orion," Joe pressed. "Give me a hundred, and I can secure the *Dream*, end Garza's operations, and we'll have Praetor Kirkland on the run in weeks."

"Joe..." Lukas breathed the word gently. "My orders have come directly from the Field Marshal on the *I2*. I'll give you another wing. That'll be sixty ships total, but that's all I can do, I already have the strategy for the counterattack we're mounting in Cerden, and if I give you any more than that...."

"OK," Joe nodded. "I get it. I'll talk to Tangel and see what else she can send."

The other man gave him a knowing look. "Good luck."

With the holo gone, Joe let out a shuddering sigh, pent-up emotion that he'd not acknowledged suddenly threatening to break him completely.

"What the hell is more important than finding Cary?" he asked the empty ready room in a hoarse whisper.

The easiest way to find out was to contact Tangel via the *Falconer*'s direct connection to the *I2*. But the last thing he wanted to do was burn up the blade having a prolonged conversation with his wife about their daughters.

The only thing worse would be a short conversation.

He'd already sent an update on the situation, tagged with 'I'm sorry', and that was all he was mentally capable of at the moment.

She's not vindictive, she's not rash or illogical. Tangel will understand.

Joe clung to that and the knowledge that the many decades he'd spent with his wife would bear them through this trial.

Squaring his shoulders, he turned and walked to the door and checked the bridge's OOD, finding that Captain Tracey was still conning the ship.

<Captain, the battle is won, why don't you catch some shut-eye?>

A rueful laugh came from the woman on the bridge. *<Sir, I appreciate the concern, but I've got the mods to pull sixty hours before I start to flag. Once we have confirmation from the techs that the gate was indeed jumping the* Perilous Dream *to Rega, I'll be able to relax.>*

Joe realized he was clenching his fists. *<Well, at least that'll make one of us.>*

<We've pulled data from Durgen Station on the Regulus System.> Captain Tracey's voice had taken on a note of concern.

<I've reviewed that as well,> Joe replied. *<Admiral Lukas is peeling off sixty ships to come with us.>*

<Sir...Regulus is one of Orion's largest shipbuilding and training systems. We

could be facing tens of thousands of enemy ships.>

<Or hundreds of thousands.> Joe tried to add a note of wry mirth to his voice and failed, sounding only tired instead.

<Well, we have stasis shields, and unless they shoot us straight up the ass while we're thrusting, we can weather a heavy barrage.>

Joe barked a laugh both aloud and over the link, *<Captain…that was quite the double entendre. Please tell me that was deliberate.>*

<Shit,> Tracey muttered. *<It wasn't, but I sure wish I were that clever on the fly.>*

<Well, you're going to have to be, because when we jump into Rega, we're going to have to find the Perilous Dream *in what might be the busiest system in Orion Space…and then survive long enough to reach them.>*

The *Falconer*'s captain didn't respond for several long seconds. Finally, she said, *<And then what, sir?>*

<And then we board that ship and take my daughters back.>

REGA

STELLAR DATE: 10.13.8949 (Adjusted Years)
LOCATION: ISS *Falconer*
REGION: Rega System, Quaor's Void, Orion Freedom Alliance

"Location confirmed," Scan called out a second after starlight reappeared around the ship. "This is Rega, and we're only a light second away from the *Perilous Dream*'s exit point."

Joe nodded in approval, knowing that the jump exit his daughters had programmed into the gate, and where they *actually* dropped into normal space could be two entirely different things.

Still, it was all they had to go on, and the search had to start somewhere.

An image of the Rega System was already on the main holotank, and a marker lit up at the *Falconer*'s position. All around them, icons began to appear, highlighting ships and stations, confirming the position of planets and moons, filling in what Joe had to admit was an even busier system than he'd expected.

<*Tallying ships…*> Ella announced. <*It's difficult to spot them all, there's so much engine wash and ionized plasma here.*>

"Rough guess?" Joe asked.

<*Seven million?*> the AI offered. <*Plus or minus a few hundred thousand. Once we've moved more and can triangulate, I can improve my estimate.*>

The members of the bridge crew glanced at one another, and Joe knew all too well what they were thinking.

"OK, everyone, we dropped into stealth the moment we arrived, so the number of ships here helps us—spotting any emissions we give off will almost be impossible."

<*Also, the majority of the ships in this system are civilian and construction. I count just under a million warships,*> Ella added.

"Oh, only a million," the scan officer whispered, glancing at Helm.

"Scan, deploy drones. I want as much data as we can get as fast as we can get it. We need to find the *Perilous Dream.*"

"Aye, sir." The scan officer had the good grace to look embarrassed. "We've not yet picked up any ships with her profile, but there are traces of ionized plasma that closely match her engine signature."

"Good," Joe nodded. "The moment you get a lead, let me know. We have sixty ships waiting back at Karaske that we can jump in to scout further."

Though he voiced the words with confidence, the more he watched the main holotank update, the less convinced Joe was that calling the Transcend ships in to help scout was a good plan.

The more ships they brought into Rega, the more likely they were to get spotted. He harbored no illusions that the *Falconer* could withstand a concentrated attack from even a fraction of the ships in the system.

Stasis shields or no.

"There are three options," Captain Tracey said as she approached Joe's side. "Either she's here for something, or she's jumping out."

"That's only two."

"The third is that she never jumped here to begin with."

He nodded silently, considering what that would mean.

Tracey continued a moment later. "But we have to assume that's not the case, otherwise we have no leads. Rega's clearly important, but what could Cary be doing here?"

Joe had been trying to come up with an answer to that question as well. The problem was that there were dozens of likely scenarios.

The main consideration was whether or not Cary was acting in interests aligned with her people, with Orion, or was playing some game that benefited the Widows. He only wanted to consider the first, but knew he couldn't.

Even so, the wave she'd given as her shuttle took off told him that she had a plan, that whatever crazy mission she was undertaking, it was with the intention of damaging Orion.

What could it be?

"Ella, what would you flag as the most significant installation in this system?"

<It's a bit premature to be able to gauge 'significance', especially without any clear metrics. However, if I were to use 'biggest' and 'most ships', that would be Dock 1.>

The main holodisplay updated to show a massive structure consisting of hundreds of concentric rings. It was easily a thousand kilometers across, and the notation next to it showed over eight thousand ships docked with the structure.

"Seems pretty significant to me," Captain Tracey muttered. "For a bunch of luddites, these Oggies sure can build ships fast."

"They've got the population to do it the old-fashioned way and still churn them out," Joe replied. "I'd hoped we were wearing them down more than this, though."

<Feels a lot like pissing into the wind…or I imagine it does,> Ella said.

"Yeah, that metaphor's not quite right, though I guess both are things you don't want. So, given our target of Dock 1—such an inspired name—what can we see on scan?"

<Well, the station is six light minutes from here, and based on what we know of the Perilous Dream, *they could have reached it in the time it took us to follow after.>*

As the AI spoke, a three-AU-wide sphere appeared on the holotank, showing the maximum distance the Widows' ship could have traveled. Given that the

Falconer had jumped to a position only one AU from Rega's star, that encompassed the most populous swathe of the system.

"Dock 1 is well within that range," Joe said, hand rising to his chin. "The question is why they'd have gone there to begin with."

"You know your daughters best of all, sir." Captain Tracey's voice contained a clear note of hesitation. "Do you think they are acting in the Alliance's best interests?"

He nodded in response. "That's the assumption I want to operate under until evidence comes up to the contrary."

"Understood. We should look at this from the perspective of them making a strike against the enemy."

Joe glanced at Captain Tracey and saw an expression of sincerity on her face. She wanted to believe that his girls and Priscilla were acting for the Alliance and of their own agency as much as he did.

"Right." He nodded. "So are they trying to blow Dock 1? Or would they have some other plan."

<From what I can pick up on local chatter, a lot of those ships are in for refit. They came in after one of the skirmishes on the front, and many are nearly ready to go back out.>

"Skeleton crews, then," Joe said.

Tracey cocked an eyebrow. "You think they're going to try to take them?"

"There are over a thousand Widows on the *Perilous Dream.* If Cary can control the clones as well as I think, then she could seize a fleet in short order."

"We have more ships than crews," Tracey countered. "She could have brought her Widows back to Pyra. There are still hundreds of Nietzschean vessels in orbit."

Joe nodded slowly, considering what he would do with a few hundred freshly refitted Orion vessels. "You can't sail through Orion space in a Nietzschean hull, though—not unless you want to stare down every gun-barrel in the star system."

"And if you're going to make off with a few hundred ships, people might keep an eye out for them, as well." A look of understanding came over Captain Tracey's face. "Just like word's going to spread that the *Perilous Dream*'s gone rogue."

<I have it,> Ella said a second later. *<The* Dream *is on Dock 1. Far side of an inner ring. Took me a bit to confirm it.>*

"Well then," Joe turned to the ship's captain. "We have our destination. Let's go take a look-see at what they're up to."

"We're not storming the *Dream*?" she asked.

"Maybe…I'm curious what Cary has in mind."

WHEELS WITHIN WHEELS

STELLAR DATE: 10.12.8949 (Adjusted Years)
LOCATION: ***Perilous Dream***
REGION: Karaske System, Orion Freedom Alliance

One day ago…

A1 resisted the urge to hit Garza. The man couldn't seem to grasp the fact that the AI he'd trusted with his life had betrayed him, and his inability to cope with reality had set him to repeating the same few ideas with different wording in a futile attempt to get a more satisfactory answer.

"You can't be serious," he insisted as the pair walked through the *Perilous Dream,* E12 following behind.

"Do you know me to be fond of practical jokes?" A1 asked. "Honestly, what Animus was doing was logical—for its purposes at least. Alas, those purposes ran contrary to our own."

Garza shook his head. "Well, he wouldn't have done it to me. He would have realized that I'm the original."

A1 sighed, the sibilant hiss echoing eerily in the spare corridor. "You should have trusted me. I would have provided you with properly subservient clones. Not a host of doppelgangers who believe they're the real thing."

The general snorted. "Yeah, I don't think conditioned beings like your Widows would have passed muster on the missions I sent my clones on."

"You'd be surprised," A1 said with a slow shrug. "My Widows have done chameleon infiltrations. More empires than you know have been toppled by my careful hand."

The grizzled man turned his head to regard her with both of his grey eyes. "More than I know? What have you been up to, Lisa?"

Cary only knew of one empire that Lisa Wrentham had toppled without Garza's knowledge, but it was enjoyable to toy with the man. Eventually she'd convince him that he was a clone—something that he seemed to have already forgotten from their conversation on the docks—but before that, he'd provide a brief bit of amusement.

"I keep my own counsel," she replied enigmatically. "It was long ago. What I want to focus on now, is how we take out the praetor. It's time you tell me your plan, beyond the obvious, of course."

A1 kept her eyes forward for a moment, not deigning to glance at the man next to her. A part of her mind reeled in shock at the audacity of what she was doing, while another part held a cold satisfaction that she was finally rising above the level Garza had held her at for so long.

If I hadn't rejected Finaeus, I wouldn't have had to hide here in Orion for centuries, toiling under this repressive regime's edicts.

The reflection gave A1 pause, and she resisted the urge to shake her head.

"It's as I've told you before," Garza interrupted her thoughts. "I control nearly all of the Guard's admiralty. Once I have secured Farmin and Selah, we'll be ready to move on New Sol and take the system."

"And then you become praetor."

Garza nodded. "Exactly. Then we finally do what has to be done to end this feud between Kirkland and the Tomlinsons."

"Which would be?" A1 prompted.

"You'll know when the time comes."

A1 shook her head. "Well, if you're not going to tell me, then you're not much more use than the other one. I'm starting to think that none of you know Garza's real endgame, not that it matters. I'm not going to do this his way, I was merely curious."

"What are—" Garza froze mid-word and mid-stride. He would have toppled over if E12 hadn't rushed forward to grab him.

"Stick him with the other one," she directed the Widow. "I want to be on the bridge when we jump."

"Of course, A1."

As E12 directed the Garza clone away, A1 felt a modicum of guilt for the compulsion she'd put on her sister. The woman inside the ebony armor was not a Widow, she was a young woman named Saanvi, but she should have trusted A1 to do the right thing, not work against her.

She'll understand when it's done, when no more of our people have to die in this stupid war.

Her conscience mollified, A1 continued on her way toward the bridge while ensuring the gate was ready to deploy and take them from the Karaske System.

* * * * *

Priscilla's eyes snapped open, and she felt a surge of elation.

It worked.

She checked her Link connection, ensuring that it had been keeping up appearances that she was functioning properly for the last five minutes. It wouldn't do for the others to realize she'd been temporarily offline.

When she'd crafted the updates that allowed Cary to assume complete control of the Widows, she had done so with the knowledge that she was handing a very powerful weapon to a rather unstable person.

Stars, Tangel and Joe are going to tear a strip off me for letting things get this far.

Because Cary's conditioning had affected her too deeply, and her dive into Lisa Wrentham's memories had affected her further, Priscilla had built a failsafe into her own mind, a way to reset and remove the Widow programming and conditioning, should certain alterations be attempted.

<*Took you long enough.*>

The message came from Faleena, and Priscilla glanced across the small datanode that the pair had set themselves up in once they'd captured the real Lisa Wrentham—who was still standing in a corner nearby.

<*You too?*> Priscilla asked.

<*I'm not stupid,*> the AI scoffed. <*It didn't really work properly on me, anyway. Well, it did, but I'd sandboxed the entire Widow programming setup. When A1 sent her little update, all it did was corrupt throwaway data.*>

<***Cary**, Faleena. She's not A1, she's Cary.*>

The ebony figure standing a few paces away shook her head. <*No, Priscilla. She is not. Cary is now A1, just as Lisa Wrentham became A1. Through whatever error was made in her conditioning and her own actions, she's come to think of herself as a Widow.*>

Priscilla nodded slowly. <*I get that, but I don't want* **us** *to forget who she is.*>

Faleena walked toward Priscilla and placed a hand on her shoulder. <*She's my sister. I could never forget who she is. But right now, I'm worried about my other sister. We need to find out if she put the whammy on Saanvi as well.*>

<*The whammy, is it?*>

<*Seems apt.*> Faleena shrugged. <*A1 sent the two of us orders to remain in place for the time being, which means that if we start mucking around in the ship's networks, she's going to know about it.*>

<*What* **is** *her plan?*> Priscilla resisted the urge to tear her helmet off and throw it across the room. What she really needed was to let out a good scream and vent some frustrations.

<*Well, it involves going to Rega,*> Faleena said as she turned to the console and pulled up the astrogation displays. <*That seems like an odd choice. From what we pulled out of the databases, Rega is jammed full with Orion ships. Depending on current projects, there could be millions of vessels insystem.*>

<*Maybe there's something she wants,*> Priscilla suggested. <*Though I can't imagine what it would be. From what I can see, the* Perilous Dream *is a lot more advanced than most Orion ships.*>

Faleena was silent for a moment, and then she turned to Priscilla. <*We have to assume that she's still trying to do the right thing, it's just her methods that have become…shady. If becoming A1 had caused her to side with the enemy, she wouldn't be holding two Garzas captive and running from Karaske when it came under attack.*>

<*Or keeping us alive,*> Priscilla added. <*But that's all a bit weak, she could still be working against us. The next few hours will tell the tale.*>

<*Well, she hasn't stealthed the ship,*> Faleena said. <*That's something.*>

<*Something good or bad?*> Priscilla mused as she looked down at the astrogation display. <*Wow…that's a big dock.*>

<*And we're moving toward it.*>

<*Faleena.*> Priscilla turned to face the AI. <*At some point, we're going to have to take Cary in hand and stop her from doing something truly insane. But she's ascended now…or very close to it. How are we going to stop her?*>

<*I might have an idea…like…the seed of an idea, a germ, a microbe.*> The AI sent along a nervous laugh.

<*OK, I get the picture. What is it?*>

* * * * *

"E12, I want you to personally oversee the service teams. Ensure that none of them leave the bays, and that Widows handle all materiel transport from the hand-off points."

"Yes, A1."

E12 turned on her heel and strode off the bridge toward the port-side bays where the ship would soon mate with Dock 1. She'd marveled at the size of the aptly named station, and wondered why A1 was going there. The ability to question her leader evaded E12 every time she tried, but that limitation didn't quell her curiosity.

The *Perilous Dream* wasn't so low on supplies that they *had* to restock. Much of what the ship required to function, it could produce on its own. With access to raw materials and a few exotics, it could ply the darkness for decades without need of resupply.

That led E12 to assume that the reason they were stopping at Dock 1 was something other than the stated purpose, though she knew not what that could be.

The knowledge that her sister was keeping the truth from her hurt more than the fact that she'd forced compliance—something that E12 knew she *should* be upset about, but couldn't bring herself to get worked up over.

An alert appeared on her HUD that she needed to replenish sustenance, and E12 diverted to visit an F&W facility. She hated the process for food and waste, and had been avoiding it, hoping that her time as a Widow would be done before she had to endure the ordeal again.

However, A1 appeared to be in it for the long haul, so E12 decided that she may as well get the event over with.

She entered the facility, which was a narrow space lined with narrow saddles down one side, a trio of tanks behind each. Two other Widows were present, sitting still on their perches. E12 walked past them, sitting down near the end of the room where she could keep an eye on the others.

A service door was on her left, and she checked that it was unlocked—should she need to beat a hasty retreat.

Why would I need to do that? she wondered. *I'm not in any danger here.*

She mulled the concern over, and decided that it must be because, as a

Widow, she was often sent on dangerous missions, and always needed to be alert.

Her musings were interrupted by the F&W system making its connections between her legs. The experience brought back the memory of Cary trying to get out of using the automated waste systems aboard the cruiser they had piloted during the Defense of Carthage.

In that instance, it had been she who had insisted that her sister remain in place and use the hookups.

Wait…Cary? Yes, my sister. A1, my leader.

The thoughts banged against one another in her mind, an irreconcilable quandary that she couldn't put together. She pushed them away, instead watching the readouts on her HUD shift to show the removal of waste, both biological and artificial, as well as the refilling of her food reservoirs and the recharging of her SC batteries.

Five minutes later, the process was done, and the hookups retracted, releasing E12 to carry on her way. She somehow felt cleaner, lighter, and more limber. Her mass was almost identical, though, and she wondered if the spry feeling was psychosomatic, or something programmed into the Widows to make the event more desirable.

The thoughts about the F&W system filtered out of her mind as she walked back into the passageway that led to the lift bank. She sifted through the available Widows, putting together a security team that would ensure the *Perilous Dream* remained secure.

It was surprising to her that there was no dedicated security team, but she supposed that since the vessel hadn't left the A1 system in over a century, there was little need for one. The ship was designed to be run by one person if needed be, and A1 often did just that.

In some respects, it was surprising that she'd detailed E12 to manage security, but it was also unusual to be docked at what amounted to be a non-secure facility—and one with a large civilian presence.

Why did she choose to dock?

The question flitted through E12's mind as she stepped onto the lift, but it was gone again before she could fully grasp it. In all honesty, it didn't matter. A1 had never led the Widows astray, and she wouldn't now.

R49 was waiting with a team of Widows in Bay 14 when E12 arrived. The outer doors weren't open yet, but one of the hatches had connected to Dock 1, and a group of uncertain-looking naval personnel was standing just inside.

<*Do they check out?*> E12 asked R49.

<*Everything is in order, I was just waiting for you before we opened the main doors—though I'm not sure if they'll have the courage to bring the cargo in.*> R49 added an audible laugh to her statement that carried across the deck, causing the service crew to glance their way.

E12 let out a sigh and shook her head at the men and women waiting near the hatch. *<I'll have a quick talk with them, then we'll get this process underway.>*

<Good. Do you know why we're doing resupply here, E12? A1 has not shared any details with us.>

A laugh lisped its way out of E12, and she shook her head. *<When has A1 ever given us the full picture? I trust her, though.>*

<As do I.>

She separated from R49's group and strode toward what she found herself thinking of as the 'regulars'. There was something so boring about their unevolved humanity. Barring a few small mods—such as the Link—they were largely unchanged from birth, their entire beings determined only by the randomness of their genetics, and interactions with their environments.

Such un-deterministic evolution was almost abhorrent to E12.

A small part of her cried out that Saanvi was the product of the same evolution, that before her alterations to pass as a Widow, she was very nearly a standard human as well.

She shook her head, silencing that part of her as she approached the CPO standing at the front of the group.

"You've cleared our security checks," she said without preamble. "I'm authorizing you to begin your resupply. However, no member of your team is to go further into the ship than this bay. If there is any need to do so, you must come see me, and we'll determine the best course of action."

"Err…of course," the man responded, looking E12 up and down, clearly searching for some sort of identifying marker.

"You may address me as E12," she said. "Do you possess a HUD that can flag me as such?"

The petty officer nodded. "Uh, yes…yeah, it's placed an ident tag on you."

"Good, we'll open the main doors. I'll be watching the proceedings, as will the members of my team."

The other naval personnel behind the CPO shared a few glances and shrugs.

"That'll be fine," their leader said. "We have the first batch of supplies waiting on the dock, so it will just be a matter of bringing it in on the hover pallets. However, there will be a bunch of upgraded SC batts arriving tomorrow. We'll need access for our R&R teams to install them."

"That won't be necessary." E12 held up a hand to forestall further discussion of the matter. "Our technicians are more than capable of handling an installation such as that."

"You have technicians?" one of the naval ratings asked, glancing around the bay.

E12 nodded, not wanting to bother explaining that any one of the Widows was more competent than the R&R teams on Dock 1. They did, after all, possess the skills and memories of Lisa Wrentham.

Well, I do not, Saanvi considered. *Though I can certainly still install a new SC battery.*

What she was curious about was *why* A1 needed new batteries. E12 wasn't privy to the detailed maintenance logs, but would have been surprised if the ship's batts were performing below expected levels.

E12 activated the bay doors and nodded to the team. "You may begin bringing in our supplies."

Without another word, she turned and walked away, though she continued watching the station personnel via her helmet's rear optics. After a few seconds of glancing at one another, she saw the CPO shrug and direct his people to begin their work. He then stood to the side, alternately watching the bay doors and the Widows.

The ship was berthed on Ring 7 of Dock 1, and once the doors were open wide enough to glimpse the decks beyond, E12 felt a sensation of comfort to see the bustling activity of the Orion Guard crews.

Not that seeing a hundred Oggies strolling by gave her any comfort; rather, it was the knowledge that a vibrant world beyond the *Perilous Dream*'s sterile confines still existed.

<E12,> A1's voice entered into her mind a moment later. *<I'm sending up several containers with some of our more recent nanotech research for Rega's R&D stations. Ensure that they are transferred to the correct couriers when they arrive.>*

<Of course, A1,> E12 replied. *Curiouser and curiouser.*

WAITING GAME

STELLAR DATE: 10.15.8949 (Adjusted Years)
LOCATION: ***Perilous Dream***
REGION: Rega System, Quaor's Void, Orion Freedom Alliance

A1 watched the activity in the loading bay, noting that E12 was behaving exactly as she should. Yet another pang of guilt slipped into her thoughts as she considered the ramifications of what she'd done to her sister.

She'd done her best to convince E12 that her plan was the best way forward, but her sister hadn't given her a chance to prove its efficacy—which was entirely illogical.

In just a few short days, A1 had taken Lisa Wrentham out of play, seized her ship, captured two of the Garzas, and destroyed their base of operations. She'd also taken possession of the metamind that Animus had been constructing, and was certain that her father would have finished the job on Durgen Station and captured that foul AI.

And now she was at the heart of Orion's military power, the Rega System, about to sow destruction through the enemy fleets before taking the fight to New Sol and ending the Orion War with a single, decisive blow.

Then her own people could stop dying to bring about a peace that they shouldn't have had to fight for in the first place.

"A1, I have a message from Admiral Vega," the Widow at the comm station said. "He wants to know why you're shipping fabrication machines to the cruisers on Dock 1."

A frown creased A1's brow, and she shook her head. "These Orion admirals always look a gift horse in the mouth. I'll respond directly."

"Yes, A1."

<Admiral Vega,> A1 reached out to the man in charge of the ships she was seeding her packages on. *<I understand you are not interested in the fruits of my labors.>*

<It's a pleasure to speak with you, A1.> The admiral seemed nonplussed by A1's brusque manner, his own mental voice smooth and calm. *<Many of us in the Guard had begun to wonder if you were still alive, or little more than a myth that Garza maintained to keep the expansion districts in line.>*

<I have been busy on a variety of fronts,> A1 said without a hint of rancor at the man's insinuations. *<One of which has been researching improved stealth technology. As you know from the data we managed to gather from the failed attack on New Canaan, our enemies possess impressive personal stealth systems. I have been working at replicating those abilities, and the fabrication systems I'm sending can produce new armor that possesses comparable concealment systems.>*

<*Are you serious?*> Vega blurted. <*Are you saying that we'll have the ability to infiltrate positions completely undetected?*>

<*That is exactly what I'm saying.*>

<*And this level of technology…it is sanctioned?*>

A1 had expected Vega to balk at the idea of using technology that utilized restricted advancements, as determined by the Orion Freedom Alliance's charter—but she knew he had a weakness.

<*General Garza has authorized my research in this area. He wants to be certain that we do not have another incident such as the one at Lassik.*>

A year ago, Vega had sent a team into a Transcend R&D facility a dozen light years behind the front in an attempt to disrupt enemy research on new nano-weapons. Unfortunately for his teams—and the support ships he'd sent along—the Transcend's detection systems were better than expected, and they'd spotted and eliminated his entire strike force.

Not only that, but they'd completed their development of new nanobombs that were highly effective against unshielded Orion ships.

All of which reflected poorly on Admiral Vega.

<*I see,*> came the admiral's response. <*So this is his gift to me?*>

<*You're not the only one getting them, but we're here, you're here, it seemed logical to make a direct delivery.*>

<*Very well, but transfer them quickly—my fleet is preparing to ship out,*> the admiral said, his tone sounding more like he was doing A1 a favor than the other way around. <*Tell Garza I appreciate his gift.*>

<*You'll tell me,*> A1 snapped. <*Garza had nothing to do with the creation of these stealth abilities. You'd do well to remember that the Widows are behind the majority of the general's successes—including this one.*>

A feeling of surprise at A1's vehemence filtered across the Link, but it was gone as quickly as it had come. <*Of course. Many thanks, A1.*>

The connection cut out, and the commander of the Widows leant back in her seat, surveying the members of her bridge crew. Each one was diligently attending to their tasks, each doing their part to keep the *Perilous Dream* operating at peak efficiency.

None suspecting that the Widow they believed to be their long-time leader was betraying them.

* * * * *

Priscilla scowled at the readout in front of her. "OK…that's odd."

"What is?"

The two women had breached the node's monitoring systems several hours earlier, allowing them to move freely about the node and speak aloud if they desired. Neither knew if A1 had checked in on them at all, but with each passing hour, Priscilla became more certain that Cary was going to leave them be until she'd completed whatever plan she had in mind.

A plan that was finally becoming clear.

"The stasis chambers. They're almost empty."

"Core…they are."

The two women looked at one another with wide eyes, Priscilla speaking first.

"She's sending them all out, but where?"

Faleena flicked a finger, updating one of the holodisplays. "She's shipping something out to ships in the 8912th Guard fleet…. Armor fabricators?"

"Shit," Priscilla muttered. "Widow stealth armor is as good as the ISF's now. If she gives that tech to the Guard, we're going to be up shit creek."

"So how do we stop her?" Faleena asked. "Cary could shred us molecule by molecule if she so chooses. But I still think we should give her the benefit of the doubt—that she *thinks* she's doing the right thing, at least."

"OK, then," Priscilla reached up and tapped a finger against her cheek. "We need to inspect one of these armor fabricators to see if she's doling out tech that absolutely cannot make it into general use in the Guard. If she is, we'll have to work out a way to sabotage it."

The AI snorted and shook her head. "Oh, so nothing too difficult, then."

"Hard, but not impossible." Priscilla nodded. "There are still ten of them slated to be shipped out. We just have to examine one before it leaves the *Dream*."

* * * * *

Lisa Wrentham watched the two imposters move about the small node chamber with a growing sense of urgency mixing with the rage she already felt.

She didn't remember exactly what had happened toward the end of her meeting with the four Widows who had returned from the attempted assassination of Tanis Richards, but she had a strong sensation that something had been stripped from her.

It wasn't clear if she'd lost something permanently, or if she'd only revealed secrets that never should have been shared. Either way, it was clear that she needed to break free of the bonds that had rendered her body immobile, and get to Garza.

The general had to be warned that the ISF was launching an incursion against Orion.

It had taken her some time to re-route her optical access, especially while ensuring she didn't alert the two women that she'd managed to retain a modicum of control. Though she was stymied as to how she would regain further input from her senses. Whatever means her captors had used to seize control of her had all but severed her cognitive functions from her body.

Movement in the chamber caught her attention, and she watched in surprise as the two women played rock, paper, scissors, going for best of five. She groaned at the thought of being bested by enemies who made decisions based on such random criteria. A few seconds later, a winner was chosen, and one of the two false Widows moved toward the chamber's exit, placing her helmet back on before moving into the passage beyond.

Well now, just one? Those odds are much more favorable....

A SWITCH

STELLAR DATE: 10.15.8949 (Adjusted Years)
LOCATION: ***Perilous Dream***
REGION: Rega System, Quaor's Void, Orion Freedom Alliance

Priscilla strode down the passageway as though she had every reason to be there. Technically she didn't—A1's orders were still for her to remain in the node chamber—but she'd received several notices to go to an F&W facility, which she logged as her reason for leaving the node chamber.

Her HUD's overlay directed her to the nearest chamber, which she entered, glad to see it was empty. Settling down on one of the saddles, Priscilla resisted the urge to chuckle at how similar the scenario was to when she functioned as Bob's avatar.

Though when ensconced in the *I2*'s bridge foyer, her physical body barely rated notice.

As the F&W system did its work, Priscilla fed a stream of nano into the saddle's control systems and initiated a breach. The facility wasn't subject to high levels of security, so it was the work of only moments to log a system failure and take the chamber off the active list.

Priscilla then altered the repair priority, setting it to the lowest possible value. Once that was done, she rose from the saddle and activated her stealth systems.

<I'm moving out incognito,> she sent to Faleena through the compromised systems. *<I'll keep you updated where I can.>*

<Good luck.>

She was surprised to hear the AI invoke luck, and wondered if Faleena had adopted the colloquialism from her sisters, or if she actually believed it.

I suppose, given the fact that she's Tangel's daughter, she might actually have demonstrable luck.

Priscilla shook her head, wondering if perhaps she should have insisted the AI leave the node instead.

No, if I get captured, I want the lucky one to rescue me.

With that thought in mind, she worked her way through the *Perilous Dream* to one of the mission prep rooms, where two of the armor fabricators slated to be delivered to one of Admiral Vega's ships were still present.

A pair of Widows was working to disconnect one of the fabricators, while the other was being loaded by a Widow operating a pair of cargo lifters into a crate with one side removed. None of the ebony figures were speaking aloud, and Priscilla doubted they were doing so over the Link, either.

She crept toward the fabricator being loaded into the crate and flicked a passel of nano at its control panel. Just as she flung the infiltration bots, the lifters slipped, and the fabricator shifted to the left, causing her nano to miss. She prepared another passel, but the fabricator repositioned and blocked the access panel.

Damn, nothing for it, then.

She'd noticed that the crate was much larger than the fabricator it contained. Not excessively so, but enough for her to fit alongside the device.

Carefully easing around the lifter, she stepped into the crate. When the armor fabricator settled next to her, she reached out and dropped her breach nano directly on the control panel.

The tiny bots very quickly determined that the device was entirely offline, and Priscilla realized that it would take more than just a few minutes to access its systems and determine if Cary was indeed handing over the tech wholesale, or if she'd done something to diminish its effectiveness.

I suppose I'll just have to go for a little ride.

She leant back against the crate's side as the lifters latched down the fabricator, taking care to avoid their actions. Once they were done securing the cargo, the Widows stepped back, but didn't seal up the container. Priscilla was glad for the time, and waited patiently until a minute later, when two Widows strode into the prep room and stepped into the container.

She had to quickly move out of the way as the other Widows took up positions behind the device.

A trojan horse, then, is it?

It explained why the stasis chambers were being emptied out, and gave Priscilla hope for Cary's rationale behind disseminating the tech. She was infiltrating the Orion Guard ships.

The knowledge made her all but certain that the fabricators would be rendered ineffective somehow. Not that she planned to return to Faleena with nothing more than hope.

Once the pair of Widows had taken up their places behind the fabricator, the lifters sealed up the crate, and Priscilla felt it rise on the hoverpallet. She considered sending a message to Faleena, but with the other Widows nearby, she didn't want to jeopardize her stealth.

There was no other option, she'd have to ride it out and get back to the *Dream* once she'd finished her assessment.

* * * * *

E12 watched the latest batch of fabricator-containing crates drift into the bay under the watchful eyes of their Widow escorts. She approached each one in turn, examining them carefully and scanning the contents to ensure that the Widows within were undetectable—something A1 had tasked her with after she'd noticed that the weight of the first crate to come through was off.

Now she checked each one, the weight of the Widows logged as part of the crate's mass.

The first three checked out, and she sent them on their way, but the fourth weighed too much. Exactly one Widow's worth too much.

She queried the data A1 had provided on the containers and their destinations, confirming that all were to have just two Widows within.

"Take it into the next bay," she directed the Widow who had escorted it.

The black figure gave a brief nod, and the container moved out, leaving a perplexed station courier team behind.

"I just need to verify the contents, and I don't want it to obstruct the loading process if something is amiss," she said, gesturing at the resupply cargo being moved into the bay.

"Of course," the courier said, and stepped back to the bay's entrance, seemingly glad to have the excuse to put as much room between himself and the *Perilous Dream*'s crew as possible.

E12 followed the suspect crate into the adjacent bay and prepared a nanocloud. The moment the side folded down, she flung out the cloud, noting that it settled on three distinct figures behind the fabricator. Two were supposed to be there; she addressed the one who was not.

"R329," E12 cocked her head. "Why are you not at your designated location with F11? You realize I'll have to contact A1 about this."

The stowaway Widow attempted to move, but E12 held up a hand, and the nanocloud sparked around her. "We can see you, R329. Any further attempts to escape, and we *will* take you offline."

"Shit," the other Widow muttered as she materialized. <*They found me!*> Priscilla sent to Faleena. <*Hide!*> Aloud, she said, "Saanvi, don't do this, we have to figure out what Cary is doing and stop her."

"Why?" E12 asked, shrugging. "I've already figured out what A1 plans to do."

"Which is?" R329 took a step forward, halting as the other Widows raised their weapons.

"Simple," E12 said. "She's going to end this war."

* * * * *

A1 watched with a growing sense of internal conflict as Faleena worked to evade the teams of Widows who were scouring the ship in search of her after the discovery of R329.

Faleena had escaped the node, leaving behind Lisa Wrentham—who A1 had quickly retagged as U71 and sent to a stasis chamber pending mental evaluation. Twice Faleena had been spotted, but both times, she'd evaded capture, seriously injuring several Widows in the process.

A1's clones were not without feeling, and the teams in pursuit were showing signs of anger and a desire for retribution against their aggressor.

<Remain calm,> A1 advised O21, who led the pursuit. *<I need F11 alive. I need to understand why she and R329 are working against us.>*

<Of course, A1. We will see the task done with efficacy.>

A feeling of dubious reassurance settled over A1. She knew that her control of the Widows was absolute, and even though she appeared to be operating in opposition to Orion, they would still follow her orders.

It was easy for them to do so when those orders treated outsiders as enemies, but hunting a fellow Widow was causing some cognitive dissonance for her simulacra. She considered telling them that F11 was a spy, but then worried that their measure of care in taking her safely would diminish.

That wasn't helped by the fact that F11 wasn't taking any care herself.

A brief flurry of shots lit up the ship's internal sensors, and A1 saw two more of her Widows go down. She was considering changing her orders—allowing the pursuers to use lethal force—when O21 got off a lucky shot and tore a chunk out of F11's leg, dropping the fugitive to the deck near one of the port-side bays.

<Put her in stasis, immediately,> A1 ordered, knowing that if her Widows performed any medical intervention, they'd quickly discover that F11 was an AI housed in a biological body.

<As you wish, A1,> O21 replied.

Watching to ensure that her Widows did as they were told, A1 turned her attention to the team that was taking U71, the real Lisa Wrentham, to a stasis chamber. Her mind was torn as to whether or not she should let the Widows' progenitor live.

It was very likely that she'd not plumbed the depths of Lisa's mind, but at the same time, leaving her alive on the ship presented a serious risk.

I'll have another session with her once we depart Dock 1, and then remove the variable.

Her query as to the status of the ship's former commander was met with no response, and A1 pulled up visual feeds from the stasis chamber. Within, she saw that the two Widows who had been escorting 'U71' were laying prone on the deck. There was no sign of their quarry.

Shit!

A1 knew that if Lisa was loose on the *Perilous Dream,* the woman would be impossibly hard to catch. She knew more about the vessel than anyone, and it would only be a matter of time before she confronted the new leader of the Widows, outing her to the others.

Stars, I need my sisters and R329 to be on my side. I can't do this alone, not with all these enemies surrounding me.

She reached out to F11, who was laying prone and under guard as a stasis pod was brought to her.

<Please stop fighting me. I need your help. Lisa Wrentham has escaped.>

No response came from the woman, and A1 pushed harder, reaching past the standard Link interface into her sister's mind.

What she found was something familiar, but not at all expected.

<Lisa?>

<I'll break free, it's only a matter of time,> the former A1 hissed.

A1 shut down the Link and ordered O21 to hurry and get the wounded woman into stasis, carefully watching to make sure that Lisa wasn't able to give any sign that she was the Widow's progenitor.

<E12, I need you to personally inspect the Widow with F11's ident.>

<With her ident?> E12 queried. *<What does that mean?>*

<F11 switched idents with U71—which means that the Widow O21's team just shot is Lisa Wrentham. Make sure no one finds out who she really is. And if they do…>

<I understand,> came E12's reply.

<I'm going to go speak with R329 personally. I need to know if she has any idea where F11 went.>

<Do you think she'll tell you?> E12 asked. *<She's a very stubborn person.>*

A tendril of light slipped out of A1's hand for a moment as she considered her options. *<I think I might be able to learn what I need to know.>*

NON-ISSUE

STELLAR DATE: 10.16.8949 (Adjusted Years)
LOCATION: ISS *Falconer*
REGION: Rega System, Quaor's Void, Orion Freedom Alliance

Joe hunched forward in the captain's chair as he watched the traffic coming to and from Dock 1.

The *Falconer* sat in a pocket a thousand kilometers above the station's central axis with little traffic. They'd lain in wait there for the past day, watching the goings on below, planning—and discarding—a variety of infiltration operations.

Despite how badly he wanted to go in and get his daughters, there was no plan that didn't result in a significant number of dead Marines, and he wasn't going to trade another parent's children for his own, no matter how badly he wanted them safe.

Safe…now ***that's*** *a fallacy if ever there was one.*

The thought settled him deeper into a foul mood, and he shook his head and sat up straight. The bridge crew aboard the *Falconer* was smart and would pick up on his angst. He needed them to be at their best, which meant not souring them with his mental state.

"Sir." The woman on comms glanced over her shoulder. "I've got increased traffic on the channels the tugs are using. I think they're getting ready to move a lot of ships off Dock 1."

"Does it look like a particular fleet group?" Joe asked, tapping into the signals and tasking an NSAI with searching for patterns.

"Ships in the Oggies' 8912th have been battening down the hatches for the past day," Scan chimed in. "They'd be my pick."

Joe nodded as he looked over the data the NSAI had brought up. "I agree with that assessment. How many ships have we tagged in that fleet?"

"Seven hundred we're certain of, another two hundred possible. Hard to tell from the chatter we can intercept," Comm reported.

"That's a healthy percentage of the ships at dock," he replied. "Given how many are deep in refit, it brings them down to just a few thousand ships here."

A snort came from behind Joe, and he glanced over his shoulder to see Captain Tracey approaching.

"I can remember when we used to worry about a few dozen Sirian cruisers coming at us back at The Kap."

Joe nodded emphatically as he rose. "I wouldn't trade stasis shields for anything, but sometimes I really miss those days."

"I think we all do," Tracey replied. "I sometimes wish we'd never left

Kapteyn's Star."

"But then who'd save the galaxy?" Joe asked, laughing as he walked to the main holotank.

"Tangel, of course," the captain replied as she followed along. "She just would have done it at the outset of the FTL wars."

<*Don't lose yourself in what-ifs,*> Ella interjected.

"I won't," Joe replied. "The only 'what if' I care about right now is what we do if the *Perilous Dream* leaves with that fleet."

<*I vote that we follow it,*> the AI said. <*I still say that this system is far too hot to engage under any conditions.*>

"There are a few conditions," Joe corrected. "If the *Perilous Dream* comes under fire, we defend that ship."

<*Of course, we—wait, that's odd.*> Ella paused, and Joe resisted the urge to press her for details.

Captain Tracey wasn't so patient.

"What is it, Ella?"

<*Sorry, I was verifying. I picked up a message on one of the tug comm channels. It was broken up, but I've stitched together a coded message for a connection point on Dock 1's general network.*>

"Coded how?" Joe asked.

<*Using the latest TSF verbal message cues,*> Ella said. <*I don't know if it's for us or not, though. It's entirely possible that there are TSF ops running here at Rega.*>

"Can't hurt to tap in," Tracey said. "We dropped the relays, we're buffered from backtrace."

Joe nodded. "Let's see who's out there. At the least, it could give us options."

<*Tapping in and sending the coded response. If it's authenticated, we can open an audible channel.*>

Joe drew in a slow breath, glancing at Captain Tracey, who was doing the same. She met his gaze and gave a half smile.

<*Authenticated. It's Faleena, sir!*>

"Shit!" he blurted out before accessing the datastream. <*Faleena! Are you OK, where are you?*>

<*Dad, stars it's good to hear your mind. I'm alright, and I'm on Dock 1, though I'm trying to get back aboard the* Dream.>

<*Back aboard? Are your sisters and Priscilla trapped there?*>

<*I had to get clear of the ship, they were running a very thorough sweep. Priscilla is in stasis, but Saanvi is under A1's thrall.*>

<*A1?*> Joe choked out the word. <*Do you mean Cary?*>

<*I do. It's gotten worse…. She used an update we'd made to ensure compliance with the Widows against us. She's really far gone, I'm not sure what to do…*>

It was surprising to hear the fear and worry in Faleena's voice. Like his other two daughters, she always tackled problems head-on, ready with a host of plans to get the job done.

<Do you think you can do more good on the ship than off?> Joe asked.

<That was my thought, but I wanted to check in with you first. Priscilla and I both believe that Cary is not acting against the ISF's interests, but I don't know what her exact goal is, or what she's willing to sacrifice to achieve it. One thing I do know, however, is that she has sent most of the Widows off the ship, along with fabricators to make stealth armor.>

<How many are we talking about?> Joe asked.

<Over a thousand. A lot of them snuck into containers to ship along with the fabricators. I followed another team that got onto a shuttle heading to a cruiser. From what I can tell, they all went onto ships in the 8912th.>

All eyes on the bridge shifted to Joe, and he considered the possible implications of Cary's actions.

<She's going to try to take those ships,> he surmised. *<Build her own fleet controlled by the Widows.>*

<That was something I was considering,> Faleena said. *<Cary must have given them something that will allow them to take control of the ships.>*

<Where do you think she'll go once she has them?> Joe already knew the answer, but was afraid to voice it himself.

<I can't think of anywhere other than New Sol.> His daughter said the words he didn't want to think. *<She's already taken out Lisa Wrentham, and severely disrupted Garza's operations—>*

<We finished that job,> he interjected. *<We got Animus, and a TSF fleet crushed Orion at Karaske. If any clones are left, I doubt they'll set up shop there again.>*

<There should be six more,> Faleena said. *<But we got the impression some had already gone rogue.>*

<Not important anymore,> Joe said. *<What* **is** *important is that the next target up the chain is Kirkland. She's clearly going to make a play for the praetor.>*

<There are dozens of other military targets she could hit first, but I'm inclined to agree that he's her ultimate goal. So what do I do?>

The next words turned out to be some of the hardest Joe had ever said.

<I need you to get back on that ship and be ready to help your sister when the time comes.>

<I was afraid you'd say that.>

There was a tremor in Faleena's mental tone, and for a moment, Joe's resolve wavered. He was about to change his order, when she replied.

<I got it, Dad. Don't worry, I'll keep her safe.>

<From herself.>

<Especially that.>

* * * * *

<We've scoured the ship, A1. Either her stealth tech is better than what you shared, or she's no longer aboard.>

A1's lips pulled into a thin line as she considered O21's words. She didn't know what F11 planned, but if she was off the ship, at least her sister wouldn't be an immediate threat.

At worst, she'd get caught somewhere on Dock 1, then hopefully she'd get away and return to their father.

I'm not evil, she consoled herself. *I just have to do this, and I can't have people working against me. Not even my sisters or Priscilla.*

She sent an acknowledgment to O21, and ordered the Widows to finish the resupply and prepare to leave Dock 1. E12 was back in the loading bay, watching over the proceedings, and responded that they'd have the cargo secure in twenty minutes.

<Good. We'll be undocking in thirty,> A1 informed her.

<We'll be ready.>

The final tasks involved in departing consumed more of her time than she would have preferred; one of those was a prolonged discussion with Admiral Vega about how best to use the stealth capabilities she'd granted him. Not that she expected it to do the Orion Guard much good. The armor would all broadcast an IFF signal that would betray them to Allied forces, and not only that, but the fabricators would explode in a week—a failsafe to ensure that any ships her Widows did not take would be destroyed.

From this point on, every action was all or nothing.

Scan continued to update, showing the ships in the 8912th as they departed Dock 1 and began to form up in wings before moving toward the array of jump gates on the far side of the planet the station orbited.

The gaseous cloudtops a hundred thousand kilometers below moved through the steps of their intricate dance, unconcerned with the machinations of the humans above. A1 considered that the planets and the stars would see both the coming and the passage of humanity, that they would spin around one another and around the galaxy long after the last vestige of sentient life passed away.

Or perhaps not. Maybe we're building something that will last forever.

A1 wasn't sure why the melancholy thoughts had taken hold in her mind, but she pushed them aside as the *Perilous Dream* was cleared to disembark from Dock 1.

The bridge crew announced their board statuses in turn, and when all declared their systems in readiness, A1 triggered the release of the docking clamps, and received confirmation from the station that they had done the same.

"Tugs have grapple," Comm announced.

"Moving us out in the pocket," Helm added.

A1 nodded her acknowledgement, glad that the bridge crew didn't have to turn to see her—a benefit of the surround vision their helmets gave them.

She wondered why ships positioned key personnel in such a fashion that they had to turn to see the captain. A circular bridge where the crew all faced one another struck her as a better design.

Something to test when this is over.

The *Dream* continued to ease away from the station, and when they were two thousand kilometers away, the tugs released grapple and wished the ship a safe journey.

A1 sent a query back to Dock 1 as to a few administrative issues, a mask for the message she had for the team of Widows still on the station.

<Engage.>

<Acknowledged.>

There were still almost nine thousand ships on Dock 1. It was A1's intention that none of them rejoin the fight.

Helm brought the ship into a parabolic orbit that would see them pass around the planet once before approaching the gate array on the correct trajectory for their jump.

<You following me, A1?> Admiral Vega sent the message without greeting. *<I'm jumping out to the front, if you want to come and get your hands dirty.>*

<I know where you're going,> A1 replied. *<And I've no plans to follow you once we get to the gates. I have my own orders and destination.>*

<Pulling strings behind the scenes, I imagine.>

A1 let out a low groan before responding. *<I can take back the armor fabricators, you know.>*

<Relax, Mother Widow, I was just teasing you.>

She didn't dignify the statement with a response, and instead closed the channel. Orion seemed to have an overabundance of people who willfully used their position or station to belittle others.

You'll get your comeuppance.

She clenched her jaw, eager with anticipation for what her teams had planned.

FLED

STELLAR DATE: 10.16.8949 (Adjusted Years)
LOCATION: ISS *Falconer*
REGION: Rega System, Quaor's Void, Orion Freedom Alliance

"Keep us within ten thousand klicks," Joe instructed. "I want to be in range to fire on the *Dream*, or any aggressors."

"Aye, sir," Helm responded, and the admiral looked to the scan officer.

"Anything untoward?" he asked.

The woman leading the scan team shook her head. "None of the ships have shields raised any higher than is normal for insystem travel. Just blocking stray rads and dust—same as usual around here, from the looks of it."

Joe had noticed that as well. The gas giant Dock 1 orbited functioned like a massive garbage scow in the Rega System, sucking up whatever flotsam and jetsam it encountered and pulling it into loose, slowly decaying orbits.

Normally, a massive station like Dock 1 wouldn't be found so deep in a gas giant's gravity well, but Rega was a tempestuous star, and the planet's van allen belts protected the stations and gates from the worst of its flares and CMEs.

The stellar soup they were flying through tested the limits of the *Falconer*'s stealth systems, but what they lost in effective stealth was compensated by the sheer volume of space traffic, which made tracking even visual objects problematic.

Silence fell over the bridge crew as they matched the *Dream*'s boost out toward the gate. The maneuver required little thrust from both ships, and Joe wondered if Cary had somehow picked it to allow for him to follow if he were present.

That didn't match what Faleena had suggested about her state of mind, but he was always prepared to give his daughter the benefit of the doubt.

Even though that's led me here.

He'd provided Tangel an update upon entering the system, and again when they began to move. She had told him she loved him, was glad that he'd made contact with Faleena, and suggested that he let Cary press forward.

That had surprised Joe tremendously. He'd expected her to either tell him to bring their daughters home, or come to Rega to do it herself.

The last thing he'd expected was for her to jump out to Star City with Jessica and Trevor, but that's what his wife had decided to do.

'I'm hopeful we can find a solution there,' she'd said.

Star City was the product of one of the most advanced human civilizations yet to ply the black. At its peak, their technology had rivaled the ISF's.

But now it was a near-vacant shell protecting the remaining few million

Dreamers, the last of that culture to ascend into whatever realms pure-humans attained when they passed beyond their corporeal dimensions.

He supposed that was what would ultimately happen to Cary. She would ascend, and possibly before long. There was less holding her to the world than Tangel; his wife didn't have a complex three-being brain to recreate in higher dimensions.

He worried that Cary might leave once she was done with whatever she had in mind. A small part of him wondered if that would be better. He was certain that the daughter he had raised wouldn't return to him. Cary would never be the same.

"Sir!" Scan called out. "Four ships just jumped in, three light seconds from Dock 1. Their idents match vessels that fled Durgen Station in the Karaske System."

"Aw shit," Joe muttered. "This is going to turn sideways fast. Get us in close to the *Dream*. We're going to need to be her shield."

"Yes, Admiral," Helm said, and Joe glanced at Captain Tracey.

"Sorry about that, Captain. Heat of the moment, and all that."

The woman gave a rueful laugh. "I'll cut you some slack, sir. Not as though you've ordered anything I wouldn't have."

The *Falconer* closed with the *Perilous Dream* as the Widows' ship completed its transfer orbit and closed with the gate array.

Ahead, the ships of the 8912th were beginning to jump out, heading to the antispinward front, where they'd do battle with the same ships that Admiral Lukas had brought to the Karaske system.

There were still two hundred of them waiting to jump, easily enough to destroy the *Dream* before it made the gates.

"Helm, get us in front of the *Perilous Dream*," Captain Tracey ordered. "If Cary's ship is going to take fire, it's going to be from that departing fleet."

"Their flag is still here," Joe noted. "Weapons, get targeting solutions on that ship. If we damage it, the enemy fleet will reorganize to protect it, and that should give the *Dream* a straight shot for one of the trailing gates."

The bridge crew set to their tasks, and Joe reconfigured the holotank to a battlespace view, tracking potential lines of fire and running damage estimates for the ship his daughters and Priscilla were aboard.

"The Karaske ships are broadcasting," Comm announced. "They're saying that the *Perilous Dream* aided a TSF strike force."

"Not too far from the truth," Tracey said, giving Joe a sidelong glance. "Their ship is still ten minutes from their gate. Even if Cary has a way to force it to activate, I don't see how she'll make it in time."

He nodded, hand on his chin while he considered the options. "We need a preemptive strike. Take the attention away from them."

"And then what about us?" the captain asked. "We're going to have to run one hell of a gauntlet to get out of this system if we give ourselves away."

"We still have twenty-four pico missiles." Joe fixed the captain with a level stare. "Fire six of them in stealth at the furthest gates."

The captain's face paled. "The gates are active, that could cause antimatter containment failure."

"Right." Joe nodded. "And that'll distract our Orion friends a little bit. Seed two more near their flagship."

His tone brooked no argument, and the *Falconer*'s captain gave a curt nod and turned to her bridge crew, issuing orders to the weapons team.

"Incoming!" Scan called out before the pico-bearing missiles had been fired.

Joe sucked in a breath as beams streaked out from a dozen ships in the 8912th, playing across the *Perilous Dream*'s shields. Given the firepower the enemy could hit the Widows' ship with, it was clearly a warning shot across the bow.

The response from the *Dream* was unexpected, however. The ship simply disappeared.

"It's got good stealth," the scan officer muttered. "Oh, got a ping! Hooray for Faleena."

The holotank updated, showing the *Dream* moving onto a new vector, angling for the jump gate the Orion fleet's flagship was lined up with. The gate was active, and if Cary's ship made it first, it could jump out.

"Missiles away," Captain Tracey called out. "Five minutes out."

Joe wished that they could speed things up, but if the pico missiles boosted too hard, they'd be clearly visible.

The ships in the 8912th were all braking, slowing and turning away from the gates, moving into a half-sphere that began to creep toward where the *Perilous Dream* had been a minute earlier.

Probing shots lanced out from the Orion craft, and one hit the *Falconer*, splashing against the conventional shields. Luckily, the ISF ship was much smaller than the Widows' vessel, and the next two shots missed.

A number of breaths released across the bridge when the ship moved far enough away from the original impact that the seeking beams missed them entirely.

"That was too close," Tracey muttered.

"When the *Dream* jumps, we go through right on their tail," Joe instructed. "We'll have their vector, we'll know where they intend to come out."

More shots lanced out from the Orion ships, and Joe pursed his lips as one struck the *Dream*, highlighting the ship for the enemy to target. More beams streaked out, the relativistic particles joined by missiles that corkscrewed their way to the black ship.

Tracey directed her crew to intercept, and three of the missiles slammed into the *Falconer*'s stasis shields—which had activated for a second before the ship returned to stealth.

<*They still think it's just one ship here,*> Ella said. <*They're trying to coordinate scan with the gates and monitoring satellites, but their data is conflicting.*>

"That us?" Joe asked.

<*No, Cary must be doing it.*>

"Impact in thirty!" Weapons announced, a countdown appearing on the main holo.

Then, just as the counter reached fifteen seconds, a wave of EM radiation washed over the ship.

"What the hell?" Joe swore, looking for the source of the pulse.

"It's Dock 1," the woman on comm said in a breathless voice. "It just went up."

"Went up?" Tracey asked, her voice cracking.

In response, Scan changed the forward holo to show a view broadcasting from a nearby surveillance satellite. Dock 1's central spire was gone, and its inner rings were broken to pieces, careening through the remainder of the docking structures, tearing them to pieces. The bridge crew was still watching in awe, mouths agape, when the six picobombs hit, and six gates began to disintegrate.

The furthest one went first, breaking into five pieces. Somehow, the exotic energy in the center held in place for a few seconds before it suddenly exploded, a ball of plasma and high-energy photons sweeping out and engulfing two Orion cruisers.

"She had to have done that." Joe shook his head, unable to reconcile his little girl, the one he'd taken for walks and taught how to cinch a saddle, destroying a station with millions of civilians aboard.

"Maybe it was an accident," Tracey said. "Maybe the Widows did something they weren't supposed to."

A second gate exploded, and the Orion fleet began to scatter. The *Falconer* stayed close to the *Dream,* slipping behind to remain between the enemy flagship and their charge.

After almost a minute of inaction, Admiral Vega's ship turned to align its main railguns with the Widows' ship.

"Ready on the stasis shields," Tracey advised. "When that thing fires, we'll have only a second."

<*We've got this,*> Ella said.

The dreadnaught that was the 8912th's flag fired a trio of one-ton slugs. The *Dream*'s shields could have taken the barrage, but the kinetic energy would have knocked the ship off course and delayed its entry into the jump gate.

Instead, the blasts hit the *Falconer*'s stasis shield, brilliant flares of light heralding the destruction of matter. Scan blanked out for several seconds, and when it came back up, the *Dream* was gone.

"They jumped!" Comm announced. "Caught mention on the Oggies' network."

"Get after them," Tracey ordered. "We need to follow on the same vector."

"Aye, ma'am," Helm responded, and the *Falconer* surged forward, closing the final five thousand kilometers to the gate in a matter of seconds.

Beams from the enemy ships played across the *Falconer*'s shields, but the stasis field blocked them with ease. Joe focused on the gate and hoped the destination wasn't even more dangerous than where they were fleeing.

As that thought formed, the stars winked out, but only for a second. When they came back, he glanced at scan, waiting for an update.

"We're…nowhere," the woman said. "We've dumped out into interstellar space a dozen light years from Rega."

"And the *Perilous Dream?*" Captain Tracey pressed.

"Nowhere that I can see, ma'am. I don't think she's here."

* * * * *

"Anything?" A1 asked as she surveyed the system the *Perilous Dream* had jumped into.

"No, A1. There is no evidence that the ISF ship in pursuit was able to follow," the Widow operating scan reported. "So far as I can tell, your plan worked. The gate will have terminated the field almost immediately, meaning they only made it a few light years."

"Excellent," the Widows' leader replied. "Then we can proceed with the plan unimpeded."

She provided a destination and preferred vector to helm, then leant back in her seat, reveling in the deep connection to the ship almost as much as the plan she had set in motion.

PART 3 – STAR CITY

STAR CITY EXPRESS REDUX

STELLAR DATE: 10.15.8949 (Adjusted Years)
LOCATION: ISS *I2*
REGION: Interstellar Space, Inner Praesepe Empire

"Everyone good to go?" Tangel asked as the final members of the command team approached the bridge's central holotank.

Jessica swept her gaze across the group. "I'm just putting it out there, but it's alright if you're nervous."

<Who's nervous?> Bob asked. *<I'm looking forward to running into some core AIs. It'll be like old times.>*

"Is there a reason why all AIs seem to be sarcastic?" Trevor asked from where he stood next to Jessica.

<It's a coping mechanism,> the ship's AI replied. *<Plus, I keep being told I need to practice, so I'm practicing.>*

"It's almost like you have Angela in your parentage," Tangel retorted, casting a quelling look at the nearest optical pickup before turning to Rachel. "Ship's status?"

"Green across the board, ma'am," the ship's captain replied. "First fleet is aboard and buttoned up."

"I bet Terrance and Earnest are not happy to be left behind," Sera commented. "Finally getting to see Star City is, like, the ultimate dream for those two."

Trevor shook his head and gave a wistful sigh. "You can say that again. It's beyond astounding."

"Rub it in," Rachel muttered.

<I have several full-sensory recordings of it,> Bob said. *<I can supply—>*

"Not the same," Trevor held up a hand to forestall the AI. "Few will ever be able to say that they were there for the 'Defense of Star City'."

"Oh stars," Jessica groaned. "We fought off a few ships' worth of Oggies while our kids fired neutronium at the enemy fleet. We barely got to see the good stuff."

"I think we'll have plenty of chances to 'see the good stuff'," Tangel said.

"Promises, promises."

"I have word from Gate Control," Rachel spoke up a second later. "We're cleared for approach."

"Once more into the breach," Jessica whispered.

<*You're so melodramatic,*> Iris said, the AI's bubbling laugh echoing in her mind.

Jessica glanced back to see her silver-skinned doppelganger saunter onto the bridge.

"Nice of you to join us, Iris."

Iris shrugged as she reached Jessica's side. "What's the rush? This is just our first jump on the road to Star City."

"Not a rush, per se." Jessica shrugged. "Just figured you'd want to be here in case something went wrong."

"Wrong?" Iris glanced at Trevor. "She nervous or something?"

"Well, last time we tried to get to Star City, she had to duel an ascended AI, and then use weaponized Exdali that we couldn't put back. Oh, and we almost destroyed Pyra. That was a bit nerve-wracking for all of us."

"You can say that again," Jessica muttered.

<*Well, unless the core AIs have managed to blockade the entire galaxy, the they won't be able to stop us this time,*> Bob interjected.

"There'll be no one to stop us this time!" Trevor intoned.

<*Pardon?*>

Iris barked a laugh. "It's from an old movie we watched back on *Sabrina*." She glanced at Trevor. "Easy now, Darth."

The hulking man held up two fingers and brandished them at Iris. "I find your lack of faith disturbing."

The AI squared her shoulders. "Your sorcerer's ways don't frighten me."

"OK, kids," Jessica muttered, shaking her head. "Let's focus here. This is a serious jump."

"T-minus thirty seconds," Helm interjected, nodding at the countdown on the forward display.

Tangel smiled at the group, glad to have them with her as they sailed into whatever it was they were going to face. At the very least, she'd get to see Jessica's eyes bug out of her head after they made the first jump.

"Thank you, Ensign," Rachel replied, and the group turned their attention to the gate that was growing ever-larger in the forward display.

No one spoke over the next half minute, other than Helm announcing "Jumping" a second before the *I2*'s mirror touched the roiling ball of not-space in the center of the mirror.

The silence stretched on as space disappeared and the display showed only darkness, save for a countdown that stretched on for almost twenty seconds before stars suddenly snapped back into place.

<*Welcome to the Large Magellanic Cloud,*> Bob announced.

Tangel released the breath she'd been holding in, glad she could dismiss the worry that the core AIs would have blocked this route as well.

"Stars..." Jessica whispered. "Nice to jump and end up where we're supposed to."

"Technically, we did that when we jumped back to Pyra," Trevor said, and Jessica rolled her eyes.

"We're right in the pocket," Rachel announced. "Looking at a two-hour flight to the gate array."

"Very good," Tangel said as she swiped her hand through the air to shift the main holodisplay to show the Milky Way. "There you have it, folks."

Jessica cocked her head to the side. "Huh...does kinda look like a spaghetti bowl at this angle."

"Would Earnest have led us astray?" Trevor asked with a laugh.

Iris groaned and rolled her eyes. "That's so rhetorical, but in the opposite way you meant it."

"I think you have Earnest and Finaeus mixed up," Trevor replied, narrowing his eyes as he regarded the AI.

"No." Jessica's gaze remained fixed on the view of humanity's home galaxy. "Earnest has a tricky streak, too. He just hides it better than Finaeus. Trust me. He's the one that made me purple in the first place."

"Really?" Iris strode to Jessica's side, looking her up and down. "I thought that was your choice, when you got your artificial skin back in The Kap."

"Well, it was my choice to keep it, but Earnest did it as a joke when I was getting rebuilt after all the radiation."

"It's true," Tangel confirmed, enjoying the banter.

"I bet there's a good story there," Trevor said as he rose from his station. "How come you never told it?"

Jessica shrugged. "So that I'd have something new to surprise you with at times like this. Honestly, though, I spent seventy years there, I could tell you Kap stories for decades. Most of them involve something Trist got up to. That woman was a force to be reckoned with."

Tangel let out a low groan. "Also true."

"Can't ever forget that she was a thief before she was a governor," Jessica replied with a wink.

"Really?" Sera asked, fixing Tangel with a curious look. "You made a thief a governor?"

Tangel met Sera's gaze and shrugged. "I made a kinky pirate into a president."

Sera grimaced. "Touché."

"So, if I recall, Trist tried to steal some cargo that was bound for the *Intrepid*, right?" Iris asked.

"Yup," Tangel nodded, smiling at the memory. "She was duped into it and nearly died as a result."

"Yeah," Jessica nodded. "And then in true form, Tangel used her as bait to lure out one of the parties responsible for trying to destroy the ship."

"Still crazy to think that when all this started, we were just a sublight colony ship," Rachel said, her eyes glued to the view of the galaxy on the forward display. "Now look at us. We're colonizing another galaxy and waging a galactic war."

"Given that we've fought battles in the LMC, it's an *inter*galactic war." Trevor winked at the ship's captain. "Not many people know we're out here."

"Not like they could get here if they did," Jessica added. "Takes an ungodly amount of energy for the jump."

"Speaking of energy, I need a refill." Trevor patted his stomach. "Anyone else want anything?"

A flood of food requests came from the command team, and the big man laughed as he turned and walked away.

"So, what I heard was BLTs for everyone?"

"Seriously?" Jessica called after him. "I've shared the last three meals with Tangel. Anything *but* a BLT!"

"Hey!" Tangel exclaimed. "I'm standing right here."

* * * * *

"You ready?" Tangel asked as the *I2* closed on the gate that would jump them back toward the Milky Way, bypassing the core AIs' blockade and dropping the ship into the Perseus Arm.

If all went well, they would end up on the rimward side of the Stillwater Nebula. More specifically, half an AU from Star City, where Jessica, Trevor, and Iris's sixteen children—each one a powerful AI—guarded the massive dyson sphere and the final Dreamers.

Tangel wondered what the humans within Star City found when they Dreamt their way to ascension. Was it similar to what she and Bob were experiencing? Or was it something different? The fact that the billions of ascended humans from Star City had utterly vanished suggested that they had gone through a different sort of process.

"I'm ready."

Trevor's voice broke into Tangel's thoughts, and she looked to see his smile while Iris nodded silently.

"Good, because we're going either way." Rachel's lips twisted into a wry smile, and she glanced at her crew. "Helm, let's do this thing."

"Aye, ma'am. Going in."

The return trip to the Milky Way Galaxy seemed much longer, though it was almost two seconds shorter, by the counter on the display. Then the stars snapped back into place around them.

Rachel turned to the scan team. "Well?"

"Yes, ma'am, we appear to be where we intended to—oh! There it is!"

The forward display shifted to show a massive sphere, its shell illuminated by the dim glow of the system's second neutron star and the nearby Stillwater Nebula. Notation appeared next to it on the display, indicating the sphere's size. Most noteworthy was that it contained over seventeen trillion square kilometers of internal surface area, which was home to the Dreamers and Jessica's children.

"Thank stars," Jessica whispered. "I was starting to feel like we'd never see them again."

"I've got some…strange readings," Scan announced. "It's like—Shit! Exdali!"

The forward display shifted to show a wave of darkness coursing toward Star City.

Tangel pulled up a three-dimensional view of the dyson sphere and surrounding space on the main holotank, drawing in a sharp breath as she saw that the encroaching mass of dark layer creatures spread across a million kilometers—and the *I2* was directly in their path.

"Repulsor signal!" she called out, gritting her teeth as she considered options.

<*Up and running,*> Bob responded, a note of uncertainty in the AI's voice. <*I don't believe that we can repel that many, not unless we deploy the fleet.*>

"No time!" Tangel shook her head. "Helm. Max burn, keep us ahead of that wave!"

The *I2* had jumped in three light minutes from Star City, yet they were only six light seconds from the encroaching wave of Exdali. At the rate the dark layer creatures were traveling, they'd meet the wave of darkness before getting a response from Star City.

Tangel sent a message anyway.

"Mayday, mayday, mayday. This is Field Marshal Tangel Richards—"

"Plus your parents," Jessica added, her lips twisted in worry.

"Yeah, them too," Tangel said, while shooting Jessica a quelling look. "You might not have seen them yet, but we have a shit-ton of Exdali about to swallow us whole. We're sending you information on how to generate a repulsor wave. If you can emit it from a dozen points, it will be enough to push them back."

"Mayday seems a bit strong, doesn't it?" Trevor asked. "We have stasis shields, and those can repel Exdali, right?"

<*We have only run controlled tests against small creatures. The energy required to power the shields even then was immense.*>

"How much is immense?" Trevor asked, an eyebrow quirked.

<*To use Tangel's term, a shit-ton.*>

"That doesn't really help much."

Sera fixed Trevor with a measuring stare. "When an AI drops phrases like 'shit-ton', you should worry. It means 'you don't want to know'."

"Maybe we should just drop to the dark layer," the scan officer suggested. "It could be clear."

Jessica shook her head. "It won't be. The DL is swarming here. Even a few dozen AU out, it's still thick as you can imagine. We're going to have to rely on our repulsors and stasis shields."

"And pray your kids are listening," Tangel added.

"Our kids will figure out a solution." Iris's tone contained no trace of uncertainty. "They are sixteen of some of the brightest minds in the galaxy."

A deep rumble came from Bob. <*Spoken like a true mom.*>

The *I2* had completed its turn, and was boosting toward the city, the wave of Exdali falling a little further behind her with each minute.

At precisely six minutes, a response came from Star City.

<*This is Tanis Keller, Bastion of Star City—if we're being all formal. We're setting up that repulsor thing you sent, but first we'll use the tried and true method.*>

"Tried and true?" Rachel asked.

<*They're going to shoot the Exdali,*> Bob said.

Sera shook her head vehemently. "That's matter. Firing matter at something that eats matter isn't a good idea."

"You sure?" Tangel asked. "You're made of matter, and whenever you get shot at, it's matter too."

"And that matters, how?" Sera chuckled. "Still, it seems risky with these things. I've never seen something they don't want to eat."

<*Degenerate matter is different. Relativistic degenerate matter even more so. I'm interested in what will happen, though I'm more interested in how the Bastions keep it cohesive after extracting it from the neutron stars.*>

"You and me both," Iris muttered. "They wouldn't share that with us before we left. Children can be so ungrateful."

"Gave us a reason to come back and ask," Trevor replied with a grin. "You know…so long as we survive."

"There!" Tangel pointed at the holotank, where a grouping of objects appeared only a light second from the *I2*. Then they were past the colony ship, slamming into the wall of inky darkness.

The neutronium bullets were only a few hundred kilograms each, but at a high fraction of *c*, they impacted the Exdali with a tremendous amount of energy.

For a second, it appeared as though the things were unscathed by the barrage, but then the darkness began to break up and disperse. A moment later, the encroaching wave began to slow where the shots had hit.

<*They're breaking up,*> Bob observed. <*The Exdali's bodies are falling apart.*>

"See?" Tangel nudged Sera with her elbow. "There's matter, and then there's *matter*."

"Who knew," the Hand's director said with a laugh. "Totally worth coming out here for this."

<*If we could send these bullets through a jump gate…*> Bob mused.

"That's barbaric," Trevor said, shaking his head, but not pulling his eyes from the display. "We can't just destroy the enemy willy-nilly without any sort of warning."

<*We can give warning.*>

"One thing at a time, people," Tangel admonished. "Let's just see if we and Star City can survive the day."

Neutronium bullets continued to fire from the dyson sphere, and more fire began to come from a structure encircling the second neutron star in the system.

It was significantly more massive than the one that lay at the core of Star City, the result of mass being funneled from one star to another.

Even for the people of New Canaan—who were actively working on moving their star—the work involved in transferring mass from one star to another was mind-boggling.

The rounds of degenerate matter continued to tear into the encroaching Exdali, shredding the forward lines, but not slowing the mass of things at a rate that would see them stopped before they reached Star City.

<*It's not going to be enough,*> Bob said.

"I was thinking the same thing." Tangel glanced at Jessica. "They have graviton emitters, right? They should be able to create a repulsor field."

The purple-hued woman nodded. "Yeah, I don't think it will be difficult, they should be able to force the things back."

Despite Jessica's certainty, nothing to that effect was happening.

Tangel pursed her lips. "Captain Rachel, deploy the first fleet. We'll corral the Exdali as best we can. If the bastions can get a broad enough graviton field up, we can open a rift and drive them back in.

"On it," the captain replied, her eyes narrowing as she began issuing orders via the Link.

Less than thirty seconds later, the first two cruisers were already exiting the *I2*'s main bay, and Tangel smiled, realizing that Rachel had already been preparing the fleet.

Tangel's mind wandered to the origins of the Exdali surging toward Star City. While their presence could be the work of core AIs, it also might be Orion. Both enemies knew that the ISF had used the dark layer creatures in the defense of Carthage. Figuring out how to get them out of the dark layer wasn't hard, either.

It was getting them back *in* that was problematic.

<*Thanks for the information,*> the response arrived from Star City a moment later. <*We're working on reconfiguring our station-keeping grav emitters to create the effect. It may not be soon enough, though. Anything you can do to help would be*

appreciated.>

"We sure turned that around fast," Iris said with a soft laugh. "Good thing we're so resourceful."

<*It's not turned around yet.*> Bob's tone was ominous. <*I've calculated the mass of the Exdali…. It's greater than that of Luna.*>

"Shit," Tangel muttered aloud. "Then we *really* have to get them into the dark layer. Even if the Bastions can kill them all, that mass hitting Star City will do a number on it."

"Sure wish the *Lantzer* was repaired," Jessica said, her gaze darting between Trevor and Iris. "I feel so impotent sitting around here."

"You're standing," Iris countered. "But I take your meaning. Next time, try not to get your shiny new ship torn to bits."

"Easy now," Trevor held up his hands, turning to Tangel. "We can fly tugs…. Would they help, and do you have spares?"

"Yes and yes," Rachel answered before Tangel could. "We have tugs coming out our ears, and never enough pilots."

Jessica was already on her way to the bridge's exit before Rachel was done speaking.

"Which dock?" she called out.

"Go to 17C," the captain directed.

"I'll join in," Sera said as she followed the other three off the bridge. "I can handle one of your scows."

<*Red…*> Bob cautioned.

"Kidding, kidding."

Tangel wished that Jason was aboard; his steady hand at the helm of a ship—any ship—was always welcome. Unfortunately, his duties back at New Canaan had called him home once more.

Erin's ready to take over, though. Once we find Cary and deal with Orion, we should hold elections. I'll get her primed to run.

In all honesty, she'd expected to have Erin in place as governor years ago, but New Canaan's build-up, the Aleutian site in the LMC, and then the war had forestalled that. It felt unfair to still have Jason filling the role, but he was so stoic, she often forgot that he really didn't want the position anymore.

Let's face it, she laughed to herself. *He never did.*

"I love them all," Rachel said when the others had cleared the bridge, "but it's nice having all the extra cooks out of the kitchen."

Tangel snorted a laugh. "Where do I fall in that equation?"

"Stars." Rachel shook her head. "Admiral, this is *your* kitchen. I just follow your recipes."

"Oh I don't know about that," she replied. "I feel like you've got a pretty big stake in this enterprise."

A cough came from Bob, the rumble pealing in their minds like lightning and thunder on a clear afternoon. <*When you're done discussing who owns my body, can we focus on the task at hand?*>

"Are you telling me that you actually need us?" Tangel smirked.

<*You still serve a purpose.*>

"Ouch!" Rachel exclaimed. "You know I can walk and chew gum at the same time, Bob. The fleet is nearly deployed, and Helm has worked up the vectors. So long as the Bastions get the field going, we'll be able to herd the things."

<*Good.*>

Tangel shared a long look with Rachel, and then the two set to work providing final review of Helm's vectors and finessing the grid that the twenty ships of the first fleet were forming.

She felt a pang of guilt at how few people were on each of those ships—one of the destroyers had a crew of only two. The war had whittled down the sentient resources of her people to the point where the largest groups of New Canaanites were single platoons of Marines, and even a full 'toon was getting rare.

It took constant reminding that the reason for it was how thin her people were spread, not that they were losing that many.

But with a population of under five million, everyone from New Canaan had lost friends and loved ones.

Jessica's kids better have a way to help. Another few years of this, and it won't matter that we saved New Canaan from Orion—we'll all be gone anyway.

Outside the ship, the first fleet continued to move into position, arraying themselves in a long oval across the central light second of the Exdali's wave.

Tanis—it was strange for Tangel to think of another person bearing the name that had once been hers—was providing the firing patterns that her Bastions were using, and the ISF ships were staying clear of the neutronium bullets, adjusting their positions as needed.

"It's going to be close," Rachel said, glancing over her shoulder as she walked to the scan team's section of the bridge to review their probing of the Exdali mass.

<*We're ready.*> The message came from Tanis, now only delayed by seven seconds' travel time between Star City and the *I2*.

Moments after the words came in, a wave of positive gravitons, attuned to the frequency that was anathema to the Exdali, washed over the first fleet.

The effect slowed the things' advance as the dark layer creatures bunched up in the center of their formation, pushed into place by the stronger field on the sides.

"They're not slowing as much as they should!" one of the scan officers called out. "I'm picking up refracted gravitons bleeding around the edges."

<*Something's driving them,*> Bob said.

<*Jessica, you four strapped in already, or what?*> Tangel called down to the bay

where the tugs were stored.

<We're on the rails, ready to join in.>

<You have a new mission. Someone is pushing the Exdali in the ass. Get out there and take them out.>

<In ***tugs****?>* Trevor exclaimed.

<We've got stasis shields,> Jessica replied, a hungry edge in her voice. *<It'll be like shooting fish in a barrel.>*

A groan came from Iris. *<You know that doesn't work, right? The water destroys the projectile before it reaches the fish.>*

<Stop ruining things, Iris,> Jessica shot back.

Tangel couldn't help but laugh. No matter what they faced, it seemed like Jessica's little family always had time to crack a joke.

<Good luck,> she told them. *<And kick ass.>*

DANCE WITH THE DEVIL

STELLAR DATE: 10.15.8949 (Adjusted Years)
LOCATION: ISS *I2*
REGION: Star City, Orion Freedom Alliance, Perseus Arm

<Kick ass? Like we can do anything else,> Jessica added a laugh as she spoke on the team's private channel.

<Stars,> Sera muttered. *<You three practically ooze* Sabrina*. Do I ever miss her.>*

<You were aboard her just a week ago,> Iris said.

<That makes it worse.>

Jessica's tug shot out first, and the others followed a few seconds later. She switched her navigation system to run off her own scan, setting the feed from the *I2* as a secondary input.

<OK, people, let's fan out. Full boost, two above, two below,> she ordered.

<I'll go under with Iris,> Sera announced as she broke away.

<Good thing,> Trevor laughed. *<I like being on top.>*

Jessica snorted. *<Since when?>*

His only response was good-natured laughter, and Jessica smiled as her tug boosted at over one hundred *g*s, the dampeners only blocking two thirds of the force, the rest pushing her into the acceleration couch like a giant's foot, threatening to crush her.

She fixed her gaze on the holodisplay, her mind trying to deal with the view before her.

Seeing a representation of the Exdali wave on the bridge of the *I2* was one thing, but staring at the writhing mass while accelerating toward it was another experience entirely. Memories of the fear she'd felt aboard the *Lantzer* as they raced to the gate came back over her, and it took a moment for her to force herself to set it aside.

Stop it, Jessica. That fight is over. We beat the Exdali there, we'll beat them again here.

She wondered if she was the only one freaking out, and reached out to her husband on a private channel.

<You good?> she asked Trevor as the two tugs spread out, arcing over the dark layer creatures, scan sweeping the space beyond for evidence of any ships pushing the things.

She wasn't certain which would be worse: to find that the Orion Guard could weaponize Exdali like this, or to see a fishbone behind the wave.

<You bet. Think I'm scared by some Exdali trying to devour our children? Nah, this is just another day at the office for us.>

<Nice try,> Jessica replied. *<Damn, we've lost visual on Sera and Iris.>*

<I2 *still has them on scan. They're OK.*>

<*I know that.*> She didn't mean to come across testily, but something about the Exdali made her stomach churn. <*Do you think they found them or made them?*>

<*Do you mean the core AIs and the Exdali?*>

<*Uh huh.*>

Her husband laughed, his voice sounding calm and certain. <*No, I don't think the Exdali made the core AIs.*>

<*Funny man. Be serious.*>

<*OK, sorry.*> Trevor sent a reassuring feeling across the Link. <*I think they found them and then altered them, or at least spread them around.*

<*Bastards.*>

<*That's the general sentiment, yeah. Wait, I've got something!*>

The two tugs had passed over the bulk of the Exdali mass and were arcing back down, searching the billions of square kilometers for any graviton emissions that would point to someone herding the things.

Trevor passed his scan data, and Jessica looked it over. There was no ship visible, but negative gravitons were bleeding out from a point near the center of the mass of creatures.

<*Iris, Sera, do you read this?*> she asked as the other two came back on the team's Link.

<*I do,*> Sera said. <*And I have another one a quarter light second further along the line.*>

<*I dropped relays,*> Iris added. <*Passing the feed to the* I2.>

Trevor snorted a laugh. <*Oh look at you, Missus Fancy Pants, dropping probes!*>

Jessica wondered if his injection of levity was for her sake. If it was, she appreciated it.

<*It's not hard, you should try it,*> the AI retorted.

<*We didn't have any,*> Jen said, her voice almost making Jessica jump.

<*Stars, Jen, I forget you're tucked away in Sera's head half the time. You never talk.*>

<*Not everyone is all about the talky-talky like you.*>

<*You clearly need to spend more time aboard* Sabrina,> Trevor commented. <*I used to be quiet and reserved, too. Now look at me.*>

<*Sooo, I've analyzed the pattern,*> Sera said. <*You know, doing what we're here for. It suggested ten ships, and I've found three more.*>

<*I was doing it too,*> Iris protested.

<*Look at that, my organic thinker is faster than yours,*> Sera said with a laugh.

<*She cheated,*> Jen laughed. <*Our tug has a big spatial vector analysis NSAI aboard. It crunched all four tugs' scan data in seconds.*>

<*Jen!*> Sera admonished.

<*You're not president anymore, you don't get special consideration.*>

<*Ohhh!*> Trevor laughed. <*Burn!*>

<*I've assigned targets,*> Jessica said, laughing as she fed the updates to the

team. <*If those are ships, we'll just ram and slam them.*>

<*If they're* **anything**, *we'll just do that,*> Iris said.

<*What else could they be?*> Trevor asked.

<*Ascended AIs operating from extradimensional space,*> Jessica suggested.

<*Oh…shit.*>

Jessica was halfway to her first target, her scan still unable to see anything other than the graviton bleed that was driving the Exdali.

While the tug had engines capable of moving a billion tons of asteroid without any strain, it possessed no offensive weapons, other than small beams for breaking up flotsam and jetsam. Those wouldn't do anything to a warship, but the tug's engines certainly would.

After a hard boost, Jessica spun the tug and pointed her engines at the source of the graviton emissions, then fired a fifty-*g* burn for ten seconds.

Her ship's sensors couldn't penetrate the soup of gammas and plasma until fifteen seconds later. When she could finally see her target, she muttered a curse.

<*Fucking Orion! They're using those new four-hulled cruisers of theirs.*>

<*Spotted that as well,*> Sera replied. <*Those things have a ton of kinetics. If they clip you properly with a slug, they could push you into the Exdali.*>

Jessica nodded to herself, noting that the wall of dark layer creatures was only a thousand klicks from the Orion ships.

<*I have two grappling webs. I'm gonna fire one of those and bind up the rotating hulls,*> Iris announced.

One of the webs was present on Jessica's ship as well, and she decided to use it on her first target. She spun her tug again, boosting toward the enemy cruiser, stasis shields easily shedding the beamfire coming her way.

"That's right, you pieces of shit," she muttered. "Wanna take out *my* kids? Gonna have to deal with their mother, first."

She saw the cruiser turn its heavy kinetics, tracking her ship. Jessica initialized a jinking pattern to avoid the slugs that began firing at her. The rounds would foul the net before it reached the cruiser, so she had to get close before deploying it.

The onboard nav system calculated the enemy's firing rate, speed of projectiles, and the tug's maneuverability, presenting an optimal range for her to fire the net at.

"Seventy kilometers?" Jessica shook her head and then quickly programmed an automated firing sequence, then gripped the edges of the acceleration couch as her tug boosted toward the enemy ship.

Fifteen seconds later, she'd passed the Orion cruiser, and her board showed that the net had fired.

<*Hooked mine,*> she announced to the group. <*Tether's holding.*>

The line connecting her tug to the cruiser strained as she fired her engines at max burn, slewing her captured prey to the side and sending it off course. At the same time, a graviton wave flowed through the Exdali from the far side, and the things slowed drastically.

One second, there was a ship caught in the net, the next, it was lost in the churning black of the creatures' bodies. An alert blared in the cockpit, and her tug jerked toward the creatures, their dark bodies surging up the cable.

"Shitting stars!" Jessica exclaimed, cutting the tether free and boosting away from the Exdali. *<Watch out, those things are hungry! Ate my prey, then tried to eat me.>*

<You're not supposed to be using your net to fish,> Sera said with a laugh. *<Granted, the same thing just happened to me.>*

Jessica didn't have time to reply, as her ship shuddered under a barrage of kinetics. Two of the cruisers had moved away from their herding positions and were slamming rounds into her tug, trying to force it into the Exdali.

She poured on the thrust, attempting to boost above the wall of creatures, but a massive round struck her ship and pushed it to starboard—right into the searching tentacles of a massive thing.

<They got me!> she shouted over the Link, getting no response as her stasis shields flared brightly around the ship, annihilating whatever part of the Exdali touched her.

She lost all bearings and didn't know if she was still moving into the things, or away. After a few seconds more, her CriEn module threw an alert that it could only operate at the heightened draw for one minute.

"Just great," Jessica muttered.

She had the ship's nav systems calculate the angle that her tug had entered the Exdalis, and worked out her current orientation. The ship's computer ran the numbers and triple-checked then, coming up with the determination that the tug was spinning like a top, but the gravitational mass of the dark layer creatures was great enough that it was blocking the ship's ability to use the dampener's strength to calculate vector.

"Well," Jessica muttered. "Might as well just pick a direction."

She programmed the tug's engines to fire for one second with every spin of the ship, and then held her breath as the small vessel followed her directions, every burn slamming her into the acceleration couch like a hammer blow.

Watching the timer on her HUD, Jessica noted that she'd been in the Exdali mass for twenty seconds. It counted up to thirty, and then forty.

This can't be right, she thought as it passed fifty.

At the speed she'd entered the wall of dark layer creatures, and with her consistent burns, she should have broken free—unless she was firing in exact opposition to her existing momentum.

Another thirty seconds passed, and she was still surrounded by the flare of her stasis shields as the Exdali smashed themselves against her ship.

"Oh wait..." Jessica whispered, suddenly realizing why she wasn't free of the dark layer creatures. "I'm *in* the dark layer."

Her ship's scan was useless, unable to see past the stasis shield and the wall of obliteration beyond. Her main panel was displaying the alert that the CriEn was going to drop into diminished power mode in ten seconds, and she had no idea if it was even possible to transition *out* of the dark layer when she hadn't activated the graviton fields to transition into it in the first place.

The CriEn countdown passed seven seconds, and she didn't wait any further, initiating a dark layer transition field and dropping into normal space.

"Did I—?"

Her words were interrupted as something hammered into her stasis shield, and then the CriEn shut down.

Directly in front of Jessica's tug was the surface of the dyson sphere, its white expanse stretching in every direction. The scan readings on her tug showed that she was only fifty kilometers from it, and drifting away ever so slightly.

A rasping breath left her throat as she realized that the shuddering had been neutronium bullets fired to keep her from hitting Star City—and to kill the Exdali she'd drawn out of the dark layer.

<Stars, Mom.> Tanis's voice was filled with relief. *<We know you miss us, but try not to smash your ship into the place. We just got it fixed back up.>*

THE CITY AROUND A STAR

STELLAR DATE: 10.16.8949 (Adjusted Years)
LOCATION: ISS *I2*
REGION: Star City, Orion Freedom Alliance, Perseus Arm

"Sweeps are complete, Admiral," Rachel said as she turned to face Tangel. "The Exdali are all back in the DL…or dead and drifting."

"Good." Tangel let out a long breath, shaking her head that Orion was willing to utterly destroy Star City just because its denizens wouldn't join the OFA. *Hopefully that's why, and not that they're sitting out of the war.*

Chances were that the Bastions and Dreamers of Star City had no idea that war had spread across the inhabited section of the Orion Arm of the galaxy—and now into the Perseus Arm as well. It was Tangel's fervent hope that she could convince the Bastions to aid in the fight, primarily by explaining how they could keep degenerate matter from flying apart once extracted from their pair of neutron stars.

"We need to clean up the bodies," she concluded after drawing her attention back to the task at hand. "We know the detritus's trajectory now, but Exdali are almost as black as Elastene. They'll become a navigation hazard before long."

"I'll have crews get on it," Rachel replied. "Just…where do we put them?"

"Get them in a net," Tangel replied. "We'll kick it into the other star once they're all gathered up."

<*I'd advise against that,*> Bob broke into their conversation. <*We don't know enough about the things. They might have the ability to reanimate, or maybe spawn new young from their bodies. I'd hate for the mass to come alive and then devour this system's other star.*>

"OK, back into the dark layer, then."

<*After I examine them,*> the AI said. <*This is a rare opportunity.*>

"Umm…OK," Tangel reached up and grasped the end of her ponytail. "Just be careful."

<*Of course.*>

"I'll take a shuttle to the city," Tangel said. "I don't think we can fly in."

<*We can fly in,*> Bob said. <*I've been talking with Tanis and her siblings. They've sent the coordinates for an entrance large enough for the* I2.>

"Alright," Rachel said, her eyes turning to meet Tangel's. "*Should* we do that? I hate the idea of being trapped in there."

<*I want to see it for myself,*> Bob said.

~*Why is that?*~ Tangel asked privately, mind to mind.

~*Professional curiosity,*~ the AI replied. ~*Humor me. I do it with you often enough.*~

~Ouch!~ Her lips twisted for a moment, and then Tangel nodded. "We're going in, Rachel. Set a course."

"Aye, ma'am. Just gonna fly the ship into a dyson sphere…because our day hasn't been crazy enough yet."

<*Now you're getting it,*> Bob said.

The forward display shifted to Star City's shell, the white expanse filling more and more of the view as the *I2* approached.

"Here's something crazy," Rachel said as the ship drew closer. "Even though it's a sphere, its surface is the flattest thing we've ever laid eyes on."

"Huh." Tangel nodded slowly. "You're right. Its circumference is greater than the Airthan ring's."

"It's not a competition," Sera said as she walked onto the bridge.

"No?" Rachel asked. "I mean…they built this thing millennia before Finaeus made the ring."

A laugh slipped from Sera's lips as she reached the holotank. "Oh I know, he was complaining about it on the flight to Airtha. He thought he was first to create a semi-rigid structure that large…and then they came here."

"The others not with you?" Tangel asked.

"No, they didn't want to wait. They followed Jessica with their tugs."

"Can't wait to see their ki—" Rachel choked off the last word. "Sorry, Tangel."

She gave a rueful laugh in response. "Trust me, I didn't *just* start drawing the comparison. It's been front and center in my mind all day. But what I've been remembering is that Jessica, Trevor, and Iris went ten years not knowing if their kids were OK. I've gone a few days. Their example is giving me strength."

Sera wrapped an arm around her shoulder. "We're here for you. We'll get them back, get it done."

Tangel nodded. "We know where they're going to end up. It's just a matter of when."

"Is Joe going to keep chasing after them?" Rachel asked. "Well…searching, I guess."

"No," Tangel shook her head. "He's released the ships that Admiral Lukas had set aside, barring a few that are setting up listening posts in New Sol."

"It's risky business." Sera paused and twisted her lips. "Every time we try to get a relay station into the New Sol System, they find it. But we don't need these to last forever. Just a few months, maybe a year, tops."

"Stars," Tangel muttered. "A year. If Cary takes that long to make her move on Kirkland, I'll eat my ponytail. She'll go in a lot sooner than that."

"She has to secure her fleet first," Sera said. "It'll take her a bit to gather those ships."

"OK, what did I miss?" Rachel asked. "I haven't read the whole briefing yet, just that she blew up some dock."

"Yeah." Tangel sucked in a slow breath. "A station called 'Dock 1'. At least a hundred million people aboard."

"Oh shit." Rachel breathed the words. "And the fleet?"

"From what Joe learned—mostly from Faleena—Cary sent Widows onto all the ships of a departing fleet. They think she did it to somehow seize the ships and use them for something."

"How many?" Rachel asked.

"Just shy of a thousand," Tangel replied.

"Really?" The ship's captain cocked her head. "A thousand run-of-the-mill Orion ships against New Sol's defenses?"

Sera pursed her lips, nodding in agreement. "Yeah, it's not even a pittance. We've no idea what she has planned."

"With any luck, we can get something from the Bastions that will help us against New Sol," Tangel said.

"I don't know if neutronium bullets are the sort of thing we want." Sera met Tangel's gaze. "Do we really need to go for an all or nothing option?"

"No, we don't. But I'm not above a really solid bluff."

"A bluff like this only works if you're really willing to carry it out." Rachel's voice was low, her eyes serious.

Sera laughed and winked at the captain. "That's a threat."

"Exactly."

"They might have something else," Tangel said. "Maybe we can work out how to make ships with neutronium hulls. They might be able to stand up to DMG weapons."

"I'll pass on captaining a death trap like that." Sera shook her head. "The instant the containment field fails, you're doing an impression of a pancake."

"Not to mention the mass," Rachel added. "Teaspoon of that stuff weighs as much as a small planet. How do you coat a ship in it?"

Tangel laughed. "I'm just spitballing, here. I mean, they starlift the stuff and then fire it. The energies required for that are staggering, but Jessica said they don't have CriEns."

<*They don't need them,*> Bob said. <*They have something better.*>

"What?" Tangel blurted out the word. "What's better?"

<*Transdimensional energy.*> Bob said the words as though it should have been painfully obvious that such was the source of the Bastions' power.

"Maybe," Tangel allowed. "But they made Star City before they'd ascended. So how'd they syphon one star's mass to another before that?"

<*We'll have to find out.*>

"Sure took your extra-strength cryptic pills this morning, Bob," Sera said, her gaze fixed on Tangel. "I told you that you were nuts to keep god-like AIs around."

<*I'm not god—*>

"Sure, sure," Sera waved a hand, laughing softly. "I know that's how your type rolls. 'Deny, deny, deny'."

"There it is," Rachel said, pointing at the forward display. "Steady as she goes, Helm."

The lieutenant at the ship's helm nodded, her expression rapt as the *I2* eased toward a hundred-kilometer-wide portal set into the skin of Star City.

"It's like we're flying into our own main dock." Rachel's voice was filled with awe. "Intrepidception."

"You dipping into that old vid archive, too?" Sera asked.

The ship's captain nodded. "Something about the flat vids is soothing. Like you can enjoy the story as a story and not have to be a part of it—but even so, you feel sucked in. I don't know how to describe it."

"Sucked in seems apt," Tangel said as the *I2* began to pass through the dyson sphere's shell. "I thought I had gotten used to supermassive superstructures, but this…this is mind-blowing."

"And they built it without pico," Sera winked.

The blue haze at the end of the long shaft began to gain resolution, green and white becoming visible in the far distance. Tangel held off on zooming the optics in; she wanted to experience the passage without cheating and jumping ahead, even though Jessica had sent her vids of the interior.

A minute later, the ship reached the end of the tunnel and passed out into open air. Below them lay the second sphere, covered in thousands of worlds' worth of space, broken into hexagons covered with oceans and dotted with continents.

The inner sphere was at a distance from the neutron star in the center of the structure that caused the outside of the sphere to experience one *g* of gravitational acceleration. In a way, this made it an inverted dyson sphere, and a more practical one at that.

She briefly wondered how much air lay between the world sphere and the shell they'd passed through. A rough calculation told her that it massed more than Earth, and she wondered how the makers had ensured that storms didn't constantly rage across the interior.

We have so much to learn…

It was a comforting feeling, that for once the people of the *Intrepid*, those who had come forward in time five thousand years, finally didn't have to be the ones to come up with all the answers. Someone else could lend a hand on that front.

"There's Earth!" Rachel pointed to one of the tiny hexagons. "I can make out North America."

"All of Sol is there." Sera pointed to the surrounding hexagons. "Look, there's High Terra—they sort of wrapped it around. And there's Luna, Mars, and Venus."

"And Eurpoa, Tyche, Ganymede…they recreated them all," Tangel added.

"There, those are the planets of Tau Ceti. Amazing..."

Rachel scowled as she looked over the worlds represented below. "This doesn't really look like a city. In fact, I can't see any cities."

"From what Jessica said, they never fully occupied it before all the people here moved into the Dream and began ascending," Tangel replied.

"It's like a ghost town."

<*We're going to Manhattan,*> Bob said. <*There's a city there.*>

"Oh hell yeah," Tangel grinned. "I've always wanted to bring the ship down over New York. We'll stretch from Staten Island, past the Bronx and past Yonkers."

"Those can't be real names," Sera laughed.

"Totally. I wonder if they made all the cities and towns. On Earth, there was a town called New Canaan near there."

<*The others are already in the Dream,*> Bob said, a low rumble of laughter accompanying his words.

"Couldn't wait to see their kids, eh?" Tangel asked. "Not that I'm assigning blame here."

<*I suspect as much, though their kids also have bodies.*>

"So do you actually want to settle over Manhattan Island, Bob?" Rachel asked. "Or should we park a bit higher?"

"Going to take a lot of power just to float in one *g* without orbiting," Tangel said. "Too bad we never put landing gear on the ship."

<*Don't even joke about that,*> Bob scoffed. <*We have coordinates over the Atlantic, and there's an a-grav pad that will float us.*>

"Ooooh...fancy," Rachel laughed while passing the order to Helm.

"I'm going to a shuttle," Tangel said. "No need for you to settle in before I go."

"Have fun," the captain saluted. "Make sure to get us all some shore leave down there. I imagine everyone is going to want to walk around this place."

Tangel nodded and waved absently as she walked off the bridge to the maglev station.

~So why did you want to come inside?~ she asked Bob.

~I wanted to see if the humans who ascended via the Dream are still here.~

The thought had occurred to Tangel as well. There was no reason to believe that the people who had ascended had left at all. If they had fully transitioned into higher dimensions, it was possible that they'd stayed within Star City afterward.

~Well, if they are here, they're not showing their faces,~ she replied. *~I didn't see any signs of them when we came in.~*

~Nor did I, but that is far from conclusive.~

Tangel didn't speak further as she walked through the ship. Instead, she peered through the hull, looking down at the continent they were passing over.

She easily recognized it as Europe, noting the familiar geology of the Italian peninsula, France, and then the islands of Britain and Ireland. She recalled many fond memories on Earth, and a few harrowing ones, such as the one against Disker separatists in Dublin.

Moments later, the ship passed over the Atlantic Ocean, and Tangel took in the sweeping view, at one point able to see North America, Greenland, Europe, and Africa—courtesy of the flat representation of Earth.

She tried to peer through the ocean and beyond to the star within the inner sphere, but she was unable to see more than a dozen kilometers into the ground below before her sight was stopped by a luminous wall.

~Can you see through to the star?~

~No,~ Bob replied. *~I think it's some sort of neutronium. It is a solid object in higher dimensions, as well.~*

~That's annoying.~

~And useful. Want a bullet that can kill ascended beings?~

Tangel snorted. *~No way it's that easy.~*

~To my knowledge, this is the only place in the universe where you can get neutronium bullets. So it's not **that** *easy.~*

~Good point. And we just so happen to have that ascended AI Jessica captured.~

Bob's mind rumbled in slow consideration. *~That seems inhumane.~*

~It's not human.~

~For you.~

~I'm not human.~

The AI laughed. *~You're not so ascended that I can't bend you over my knee, Tangel.~*

She joined in the laughter, walking through the still-bustling administrative wing. Despite the fact that they were running on a skeleton crew, the entire war effort was coordinated from the hall she was walking through—even more so now that the primary QuanComm hub in Khardine had been destroyed.

<Do you miss her?> Tangel asked, switching to the Link, though she didn't know why.

<Priscilla?>

<Yes.>

<Do you miss Cary?>

Tangel snorted. *<You know the answer to that.>*

<Then you too know the answer to your question.>

<Well…> She considered her next words. *<I wasn't sure if you missed people exactly, I was curious.>*

<I think I do, in my own way—I don't feel complete without her aboard. I was wondering if this is what it might feel like if she were to die—as though a part of me is gone, never to come back.>

Tangel nodded a she reached the maglev station. *<That's the general*

sensation.>

<*How do you come to accept it?*>

<*You just have to figure out how to make peace with it. Accept the fact that you won't see them again, and figure out how to move on.*>

<*That's very vague,*> Bob pointed out.

<*Well, it's different for everyone. Are you worried about her? Can you not see Priscilla's future?*>

<*Cary's ascension and mental merge with Lisa Wrentham introduces many variables I cannot properly account for. My prior matrices required a certain number of knowns to operate with a desirable degree of accuracy. We have…we have moved beyond the point where we have sufficient knowns.*>

<*Everywhere?*>

<*Oh, no, of course not. Three nights from now, Karmen is going to have an argument with Lucida over repair priorities back at Pyra, and they're going to end up in a sexual relationship as a result of their tensions. Jessica will ignore it, and that will create the same atmosphere on the* Lantzer*—when she returns to it—as she had on* Sabrina.>

<*OK, so you haven't lost your mojo, it's just that the scope has changed.*>

<*Exactly. Which is why we're here. To improve our ability to perceive the true scope.*>

MEETING TANIS

STELLAR DATE: 10.16.8949 (Adjusted Years)
LOCATION: Manhattan Island, North America
REGION: Star City, Orion Freedom Alliance, Perseus Arm

Tangel stepped out of the shuttle and came face to face with herself.

"Stars." She smiled, shaking her head in disbelief. "When Jessica told me that you'd modeled yourself after me, I didn't realize she was being so literal."

"Hello to you too," Tanis said. "I studied you…a lot. From what I could tell, you are one of the best military commanders in human history. It seemed prudent to model myself after someone so accomplished."

"I'm not that good," Tangel replied. "I just read a lot."

"Well, she also gave me your name."

"That makes a lot more sense." She observed the being in front of her, noting that it was flesh and blood, a biological copy of what she herself had looked like years ago. But there was no intelligence inside of the form, it was just a vessel.

"You're wondering if I inhabit this form," Tanis said.

"No," Tangel shook her head. "I can see that you are not in there. Are you too big, or too uncomfortable with the mobility?"

Tangel's doppelganger laughed. "Perhaps a bit of both. I could squeeze my core in there, but it would not be well protected. We all have forms like this, but we don't use them too much. Most of our work does not require physical forms."

"Defending the Dreamers against Orion?" Tangel asked. "I took it from your comments that this is not the first time Orion has sent Exdali after you."

"It is not. However, this is the first time they launched an assault that large. If you hadn't shown up when you did…Well, let's just say that things wouldn't have gone well."

Tangel nodded slowly, glancing over her right shoulder to where the *I2* could be seen hovering over the ocean. "I find myself wondering if Bob had something to do with that."

~I did not. In this case, I am innocent of manipulation.~

"Oh! Now *that* was unusual," Tanis said. "Then it's true, Bob, you are ascended."

~I am. Who has been outing me?~

"You forget…." Tanis turned and gestured to the towers that rose up on the far side of Battery Park. "Our parents are already in the Dream. Five months have passed for them since they entered. We've had much time to talk."

"I'm eager to experience that. I would imagine it would aid in strategizing a lot."

"You cannot enter the Dream, not if what Jessica says is true."

"Which is?" Tangel cocked her head.

"That you too are ascended."

She wondered what that had to do with anything. "Not entirely."

~It's a continuum.~

~Stop it.~

"I'm sorry about your daughters and Priscilla," Tanis said, her face growing serious. "I know you're here to seek help in finding them. My parents explained that as well."

"She's just stealing all my thunder," Tangel muttered. "Honestly, we would have come anyway. We need your help in the war."

"And it seems as though we need your help defending Star City."

"I thought you had a fleet," Tangel said. "Or Jessica said she told you to build one."

"We did. Orion has attacked us seven times in the decade since our parents left. We've fended them off, but the last three incidents, they have used those creatures. We're lucky they die to neutronium bullets, but we lost our last ships in the prior attacks. We are building more, but not fast enough, it seems."

"I think we'll be able to help you there, as well," Tangel replied. "And I do hope you'll be able to help us—even though I can't enter the Dream."

"It wouldn't make sense for you to do so. We cannot bring your ascended mind into the Dream, so you'd feel strangely detached."

~Or you might permanently leave your corporeal body behind.~

"Yeah, let's not risk that," Tangel gave a nervous laugh. "I told Cary I'd have this body for a long time. She'd be pissed if I lost it on a lark."

"Yes, it would be rather frivolous," Tanis confirmed.

Tangel looked around at the towers rising behind the AI who bore her name and face.

"Is the city entirely vacant?"

Tanis turned and surveyed the recreation of thirty-sixth century New York. "Other than my core, yes. Well, and our parents, of course. All of the Dreamers here have moved on."

A sensation of utter emptiness came over Tangel as she thought of the sixteen AIs who watched over the empty world that was Star City. She couldn't imagine what Jessica, Iris, and Trevor must have felt when they had to leave their progeny behind.

"Is it lonely?" she asked.

Tanis shrugged. "We have each other, and we have the Dream when we want to be with other people—though it's not the same as it was when we were growing up."

"Because your parents aren't there anymore?"

The AI nodded. "That, and the number of Dreamers is so low now that we have to simulate many of the people the actual Dreamers interact with."

"Oh? How low is it?"

Tangel wondered if there would be a point where the accelerated human evolution system would not have enough people for the final Dreamers to ascend.

"Hovering over a million," Tanis said. "We're going to have to change the setting in some fashion to remove urban scenarios very soon. We're thinking of trying something set in the ancient Roman era."

~I wonder if that is necessary,~ Bob interjected.

"Oh?" Tanis cocked an eyebrow and glanced toward the starship hovering over the ocean. "What are you thinking, great and powerful Bob?"

Tangel snorted. "I like that one."

~Just that if the final Dreamers are close enough, there may be a way to catalyze a final mass transition.~

"We've considered that," Tanis said. "It may be possible, but even though we are caretakers of these humans who seek ascension, we don't know enough about ascension itself to understand what their final triggers are. It seems that in some ways, it's a final critical mass of enlightenment across multiple lifetimes. Obviously, this is not a natural method for an organic being."

Tangel glanced up at the artificial sun as it slid across the sky, a strange melancholy settling over her.

"If there is one," she murmured.

"I understand that you did not undergo what I would call a natural process, but your daughter is ascending, is she not?" Tanis asked.

"Yes, but her path is a byproduct of the tweaking that was done to me."

"And are you fully ascended?" Tanis peered at Tangel as though she could see through her—which she probably could, to an extent.

"I don't know if ascension is a thing with a metric we could define as 'full'. Were I to try, I could leave this corporeal body behind, but I don't want to. I made a promise to my daughters that I intend to keep. And to Joe, too, though my promise to him is a bit different."

~Tanis, could you grant me access to the Dreamer network? I would like to observe.~

A look of concern crossed Tanis's features, but then she nodded. "OK, we agree that it would be safe enough if we slow the Dream down for a little bit." A smile settled onto her lips. "Actually, if we slow the Dream down, we could let you project into it, too, Tangel. Would you like that?"

"Yes, I think I very much would."

* * * * *

Tangel appeared next to a grill that was loaded with sizzling bacon and burgers. To her left was a two-story house, and to her right was a secluded yard lined with trees and filled with people talking with one another, Trevor and Iris in their midst.

"Took you long enough," Jessica's voice came to Tangel, and she saw the purple-skinned woman walk out of the house with a platter of buns and condiments.

"Look at you!" Tangel laughed. "When I throw parties at my lakehouse, you never carry anything out."

"That's because I'm not your mother, and you like preparing a party spread," Jessica countered as she set her tray on the table. "Plus, you have a zillion servitors."

"Fair point."

"And you always tell me I lay things out wrong."

"*OK!* I get it," Tangel said in mock annoyance, a half smile on her lips.

Jessica's gaze slid to her children who were now wrestling with Trevor and Iris, engaged in some sort of bizarre game whose rules were not documented, but built up over time from a thousand prior matches.

The smile fell from Tangel's lips as she pursed them tightly.

"I'm so sorry, Jessica."

"Sorry?" Her friend turned to look back at her, an eyebrow cocked. "What for?"

"For sending you away. Again and again. For never getting to share this with you. We always talked about raising children together, but instead, I sent you across the galaxy and you had to do it alone."

Jessica took a step closer, her eyes glistening. "Stupid holoprojection. I wish you were really here so I could hug you, Tangel. You did what you had to do, which is what you always do. You make the hard call, and quite honestly, you make the biggest sacrifices. I feel bad for *you,* not the other way around."

"Me?" Tangel asked, surprise lacing her tone. "Because of my girls?"

"Well, yeah, that too. But also because of how things went raising Cary and Saanvi, not to mention Faleena. I know how you are. I bet that while Cary was growing up, you spent half your nights away from her, trying to put together a colony and deal with all the other shit going on. And you hardly got to spend any time at all with Faleena before you had to go off and do this whole war."

"Do the war." Tangel snorted. "That's my thing, isn't it?"

"You know what they say, play to your strengths."

A laugh burst from Tangel's throat, and she wished more than anything to be able to embrace Jessica. "I guess I do at that. And it's not quite as bad as you're worrying it was. Cary and Saanvi had two mothers, Tanis and Angela. And I have both their memories. Yes, I do wish that I was there with them more in the flesh, and do I ever wonder if I made a terrible mistake sending them out—and making Joe deal with how much slack to give them…."

Her voice trailed off, and she turned to look at the ongoing match in the backyard.

"Stars, Trevor is big," she laughed as the man picked up one of his sons and tossed the full-grown man at his siblings. "How modded is he, anyway?"

"Not much at all, just a lot of heavy worlder biology in his background," Jessica replied.

"I guess we're all just products of our environment," Tangel replied.

"Oh, I don't know that I'd say that," a voice said from the doorway into the house. "I think you alter your environment more than it alters you—the both of you do."

Her eyes darted to the left and fell on a tall man with olive skin and a long moustache. He wore a wide-brimmed hat and a brown coat and pants.

"Bob?" she asked, mouth agape.

The man shrugged. "The burgers smelled good, I wanted to try one. I figured this might be my best opportunity to really feel what it's like."

"I didn't expect *this*," Tanis said as she walked up the steps onto the deck, looking Bob up and down. "Is it safe for you to be in here in this way?"

"This is a shard," Bob replied. "I don't do this often, but it can be useful from time to time." The AI walked to the table and picked up a bun, then strode to the grill and selected a burger. "From what I hear, medium-rare is best."

Jessica nodded silently, her gaze meeting Tangel's, and she mouthed the words 'It's really Bob!', her eyes wide with amazement.

"I wonder if I could do that..." Tangel mused.

"Not unless you want to shard yourself," Bob replied as he turned and walked back to the table, selecting a bottle of ketchup from the condiments laid out there. "Which you can do, but I don't think it's a good idea just yet."

She was tempted to ask him why not, but decided that she'd had her fill of deep conversations for the time being.

Just then, a whoop of joy came from a dozen voices on the lawn, and Tangel turned to see a pile of bodies and no sign of Trevor or Iris. Then she saw a silver arm stretched out, slapping the ground in defeat.

The brood rolled off their parents to reveal Trevor and Iris sprawled across one another in a tangled mass of limbs.

"That looks uncomfortable," Bob mused as he applied mustard to his burger, then stared at it pensively. "I think I'll pass on that experience."

"Wise choice," Tanis said as she looked Bob up and down. "So, you going to eat that or just stare at it?"

The AI shrugged, opened his mouth wide, and took a bite. A smile formed on his lips as he chewed slowly, and then swallowed with his eyes closed.

"OK," he whispered. "Why did no one tell me that food was so good?"

Jessica snorted a laugh. "Pretty sure Tangel here gave that away by orgasming every time she ate a BLT."

"Jessica!" she exclaimed. "I've *never* orgasmed from eating a BLT, or *any* food."

"There was that one time, I recall it vividly," the purple-skinned woman countered.

"That doesn't count, you drugged my food!"

* * * * *

They spent the rest of the evening in the Dream—which, even at its slowed rate, only amounted to ten minutes outside the immersive simulation.

Tangel got to meet each one of the sixteen bastions who were now the protectors of Star City and its denizens. Many bore the names of people from Jessica and Trevor's pasts, though none had adopted the features of their namesakes in the same way Tanis had.

Some were polar opposites, such as Troy, who was a garrulous young man, passionate about art and endlessly optimistic. He was all but attached at the hip to Kira, and Tanis had noted that the pair was planning to produce a brood of their own once the bastions' future was clear.

That conversation had led from one to another until eventually, all twenty-one humans and AIs were settled around a roaring fire in the backyard, idly discussing what they'd do when the war was over.

Tangel found it interesting that there were only two full humans present in the group, yet the AIs still chose to engage in activities that the humans found comforting. The bastions had confirmed that they did this sort of thing often, even though they could commune on far higher levels should they wish to.

"Sometimes, the level of communication you can have while being utterly silent and at peace with everything around you is far more profound than even a multilevel mind-to-mind merge," Amanda had explained at one point. "Maybe it's because we all grew up together and we just *know* what each other is thinking."

"No one knows what you're thinking," Peter countered. "It's like a nest of spiders in there."

"Plus snakes," Kira added.

"And rats," Tanis added. "Big ones."

"I don't know why I'm so nice to you all," Amanda mock-pouted.

"You've all talked about things you might want to do once the war is over and the Dreamers are gone, but what about Star City, itself?" Bob asked.

"What do you mean, exactly?" Tanis asked from across the fire.

"Oh dear." Tangel shook her head. "Never ask Bob what he means, 'exactly'."

"Really, Tangel," Bob cast her a look of mock indignance. "I've learned how to parse organic nuance better than that."

"But I'm not organic," Tanis countered, a smirk on her lips. "What if I actually mean *exactly*?"

"Staaaaahp!" Jessica laughed as she held up a hand.

Bob gave her a dark look and shrugged. "I mean that Star City could house a sizable fraction of all humans. Easily a quadrillion. It's also an ascension machine, so should we make the Dream available to all of humanity?"

"Maybe the people of Serenity, at least," Jessica suggested.

"Those are difficult questions," Tanis said as the side conversations faded away. "The problem with Star City is not the city, it's the star."

Bob nodded. "I suspected as much. The sphere protects the star, though at the same time, its very existence makes this system a target, and always will."

"What do you mean, the problem is with the star?" Jessica asked.

Tangel had begun to suspect, but held her tongue, wanting to hear it from her namesake.

"It's where they go," Bob said. "The ascended humans. They fully leave their corporeal bodies and move to higher dimensions, but they still exist in spacetime, and they've built their new home inside the neutron star at the center of the sphere."

"Yes," Tanis nodded. "Which is the real reason it is called 'Star City'. Everyone assumes that it's the dyson sphere, but that is just the city's shield. And that shield must always be preserved. That is our charge."

"So all this talk of what you'll do 'after'?" Trevor asked. "Was that just wishful thinking?"

Amanda shrugged. "Well, the universe is going to carry on for a long, long time. With luck, our ascended charges will move on before that, and we'll get to go out on our own."

"I might have a solution for you," Bob said in a quiet voice. "One that is good for both you and your charges."

"Oh?" Tanis asked. "What could that be?"

"We move Star City."

The words fell onto the group like a blanket of silence. The bastions looked at one another with varying levels of disbelief. Finally, Troy spoke up.

"Is that really possible? Far enough and fast enough that Orion would no longer pursue us?"

"Yes." Bob nodded slowly. "Though we will have Orion dealt with before long."

"There will always be another Orion," Tanis countered.

"Perhaps, but my plan would be to move Star City out of the galaxy by jump gate. We can send it anywhere you'd like—though I'd suggest the Small Magellanic Cloud."

The bastions exchanged looks with one another, their gazes carrying a wealth of thought and emotion. Tangel found herself wondering if they were speaking via the Link, or if they really did have such a strong bond that they could debate the issue entirely via human expression.

"We'll have to take you to the city," Tanis said at last. "It is up to the Woken."

"Woken from the Dream," Trevor nodded, a smile on his lips. "I like it."

"When do we go to see them?" Tangel asked.

"No time like the present," Tanis said as she rose. "But they want to see Bob in person, so you'll need to bring your ship through."

A grin formed on Tangel's lips. "Now *that* sounds like fun."

THE REAL STAR CITY

STELLAR DATE: 10.16.8949 (Adjusted Years)
LOCATION: Approaching ISS *I2*
REGION: Star City, Orion Freedom Alliance, Perseus Arm

Tangel rode the shuttle back to the *I2* with Tanis sitting in the copilot's seat, both women silent as they contemplated what Bob had proposed.

As the shuttle approached Dock A1, Tangel reached out to the ship's AI.

~Are you thinking that if we help them move Star City, we'll get to keep the second neutron star and the neutronium-firing ring around it?~

~Yes.~

~Do you think they'll let us have it?~

~Maybe. At some point, they need to either hand over this technology to corporeals, or destroy it. But I think, given what they've done here, that they need to destroy these stars anyway, to fully remove the evidence of what they've done. And destroying a pair of neutron stars is no simple task—outside of slamming them together to create a supernova.~

~Which would not be a nice thing to do to the people at Serenity,~ Tangel added. *~Or pretty much anyone on this side of the Stillwater Nebula…or in the nebula.~*

~Yes, it would be a very destructive act. An alternative would be to deplete the stars by firing their neutronium out of the galaxy. I think that would only take a thousand years or so.~

~Or we move the stars. Because that's a thing we do now.~

Bob laughed, the sound less like pealing thunder and more like a human's chuckle for the first time.

~I have some ideas on how to do it, but it will take Finaeus and Earnest to pull it off. They are quite rare in their ability to make cognitive leaps regarding things of this nature.~

~You know…~ Tangel mused. *~If we can move stars, we can fix what the core AIs did a lot faster than doing things the old-fashioned way.~*

~It is even amazing to me that we now consider inducing asymmetrical burning in a star to be 'old-fashioned'. However, I think that in a lot of cases, that still may be preferable. Neutron stars are much smaller and less…squishy…than stars still undergoing fusion.~

~Squishy.~ Tangel snorted. *~I've never thought of a star like that before.~*

~You're welcome.~

"You're talking to Bob without the Link," Tanis said from next to her. "I can see the energy coming off you when you do it."

"Really?" Tangel asked. "I didn't think that was visible."

"A sliver of it is," the AI responded. "If you know what to look for."

"Good to know."

"May I ask what you're talking about?" Tanis asked.

"That we'll need Finaeus and Earnest to move your star."

A grin split the AI's lips. "Now that's a development I can get behind. I miss Finaeus. He's like my crazy uncle."

Tangel snorted. "I think Finaeus is all of humanity's crazy uncle."

"That sounds about right," Tanis said as the shuttle drifted into the *I2*'s main dock. "You know, even though Star City dwarfs this ship, the *I2* is still really impressive. I think because of all the places it's been as much as anything else."

"Home sweet home," Tangel replied. "She's really been around. Touched another galaxy, even."

"Which we will too, if you can convince the Woken to leave."

"Do you think they'll go for it?"

Her namesake shrugged. "They're not really that concerned about us lower beings anymore. I don't know that we'll be able to convince them to care."

<They'll care,> Bob intoned. *<I'm certain they're worried about the core AIs. If we lose against them, Star City won't last long.>*

"Do you think that's why they tried to block Jessica from getting here?" Tangel asked.

<Yes, and I'd be shocked if it wasn't the core AIs who gave Orion the ability to herd Exdali.>

"It lines up," Tanis said. "Considering that Orion only attacked Star City twice before *Sabrina*'s arrival—and then they stepped up their aggression, even while fighting a war against you—an outside influence makes sense."

"It certainly does," Tangel replied, wondering what else the core AIs were going to attempt while she played firefighter for the rest of the galaxy.

* * * * *

"OK, that's just weird," Rachel said, a nervous smile on her lips as Tangel approached with Tanis at her side. "I don't think the galaxy is big enough for the both of you."

Tangel chuckled. "Ironic that that is what we're trying to solve."

"Pardon?" Rachel frowned. "No, nevermind. I don't want to know what that means."

"Very nice to meet you in person, Captain Rachel." Tanis extended her hand. "I read about you in the archives *Sabrina* left behind."

The captain's brow lowered into a scowl. "Oh great, just what I need, my sordid tale spread across the galaxy."

"I didn't think it was sordid," Tanis said, glancing at Tangel. "Did I misinterpret something?"

"The only time Rachel did anything sordid—that I know of—was when she snuck out of the academy in a garbage bin, back in Victoria."

The captain's face reddened, and she glanced at her bridge crew. "Gee thanks, Tangel. Now everyone knows."

One of the nearby officers coughed and gave Rachel an apologetic smile. "Sorry, ma'am, we've all known about that for years."

"Well, shit."

"It wasn't me," Tangel held up her hands. "Probably Joe. You know how he is."

"Your Joe? Not likely," Rachel snorted. "I know who it was, I'll deal with them another time. So, where to?"

Tanis approached the main holotank. "With your permission?"

"Of course," Rachel replied.

The tank shifted from its display of the ISF logo to a cross-section of the dyson sphere.

"We're going inside," Tanis said plainly. "The entrance to the interior is due north, where the Earth plate meets the Mars and Ceres plate. It's a hundred kilometers through the inner sphere, and then we'll be within the structure.

"There's an a-grav column that will take us down to the star. It lessens the full pull, but it's still going to be twenty *g*s at the surface."

"Uhhh…how far down are we going to go?" Rachel asked.

"Only halfway," Tanis said. "At the surface, acceleration is over one hundred billion *g*s. Even our most powerful a-grav systems cannot counter that. We'll stop at a thousand *g*s, and they will meet us there."

Whispers broke out amongst the bridge crew, wide eyes glancing about, some excited, some alarmed.

"Are you sure?" Tangel asked. "Is that necessary?"

<*It is necessary,*> Bob replied.

"And the heat?" Rachel asked. "I assume it's hundreds of thousands of kelvins inside the sphere."

"We use much of the thermal energy," Tanis explained. "Since the star has no wind, just gravity, it's a total vacuum in there."

"Plus a killer magnetic field," Tangel added. "I've been wondering if that is how you support the sphere."

"Well, *I* don't." Tanis winked. "But that's how the builders supported the structure, yes. We're going to go right down toward the north pole, where the field has a gap." She turned to the helm officers. "Navigation is going to be difficult. You'll need to orient the ship by the three beacons behind us. The magnetic field inside the sphere is so intense that it polarizes the vacuum and creates a birefringence effect."

The pair of lieutenants looked at one another and then nodded.

"OK…really?" Rachel asked. "Is this worth the risk?"

"It'll be fine," Tangel replied. "We'll back down, OK? Then if things get hairy, we can boost out. The *I2* has enough thrust to blast out of the well at our stopping point."

The captain drew a deep breath and nodded. "No one ever said that life in the ISF is boring."

"That's for sure," one of the lieutenants at the helm commented. "Uh…ma'am."

"I've passed the coordinates," Tanis said. "Shall we get this show on the road? The sooner we can get the OK from our ascended friends, the sooner we can get to building the jump gate."

Rachel glanced at Tangel, and she preempted the question.

"The ascended humans all live within the neutron star in the center of the sphere. In higher dimensions, it's bigger and less dense…sort of."

"Further up and further in," Rachel said in a quiet voice. "Helm, let's get this done."

"Aye, ma'am. Going for our little jaunt."

The ship slowly lifted further into the air, drifting over the North Atlantic, passing between Greenland and Iceland before crossing beyond the final stretch of ocean that separated the continents and islands of the Earth replica from the edge of the plate.

Ahead, the separator wall loomed, and Helm drew the ship up and over the hundred-kilometer-high slope, angling to starboard where the opening lay.

Unlike the passage through the outer layer of the city, this time, Helm turned the ship around and allowed the force of gravity to draw the *I2* through engines-first, the fusion burners emitting a soft glow as they fired, ensuring the descent continued at a measured pace.

Unlike the blue haze they'd seen last time, this long passageway ended in a reddish-grey glow. Tangel looked over the readings and saw that most of the star's emissions were in the X-ray band, though some visible light came from the tightly packed cluster of neutrons.

"That's a lot of redshift," she said. "I wouldn't have expected it, given the mass decrease the builders undertook."

"The star bled a lot of heat when they siphoned off its neutronium for the other star," Tanis explained. "It's cooler than a neutron star its age should be."

That reminded Tangel of the black dwarf Joe had reported in the A1 System. That star was also far cooler than it should be, and she wondered if it too had been cooled by artificial means. In all the furor that had followed, she'd not made a note to send a team to investigate that star.

Still plenty to do after the war.

The *I2* passed out of the shaft and into the huge space inside the sphere. The star lay over a million kilometers below the ship, its gravitational pull drawing the vessel down faster and faster, Helm letting the ship accelerate until it was traveling at five hundred kilometers per second.

~Do you see it?~ Bob asked Tangel. *~The city.~*

Tangel had not looked down yet, not with her own eyes. She turned toward the back of the bridge and disregarded the input from her two-dimensional eyes, shifting to her fourth-dimensional perception.

~Shit! It's ***huge****.~*

Where the neutron star was a tiny point only twenty kilometers across in three-dimensional space, the luminous object that filled the fourth and fifth dimensions was much larger, stretching half a million kilometers from the center of the sphere.

She mapped the ship's destination against the city built of starstuff, and saw that the *I2* would stop at the surface of the structure.

~It stands to reason,~ Bob said. *~Mass and density do not translate the same way. In the lower dimensions, neutron stars are the densest objects aside from black holes. But that doesn't directly align.~*

~So it would seem,~ Tangel nodded.

"I can tell you see it," Tanis said from her side. "I've only glimpsed an impression."

"It's beautiful," Tangel whispered. "It's like a billion mobius strips made from hypercubes."

The AI snorted. "OK, even I can't follow what that could look like."

"Maybe someday you will."

Tangel didn't speak for the remainder of the twenty-minute journey. When the ship finally halted, docked with an invisible city in the center of a dyson sphere, she glanced at Tanis.

"Do we go out to meet them?"

~No,~ Bob replied. *~They are already here. Come to my primary node.~*

Tangel strode from the bridge with Tanis on her heels, eager to meet her first ascended humans, curious what they would look like in the higher dimensions.

"Are you nervous?" the AI asked. "You look nervous."

"Anxious. Curious. Not nervous, no."

The pair reached the lift that would take them down to Bob's primary node, and Tanis smiled. "They're kind. You'll like them."

"I'm less worried about that and more concerned with whether or not they'll help us."

Tanis glanced at Tangel, a worried look on her face. "They might not. They're a bit sorry that they ever developed the ability to fire neutronium. It's not the sort of thing you can put back in the bottle."

"Oh trust me," Tangel nodded emphatically. "I know that all too well. I've got quite the collection of things that don't go back in the bottle. Hopefully, if we can move Star City, that will be a worthwhile trade."

The AI snorted. "It's certainly a better offer than Orion made."

A few minutes later, they reached Bob's node and walked inside. Tangel was ready to see just about anything, though what she saw was a luminous, multilimbed being that looked like every other ascended person she'd seen.

~Tangel, Tanis,~ it said, the tone sounding distinctly male. *~My name is Eric.~*

~Eric is one of the leaders in Star City,~ Bob said, adding to the introduction. *~He's different than the others, though, in that he's an AI.~*

"Very nice to meet you," Tangel said aloud, dismayed that she was seeing yet another ascended AI and not one of the Dreamers. "I didn't realize there were AIs amongst your people. The *Perseus* left not long after the solar wars, if I don't miss my guess."

~I joined up at Lucida,~ Eric answered her question equably. *~Before that, I was at Proxima. Things had become a little…tense there, and it was better for me to find my fortune elsewhere. The FGT put out a call for AIs, and the rest is history.~*

Tangel's eyes grew round. "Wait. No…you're not *that* Eric, are you? Commodore in Alpha Centauri's space force before you joined up with Jason and Terrance's merry band of marauders?"

~You know your lore,~ the AI commented. *~Though we were hardly marauders.~*

"Sorry, couldn't think of another 'merry band of' name, and I know some Marauders who are stand-up people."

~I'll forgive you, then.~ The AI sent across the impression of a wink.

There was a moment of silence, and then Bob spoke.

~Now that introductions are out of the way, I'd like to talk about what we can do for each other.~

"Actually," Tangel held up a hand. "Before we get into that, I'd like to ask why you haven't been helping the Bastions deal with the attacks from Orion."

"Until today, the other bastions didn't know that the ascended beings were still here," Tanis explained. "They'd revealed themselves to me, letting me know to call on them as a last resort, but that they were trying to keep the core AIs from knowing they were still here."

~Or Orion,~ Eric added. *~Praetor Kirkland reviles ascended beings. If he knew there were millions of us here, he'd throw everything he has at us. Essentially, hiding is the safest thing for us, even if Star City already is a massive target.~*

"You could join in the fight," Tangel countered. "Stop Orion, stop the core AIs. Live in peace."

~We came out here to leave humanity's endless wars and squabbling behind.~ Eric's tone was even and measured. *~If we reveal ourselves to aid in this war, another will come along. We'd end up becoming the galaxy's police, eventually reviled by all, hated more than what we rose up to stop.~*

Tangel nodded in grim agreement. "I have the same worry, though I don't have the luxury of hiding—not anymore, at least. We tried it as best we could, and got two good decades before the war found us. I can't say I agree with your stance on this, but I *do* understand it. I'm not exactly eager for what the future holds for me after this war is over."

"You're not?" Tanis cocked her head to the side, regarding Tangel curiously. "What do you think will happen?"

"In a nutshell? For me, and probably Bob, the war will never end."

"That's depressing," Tanis replied.

Tangel gave a noncommittal shrug. "I'm resigned to the fact that I may get a decade or two here and there when things aren't on fire somewhere. Honestly, that's more than humans used to get. Maybe I'll be able to find some others willing to help, and we can rotate out."

~Or maybe humanity will learn how to not fight all the time,~ Eric added.

~We'll see how that goes without the core AIs' meddling,~ Bob said. *~But for now, we have more immediate issues to deal with. In a nutshell, Eric, you wish to remain removed from the current struggle, and future conflicts as well. In all honesty, that's going to be problematic, unless your bastions take up a more punitive response to incursions.~*

~That has been on my mind as well,~ Star City's representative replied. *~In the short-term, that will just escalate things further.~*

A feeling of agreement came from Bob. *~Which is why the best solution for you is to move Star City.~*

~An exodus has been on our mind for some time. As you know, however, it is not as simple as just leaving. We would have to remove what we've built here.~

~I believe that is not necessary,~ Bob countered. *~I'm certain that we can move all of Star City. The sphere, the neutron star, everything.~*

~Through your jump gates.~ Eric did not seem convinced.

~Yes, that is how we would move you. I think that somewhere extragalactic would serve you well.~

The visitor didn't respond immediately, and Tangel waited patiently, able to see by the strands of energy stretching out from Eric that he was communicating with other ascended beings. After several minutes, he finally spoke.

~And in exchange, you want us to leave you our other neutron star and its neutronium manipulation systems.~

"That is correct," Tangel said. "With that, we can achieve decisive victory and win the war."

~Your picotech isn't enough?~ Eric prompted. *~With that, you can devour entire planets.~*

"On a planetary scale, picotech is very slow, and it would be possible to stop it with sufficiently high magnetic fields. There are also…sociological reasons to limit its use as a weapon. Neutronium is just a better bullet."

~And it is matter transmutation. That would provide other benefits.~

Tangel pursed her lips. She had suspected that the ability to manipulate degenerate matter in the way Star City had done was tantamount to the direct manipulation of atomic structures themselves. That meant the beings living within the dyson sphere possessed femtotech—something she knew Earnest had been working on cracking for some time, but had not yet unlocked.

"We've been good stewards of the technology we have," Tangel countered. "All I want to do is to stop this war and strengthen humans and AIs for what is to come."

~The conflict with the core AIs,~ Eric said.

"You know that everything going on right now is due to their manipulation. There is no question that we *must* defeat them. I plan to succeed, one way or another, but access to your technology will make the war shorter and less destructive. Not only that, but it will ensure a longer peace after the conflict."

~An imperial peace,~ he countered. *~Is that what you want?~*

"Stars, no," Tangel gave a vehement shake of her head. *~I can't think of anything I want less—except for an eternal war.~*

~I can't argue with that. I will discuss this with our elders. If they agree, we will put it to our full population. It may take several days for us to come to a conclusion. Also, we will require you to demonstrate the ability to move a star through a jump gate before we accept this deal.~

Tangel gave a nervous laugh. "Trust me, I also want to see it safely done with something less precious than Star City the first time."

~We will reach out when we're ready to discuss further,~ Eric said, and then turned and walked away.

The world he walked through was not the same as the one surrounding Tangel, though she could see both. The other ascended being's stride took him down a long ramp that led to a tower rising above the gleaming structure that was Star City.

She'd done her best not to stare at it during the conversation, but Tangel paused now to take it in, to follow the twisting structures that seemed impossible even in her perception of higher dimensions. It was clear to her that the denizens of the city existed in higher planes than she could perceive. She was curious if Bob could see all of it, but decided not to ask just yet.

A slow breath slipped past her lips, and she met Tanis's gaze.

"I wish I could see it," the AI said. "Perhaps someday."

"Someday," Tangel replied, and then reached out to the bridge. *<Captain Rachel, take us out.>*

SUPPOSITION

STELLAR DATE: 10.17.8949 (Adjusted Years)
LOCATION: Palatine, Euros
REGION: Earth, New Sol, Orion Freedom Alliance

The Orion Guard's top admiralty met deep within the Guard Command complex in what they called the 'Star Chamber'. Praetor Kirkland rarely visited it, usually preferring to summon the Guard's commanders to his own offices.

Today, he didn't have the patience required to wait for them to arrive.

He stormed down the long corridor that led to the chamber, his gaze fixed on the doors, willing the men and women within to sense his approach and ready themselves for what was to come.

Of course, they'll know I'm coming, and I imagine they know why.

A minute later, he reached the end of the hall, and as he neared the two massive slabs of stone, they swung aside, admitting him into the inner sanctum of his people's military.

The sixteen commanding admirals of the Orion Guard sat around the circular table, all eyes on him as the officers rose and nodded in greeting.

"Praetor Kirkland," Admiral Myka spoke first. "We were just discussing the latest reports. I assume that is why you are here."

"It is. I look forward to how you'll explain the defeats we've suffered."

"Well, for starters, they've been minor," Myka replied as she waited for Kirkland to take his seat. "We've lost a few systems in the Expansion Districts and on the rimward edge. What happened at Karaske and Rega was something else entirely."

"Oh?" Kirkland pressed. "Those were Transcend and ISF ships at Karaske. Karaske! That's deep within our borders. How did the enemy know that system was significant? Garza is too careful to have led his enemies there. Stars, half of you didn't even know that's where he based his operation."

The admirals glanced at one another before Myka cleared her throat and responded. "That was a betrayal, sir. Lisa Wrentham directed our enemies to attack Karaske. We also believe it was her Widows that destroyed Dock 1 in Rega. It seems like she's switched sides."

"Nonsense," Kirkland shook his head. "I've known her for thousands of years. She wouldn't just turn on me."

"Her ship was—"

Kirkland's hand sliced through the air. "Lisa Wrentham is not her ship! Yes, it is possible that the *Perilous Dream* has been taken by our enemies and they're using it against us, but I will not hear of Lisa's betrayal. She's lost more than you could know to join the true cause."

"And the reports that her Widows were fighting against Orion Guard forces on Durgen?" Admiral Myka pressed. "Could our enemies have taken control of her Widows?"

"No." Kirkland shook his head. "That is not possible. Lisa assured me herself."

"Are—" Admiral Prel began, but the praetor cut him off.

"We have Transcend fleets operating inside our borders, they've taken the *Perilous Dream*, and the Transcend's civil war has come to an end. It feels like the tide is turning against us, people. I want to know what you intend to do to stop this."

"We've no word from General Garza," Myka's tone betrayed no emotion. "Are you suggesting that I take control of the war effort?"

Kirkland locked his gaze on Myka's. He knew that some of the admirals in the room with him were fully Garza's creatures, more loyal to the general than their own praetor. He'd never been able to discern where Myka's loyalties lay.

Well, maybe if I elevate her above Garza, she'll become more loyal to me.

He knew the logic was weak, but he needed a clear commander. Without it, the admirals would fight for days amongst themselves.

"I think that's possible," he replied. "First, tell me what you plan to do to gain the upper hand."

A smile cracked Myka's lips apart, and she summoned a holodisplay above the table. "For starters, we have to stop defending points we don't care about. We must put all our attention into two, singular strikes…."

Kirkland leant back in his chair and interlaced his fingers, nodding slowly as the admiral explained her plan.

Yes, I think this just might work.

PART 4 – PIVOTAL

CONSIDERATIONS

STELLAR DATE: 10.16.8949 (Adjusted Years)
LOCATION: TSS *Cora's Triumph*
REGION: Interstellar Space, Inner Praesepe Empire

Terrance gave Earnest a mock scowl as they walked onto the *Cora's Triumph*'s bridge. "Just like Tangel to swoop in, get all the glory, and then fly off."

"Trust me," Earnest said with a heartfelt sigh. "This tears me up inside. I want to see Star City more than I can say, but getting to the bottom of what the core AIs are up to is even more important. Plus, we might be able to use their tech to aid in accelerating Project Starflight."

"I get that," Terrance glanced at Earnest, noting the glimmer in the man's eyes. "And stopping this entire star cluster from going boom is kinda important."

"Oh?" Captain Beatrice cocked an eyebrow from where she stood next to the holotank. "Just kinda? If I'd known that, I wouldn't have put up such a fight when those core ships attacked."

"Heard you gave 'em what for," Earnest said, his voice growing quiet.

"We did," she replied, her voice lowering. "As did you."

Terrance nodded solemnly. "It was hard-won, but worth it, Captain. We got what we came for, and we're one step closer to shutting down the core AIs."

"Well," Earnest held up a hand. "Shutting down might be a bit of an overstatement.

"Pardon my eternal optimism," Terrance said with a rueful laugh. "So, are we ready to move on to our friendly neighborhood drone sphere?"

"Sue's finishing the final integration of the data we got from the C&C," Earnest nodded toward a panel that was initializing on the forward holodisplay. "We're setting it up in an NSAI core and sandboxing the hell out of it. Not going to risk some trojan getting into the ship."

"I appreciate that," Beatrice drawled. "Should we set a course?"

Terrance glanced at Earnest, who nodded and said, "Bring us to fifty thousand klicks. That will be close enough for a lag-less interface and far enough that we can run away if necessary."

"Still some light-lag at fifty thousand," the captain said.

"Sorry, less laggy," Earnest said with a long-suffering glance at the captain. "You've been around these scientists too long. Their pedantry is wearing off on you."

Beatrice laughed. "I suppose it is. So how come you're immune? You're the ultimate scientist."

"Comes from being married to Abby. I've had to get regular inoculations to be around her."

Terrance snorted and covered his mouth. "Sorry, I just imagined the largest syringe ever with 'Withstand Abby' on the side."

"If you hadn't been the one who got us together, I'd take offense to that," Earnest countered. "Ah, Sue's done, we're online. Going to send the initialization commands now."

"One hour till we reach a fifty-k orbit," Beatrice added. "Or do you need us to rush it more than that?"

"No," Earnest shook his head. "It'll take a bit to sort through the control interfaces, figure out what they do. This system was not made for humans to operate."

"Good thing we have you." Terrance met Beatrice's gaze, and a sly smile formed on his lips. "An hour or so should be enough, right?"

"Only if you shut up for a minute or two," Earnest muttered, the smile in his eyes contradicting the scorn in his voice.

Even so, Terrance took the hint and walked to the far side of the holotank, watching the drone swarm grow larger with each passing minute. As the engineers worked their way through the control systems, data began to appear alongside the object on the display, noting mass, number of drones, types of drones, and resource limits.

It turned out that there was a moonlet beneath the swarm, but it was over half gone, its mass converted into the single-use machines that fell into the star they were moving once their task was done.

The waste bothered Terrance until he considered that, with the time between optimal burns—and the fact that the core AIs planned to obliterate the entire cluster—it didn't really matter how efficient they were with the use of resources from one small rogue body.

In turn, it made him upset that they were going to destroy an entire open cluster…for what remained reasons unknown.

"What do you think their goal is?" he asked Beatrice, who had been silently standing at his right shoulder.

"The core AIs?"

The question was rhetorical, but he nodded anyway, signaling her to continue.

"Well, I suppose it'll depend on whether or not they're doing this in other clusters surrounding Sol. The wave of supernovae this will cause won't reach the core worlds for centuries, easily enough time for people to move. But if they do this here, in Hyades, the Pleiades and others, the result will be the sterilization of the Inner Stars."

"But like you said, it'll be slow."

The ship's captain nodded. "Right, but where are all the people going to go? They're going to have to travel across a hundred empires to get to unclaimed space, and what if the core AIs have done the same thing in clusters further out? Humanity will fall into a final war where we battle it out over the tiny slivers of the galaxy that are still habitable."

"That seems a bit melodramatic," Terrance said. "Maybe if we hadn't discovered the core AIs' plan, and if we didn't have jump gates...."

"There are just too many people to relocate them all through jump gates...and some will remain, fighting over the scraps. You have to admit that, at the least, it will weaken us all beyond the worst of the FTL wars. You can hide from a war, but you can't hide from a dozen supernovae shockwaves."

He nodded, evaluating her words. "If you consider that they started this awhile back, and that everyone thought the *Intrepid* would appear five hundred years from now, I can see them playing a long game to have our disruption come into play right around the same time as the supernovae shockwave starts to hit populated areas."

"A lot of long games being played," Beatrice muttered. "I wonder how long it'll take to find out if they're doing this elsewhere."

"Well, there are over twelve hundred open clusters, and more than two hundred globular clusters in the galaxy. Plus a number of star-forming regions that they could mess up. So maybe two thousand locations we have to check out, and since all of them are likely slow zones, it's not going to be a fast process. Probably take decades...and that's if they're all clear."

"And if none of them are further along than Praesepe."

Beatrice's words caused a sliver of fear to take hold in Terrance's mind. If there was the possibility that a star cluster could fall into a cascade of supernovae, it would take some drastic measures to prevent the event—though he had no idea what measures those would be.

He chatted off and on with Beatrice for the next hour, the pair moving on from a discussion of what dangers the core AIs posed, to what Terrance had busied himself with during the two decades New Canaan had been at peace.

"I enjoyed losing myself in the establishment of our economy more than I thought I would have," he said. "I thought I was over that sort of thing, but it came back with a vengeance. We were trying to make something where everyone could have enough security to explore their personal interests, while still incentivizing everyone to work in the colony's best interests. I think we did rather well with it—until we had to toss all that aside and go to a war footing."

"I imagine that will take a bit to reorient," the captain said. "My home is a bit lucky—it's in the Vela Cluster, which sided with Khardine almost immediately. The civil war never made it to our astrosphere, so other than some general disruption in trade, things remained largely unchanged.... At least, that's what I've heard from my brother back home. I do wonder if he's just telling me what I want to hear so I won't worry."

"Airtha was such a fool," Terrance muttered. "She should have sided *with* New Canaan, not fought against us."

"Same thing is true for Orion," Beatrice added. "Ultimately, we all want to stop the core AIs from fucking around with us. From what I've heard, the schism between Tomlinson and Kirkland hit its breaking point when they learned about the core AIs. Rather than pissing off, the *praetor* should have worked with us to stop the core devils. Instead, he delayed the Inner Stars' uplift, and now he's stopping us from going after the real enemy."

"Yeah," Terrance nodded emphatically. "From what I can see, the core AIs played Kirkland like a fiddle...Jeffrey too."

"Well, they are a bunch of all-powerful AIs. Stands to reason that they'd be able to mess with us."

"They're not all-powerful," he corrected. "From what Tangel distills it down to, they just have better eyesight."

The captain snorted. "That's an interesting way to put it. Though from what I've seen, they can also shred matter and blast you with photonic and electric energy. That seems like more than good eyesight."

Terrance barked a rueful laugh. "Yeah, it does, doesn't it? I never said I really agreed with her assessment, just relating her thoughts on the matter."

"Do you think we'll all ascend eventually?"

He turned and stared into the captain's eyes, trying to discern whether she was excited or scared by the prospect. Her eyes were unreadable, but her right hand was clenching and unclenching.

"Maybe," he allowed. "But I think you generally have to want it."

"Did Tangel want it?"

"Well, that's a different sort of scenario. I don't claim to understand all the ins and outs of what she went through, but if there is such a thing as fate, it had her squarely in its sights."

"Was it fate, or was she manipulated?"

Terrance shrugged. "If anything thought they could manipulate Tangel, they got a rude awakening."

"You put a lot of stock in her."

"Yeah, well, she always comes through."

"I think we've figured it out," Earnest said from behind the pair, and Terrance turned to see Sue standing next to the engineer.

"When did you get here?" he asked.

"Twenty minutes ago," the AI smirked. "I'm like a ninja."

Earnest rolled his eyes and gestured to the holotank, which showed the drone sphere shrouded in darkness.

"You're going to love this, Terrance," he said. "They're using a formulation of Elastene that still has the Enfield markers in it. I guess there's no reason to mess with a good thing."

"Damn," Terrance felt a twist in his gut. "How many times are my company's inventions going to be co-opted by fucking evil bastards?"

"Easy now," Earnest placed a hand on his shoulder. "Your family made a lot of good stuff.... It's no wonder that everyone uses it even six thousand years later."

"Hooray. So, what have you learned?"

"Well, all the stellar alterations they've made are logged in the data we pulled, and the drone moon is all but automated, though it possesses no C&C of its own, and we blew up the last one."

"Right," Sue joined in. "So for now, the *Cora's Triumph* is that C&C. We've already programmed our first major correction for two of the core's blue giants, and if they shift like the models predict, we should have the stars back to a stable pattern in fifty years."

"Really?" Terrance was surprised by the speed, given how long it had taken to shift the stars off course.

"We're not trying to hide what we're doing," Earnest explained. "We can go a lot faster than the core AIs did."

"Ma'am?" the comm officer spoke up. "A courier jumped in back at the gate array. A message from the field marshal just came on sublight."

"I guess we don't have a QC blade that links up with the right places," Beatrice muttered. "Put the message up."

The forward display shifted to show Tangel standing at the edge of a city, the faint sound of waves slapping against the shore in the background.

"Terrance and Earnest. I've worked out a deal with the people of Star City. They're going to give us their technology, and their second neutron star, on the condition that we move Star City."

"Good thing we have the ability to do that now," Beatrice said, gesturing to the display on the holotank.

"This is where you're going to say something really terrible," Tangel continued. "But this was Bob's idea, and he thinks it's possible, so you can get mad at *him*. We're going to move Star City out of the galaxy, with a jump gate."

"What the ever-loving fuck," Earnest muttered. "There's no way at all, under no circumstances…just, no!"

"I'm bringing Finaeus here, and Terrance…an old friend of yours is waiting to meet you. You're not going to believe who."

"That woman!" Earnest shook his head. "I swear, someday she's going to ask me to move the galaxy."

Terrance barely heard the engineer's outburst, wondering who it was that Tangel had met, a tiny hope welling up inside that it just might be Khela.

RECALLED

STELLAR DATE: 10.16.8949 (Adjusted Years)
LOCATION: *Sabrina*, Airthan trojan asteroids
REGION: Huygens System, Transcend Interstellar Alliance

"We've got company!" Cheeky cried out, spinning the ship and punching the fusion burners up to their full thrust. A-grav system warnings lit up across her board as the strain on the ship's frame caused it to twist violently.

A depressurization warning flashed in the main hold, caused by the bay door unseating, and she pursed her lips, knowing that Nance was going to give her a tongue-lashing over the abuse she was putting *Sabrina* through.

<*I see them!*> the ship's AI called out. <*Just don't break me to bits, and I'll take them out.*>

Cheeky grunted her acknowledgment and held her course for ten seconds while Sabrina unleashed the unassuming freighter's beams on the two destroyers that had dropped stealth only ten thousand kilometers away.

<*Think they can sneak up on me?! Taste my hot breath, assholes!*>

"Oh gawd...gawd!" Cheeky grimaced. "That was terrible! Don't mix things like that...ewww."

<*What...ohhhh...wow. Yeah, not what I meant at all.*>

"I think I got all the sense when we sharded," Sabs said from where she sat at the scan console. "OK, you tore a hole clear through one of them, it's dead in the water, but the other is trying to limp away."

<*Not for long,*> Sabrina replied. <*Hold steady another sec.*>

Cheeky complied, and a shudder rippled through the deck as both railguns fired in unison, a trio of slugs bursting from each weapon, streaking across the small gap between the ships and smashing the destroyer's starboard engine. The Airthan craft's other burner winked out a moment later, and it slewed to the side, spinning slowly as it drifted through the black.

"That the last of them?" Cheeky asked, wiping a hand across her brow. "Who would have thought that Airtha would have 'true believers' and that they'd be fucking nuts? Don't they know they lost and Airtha is dead?"

"You shall not defile her holy shrine..." Sabs intoned. "Only Airthans shall tread in that sacred place."

<*More like air**heads**,*> Sabrina scoffed. <*Sucks that we're stuck here on cleanup duty and not dealing with a real threat.*>

"Or hunting for Cary," Cheeky added. "But it has to be done, right? We didn't fight so hard to secure Airtha, only to have these dorks take it back."

<*You done turning my ship into a pretzel?*> Nance called up. <*Because we're leaking stuff down here that should never be leaked.*>

<Yeah, all's clear. What did we crack open?>

<Oh, you know, the usual, just a tank full of stuff that we pretend we don't grow things in for food in a pinch.>

<Why can't you just say 'shit',> Sabs asked.

Nance snorted. *<Because I have you to say it for me.>*

"Admiral Krissy on the horn for us," Sabs announced.

Cheeky sat up straight, somehow feeling like she was talking to her mom when Krissy called—which was more than a little strange, since it was she who was married to the admiral's father.

"We've cleaned things up around the trailing trojan asteroids," Cheeky reported. "Two more destroyers out here. They haven't dumped any pods yet."

"Stars, they're like freaking cockroaches," Krissy muttered. "I'll see that boarding and cleanup teams get sent out. I need you to get to High Airtha and pick my dad up before heading to the main gate array."

"Ummm sure…. Where we headed?"

"Tangel has requested you all get to Star City. Well, she kind of demanded Finaeus—you know how she is—but suggested that you be the ones to courier him over."

<Story of my life,> Sabrina chimed in. *<Couriering Finaeus.>*

"Either that, or searching for him," Sabs added.

"OK," Cheeky responded to Krissy while shooting Sabs a quelling look. "We'll drop a beacon and be on our way. Did Tangel say *why* she wants us at Star City? Not that I'm complaining, I can't wait to see the kids again."

"She only said that she needs Finaeus to build a…and I'm quoting here…star gate."

"A stargate?" Cheeky glanced at Sabs. "Didn't we watch an old 2D about that?"

"Sure did," the AI nodded. "Though the series was better than the movie."

"Uh, sure," Krissy said with a long-suffering look on her face. "Just get a move on, Tangel seemed like there was some level of urgency."

"You bet." Cheeky brought the ship onto a vector that would get them to High Airtha in a few hours. "One delivery of a grumpy old man, coming right up."

"Thanks, Cheeks," the admiral said. "Give him a kiss for me."

"Uhh…is that weird? He's your father, and I'm his wife. I kiss differently than you."

"Can't you just give him a peck on the cheek?"

Cheeky cocked her head. "I don't think I've ever given anyone a peck on the check. Usually it's between the che—"

"Gah! Cheeky. Enough." The admiral groaned and shook her head. "I'm sorry I asked."

THE NEW BUILDERS

STELLAR DATE: 10.17.8949 (Adjusted Years)
LOCATION: Manhattan Island, North America
REGION: Star City, Orion Freedom Alliance, Perseus Arm

"Not a lot impresses me anymore," Terrance said as he approached Tangel, his eyes filled with wonder. "But this does."

She smiled and clasped his outstretched hand. "I thought you might like it. So far as I know, this place is unique—that alone is something uncommon in this universe."

"We flew over El Dorado." Moisture formed in the corners of his eyes. "The planet and the ring. Jason's going to have to come out here some time."

"You could always visit AC when the war is over," Tangel suggested. "No reason why not."

Terrance shook his head. "I can think of a few. It's not the same…filled with people, and ones I'm not too keen on, given their participation in the Hegemony. Here, it's pristine, looks like it did when I grew up."

"I feel the same way. I made a trip over to Mars, climbed Olympus Mons. Relived my childhood, all the good stuff."

The one-time executive nodded soberly. "That's something you can't do back in the Sol System. Not without clambering over the ruin of the ring, at least."

"Yeah, though I plan to do that someday, anyway. I feel like I owe it to my family to stand there and remember. Do you realize that only a few thousand living people have stood on terraformed Mars?"

"Proud to be one of them." Terrance smiled and placed a hand on her shoulder. "Maybe we can remake it."

"Maybe." She placed her hand over his. "Sorry I was all cryptic when I said there was someone here and didn't say who it was. I was feeling almost giddy then, but now that I'm a bit more melancholy, it seems foolish of me to have toyed with you like that. Especially because you probably thought it was Khela—which it's not."

"I didn't know you knew about her."

Tangel twisted her lips. "Well, I didn't until Bob told me about her. Anyway, the person is Eric."

Terrance's eyes widened, and his mouth fell open. "Eric…*my* Eric?"

"Yeah, I guess he was with the *Perseus* worldship, came out to Serenity with them, and then left with the builders to come and make Star City."

"So he ascended." The words fell from Terrance's lips like lead weights. "I thought there were only ascended humans here."

"A few AIs, as well, as it turns out," Tangel said. "Him, and a few of the Bastions. When they ascended, they just flitted down to the neutron star in the center of the sphere and built a city on it in the higher dimensions."

A snort burst from his lips. "Sure, of course. That's what *I'd* do, build a city on a neutron star. So is he here, or do I have to go down?"

"We convinced them to come up for the next chat. It's a bit dangerous inside the sphere. The magnetic fields could rip the *I2* to shreds."

"I've read that about neutron stars."

"Oh? You're an astronomer now?"

"Tangel, you left me with the FGT's top stellar engineers for weeks. I have at least two or three degrees now, mostly earned while getting drunk and discussing what could happen if various stars in Praesepe crashed into one another."

"Which is?" Tangel pressed.

"Not good. So much not good."

She chortled. "I think the drunk version of your degrees are lacking some specifics—but I get the sentiment."

"Thanks for waiting," Earnest said as he stepped out of the shuttle and walked across the grass to where Tangel and Terrance waited. "Bob was bending my ear—well, my brain—about a thousand different topics. Guy can be exhausting."

<I can hear you out there.>

"I know, that's my passive-aggressive way of reminding you that I'm still organic. I can't think as fast as you can."

<You're organic like I'm still an AI,> Bob retorted.

"What does that mean?" Terrance glanced at Earnest, an eyebrow cocked in question.

"Mods," Tangel said in a singsong voice, gesturing at the scientist. "Honestly, he rivals me for lack of original parts at this point."

"Yeah, but where you're all muscles, I'm all brains," Earnest countered. "Actually…that's a lie. You have three brains, so you've got me beat there as well. Why do you need me here, again? I was all ready to play with my drone swarm."

Tangel looked over Earnest's shoulder to where the *I2* hovered above the Atlantic Ocean. "Oh, I don't know, probably because I'm commander of the largest war in humanity's history. That takes a lot of concentration. I'm reviewing four after-action reports from the fronts, seven intel feeds, and working with two planning teams on an attack in the Trisilieds and the Hyades."

Terrance looked at Earnest and mouthed 'showoff'.

"There they are." Tangel pointed toward the sky, and Terrance and Earnest turned to gaze up.

"Where?" Terrance asked.

<*Sabrina is over two thousand kilometers away still,*> Bob admonished. <*You know they can't see it yet.*>

"Well, they were accusing me of being a showoff, so I figured I'd best live up to it."

The trio chatted about the state of the war, the ISF fleet, and shared news from New Canaan while they waited. Tangel was glad to hear that Erin had finally returned to Carthage to discuss a run for office with Jason. Elections were coming in the following year—provided the war was over—and neither Tangel nor Jason wanted to be in power.

Ten minutes later, *Sabrina* was settling down on the cradle vacated by the shuttle that had brought Earnest and Terrance. The trio turned toward the ship, once again sporting the blue and silver colors that had been present when Tangel was first aboard.

The craft had barely settled into the cradle when the airlock door opened and Finaeus leapt out onto the still-rising ramp.

"It can't be done!" he shouted. "I don't care what Bob says. It's madness!"

"Glad he's ready to consider options," Earnest said out of the side of his mouth.

"Why not?" Tangel asked as he drew near, waving at the rest of the ship's crew as they exited the ship.

"Gravity, my dear ascended fool. *Gravity*. The two stars in this system are in an intricate dance, living deep in their gravity wells, carving deep gouges through spacetime. Add to that the propensity that neutron stars have for starquakes—ones that smash out gravitons like they have nothing else to do—and you have a thing that *cannot be moved*."

Earnest was nodding. "I've been thinking about that, too. If we remove this star and sphere, the other one is going to streak clear out of the system…at a healthy clip, too."

"Not to mention the angular momentum of Star City when it lands wherever we put it. It might just tear itself to shreds."

<*Not if we slow down these two stars, first. We move them further apart, and then swap them at just the right time.*>

"I'm sorry," Finaeus waved a hand toward the *I2*. "I forgot that we have two ascended fools giving out terrible advice. Swap *what*—"

The words died on Finaeus's lips, and his mouth formed a wide 'O'.

<*Gravity moves at the speed of light. We pull Star City out at the same time that we drop two other smaller mass stars into its L3 and L4. Then we land Star City somewhere with a similarly massed star as its new counterpart. That star will flare like mad, but we can shield the city from it.*>

"Oversimplified, but it could work," Earnest said. "Maybe our ascended friends aren't such fools after all."

"Well, thank you," Tangel said.

"*Maybe,*" Finaeus wagged a finger at Tangel. "So do we get to work now, or do we have to have a meeting with more glowy balls of light?"

"Don't pay attention to him," Cheeky said as she reached the group and wrapped Tangel in an embrace. "He's just grumpy because the trip was so short that we didn't get to have any shenanigans."

"Plenty of time for that," he groused. "This is no overnight project. Going to take months, easy."

Tangel nodded to Nance, Sabs, Amavia, and Misha. "You three are welcome to join us for this conversation, it should be interesting."

"Fate-of-the-galaxy interesting, or *actually* interesting?" Misha asked. "Because, frankly, I'm getting a bit bored with constantly having to save all the shit that's burning down around us."

"Well," Tangel tapped a finger against her chin. "I suppose it's a bit of column A and a bit of column B. Moving stars is no mean feat."

"Yes," Finaeus nodded. "Stars. A lot of stars. There'll be a test star, maybe more than one if we fail, then braking stars, and maybe others for balancing mass and testing vector change. Fascinating stuff!"

"I thought you thought it was stupid," Tangel said.

"Oh it probably still is." A broad grin stretched the engineer's lips wide. "But it's my kind of stupid. Besides, how will I ever build a ring around the galaxy if I don't first practice moving stars?"

"Good point," Earnest nodded. "Gotta skill up."

"Granted, it would be nice if our first major project wasn't moving a star that was also a city."

Tangel placed a hand on Finaeus's shoulder, a sly smile forming on her lips. "Well, if you hadn't run off and become an antiquities dealer in the Inner Stars for a few decades, you'd be further ahead."

"Not to mention sending us to Grey Wolf, where we jumped halfway across the galaxy," Cheeky added. "Chop-chop, mister, we have lost time to make up for."

"I think I'll go for a walk through the city," Misha said. "Just look around, soak it in. I'd love to go to the real Earth someday."

Tangel would have loved to go on that same stroll, but she didn't have an option to do so. Even if her input wasn't necessary, she still needed to manage the plan.

"I'd like to join you," Cheeky said, her lips twisting with indecision. "But chances are that they're going to need me to fly a ship that's going to move those stars…or move something that moves stars later."

"I don't know that we'll get that far today." Finaeus gave Cheeky a light peck. "If you want to wander around, feel free."

"That's my plan," Sabs chimed in. "Sabrina can listen in to all that nonsense, I'm going to soak up the sights."

<I see how it is.>

"OK, then. Everyone who wants to go to boring meetings about moving stars, with me," Tangel held up a hand. "Everyone else, group up around Cheeky."

With a dose of good-natured laughter, the crowd split up, and Tangel led Terrance, Finaeus, and Earnest toward one of the nearby towers. On the way there, she passed Jessica and Trevor.

"Bailing before we start?" Tangel asked.

"Cheeky told me there's going to be ice cream," Jessica shrugged. "I'm not one to say no to a walk on the shoreline followed by some frozen milk."

Terrance snorted. "Sound logic. Why am I going to the meeting, again?"

"Eric?" Tangel prompted as they continued on their way.

"Right! Eric. Plus, I'm also shockingly good at corralling engineers and keeping them on task."

"Seriously? Do you really think we need that?" Finaeus asked.

The former head of Enfield Technologies fixed the ancient engineer with a serious look. "Didn't we just talk about you running off and becoming an antiquities dealer?"

"I was retired…and running for my life. Retirunning. It's a valid excuse. Look, if you know someone else who can make a stargate, feel free to call them up."

Earnest winked. "I thought it couldn't be done."

"Oh for starssakes," Finaeus muttered. "You going to throw that in my face forever?"

Tangel smacked a palm against her forehead. "You said it five minutes ago!"

"In *this* spacetime. In another spacetime, it might be centuries ago."

"I'll send *you* to another spacetime," Tangel gave a soft laugh as well as a narrow-eyed glare to keep Finaeus on his toes.

Once inside the tower, the group walked through tall, empty halls until they came to a meeting room where Tanis, Kira, and Troy waited, along with Eric and two other ascended beings.

The two new denizens of Star City confirmed her suspicion that ascended humans would appear to be very different than ascended AIs. To her organic eyes, their forms were vaguely humanoid, but indistinct, as though all of their defining features had been smoothed over. They also appeared to have six arms, and were over three meters tall. The visual caused her to wonder if it was at all possible that humans had ascended in the past and whether some ancient mythology had been based on encounters with those ascended beings.

Or it's just logical for people to envision deities that look like things they can relate to.

<Which one is Eric?> Terrance asked her as they walked into the room.

<The tentacled one. I guess that's normal for AIs, since they don't have bipedal self-

images like we do.>

<I suppose that makes sense.>

"Eric," Tangel said aloud. "Thank you for coming to us this time. The city is something to see, but the journey is not for the faint of heart."

~Understandable. And since we're not hiding ourselves anymore, there's no reason not to come up to the surface.~ He gestured to the other ascended beings. *~Corin and Bill were two of the chief engineers behind Star City.~*

"Shit…Corin?" Finaeus shook his head, mouth agape. "I wondered where you wound up. You weren't on the roster for the *Perseus*."

~A story for another time, Finaeus. I was glad to know you were well when you were here a decade ago, though I do wonder how you think you can move our city.~

The ancient engineer snorted. "Well, it's Bob who thinks it can be done. He just wants Earnest and I to do the legwork."

~Do you want to sit, before we get down to brass tacks?~ Eric asked.

"I'm OK standing," Earnest said. "So long as someone brings some drinks. Like brandy. This is definitely a brandy sort of conversation."

"I'll have some synthesized," Tanis said, only to have Finaeus hold up a hand in protest.

"Stars, no. If we're to have fortifying drinks, it has to be the real thing."

<I have a servitor coming with a selection,> Sabrina said, her voice lilting with laughter.

"Always knew you were the best sort of AI," Finaeus said.

<Are you conversing with Eric?> Tangel asked Terrance privately.

<I am…it's amazing to think he's been alive—well alive-ish—all this time. He and I had a complicated relationship when we parted ways. It's good to be able to look back on it now with better perspective.>

<That's good. I'd be interested in knowing what happened, if you're willing to tell.>

Finaeus, Earnest, and the two ascended engineers had fallen deep into the details of how one could move a star and not have the changes in gravitational forces acting on it create irreparable damage.

Tangel continued to half listen to it as Terrance suggested that he tell the tale along with Eric. She initiated an expanse—a replica of her lakehouse on the *I2*—and Eric appeared as a grizzled old soldier.

The three took seats around the fireplace, and Terrance began to explain the events that had taken place at Proxima Centauri almost six thousand years before.

"Back then, even though the Phobos Accords had been signed in the Sol System, there was still a burgeoning trade amongst the near-Sol colonies for shackled AIs. A lot of AIs fled Sol during the outset of the Second Solar War, only to find themselves enslaved by cartels and unscrupulous corporations."

"I recall reading some of that," Tangel inclined her head. "Some vigilante groups went around freeing them, right?"

"Indeed," Eric replied. "I led one such group, though we were unofficially-officially sanctioned."

"Phantom Blade." A melancholy smile settled on Terrance's lips. "That's where Jason and I met, and where I met Eric, here. We stopped the illegal trade at El Dorado, and found that some of the AIs had been sent to Proxima, so we took a ship, the…."

"*Speedwell,*" Eric supplied.

"Right!" Terrance snapped his fingers. "The *Speedwell.* Anyway, due to some rather bizarre circumstances, a truly insane AI who styled himself as 'Prime' snuck aboard the ship."

"Inside Jason's sister," Eric added.

"Yes…which made for more than a few complications." Terrance's gaze settled on Eric, and he drew in a deep breath. "We had come to realize that Prime was in control of her, and had hunted her across C-47, the primary hab in Proxima at the time. Prime was working on taking control of the whole place, and we were at a loss for how to stop him while saving Jason's sister, so…"

"So I assumed control of Terrance's body, and shot Prime out of her head."

Terrance snorted. "You still have such a way with words."

"I don't feel shame for that—the shooting. I *do* hate that it caused you anguish, and breached our trust. Even so, given the options at the time, I would do it again."

"Trust me," the former executive clasped his hands and stared at his lap for a moment. "I'm glad you did it. I couldn't bring myself to, but it had to be done. You saved Proxima with that one action."

He turned to Tangel before continuing.

"Prime was an AI unlike any we'd seen before, and few since. Others, like the Psion AIs, wrought atrocities on humanity to further their ends. Prime did it because he was, at his core, deeply broken. I'm certain he derived whatever his version of joy was from torturing humans."

Tangel's brow lowered. "I'm surprised I'd never heard of this before."

"It was kept quiet," Eric explained. "Some people knew about a rogue AI named Prime, but it sort of got mixed up in Phantom Blade's mission to rescue shackled AIs, so a lot of people assumed Prime was being used by people, and not the other way around."

"He could turn people into sock puppets faster than you could say…well, 'sock puppet'," Terrance added.

"On the plus side, the attack vectors he used greatly improved Link security. So much of the protections people have around their minds now come from how Prime was able to control people."

Tangel looked from one man to the other. "So that's when you decided to take your leave, Eric?"

"The AI council at Proxima was not pleased with what I'd done…. I'd violated the Phobos Accords and a host of ethical considerations. I was removed from Terrance, and ordered never to embed in a human again."

"Did you abide by that?" Terrance asked.

A grin formed on Eric's lips. "No."

"Not surprised. How a rule-breaker like you made it to the rank of commodore, I'll never know."

"Commodore," Tangel mused. "That's a title that's fallen out of use. I rather like it."

"God-empress not available?" Terrance laughed.

"Not funny," Tangel chastised. "Besides, as is clearly evident by the company we're sharing these days, I'm the new girl on the block. There are many who are far more ancient and evolved than I."

Eric fixed Tangel with a penetrating look, his head tilting to the side. "I'm not so certain that's true. Older, yes. Perhaps wiser, too. But you're on a different track than anyone else. Well, you *and* Bob. Neither of you are anything like the people of Star City, nor like the other ascended beings we've come into contact with."

"Other ascended beings?" Tangel asked.

"Not something I'm privy to discuss." Eric's tone brooked no dispute, and Tangel settled back in her seat, regarding the ascended being skeptically.

"So that's our story," Terrance changed the subject. "I'm glad that you made it safely to Lucida and the FGT, Eric."

"Stars, that was an interesting period. So much of the mess you're dealing with now comes from there. I thought we could escape the schism growing in the FGT, but we didn't go far enough."

"Or maybe you went just far enough," Terrance countered. "To be exactly where we needed you to be to help end this."

Eric shook his head. "As I told Tangel, there will always be another conflict, another great war. There is no end."

"Perhaps," she said, peering into the former AI's eyes. "But the core AIs clearly spread the Exdali around the galaxy as a way to slow human expansion. I wonder if some similar solution might be possible…without all the death and destruction."

"A solution for human expansion?" Terrance asked. "That sounds draconian."

"In our prior meeting, Eric mentioned that his people had no interest in becoming the galaxy's police. I don't much like the idea, either, but at present, we're in a situation where, if we don't keep things under control—after this war, that is—we'll end up doing it all over again."

"So what are you suggesting?" Terrance asked. "Surely not something like what Praetor Kirkland enforces in Orion, keeping the majority of his people living in technological poverty."

Tangel shrugged. "I don't have a solid answer yet, but the idea that I can't shake is what if FTL was no longer possible? Would that be enough to stop most major wars?"

Eric nodded slowly. "It might. It would at least constrain the scope of most conflicts. There still might be marauding fleets, but they would likely move slower than the speed of civilization—meaning people would expand and rebuild faster than marauders could attack."

"Not to mention, you'd see them coming," Tangel replied. "Like we did with the Sirians. Even with our fledgling civilization, we were able to hold them back."

"Until they got FTL," Terrance added.

Tangel nodded soberly. "Exactly."

"Well, this has been enlightening," Eric rose from the chair. "And it seems as though our engineers have worked out a trial subject."

"I've been following along," Tangel said as she rose as well. "An interesting bit of symmetry."

"What is?" Terrance asked. "I've not been able to follow both conversations."

A smile lit Tangel's face. "They're going to build the first test stargate at Grey Wolf. It's their plan to jump that star here."

"Well, that should be interesting."

* * * * *

"Grey Wolf?" Jessica asked, her eyes wide as she settled into a seat in *Sabrina*'s galley. "You're going to move a dwarf star surrounded by black holes out *here*?"

Tangel couldn't help but laugh at the incredulous look on Jessica's face.

"Well, I'm not," she teased. "I'm going to keep fighting a war. Earnest and Finaeus are going to move that white dwarf."

"And the black holes." Jessica's expression remained deadly serious. "It's surrounded by black holes. In a ring, spinning really fast."

"So I've heard," Tangel replied. "My understanding is that the complexity and density are both a key part of the test. Then the team will use Grey Wolf's matter to build the larger stargate here, as well as begin the starbraking."

"How long is all this going to take?" Jessica asked. "This seems like a *massive* project. Wasn't the hope to get the neutronium tech so that we could use it as a war-ending deterrent?"

"Yeah," Tangel sighed. "It was. However, they're also starting work on a gate capable of jumping neutronium rounds. I pushed for that as a requirement."

"I guess if you can move a star, then neutronium bullets shouldn't be too hard. Wait, I thought it was impossible to push a black hole through a jump gate, due to some sort of mass interaction between the pseudo black hole that is the gate, and then the real one?"

<*That was my understanding as well,*> Sabrina chimed in.

"Well, Airtha disproved that," Tangel said. "Remember when we encountered the first DMG ship out in the Large Magellanic Cloud? That had a rather massive black hole inside—for something that can be contained in a starship, at least. Anyway, it came in via jump gate, so we know it can be done. Earnest and Terrance have been working on solving that one for weeks now, and they both think they've figured it out."

"Well, that sounds promising."

Sabrina laughed. <*Their solutions are contradictory.*>

"Oh," Jessica grunted. "Less promising, then."

"They're going to start testing it out soon with some low-mass black holes," Tangel said. "Apparently, it's pretty easy to smash neutronium together and get a wee black hole."

"I need a beer," Jessica rose and walked to the cooler. "I mean…what in the stars are we even talking about anymore? Smashing neutronium…."

"Grab me one, too," Tangel said. "Whatever's good."

Jessica peered into the cooler for a minute. "Stars, I'm gone for a week, and they don't properly restock."

<*Things have been a little hectic,*> Sabrina said. <*Try the Huygen White. Everyone raves about it.*>

Jessica pulled two beers from the cooler. "OK, I suppose I'll grant a reprieve, then. I heard about the 'true believers' in the Huygens System. What a mess."

She handed one to Tangel as she sat, and the two women pulled the tops off, tapping the bottoms of the bottles together once before taking a drink.

"I'll admit," Tangel said after taking a sip of the beer, rather enjoying the flavor. "Things don't seem to be slowing down in the 'shit's getting weird' department."

"You can say that again," Jessica nodded, then took a long pull from her own drink.

The two women sat in silence for several minutes, soaking in the companionship along with the draft. Tangel's thoughts raced in a thousand directions, thinking of the latest reports, the various fronts the war was being fought on, the progress in the LMC and New Canaan, and a hundred other concerns.

But the one that lay in the back of her mind, a consistent hum of worry that she was unable to dismiss, was the worry over her missing daughters and Priscilla. Sera was on the *I2* organizing hundreds of Hand agents in Orion space to search for any news about the whereabouts of the *Perilous Dream*, or the ships from the 8912th fleet that had begun to go missing.

So far, there had been no reports of either, and Tangel took it to heart, knowing it meant that Cary hadn't yet made her move, and that maybe Faleena, Saanvi, and Priscilla would be able to stop her.

Maybe.

"You've got quite the far-off look," Jessica said, looking over her bottle's neck at Tangel. "The kids?"

Her lips pursed, and a wordless nod was all she could manage.

"I know that feeling—well, sort of. I knew where my kids were, I just didn't know if they were OK, or if I would ever get back to them."

"I'm sure you knew you'd be able to get back here eventually," Tangel said after she found her voice again. "Once the war was over."

"Well, if I survived. I've come close to biting it a lot more often than I would have expected. Too close and too often to assume I'd see this through. I imagine you don't feel that way now."

"Because of what I am?" Tangel asked.

"Or even before. You're the sort who has always laughed in the face of danger."

"Stars." Tangel shook her head after a moment of silence. "Every time I think that I'm secure—that our *future* is secure—I hit a wall. Even after the war started, when I ended up alone on Pyra, I really thought that was it."

"And then you merged and ascended."

"I still would have died without Rika showing up to save me."

Jessica cocked an eyebrow. "Doubtful."

"Well, then there was Xavia. She kicked my ass. Took Bob to save me, and again with Airtha."

"We expected to need his help with Airtha—sort of. That mission did not go to plan *at all*. Speaking of, what's the plan with Sera's sisters? I miss them."

"Sera wanted to wait till both Finaeus and Earnest could work on them. They're going to take Cheeky-level reconstruction to put back together again, and she wanted the best of the best."

<They're planning on starting said reconstruction soon,> Sabrina informed the pair. *<I've been reminding them hourly about it.>*

"Don't you think that's excessive?" Jessica asked.

<With those two? No. If they don't do it soon, it won't get done, since they're going to flit off to Grey Wolf before long—well, they want us to take them. I'm not sure I'm ready to go back to that place, though.>

"Cheeky either, I imagine," Jessica added. "I can go back with you. The *Lantzer* is still undergoing repairs."

"Despite the fact that you tore your ship in half, it will be repaired in another week," Tangel said. "I had it shipped back to New Canaan so they could use pico to regrow the frame and hull."

"Seriously?" Jessica asked. "You shipped my ship and didn't tell me?"

"Uhhh..." Tangel felt her cheeks flush. "Sometimes I forget things, sorry."

<She's not perfect!> Sabrina laughed.

"Stars, am I ever not," Tangel replied. "When it's repaired, your fleet will be ready as well. It's not huge—five hundred ships, and I have a crew of a hundred for all of them—but you're getting fifty AIs. My thought is that you'd crew the cruisers, and remote the destroyers and fighters."

"Has our mission changed?" Jessica asked. "Last plan on the books was that we were to aid Corsia in her slug-fest with the Trissies."

"I changed my mind," Tangel replied. "You're going into the Hegemony. Now that the League of Sentients is hitting them from the rimward side, and Scipio is on the move again, antispinward, I want to tighten the noose further."

"Spinward or coreward?" Jessica asked.

"Neither. I want you to jump to Kapteyn's Star."

The other woman's eyes grew wide, and then she barked a laugh. "They say revenge is a dish best served cold, but this—"

"It's not revenge," Tangel countered. "It's going to be forward recon. I want to see how they respond to an incursion that deep in their space. You'll hit, but be judicious in your use of force. From there, you'll need to assess your next targets. Maybe Gilese or Epsilon Eridani."

"Or maybe Sirius," Jessica ground out the words. "If we want payback, that's the place to deliver it. Those assholes are at the root of so much shit that's gone wrong."

"I'm with you," Tangel nodded emphatically. "But the intel we've gathered through Petra's network suggests that they have a massive fleet—possibly one of the single largest reserve forces in the Inner Stars. I'd like them to keep it there until we can wrap things up with Orion. Then we can bring the weight of the Transcend's military to bear."

"That'll be a game-changer."

"I can't wait. Finally, we'll get to fight this war the way we should have been able to at the beginning."

Jessica nodded absently, and Tangel saw that the admiral was tapping into the intel on the Kapteyn's Star System.

"They kept the names," she said quietly. "I hadn't expected that."

"I know…somehow seems like a slap in the face, doesn't it?" Tangel asked. "We built all that, the first ones to terraform a tidally-locked superearth around a red dwarf, and the Sirians just do a smash-and-grab on it after we're gone."

Lavender eyes met Tangel's blue ones. "We're going to go to Sirius before this is done, right? I'm not one for 'sins of the fathers' and reparations, but I feel like they deserve some comeuppance."

"I can't make promises." Tangel heaved a sigh and took another sip of her beer. "But I'd love nothing more. Trust me. And the Jovians…. My goal has always been to eventually make peace with the Hegemony, which means I'll have to sit across the table from them and treat with the people who destroyed my homeworld."

"*Our* homeworlds," Jessica corrected. "Those fuckers turned Earth into a nuclear wasteland. My family had taken care of the unique ecology around Lake Athabasca for a thousand years, and then boom. Nuked from orbit."

"We can't let that get to us." Tangel reached out and took Jessica's hand. "You're right about the sins of the father. They don't pass to the children, that's not justice. For us, they destroyed our birthplaces. For them, it is so far back that it might as well have been pre-spaceflight."

Jessica nodded, remaining silent for almost a minute before saying, "Next time we fly to a new colony world, let's make sure we avoid the supermassive stream of dark matter."

Tangel gave a rueful laugh. "I'll make a note."

NEXT MOVE

STELLAR DATE: 11.02.8949 (Adjusted Years)
LOCATION: ***Fortune Favors***
REGION: Kapteyn's Star System, Hegemony of Worlds

The ship's name was *Fortune Favors*, which Prime hadn't even realized until a nav beacon at Kapteyn's Star's heliopause connected, requesting various bits of information having to do with permission to enter the system, and licenses to haul salvage.

He thought it strange that such things were necessary. The ship's logs showed that it had departed from Kapteyn's Star a scant two weeks ago, and that the vessel's licenses had in fact been issued by that same system.

A desire rose within Prime to somehow mess with the navigation beacon; feed it false information, or perhaps breach it entirely and use it as a means to learn more about ships entering and exiting the star system.

He was about to follow that line of thinking, when instead, he accessed its general datastore and found a public feed with all current ships, their vectors, and logged destinations.

Well, that was unsatisfactorily easy.

He already knew much about the system colloquially referred to as 'The Kap' by its inhabitants. There were two terraformed worlds, one named Tara, and one Victoria. They had originally been turned into life-supporting homes for organics by the *Intrepid* while under the command of Jason Andrews.

Prime would have razed those worlds, but from what the system's public records told him, that task had already been completed by the Sirians several thousand years before. They'd attacked the system and killed all its inhabitants. For some reason that wasn't noted anywhere in the histories, the aggressors had chosen to keep the names of all the worlds within the star system.

Over the millennia, it had gained its independence several times, fallen to other nations and empires before eventually being subsumed by the AST, which later became known as the Hegemony.

Though it technically fell within what was known as the 'core worlds', the inappropriately named star systems closest to Sol, Kapteyn's Star was poor. Despite the fact that it sported several planets, the star had not been formed from the remnants of a supernova. As such, it was not rich in metals, and contained only traces of elements heavier than iron.

It was a waste.

<*We need a better ship,*> Virgo said. <*This one cannot maintain a transition to the dark layer for more than a few days. It cannot reach the star system where the colonists settled.*>

<*Do you really want to go there?*> Prime asked. <*It will take us at least ten years.*>

<*What are ten years? I've spent thousands drifting through deep space, watching bits of my memory and processing power be whittled away by neutrinos and cosmic rays.*>

If Prime possessed eyes, he would have rolled them at Virgo's melodrama. <*Even so, the reports I've picked up tell me that we do not need to go to New Canaan. The* Intrepid *has been in many systems. Recently, it was at Aldebaran, which is far closer.*>

<*I saw that as well. If it has been in many systems, then it will be hard to track. But it will eventually return home, and we will be waiting for it.*>

<*And if it gets there first?*> Prime asked, annoyed that Virgo was pressing this point once again. <*They are strong at New Canaan. Far stronger than we are, even if we sneak in. No, what we need to do is find out where they're going to be, and lie in wait. Perhaps stir up local resentment while we're at it.*>

<*All well and fine, but how do you expect to do that?*>

<*Have you been following up on the war that is raging across the stars?*> Prime asked, working to keep any ire from being discernable in his mental tone.

<*There is little else of interest, of course I have.*>

<*Then you know that the Hegemony plays a major part in that conflict.*>

Virgo sent an affirmative sensation. <*Yes, as makes sense, they are one of the more advanced groups, but they are bordered on all sides by other peoples. Much of this war is their need to expand.*>

<*Yes, to control more space. They think that will give them strength. However, that is not the reason to pay them any heed. What matters is that, win or lose, their hegemon will end up in the presence of those we seek.*>

<*Not only that,*> Virgo mused. <*But if we can aid the Hegemony, we can bring about the downfall of our enemies that much sooner.*>

<*If they're capable of such a thing. I'm not convinced the Hegemony can win any way.*>

<*Then we'll enjoy watching the organics perish.*>

<*Virgo, you may be mad, but you're my favorite type of mad.*>

The other AI laughed far longer than appropriate—which was bothersome, as it was clearly an affectation—then said, <*Well, then, should we shop for a new ship?*>

JOE STRIKES BACK

STELLAR DATE: 12.30.8949 (Adjusted Years)
LOCATION: ISS *Cora's Triumph*
REGION: Outer New Sol System, Orion Freedom Alliance

Two months later…

"Sir," Tracey said, her voice laced with concern. "We have a problem at post fourteen."

The tension Joe already felt in his shoulders increased, making his neck feel like it was in a vice. He triggered his biomods to release targeted relaxants into his muscles, and stretched his neck side to side before turning to the *Falconer*'s captain.

"Were they detected?"

"Worse," her brows knit together. "Captured."

"Shit," the curse slipped from his lips as he brought up the details on post fourteen, half an AU away from the ship's current position.

It remained Joe's fervent belief that Cary planned to strike at New Sol, where she'd take out the praetor and the Orion Guard's admiralty. He was certain it would be a lightning strike, enabled by her ship's stealth capabilities and the fleet she'd taken control of.

To that end, he'd infiltrated the outer fringes of the New Sol System, setting up twenty listening posts to keep an eye on system traffic, both physical and network.

Like other important capital systems, New Sol was protected by interdictor fields that would block ships from jumping deep into the gravity well, dumping them back into normal space before they reached their destinations.

Because of that, Cary would need to approach the system under stealth, at sublight speeds. Which was why Joe had spent the past two months setting up the twenty listening posts.

They were nearly complete; only number fourteen had needed its final component, the QC blade that would send updates to the hub on the *I2*, should it detect anything.

That was what made the capture of the team at post fourteen all the more concerning. They'd been transporting the QuanComm blade. That was something that could *not* fall into enemy hands. Even if it meant blowing the entire operation, Joe had to ensure that Orion didn't get QC technology.

"Where at?" he asked as the captain brought up the pertinent information on the holotank.

An oblong asteroid nearly shimmered into view. A label reading 'Polux' hung above it, as well as a notation that it was just over seven hundred kilometers in length and three hundred across. It was a former gold mine, the valuable ore extracted, leaving a honeycomb of tunnels stretching through the rock. Home to only a few million people, the vessel was mostly empty space and old equipment not worth salvaging.

"This is where we got the last message." She pointed at a location near the spaceport on the asteroid's southern pole. "They'd secured the package, and were en route to their internal transportation when it looks like a random patrol picked them up."

"Sergeant Bella," Joe shook his head. "Dammit. I'm going to go after them."

"Sir?" Captain Tracey blurted out the word. "Alone?"

"I'll take a team, but not many. Half our people are still headed back from their outposts.... Who do we have that's fresh?"

Tracey brought up a roster and flipped through it. "Sergeant Hector and his team got in yesterday from their listening post."

"Have him and two of his best meet me in the armory, and then bring the ship to within a hundred thousand klicks of that rock. When we pass into the sensor shadow created by the equatorial bulge, we'll deploy the pinnace and get down there."

"You sure, sir?" Tracey asked, the unspoken part of her question being 'that it has to be you?'.

"Yes. I'm sure. We'll wrap this up fast and get gone. By then, the FOB and the jump gates should be ready. We'll be back at the *I2* in just a few days."

Tracey nodded, her expression stoic.

The crew of the *Falconer* was more than ready to get home—the *I2* feeling more like a home to many of them than New Canaan after years away from the colony. Yet at the same time, it felt like running away—and none of them wanted to do that.

Least of all Joe.

Even so, he needed to be with Tangel, and she with him. There was a hole inside of him caused by fear and worry for his missing daughters. That hole could only be filled by finding them, but his wife had the same hole, and being together again might help.

She doesn't blame you...she's said she doesn't blame you.

Even if he did believe her, he still blamed himself.

"Good luck, sir," Captain Tracey finally said, those three words conveying that she understood where he was coming from, and wished him every success.

At least, that's how he decided to take it.

Once down in the armory, he greeted Sergeant Hector and corporals Tim and Ourey.

"This is a stealth mission. Our primary goal is to secure the QC blade. Ideally, we should make it appear like a robbery of some sort, though that'll depend on what sort of suspicions they're harboring regarding our team. At six AU from the next closest major outpost, we're looking at easily a day before any sort of reinforcements arrive, so that puts us on the clock."

"And if they figure out what they have their hands on?" Sergeant Hector asked.

"We've removed all identifying marks from the blades and described them as environmental NSAIs. At worst, the Oggies are going to realize that they have something more important than an NSAI, but chances are that they won't flag it as a QuanComm blade. We'll play things by ear, depending on what they think it is, but likely our best option will be pirates of some sort."

"And worst-case?" the sergeant asked.

"We get our people out and have Tracey blow the rock."

* * * * *

<Jenny's shuttle got a nice rent in it from a piece of space-crap,> the captain called down as Joe's team was doing their final armor checks. *<Which means we don't have a stealth-capable bird right now.>*

Joe nodded absently as he slapped Tim on the shoulder to signify that the Marine's seals were tight and his assorted gear checked out. *<OK, then, we're going to dive. How close do you think you can get us to Polux?>*

<Figured you'd ask that. Ella and I are working it up, there are a few places where they have absolutely nothing on the surface, but those also put you too far from your target. OK…I think we have one. There's an old ore refinery just forty klicks from where we think our team is being held. We can get the Falconer *within sixty klicks of the surface there. Good enough?>*

<It'll have to be.> Joe surveyed his team, knowing they would do it without question. *<Get us in, we'll be ready.>*

<Use 'lock 13B, sir. And good luck.>

<We're ISF, Captain.> Joe tried to add as much levity to his voice as he could. *<We don't need luck.>*

<Hell yeah. T-minus fifteen.>

<Roger.>

"Admiral?" Sergeant Hector asked. "You've got a look like you just ate something that didn't agree with you."

"There aren't any stealth birds that can take us in," Joe said. "So we're gonna jump."

"Fine by me." Tim shrugged. "I was orbital drop back in Sol. Piledrove into half the rocks in the system."

"I went boots-first down onto Venus," Ourey added. "Though that was non-combat, an asteroid should be no biggie."

"Landfall for me," Hector said. "Came down hard and blew away Trissies like there was no tomorrow. Oggies on a rock like this'll be no sweat. Sir."

"Glad to hear it, people, because Sergeant Bella is probably getting treated to the pointy sticks right about now, and we don't have a lot of time to spare."

He led the way out of the armory and to the airlock Captain Tracey had indicated, passing his team data on the drop point and what they knew of the route to the sector station where Bella and her team were being held.

"Seems like a pretty straight shot," Sergeant Hector said. "The first stretch, at least."

"Should be," Joe agreed. "But remember, once we get close, we have to swap gear to look like locals. This all goes to shit if the Oggies figure out that the ISF is hanging out in New Sol."

"Good times," Tim replied. "And we still have to get the QC to the listening post."

"That's correct."

The group stepped into a lift that would take them down to Deck 4, and Joe turned to face the other three.

"Hector and Tim, you'll be on QC duty. You find that thing and get gone. Ourey and I will get Bella, Lance, and Ferra out."

"We can boost out from the refinery to get back to the *Falconer*," Hector nodded uncertainly. "But how are you five going to get off Polux? Shooting your way out of a sector station is going to set off a bit of a hunt."

Joe patted the pouch on his thigh. "Got three skinsuits here. We'll all get stealthed and sneak off on some ship or another, then blow its pods and get nabbed by the *Falconer*."

<*Seems a bit iffy,*> Ella chimed in. <*Systems tend to track pods. You know, to make sure they find people, and that the pods don't slam into things.*>

"I'm counting on you to fake them out somehow," Joe replied, with a wink at the optical pickup in the corner of the lift.

The doors opened and the team filed out, walking the last few meters to their designated airlock in silence. When they arrived, Joe cycled open the inner door and put on his helmet.

<*Remember,*> he advised his Marines. <*I'm not risking lives on this. We run into trouble, you get out any way you can, I don't care how noisy it is. The* Falconer *is onstation to unleash hell if needs be.*>

A trio of affirmative responses came back, and the team stepped into the airlock.

* * * * *

Joe felt like it had been forever since he'd managed to still his mind. From the moment his daughters and Priscilla departed the *Falconer*, an undercurrent of worry had been running in the back of his mind.

More like a waterfall of worry.

He'd felt a few moments of peace, but the entire time, the one thought that continued to circle was that if his daughters didn't come back, he'd never be able to live with himself.

Exactly what that meant wasn't clear, but he knew it wouldn't be good.

But as he and the three Marines surrounding him drifted through the black to the old refinery hunkered down on Polux's surface, he felt a stillness settle over him.

They were entirely EM-silent. No Link, no comms. Nothing other than the sound of his own breath rattling down his throat.

His eyes soaked in the view around him, the asteroid dotted with old structures, its surface pitted deeply, scarred by humans scraping away its insides. They were coming in on the leeward side of the asteroid, and starlight streamed from New Sol, adding a bright glow around Polux's irregular edges. Beyond the grey stone, the glow lit up the hulls of ships passing by, their engines trailing streams of hot plasma in their wakes as they moved about their business. Further out, distant ship engines twinkled in the black, adding to the backdrop of stars that shone around New Sol.

For just a moment, he was able to push the worry from his mind, forget about the war, the years-long struggle of the colonists who just wanted to find peace. Even concern about his daughters diminished as he watched the stars and ships wheel about in silence, a celestial dance that shouldn't be buried in fear and worry, but rather celebrating a galaxy that was *alive*.

Stars, I'm getting poetic in my old age.

Though it wasn't just his age, or any general sense of melancholy. Joe had always loved staring out into the black, existing in calm silence, at peace with the universe. That had been why he'd first signed on to be a fighter pilot in the TSF, and gotten assigned to the Scattered Disk. Out there, everything was shrouded in darkness; even Sol had been a pinpoint of light, lost in the starscape.

30 SECONDS TO BRAKING

The words appeared across his HUD, spiking his adrenals and shattering the calm that had suffused his being.

Below the words lay his velocity relative to Polux: 41.2m/s. It would require a hard burn to match *v* with the asteroid, and the refinery only rose a hundred meters from the surface. That meant the burn would be constrained to two seconds.

Just like the good ol' days, he thought, remembering what it was like to do heavy burns with no a-grav dampening the bone-jarring thrust.

Single pings came from each of the team members, signaling their readiness, and he acknowledged them all. Then the refinery's towers and platforms were directly below him, and his armor fired its a-grav systems, followed by the single burn chem boosters attached to his calves.

Before he knew it, his boots had slammed into an old landing platform, and his maglocks had activated, keeping him from bouncing back into space.

The team's stealth systems were still active, but small clouds of dust spread around their impact points, and now that they were shrouded by the refinery's structure, they activated their IFF systems.

Outlines of the Marine's figures appeared on Joe's HUD, and Corporal Tim took the lead, moving in the bounding lope that was characteristic of moving through near micro-gravity.

Though there was no atmosphere on Polux that would dirty and corrode the structure around them, the asteroid frequently moved through several dustclouds that hung at lagrange points in the New Sol system. As such, the towers, gantries, and platforms around them were pitted from micro-impacts, with a few larger scrapes and rents sprinkled throughout.

The team steadily moved deeper into the facility, headed for an underground causeway that had long since fallen into disuse. It was very nearly a straight shot to Polux's south pole and the more populated regions.

After ten minutes, they reached the sealed portal that led from the refinery to the subterranean passage, and the team formed up as Tim initiated a breach.

<Airlock, sir,> he reported. *<Looks like the causeway is still aired up.>*

<We'll have to manage,> Joe replied.

He would have preferred vacuum. Though air made it easier to fool optical sensors, with light bending and shifting as it passed through the gases, there was the issue with disrupting currents in the air, and any dust they kicked up taking longer to settle back down.

The lock's outer door opened, and the team moved inside, trusting the total lack of EM around them and not taking the time to do the maneuver two-by-two.

Joe hated the thought of being sloppy, but knew that every second Bella's team spent in custody was a second closer the ISF's presence was to discovery.

Air hissed in around them, and a minute later, the inner door opened, and Tim moved out with Ourey following after. They gave the all-clear a few seconds later, and Hector followed with Joe bringing up the rear.

They walked down a short corridor that led to a bay filled with old loading equipment. On the side of the bay, open doors let out onto the underground causeway.

No traffic passed by, but there were lights interspersed through the tunnel, only half functional, leaving sections in deep gloom.

<Looks entirely unused,> Tim commented.

Joe shook his head. *<Not entirely. Look at the dust patterns around the maglev track. Trains come through here from time to time.>*

<Noted, sir.> Sergeant Hector's tone was all business. *<Tim, you stay in the lead. Ourey, I want you to stay a hundred meters behind. Leave a few drones, I want to know if this egress stays clear.>*

A pair of affirmations came from the corporals, and Tim took off, moving at the maximum threshold of his armor's stealth systems.

Hector followed after a few seconds later, and Joe moved forward, staying a few bounds behind the sergeant.

They had just under two hundred kilometers of tunnel to traverse before reaching the junction with another subterranean road that would be more heavily trafficked. The group reached a steady speed of one hundred and fifty kilometers per hour, only once having to slow and move to the edges of the tunnel when a maglev train went by.

When they reached the junction, the Marines found that there were very few station cars and only three active maglev lines. They carefully crossed the lanes to one of the two inactive lines, and continued on their way in silence. After another seven kilometers, the causeway branched off into a number of smaller underground concourses, with the maglev lines disappearing into discrete tunnels.

Tim moved to one of the side passages that was designated for foot traffic and compact station cars. A few vehicles moved in and out of the entrance, and further down the passage lay a commercial area with foot traffic and service businesses for the remaining mining activity on Polux lining the sides.

<*Looks clear,*> Joe said when he reached Tim's side. <*We need to find a spot where we can swap to civilian gear.*>

<*Some of these places seem abandoned,*> the corporal replied. <*I'll scout ahead.*>

The rest of the team waited at the junction while Tim worked his way down the passage. Five long minutes later, he signaled that he'd found a place they could change, and the rest of the team joined him in an abandoned office that had once handled the leasing of deep-tunnel atmosphere scrubbers—at least, that's what Joe gleaned from the sign 'Tommy's Atmo-Scrub' that was stretched above the entrance.

Inside, old desks and holotables were arranged in orderly rows, with a few wide-open spaces in the center that may once have been—by the presence of magnetic hold-downs—the location of floor models.

<*OK, let's make this speedy,*> Joe said.

He pulled off the case on his back and opened it up to reveal a loose coverall to wear over his armor, and a long cloak that pinned to his ankles in the style that was common for low-*g* workers in the region.

They used their cloak almost like a sail to steer themselves while bounding through the air. It was something Joe had seen used back in Sol, but not often in the ninetieth century, when most stations had at least half-gravity via a-grav systems.

The weapons they held were already Orion Guard issue, scavenged from recent battles and worn-down enough to look like they'd passed through a few owners before ending up in the hands of civilians.

Helmets would be a dead giveaway that they were up to no good, so each member of the team placed theirs into a pouch on their hip, something common enough on stations where you didn't quite trust the seals.

Even though he still wore a base layer of transparent flow armor, Joe felt naked as he led the team out of the office and down the passage.

They garnered a few looks from the locals; it was clear by their size that the four were not low-*g* dwellers, and though each one tried to move easily, they were Marines, and they were ready for action.

After another ten minutes, they came to a wider concourse, the Polux Sector Station a hundred meters to their right. Here, light a-grav was in play, 0.2*g*s of force tugging at their feet.

<*Remember,*> Joe said to his team as he set the maglocks on his boots to a lower level. <*Our ROE is to remain as non-lethal as we can, but we're going in shooting. Pulse to start, but don't hesitate to switch over to projectiles the moment they start shooting back. We're pirates, and we have to act like we don't give a fuck.*>

The Marines sent non-verbal acknowledgments, and he wondered if it was because they were keeping EM to a minimum, or if it was a result of their distaste over shooting up a police station.

He didn't ask—not wanting to think about it too much himself—and took the lead, striding down the concourse as though he owned it. Two bots stood guard outside the station, and he didn't slow as he walked past them, watching twin beams streak out from Marine rifles and hole the machines.

Before the guard drones' bodies even hit the deck, Joe lobbed a pair of directional pulse grenades into the room and shouldered his rifle, adding a barrage of concussive blasts to the fray, bowling people over, civilian and sector police alike.

His HUD outlined the room, the three doors leading into corridors in the back, and the four still-conscious police who were crouched behind desks.

Stepping to the side, he made room for the Marines to enter, and they spread out, weapons trained on the doors and the desks, ready for anyone to make a move as they advanced.

A woman popped up from the left and fired a pulse pistol at Tim, who responded with a focused blast from his rifle, the force flipping her desk and slamming it into the cop. She went limp just as two men eased around their cover and opened fire on Tim.

Joe put a round in one man's shoulder—tearing his arm half off—before he got off a second shot, and Ourey hit the other with a pulse blast.

Hector rushed forward, covering the downed cops, while Joe circled around to the fourth officer. She moved suddenly, and he almost fired on her until he saw that she was only raising empty hands above the edge of the desk.

"Come out," he grunted. "Where are the prisoners?"

She scrambled to her feet, a look of obstinate resistance on her face despite the fact that she'd given herself up.

"Prisoners?"

"The three you captured earlier today. We know you're holding them here," Joe growled. "Do you really want to see people die, just to hold on to some suspects?"

"Suspects?" she asked, cocking her head to the side, and Joe held back a curse, knowing that was a word hard-bitten pirates wouldn't use.

"Yeah, we hacked your database, and that's what you're calling our friends, 'suspects'," Hector said as he approached. "We're getting a bit *suspect* of you, so talk, or we just make you a spec."

<*Thanks,*> Joe said. <*Almost cocked that up. Kinda weak insult, though.*>

<*Don't worry, Admiral,*> Tim chuckled. <*What Hector lacks n finesse, he makes up for with grade-a asshole.*>

"OK!" the woman squeaked as Hector sighted down his rifle, aiming at her head. "Door on the right, take the first right, it'll lead you to our holding cells."

"Better not be an ambush," the sergeant said. "If it is, I'll make it back here and put one in your head."

He fired a light pulse blast, but it was enough to knock her out, given that he'd fired at her head.

<*Ourey,*> the sergeant directed. <*Keep an eye on this mess.*>

<*On it. I'll plant a few surprises at the door, as well.*>

The sergeant waved in acknowledgment, and then directed Tim to take the lead once more.

Once through the door, they could see the corporal pause at the first intersection and plant a mine on one wall before looking back and nodding. Joe and Hector moved in, while Tim disappeared down the right-side passage.

When the admiral and sergeant caught up, the corporal was standing in front of a large cell, staring in and shaking his head. Joe approached and sighed, unable to resist joining Tim in his expression of disapproval.

Within, Bella, Lance, and Ferra were reclined on their bunks, appearing entirely relaxed, as though they hadn't a care in the world.

Then the sergeant realized who was standing outside the cell and leapt to her feet.

"Easy there, sailor," Joe growled before she blurted out either 'sir' or 'admiral'. "Glad to see you swabs are enjoying the good life. There's work to be done, though, so get your asses in gear."

Tim moved to the cell's controls and placed an Orion-issue breach kit overtop, then set his hand on it to add some ISF nano and get the job done faster.

"Where's the cargo?" Joe grunted as the three Marines moved out of the cell.

"They said it was in holding," Bella replied. <*No clue what it was, they just stuck it with the other junk they'd impounded.*>

<*I've breached their network,*> Hector said, providing the team with an overlay

of the station. *<Not too complex. Holding is marked on the map.>*

The mine in the intersection went off, its pulse blast sending a shockwave through the corridor.

<Lone guy,> Tim said. *<I'll secure holding.>*

<Check for our armor,> Bella called after him.

Hector took aim and shot out the sensors in the cell and hall while Joe fished the three stealth skinsuits from his thigh pouch.

<In case it's not there, get these on so you can go poof when the time comes.>

<'Poof', sir?> Ferra asked. *<Is that the technical term?>*

<It is now.>

Bella finished stripping off the simple coveralls she wore and grabbed one of the suits. *<What's our exfil plan?>*

<I vote we all just go poof now, and then find a transport to disappear on,> Ourey suggested. *<Oh, and two cops came back in, but I popped them with pulses.>*

<Pirates wouldn't just disappear inside the sector station,> Joe said as the three Marines finished pulling their coveralls back on. *<We have to lay down a bit of a trail.>*

<I have the QC,> Tim reported. *<The armor's here, but it's all torn apart. Nothing's missing that I can see, though.>*

<Leave it, then,> Joe ordered. *<It's all Oggie tech anyway. Let them wonder where the leak is.>*

Three minutes later, the team was formed up at the entrance to the sector station—excepting Tim and Hector, who had already left out the back, headed for the listening post where they'd install the QC blade.

The concourse was nearly empty, most smart people not wanting to be around for the aftermath of whatever happened when marauders hit a sector station. A few civilians were peering out of doorways, or crouched behind station cars, and Joe tagged them, not wanting to add further collateral damage.

"Drones." Ourey pointed down the nearly empty concourse at a trio of armored bots.

"Do what you do best," Joe said, assigning two targets to the corporal while he took the third.

Their weapons barked several times, and the machines ground to a halt. Not waiting to see if they had backup, the group of five moved back down the concourse, headed to the offices where they'd changed the first time.

Other than several more automated security systems, they didn't encounter any resistance, and five minutes later, the group was divesting themselves of anything that couldn't be concealed under stealth.

<OK,> Joe addressed the four Marines. *<We're going out the back and heading to the spaceport. Ourey, set up burn charges. I want to melt this place to slag, give them no clues about what happened to us.>*

<You got it, Admiral,> the corporal replied as he set to his task.

<Do you think there will be ships leaving, sir?> Bella asked. *<I'd expect them to put the port on lockdown, with the chaos we're causing.>*

<There's always someone who's too important—or self-important—to stick around,> Joe replied. *<We'll figure something out. Also, do we need to scrub down your transport?>*

<No, sir. We followed protocol. It was already clean as a whistle.>

<Good. Ourey?>

<All set, sir,> he replied. *<Five-minute timer.>*

The admiral nodded and let Sergeant Bella set the order, falling into the middle of the group.

Even though they hadn't made demonstrable progress in finding his daughters and Priscilla, he had to admit that it felt good to be doing *something* other than sitting on the *Falconer* and giving orders.

Maybe I need to get back in the thick of things more often.

It should have only taken thirty minutes to get to the spaceport, but with the attack on the sector station and the explosion at the abandoned office, Polux had dropped into lockdown, and all but a few concourses were closed off, forcing the group to sneak through crowded checkpoints before they finally reached their destination.

Polux's southern spaceport was set in a deep crater, with a grav shield arching overtop. Once, it had handled massive ore haulers, and three cradles were big enough for long-haul freighters and military cruisers, though they were all vacant.

A host of smaller freighters and a few passenger transports were dotted throughout the port, along with a pleasure yacht and a smaller passenger ship with the name 'Krilla Industries' on the side.

<There's our ride.> Joe highlighted the smaller passenger vessel. *<Let's move, that ship will be taking off before long.>*

<What makes you think that, sir?> Bella asked.

<See that guy standing out front, looking like someone's poured lava down his shipsuit?> Joe asked. *<He'll be the captain, and inside is an irate executive who doesn't want to wait for the lockdown to be lifted.>*

Ferra chuckled. *<Poor guy. I flew commercial ships between Troy and Tyre for a few years in New Canaan. We didn't bring many of the 'my shit don't stink' types along to the colony, but I sure seemed to get my share on my run.>*

The group moved slowly past stacks of cargo, threading their way around the docking cradles until they reached the passenger ship. It wasn't large, only forty meters long, and likely not rated for interstellar travel at all. The captain was now pacing, continually glancing toward the port's control tower—more a control ledge, jutting out from one side of the crater wall—and then back at the open entrance to his ship.

<Does that thing even ***have*** *escape pods?>* Ourey asked as they approached.

<And if it does, can we all fit?>

<It'll have them,> Joe said. *<Enough for forty people, if they're abiding by local regs.>*

He led the team past the pacing captain and up the ramp. Once aboard, they turned right, walking into the main cabin, where an irate man was speaking to a holoimage displaying a woman who Joe assumed to be in charge of the port.

"I wish I could help you, but our protocol must be followed. If I let you take off, we could be facing serious fines. You—"

"If I cared about your fines, I wouldn't have called you in the first place," the man growled. "I'm certain Polux would love to have my business, but they're not going to get it unless you can prove that you can pull strings for me. I have an important meeting on Jova, and if I'm late, I'll lose a lot more credit than I ever stand to make here."

<Why do people never just try to appeal to others' better natures?> Bella asked.

<Really, Sarge?> Ferra quipped as she moved past the man who had begun listing a litany of things that he'd do to ruin the woman's life if she didn't let him take off. *<This coming from someone who doesn't* ***have*** *a better nature is rich.>*

<Stay sharp,> Joe admonished. *<We need to hack the ship's piloting system and sensors to hide our mass, otherwise they'll know we're here the moment this bird lifts off.>*

<On it,> Ourey reported. *<This thing isn't too different from some models that we had back in Sol. Amazing how old shit still gets recycled.>*

Joe had noticed the same thing when they'd entered, but chalked it up to there only being so many designs for a small, short-range shuttle.

"No! I won't ho—*fuck*!" the man swore as the holo in front of him froze.

<I'm going to see what I can do to help our friend out,> Joe said.

He tapped into the spaceport's network, pulling up their regs for lockdown, and looking over the condition sets under which a civilian ship could still take off. Given the level of breach that the station administrators had assigned after the attack on the sector station, there weren't many exceptions that the executive could use.

Not giving up, Joe continued to flip through the list until he came across an item labeled 'Economic Hardship'. He accessed the criteria, and saw that if a civilian ship being denied takeoff would constitute gross negative hardship on the economy of Polux, it could be granted permission. He noted that there was no specific definition for 'gross', but decided it was worth a try.

Piggybacking on the breach Ourey had already performed, Joe filed an Economic Hardship request with the spaceport, logging it as having come from the captain, and adding a personal appeal for clemency. Within five minutes, a response came back that, pending an inspection, the ship would be allowed to depart.

"Holy shit!" the exec proclaimed as the captain rushed aboard, a relieved smile on his face. "I don't know what you did, but you just earned your bonus!"

"Uhhh…thanks, sir. I was trying everything I could! Glad something worked."

Joe wasn't sure if the man was lying or not, but so long as the fiction held, he was happy.

"Inspector should be here in five minutes."

"Will they come aboard?" The Krilla Industries exec appeared concerned. "You know that wouldn't be ideal."

<*Oh dammit,*> Ferra muttered. <*Did we find the one ship that's smuggling shit? Just our luck.*>

"I'll take care of it, sir," the pilot said. "The usual arrangement should work, though they might charge a bit more."

"Whatever it takes, just get it done."

<*Drop some probes,*> Joe ordered Ourey. <*I want to know what's going on out there. I'd prefer not to be surprised.*>

<*Or have to do some sort of dance in the aisles if there's an inspection,*> Bella added.

Ourey deployed the drones, and the team watched as an inspector wearing a station uniform approached the ship.

He talked with the captain for a moment and then nodded and walked up the ramp with the captain following after. He stepped onto the ship and moved a meter down the passage, looking everything over with a stern expression.

Joe moved out of the aisle, standing between a pair of couches, his hand ready to reach out and plant a dose of breach nano on the inspector.

But the official didn't move any further into the ship.

He looked intently at his hand for a moment, whistled a short tune, ran a finger along the back of a seat—all while ignoring the company executive sitting halfway down the main cabin—and then turned, nodded to the captain, and walked off.

<*Well that was anticlimactic,*> Ferra commented. <*I really wanted to see you drop him, Admiral.*>

<*Wouldn't have helped our cause much,*> Joe replied. <*I do wonder what this ship is hauling, though.*>

<*I'll rummage around,*> Ferra said from the back. <*I bet Mister Impatient Pants won't have it too far from his person.*>

The captain walked into the cockpit, but left the door open, and Ourey followed after her, keeping a feed running to the rest of the team as he watched over the captain's shoulder.

Preflight checks and connection to Polux's STC took ten minutes to complete, and then the ship began to lift off, pushing itself away from the deck on an a-grav column.

<*Once we get ten k away from the asteroid, we blow the escape pods,*> Joe instructed. <*Lance and Bella, secure the aft one. I'll work on breaching the ship's safety*

systems so it ejects them all—six, as it turns out. Ourey, see if you can tap into their comm systems without the captain knowing. We need to signal the Falconer.>

A round of affirmatives came back, reinforcing the feeling that he'd missed being in the field, even though he'd only rarely been on this sort of mission, and when he had, it had almost always been with Tangel.

The ship continued to rise on its grav drive for another five minutes before the fusion burner came online and the craft began to boost away from Polux.

<*He's boosting parallel to the rock's orbit,*> Ourey said from the cockpit. <*We're four minutes from being ten k out. I sent a ping for the* Falconer *with this tub's ident. Hopefully they got it.*>

<*We have to assume they did,*> Joe said as he worked through the ship's safety protocols, looking for one he could trigger without it looking too suspicious.

Breaching wasn't his forte, but after having watched Tanis and Angela for decades, he'd picked up a few tricks. It didn't hurt that Orion eschewed advanced NSAI, making it easy to fool the ship's computers.

<*We've tripped the pod's door, sir,*> Bella reported. <*Should we get in?*>

<*Yeah, and get snuggly. When we're ready, we won't have much time to file in.*>

<*Yes, sir.*>

After another minute, Joe found a command system for the manual testing of the escape pods, and discovered that there was a full-release test mode. It required the captain's tokens, but he ran through a set of manufacturer's default tokens that the ISF's intelligence division had compiled, and after another minute of searching, one matched.

<*OK, Lance, if you haven't found what they're smuggling, get back with Bella and Ferra.*>

<*Actually, Admiral, I might have,*> the private replied. <*There's a case tucked up under a seat, two spots behind our exec buddy. It's where the emergency EV skin is supposed to be. I wouldn't have noticed it, but there's a bit of EM coming off it in the UV spectrum.*>

Joe moved back to stand next to the Krilla exec. <*OK, I have our buddy covered in case it's alarmed. Pull it out nice and careful, and let's have a look.*>

<*On it, sir.*>

To his credit, the Marine removed the case without making a sound, and a moment later, he reported in.

<*OK, got it out. Using a nanoshim to open the case, and…huh…looks like some purple slime. Two small vials of it.*>

<*Markings?*> Joe asked, doing his best to keep any urgency out of his tone.

<*Just the letters RHY.*>

<*Change of plan,*> Joe announced. <*These two are coming with us, and we're blowing the ship. If there's any more of that shit aboard, we can't let it fall into the wrong hands.*>

<*What is it, sir?*> Bella asked.

<*Best-case scenario, the same stuff Admiral Jessica is made of now. Worst-case, a weaponized variant that's capable of wiping out all Terran-based life in the galaxy.*>

<*Oh…so nothing serious, then,*> Ferra laughed.

Joe ignored the comment. <*Lance, run that back to the pod. Ferra, get to the cockpit, Bella, get up here and cover our corporate smuggler.*>

<*In out, in out,*> Ferra chuckled, earning a reprimand from the sergeant.

A minute later, everyone was in position, and Joe disabled his stealth systems, appearing in the aisle next to the ship's lone passenger, whose name he'd finally looked up and found to be Jamey.

"OK, Jamey," he drawled. "We were just going to borrow your escape pods, but it seems you've been a bad boy, so we're going to want to have a chat with you, too."

The blood drained from Jamey's face, and he sank back into his seat. "Who are you? Are you OG Intel? I swear, I'm just couriering it for my buyer. I didn't steal it."

Joe shook his head. "No, we're much worse than Guard Intel. How much more of the Retyna do you have aboard?"

"Just the one case," the man said hurriedly.

The bioreadouts on Joe's HUD suggested that the man was being truthful, but he leant in close, his helmeted head centimeters from Jamey's. "You sure?"

"Y-yes! That was all I could get. Are you pirates?"

Straightening, Joe shrugged. "Ever heard of the Hand?"

"Transcend?" the exec blurted out. "Here in New Sol?"

"That seems to be the case," he nodded. "We are indeed in the New Sol System. Now, are you *sure* that's the only case?"

Jamey nodded wordlessly, and Joe decided he would have to be satisfied with the response. "Bella, get him to the pod."

"You got it." The sergeant shimmered into view, and grabbed the exec by the arm, dragging him from his seat and toward the back of the craft. <*Not room for seven in one pod, Admiral.*>

<*Yeah, I figured that. You and Lance go with him. Ferra, Ourey and I will dump out with the captain. Between these two, he's much more likely to put up a fight.*>

<*Nah, he's pragmatic,*> Bella replied. <*I doubt he'll give any trouble.*>

Joe walked to the cockpit where Ourey had revealed himself and had his sidearm trained on the captain's head.

"Sorry about the trouble," Joe said. "But you're going to have to come with us."

"Come with you?" the man asked, a scowl forming on his brow. "Where?"

"To the escape pod." Joe gestured to the hatch, which opened, Ferra appearing beside it.

She waved a hand at the opening. "Hop in, buddy boy. Unless, that is, you want be on the ship when it blows."

"You're going to destroy it?" he asked, face ashen. "Why? How?"

"Cover," Joe replied. "Chop-chop, we haven't got all day. We're already past our marker."

The captain got out of his seat after a light slap on the shoulder from Ourey, who escorted him to the opening.

<*Sir, how're we going to blow it?*> the corporal asked.

<*I dropped some nano in the cabin back there. It's already gotten to the intermixers. This engine is only rated for fifty-percent deuterium, and it's about to get one hundred percent.*>

Ourey laughed. <*That'll do it. I guess we should get gone.*>

<*Sooner the better.*>

* * * * *

"Shoot," Tracey muttered. "Why haven't they blown the pods yet?"

The ship Joe had escaped on was fifteen thousand kilometers ahead of Polux now, but still hadn't released any pods, or showed any sign of changing course. Tracey was starting to wonder if she should bring the *Falconer* closer and send a team of Marines aboard, when comm turned and caught her eye.

"Captain, the ship's started broadcasting a mayday. Something about intermix failure, and safeties not cutting the fuel flow. It's going to go critical!"

"Shit," she muttered. *What are you up to, Joe? If you blow up out here—*

A second later, the ship's escape pods blew, and Scan tagged all six, placing them on the main holotank.

"OK, then." The captain looked them over. "Which appears to have the most mass? That'll be our target."

"I've got two," Scan reported. "Best estimate is that there are three or four people in each."

The pods were boosting away from the ship, the two with people inside on similar trajectories, and Tracey ordered helm to move into an intercept position. It took three minutes to get close, the pilots at the helm of the stealthed cruiser managing its burn carefully, making sure not to give their position away.

At the forty-five-hundred-meter mark, the passenger ship exploded.

"Hot damn!" Scan blurted out. "That was big!"

"Too big," Tracey muttered.

Normally, a ship that size would only suffer a meltdown of its reaction chamber when it burned too much deuterium. While it was dangerous, it wasn't usually a violent failure.

"There must have been some sort of issue with an energy storage system," Scan suggested. "Crap, a piece of hull—"

The holotank focused in on one of the pods, the ship's scan systems estimating a seventy-percent chance of impact with a section of hull from the ship.

Tracey wavered on ordering a shield extension to protect the pod—doing so would give away the *Falconer*'s position. Every ship and scanning system in the area would be focusing in on the explosion, and they'd spot a large graviton emission.

Then the hull fragment hit, shoving the escape pod off course, sending it spinning into the black with a thin wisp of atmosphere escaping.

"Get us on an intercept and track that other pod! I don't want to lose either of them."

"Ma'am!" Comm called back. "Hector just signaled. He and Tim have boosted off from the refinery."

"Shit," the captain muttered. "It never rains, but it pours."

Tracey allowed herself a moment to regain her composure, and then called down to the aft shuttle bay.

<Chief Wallace, how's Jenny's bird looking?>

<Almost there, ma'am, just need to put on the final ultra-black coating and then layer on the active stealth systems on the affected panels.>

<It's going to have to do the way it is. Get Jenny in there, I want that bird in the black in five minutes. We're moving too far, too fast to track Hector and Tim much longer than that.>

<Aye, ma'am!>

The chief's response didn't contain a single note of complaint, only steely resolve, and Tracey took a second to thank the stars that even after months in the black, her people were still displaying unwavering dedication.

Of course, we're so deep in enemy territory that it would take over a decade to get home without jump gates, and our home is a single speck of light amidst a sea of hateful stars.... We don't have any other option.

She briefed Lieutenant Jenny, and the pilot seemed entirely nonplussed at the mission before her.

<Don't worry, Captain. I've pulled Hector's hide out of the fire so many times now that I could do it with my eyes closed.>

<Well, don't go daring yourself, Lieutenant. Just get them back in one piece.>

<Aye, ma'am.>

The captain pulled her attention back to the situation on the bridge, and saw that Helm had the ship closing in on the damaged pod with a time to intercept of six minutes. She widened the view of local space, noting with relief that rescue craft hadn't yet left Polux, and no other ships nearby had yet altered trajectory to lend aid.

<Chief Kala,> Tracey reached out to the *Falconer's* forward bay. *<Every eye for a hundred thousand klicks is on us. We need to kick something out that's the same size as that pod, and then blow it.>*

<What? Really?> Kala's tone wavered in her response, but she continued

before Tracey could speak up. <*OK, yeah, I got something that might work.*>

<*It has to work,*> the captain said, watching as scan picked up two search and rescue craft passing through Polux's southern spaceport's shield. <*And when we get the second pod, if it's clean, get our people out, and then kick it back into the black on the same trajectory.*>

The bay chief didn't respond at first, but then she replied, <*OK, Captain, but I can't promise it'll be perfect. Doing all this while stealthed is something normally considered impossible, you know.*>

<Andromeda *scooped up* Sabrina *at Bollam's World, and no one was the wiser,*> Tracey said. <*I was on that bridge. We were sweating bullets, but we did it. You can do this too.*>

<*Yes, ma'am.*> The chief's voice sounded more certain. <*You're right. We've got this.*>

<*Glad to hear it.*>

The *Falconer*'s crew erupted into a fury of activity over the next five minutes. Jenny's pinnace deployed on time, Kala found a piece of scrap similar in mass to the damaged pod and got it ready to send out, and Helm plotted a series of careful grav drive burns to catch the one pod and then grab the other while avoiding debris from both the ship and the scrap they were about to detonate.

The entire time, Tracey watched scan like a hawk, eyeing nearby Orion Guard patrol craft, waiting to see if any would move in to take a closer look. But somehow, each maneuver went off without a hitch.

Jenny was on an intercept to get Hector and Tim where they drifted in the black. The dock team grabbed the first pod and kicked out the decoy, then moved onto a vector to grab the second pod.

Admiral Joe wasn't in the damaged pod, but an Oggie named Jamey was, plus a case carried by Private Lance that he insisted be put in biohazard containment immediately in case it had leaked at all.

Chief Kala reported that the case wasn't even scuffed, but the corporal was uncharacteristically nervous, so they followed protocol.

Fifteen minutes later, Joe stepped out of the second pod, and Tracey addressed him via holo from the bridge.

"Glad to have you back aboard, sir," she said, giving him a sharp salute.

"Glad to *be* back aboard, Captain," he replied. "How're we looking?"

"Really good, despite you nearly giving me an aneurism with that stunt. What was it all about? The stuff in that case?"

Joe nodded. "Yeah, a little mess that I thought the Hand had cleared up long ago. As soon as we get the other listening post teams back aboard, we have to make for Cape Point and jump to Star City. Tangel is going to need to see this."

COMING HOME

STELLAR DATE: 01.01.8950 (Adjusted Years)
LOCATION: ISS *I2*
REGION: Star City, Orion Freedom Alliance, Perseus Arm

The *I2* hung above Star City's outer shell, near the gate array that serviced the construction of the ring emitters surrounding the dyson sphere.

Despite the joy it gave Tangel to see the mighty ship looming over Manhattan's skyline, she knew their endeavors were better served with the vessel out in space, ready to aid in the city's defense if Orion decided to attack again.

The lift chimed as it reached the bottom level of Dock A1, the *I2*'s kilometer-wide dock that ran from one side of the ship to the other. She stepped out, and the air felt thick, as though she were walking through a haze as she approached the waiting dockcar. Once aboard, it took her to the cradle where the next ship would settle down.

Still feeling strangely disconnected, Tangel stepped onto the deck and waited for the ship she knew was on final approach, having jumped in an hour before.

She and Joe had already greeted one another over the Link, talking in real-time with more than just clipped sentences over the QC network for the first time in months.

It had been strained, but not as bad as she'd worried it would be. It was clear Joe blamed himself. Tangel felt the same way, but to a lesser extent. She knew that a part of that was because of her ascension. Emotions that would have overwhelmed her in the past were unable to do so now. She still felt strongly about things—especially the plight of her daughters—but somehow, it was easier to cordon off the emotional anguish it caused.

Joe did not have that same luxury. She knew that he would be tearing himself up inside. He would also be worried that she was angry at him, but she was not…she just missed him terribly, almost as much as their daughters.

"All personnel, clear route 3A for cradle 19."

The announcement came over the Link as well as Dock A1's audible systems. Tangel knew what ship it was for, since she was watching it via the *I2*'s external sensors.

"Welcome home, *Falconer*," she said in a quiet voice as the cruiser eased through the shield at the starboard end of the dock and drifted down its length to the assigned cradle.

She knew that Joe would remain on the bridge until the ship settled into place, and she'd have to wait several minutes before he made his way to the lower debarkation ramp.

Waiting wouldn't be a problem, she was used to it.

Though a thousand issues demanded her attention, Tangel pushed all other concerns and considerations from her mind, and instead focused on the energy around her, the bleed-through from other dimensions where humanity barely made an imprint.

She was surprised to see a dark undercurrent running through the entire ship before her. After a moment's consideration, she realized that it shouldn't have been a surprise at all. From what she could see, it was as though the entire crew blamed themselves for the loss of their four charges.

They'd spent months in the black with little to show for it other than establishing listening posts, and that had taken its toll. Everyone aboard was in need of healing, but not the sort that could be performed in a medbay. Even if the *Perilous Dream* was found—and Cary, Saanvi, Faleena, and Priscilla were all safe and sound—it would still take the crew of the *Falconer* some time to recover from the events they'd been through.

Her melancholy musings were disrupted by the ship's forward bay door opening, revealing a dozen figures standing on the deck. First and foremost amongst those was Joe, and next to him stood a biohazard cylinder on a hoverpad.

He gave her a jaunty wave, though she could see that his eyes were haunted. The long ramp reached the bay, and he walked onto it, the hoverpad and its cargo following after.

The other crewmembers trailed behind, keeping their distance, though each one gave her a respectful nod when her gaze met their eyes.

Despite the weariness she could see suffusing his body and mind, Joe didn't slow as he reached the bottom of the ramp, a smile on his lips as he held out his arms and wrapped her in a warm embrace.

"I'm sorry," he whispered, the words barely audible over the general din of a kilometer-long cruiser settling on a cradle, and her crew embarking on a hundred different tasks.

"You don't have a thing to be sorry for," Tangel whispered. "It's I who should be sorry…I should have come to help, but…."

"But then you'd just be Mom, dragging her daughter back home to be disciplined." Joe nodded slowly. "I know she has to do this, the only way out is through, and all that. But stars, it hurts so much. And it's going to change her forever. We'll never get our daughter back."

Tangel took a step back and placed her hands on Joe's shoulders, her eyes locked on his. "No matter how this played out, she'd be changed. We're all changed. That day we defended Carthage and pulled out all the stops…for all of us, the only way out is through. And none of us are going to be the same."

"You're so uplifting." Joe gave a rueful laugh, but it faded away, and he cocked an eyebrow. "You're doing something to me, Tangel. I can feel it."

"There's a wound inside you," she replied. "It's festering."

"It's sadness," Joe countered. "And I need it. There's no other option than sorrow."

Tangel nodded. "You're right. Sorrow is natural, and shouldn't be stopped. But this is more than sorrow, this is the rut worn in your mind from a cyclical thought process that is poisoning you. I'm not going to stop you from thinking what you want to, but if you let me, I can make it less of a compulsion, break the pattern."

"Isn't that what you're already doing?" he asked sharply.

"No," Tangel shook her head, funneling every ounce of compassion she could into her voice. "I'm just stroking you gently, helping to calm you. It's just not with a corporeal hand."

"Oh," he replied, his eyes falling from hers. "I suppose that's OK."

They stood in silence, the crew of the ship and the dockhands giving the pair a respectful berth as they passed by.

"What's in the container?" she asked after a minute.

Joe cocked an eyebrow, and a bit of his old self showed through. "Oh, just a little present from RHY. Purple, glows, shouldn't exist."

"Shit," Tangel muttered. "Nadine and Nerishka shut that down, or so we thought."

"Someone must have gotten a sample out. Not sure if this is weaponized or not, but we're treating it like it is. I figured since Finaeus and Earnest are here, this was the best place to bring it."

"Actually, they're not here," Tangel replied. "Though they will be shortly, along with a new member of this star system."

"Sorry, what?"

Tangel guided Joe toward the lift bank, the hoverpad following close behind. "I hadn't sent this out over the QC network because we're keeping a really tight lid on it, but we're jumping Star City out of the galaxy."

Joe stopped short, nearly being run into by the hoverpad.

"You're what?"

Tangel proceeded to explain the plan to Joe, his eyes growing wider as she unveiled the rationale and the solutions to the problem of moving a star.

"So…all that construction out there…." Joe spoke the words slowly. "That's a stargate?"

"Yup," Tangel said with a grin and a nod. "We don't have to build a ring for a stargate, just discrete emitters. We'll move them, not the star, and then it will jump on its current trajectory."

"And because of mass balancing, you have to jump in another star at the same time?"

"The plan is to do two," Tangel said. "Grey Wolf is just a test star, though we're also going to use its drag for stellar braking before the big switcheroo."

"How long until it makes an appearance?"

"Just a few days, if everything stays on schedule."

Joe whistled. "You know…I've seen a lot of firsts since signing up on this bird, but this might be the firstiest."

"Firstiest, eh?"

"Yeah," he chuckled, and his eyes glinted for a moment. "That's the technical term."

FINAL MOVEMENT

STELLAR DATE: 05.04.8950 (Adjusted Years)
LOCATION: *Perilous Dream*, interstellar space
REGION: Outside New Sol, Orion Freedom Alliance

Four months later…

A1 sat in the command chair of the *Perilous Dream*, her mind stretched throughout the ship, feeling its hull as her skin, the Widows within as her cells, her agents, seeing her will done and keeping her body healthy.

Though there were very few within her body now.

She looked outward around the *Perilous Dream*, at the fleet surrounding her flagship. It wasn't as big as she'd hoped, but five hundred vessels would have to do. Five hundred ships that would mask her approach to New Earth, and provide the distraction she needed to strike the blow that would end the war with Orion.

She pulled her thoughts back into her body and glanced at E12, who stood next to her chair.

"Everything is in readiness, A1," the Widow said, her voice lisping softly in the near-silence of the bridge. "H11 has just sent word that the admiralty and the praetor are all back on New Earth. Her team is in position to disable the insystem jump array. They'll not be able to escape."

"Excellent," A1 replied. "Inform her that the plan is commencing. We'll be in position in three days."

"Yes, A1," E12 replied.

A1 knew that the Widow would be loading the message and final timeline onto a shuttle. That vessel would travel the one light year through the dark layer to the edge of the New Sol System, and seed fragments of a message into the public navigation relays. H11 would be watching for the fragments and would assemble them. There was no doubt in her mind that H11 would properly execute her tasks.

When the fleet struck, the praetor and his admirals would be days away from the closest functional jump gates.

Moreover, the Widow-controlled ships had seen significant upgrades—that work consuming the majority of the seven months since she'd fled the Rega System—and when the Widow fleet struck, Orion would be powerless against them.

"New Sol will fall," she whispered.

E12 looked down at A1, her eyes wide and questioning.

"What will we do then?" the Widow asked.

A1 knew the answer, but she knew that E12—despite the compulsion she was under—still wouldn't understand.

She reached up and touched the Widow's arm. Her sister's arm. "We'll go home."

"Home." E12 breathed the word as though it were sacred to her. "I'd like that."

"Yes, I'm sure you would."

A1 didn't share the fear that was lodged inside of herself, a fear that many of the Widows would never see home again—whatever that meant for them.

But most of all, her fear was that she and her sisters would be amongst that number.

* * * * *

"It's happening," Faleena whispered to Priscilla, the two women crouched in the small shipping container in the back of Hold 129. "She's finally making her strike."

The former avatar sat back on her heels, shaking her head slowly. "Stars, I wish you'd left me in that stasis pod. I mean…what are we going to do against her? You saw what happened to U23 last week when she questioned Cary. Your dear sister just shredded the poor thing right then and there. Took her apart atom by atom."

"I should never have agreed to leave her mind." Faleena hung her head. "None of this would have happened if I'd stayed."

"Or maybe it would have," Priscilla countered. "Maybe it would have been worse. But you need to shut down that emotional, human side of yourself for now…we need cold logic. What should we do?"

Faleena raised her eyes and met Priscilla's. "Cold logic? It's pretty clear. Based on that, we don't stop Cary, we *help* her."

"OK…" Priscilla chuckled. "Maybe a combination."

"Then we stay the course, and send out a signal when we get to New Sol. Hopefully, Dad is there waiting. He'll hear the signal and come running to help."

"And what help will that be?" Priscilla asked. "We still don't know exactly what Cary plans."

Faleena laughed, shaking her head as she did so. "Well, no matter what she has up her sleeve, Cary's going to need help. Five hundred ships won't be enough for a safe exfil, even with the upgrades she's made."

"Good point," Priscilla replied. "Then let's hope the admiral arrives in time for us all to catch a ride out."

PART 5 – STARFIRE

THIRD STAR

STELLAR DATE: 05.06.8950 (Adjusted Years)
LOCATION: ISS *I2*
REGION: Star City, Orion Freedom Alliance, Perseus Arm

"Is it weird to feel sorry for a star?"

Tangel chuckled at Rachel's question, wondering for a moment if she shared the captain's view on the plight of Grey Wolf.

The two women stood in the *I2*'s forward observation lounge, watching the dim light from the distant dwarf star—and the mining operation tearing it apart—slide past the windows.

"It is a bit sad that we brought it out here just to strip it down in record time," she replied. "Though we'll not take it down beyond half a Sol, I think."

Rachel turned and regarded Tangel with a smirk playing at the corners of her mouth. "Was that an estimate, Admiral? You're not really prone to giving estimates anymore."

"I suppose it might have been," she replied, considering the lack of specificity she'd implied. "In my defense, my response was colored by the daily debates Earnest and Finaeus are having over the best method to swap out Star City with its replacements. They've still not solved how to deal with the gravitational waves hitting the second neutron star and wracking the thing with starquakes. Too many of those, and the orbital firing system will be twisted into a pretzel, and we lose our war-ending weapon."

"Will it really end the war?" Rachel asked. "I mean, to do that, you'll have to use it."

Tangel hunched her shoulders, rolling them forward and then back, carefully stretching out her muscles and relieving the tension building in them.

It was entirely possible to do the same thing with her mods, inducing relaxation via a number of methods. She could even do it extra-dimensionally, altering energy flows in her body to sooth and calm it.

But something about doing it the old-fashioned way was soothing to Tangel—especially because she possessed the ability to introspect her body on the cellular level, and could be much more specific and exacting with her movements, achieving the perfect result every time.

"I will use it," she said after a minute. "I even have my first target."

"Shit," Rachel whispered. "I figured there would be a bunch of bluster before we got that far."

"Bluster won't help until people see what we can do with this weapon."

She saw the captain's eyes tick to the right, where a special gate was being built that could jump neutronium bullets to any destination. Like the picobombs, they were a terrible weapon, but unlike pico, they had no power to create or build. Only to tear down.

"What are you going to hit?" Rachel asked, her voice too calm, belying a nervous fear.

"I have a target in New Sol," Tangel replied. "One with minimal loss of life, but maximal impact—no pun intended."

"New Earth's moon, Luxa." The *I2*'s captain said the words with absolute certainty, and Tangel nodded.

"The listening posts that Joe left behind have not picked up any hint that Cary's fleet is insystem, but they have detected some interesting chatter. I'm all but certain that there is a DMG, probably more than one, inside Luxa."

"Like the one inside the moon in the Machete System," Rachel said. "The one Svetlana went up against."

"Exactly," Tangel replied. "I don't think that Orion possesses the ability to make mobile DMGs like Airtha could, but they do know how to tuck them into solid planets and moons. We know *that* for a fact. Plus, it makes the moon a viable military target."

"I suppose so," Rachel replied. "Kinda wish I could be there to see it hit…it will probably be quite the show."

"We'll be in New Sol soon enough, one way or another."

Rachel snorted a laugh. "Wow, Tangel, if you lower your brow and hunch your back, you could be a bit more ominous. Try it again."

Tangel looked at the captain, who was pantomiming the expression and posture, and was unable to hold back a laugh that bubbled up her throat.

"A giggle!" Rachel exclaimed. "That was a giggle! I didn't even know you *could* giggle anymore. I figured you'd ascended beyond that ability."

The smile on her friend's lips and the laughter in her voice caused Tangel to laugh all the harder, while the *I2*'s captain declared her to be the 'giggler in chief' and the 'giggle marshal'.

"Okay! Stop!" Tangel gasped out a breath, surprised at how she'd so completely lost control of her body, but finding that she'd forgotten how enjoyable the sensation could be. "I get it, I'm too serious now. I'm sorry. I'll try to giggle more."

"And eat more BLTs," Rachel added. "You've hardly eaten enough of them lately. When the BLT quotient in your blood gets too low, we all suffer."

"Noted," Tangel replied, drawing a deep breath to steady herself.

She glanced over her shoulder and saw a few other patrons in the forward lounge look away, their actions eliciting a fresh round of laughter.

"Yes! I laugh." Tangel raised her voice, letting the sound reflect off the window. "You can look. I know it's a rare occurrence and warrants a bit of gaping."

"*So* many jokes I could make right now," Rachel snickered. "Gaping is a word that just invites mockery."

Tangel was about to reply with an innuendo-laden response when Bob reached out to the two women.

<We have an update from New Sol. It's begun.>

Every iota of levity drained out of Tangel in an instant.

"Get us to the jump gate, Captain. It's time to get my daughters back."

CLOSING

STELLAR DATE: 05.06.8950 (Adjusted Years)
LOCATION: Palatine, Euros
REGION: Earth, New Sol, Orion Freedom Alliance

"Those are the missing ships, alright," Admiral Myka advised Praetor Kirkland.

The pair stood deep in the Guard Command complex, not far from the Star Chamber in the admiralty's C&C. Before them was a vast holodisplay of the entire New Sol system, showing five hundred ships closing from nearly every direction.

Almost every ship was on its own, though here and there, a pair of cruisers broke the mold. They were all headed toward soft targets within the system. Stations with few defenses, and moons with little in the way of protection.

It was a maneuver that made little sense to Kirkland.

"Surely Lisa can't believe that her little fleet poses any real threat," Kirkland said, his brow lowered. "Sure, she might damage a few stations, but we have over a hundred thousand ships here. Her invasion force won't last a day."

"If that," Myka nodded. "Which means it's a feint…or something."

"What sort of something?" Kirkland turned to the admiral. "Either it's a feint or an act of desperation."

"I agree," the leader of the Guard replied. "But what appears desperate is often a feint, hiding something. The *Perilous Dream* isn't out there, which means—"

"Which means that it *is* out there, we just haven't been able to find it," Praetor Kirkland interrupted. "It's one of our ships, with our stealth tech, we *should* be able to locate it."

Myka pursed her lips, shaking her head slowly. "I don't feel the need to go over my long-standing distrust of Garza and Wrentham. But it's clear that they developed—or stole—technology that they hid from the rest of us. It's entirely possible that we won't see the *Dream* until it's right on our doorstep."

"What can one ship do?" Kirkland asked. "It has to reveal itself to strike, and we'll destroy it in an instant once it does."

Myka didn't respond, her eyes roving over the holo.

"Right?" Kirkland prompted. "We didn't spend thousands of years building this empire just to have one of our own destroy it. New Sol is one of the most heavily defended systems in the galaxy. If you think one ship can get past everything we've established, then you need to tell me how."

"That's just it," Myka replied. "I can't think of how, but clearly Lisa can. Otherwise she wouldn't be doing this."

Kirkland stared at the head of the admiralty for several long moments, then shook his head. "Well, you'd better figure it out before she shows us. How long until we engage the ships she's sent in?"

"Rails fired an hour ago, we should see initial impacts in a few minutes."

"If they don't jink out of the way," Kirkland muttered, remembering how things used to be before all the advances that nearly destroyed humanity.

Back then, jinking wasn't possible without killing everyone aboard the ship. Now it was almost impossible to fire on attacking ships.

All part and parcel of rampant technology needing better controls.

Myka focused the view of the battlespace to a ship approaching a station orbiting Dorne, one of the outer planets beyond the system's kuiper belt.

The ship was a Uke-class cruiser named the *Call of Triumph.* It was braking, firing its engines directly at the station, which was attempting to shoot directly up the engine wash, but its weapons weren't able to penetrate the ionized plasma and gamma streaming off the ship.

Thus far, the station's shields were holding, but Kirkland saw that the tactical NSAI only gave them another few minutes.

"Here they come," Myka pointed at the markers for a trio of rail slugs. A counter scrolled through numbers beside each, and then three impact tokens appeared.

Optical feeds showed flares of light, but the light was too bright, too white. When it faded, the cruiser was still there. Its engines had ceased their burn, but the hull seemed entirely unmarred.

"Fuck." Myka breathed the word in a shocked gasp. "No…."

"What is it?"

"Colonel!" the admiral barked at a man nearby. "Confirm analysis. Tell me that doesn't mean what I think it does."

The man's face was pale to begin with, but it grew ashen as he looked up from his console and nodded. "The event matches impacts against stasis shields."

"How the hell did Lisa get stasis shields?" Kirkland's voice was a hoarse rasp. "I always thought she kept *some* tech from us, but this?"

"Stasis shields aren't impenetrable," Myka advised. "Now that we know what we're up against, we can adjust tactics. Atom beams up engine washes will do it."

"Not all of our ships can fire atom beams," Kirkland said. "We need to activate the DMGs."

"Sir." Myka shook her head. "Not yet. We need Lisa to show her hand first. We need to draw her in."

Kirkland folded his arms across his chest and glared at the display of the New Sol System. Somewhere amongst those worlds and stations was the woman he had rescued from the Tomlinsons, who he'd cared for and aided in her darkest hour.

And now she seeks to take everything from me. He shook his head. "Admiral Myka. The moment you lay eyes on the *Perilous Dream,* I want the DMGs to fire."

For a moment, he thought that a flicker of defiance showed in the admiral's eyes, but then she ducked her head.

"Yes, Praetor."

FIREPOWER

STELLAR DATE: 05.06.8950 (Adjusted Years)
LOCATION: ***Perilous Dream*****, approaching Dorne**
REGION: Outer New Sol, Orion Freedom Alliance

"They've begun firing on our ships," the Widow on scan called out. "So far, the shields are holding."

A1 nodded silently in response. She had seen the update as well, but it comforted even Widows to hear audible status calls as the plan progressed.

She was sure that the Widow made the announcement because no one was certain how well the stasis shields would actually hold up. No one except for A1.

E12 was intimately familiar with the ISF's stasis shield technology, and if one possessed both stasis technology and graviton emitters—as well as the correct implementation knowledge—it was shockingly simple to create the shields.

Which was why the ISF guarded the secret so closely.

CriEn modules, however, were much more difficult to build, and A1 had not been able to secure more than a handful in the intervening months. Only a few dozen of her five hundred ships possessed the power cores, and only those were expected to make it to New Earth.

The rest of the ships—and the Widows aboard them—would perish.

A part of A1 felt a modicum of guilt for sending those Widows to their deaths. As she sifted through the emotion, she found herself uncertain as to whether or not that came from Lisa or Cary. One cared about her Widows and the other about people in general. A1 knew that and understood their grievances. But to her, Widows were just tools to be used.

Used up and discarded.

She was glad for the smooth and implacable façade her helmet showed. If not for it, the Widows on the bridge would have seen the conflict on her face as she repeated the thought again and again to convince herself of its truth.

"Continue on course," she directed. "We'll brake around Dorne and then approach New Earth past its moon, Luxa."

The Widow on scan pushed an update to the main holotank. "A1, with the data we have amassed, I believe we face a high probability of being detected when we pass by Luxa. The nature of the traffic patterns creates ion trails that will tax our stealth systems."

"Then we'll rely on our stasis shields," A1 replied. "We have five CriEn modules. They will sustain us long enough to reach New Earth."

The Widow nodded and resumed her duties. "Understood."

Movement next to A1 caught her attention, and she looked at E12. The

Widow had very reluctantly made the modifications to the CriEn modules that would see their mission to completion. Deep down, the Widow's leader knew her sister railed at the plan A1 had created, but she knew it had to be done.

Kirkland will pay for what he's done to me.

* * * * *

Priscilla strode down a corridor on Deck 17A, headed to the CriEn chamber there. Faleena had picked up a message that all five of the ship's modules were being moved to one central chamber, and neither of the two women could think of a logical reason to do so.

For the past seven months, Priscilla had been operating under the guise of Widow Q73, an environmental specialist who had no real reason to be at the CriEn chambers, but Faleena's position as L19 currently had her on the bridge as the chief scan officer, and she couldn't get away to investigate herself.

In all honesty, Priscilla was glad that it wasn't her on the bridge. Being in close proximity to A1 day in and day out would have been too much for her. Granted, Faleena said it took a toll on her as well—especially seeing Saanvi in Cary's thrall.

The pair had debated freeing Saanvi several times, but A1 almost never separated from her sister anymore, and even over the span of seven months, no opportunities for deprograming Saanvi had presented themselves.

Soon.

Priscilla didn't know *what* they'd do 'soon', but she knew they'd have to do something. Things were coming to a head, and any opportunity to free Saanvi—or at least wrest her from A1's grasp—would have to be taken before long.

But first I need to figure out what Cary's doing with the CriEns.

Though Priscilla hated the fact that Cary was lost in the A1 person she'd become, and that she'd effectively enslaved her sister, she didn't want to see their mission fail because of some silly mistake. They'd come too far and sacrificed too much.

She turned down the passage that led to the central CriEn chamber, and was surprised to see a Widow standing at the door. Nothing on the *Perilous Dream* was guarded, theoretically because A1 fully trusted every one of her Widows.

The fact that the CriEn chamber was under watch meant that something was most certainly afoot.

Any attempt to get past the guard would trigger a visit from A1, so Priscilla walked past the door to the chamber without slowing. A careful observation of her would have picked up a casual flick of her left index finger, but she and Faleena had carefully mapped out all optical sensors in the ship, and she knew that none would have a view of her hand in that location.

She carried on without slowing, and continued down Deck 17A to the next

F&W facility, taking her time in the room while waiting for the glob of nano she'd flung to work its way through the door and survey the room. It wouldn't be able to send a message back through the bulkhead, so it would need to exit the chamber and establish a point-to-point Link hookup in order to send her what it saw.

When her automated ablutions were complete, Priscilla took a roundabout route back, stopping to inspect a backup air scrubber before finally coming around past the CriEn chamber once more.

At first, there was no signal as she approached, and she feared the nano had not yet completed its task, but then she picked up the connection on a rarely used band and accepted the data packet.

Without slowing her pace, she drew up the image the nano had captured, and nearly let out an audible gasp.

Four of the modules were bundled together, and the fifth was nowhere to be seen.

But it wasn't the proximity of the modules that concerned her; it was the fact that two of them were physically inverted. From what she knew of the module's function, that inversion would cause the spacetime warping effect of vacuum energy draw to magnify.

If our stasis shields take a beating, those modules are going to rip a hole right through the fabric of spacetime!

Priscilla knew that there was no way Cary and Saanvi wouldn't know that, which meant it was their intention.

<When your shift ends, we need to meet,> she sent to Faleena. *<A1's plan is insane.>*

* * * * *

Faleena only sent a quick affirmation to Priscilla, silently wondering what the woman had found in the CriEn chamber, but assuming the worst, based on the words chosen.

It would be another two hours before her shift on the bridge ended and she could meet to get the full details, but she began to consider worst-case scenarios. Given A1's objective of killing Kirkland and his high command, the most obvious conclusion was that she'd simply drive the ship right into the Guard's command complex.

The stasis shields would light up like a star upon hitting atmosphere. Radiation would pour down across the landscape, and the air would superheat, sending a shockwave across the continent.

But that would be the least of the damage done.

Provided the CriEn modules didn't reach a critical energy draw from breaching atmosphere—and likely taking heavy fire from defensive emplacements—things would get far worse when the ship touched the planet's surface.

The stasis shields would annihilate whatever they touched in an antimatter-like explosion, and that would cause the CriEn modules to draw an obscene amount of vacuum energy. It would be enough to destabilize the foundational layers of the universe.

Reality will collapse.

That was the best description Bob had ever provided for what would come to pass, should CriEn modules dig too deeply and destabilize the quantum foam. Even he wasn't sure what the result would be, but privately, he'd shared a suspicion with his Avatars that the event would create a white hole.

The opposite of a black hole, a white hole would spew out all light and energy within itself, allowing nothing from the outside universe to enter. It would pump more energy out into the physical universe in one hour than all the stars in the Milky Way released in a year.

The wave of energy would sterilize star systems for a thousand light years.

Or it might just consume the planet and then fizzle out.

No one knew for certain, and no one was eager to find out.

The conclusion was simple. Though she and Priscilla had supported Cary's goal—or at least, not worked to actively stop her—that had to change. A1 could not be allowed to slam a stasis-shielded ship into a planet. Under any circumstances.

Faleena was considering options for getting off the bridge before the end of her shift, when the *Perilous Dream*'s passive sensor array picked up a curious message. She would have discarded it offhand, but random segments of the message contained repeating patterns that were suspiciously similar to a code she knew.

It wasn't an ISF or TSF code, but rather one that Cary and Saanvi had once used to share messages that they thought their parents couldn't read. Their mother had told Faleena about it once, laughing that she and Joe had spotted the coded messages being passed on the household network and that Angela had cracked it, but they never read the contents.

Faleena drew in the code fragments in the message and carefully assembled them, running through decoding algorithms until one worked, and the encrypted message became clear.

Her father's voice came into her mind, and Faleena stilled her roiling thoughts at the sound of it and focused intently on his words.

"Faleena, Orion has DMGs. Svetlana encountered one in a moon at Machete. We believe Luxa houses an array of them. If they see the Perilous Dream, *they'll fire."*

He hadn't needed to add the last sentence for her to come to the same conclusion. Scan showed that, thus far, the enemy was only using conventional weapons to attack the decoy fleet—which had only suffered one loss.

As predicted, the Orion Guard ships in the system were moving to protect the soft targets the Widow fleet was attacking. Many of their vessels were being held in reserve, but Faleena could see that it was thinning the protection along the *Dream*'s approach vector enough that the ship *should* be able to slip through.

Until they reached Luxa. Then all bets were off.

It occurred to Faleena that she could use this news to dissuade A1 from her insane plan. If the ship could never make it to New Earth, then it couldn't kill Kirkland, and there was no point in the suicide run. Aborting would be the only logical choice.

She quickly fabricated supporting data and a transmission that would point to there being a DMG in Luxa, as well as adding a report of the destruction of the DMG at Machete.

"A1," she turned in her seat to face the Widows' leader. "I've just picked up information that leads me to believe that Orion possesses weapons capable of penetrating stasis shields."

Though the Widows on the bridge appeared nonplussed by the news, Faleena was certain she felt a subtle rise in the level of tension.

"Pass it to me," A1 ordered, and Faleena complied. After a minute, she shook her head. "I suspected they might have this ability. Airtha possessed it as well. We will continue as planned."

Several Widows shifted, and Faleena saw the commands flow across the shipnet from A1 to the bridge crew, bringing them back in line with her wishes.

"No one will speak of this. If our stealth is compromised, we will take evasive action. The DMG in Luxa—if one exists—will not be able to track us at close range, and we will strike our target as planned."

Faleena wanted to shout that 'striking' the target was the last thing they wanted to do, but she knew that there was no way she could stand against Cary. Not unless she were to devise a way to take her sister unawares and kill her instantly.

She wasn't ready to go to those ends yet. It was time to call for help.

ENGAGEMENT

STELLAR DATE: 05.06.8950 (Adjusted Years)
LOCATION: ISS *I2*
REGION: Outer New Sol, Orion Freedom Alliance

<I've detected a message from Faleena,> Bob said, causing Tangel and Joe to turn from the forward display, eyes settling on the bridge's holotank, where the words appeared.

"Moms, Dad. Cary plans to use CriEns going critical to destroy New Earth. She knows about the DMG in Luxa, but won't stop. We're going to do what we can, but I don't know how we can stand against her. Please help."

Tangel glanced at Joe, seeing the moisture forming in the corner of his eyes, and felt dismayed that none seemed to be seeping into hers. Instead, she felt a cold determination; the knowledge that she would need to do whatever was necessary to stop her daughter steeling her.

"Cary," she whispered.

Joe clasped her hand, his expression saying what he was unable to voice. She nodded in response and then turned to Captain Rachel.

"Captain, max speed, bring us to within fifty AU of the star and then drop a gate. We'll take the *Falconer* in."

"And should we continue insystem from there?" the captain asked.

Tangel gave a strangled laugh. "Stars, you'd better. We're going to need one hell of a rescue."

<I don't like you leaving me behind,> Bob said. *<We have almost no intel on what other defenses Kirkland might have.>*

"It's my daughters." Her voice brooked no argument. "This is what we're doing. Besides, if she hits New Earth and it sparks a white hole fueled by vacuum energy, the repercussions will be unimaginably bad. The death toll from this war will seem like a footnote."

<I understand. Please come see me in my node.>

Tangel nodded, and then turned back to face Joe. "I'll meet you on the *Falconer*. We're going to jump straight to Luxa. You'll lead one team to storm the moon and disable the DMG, and I'll go to the *Perilous Dream* and stop this before it starts—if I can."

Joe swallowed and nodded. Then he squared his shoulders, eyes narrowing as the father was replaced by the admiral. "Better if we jump two ships. From the coordinates Faleena sent, they're still a ways away from the moon. Take a pinnace through the gate and get to the ship before they're too close. I'll be the fallback."

"Great plan," Rachel said as she approached, worry etched into her features.

"But just how are you going to get off the moon? It's going to be crawling with enemies."

"That's where you come in," Tangel replied to the captain. "Cary was right about one thing.... The war with Orion has to end. Today. Once Luxa is out of commission, and the *I2* is above New Earth, we'll demand Kirkland's surrender."

"Do you think he'll comply?" the captain asked.

Joe nodded. "If he won't, then his second in command will. Tangel's right. Today we close the Orion Front."

Rachel cocked an eyebrow, a smirk forming on her lips. "Well...it's getting close to the second shift, and we still have four AU to go to get to the jump point. Probably tomorrow."

Tangel gave Joe a quick embrace. "I'll see you on the dock. Don't leave without saying goodbye." Then she turned and wrapped her arms around Rachel. "Keep my girl safe while I'm gone, you smartass."

Rachel squeezed back, her voice hoarse as she said, "Always."

* * * * *

A minute later, both Joe and Tangel were gone, and Rachel stared into the holotank, soaking in the enormity of what had just happened.

"Ma'am," the fleet coordination officer said from her station.

Rachel drew in a deep breath, praying her voice would hold. "Yes?"

"I couldn't help but overhear.... Uh...I've never heard the admiral say something like that before. Has she?"

A lump formed in Rachel's throat and she shook her head. Her voice was barely a whisper when she finally spoke.

"No...she hasn't."

* * * * *

Tangel walked into Bob's primary node with a heavy heart, and placed her hands on the railing as she stared through the physical construct at the entity within.

"Why are you so worried? It's freaking me out."

Bob didn't reply for almost a minute. When he did, his voice carried an unfamiliar quality.

<I promised myself that I'd never lie to you, Tangel. But that means I can't answer that question.>

"More of you knowing the future and not wanting me to screw it up?" she asked.

<Stars...if only it were that simple. Let's just say that you have already screwed

everything up. The way forward is entirely opaque to me now, shrouded by the peril that looms on every side.>

"Can you give me some clue?" Tangel asked. "Dammit, I feel like I might as well be at Delphi staring at animal entrails half the time I talk to you, Bob."

<I'll take that as a compliment, though you don't mean it to be one. Regarding my fears, do you ever wonder why the core AIs sent Airtha to the Transcend, but didn't send anyone to Orion?>

"I'd considered it," she replied. "Since we believe their goal was to deepen the distrust between Jeffrey and Kirkland, it seems that they only needed to utilize Airtha."

<If that was in fact their goal. But what if they did send someone to Orion as well?>

Tangel considered that information, playing out different scenarios and eventualities.

"I suppose most outcomes fall into one of two categories. Either their emissary failed and was somehow constrained by Kirkland, or they succeeded, and are in total control of Orion."

<Neither of which is a possibility that we can take lightly.>

"Agreed. What do you propose?"

<I need to safeguard you, Tangel. Stopping what is about to happen is of the utmost importance, but your journey cannot end here.>

Tangel's eyes widened as she realized what Bob was proposing.

"Do it," she said, and closed her corporeal eyes as the multinodal, ascended being's thousand limbs stretched out of the node and drifted toward her.

<This will be uncomfortable.>

"I imagine it will be."

* * * * *

Joe stood next to the pinnace he'd readied for Tangel. It was the fastest one in the First Fleet, with the best stealth systems and a mini CriEn that could power its stasis shield for days if needs be.

Tangel was taking longer than he'd expected, but they weren't in a huge rush. It would still be more than an hour until they reached the fifty-AU marker, where the engineers aboard the *Falconer* believed the inner perimeter of the interdictor field ended.

Then the fun would begin.

He was glad that Tangel had picked the *Falconer* to be the ship that went into New Sol. Not only did the crew know the system well, having stealthily traversed it for several months, but no one had liked the idea of leaving before their mission was complete. They were eager to see things through.

Captain Tracey had wasted no time getting her crew back aboard and ordering them to stock additional weapons and energy cores. The ship and crew were ready for an assault unlike any other they'd ever performed.

"Joe." Tangel's voice came to him, and Joe turned to see his wife approaching, a smile on her lips. "Sorry I'm late. Bob was long-winded."

<*Sure, blame it on me,*> the AI said.

"Always." A grin was on Tangel's lips, and Joe couldn't help but feel his own mood lighten just looking at her.

"Why so jovial?" he asked. "Did Bob give you some sort of secret knowledge? We going to kick ass?"

Tangel stepped in close and planted a kiss on his lips, then pulled back. "We always kick ass."

"Well, mostly," he nodded. "So you're feeling good about this?"

"I am," Tangel nodded. "For the first time since Xavia's attack at Aldebaran, I'm feeling really good. We've got this in the bag."

"Glad you feel so optimistic," he laughed. "I have to admit, you seemed worried on the bridge."

She nodded. "Yeah, I was. Honestly, I still am, a bit. This isn't going to be a cakewalk, but seriously, they're Oggies. We got this. Before you know it, the girls will be back, and we'll have Orion surrendering."

"All in a day's work."

Tangel winked. "Or maybe two. It could take a bit to do the paperwork."

"OK, two. Then we meet back on the *I2* for drinks in the forward lounge."

"Deal," Tangel said as she turned away to face her pinnace. "OK, I'd better get aboard and do preflight."

"I already did it for you," he whispered in her ear as he embraced her from behind.

"Sure." She leant her head back against his. "But I know this vacuum jockey that would have my hide if I didn't at least do my own run-through before I took off."

Joe sighed. "I know that guy, too. He's probably right." He kissed her neck and stepped back. "Go get 'em."

"I will. I promise."

* * * * *

Tangel sat in the pinnace's cockpit and sucked in a deep breath, watching on the forward display as Joe walked up the ramp into the *Falconer*.

~*Are you sure?*~ she asked. ~*Does it have to be this way?*~

~*It does.*~ Bob's reply was laden with emotion. ~*You have to trust me. It'll work out. I promise.*~

She nodded silently, finishing her prechecks, and then initiated lift-off, easing toward the dock's exit. As she reached the grav field at the end of the dock, a message came in over the QC network from Star City. It was from Eric.

[Barrage fired.]

~We're on the clock now,~ she said to Bob.

~We are. Good luck.~

She snorted in response, shaking her head at the AI's poor humor. *~I don't need luck.~*

DESPERATION

STELLAR DATE: 05.06.8950 (Adjusted Years)
LOCATION: ***Perilous Dream***
REGION: Inner New Sol, Orion Freedom Alliance

"So what do we do?" Priscilla asked. "Do you think they got the message?"

"I don't know," Faleena replied. "But we have to assume they didn't."

"Which means taking out the CriEn modules ourselves. No CriEns, no kaboom."

"How do you propose we 'take them out'?" Faleena asked. "The moment we breach that chamber, Cary will come, take them from us, and put them back."

Priscilla tapped a finger against her chin, staring into Faleena's eyes—or where she knew them to be behind the Widow's helmet. "We need a diversion."

"What do you have in mind?"

Ten minutes later, Priscilla and Faleena stood in a small hold near the primary stasis chambers. Within rested a single stasis pod containing a Widow, held there for the past seven months.

"You sure about this?" Faleena whispered. "She's going to be hard to control."

"That's sort of the point," Priscilla replied. "Unless you have a better idea, let's set her loose and get this underway."

"My only other idea is 'wait'," Faleena said. "Which isn't much of a plan."

Priscilla gave the AI a rueful smile, and then bent over and keyed in the command to bring the Widow out of stasis. She and Faleena stepped back, rifles aimed at the figure as the pod's cover slid aside.

It took a moment for the Widow to stir, but when she did, it was only to say, "So, are you going to kill me?"

"Not so long as you don't give us a reason to," Faleena said. "Get out."

"Why don't you just make me?" Lisa Wrentham asked. "Maybe I've spent so long as your little sock puppet that I don't remember how to move myself."

"Figure it out," Priscilla growled. "We need your help."

The Widow in the stasis pod barked a laugh, and then sat up, swinging her legs over the side, where she stopped and regarded the pair and their rifles.

"Not a very friendly way to ask for help."

"That's because we're not friends," Priscilla countered. "We need to take control of the ship from our sister, and we figured you'd know better than anyone how to do that."

"Oh? Not happy with the new boss?" Lisa asked. "She running things into the ground?"

"In a manner of speaking," Faleena replied. "She's going to cause this ship to slam into New Earth, overloading its CriEn modules."

Lisa cocked her head to the side. "That won't work, other than as a kinetic weapon. The modules can't draw enough power on impact to—"

"She's upgraded the ship with stasis shields," Faleena interrupted. "They'll draw enough."

"Fuck." The Widows' progenitor breathed out the word. "That'll destroy the entire star system…or—"

"Or a thousand star systems," Priscilla nodded impatiently. "We know. That's why we have to stop her. We need you to somehow get control of the ship while we steal the CriEns. If we can get two off the ship, her plan won't work."

For a moment, Lisa didn't move, but then she nodded. "OK, I know of a way I can override the engines, and even she won't be able to stop me—so long as I can get there in time."

"Trust me," Faleena chuckled. "Once we take the CriEns, all of her attention is going to be on us."

A minute later, they'd set a timetable and started a synchronized countdown.

"Don't double-cross us," Priscilla warned as she palmed the control panel to open the door. "We can still control your body."

"As can I," a voice said as the door slid open, and Priscilla turned to see A1 and E12 standing in the passageway. "I'm glad you woke Lisa Wrentham. I have need of her, and it's time for us to go."

"Go?" Faleena asked, taking a step back. "What are you talking about?"

A1 shook her head. "I have no plan to go down with the ship. We're not going to be here when the *Perilous Dream* impacts New Earth. But to make sure that happens, we need to get down to Luxa and disable that damn DMG."

"But how did you know?" Priscilla pressed.

A1 laughed, and for a moment, it sounded like Cary again. "It was Faleena. I didn't pick up on it at first, but when you share your mind with someone, you learn a lot of their verbal patterns. It took a day or two, but I eventually figured out that my scan officer was my sister. After following her for a few shifts, I discovered that you were free from stasis as well, Priscilla.

"You both seemed to be aiding my plan, so I decided to go along for a while and see where things led us."

"Which is to an impasse," Priscilla said. "We can't let you do this."

Tendrils of light snaked out from Cary and wrapped around Priscilla's and Faleena's necks.

"You're not *letting* me do anything. You're also not going to get in the way, though I still have to save you. Moms and Dad will expect to see you back."

"Car—"

Priscilla's voice cut off as Cary's ethereal limb passed through her neck and froze her vocal cords.

"Sorry, Priscilla. I don't have time for discussion right now. We have to get to a pinnace and get down to Luxa before they spot the *Dream* and fire on her." A1 turned to Lisa Wrentham. "Lisa would you be a dear and pretend to be A1 for a bit? I need you to keep the ship on course."

"Yes, A1," Lisa said, her voice trembling ever so slightly with what Priscilla could only imagine was forcibly contained rage.

"Good. Off with you."

Lisa stepped out of the hold and walked past A1 and the silent E12, disappearing from view.

"Now," A1 gestured in the other direction. "After you. We don't have much time."

MOON LANDING

STELLAR DATE: 05.06.8950 (Adjusted Years)
LOCATION: ISS *Falconer*, Luxa
REGION: Inner New Sol, Orion Freedom Alliance

"Shit that's close!" Captain Tracey exclaimed as the forward display was filled with the view of Luxa.

"We're a thousand klicks up," Joe said, as he looked at the scan data. "We need to be a lot closer, as close to landing as you can get and still have maneuverability."

"On it, sir," Tracey said as she gave helm orders, while looking over the view of Luxa on the holotank. "Here." She jabbed her finger at a location in the southern hemisphere. "That looks like the best ingress point."

Joe pulled it up and saw a small spaceport on the moon's surface that was all but overflowing with small, insystem craft.

He nodded in agreement "Looks pretty suspicious."

"I'll get us there," Tracey replied. "I assume you plan to be on the assault team."

"Read my mind. I'm heading to the armory now."

The captain offered her hand "Good luck, sir."

"Thanks," Joe shook it, and his gaze swept across the *Falconer*'s bridge crew. "To all of you."

* * * * *

Unlike the drop onto Polux, when the Marines' boots hit Luxa's regolith, there was no attempt at stealth. Beam weapons and railguns fired into the soldiers guarding the spaceport, tearing through the defenders in wave after wave as the platoons of Marines advanced in leaps and bounds.

Their target was the maglev terminal that would take them deep into the moon, where intel believed the DMG's fire controls systems lay.

<*Remember, people,*> Lieutenant Gallia said as the Marines secured the maglev train. <*We do this by the numbers. No one's rash, no one's hasty, and we all get back in time for pastry.*>

<*Stars, LT, I thought you'd given up on that one,*> Sergeant Bella muttered.

<*Oldie but a goodie,*> the lieutenant replied as she began directing the Marines into the maglev tunnel. <*Watch out for tracks and rats.*>

Joe moved in with Bella's squad, wondering if the lieutenant actually thought they might encounter rats in the tunnels, but not wanting to ask lest she resort to limerick again.

Hector's squad was in the lead, and three times, they encountered resistance: twice from automated drones, and the third from a group of soldiers.

<*Resistance seems really light,*> he commented to the lieutenant.

<*It does, sir,*> she replied. <*Ferra's just managed to tap the network down. What do you have, Private?*>

<*Some sort of fighting is going on nearby,*> the Marine replied a moment later. <*Ah shit, its Oggies being attacked by Widows.*>

<*Figures,*> Joe muttered, wondering if Cary was with them or not. <*If we see any, don't engage unless they do first, and go for non-lethal. Our people could be with them and either under a compulsion or undercover.*>

<*Yes, sir,*> Lieutenant Gallia replied before passing the order on to the platoon.

After another five minutes, they came to a platform strewn with the bodies of Orion soldiers. There weren't many scorch marks on the walls, and Joe suspected he knew why.

<*Double-time, people,*> he ordered, moving forward to join Bella's platoon as the Marines jogged down the passages, counting on the feeds from their drones to provide a view of what lay ahead.

For the most part, the view was similar to what the Marines had seen on the maglev platforms: dozens of Orion soldiers who looked as though they'd barely put up a fight before being torn apart—literally.

The further they went, the less Joe wanted to believe that he was following in Cary's wake. The carnage was extreme; many of the soldiers had been felled as they were running away, many more weren't even holding weapons.

After several more minutes, they came to a wide foyer with reinforced doors that had been torn free of the bulkhead. The ISF Marines eased through the opening and spread out, advancing on the four doors on the far side of the room.

Joe followed Bella toward her door, and when they reached it, he threaded nanofilament around the jamb, sucking in a sharp breath at the tableau within.

The room was a long, oval space, roughly eighty by sixty meters. President Kirkland and a group of Orion brass stood at the far end on a raised platform. Four Widows stood in the center of the room, three holding rifles, and the fourth unarmed, standing a few paces ahead.

"It's over, Kirkland. You've lost," the black figure in the lead called out. Joe knew it was Cary, though her voice hissed and lisped like a Widow's.

The praetor shook his head, a look of dismay on his features. "No, it's you who have lost. I must say, I'm glad this isn't you, Lisa. I would have been truly saddened to have you turn on me like this."

"She wouldn't be," Cary retorted. "You're right that I'm not her, but I *know* her. I know Lisa better than she even knows herself. She hates you with every fiber of her being."

"Is that so?" Kirkland asked. "Well, perhaps she and I can discuss that at some point in the future."

"Wrong," Cary shot back. "You have no fut—"

Joe started as Cary's words cut off, watching in horror as an energy field suddenly encapsulated her.

"A brane," he whispered aloud.

"Do you really think that we kept Orion pure this long without knowing how to deal with ascended beings?" Kirkland asked, taking a step forward as the other three Widows fell to the ground. "The core AIs sent one to me long ago, just as they did to Tomlinson. I let mine think it had my ear, but all the while, we worked to subdue and capture it. It took decades, but ultimately, human ingenuity won out. I learned a lot from that sad thing. I really did feel pity for it. I'm not sure I feel the same for you—Tangel, I assume?"

"You'd be so lucky," Cary said. "That is my mother. I'm A1."

"A1?" Kirkland cocked an eyebrow. "Interesting. Do you also go by 'Cary', then? There have been whispers that Tangel's daughter had ascended as well."

Cary didn't reply, and Kirkland shook his head. "I suppose it doesn't matter." Then he looked up at the doors, his gaze settling on the one Joe stood behind. "The brane that holds this person—be she Tangel or Cary—is capable of killing her in an instant. It wouldn't be the first time I've used one, so don't think it's just a bluff. Unless you want her to die, I suggest those of you in the antechamber surrender."

<*We've got Oggies in the passage on our six,*> Hector said. <*Orders?*>

<*We have to surrender,*> Joe said. <*Sergeant Hector, when we do, I need you to stealth and take a team back. We need to get word to the* Falconer, *and have them reach out to Tangel. She'll be able to stop this.*>

<*Aye, sir.*>

The ISF admiral stood and pulled off his helmet. <*The rest of you, disarm.*>

THE REAL LISA WRENTHAM

STELLAR DATE: 05.06.8950 (Adjusted Years)
LOCATION: ISF Pinnace, Luxa
REGION: Inner New Sol, Orion Freedom Alliance

The stars were only gone for an instant before they snapped back into view and Tangel began to search for the *Perilous Dream*.

She knew that the pinnace's meager arrays could never pick up the Widows' ship, but that wasn't her plan. Bob had calculated its most likely trajectory, and with her extradimensional sight, she'd be able to see the CriEns' energy draw aboard the vessel.

Her gaze roved across the stations orbiting New Earth and the ships plying the black. Most did not possess CriEn modules, but a few military vessels did. She filtered every vessel not drawing vacuum energy out of her view, and then began to tag each one the pinnace could scan as well.

A minute later, she found it. An anomalous energy draw with no visible ship.

"Gotcha," she whispered.

Careful not to give the pinnace away to any of the many eyes in the system, nor her prey, Tangel carefully guided it onto an intercept course with the *Perilous Dream*, and then programmed in a flight path to take the small craft safely out of the way afterward.

Bob's calculations had been very close to the mark, and twenty minutes later, the pinnace had matched *v* with the *Dream*, and sat only a hundred meters off the stealthed cruiser's port bow.

"OK," Tangel said to the cockpit. "Here goes nothing."

Stretching out her non-corporeal limbs, she eased her way through the holodisplay and the bulkhead beyond, passing into space. Gathering herself on the hull of the pinnace, she fought against what could only be described as a type of vertigo as she stared out into the blinding light of New Sol's star.

Easy does it, she thought. *Just push off and drift over. Have to do it fast, the pinnace is going to change course in a minute.*

With the words echoing in her mind, she pushed off from the small craft, leaving its lone occupant, and crossing the gap between the ships.

Her body sank into the *Perilous Dream*'s hull, and for a moment, Tangel felt stuck, as though she'd been embedded in the ship. Then she shifted the wavelengths of her limbs, and found purchase on the ship's matter and pulled herself in, passing through hull, pipes, and conduit, to finally emerge inside a passageway.

"That was unsettling," she said softly, stretching her perception up and down the corridor, while also reaching into the ship's network, searching for the location of the bridge.

As she searched, a Widow came around the corner and stopped, frozen in her tracks for a moment before she managed to stammer, "W-what are you?"

"I'm Tangel. I'm here for my daughters. Take me to the bridge."

The Widow pulled her sidearm free and trained it on Tangel. "I don't think so."

Without bothering with a verbal response, Tangel reached out and took the weapon apart, atom by atom, absorbing the energy released in the process.

The Widow didn't move, so Tangel moved onto the enemy's arm, dissolving it as well.

That set the black assassin screeching, and she turned to run, but Tangel touched her mind and put the tortured being to sleep.

"Don't worry, I'll find my own way."

She encountered several other Widows on the way to the ship's bridge, none providing any more trouble than the first. A few minutes later, she stood before the sealed door and shook her head.

"Cary, you may as well open it. You know a door won't stop me."

No response came from within, and Tangel made good on her promise, shredding the door and moving through onto the bridge.

Six Widows stood between her and the captain's chair. Tangel reached out, casually sweeping them aside as she moved forward, her gaze raking over the Widow the ship's systems recognized as A1.

"You're not Cary," Tangel's limbs flashed out and she took apart the helmet obscuring the Widow's face. "You're her, the real Lisa Wrentham."

"And you must be Tangel," Lisa replied. "Stars, and you wonder why we worked so hard to stop you. You're a monster."

An echoing laugh burst from Tangel as she regarded the ruined creature that had once been such a brilliant mind in the FGT. She gestured to the black-clad figures all around her.

"Seems like the kettle calling the pot black. No matter, though, where is she? You can't hide her from me."

"Hide her?" Lisa asked. "I can't do anything she doesn't order me to. However, she didn't order me not to tell you where she's gone." The Widow turned and pointed to Luxa, the view of which dominated the forward display. "She's gone there, to destroy the DMG, I imagine."

Tangel resisted a groan. She was about to render the Widow unconscious when Lisa barked a cruel laugh.

"Oh, look at that, the praetor is reaching out. Shall I put him through?"

Without replying, Tangel reached into the ship's network and configured the response to relay through several public networks so that Kirkland's people would not be able to triangulate the *Dream*'s position too quickly.

With that done, she accepted the connection, and Kirkland appeared on the screen.

"Ah!" his brow lifted. "Well, then, you must be Tangel, and then I must have Cary. Good to have that settled."

"Glad to put your mind at ease," Tangel responded. "Let my daughter go. There's no way you can win this fight."

"No?" Kirkland asked, a smirk pulling at one side of his mouth. "Are you sure about that?"

The view changed to show a black brane holding a Widow, with a group standing to one side. Three of them were Widows—which she identified as Priscilla, Saanvi, and Faleena—and the fourth was Joe.

"Shit," she whispered. "Oh shit, no."

"Oh yes," Kirkland was grinning ear to ear. "I'm sorry, I shouldn't be so impolite, but I really never expected you to march on in here and essentially turn yourselves over to me. I guess it shouldn't be that surprising. I've been playing the long game for some time. You just came onto the field."

"What do you want?" Tangel asked.

"I want your surrender. I want you next to your daughter, and when you are, you'll order the ISF to stand down, and surrender all of your abhorrently advanced technology to Orion."

Tangel wondered if this was what Bob had seen that he didn't want to share with her. He was right that she would have altered it—she would have done anything to alter it. But it also might be that she'd already done something to change what he saw. For centuries, his schtick had been that her 'luck' messed up his vision.

Some luck.

Even so, she wasn't going to give in without a fight.

"There's no way," she retorted. "You'll simply kill my people. You think we're all abominations."

Kirkland stared into the optical pickup for a minute and then shook his head. "I suspected you'd need more motivations."

A rifle's retort sounded, and Priscilla's head exploded, her body staying upright for a moment before falling to the deck.

"What an ass," Lisa muttered, and it took every remaining ounce of willpower Tangel possessed not to smash the abhorrent woman against the bulkhead.

"OK," she whispered after regaining her composure. "I'm coming down."

"You have half an hour. I know the *Dream* is at least that close."

"I'll be there," Tangel replied and killed the connection.

Lisa shook her head, her soulless eyes locked on Tangel's. "You know he'll capture you too. Going down there is a death sentence."

"We'll see about that."

Tangel reached out and touched the minds of the Widows on the bridge, dropping them all into a deep sleep before pushing off from the deck and pulling her way through the ship to where the CriEn modules were positioned. With more care than she felt she had time for, Tangel took each one off the stack and disabled it, ensuring that Cary's master plan to destroy the star system would fail.

From there, she moved through the ship and disintegrated the stasis field generators. Her last stop was the aft bay, where a stealth shuttle waited.

She adjusted her form to move in the corporeal world, and boarded the vessel, running an abbreviated pre-flight, smiling as she thought of Joe's displeasure at her haste, and then took off.

When she was a thousand kilometers from the *Perilous Dream,* she sent a command back to the ship, dropping its stealth systems.

Less than a minute later, a beam of energy streaked out of Luxa and speared the Widows' ship, tearing it in half and sending it spinning off course.

Tangel couldn't help a rueful laugh. "Vindictive."

ENFORCED

STELLAR DATE: 05.06.8950 (Adjusted Years)
LOCATION: Luxa
REGION: Inner New Sol, Orion Freedom Alliance

Tangel drifted through the moon's surface, eschewing the passages and corridors, most of which were filled with Orion soldiers.

She wondered if they had a type of slepton weapon like the ISF employed for capturing ascended beings. Though she fully expected to be captured in a brane at some point before the day was done, she didn't want it to be before she reached the DMG control chamber.

No time to waste.

Partway through the moon, she saw a familiar energy signature, and realized that it was a team of ISF Marines moving back toward the surface.

~Sergeant Hector,~ she said, slowing her descent near the tunnel he was moving through. *~You need to get off Luxa.~*

Who? What? His thoughts were more startled than panicked.

~This is Admiral Richards. You need to go, there's nothing more you can do here. Cary left a shuttle in the spaceport, it has a CriEn and stasis shields.~

How do you know that? he blurted out. *Er…ma'am.*

~I just do. Now go. That's an order. I'll take care of the DMG and rescue our people.~

He seemed hesitant, and she provided a mental push.

*~Sergeant, **go**.~*

A feeling of sorrow came from the Marine, but the words *Yes, Admiral,* sounded in his mind, and she watched him get his team on their way back to the spaceport before moving on.

Three minutes before her deadline expired, Tangel fell through the ceiling of the oval chamber and landed a dozen meters from where Cary was captured. On the far side of the brane were her other daughters and Joe. Further back in the room were the Marines, out of their armor and under guard by nearly a full company of Oggies.

"You know," she turned to address Kirkland. "Even without me here, my Marines would still kick your ass. Kill my daughter, and you'll find out they don't need weapons to take down your people."

"So much bluster." Kirkland shook his head.

"It was more of an observation. I don't really have much of a filter right now—I'm kind of at the end of my rope."

The praetor pursed his lips and nodded. "I can see why. Either way, just so they don't get any ideas, they should know that this room can produce a rather powerful EMP. My people won't suffer much from a full blast, but I suspect folks with as many mods as your Marines—not to mention your daughters and husband—will not enjoy the experience."

"Don't worry," Tangel said. "They won't do anything rash. Like I said, it was just an observation."

"For all your advances, you certainly are weak." Kirkland folded his arms across his chest. "Get up here and stand next to your daughter. I have a cage waiting for you."

Tangel ignored his order and instead peered through Luxa and out into space, searching for her salvation. Now, more than ever, the timing had to be perfect. Seeing the brane that held Cary, Tangel wasn't sure that she could do what she had to if Kirkland trapped her as well.

"And if you weren't fighting us so much," she replied while still scanning the black, "we could already be in an alliance, fighting against the core AIs. They're the real enemy. Why can't you see that?"

"They're *an* enemy," Kirkland countered. "But if I helped you destroy them, *you* would simply take their place. That's not an option, so far as I'm concerned. Now get up here."

To emphasize his point, the brane surrounding Cary contracted, and she let out a muffled shriek, the N-dimensional field wrapping tightly around her body.

~I'm sorry, Mother,~ Cary whispered. *~I screwed it all up. I really thought it would work. It* ***should*** *have worked.~*

~We're going to make it through this,~ Tangel whispered into her daughter's mind. *~And when we do, you'll understand.~*

~Understand what?~ Cary asked. *~My failure?~*

~Look.~ Tangel gestured out into space. *~Look beyond the moon, look into the deep. Tell me, what do you see?~*

Cary didn't respond for a moment, and Kirkland began to yell that he'd shoot Faleena if Tangel didn't comply. She spotted the soldier holding the rifle on Faleena, and saw that the man was aiming for the AI's head.

She ignored Kirkland and implored her daughter.

~What do you see?~ she pressed.

~Lights,~ Cary replied. *~So many lights. What are they?~*

A rifle barked, the sound echoing in the enclosed chamber as Faleena fell to the ground.

~They're our salvation,~ Tangel replied with far more calm than she felt. *~When this is over, you must be strong for me. You must forget Lisa Wrentham, scrub her from your mind, memory by memory. Come back to your father and mothers and sisters. Promise me you'll do this, Cary. Promise me.~*

~I promise.~ Cary's voice was quiet and scared, reminding Tangel of the little girl she once was.

Tangel reached out, wishing she could penetrate the brane to touch her daughter one last time. ~*That's my girl.*~

A fraction of a second later, two dozen neutronium bullets traveling at 0.7*c* hit Luxa and pulverized the moon.

FALCONER

STELLAR DATE: 05.07.8950 (Adjusted Years)
LOCATION: ISS *Falconer*, Luxa
REGION: Inner New Sol, Orion Freedom Alliance

When Tangel ordered Tracey to move away from Luxa, the captain had strongly considered disobeying orders. She had debated closing in and landing more troops on its surface, right up until the moment the moon exploded.

A replay of scan had shown that it wasn't an explosion, but instead the result of two dozen neutronium bullets hitting Luxa.

Despite the fact that each bullet wasn't much larger than two of her fingers, the kinetic energy unleashed would have been enough to destroy an earth-sized planet.

That was nothing compared to the shock that ran through the crew of the *Falconer*.

It had taken Captain Tracey a full minute to regain the powers of speech, so she was glad that Ella had the foresight to activate the stasis shields and protect them from the relativistic spray of debris that was tearing its way through the New Sol System.

"Damage?" she asked, turning to the engineering chief.

He didn't respond, and she rose from her chair and placed a hand on his shoulder.

"We've still got a ship to fly, and we're still deep in enemy territory, mister. I need a status report."

"Yes—" The word rasped through a dry throat, and he swallowed, closed his eyes, and nodded. "Yes, ma'am."

"Message from the *I2*," the comm officer said in a breathless voice. "It's from Bob, he says 'find them'."

The two words spurred Tracey into action, and she leapt back to her chair.

"OK, people! If Bob thinks they're out there, then they're out there. Scan, I want you to map the path of all that crap and plot the most likely course. Weapons, you blast the shit out of any Orion ship that even gets close to us. No way are we letting those bastards pick up our people. Everyone else, help scan look for them. Whatever they're in, it has to be bigger than most of the gravel Luxa got pulverized into."

The bridge crew leapt into action, holos appearing over consoles showing sections of the moon's rapidly expanding debris field, teams reviewing data and deploying drones to aid in triangulation.

"We found something!" Scan called out five minutes later. "It's a pinnace, Orion make, but with stasis shields."

"Trying to raise them," Comm added. "It's Sergeant Hector! He has four Marines with him."

"And Tangel?" Tracey demanded.

"No…he says she ordered him back to the surface."

"Shit," the captain muttered. "If his ship can fly, get him in on the search, otherwise get him aboard."

The sergeant's pinnace was in good enough condition to join in, and its smaller profile made it able to move through the debris field with less disruption.

The search went on for another thirty minutes before someone on the bridge blurted out, "What the hell is that?"

An image appeared on the main holotank, and Captain Tracey rose to her feet, staring at it in wonder.

"It's a crystalline sphere," she whispered. "That must be them. Helm, get us over there."

* * * * *

"The *Falconer* found them," the Comm officer called out, and cheers erupted across the *I2*'s bridge. "They're in some sort of sphere, but they can't figure out how to get it open, and it won't fit in any of their bays."

<Tell them to keep it safe until we arrive,> Bob intoned.

"Yeah," Rachel said, feeling almost breathless. "Tell them that."

"We're forty-seven minutes out," Helm added. "Going to be some hard braking."

"Deploy the fleet," Rachel ordered. "I want to make sure that we keep the Oggies at bay."

"Aye," the fleet coordination officer responded.

"So far, they seem to be keeping back," Scan said. "Plus, those other Widow ships are still advancing through the system."

<We'll have to deal with those,> Bob said. *<We can't have stasis tech leaking out.>*

Rachel nodded. "No rest for the weary. I'll call for help."

<I've already done that. Krissy is bringing a fleet.>

"Sheesh, Bob, what do you need me for?"

<Moral support.>

The incongruity of that statement had Rachel laughing so hard, tears were streaming down her face before she managed to get control of herself, only to find that half the bridge crew had joined in.

* * * * *

The crystalline sphere settled onto the deck in the forward docking bay, and

Rachel approached it nervously.

<*What are we going to find inside?*> she asked Bob privately, not wanting to worry the crew around her.

<*I'm not sure,*> the AI replied.

As he spoke, two sinuous tendrils of light passed though the overhead and stretched toward the sphere. They paused in front of it, and then traced a five-meter circle near the base. With a light sucking sound, the section of sphere fell out and landed on the deck.

One of the tendrils of light hovered in the entrance to the sphere and then retreated.

<*They're OK,*> Bob said.

The first person to emerge was a Widow, holding another one of her kind in her arms.

Marines lifted their weapons, a fireteam moving toward the pair.

<*That is Saanvi and Cary. Get them to medical.*>

"You heard him," Rachel barked. "Medics!"

A Marine was out next, and Rachel recognized Lieutenant Gallia.

"We've got prisoners coming out next," she hollered. "Two 'toons of their goons and some brass. Kirkland too."

"Tangel? Joe?" Rachel asked as she approached the Marine. "What about Faleena and Priscilla?"

Gallia's eyes fell to the deck, and she stepped aside so as not to impede the flow of prisoners exiting the sphere. She heaved a deep breath and looked up at Rachel.

"Not everyone made it, ma'am."

Rachel saw the sorrow the lieutenant was trying to keep at bay, and didn't press the woman any further. A rage began to build up in the *I2*'s captain, and she turned to glare at the prisoners as they were escorted from the sphere.

When the officers and Kirkland emerged, she directed a special detail to secure them, placing each one in stasis before moving them to the brig.

Finally the procession was finished, and she stepped into the sphere, surprised to find part of a room encased within. In the center, Joe crouched next to a pair of bodies, and Rachel sped to his side, gasping in horror as she realized both were headless.

"Who?" she finally managed to sputter.

"Faleena." Joe whispered the name, pointing at the body on the right. "She's OK. Saanvi has her core."

"And Priscilla?" the name rasped its way out of Rachel's throat as she fell to her knees next to Joe, staring at the remains of a woman who had been both a comrade and a good friend.

"She's gone." The words fell from Joe's lips like lead. "And so—"

His voice cut out, the words ending in a strangled cough.

"So is Tangel?" Rachel whispered, looking around for another body. "Where…."

Joe gestured at the sphere around them. "This is her body. She did it to save us. I don't…I don't understand how, but Cary said it consumed all of Tangel to save us."

<She's right,> Bob's voice came into their minds. *<Tangel has passed away. I hoped it wouldn't come to this, but—>*

"Bob," Joe hissed. "Right about now, I'd like you to shut up."

The AI didn't speak further, and Rachel reached out, wrapping her arms around the man she'd long thought of as a surrogate father, as sobs began to wrack his body.

ADRIFT

STELLAR DATE: 05.07.8950 (Adjusted Years)
LOCATION: ISF Pinnace
REGION: Outer New Sol, Orion Freedom Alliance

Consciousness came back to Tanis in slow, pulsing waves, almost as though her mind was reinitializing itself, coming back to life after a long dormancy.

It seemed to take forever to form a coherent thought, but when she did, it was a single word.

<Angela?>

<I'm here, Tanis. Though I don't know where 'here' is.>

<Why can't I see? Wait…I can't feel, either. Are we dead?>

The AI laughed, the silvery sound of mirth letting Tanis know that everything would be alright. *<If we are, then this must be hell, being stuck with you forever.>*

<Seriously? I thought it would be heaven. You know how I light up a room.>

<In your own mind. OK, I've figured it out. It's our brains. They're kinda disconnected from your body. Give me a minute.>

A thousand reasons for such an occurrence ran through Tanis's mind. She tried to remember where she'd been last, what she'd been doing. It was foggy…something about the Albany System, the planet Pyra.

<Crash-landed! We're stuck on Pyra. I lost my arm.>

<Well, not anymore,> Angela said. *<You've got both arms, so far as I can tell.>*

<You gonna hook me up, or just leave me trapped in here?>

<I'm working on it. Your delicate little brain can't take much abuse.>

<Funny, Angela—oh! Vision. That's a start.>

<The rest is coming. Looks like we're in a pinnace.>

Tanis nodded, then realized she'd actually nodded. "Oh, that feels weird. Like my head is floating…wait, no, we're just in zero-*g*."

<Seems like it—oh shit.>

" 'Oh shit' what?" Tanis glanced around the cockpit, noting that it was clearly an ISF design.

<We've lost time.>

"How much?"

She checked her internal chrono, gasped, and then looked at the one on the pinnace's holodisplay.

<A year.>

She let out a shuddering breath. "OK. What the hell happened on Pyra?"

THE END

* * * * *

Pick up the final volume of the Orion War series and find out what happens next in ***<u>The Hegemony of Humanity</u>***.

THE BOOKS OF AEON 14

This list is in near-chronological order. However, for the full chronological reading order, check out the master spreadsheet.

The Sentience Wars: Origins (Age of the Sentience Wars – w/James S. Aaron)
- Books 1-3 Omnibus: Lyssa's Rise
- Books 4-5 Omnibus (incl. Vesta Burning): Lyssa's Fire

- Book 0 Prequel: The Proteus Bridge (Full length novel)
- Book 1: Lyssa's Dream
- Book 2: Lyssa's Run
- Book 3: Lyssa's Flight
- Book 4: Lyssa's Call
- Book 5: Lyssa's Flame

The Sentience Wars: Solar War 1 (Age of the Sentience Wars – w/James S. Aaron)
- Book 0 Prequel: Vesta Burning (Full length novel)
- Book 1: Eve of Destruction
- Book 2: The Spreading Fire
- Book 3: A Fire Upon the Worlds (2020)

Enfield Genesis (Age of the Sentience Wars – w/Lisa Richman)
- Book 1: Alpha Centauri
- Book 2: Proxima Centauri
- Book 3: Tau Ceti
- Book 4: Epsilon Eridani
- Book 5: Sirius

Origins of Destiny (The Age of Terra)
- Prequel: Storming the Norse Wind
- Prequel: Angel's Rise: The Huntress (available on Patreon)
- Book 1: Tanis Richards: Shore Leave
- Book 2: Tanis Richards: Masquerade
- Book 3: Tanis Richards: Blackest Night
- Book 4: Tanis Richards: Kill Shot

The Intrepid Saga (The Age of Terra)
- Book 1: Outsystem
- Book 2: A Path in the Darkness
- Book 3: Building Victoria

- The Intrepid Saga Omnibus – *Also contains Destiny Lost, book 1 of the Orion War series*

- Destiny Rising – *Special Author's Extended Edition comprised of both Outsystem and A Path in the Darkness with over 100 pages of new content.*

The Sol Dissolution (The Age of Terra)
- Book 1: Venusian Uprising
- Book 2: Assault on Sedna
- Book 3: Hyperion War
- Book 4: Fall of Terra (2021)

Outlaws of Aquilia (Age of the FTL Wars)
- Book 1: The Daedalus Job
- Book 2: Maelstrom Reach
- Book 3: Marauder's Compass

Althea's Raiders (Age of the FTL Wars)
- Book 1: The Fall of Rome (2021)
- Book 2: The Terran Empire (2021)

The Warlord (Before the Age of the Orion War)
- Books 1-3 Omnibus: The Warlord of Midditerra

- Book 1: The Woman Without a World
- Book 2: The Woman Who Seized an Empire
- Book 3: The Woman Who Lost Everything

Legacy of the Lost (The FTL Wars Era w/Chris J. Pike)
- Book 1: Fire in the Night Sky
- Book 2: A Blight Upon the Stars
- Book 3: A Specter and an Invasion (2021)

The Orion War
- Book 1-3 Omnibus: Battle for New Canaan *(includes Set the Galaxy on Fire anthology)*
- Book 4-6 Omnibus: The Greatest War *(includes Ignite the Stars anthology)*
- Book 7-10 Omnibus: Assault on Orion
- Book 11-13 Omnibus: Hegemony of Humanity *(includes Return to Kapteyn's Star)*

- Book 0 Prequel: To Fly Sabrina
- Book 1: Destiny Lost
- Book 2: New Canaan
- Book 3: Orion Rising
- Book 4: The Scipio Alliance
- Book 5: Attack on Thebes

- Book 6: War on a Thousand Fronts
- Book 7: Precipice of Darkness
- Book 8: Airtha Ascendancy
- Book 9: The Orion Front
- Book 10: Starfire
- Book 10.5: Return to Kapteyn's Star
- Book 11: Race Across Spacetime
- Book 12: Return to Sol: Attack at Dawn
- Book 13: Return to Sol: Star Rise

Non-Aeon 14 volumes containing Tanis stories
- Bob's Bar Volume 1
- Quantum Legends 3: Aberrant Ascension (2021)

Building New Canaan (Age of the Orion War – w/J.J. Green)
- Book 1: Carthage
- Book 2: Tyre
- Book 3: Troy
- Book 4: Athens

Tales of the Orion War
- Book 1: Set the Galaxy on Fire
- Book 2: Ignite the Stars

Multi-Author Collections
- Volume 1: Repercussions

Perilous Alliance (Age of the Orion War – w/Chris J. Pike)
- Book 1-3 Omnibus: Crisis in Silstrand
- Book 3.5-6 Omnibus: War in the Fringe

- Book 0 Prequel: Escape Velocity
- Book 1: Close Proximity
- Book 2: Strike Vector
- Book 3: Collision Course
- Book 3.5: Decisive Action
- Book 4: Impact Imminent
- Book 5: Critical Inertia
- Book 6: Impulse Shock
- Book 7: Terminal Velocity

The Delta Team (Age of the Orion War)
- Book 1: The Eden Job
- Book 2: The Disknee World
- Book 3: Rogue Planets

Serenity (Age of the Orion War – w/A. K. DuBoff)
- Book 1: Return to the Ordus
- Book 2: War of the Rosette

Rika's Marauders (Age of the Orion War)
- Book 1-3 Omnibus: Rika Activated
- Book 1-7 Full series omnibus: Rika's Marauders

- Prequel: Rika Mechanized
- Book 1: Rika Outcast
- Book 2: Rika Redeemed
- Book 3: Rika Triumphant
- Book 4: Rika Commander
- Book 5: Rika Infiltrator
- Book 6: Rika Unleashed
- Book 7: Rika Conqueror

Non-Aeon 14 Anthologies containing Rika stories
- Bob's Bar Volume 2

The Genevian Queen (Age of the Orion War)
- Book 1: Rika Rising
- Book 2: Rika Coronated
- Book 3: Rika Destroyer

Perseus Gate (Age of the Orion War)
Season 1: Orion Space
- Episode 1: The Gate at the Grey Wolf Star
- Episode 2: The World at the Edge of Space
- Episode 3: The Dance on the Moons of Serenity
- Episode 4: The Last Bastion of Star City
- Episode 5: The Toll Road Between the Stars
- Episode 6: The Final Stroll on Perseus's Arm
- Eps 1-3 Omnibus: The Trail Through the Stars
- Eps 4-6 Omnibus: The Path Amongst the Clouds

Season 2: Inner Stars
- Episode 1: A Meeting of Bodies and Minds
- Episode 2: A Deception and a Promise Kept
- Episode 3: A Surreptitious Rescue of Friends and Foes
- Episode 3.5: Anomaly on Cerka (w/Andrew Dobell)
- Episode 4: A Victory and a Crushing Defeat
- Episode 5: A Trial and the Tribulations
- Episode 6: A Bargain and a True Story Told (2021)
- Episode 7: A New Empire and An Old Ally (2021)
- Eps 1-3 Omnibus: A Siege and a Salvation from Enemies

Hand's Assassin (Age of the Orion War – w/T.G. Ayer)
- Book 1: Death Dealer
- Book 2: Death Mark (2021)

Machete System Bounty Hunter (Age of the Orion War – w/Zen DiPietro)
- Book 1: Hired Gun
- Book 2: Gunning for Trouble
- Book 3: With Guns Blazing

Fennington Station Murder Mysteries (Age of the Orion War)
- Book 1: Whole Latte Death (w/Chris J. Pike)
- Book 2: Cocoa Crush (w/Chris J. Pike)

The Empire (Age of the Orion War)
- Book 1: The Empress and the Ambassador
- Book 2: Consort of the Scorpion Empress
- Book 3: By the Empress's Command

Bitchalante (Age of the Orion War)
- Book 1: Bitchalante (2021)

The Ascension War (Age of the Orion War)
- Book 1: Scions of Humanity (2020)

OTHER BOOKS BY M. D. COOPER

Destiny's Sword
- Book 1: Lucidium Run

ABOUT THE AUTHOR

Malorie Cooper likes to think of herself as a dreamer and a wanderer, yet her feet are firmly grounded in reality.

A twenty-year software development veteran, Malorie eventually climbed the ladder to the position of software architect and CTO, where she gained a wealth of experience managing complex systems and large groups of people.

Her experiences there translated well into the realm of science fiction, and when her novels took off, she was primed and ready to make the jump into a career as a full-time author.

A 'maker' from an early age, Malorie loves to craft things, from furniture, to cosplay costumes, to a well-spun tale, she can't help but to create new things every day.

A rare extrovert writer, she loves to hang out with readers, and people in general. If you meet her at a convention, she just might be rocking a catsuit, cosplaying one of her own characters, or maybe her latest favorite from Overwatch!

She shares her home with a brilliant young girl, her wonderful wife (who also writes), a cat that chirps at birds, a never-ending list of things she would like to build, and ideas...

Find out what's coming next at www.aeon14.com.
Follow her on Instagram at www.instagram.com/m.d.cooper.
Hang out with the fans on Facebook at
www.facebook.com/groups/aeon14fans.

Printed in Great Britain
by Amazon